WHAT LIES WITHIN

Masks & Shadows

NICOLLE MAY

To those who find their prince charming in all shades of morally gray.
You know the ones.
The crooked grins. That dangerous voice.
The ones that make your breath catch when they say, "Hello, darling."
Or the way they uses their ... sword.

To the villains who find their darkened soul
awakened by a spark of light.

To those who don't think they're worth it.
You are.

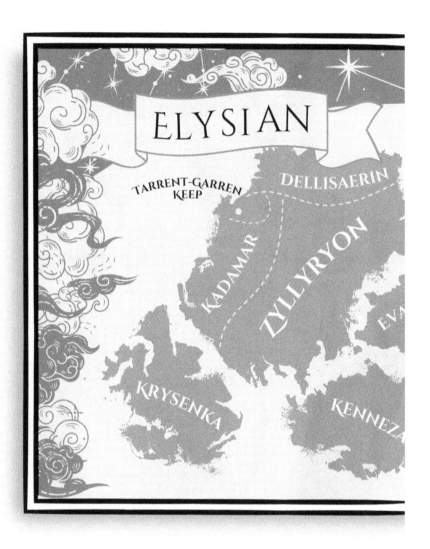

By royal decree of High King Magnelis,
any unauthorized subject found in
possession of an Elysian map will be
tried for treason and sentenced to death.

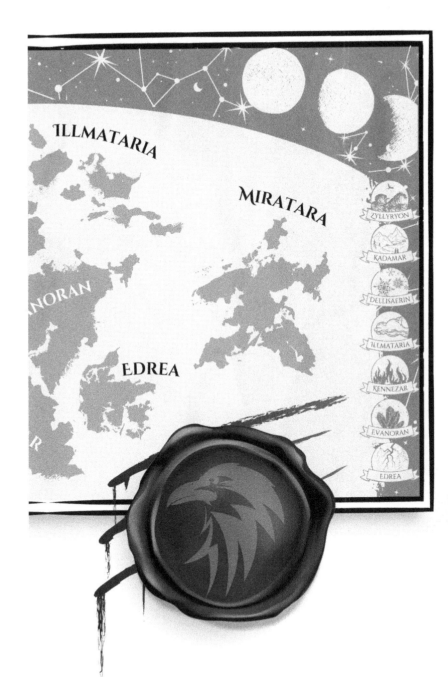

ILLMATARIA

MIRATARA

NORAN

EDREA

ZYLLYRYON

KADAMAR

DELLISAERIN

ILLMATARIA

KENNEZAR

EVANORAN

EDREA

THE KNOWN KINGDOMS OF
ELYSIAN

 ZYLLYRYON KINGDOM OF MIST & SEA

KINGDOM OF LAND & GROWTH **KADAMAR**

 ILLMATARIA KINGDOM OF AIR & WIND

KINGDOM OF FROST & ICE **DELLISAERIN**

 KENNAZAR KINGDOM OF FLAME & FURY

KINGDOM OF CRYSTAL & GLOW **EVANORAN**

 EDREA KINGDOM OF POWER & FLOW

TARRENT-GARREN KEEP
TERRITORY OF THE GUARDIANS
GOVERNED BY NO KING

THE UNKNOWN LANDS
KRYSENKA DARKNESS REIGNS

STARLIGHT's CAGE **MIRATARA**

PLAYLIST

ALORA

You're On Your Own Kid - Taylor Swift 🖤

Face Down - The Red Jumpsuit Aparatus 🔁

Bigger Person - Lauren Spencer Smith 🖤

Control - Loveless 🖤

Would've, Could've, Should've - Taylor Swift 🔁

TRUSTFALL - Pink 🖤

Waking Lions - Pop Evil 🖤

Unbreakable - Citizen Soldier 🔁

Ignite - Skillet 🔁

Burn - 2WEI & Edda Hayes 🖤

Warrior X - Beth Crowley 🖤

Little Girl Gone - CHINCHILLA 🖤

Plot Line - Emlyn 🔁

What Do You Make of Me? - Beth Crowley 🖤

Just a Kiss - Lady A 🖤

GARRIK

🖤 I Didn't Ask For This - Beth Crowley

🔁 Evil - Letdown

🖤 Monster - Hidden Citizens & Ryan Innes

🖤 You'd Never Know - BLU EYES

🔁 Never Ending Nightmare - Citizen Soldier

🖤 Bad Liar - Imagine Dragons

🖤 Numb - Ryan Oakes

🔁 Invisible - Citizen Soldier

🔁 This War - Ascendia

🖤 Empty - Letdown

🖤 Weight of the World - Citizen Soldier

🖤 Harder to Breathe - Letdown

🔁 Evergreen - Arankai

🖤 Prisoner - Raphael Lake

🖤 Through Hell - Melrose Avenue

FIND THE COMPLETE PLAYLIST WITH MORE SONGS HERE:

PRONUNCIATION GUIDE

NAMES:

Garrik - Gar-rik - Shadow Daddy is also acceptable.

Alora - Uh-lore-uh

THE SHADOW ORDER:

Thalon - Thal-in
Jade - Jay-d
Aiden - A-din
Eldacar - El-duh-car

OTHERS:

Kaine - Piece of shit - otherwise pronounced as Kay-n

Magnelis - also a piece of shit - otherwise pronounced as Mag-nel-iss

Malik - Mal-lik
Brennus - Bren-iss
Nevilier - Nev-uh-lear

She - Snake bitch - aka the absolute worst EVER who deserves a horrible death.

Rowlen - Roe-lin
Emeline - Em-uh-leen
Nadeleine - Nad-uh-leen
Deimon - Day-muhn
Draven - Dra-ven
Calla - Call-uh
Allseeah - All-see-uh
Kerimkhar - Ker-im-car
Airathel - Air-uh-th-el

PLACES:

Elysian - El-iss-ee-in
Telldaira - Tell-dare-uh
Alynthia - Uh-lin-thee-uh
Galdheir - Gal-d-air
Maraz - Muh-raz
Lirazkendra - Ler-az-ken-druh
Tarrent-Garren - Tar-rent Gar-ren

KINGDOMS:

Zyllyryon - Zeh-leer-re-on
Dellisaerin - Dell-iss-air-in
Kadamar - Kuh-adam-are
Kennazar - Ken-uh-zar
Ilmataria - ill-muh-tar-ee-uh
Evanoran - Ev-uh-nor-in
Edrea - Aye-dree-uh
Krysenka - Chris-en-kuh
Miratara - Meer-uh-tar-uh

TRIGGER WARNING

(THESE ARE ALSO SPOILERS)

This book contains very dark triggering situations such as domestic violence (these scenes are detailed) and fade to black / insinuated rape / sexual assault flashbacks / nightmares. There is also graphic violence and gore, torture, sexual assault, kidnapping, psychological abuse, physical abuse, mental abuse, alcohol abuse, mentions of magical drugs, explicit sexual situations, and severe PTSD.

Your mental health matters.

For those of you who wish to go in blind, remember, this fantasy 'traumance' (trauma and romance) is a work of fiction, and I do NOT condone any situations or actions that take place between the characters. Continue to Chapter One.

If you do NOT want to go in blind, I do want to give you the opportunity to know what is coming. Please feel free to visit my social media or visit the link below for the chapter by chapter content guide.
https://claims.prolificworks.com/free/GBh5zzPG

YOU ARE NOT ALONE.
YOU ARE WORTH IT.

United States:

Domestic Abuse Helpline: 1-800-799-SAFE (7233)
Suicide Hopeline: 9-8-8 (Text or call)
Sexual Assault Helpline: 1-800-656-HOPE (4673)

Canada:

Domestic Abuse Resources per province:
https://www.canada.ca/en/public-health/services/health-promotion/stop-family-violence/services.html
Suicide Hopeline: 9-8-8 (Text or call)
Sexual Assault Helpline: 1-877-392-7583

United Kingdom:

Domestic Abuse Hotline: 0808-2000-247
Mental Health Support: 85258
Sexual Assault Helpline: 0808-500-2222

Australia:

Crisis Suicide Helpline: 13-11-14
Sexual Assault, Family & Domestic Violence Helpline: 1-800-737-732

Please Note:

These resources are to the author's best research capabilities.
For current and up-to-date websites and phone numbers, please visit
your country's government website.

AUTHOR'S NOTE

You are entering the darkened world of Elysian.
(Minor spoilers below)

I hope that you enjoy reading, the characters, the magic, the found familial bonds,
and especially the tense relationship between the Savage Prince and Alora.

Some may find the earlier actions of the Savage Prince to be menacing,
brutal, and morally gray. For those who love the villain more than prince
charming,
I'm excited for you to read the first words that make his victims beg for mercy.
But to some, his actions are dark, ruthless, sadistic, and unforgiving.

Garrik has a *dark* past.
Give him time to peel back his tormented layers and share his darkened world.

With this in mind ... "Is it spicy?"
Listen. I'm not a fade to black girl. (It's just not the genre style *for me*.
You do you! I'd never yuck anyone's yum.)
This is a slow burn. If you're looking for a book where they smash
their genitals together for an unemotional quickie, this is not it.
There is delicious sexual tension and detailed steamy scenes,
but due to major trauma, their 'release' isn't in book one.

Please consider being patient.
This book is heavy on trauma healing before the deed is done.
When I started writing their stories, thinking they would have their moment far
sooner, it became quickly evident that neither character was ready yet. I promise
you, if you follow their journey, if you fall in love with them, the way they both
do, you will be satisfied. Garrik is ... well ... it will be worth the wait when the
Savage Prince,
Lord of Darkness, gives his heart, and that incredible body, away.

Please take the trigger warnings seriously.
There are very dark themes. Some may not understand the actions and responses
of characters and find them odd, perhaps annoying, or incredibly frustrating.
Please, give them a chance to heal. Remember that everyone has a silent battle,
no matter how small. Mental health and trauma affect the mind and body
differently. These characters are no different. At times, you may hate someone
and not understand their reaction unless you have experienced trauma, too.
And for that, I am truly sorry.

So without further ado ...

WELCOME TO ELYSIAN.
WELCOME TO WHAT LIES WITHIN.

CHAPTER 1

What could be worse than Death?

It was simple, wasn't it?

She rubbed her chest as the answers to that tiny question gathered like storm clouds in her mind. The pulse of her racing heart mirrored the rolling beat of thunderous cloud cover.

Releasing the ground-rattling power of branches of lightning dancing in the distance—outside the southernmost walls—a terrible storm was dawning. And she wasn't sure which would be worse—the sky or the betrayal behind mahogany eyes waiting in the west.

Worse than death? *Nothing was worse than death.*

And she had spent her entire life hiding from it. She'd been lucky—if you could call the constant bruises and broken bones *lucky*.

Not so lucky were the two decaying carcasses that were once breathing, worthless heaps of males, now stenching up the alley. Although no one in this part of Telldaira cared. Just another deal gone wrong. A fight over something as simple as a slice of bread. A mistress who had caught her husband with another female. Someone who needed to be disposed of.

It didn't matter.

She bit back the nausea rising in her throat. No stranger to corpses, the putrid stench of rotting decay was still never easy to inhale no matter how long they had lain there. And these two smelled like a sea of rodents that had boiled in the sun for a week and looked like they were tossed in a stale swamp before being dumped in a city's worth of defecation.

Blinking back the burning tears filling her eyes, she covered her mouth with her cloak. Looking past the bodies out onto the street.

It wouldn't smell much better out there.

Faeries didn't come to these markets for reputable reasons. In fact, there was really *no* good reason to be there at all, unless they were actively seeking something dark and depraved. And the Telldairan guard long since gave up on policing them. It was an easy way to rid the city of the untouchables. The unwanted. The screw-ups and lesser-thans. The ones who sucked society dry and mucked up the city's pristine streets that were too perfect for the underclass degenerates to tread on. It offered the perfect solution to ensure they never did.

So why in Firekeeper-filled-hell was she—a lord's betrothed—there?

Perhaps it was because no matter what gaudy fabrics of silk and lace she wore or how often they schooled her sharp tongue to please nobility, she still belonged there. The only place she knew to turn to. Outcastle Alley accepted anyone. Death didn't discriminate.

In the end, no matter who you were, everyone ended up either buried in Elysian dirt or their ashes spread across it all the same. She would be no different.

Every time she found herself standing in that very spot, the experience was always the same.

Her breathing grew shallow. Heart filled with a deep ache as her hands gripped the dark cloak around her long, wavy white hair and kept the wind from biting her quaking shoulders. And then her boots would beg to remain motionless. Or perhaps that was the comforting darkness choking around her every step, inviting her to turn back. Each time knowing how incredibly foolish it was to be there.

The cover of the alley offered safety. Then again, how safe could an alley with two dead bodies be?

What was behind her was safer.

She almost laughed at that thought, rolling her eyes at the irony and pulling her cloak tighter.

Safe. Would there ever be anywhere truly *safe?*

2

When she was young, she'd often hear whispers of a ruthless king whose claws were etched into the entire realm of Elysian. Bloodthirsty. Power-hungry. Merciless beyond all measure. Those rumors were a bedtime story, a tale spun by older younglings to scare siblings. A threat given by parents to force compliance. But for others ...

They were real.

A testament to their past. A folk tale passed through the generations. Or a scar left on the bloodline.

She'd never believed them.

Not until it was her bloodline.

Not until she was left with a gaping wound. Bruised and bleeding, unending agony coursing through her veins like that surrendered by the rip of a blade through flesh and bone. The vibrations tearing through her body long after it relinquished the last drop of misery. And when the pain subsided, the only comfort left resided in darkness.

Until that darkness surrendered to something anew, shattering the world beneath her feet. Only then did she realize that what once was would never be again.

That was long ago. Too long ago.

And this was now.

Feet shifting, she looked out onto the street again.

No point dwelling on a life lost to the past, she thought while lifting her black riding boots over the dead bodies, stiff and rotting in their filth. They looked young. *What a shame.* Younglings didn't live long in Telldaira. She should know. She was one of the lucky ones.

Another crack of thunder rattled the decrepit, red-bricked buildings around her, flaking off pieces of the brick to fall to the stones below. This place was a shit-hole. No wonder the markets were held there.

The amethyst glow of lightning flashed across the damp street ahead. She stepped out of the whorling darkness and raked her sapphire eyes over the vendors. Not much had changed since the last time she'd visited. A few condemned market stalls had been ransacked, leaving broken wood from tables, shattered goods, and the ripped fabric of canopies to prove someone had once held business there. The owners were now long gone. Perhaps dead in another alley for all she knew.

At first, this started as a rebellion. A means of escaping her brutal reality, if only for a few hours. Now a means for salvation, it was still a generous risk to be missing so early. An even bigger risk venturing to the forbidden markets.

But the danger didn't matter. She didn't need flames to suffer the anguish of burning, and this seemed to be her last choice. No one was coming to rescue her. No one ever came to her aid. She'd do it herself—had been doing it herself for her entire life. Why would that change now?

Some would call her foolish, but even so, her black boots stalked further down the street, lined wall-to-canvas-wall with booths. Inside the echoes of desperation and poverty, crowded by a considerable stench of thick decaying meats, and mildew, mixed with the aroma of souring unwashed bodies and coital agreements.

Bile burned in her throat with every passing step.

Today, she needed to be there. Her escapes were no longer about choice but survival—a necessity. Nothing would stop her as she mercilessly trained her eyes on the stones of the street beneath her moving feet. Not even the unwavering feeling of a dark presence stalking her could make her turn around and leave. It was best to bind her eyes elsewhere for now. Turning back only offered more of the same.

Glimpsing inside stalls that she hadn't intended as her destination could result in something far worse than the desperation that brought her there. To that specific stall. Risking everything for ...

Was it even worth it?

Again. It didn't matter.

Only ten more steps. You can do this. Get in. Strike a deal. Get out.

Knocking into her shoulder, someone hissed to her left.

They tempted a look, but only a returning hiss released between her gritted teeth as she continued moving.

Don't show any fear. They would use it against her.

Weaving around the dingy garb, the conniving eyes and brazen grins of faeries congregating on this incoming stormy morning found her. The eeriness brought a chilling sense that someone was following behind her again.

Darkness—a shadow—had stalked her since the alley. She could feel it. Whoever it was.

She dared not turn. *Here, you do not stop. Not for anything. Not for anyone.*

So, she didn't.

Through the smoke and fog-covered stones beneath her boots, the familiar black and red canopy erected ominously in her side-view. Its viridescent hissing cobra emblem should have been warning enough to turn away, but like the shadows pulling at her boots and stalking behind her, nothing could deter her.

Go back, starsdamnit, her mind coldly growled. Sending her skin pebbling under the warmth of her dark cloak.

She ignored it.

Movement inside the dismal stall gripped her already thundering heart in a panic. Shifting toward the back that split into rooms made of canvas. The creature most likely lived there.

She stood outside, a mere footstep from crossing the threshold, refusing to pass any further. Any closer.

Damning, crimson serpent eyes within the Cimmerian stall cascaded through the darkness until sickly green scales caught the dreary light of morning, and rotten razor-sharp teeth peaked through a wicked grin.

"I didn't expect to see you back so soon, girl," the words slithered from it like venom constricting inside veins.

Her shoulder found a wooden post and dug into it with the weight of her body, crossing her arms with a matching grin to conceal her molten nerves. An illusion—a familiarity she could settle into. "Seems you've underestimated me."

"You brought it?" The creature hissed, weaving its serpentine tail around the dirt until it met the table.

With a sharp flick of her wrist, an old brown leather satchel dropped on the wood. She arched a brow, cocking her head with a wry grin.

Being an orphaned faeling had taught her many skills. The art of acquiring items that didn't belong to her was one—and nobility were none the wiser at certain social events. No one watched for a lord's betrothed; no one expected her to steal away into their pockets and relieve them of such obnoxious possessions.

She glanced at the counter. This one was almost insulting for how easy it was to thieve.

"The item, as discussed," she dryly stated, as if she couldn't care at all. "Now, give me what I bargained for or I'll find another who has use for it." White hair fell loosely from her hood in waves as she took a measured step forward, gripping her palm around the bag. Demanding sapphire eyes locked onto the green faerie's claws that tapped one by one on the table.

Its eyes narrowed. "The fiancée of Kaine Dralkin, returning to make a deal? Tell me, does he know where his"—pausing and raking over the curves of her figure, those crimson eyes flashed from her black boots all the way to the cloak's hood—"*property* is today?"

Glass shattered to her left, jerking her shoulder from the post, and she stiffened.

Three High Fae males with rippling muscles toweled by the cover of dark cloaks stood over a vendor. Likely hitmen. One forced and buried his knee into the vendor's chest while silent chokes for air heaved from his lips. Gripping his throat with a raised fist while the others snickered.

Jasmine eyes raked over to her, and she quickly withdrew her gaze. She needed to get out of there. The clock was already ticking, along with the raindrops beginning to spit. And now she was in the midst of witnessing a possible deal gone wrong. She needed to leave before they had finished and quite possibly followed her out.

And if the High Fae males were not enough to send her nerves into an overwhelming panic, *his* name was.

Lord Kaine Dralkin.

If any name could freeze over Firekeeper's realm, that was it. It sent roaring rage tearing through her bones and a deep shudder across her skin. Instead of allowing him another moment of control over her body, she gritted back the warmth building in her palms and leaned forward with a snarl. "Stop *wasting* my time. Either take it or I'll find someone else."

A wicked laugh echoed inside the canvas walls. Obviously amused at the nerve struck. Widening its smile, a taunting tone slithered from serpent lips. "My, my. How demanding... Very well. Ten coins, if it's truly as you say it is."

Just as expected. The incredulous snake was known for its shady deals and had offered an insulting proposition. Nobody honorable dealt business there. That wouldn't prevent her from obtaining what she was promised. "It's worth double that and you know it."

"Yes, but seeing as you're so deliciously desperate, that is my price. Take it or leave it. It makes little difference to me." A green barbed tail swayed in front of the creature, its razor-sharp tip constricting around the satchel in her hand.

As she ripped the satchel away from it, she almost stumbled backward onto the street and noticed it beginning to darken with raindrops.

"Do you know what I had to risk to get this?" A foolish question. This faerie wouldn't care. "Twenty coins. I'll take no less." She pinched her eyebrows, curling her lip to show gritted teeth. Taking less could not be a possibility. This was her last chance. If the deal fell through, there would be no hope—no escape.

Take the deal. Take the damn deal.

Walk away, now, her mind coldly growled. Laced with a gentle tingle, it caressed the endless walls of her mind like smoke dancing across the night sky.

"Fifteen." Rain hammered against the roof.

"Twenty." Thunder shook the stones beneath her feet.

"Seventeen—"

"Twenty-five"—a cunning grin—"and that blade. For wasting my time." She gestured with a nod at the wall behind, flooded with various odds and ends that she didn't care to know about. A black-bladed dagger hung. There was really no reason for it, but it amused her to see just how far she could push.

The faerie roared with laughter. "You have a spine on you, girl." Claws tapped the table as crimson eyes speared her sapphires. "Very well." It snatched the satchel from her hands before throwing a purse on the table. Then its barbed tail slid the dagger forward, coming to a stop before the table's disintegrating edge.

She snatched what was owed to her so quickly her nails etched grooves into the wood. Shoving the dagger into her riding boot, the purse was shoved deep into the pockets of the leather pants next; she only wore such an *unbefitting* item on outings such as this.

Without another word, her feet pivoted back to the busy stones of the rain-covered street and began to hustle away—

"One last thing," the faerie hissed.

But she didn't turn back. Rain pelted her hood as she growled low. "The deal ... is *done*."

"Is it?" A devilish laugh escaped its lips. "If you wish to walk out of here unannounced, as if you were never here at all, a future debt will be required. Whenever I call, wherever I will it, you will return here until what I deem is done. Swear it. Or your betrothed will learn of your activities."

She glanced at the High Fae males ripping apart the stall down the street, avoiding the jasmine eyes of the one who simply stood and watched. "The deal is done." Something like sparks lit in her eyes when she whipped her head over her shoulder, the movement catching the wind to disturb her white locks peeking out.

The serpent snickered. "I can sense your desperation, girl. I'm sure if Lord Kaine learned as to why you're in the forbidden markets, he'd have you marked and thrown to the wolves. Or have you hauled off to the High King. Tell me, does he know that you're a—"

"*Deal*. It's a deal." A strong smell of smoke crossed her path as the green faerie grinned in delight. The shadows in the stall grew darker. And her blood threatened to empty.

"Smart girl." It swayed its tail over the wooden table and rubbed against her upper left arm concealed under the cloak. "Best keep this hidden. Wouldn't want you dying before you can complete what's owed to me."

"Finish the deal, snake," she hissed, batting the tail away. She knew the reputation of the green faerie, yet she'd still come there.

Deals were more than an exchange of words, rather unspoken promises and underlying statutes hidden between breaths. She knew of how this creature acquired things no one had ever voiced; she'd thought the High King's army stories were just that—over-embellished recollections. This faerie was everything those fables spoke about, though.

And now ... it knew her secret.

Her hand reluctantly extended to the creature's tail, body growing taut when someone brushed too close behind her as they passed, leaving the strong stale stench of whiskey against her cloak. Which was utterly *perfect*. Because Kaine didn't drink whiskey or allow her the privilege, but he would smell it. And she would certainly suffer for it.

But there was no choice. It was either make a deal with this devil or forever remain with the monster she knew so well.

She clasped her hand around the razor-sharp edge and trembled. Before she could release her hold, the faerie wrenched itself from her grip, leaving a stinging, dripping wound in its wake.

The deal was done.

"Whenever I need you, *Alora*, you will bleed again. Watch for my call. Hold on to my knife for me. I may want it back one day." The serpent turned into its darkened stall. "Now run along, little lion cub."

Her name in the creature's mouth sent a chill down her stiff spine. The wound on her palm uncomfortably tingled as it surprisingly closed itself back up before her eyes. Her High Fae blood wouldn't seal a wound that fast. It had to be ... magic.

What did I agree to? The thought burned bile in her throat.

Get out of there.

The voice was right. She'd think about this later.

Thunder became her footsteps' companion of concealment. The rain was ruthless, pouring down like a vicious waterfall, an utter downpour that allowed her to escape undetected. She had never been more thankful for a storm. Usually, poor weather served only as a punishment, locking her inside with *him*, but today Maker of the Skies seemed to be her ally.

The streets had cleared too, leaving her boots a quick and clear path of escape. Alora rushed over puddle-soaked stones back toward the awaiting entrance of the alley. Back to the dead bodies now being washed clean of their stench until the blistering sun would scorch their putrid odor once again.

The dark shadows wrapped around her gaunt figure the moment she leapt over them and sprinted inside.

Alora inhaled a shaken breath; relief bubbled inside from the hidden refuge in the shadows. Her secret getaway, an unseen escape back to her side of the city. The darkness covered her as she knelt down under an awning, emptying the contents of the purse into her hand.

Twenty-five coins.

Twenty. Five. Coins.

It seemed impossible.

Utterly speechless as she sucked in a shallow breath, she allowed herself to feel the hope sitting in the palm of her hand. The deal was a success.

Alora pressed against the wall, drawing the other gamble from her boot. She clenched the onyx leather in her hand. By the mercy of lightning billowing across the sky, a crystal gemstone on the hilt reflected the flashing amethyst glow as she stood to inspect it. She had no specific reason to ask for it. It could prove useful for her personal safety—at best. Nothing more than a silly little knife.

But something like a coiled tether called to her when she glimpsed it. She could have happily walked away without it.

Perhaps she should have.

Alora twisted it between her fingertips, examining the exquisite craftsmanship. It was something magnificent, certainly. The shining night-dark blade wasn't straight as expected but had a serrated wave like a winding river instead. No more than maybe nine inches in length from hilt to sharpened tip. Whorls of matte-embossed smoke-like tendrils accented the obsidian blade until it settled at the spiraling black leather handle.

Her thumb traced the single, opalescent, star-shaped crystal jewel that rested perfectly near the top of the hilt, encased in the leather. Dragging the pad across the raised ridges of the stone and down until it dipped into two empty settings below, her eyes followed as she traced it.

Of course...

Typical snake. It gave me a damaged knife. Alora exhaled a vexed sigh.

Still, the slithering hiss of the green faerie echoed in her mind. *'Hold on to my knife for me. I may want it back one day.'*

Alora scoffed, wrinkling her rosy porcelain face. If the green faerie thought it could cast another veil over her life, it was highly mistaken. She had lived her entire life in the shadows. They didn't scare her anymore.

No more deals.

No more broken promises.

No more painful days or endless nights.

It all ends—and *soon*.

Free. She would finally be free. And no one from Telldaira could stop her.

Alora shoved the dagger back into her boot and rose. *I'll do what I damn please.*

CHAPTER 2

Running away wasn't nearly as easy as they say. It sounded simple enough. Breathe through the fear; walk through the fire. Get burned along the way. Then, once through the flames, turn back and watch everything fall to ashes.

Everyone said it. Then again, not everyone had to live like she did.

Not everyone had their legs quaking, blood draining from their face with every step on the soaked stones of the street. Not everyone struggled to determine the roaring of thunder from their own thoughts because their own personal Firekeeper-filled-hell lay ahead.

Claws waited to rip her apart.

Alora's nails dug into the purse inside her cloak for fear it wasn't real. She loosened a calm breath when the cold metal kissed her fingertips.

Twenty-five coins.

It was real.

For years, she'd fantasized about running away—escaping—a new, peaceful life. Never more than hopeless thoughts and useless wishes.

Dreams to brighten her never-ending nightmare. She survived, had a decent life, and was accommodated with life's necessities. Bruises had meant nothing for a while. Kaine promised he'd stop, and she even believed him for longer than she should have. At least she was alive. Didn't need to suffer through hunger anymore, or the humiliation of tattered and torn clothing. She was a *lady* for-stars-sake.

Many would envy her. Say that the stars had blessed her with her life. But no one saw what was behind the closed manor doors. No one heard the shouts. No one felt the tremble in her body when he came near. Saw the fear in her eyes when his palm would lift to caress her cheek in public but wound it in private, illusioning himself as the perfect lord.

That was not a blessing.

That was not living.

The stars would never gift such torment.

Warmth bit inside her shaking fist like a star ready to burst as she quickened her steps.

Good. Get angry. Let the anger drive you.

The voice was right, like usual. She was angry but also wholly terrified. A constant balance these days. But in only a few days, her suffering would be ashes in the wind.

A chilling northern breeze whipped her face, spraying beads of water that had collected on rooftops over the wool of her cloak.

She'd taken the alleys from the south. A labyrinth of routes that only those who grew up on the streets knew about. Coined as the 'underground', it stretched from the southern walls until it reached the smuggler caves of the northern cliffs, an easily accessible maze to bypass the guardsmen who stalked the streets. Keeping gutter rats like her out of the most extensive and illusive parts of Telldaira. She knew the way like she knew her own heartbeat. Only one more alley would leave her jumping down into a tunnel, and a short incline at the end would welcome her into a lush garden in the west. The *privileged* section of the city. Home to nobility—and the rich.

Alora hesitated.

Just as she was about to cross into another alley of back-to-back run-down structures, on the main street, the shrieks of an elder male echoed off the buildings. His desperation tore a deep gash in her heart.

Gripping the condemned wooden building under her palm, splinters threatened to spike her skin as she strained to hear. Though he was shouting, he was still far away. Likely down the street a ways from the echoes. But his cries were earth-shattering all the same.

So, Alora stepped forward, down the alley, letting the peaking sun through the drifting storm clouds warm her face.

The main street housed businesses for the lower class. Unlike the shops in the north and west, these storefronts were mostly the same. Earth tones, dusty brick, or rotting wood held together by poor patch jobs and prayers. Little shrubbery or pots of flowers to brighten any frowns due to empty pockets and ruthless hunger. Most couldn't afford their businesses, let alone decorations.

That all changed the moment the inner southern gates met the rest of the city.

Telldaira had all but given up on the south, and the guarded gates let the faeries who could only afford to live there know it. No one could pass through unless given special passes. No exceptions. No pity. She held one of them but had never needed it, thanks to the underground.

Careful to keep her hair hidden in her hood, Alora poked her head around the corner, raking her eyes over the main street.

Nearly ten yards over, stumbling into a crowd outside a tavern whose night lanterns were still burning on the rusted iron hook, a silver-haired male with broken and shredded membranous wings desperately clawed at a female. Her sun-bright hair waving down her back caught in his grip as he shrieked in her face with terror and tears streaming down his own.

Alora could hear him then. His desperate pleas for someone— *anyone*—to listen to him.

Every face in the crowd turned from him. Dismissed him like breath on the wind.

But even when he landed on his knees, still, he pushed himself up and found the next. Crawling closer and closer to her.

Likely a drunken fool.

His choked voice rippled to her ears, never cracking the desperation. "Please! They're coming. *They'll kill us all.*"

Her ears perked.

"The gray-haired demon of Elysian rides to our border!" he beseeched.

Not this again, Alora thought as she heavily sighed. *The gray-haired demon of Elysian.*

More stories. Myths spread through the kingdoms and spun in the markets from weary travelers of their crossings with the fabled force. No one there believed them. The High King's army hadn't been in Telldaira for nearly twenty years. And Kaine was meticulous with his guardsmen; they scrutinized every single faerie who crossed the gates. Allowing no one with a magical mark on their left upper arm—no Marked Ones—

13

through the walls. No one was foolish enough to try. The fear of being imprisoned and carted off to Castle Galdheir prevented anyone from attempting it.

Unless they were a Marked One born inside the walls.

Like her. Like—

Wrinkled palms gripped her shoulders. "Please ... *please*! I watched from the ashen earth as my mother, my sister, was burned in our home so long ago. The demon stood in the shadows of the rubble, his eyes of death watching everything I loved turn to dust. And he's coming! *He's coming!*" The elder's face twisted in grief when she opened her mouth to speak, but his wails interrupted her. "The High King's army stomped over their corpses, leaving our smoldering town behind. There were no survivors. Please, you have to listen to me!"

The male released her, and she watched as he stumbled up the street, repeating his story to the next.

No one believed him. Not even her.

The gray-haired, smoke and shadow-covered, faceless demon, who single-handedly leveled cities and feasted on faelings alive?

They were all spineless stories. Myth. Nothing more, surely ... right?

"Before this night is over"—the male swatted away another male's hands as the heavy rumble of footsteps drew closer—"you will see! You'll all see. Get out before it's too late!"

The sound of boots on wet stone drowned out his voice.

Telldairan guards were coming. She needed to leave. Being the only white-haired in the city, everyone knew who she was. Who she belonged to. Whose property she was.

Alora clasped the cloak around her body tighter. *Just another story.* And turned back into the alley.

By the time she made it back to the manor, the servants were out tending to the landscape. Which made her return more treacherous. Many loved her, but Kaine still paid them. They were his. And no one wanted to risk losing their wages or status to keep their lips sealed.

She couldn't blame them. Working for Kaine was a luxury of its own. The fae-made forest, where she stood and carefully concealed her dagger, offered a view that was so captivating that it could easily leave anyone in a state of wonder.

The manor itself perched on a small incline in the western part of

Telldaira. White-painted iron gates lined a marble-chipped walkway. Sparkling and glistening in the morning sun. At its end, six pillars of marble connected an obscene balcony above a long, welcoming ramada of the fifteen windowed front. Kaine had it fit for a king's entrance, made to welcome his multitudes of guests for outside celebrations.

Below it, extending across the estate, twisted trees with green leaves and lavish shrubbery beautifully landscaped the view from the secluded street far below. The next nearest manor was no less than five hundred yards away in every direction.

In the front, the ten-foot-tall windows sat built into the three-story monstrosity. Curtains of the finest fabrics hung behind the glass, making the inside appear dim in the bright morning light.

It was indeed a statement of luxury, wealth, and high status. Fit for any nobleman. Its beauty was the envy of the city. A place everyone wanted to own. A place that was said to hold the brightest of memories, beautiful dinner parties, integrous business deals, uncontrollable laughter, passionate love, and hope for the future.

It was none of those things.

Not a starsdamned one.

Alora held back the nausea as her black boots stained the marble beneath her feet with thick mud. She had spotted golden hair beaming under shards of sunlight. *Taryn,* one of Kaine's most trusted female servants, was working the grounds. The one she often caught leaving the second floor of the manor with a smirk and a blush warming her cheeks.

Taryn could clean the mud, she decided. Otherwise, Alora would have happily slipped through the shrubbery to prevent more work for those she cared for. And as long as she could slip unseen, no one would know who the muddy footprints belonged to. She could be revengeful without being reckless.

Kaine's proclivities the night prior would render him a long, restful morning until a stabbing headache wakes him. Allowing her time to breeze through the front door, make her way up to his bedchamber on the second floor, and undress to lie naked, as he commanded, before softly settling under the silken sheets beside him.

Every nerve in her body fired on edge as the monstrous green front door slid open easily. She had taken time to use pearlsea oil, a glimmering white flower only found in Zyllyryon, on the hinges days prior to avoid any unwanted creeks alerting Kaine's servants.

Her boots crossed the threshold of their—

She scoffed.

—*Kaine's* ridiculously elaborate manor.

Kaine was rich ... *filthy* rich. He owned two-thirds of the businesses, lodgings, and infirmaries in Telldaira. Name it, he undoubtedly owned it. Kaine's newest conquest: a wealthy clothing corporation located in the northern part of the city, exclusively for the nobility and royalty of Zyllyryon. Even the High King was known to wear the fineries sourced there.

Most lords govern their cities, keeping the title within the family. Kaine just so happened to be at the top of the lineage when the last lord mysteriously died. He wasn't born to hold Telldaira in his palm, but High King Magnelis was strategic with whom he appointed to run his slums—nothing compared to Castle Galdheir, of course. And like must call to like because Magnelis's malevolent heart had appointed one just as evil.

From then on, Kaine was as close to a king as any in all the kingdoms could be. The head of the local garrisons bent to his every word. He never paid for anything—never needed for anything. Remaining on his docile side meant future wealth for you ... if he tolerated your lavishing, praise, and fealty. Everyone knew him, wanted him to know them, or wanted to trade with him. Faeries of all kinds wanted to be with him, though he was already betrothed to her.

Like that mattered, though. Kaine's fantasies were always satisfied, no matter which female he got pleasure from.

Disgustingly enough, she was the *lucky* one to be in his bed.

Or so everyone said.

If they only knew ...

Alora stalked through the open foyer, as big as an elegant ballroom, large emerald vases of ivory delphinium, creamy dahlias, painted ferns, and a hint of lush greenery adorned it. Paintings of her betrothed lined the walls to greet the eyes of those fortunate enough to be invited in. After spending so much time there, she hardly noticed them anymore.

The wooden floors were lined with ornate emerald rugs splashed with golden threads on the edges. She had loved the color once, green, like the eyes of her father, who had now become a faded memory. Not anymore. Not with the belongings Kaine crowded his home with.

It all made their guests gawk in awe.

It made her want to vomit.

Alora latched the door behind her and made sure to scuff the mud off her boots in front of one of the paintings—*Taryn could clean that, too* —greeting the painting with a middle finger before steadily moving her feet toward a grand staircase twenty feet before her.

Three hallways sat at its top before spreading both directions into two mezzanines, each lined with closed oak doors, green cushioned benches, and various paintings that surrounded the foyer in a railed square. Two open-door frames sat on the ground floor, flanking the staircase, leading out into a lush garden courtyard. Beyond the courtyard, a wall of doors sat. Each contained a small room for servants to live in.

Her eyes caught the flickering glow of candlelight from the middle of the three at the top, lighting the hallway to the end where her—Kaine's—bedchamber awaited. She toed the heel of her boot, slipping it off, then the other, and placing them beside the staircase where she knew one of the housemaids would tuck them away.

Heat flushed her face. It was always too hot there. She was always too hot. Nothing in the manor could cool her. No windows were allowed open, fires constantly roared in the hearths. Kaine didn't care or try to make her comfortable. Not anymore. The fire that lay dormant inside her fanned a permanent trace of embers across her skin.

And the sight before her didn't help with that.

The staircase. She hated the staircase.

Hated every irritatingly beautiful piece of redwood board, every deep curve in the shining smooth handrail, each over-decorative spindle connecting the white marbled steps to her tightened grip. She hated that it held so many painful, bloody secrets. Each guest that ascended the abomination would never know the dark secrets it shared with her and everyone in his house.

Prison.

How many times would she stand frozen to the emerald rugs below the first marbled step? How many times would her knees quiver and fingertips ache as she pushed herself up one by one, as she did right then? Each memory fought to win the battle of her nerves with every step of her feet. Taunting her. Laughing at her. Pulling at her heart until she would reach the top. And once there, her vision would blur and her heart would thunder. She would run to the hallway threshold, gripping the wood until it threatened to splinter, just to stay upright before looking back to prove to herself that she made it to the top without being thrown back down it.

You're at the top. You're safe. The lies she repeated to herself just so she could steal a heaving breath. So she could calm her nerves from the panic because lighting her prison on fire would bring even worse repercussions.

Her thin, aching, pale fingertips lightly brushed new imperfections and dents in the wall atop the grand staircase as sapphire eyes raked down the dim hallway in the middle. Walking on the balls of her feet to avoid the cracking of floorboards, she passed two more walled staircases on either side leading to the third level of the manor that housed Kaine's study and business rooms.

Everything was quiet. Almost peaceful—almost.

The crystal sconces and jeweled chandeliers of glowing candles lined her path, giving off an ominous smoke aroma as she descended it.

Oftentimes, she'd wonder if the smoke and shadows were a warning. 'Don't go in there. You know what waits for you,' it'd indicate. But that was foolish thinking. What could smoke and shadows do? Nothing. Then her feet would simply keep moving.

The same emerald rugs guided her steps past six more doors. And at the end, one short left turn gave way to her darkened bedchamber. Where her *betrothed* would be sleeping.

The shadows outside the door danced a little darker that morning as she listened for his heavy breathing.

Only a few more steps.

She paused, toes digging into the floor, and her eyes drifted left to a different darkened room. No longer did light fill the once calming space, though it held a tall window facing the north. Long since boarded up, the white curtains torn from the wall. Peaceful—heart-wrenching—cold memories of the stunning views it once yielded haunted her with every passing second. A simple redwood chair with parchment and a pen resting atop it and a shelf blessed with books under its daily sunlit glow sent her heart a pained ache.

She quickly tore her eyes away before the tears burned.

Focus. You can do this. Closing her eyes, Alora inhaled deeply and gripped her cloak.

At last, her feet silently rested at the threshold, her sleeping betrothed unknowingly waited beyond. The waves of her white locks fell around her shoulders as her body pivoted into the entryway of her bedchamber—and slammed face-first into a bare broad chest.

Then blistering-hot hands clamped around her tense shoulder and neck.

Fingers sought purchase against her flesh like they molded clay.

His voice came next, a tone of damning torture. "Where in Firekeeper-filled-hell have you been?"

Panic thrashed down her body. Too frightened to speak.

Kaine's grip tightened around her as she tried to pull back from his reach. He towered over her even as she stood upright. The build of a man who could kill with his bare hands. His mahogany eyes were filled with a villainous rage trapped behind jaw-length ebony hair. Everything about him commanded great authority.

A beautiful face and a decent physique clothed in expensive finery. But a true demon lay within.

"You've been out with *him* again, haven't you?" Kaine forced her into the hallway, pushing her into the open doorway of the dining room across from his bedchamber. His powerful grip held firm as his corded arms slammed her onto a long redwood table inside. The flaming candles rattled; smoke whirled from the lit wicks as they balanced and steadied.

Flat on her back, Alora's hands clamped around his wrist. Digging into his tanned skin with no hope of releasing his clasp as terror-filled eyes flooded and smoke from the candles burned her nose. "No, I wasn't. Kaine, please—" *Please.*

"When I wake in the morning, the first sight I should see is my fucking wife naked, by my side, to tend to my needs." Spit pebbled across her face. "Not an empty bed," Kaine seethed.

Wife.

The title he used to assert ownership of her. They hadn't had the ceremony yet, but by all technicalities, it wasn't required. By Elysian law, being a betrothed was as good as married. But she'd never call him her husband. She'd make sure of that.

Kaine released his grip around Alora's throat, only to reposition himself on her arms. Pinning them beside her head, he lowered his rippling form up onto the table, forcing himself against her squirming body.

She had been there many times before. Years of this *generous* attention. His expectations, her 'disobedience.' Her body was a canvas. And his hands held the tools to paint what his eyes craved. Rich tones of violet and deep navy, dark hues of emerald and chestnut that slowly faded away. Fresh ebony and ash strokes painted under her clothing.

This was normal.

Kaine lifted a hand, his palm positioned to collide with her face. The movement caused enough wind that the candles, filling the space around them with a steady stream of smoke, flickered out. She hoped the heavy scent would cover up her own.

The wick's heavy smoke connected to the other lit candle beside it and, with one dance of its flame, ignited along the path.

The flame traveled through the smoke's whirl, circling Kaine's lifted hand before the flame scorched his perfectly smooth skin.

He flinched away with a shriek, violently shaking his hand.

Alora threw every ounce of fear and resentment into her legs. Jerking her knees up and jabbed hard into his gut, forcing him to release his hold and slide off the table in an enraged growl.

"You *promised* you wouldn't do this again!" Alora slowly backed toward the door of the dining room with liquid flooding her lower lashes. Her hands hovered in front of her. A useless barrier that would protect her like a piece of tissue would. Pointless.

A clash pierced her ears. Glass shards peppered her face and the white of her rib-length hair. The remnants of Kaine's decanter littered the floor and cracked beneath her retreating feet.

"Get the hell back here or I promise what comes next will be much worse." His nostrils flared as one hand gripped his gut.

Run. Get out of there.

A chair soared across the room. Shattering a silver-leafed, floor-to-ceiling mirror.

"*Now!*" Kaine's anger rattled the candles as much as her bones.

"Okay," she breathed, "just please—*please* ... don't." Knees buckling, Alora hesitantly maneuvered forward to the table where Kaine stood, avoiding the glass shards under her feet before carefully pulling the cloak from her shoulders, pooling it on the emerald rug. The floor that held countless brutal memories. The wooden floorboards she'd grown accustomed to kissing, laying on, covering her face to block incoming blows. His favorite place to see her now collected the evidence of where she had been that morning.

Kaine paid no mind to her cloak. His darkened eyes tracked her every step, then he locked his palm around her wrist. Wrenching her into his body, twisting her wrist as he pushed her to her knees and caused her to shriek in agony.

"*Quiet,*" he barked. A brutal slap to her cheek accompanied his demand. "Give me one damn good reason why you left this morning without my permission." Twisting her wrist for emphasis.

"I—" Her arm twisted again. She screamed in pain. "Kaine, please. I'm sorry—I'm sorry! I couldn't sleep. I just needed to go for a walk. I didn't mean to upset you. *Please.*"

A deep rumble filled his chest, and he threw her arm back into her body before crouching down. That broad hand gripped under her chin, pulling her gaze to meet his glaring eyes.

"Make it up to me." Those darkened eyes turned predatory as his legs pushed his lithe figure upright. Kaine unbuttoned his dark verdant pants, stroking his hardened mediocre cock inches from her face. A bead of precum waited on the swelled head. "Show me what a good *wife* you can be."

What Kaine lacked in length was overcompensated in wrath and pain. There were few moments when he wouldn't harden as he beat her. This time was no different. And there was no doubt in her mind: if she didn't do what he demanded at that moment, her treatment would end soaked in more than just his release.

The bruises would be much worse because the beatings had escalated. The bruises were harder to hide; her shattered belongings resigned to burned piles scattered in his dumping plants throughout the city. Everything she loved, destroyed. Each hand he laid on her was one step closer to her death.

Not a fucking chance, the voice inside her mind whispered.

She raised her head.

Death would not come for her today.

"Prove to me that you're mine and mine only. Then I'll forget this ever happened." His hand brushed back a lock of her white hair behind her ear.

Alora hated that gesture but didn't resist as he gripped her throat and pulled her closer.

"Good girl."

She could have sworn she heard a low, vicious growl reverberating in the depths of her mind as she focused on thick smoke whirling above the table and around Kaine.

Then her mouth closed around him.

ALORA LAY in the comfort of darkness after what seemed like unending torture for his pleasure. The tousled dining room held little satisfaction for Kaine and went even less toward proof of her loyalty. She hadn't screamed in agony.

It was only after he had brutally dragged her from the floor and forced her into the sunless bedroom that he found what he was looking for. Her compliant screams that led to his release, high on the ecstasy of her pain.

He wouldn't leave her merely existing there. Bruised and incredibly exhausted as he pulled his pants on and finished dressing in that which a lord was expected to flaunt.

Oh, how easily he slipped on the face of perfection and grace as a sigh of deep pleasure and satisfaction escaped his repulsive lips, knowing that he once more forced what he desired from her and left her alone and broken to pick up her shattered pieces. When Kaine fucked her mouth, he was not any sort of gentle. The gurgled chokes brought him some pleasure—her throat sore from the beating it took.

Alora rolled away from his direction.

Without a word after, Kaine escaped through the dimmed doorway. Finally leaving her to fade into the harrowing cage of her own tormented thoughts.

'Tell me you're mine.'

'Say it again.'

'Scream it.'

'Whose are you?'

'Louder.'

His handsomely evil voice rang in her head like shackles upon her skin as she pulled her knees into the scorch of her bare chest. At least shackles left scars to see. Hers were ruthlessly hidden, concealing the pain inside her tattered mind. And because of her High Fae blood and their healing qualities, Kaine was sure to be just as *kind* to her body tomorrow. And the next day. And the next...

Bruises. They didn't heal as fast as a bleeding wound. And Kaine loved painting his canvas as much as she had once loved music.

There was a time she loved him. *Truly loved him.* His voice. The soft caresses down her spine with a feather-light touch. The kisses he once showered her with. How his hands lovingly proved how much she meant to him. A time when he'd carefully consider her needs and wants and every desire. A time where she'd do anything for him and with him. When she enjoyed spending these kinds of moments in his arms, feeling his body against her ... inside her.

Her hands tightened around her legs.

That ended so long ago.

Today's submission was a sacrifice for survival.

And even that would come to an end.

Soon.

She stared across the bedroom. At their disheveled emerald sheets that were much too warm for her skin, draped and pooled on the floor at the foot of his bed. Glared at the coarse ropes on the headboard. At his empty glasses of liquor atop the redwood side tables. Her heart in her throat at her ripped clothing sprawled across the rug-covered floor. She hadn't been wearing something Kaine had forced her to wear. *Of course he'd had to destroy it.* Another piece of her gone.

Alora pulled her palms to her upper arm and stroked her thumb over her death mark. In the darkness, she imagined it. Her death sentence gifted at her birth by Destiny alone. Magically inked dancing flames licked up her flesh as sparks exploded in bursts of black swirls and perfect beams like flares of starlight. The flawless depiction of her unused power. It lay there, as dormant as her magic. Utterly useless other than to be a beacon of her unwilling treason.

She would thank the stars for a lot of things, but never ... *this*.

Her vacant sapphires stared into the cooling darkness caressing her pale, bruised skin. She found comfort in it—the moving darkness—a place she could always hide. Sometimes she could even feel it's cold, refreshing touch against her burning skin. It brought the scent of warm vanilla and oak on a soft, winter wind, leather and metal in a spring meadow.

The smell of pure comfort.

Whenever she needed it, it was there. Even in her dreams, *after*, it met her there. Where others would find monsters, horror, Death, even evil in the darkness, she felt safe there in the shadows. Like they understood her pain. Like they listened. Knew what she needed.

Such beautiful shadows, she thought, dancing her fingers in the darkness and wishing she could feel it. Those beautiful shadows swirled around her until they carried her into a calm slumber.

KAINE SAT at the head of the long oak table when she slipped back inside the dining room's doorway, carrying breakfast on a silver tray. Every servant knew of his outbursts and how he liked to use his *wife* in degrading ways. It was expected of her to serve him—even in front of those considered lower in status.

What was left of the mirror had been removed. The broken chair gone, and likely being mended. No shattered shards of glass remained from his enraged display of power. Almost like it never happened.

A new crystalline decanter of scarlet liquid was perched in front of a substantial pile of paperwork. Kaine's pen feverishly scratched across the surface of one and a fresh glass strained within his agitated grip. Beside him lay a small, wrapped bundle of flowers.

Red roses.

It was always the damn red roses.

The color of blood. Her blood. The sight of them forced her right back to the moments of it spilling onto the hardwood floor. Dripping from her lips. His knuckles. Down that staircase.

Wrapped with a small tag that had her name scribbled on it, the petals were droplets of her blood collected, scraped from his wooden floors, and made pretty. A promise of 'never again.' *Or soon.*

Her lip curled at them.

She hated flowers.

Hated what they stood for. The lies and half-assed apologies that surrounded them. The sight of them made her palms warm with heat. She knew what would come next. It always did.

"You know how on edge I've been." *There it was, like always.* "You can't do things like that to set me off. You ... affect me deeply, Alora. That's why things like what happened this morning take place. You know I don't mean to, right?" He stretched his hand to her as she set the breakfast tray beside him. He, in turn, pushed the flowers toward her with a lazy nudge without peeling his eyes from his paperwork. "I have a damn city to care for. You can't do those things when I have so much to deal with. Understood?"

Her hand was suddenly back in his as he gripped it, rubbing the top with his calloused thumb. Almost like attempting to soothe with a kiss the stinging cheek he just slapped. It meant *nothing*.

"I understand..." *That I want to take my dagger from the forest and shove it into your worthless neck.* She forged a grin, looking into his unapologetic eyes that had lifted to the swell of her breasts. *How beautiful my black dagger would look protruding from his neck*, she silently hummed.

How starsdamned beautiful indeed.

CHAPTER 3

The downstairs foyer had burst with life. Servants had turned over the vases, arranging fresh flowers and greenery, swept the marbled floors, and traded out the rugs for new emerald and gold designs—as was their daily routine. Kaine cared little for the mundane. And his wealth far exceeded any limit preventing him from brandishing the manor with new furnishings every day.

Somehow, Alora stepped from the last level of the staircase without incident. Avoiding trampling her ridiculous skirts—that she had changed four times because of Kaine's disapproval—underneath her jeweled slippers, she measured her steps. To hesitate in front of a perfectly pristine display of revolting power and seamless grace would be an embarrassment to Kaine.

Kaine wore noble finery, free of blemishes and wrinkles, and exuded high privilege. His boots reflected the sunlight from the windows, so clean they could be licked without repulsion. A lord amongst the rabble. And she noted how he took great care to sweep his eyes to the staircase. Reflected in his visage: a vicious evaluation of what was his.

Alora.

Like a piece of furniture, she too was required to be an epitome of his tremendous status. Standing there in a dress that was too extensive for her to run and too expensive to be seen as anything but a trophy for his arm. Like a wilted flower that thirsted for a drop of water; his hand was the only one to provide a taste.

He stepped forward, still evaluating her when his eyes became critical of something. She didn't know what of but felt the vicious disappointment rolling off him.

Kaine lifted a hand, took another step through a tendril of smoke from a nearby candle, and tripped against the rug's edge.

She flinched. The movement was entirely outside of her free will. Yet his face pulled taut, and his jaw set as he reset himself and stiffened. If they were anywhere alone, that hand would've done more than stuff inside his pocket, looping his thumb to the outside before pacing to cover his stumble.

Maybe she enjoyed those hideous rugs after all.

"You won't go anywhere until I return. No visitors. Stay inside the manor. Do not leave," Kaine merely said, stopping her heart hammering against her chest.

Alora forced herself to meet his glare, eyes widened, but she shouldn't have been surprised.

The manor? Not even permitted to stroll the grounds or to enjoy a ride through his forests?

His instructions were painfully clear. *'Stay inside the manor.'*

There was no point in asking why. She already knew he wouldn't answer. And even if she did speak up, a backhanded sting would collide with her cheek or mouth, lingering for hours as a reminder of her insolent tongue. What property deserves the right to question its owner, after all?

Kaine didn't so much as glance back as he passed through the front door. Taking the time to side-eye a short, golden-haired servant, and flash her a primal male grin. Despite the audience, he slowly raked his eyes over her before his heavy footsteps padded down the marble-chipped stones and a male servant opened the door to Kaine's awaiting carriage. One of his many symbols of high class and nobility.

It clattered away with immaculate grace, leaving the grounds through the white-painted iron gates and shrubbery.

Taryn lingered a little too long for their connection to go unnoticed. Catching the astonished and envious glares and collecting whispers from the maidservants before her gaze met Alora's with brash inconsideration.

Only a few more days, then Taryn could have him.

Alora lifted the skirts of her silken emerald dress ornately crested with fine golden threads as hideous as the rugs she scuffed her jeweled slippers on, turning toward the open door of the courtyard and the servant quarters beyond.

She was caged. Shackled like a wild animal. For whatever Kaine's reason.

Only ... her shackles were as illusioned as the finery she wore. And Kaine would learn something very critical, very soon. Caging an animal only fueled its ambition to escape. And he left the doors unlocked, wide open, envisioning nothing but his cruel voice to seal her in.

Alora forced back the boiling blood in her veins and slipped through the courtyard door.

Stay inside the manor?

Do not leave?

Watch me.

THE DAWNWOOD BRANCHES HUNG LOW, caressed by the light winds that blew in from the north. Alora pulled up the collar of her navy tunic and stopped at a tree carved with a symbol that indicated mass remembrance. The beauty of Rhidian Forest would've been enthralling had it not been for its sobering reminder of the past. Even now, two hundred years later, the ground wept for the lives ended within its embrace. The cries of the meek and powerless seeking swift refuge within its solace were still echoed in every bristle of the leaves. Singing unnerving melodies of steel and bloodshed.

Crisp, cool wind tore at her, drawing her attention to the north, toward the smuggler's caves where she last laid eyes on her parents. Another similar series of carvings marked the stones there. A symbol by her own hand.

Alora laid her palm on it. The rigid indentations scratched against her skin when she traced the grooves with her fingertips.

The High King's army was to blame for this injustice. Those stories were true. She had lived through it. Had fled through those same trees after days hidden inside the caves after his armies came and laid waste to Telldaira so long ago, ruthlessly killing for the sake of two Marked Ones that he never found—or that's what the rumors said. And in his devastation, thousands suffered for it. Not just her.

No stranger to this oasis, the earthy forest scent, strong with moss and damp dirt on its floor, welcomed her. She closed her eyes, thanking the forest for its refuge, and weaved through the tree line.

A calming darkness danced around her feet, whispering around every branch and misting beyond the leaves. The sun's positioning suggested some time in the afternoon, carrying its own warmth in its rays, but this time of year, the wind blew with a bite against her body. A corset vest wrapped her body and flowed loosely in the back, down to her knees, but fell short in the front. The leather hugged over a long-sleeved navy tunic, almost too warm for her to bear, and cinched tight around her waist by a three-strapped leather belt.

Normally this form of rebellion was used for refining learned skills. Sword work. Bow and arrow accuracy. Hunting and tracking. Sometimes sleeping or foraging. Real and true rest could be found out there when she couldn't obtain it in the manor.

But today, she didn't seek sleep.

With the obsidian jeweled dagger nestled inside her boot, and a blade sheathed at her side, she climbed a steep wooded incline into the boundless forest beyond the meadow and Telldairan walls. A thick labyrinth of leaves snuffed out most of the sunlight, but she knew the route without its glistening aid. The darkness within weighed heavy against her shoulders, forcing pinpricks of aching nerves to fire inside her legs when she glimpsed her bruised wrist. Alora's breath caught at the sight. Her mind awakened, replaying moments of brutal hands of betrayal.

She could feel it brimming.

No, not now. Please, not now.

Her heart began to beat faster.

Not now, please!

And then, it wasn't trees surrounding her—it wasn't a forest at all.

Suffocating ivory walls faded into view.

Bloodstained rugs of emerald and gold, shattered glass peppered across hallways, dining rooms, and bedroom floors.

Broken handrails upon a grand staircase. Blood dripping down every redwood step. Cracked marble, shattered mirrors, punctured holes on wood-paneled walls a head width apart, shattered belongings. A boarded-up window.

The forest wasn't there at all anymore. Even the darkness couldn't persuade her to break the cage of her broken mind. Everything closed in. She couldn't feel the air around her. Couldn't breathe. Not fast enough. Her insides burned, pleading for comfort. Pleading to get out, to run, to escape, to—

Alora gasped. Unable to fill her lungs.

That hammering heartbeat thundered inside her aching, taut chest.

Without any recollection of her steps, she found herself feet from a ledge. Overlooking a deadly drop into the valley floor.

Burning fists balled tightly by her side. Her bruised wrist ached with the tension. Each phantom touch of Kaine's hand invaded her body as she gripped her fists tighter. Nails digging sharply into her palms as a strong heat flared through her face, radiating to her core, her center, to the sturdy feet beneath her.

Time seemed to slow to a series of imperceptible gasps.

Please don't do this. Not again.

Every starsdamn thing he had ever done to her constricted her veins. Every painful memory, every lie. Every thoughtless, half-assed apology that the scent of red roses clung to. Each earth-shattering blow against her. The broken bones and bruises. All the moments he had thrust her down the marble of the grand staircase, burned her with the dining room candles, or cut her with shards of glass. Every moment waking on the floor beneath his boots or in his bed.

Burning tears flooded down her rosy cheeks.

It was too hot. She was too hot. Always too hot.

Her throat constricted.

She'd had *enough*.

Enough.

Enough.

Enough.

White flames detonated...

She was on fire.

Nothing mattered, nothing at all. Her skin glowed with white flames that didn't burn her. Snowy hair radiated in a raging glow. Sapphires turned to embered eyes, and fire singed through every vein.

Then glimmering sparks burst inside the flames around her.

Alora unfurled her numb fists by her side and released an unbearable scream.

She was not the darkness she endured. She was the fire. The whole starsdamned roaring inferno. A deathly explosion of destruction.

Body buckling beneath the wounds deep in her heart and the scars covering her mind, her knees slammed into the ground. It happened with such force that the dirt scattered and sprayed out around her. She fisted her aching fingertips into her hair, pulling tightly.

And screamed, again. Releasing another powerful eruption.

Higher, higher, higher.

Further and further.

She wailed until her lungs turned to ash.

Someone cried out to her, deep in the depths of her mind.

Another voice echoed from the forest behind, but it was nothing more than a whisper. "Alora, stop. You can't do this. *Someone could see!*" The voice grew closer.

Alora's back buckled as the seemingly unstoppable tears ruthlessly plummeted down her face. She slammed her fists to the earth, sparks exploding inside the flames. Heavy sobs choked the air from her throat. Each gasp of air harder and harder to collect as her vision dotted and blurred.

Barely feeling anything, satin hands cupped her stinging cheeks, the flames scorching perfect aristocratic skin. And that usually silvery voice shrieked in agony the longer they held there, *"Alora, please!"* The tone as brutal as the heat around them.

Even if she wanted to, the flames wouldn't die. Not until every memory of what Kaine had done was burned away.

She whipped her head up from the ground, opening her blurred eyes, seeing nothing but the hazy, dancing white.

The hands released her and pulled out of the firestorm, calling to her above the roar instead. "You need to stop! The forest, it'll catch fire!"

You can do this. The voice ... it was there. *Just breathe.*

One breath.

Two.

Then three.

With each inhale, her inferno diminished, until minute smoldering embers were left in her shaking palms. Thick smoke wrapped her firmly, making it impossible to see anything beyond it. She looked into the whorls of gray tendrils and clouds of darkened ash, slowly focusing on a tall figure's ringed hand reaching through the swirls. Close enough to smell leather and metal.

Black clothing blended in with the wisps as hair, masked in the shade of the smoke, swirled around troubled, colorless eyes.

You are alright. The voice comforted. Her breaths deepened. *Keep breathing.*

She blinked through the remaining tears spilling over her bottom lashes and reached out as the diminishing smoky cage began to fade away. Her hand grabbed a blistering, burned palm, and then it was pulling her from the ground. The smoke disappeared like a ripple in a lake, and she glimpsed the sun, the cliff edge, and the green valley beyond.

Standing inches from her, a male in burned navy clothing gazed with widened, ice-blue eyes. Disheveled, light golden hair twitched in the cool breeze as he clasped his blistered hands around her shoulders. "Are you okay?" he asked, carefully raking his eyes from her white hair to boot tips.

Not entirely sure how to answer that question, Alora pulled away from his grasp, no matter how gentle and reassuring it felt.

"I'm"—she gasped—"I'm so sorry. I was ... I ... Kaine." Her voice caught in a whimper.

"It's fine. You're fine," he breathed. A seared hand reached for her again. Guilt followed it.

Alora's lips quivered, unable to speak. Unable to gather a single sound thought. Her shaking hand brushed down her fingers, pulling them each tight to relieve a painful ache. It was all she could do. Find the ache, relieve it, and travel back up her arm, pulling her blue sleeve with the movement.

"I'm so sorry, Rowlen," she repeated.

Ice-blue eyes narrowed on her sleeve. On what had been hidden underneath. Rowlen puffed his chest, gritting his teeth as he swore under his breath. "I'll kill him."

"No. You can't," she rasped. Her heartbeat quickened, threatening another firestorm while the warning spark of embers lit her palm. *Please, don't start again. Not again.*

"I'll rip his starsdamned head off."

"Rowlen, no." It wasn't a suggestion.

"I can't stand to see you like this any longer." Rowlen's voice rose. "You need to leave him before it's too late."

Before he kills you. She could interpret his tone. And he was right.

"I know," she breathed. "I need a little more time."

Rowlen stiffened, crossing his arms in front of his chest, disturbing the fine navy fabric. "More time for what? You *know* I will help you."

Of course he would. He always had.

From the moment they met, Rowlen had taken care of her. Living in crates and wearing rags, she spent years as an orphaned faeling running through the city streets. Rowlen and his family were well off and his mother was of a noble bloodline. They wisely invested her inheritance in building an even bigger empire, leaving their son to want for nothing for the rest of his life.

And one rainy afternoon, he caught a streak of white hair dashing into the bushes of his father's estate, only to find a dirty and starving female, much the same age as himself, hiding within. It was only a matter of time before he found her an apartment, helped her acquire a living. Lavished her with necessities until she refused not one more gift other than his gracious friendship.

Now the stakes were higher. And she wouldn't chance the opportunity for Kaine to lay devastation upon Rowlen—or his family.

"And what if news of you aiding me reaches Kaine? Your father's business will be in ruins... No, I can handle this myself. I need a few more days. Then I'm done. I'll be out." Alora gently grabbed his wrists as nausea formed in her gut, realizing the wounds she had caused. "Rowlen. I'm sorry..."

But his face was soft when he gazed down at his hands. Almost as if he had forgotten.

Before she could say anything, pure glistening light glowed from his hands, revealing the secret they were bonded by.

Where the bleeding and blackened edges of peeled blistering skin had been, now was restored perfectly smooth.

She rubbed over his ringless fingers. Grinning and rotating his palms to inspect for any lingering wounds. His abilities had always amazed her; he was gifted with impressive healing magic.

"Don't be sorry." Rowlen brushed his hands through his golden hair. "I don't like this, Alora. He could do this to you again, and next time, you might not walk out alive." He carefully took her wrist and examined it. "Let me heal this, at least?"

The white glow began to beam, but Alora tugged her arm away.

"Leave it. Let it be the proof I'll need when I leave him. Others need to see what he has done to me."

THERE, in Rhidian Forest, on the edge of something that could easily turn final, it was only the flash of her blade and the whistling of his sharpened steel that served to remind her of what was pretend and what was reality.

Alora positioned her sword and aimed for the soft flesh and dip below Rowlen's neck.

With impeccable focus, her blackened boots slowly cross-stepped across the mossy forest floor, still damp from the morning thunderstorm. Each footfall was maliciously measured, allowing her to maneuver in a half circle that Rowlen defensively mirrored.

The true reason for today's rebellion.

To train with Kaine's rightful suspicion—*him*—Rowlen.

The only other male in her life. The only one who cared.

Kaine didn't approve of most of the things Alora wished to do. But

WHAT LIES WITHIN MASKS & SHADOWS

this *especially* was one that he would never allow. Never anything that she could potentially use against him. And magic? That went without question.

He knew what she was—an outlawed Marked One as deemed by High King Magnelis—and forbade her from using her powers. To protect himself from certain death if anyone learned of her power, he would deny ever knowing. Even harboring the identity of a Marked One, a fugitive, rendered a painful death that the High King's army would happily enact.

It's happened before. Alora pictured the symbol etched in the tree and shivered.

One of the earliest memories of her abuse was the day she confided in Kaine about her magic. He'd witness the evidence of it eventually. Impossible to hide, it was permanently illustrated on her upper arm. If she had a marriage bond with him one day, he would've discovered it anyway, and she had wished against holding him at risk of the High King's pleasure.

'Dammit Alora. How could you do this to me? To me!' Her mind filled with the memory. Kaine had pushed her away in terrified panic and paced the redwood floor of the manor's servants' kitchen.

Glowing molten metal, engulfed in white flame, had melted against the marble countertop. A square-cut emerald rested beside it, sparkling with the reflection of her flames. It was her favorite color—his, too.

In a precise movement of sparks and flame, both items had lifted into the air as she formed the silver into a ring and nestled the emerald inside.

As an innocent, her tenderhearted gesture was ill-received. A skill that she had possessed as her birthright, secreted away until she conjured the courage to reveal it only to those she trusted most. Like Rowlen, and who she thought was also Kaine. Only he didn't accept it as anything special. No exchange of kind words, no form of understanding. He didn't fall awestruck at what she had trustingly performed. Only unsettling distrust crossed his face as he jerked back from the counter, staring at her like she had committed the most unforgivable crime in Zyllyryon's history.

'I could die because of you! You know what happens to those who harbor Marked Ones. That's what happened to your parents, isn't it? They died to protect you. You're going to get me killed.' Kaine's hand had risen and viciously slapped across her cheek, tearing into soft skin. *'How could you keep something like this from me?'*

Maybe if she had left him then, things would have been easier. Then again, he now carried the secret to manipulate her imprisonment. To keep her caged, with nowhere to go. One word and the High King's army would collect her. And if she acted without preparation, it was certain that her fate would end in Magnelis's hands.

Rowlen's eyebrow lifted with a mischievous gleam in his eyes. He placed one brown boot behind and leaned forward, bending his knee. The pommel of his sword came to hover near his ear. Leaving the blade to rest on an outstretched arm, the positioning was perfect. There he stood, ready to fight after an hour of respite.

"Fancy knife. I win, it's mine."

"You won't win." Alora grinned, and he scoffed before she sheathed the obsidian dagger back inside her boot.

Straightening, Alora adjusted her footing and positioned her sword, just as Rowlen had taught her. "You know I could knock you on your back where you stand. I wouldn't be too eager to have my blade cross yours," she taunted.

It was true. She had perfected her blade skills over time.

Yet, knowing this, he still scoffed and said, "I'd like to see you try."

Foolish male pride. She almost laughed. Smugness was something she adored in him. Ravenous excitement glistened in her sapphires against the glow of his taunting blues; their eyes locked with intensity and sharp focus.

The forest fell quiet. Anticipation stirred.

A sharp snap of a dried branch announced Rowlen's charge. He sliced his sword through the space between them, forcing Alora to defend the advance.

Her sword swung with practiced precision, catching the edge of his blade with an explosion of sparks. Then, with one swift kick to the gut, she pushed him back.

Rowlen lost his footing. Ultimately spinning him backward, he drove his palms into moss where he flipped up to his feet, sword positioned at his front.

"You can do better," Alora goaded with a wry grin.

"I wouldn't want to mess up your pretty hair!" He swung again, this time at her feet.

She leapt, barely escaping the edge of his blade to the side of her boot. Before her feet planted back on the ground, Rowlen's elbow caught the side of her face, and she fell to her knee in the dirt.

"Had enough?" Rowlen dropped his blade in an act of mercy and extended a hand.

Her face stung. A small cut leaked blood before her blue tunic sleeve wiped it away. Rowlen was too kind-hearted for his own good. Perhaps that was why Elysian bestowed upon him healing magic.

Alora's eyes sparked with feral excitement. "Not even close!"

Rowlen's sword rushed out of his grip. Turning on him, now engulfed in roaring flames.

As it hung in the air between them, Alora pulled herself to her feet and repositioned her own blade. She advanced as his fiery sword slowly moved to his heaving chest.

Sapphire eyes gleamed with embers as she stalked forward; her porcelain face captured a feline grin. "Got you," she snickered between breaths.

With a frustrated sigh, he replied, "Yes, it would seem you have." Rowlen lifted his palms in surrender. "Last time we dueled, you weren't this skilled. I'm impressed." And grabbed his sword that had fallen to the moss and sheathed it.

The afternoon sunlight had breached through the canopy above. In the shadows of the forest, Rowlen led them through the brush until they settled in the grasses of a familiar glade.

Without intending to do so, Alora couldn't contain her excitement. Toeing off her boots, she dipped her aching bare feet into the cool waters of the nearby spring. And she didn't miss the small chuckle behind her before Rowlen's feet created gentle rapids around his ankles too.

It was peaceful there.

Almost enough to allow her to forget what waited in Telldaira.

Rowlen laid back on the grassy reeds by the water's edge and crossed his hands behind his head. His ice-blue eyes fell heavy and closed.

She often wondered, if their lives had been different, would she have ended up with Rowlen instead? She wasn't blind to his subtle advances. The look in his eyes. The care he held for her. He expressed it to her once. His ... feelings. Still, she was faithful to Kaine. And after their betrothal, there was nothing else that could be done by Elysian law. And no status of royalty would entertain an audience with someone like her to nullify it.

Even so. That didn't stop her when her own eyes became heavy from consciously laying down beside him, resting her head on his shoulder.

That also didn't stop her mind from wandering...

Perhaps Rowlen could run with her too.

"IT'S GETTING LATE."

There was no easy way to say it. Another day had almost passed in

35

the skies. Another day closer to her escape. Another day closer to leaving the place she once called home.

Another day closer to leaving *him*.

Alora warred off a sudden spike in her chest, sitting up to massage an ache in her neck as she rolled the tension from her shoulders. Unable to accept that hole growing in her heart, her gaze fell to find Rowlen wide awake and frowning up at her.

He must have felt it, too.

"I need to head off to work. Will I catch you at the High Queen's Candlelighting tomorrow?" Her aching knees groaned as she stood facing the east. Facing Telldaira's towering western gates—and walls that stretched far beyond where the eye could see on a clear day.

Rowlen sighed. "No. Father and I will be leaving in the morning. We have orders to deliver to Maldekka. Nobility needs their finery in case the High King graces their vigils." He rolled his eyes. "We'll return in two days."

At least she would see him again.

Rowlen pushed himself from the grass, standing inches from her. But that unamused expression fell to something that sent a shudder through her veins, and his voice dropped low in a vigilant whisper. "Please, be careful."

"You too," was all she could rasp out. If she said anything more …

With one last devastating smile and a squeeze to his wrist, Alora grabbed her pack, and before she could convince herself otherwise, weaved inside the shadows dancing at the forest edge. Leaving her aching heart to curse every step.

It wasn't long before she encountered the burst of light beams around darkened silhouettes that was the western tree line. Squinting from the change, Alora brushed her palm to the symbol on the dawnwood tree before stepping into the once flower-rich lush meadow, now replaced with tall stocks of seeds that danced and swayed in the breeze.

Beyond, the city walls—her prison—brazen in earthy tones of clay and stone, awaited. The color suited. Nothing about Telldaira was welcoming.

Not anymore.

Yet she forced herself through that meadow regardless of the unnerving tension coursing through her body and ignored the chilling, invisible force coaxing her to turn and vanish inside Rhidian.

Only a few more days, she reminded herself. *Then you'll never have to see this again.*

She had progressed halfway toward the unguarded gate when steady, rushed steps disturbing loose pebbles crossed her path.

Alora dropped low in a crouch in the middle of the meadow, concealed by the tall stocks of drying grass as the sound of slowing hooves traveled louder and louder.

Closer.

And closer.

To her wavering disbelief, four riders crested the top of the hill, flanked by Rhidian to the north.

They descended the hill, and her muscles stiffened.

No one ever uses this gate, she thought as a shudder of worry burned her palms. If she wasn't careful, the entire meadow would ignite into a wildfire. Alora narrowed her eyes, raking the riders from head to boot as they traveled closer to the gate.

By some mercy, not one noticed her crouching in the grass.

Alora's eyes fell on the one who led them.

And she nearly lost her breath.

It wasn't the impressive battle-black scaled leather armor, nor the way every step of his pure white horse perfectly complimented his incredible authority. It wasn't even the power rippling from his sheer presence.

But his eyes ...

The way the shadows from his hood swirled in them.

A night-dark cloak draped over his broad shoulders, adorned with an incredible silver clasp that mirrored the glow in his eyes. Formed in the shape of a dragon's roaring head, it rested to the front of his left shoulder, securing the cloak around his neck. And peaking beneath that cloak, fine wisps of matted, obsidian flourishes covered his armor. Connecting in the middle of his chiseled chest.

A flash of red tore her awareness from him.

In tight formation, three riders trailing close behind were decorated much the same. Only, upon closer inspection, their only recognizable difference was the bright crimson cloaks fashioned around their necks and hoods over their heads.

An icy chill shattered through Alora's entire body.

The intensity in the stranger's gaze ... it no longer speared the western city gates.

To her horror, that cold attention had drifted.

And now stared at her. Burning shards of ice directly into her eyes.

Her jaw clenched so tight it trembled. There was a moment where she could have run. Long before they had crested the top of the hill. Too slowly, she realized that. And now, there would be nowhere to escape. Not with them on horseback and her aching legs being her only hope.

But the stranger didn't withdraw his gaze. Not even as they passed by her in the meadow. His muscles rippled with the seemingly effortless movement of shifting in the saddle to peer over his shoulder. The darkened cloak outlined his face, enough that his colorless eyes pierced her. And those eyes never once left their target—her—not until they reached the western gates and disappeared into the city.

CHAPTER 4

Telldaira's northern streets were crowded in preparation for the Candlelighting: a festival in remembrance of the late High Queen of Elysian, Airathel.

Not much had changed since the first mourning. Zyllyryon's Queen of Mist and Sea, who was tragically lost nearly sixty years passed, was remembered by pearl-petal flowers. Shaped like a crashing wave, they were draped in lush garlands high above the streets and connected to every flaming street torch. In every windowsill, luxuriant vases filled with the same flower were full and lush and beautiful.

Even after all these years, Alora still marveled at every step down the streets. Banners with the High Queen's likeness fluttered in a warm breeze. Each one a perfect depiction of her kind spirit and generosity. The love for her people gleamed in the brush strokes of teal eyes beaming with flecks of glistening turquoise. With a beauty of no comparison, the envy of golden waves, bright as the sun, curled in long, luscious tendrils around porcelain shoulders adorned in sea-blue lace and silk, gracefully carrying the golden crown molded like waves on her head. A true jewel lost too soon, leaving an entire world to suffer for it.

The entire kingdom, Alora was told, celebrated in such ways. Though she'd never traveled out of Telldaira during the festival to know if it was true. On the anniversary of the High Queen's passing, the pristine streets of the city would flood with the petals while pyres of sea-green smoke would rise to the night sky. Wishing for another year of bliss in the Stars Eternal and condolences for the life lost.

Alora would sit on the highest hill of Kaine's estate and gaze out into the distance, searching for the smoke of nearby towns and cities filling the sky.

Tonight, the pyres would be lit. The street would fill with pearlsea petals. And Alora would be stuck inside a filthy tavern stenching of ale and male odor.

At least it was better than being at the manor. The tavern was one of her places of refuge. She was free from Kaine, who would never again step a polished boot inside the threshold, surrounded by faeries to keep her lonely mind occupied. A form of freedom, unshackled from the overpriced prison of finery and luxury, and the only last connection to her old life. This made it even more surprising when Kaine, in recent years, purchased the establishment and allowed her to continue waiting tables. The betrothed of a lord—*Telldaira's lord*—working a lowly job such as this? It was scandalous. But despite her disbelief, it quickly became clear that even if she wished to quit, he would never grant it.

It was quite simple.

The males who visited the tables were all the ilk who were easily influenced and manipulated, to which Kaine could use for his benefit without dirtying his ... *flawless* character and expensive attire. Some were wealthy business owners, others of small mind, but all had easy pockets to be filled in exchange for services Kaine would never befoul himself with. Best to let the swine bathe with swine.

Luckily, tonight, none of those *swine* were visiting the tavern. None that she recognized. Any one of those on Kaine's payroll would loosen their lips about her presence for a payout. But if she had any hope of securing extra coin to aid her escape, tonight would be the last opportunity.

High Queen Airathel's Candlelighting offered more patrons than most nights of the year. Which is why when Alora pushed through the swinging doors into the kitchen, she held a charming smile across her face and intended to flutter her eyelashes like any clever barmaid.

"He's back, Emeline." Alora dropped her illusive grin with a throaty groan. She walked across the kitchen floor, feeling her obsidian dagger shifting inside her boot, settling three empty tankards in the sink, before twisting, and leaning against the counter with arms crossed.

Emeline, a young and petite golden-haired High Fae, weathered Alora's side-eye, preparing a simple plate of assorted, thinly sliced meats and an array of crumbled cheeses.

Alora couldn't help but brush her palm along her tunic, wrinkling the fabric as her stomach announced an annoying beat of hunger. Before long, she glimpsed the street glowing with dusk's falling golden rays outside the small window above the sink.

"Brassard?" Emeline abandoned the plate, filling two tankards with ale from the wooden cask.

Alora nodded. "He reeks as if he's been drinking since first light. I have a feeling a fight may erupt tonight."

"Perhaps a song would lighten the mood? Shall you sing for us tonight, like old times?" Emeline's smile widened as her eyes glistened with excitement, handing Alora two tankards before strutting toward the door with the tray of food, her amethyst dress fluttering with each step.

Alora sighed and rolled her bottom lip between her teeth. "You know I don't do that anymore." Her eyes found a small crack in the wall to examine as Emeline grumbled. Ignoring her, Alora pushed from the wall, carrying the tankards with her. "Draw sticks to see who serves Brassard?"

Emeline's face twisted sourly. "It's your turn."

Knowing Emeline was right, Alora pushed up on her toes, scanning the tavern over the swinging doors. She considered one table in the center, illuminated under the wheel chandelier, closely. Though the room was crowded, the greasy hair and plump belly were disgustingly obvious. Her empty stomach churned, imagining the stench and Brassard's dirty hands. "Fine. But you owe me for this one. If he grabs me one more time, he'll find my fist somewhere unpleasant."

That granted her an amused chuckle. "Go on, get out there! And when you come back, I want to hear the tale of the lovely male who swooned at you the other night. I heard he was rather fetching!"

Alora hummed and grinned as she pushed through the doors.

Weaving between the sticky, round tables, she carried the drinks and settled one down on a table in front of a familiar face. Then her eyes shifted around the room, avoiding Brassard's table. There would be time for him later. *Much later*, if she could help it.

A shadow caught her eye.

In the corner, under darkness and cloak, sat a half-covered face.

Alora's eyes flicked down. A silver dragon clasp rested below the left shoulder.

41

Her body lost all function. Denying to move. To even breathe.

The cloaked stranger ... the one who rode into Telldaira's western gate a few hours before. Without a doubt, she knew it was him. Only this time, he was alone, and his illustrious armor had been replaced by a simple, black tunic tucked into black pants. The dark hood covered most of his eyes as he slouched back in his seat, chair lounging against the wall. His muscular legs were spread wide apart, one arm on the table, the other draped with his palm upon his knee. Ringed fingers tapped in a rather agitated rhythm as silver eyes, under shadow, burned into a banner of the High Queen outside the window.

Slowly, as if he could feel her stare, those eyes pivoted. To hers.

An eerie sensation rippled down her spine. It wasn't the black cloak or colorless eyes that sent the uncomfortable chill across her skin, but the wicked smirk that crept up his face when he discovered her utterly enthralled by him.

Alora's breath caught. If it wasn't for an awaiting table of males calling that moment, she may have stood staring for stars-knows how long.

"Barmaid"—Alora blinked, and the cloaked male's focus remained— "are you bringing me an ale or what?" Banging his hand on the table, he lifted his hand in the air and demanded her attention.

The stranger's eyes tracked her every movement and uneven breath as she weaved around each filled table. Remembering that illusive grin and fluttering eyelashes, Alora fought off her unsettling curiosity and turned her attention to the table of males.

"Your drinks—"

Hands greedily claimed her waist, forcing her to cry out. A sweat-covered body pressed to her back, and she realized that he'd stood.

The tankards in her hand spilled over the edges as a result, dumping half the ale on her tunic and corset before she slammed them on the table.

The disturbance caught the attention of the tavern. Most of the voices had grown quiet with the scraping of chairs against the wooden floorboards. Some snickered, others laughed. But she ignored them, squirming in his unrelenting hold.

His thick fingers dug into her hip bones, sending a sharp pain through her body from a hidden bruise left by Kaine.

It was enough to have her vision spotting. The all-too-familiar twinge of panic enveloped her senses. In that panic, her eyes found the flicker of a candle, focusing on a tendril of smoke drifting to the ceiling, as she did with Kaine, before her eyes closed and found the strength to calm her racing heart.

Brassard wasn't Kaine, though.

She could fight back.

The putrid stench of his warm breath drenched her neck as he slurred, "You're looking fine this evening. Why don't you sing us a song from my lap?" He tightened his grasp, driving burning tears into her eyes.

She could have managed a strong blow to his face ... if it wasn't for him forcing her onto his lap when he dropped back to the chair.

"*Brassard*, get your dirty hands off me!" Digging her nails into his grip, Alora slammed the heel of her boot into his toes, rendering a pleasing shriek from him, allowing her to stand and move away. "Hasn't anyone ever taught you how to treat a female?"

Brassard twisted his face in a contorted expression, and without giving her a chance to respond, he stood and forcefully seized her bruised wrist. Sending another shock of pain through her arm and causing Alora to hiss at the pain.

But a deep voice called from the shadows.

The voice, icy, like cold death itself.

"If you value that worthless hand," he said in the corner by the window, pulling a dagger from his belt and twisting the sharpened tip between two fingers, "remove it from her. Now," and leaned forward, resting elbows on bent knees.

The room ... it darkened. Every candle flickered down to glowing wicks.

Primal male arrogance surged through Brassard. "Who the hell do you think you—"

The cloaked stranger appeared at Brassard's side with seemingly impossible speed. By his perch across the room, no one had seen him maneuver around the tables, not even her. The shadows in the tavern danced around him like ink in water.

With lethal power, his fist slammed into Brassard's chin, sending him flying back on top of the table with a crack of splintering wood.

He tried to recover, pulling himself up with the desperate clawing of his hands to an upright table. But ringed fingers slammed the dagger deep into the palm of Brassard's hand, splattering blood across the wood. The stranger's grip remained on the handle as his body towered over him, leaning close to his half-conscious face that was dripping with blood from his nose.

"I do not"—the stranger's jaw flexed—"ask twice."

Brassard screeched in pain as the stranger drove the knife deeper into the table.

His eyes met Alora's. Wisps of short, wavy gray hair peeked out from the hood. His defined jawline tensed again as he turned to her, the muscles and veins in his arms bulging and his chest tight, nostrils flared with rage.

The males sitting around the room stood from their tables, approaching for a fight.

Gaze cold and dismissive, the stranger never removed it from hers as he growled, "Walk away. Unless you care to join him." A broad hand drifted inside his cloak and drew a sword halfway from its sheath.

Unmistakable terror ran across their features. They did the only intelligent thing any faerie in their position could do with drunken nerves and little weaponry. The males backed away, stumbled over their own boots, and returned to the table they were previously assembled at.

Whispers filled the room as an invisible force carried heavily in the air.

Metal slid against leather. The sword slipped back into its sheath. She barely registered what had occurred when his voice, warm as honey, broke her trance. "Are you alright?"

Up close, Alora could see his eyes. They appeared darker in the absence of candlelight. Like a night sky. They reflected the flames that returned to a low flicker on the tables and wheel above them.

Alora brushed her hand delicately across her bruise, thrumming with an uncomfortable pulse.

The stranger's stare wavered to her movement, then back to her face. His lips pulled taut. A muscle feathered in his jaw before he reached to her, opening his mouth to speak ... but something inside her had begun to spark.

She surveyed the room—*Kaine's tavern.* Every single thing that occurred there would be detailed to him upon his return. And she would be at the brunt of his displeasure. He wasn't supposed to learn that she had come to work tonight. But with Brassard squirming on his knees beside the table, the blood dripping from his hand pinned by the dagger ...

Some of the tables had emptied too, ultimately costing her coin as well. The mess. The tales to be told ...

What was she supposed to feel? *Gratitude?*

"I could have handled this without your help if you would've given me the chance. I know how to take care of myself." That spotted vision had surrendered to a shade of crimson as she denied his extended hand. Alora grabbed the spilled tankards and began to turn away toward the kitchen, expecting silence.

Instead, he amusingly scoffed. "Clearly."

This time when she met him, his impressive arms crossed and eyes taunting, hers brightened with a spark of embers before she forced the billowing rage deep down inside. The last thing she needed was to burn the tavern down. But it wasn't enough to prevent the room from growing warm with her concealed power. It also didn't stop her from picturing him with a fire lit on his ass.

"Count yourself lucky the High King's Ravens aren't around, or I would call them in here to remove you. Who do you think you are?" She wanted to jam the tankards into his abdomen but refrained. "Remove the dagger from him and *get out.*"

His mouth twisted into a grin as his arms fell beside his body. With an air of grace, he pulled a chair to the table, merely kicking Brassard's feet before he sat down. After a measured expression at the blood dripping to the floor, he darkly laughed.

Instead of removing the dagger, his broad hand closed around the half-spilled tankard meant for Brassard, drew it against his lips, and downed it whole. The tankard slammed on the table. In a slow, agonizing pull, the stranger eased the blade from Brassard's hand, drawing strangled pleas for mercy from his pale lips.

Silver eyes brightened with the begging.

Alora's blood boiled with fire. *He's enjoying this.*

"*Leave,* before I decide to take your hand as a trophy," the stranger growled.

Brassard, too wounded and weakened by blood loss, was hauled from the floor with the help of a few males and taken outside the entrance and out of sight.

The stranger watched with a cold expression, as if he couldn't care to even breathe in their direction, before settling back in the chair. Adjusting the black tunic fabric at his abdomen before propping his arm across the table, he said, "Your savior could use another drink." With an amused grin, he gestured toward the empty one beside him.

Smug bastard.

Everything in Alora desired, desperately, to command her powers and knock the tankard into the stranger's irritating face, but the painful reminder of what happened to Marked Ones tethered her from such suicidal impulses. And besides, he wasn't worth it.

"What. Will it. Be?" Sneering at him as if he were a simpleton made it easier to bite down the roaring anger through gritted teeth.

His silent stare captured the last edge of her sanity.

She raised an eyebrow and hissed, "*Enjoying the view?*"

Those silver eyes didn't move from her burning irises. Something unreadable crossed his face before his voice flattened. "Bourbon." He gestured against the tankard for two knuckle lengths of liquid, the silver of his ring glinting in the candlelight. "If a place like this has it."

A place like this. Alora scoffed and turned. Storming between the empty tables and into the kitchen. Away from him.

Emeline's wide amber eyes welcomed her. "What on Elysian was *that?*"

Alora threw the empty tankards in the sink and ran her hands down her face, ignoring Emeline's question. "Give me an ale."

The mighty bastard could drink piss water instead.

THE STRANGER'S body sat rigid and tense, a contrast to his previous temperament.

Alora scowled as she approached. Scowled because where the table had sat empty before, with only his arm lain across it, was now crowded by the muffled whispers of three figures adorned in bright crimson cloaks.

She debated on interrupting them. Debated knocking between their shoulders to slam the drink down and retire before the stranger could mutter a word. But those cloaked figures turned at a lazy wave of his hand.

Of the three, the smallest, clad in a vicious snarl, arranged green eyes in her direction, letting out an unpleasant hiss before walking away.

But the other two...

By their considerable builds, they were male. Both were muscled, though she couldn't quite see the extent because their bodies were covered in battle-black armor and hidden by bright fabric. On close inspection, their armor was intricately designed. The leather appeared scaled like that of a dragon—the likeness a best guess, surely. Dragons were myth—legend—tall tales, and they both wore the tribute to the creatures well.

The larger of the two, with beautiful dark brown skin, motioned to the doorway with an outstretched tattooed hand beside the shortest one. They both crossed the threshold, vanishing onto the street.

The other, tanned like the seated stranger, with waved ebony hair spilling around his stubble-shadowed jaw, hovered in place. Under that crimson hood, a wry smile captured his well-favored, rough face.

Much to Alora's surprise, he ... winked.

Behind him, the stranger cocked his head, silver eyes unamused, and cleared his throat and an unforgiving expression on the elegant planes of his face.

But unlike the other two soldiers, this one slightly bent at his waist, blaring his seemingly gray, almost blue, eyes at her through his top lashes before his palm collided with his temple. That rough face grimaced before he stiffened upright. Without a word, and with a short glance over his shoulder, his boots fell heavily to the floorboards, and he, too, found his way outside.

"Try not to take offense," the stranger taunted. "I thought it best if my friends were not endangered by the ... *charming* barmaid who can handle herself."

"Friends?" Alora snorted. "I should think someone like you wouldn't have any friends. Maybe if you weren't so unconscionably smug." She paused and realized the scheme she was playing into. Alora met his gaze, finding his growing intrigue, and didn't care to indulge him any longer.

He lifted his head enough that the cloak slipped back slightly, and the corners of his mouth twitched. "If I were not so unconscionably smug... Do go on." Arching a brow, his smile grew sinister.

She slammed the tankard on the table. The contents splashed out; beads of ale splattered the stranger's cloak and pants. *Satisfying, to say the least.*

"I'm not doing this with someone whose face I cannot even see. Take off your cloak."

"No." *As if she'd expected any other answer from him.*

So she pressed with baiting amusement. "Why? Are you dreadfully hideous?" Grinning, she crossed her arms, the leather of her corset groaning at the contact.

The stranger remained a solid wall of effortless composure. Then his gaze drifted to the tankard, releasing a breathy chuckle at the absence of bourbon, and he merely focused his gaze back on hers. "Quite the contrary. I am afraid, should I remove my hood, you will be stealing away with me in the night."

Alora tossed her long hair over her shoulder and made sure to kick his boot *accidentally* as she passed him by. "Drink your damned ale and be on your way."

"As you wish, Your Majesty," he called, before lifting the tankard and draining it whole.

CHAPTER 5

He lingered in the chair far after his ale had been emptied. Watching dusk be captivated by a shimmering night sky through the windows and striking his gaze on the shower of pearl-petal flowers flooding the street from those who bore wings. When he had finally glided through shadows out the door, dark cloak flowing in the wind he created, the tavern turned a shade brighter. And the remaining memory of his presence was carried by a small note on his table, under the empty tankard, and a pearlsea of perfect proportion rested beside that.

Written in smooth penmanship on white parchment that smelled of old books and wasted dreams was a note.

Thanks for the entertainment, Your Majesty.

Alora offered it a middle finger before she shredded the page and burned it over the lonely candle melting on the table. The ash dusted to the floor below, and she watched as the smoke circled the specks on the wooden floor.

Entertain this, Bastard.

Patrons cleared out not long after, leaving the tavern empty in the late hour. Emeline's shift had ended, leaving Alora to finish cleaning before she would lock up and return home.

Not home—Kaine's home—where she merely existed and slept.

Home...

She couldn't call anything a real home since her parents died. Never belonged anywhere after. Not as an orphaned faeling surviving on the streets; not in the hovels she had dwelled in. Certainly not with Kaine.

Her eyes periodically drifted to a small dusty upright piano in the corner. One she so long ago played and sang at. The very same piano that Kaine had introduced himself at—with a drink in hand. His smile, the way he watched her, the way he spoke. Unlike anyone else who visited such places as that, it set her heart ablaze.

A wasted memory.

For a moment, she considered sitting down. The ivory now caked with dirt, dust, and shadow. Lonely from years of neglect. Lonely like her. She was the last to trail fingers across its smooth surface. The last to sing with its beautiful notes. That desire forgotten long ago, stripped—beaten—out of her. Her very own piano at the manor had been crushed to tiny bits, shards of wood and broken keys destroyed on a rainy afternoon when Kaine demanded silence and she had played a level below his office.

Once, he had loved her playing and singing. The harmonies bewitched the cruelest of hearts.

Then he loved seeing her blood drip across the shattered destruction.

With a deep breath, her eyes drifted from the piano, and all the pieces of crippled desire to play faded as she turned to the table the stranger had sat at. He possessed an unsettling familiarity in his voice. So much that she paused sweeping and pictured him in her mind.

She couldn't determine what it was that was so familiar. Had she heard his voice before? Perhaps he wasn't a stranger to the city after all. She'd barely traveled beyond Telldaira, save for the forest, smuggler's caves, and on rare occasions, Castle Galdheir when Kaine was summoned. And if she had the slightest inclination that he was indeed someone she had met previously, then perhaps he was one of Kaine's business acquaintances.

Panic constricted her breath.

If that was true ... if he knew Kaine—

A shrill scream intensified her dread.

Alora rushed to the front door, scanning through unsettling shadows and swirling clouds of ash to what should have been, by now, an empty street.

Soldiers clad in silver armor, covered by purple cloaks and the glow of torches, were ripping open locked doors. They forced sleeping faeries from their homes. Wielded swords with ruthless force.

The few on horseback pulled males by their hair; females and younglings cried out in pain. Most that she could see suffered horrendous wounds, plagued with unadulterated horror.

And then she saw it.

The amber glow in the sky.

Her eyes burned from the heavy smoke drifting inside.

Telldaira had ignited in bursting flames.

Moment by moment, relentless screams broke through the marching of an army. From both near and in the distance, they were soon drowned out by the pleas for mercy amongst the destruction.

The male at the southern gates ... was right.

The High King's army had come.

"We know there's a Marked One around here. Tell us where they are and we might spare your life," one soldier threatened from beneath his helmet, caging an older male's charred tunic in his grip.

Panic reamed through her, stiffening her bones.

Alora was frozen, unable to speak, unable to breathe. Everything she had worked for. Her entire life, successfully concealing who she was, what she was forced to be. Where she suffered through cruel nights and endless days under the false security of the city and its lord, came down to a thin wooden door and glass as her last hope. Her last chance.

Death would have to wait—*the High King* would have to wait.

By the time her body wrenched away, a sharp bang slammed against the tavern's locked door. Inches beyond the glass, a torch waved through blinding shadows, growing darker with each flick of the flame.

Another bang.

Two.

They would break through that door. There was no time left. She needed to move. Needed to—

Run. Get to the alley! It was the voice, and she trusted it wholly.

Alora threw her gaze around the room. If she had more time, every table would become an obstacle, stacked in front of the doorway. Instead, her hands clasped every chair in her path, knocking them to the floor in an attempt to hinder the soldier's pursuit. It wouldn't be much, but it was something.

Her mind ... what a wicked thing it was, because, as her boots carried her to the back door, it warned of the events that were sure to come if she fell into the hands of the army. Her wrists in shackles, hair ripped out, skin flayed as she was thrown in front of the High King for his pleasure.

She held back the vomit building in her throat.

And, as if the stars themselves heard her desperation, in a burst of smoke-filled wind, the back door flew open.

Her feet slid to a stop, half expecting soldiers to storm in from the darkened alley. But there was no gleam of polished silver, no ruffle of purple fabric. No one surged inside.

Instead, only an empty alley stared back at her as she lurked around the threshold, surveying for dangers.

Enough stopping, get out of—

The front door ruptured in on itself. Misting into dust and splinters and broken shards of wood.

Alora's feet were running down the alley before the last speck hit the floorboards, an arm over her head to defend against the spray of debris. Shadows danced around every step. Disturbing the darkness as she ran. Her vision tunneled, narrowing on every object in her path. Jumping over barrels and crates, sliding around corners, and carefully setting her boots across loose cobblestones. She'd have to survive two miles of this before a small, cracked hole in the northern city wall offered her refuge in a hidden section of the smuggler's caves.

I can make it. She could—would. There was no other option. She wanted to escape Kaine. The only problem: she didn't expect a force of hand. But that didn't matter now.

So, Alora ran.

Every passing building was a blur. Until, ahead of her, the end of the alley opened into the main street connecting the two core gates of the city. If she could slip across unseen, she'd be clear to follow alleys and back roads to the refuge of the caves.

So close.

An amber glow of firelight filled the street ahead, crippling every last shred of her hope.

The soldiers were there.

Alora skidded along the dirt, stopping at the alley's edge. She crouched down against a crumbling wall. The sound of soldiers' voices, rushed footsteps, and horses stomped down the street to her right. Wavering hope bubbled in her chest once again, watching their retreat. Her feet shifted on the dirt, preparing a sturdy foothold as she jolted up.

She moved to step out onto the street, now surrounded by darkness, but her boot protested the movement, confining her in place.

Wait. Listen to what is around you.

Alora gripped the stones of the wall, not daring to move. The thrumming of footsteps, callous laughter, and horses echoed to her left. They were leaving. She pinched her eyebrows, unsure of the voice's meaning, when soldiers suddenly flooded the street to her right. If she'd taken a step, they would have discovered her.

"There's Marked Ones to the north. Get off your pathetic asses and find them!" ordered a short, red-headed, bearded High Fae on a black horse. A long scar of battle-worn years cursed his left eye, whitening it out entirely. His face could be the bane of Elysian nightmares; when she looked at him, a shuddering shiver rippled down her spine.

Her limbs went numb.

The north... There was only one other Marked One she knew of in the north.

Rowlen.

Alora's palm lit with white embers, threatening to ignite. The brickwork of the building began to smoke. She had to get to Rowlen. Maybe she could leap from rooftops, get to the tunnels, run to the—

The air fell cold despite the blistering heat of the burning city. A voice like eternal nightmares shook the stones beneath her feet, rattling every brick of the buildings. A voice so cruel and vicious and heartless, it belonged in the depths of Firekeeper's realm.

"My patience draws thin." The air seemed to suck from her lungs.

Do not move, the voice in her mind growled in lethal warning.

She wisely complied.

Darkness swept across the street as every soldier quaked. No one moved, no one *dared*. Any ounce of light was engulfed by the billowing night, shrinking away to only the glowing ash on flameless torches.

Through the sea of silver, she glimpsed ... *him*. A rider, adorned in black armor, stalking like a beast ravenous to devour its kill. A chilling gust swept through the street, disturbing his short gray hair, and atop it, an obsidian spiked crown emerged, glistening even in the absence of the fire's glow. And his face ... a thing of death itself, unlike any faerie she had ever seen. Sharpened bones like a beast, as sharp as the pointed teeth glistening under a snarling lip. His cruel expression only mirrored the black, soulless eyes surveying every trembling, worthless piece of armor unfortunate enough to cower in his path.

It can't be.

He was a myth. The monster caged inside dreams, a thing of

merciless nightmares. Black as the night, turning whispers into screams. *He wasn't supposed to be real.*

And she remembered the words spoken. *'The gray-haired demon of Elysian.'*

He had come—for her.

His roughened voice thundered. "Your incompetence has provided the Marked One with an escape. Insulting our High King and making a mockery of his efforts." Blackened eyes grew impossibly darker, and she tried not to shudder at their intensity. "This will not stand unpunished."

Something like a crack of burned wood resounded.

Then another.

Across from her, a heap of silver armor plummeted to the street, neck twisted at an odd angle.

Whorls of darkness drifted into the amber glow of the night sky from where the soldier had once stood. As if he'd been shot by an arrow from a great distance, no one had touched him, none that she'd seen.

Another, to the far right, clattered to his knees before falling flat to his face. His neck, too, twisted.

The picture of Elysian nightmares towered in his place, claiming the darkness that menacingly tendriled around him like smoke.

"Find them." The relentless darkness burst around him, colliding against every surface and body like a rippling explosion, and the torches burst back into flames. He bared his sharpened teeth. "Do not disappoint me again." And then ... he was *gone*. As if he had never existed. The space he tormented wholly empty, offering nothing but tendrils of smoke and shadow.

Chaos erupted with her next breath. Every soldier moved in a rush of sharpened swords and rushed feet. Dividing their lines into smaller parties and splitting into uncountable directions, barking orders and trajectories.

The Marked One—she could see the words taunting their eyes. A game to be played; her life as the prize.

If they believed her to be the prey in this hunt, they were decidedly mistaken.

Alora lifted her head to the north, closing her eyes. *Rowlen. I'm coming for you.* And waited until the torch light faded, disappearing into the darkness.

THE PATH through the city remained difficult, but not impossible.

She was exhausted. The screaming of her legs pleaded for rest that she couldn't risk. Despite the pain, her head was entirely clear. Spurred by purpose and focus, not the stumbling ineptness she carried before.

Each turn in her path, every burned building or charred body scorched her senses and forced tears to cloud her eyes. Still, that didn't stop her. It only made it even more difficult to attempt a straight path north. And when she recognized glimpses of hope—open doorways or rubble to hide within—soldiers would inevitably be patrolling or dragging a Telldarian by their night clothing. Most times, it was too late for her to intervene. Them snickering; her blood boiling at the horrendous deaths they caused.

Everything the devastation threw at her, she weathered—would weather until Rowlen was with her, and they would escape. And some vital part inside her could feel it. Knew that he still remained whole. Alive. Somehow, she *knew*.

Alora rounded the corner of a graystoned building, sliding to a stop when met by blistering-hot torches illuminating her face. She gasped in time for ten stone-faced soldiers to turn, their expressions shifting to wanton delight when they surveyed who they had discovered straying.

There was nowhere to go.

Behind her, the marching echoed along the alley. She had only just escaped across a small back street when soldiers flooded it mere seconds behind her evasion. Forward or back, both ended in the same circumstance—bound and carted off to Galdheir.

So, this was it. Alora's heart ached. The moment she had been running from her entire life had arrived.

Silence fell, and she wasn't entirely sure they couldn't hear her racing heartbeat. One bearing a patch on his purple cloak, signifying an honored rank, stalked between the crowd, and she stumbled a step back.

"Well," the commander snickered. "What do we have here? A pretty female to keep us company tonight?"

Alora found the alley cold and menacing as they circled her. Their faces, without any doubt, looming with every thought and desire they possessed.

How could she have let this happen? If she would have only listened to Kaine—

A warm grip sent rippling pain tearing through her arm, pulsing from her bruised wrist. From behind, a male pinned her arms against the sides of her body. Caging her.

Reverberating a sinister hum against her back, the stench of his sweat cocooned her as he stole a greedy sniff. "Mmm, she smells of ale and sweet honey." Licking the side of her face, he darkly chuckled and said, "Tastes like it too."

Two soldiers closed in, scraping calloused fingers along her arms and fisting strands of her hair for their own amusement.

"Get your damn hands off me!" She struggled.

Another, adorned in the same rank patch, gripped the front of her navy tunic. "Let's see what's in there."

"No!" The way they held her betrayed them. Alora lifted her legs off the ground, hovering from the male's hold. With great force, she aimed her boots perfectly at the groin of the soldier.

A hit.

His knees pounded into the dirt, clenching himself and grimacing in pleasing pain from the impact.

But it wasn't enough.

He stood, still clenching himself. "You little beast." The sting of his backhand convulsed across her face. Without a moment to compose herself, he continued his original intention. Alora's tunic in hand, he tore it open, down her shoulder, as the eight others advanced inward. "I'm going to enjoy—*what's this?*"

They saw it.

Her death mark.

Something pricked her skin. Her gaze fell to the thin needle, stabbed in the center of her mark. And where warmth once boiled through her veins, a chilling stream of ice now cascaded.

Perhaps if she had perfected her powers. Perhaps if she hadn't been so panicked, the thought would have occurred to her to have used her fire. But now ... it was too late.

The commander rubbed his fingers over the bubbling puncture of blood, smearing a small amount over the magical ink. But Alora thrashed enough to break from his touch.

It only provoked him to grab her chin, wrenching her face to the side before his body pressed against hers. "Looks like we're getting lucky tonight. The High Prince can take her when we're done."

That kernel of hope, the one that drove her through the city, snuffed out. Her throat constricted as she tried to scream. But she couldn't form any sort of sound. She had fought against Kaine for so many years, and now she would be taken in every sense of the word, only to find her inevitable doom at the High King's hand.

Alora found the night sky, the comforting darkness. Tears streamed down her face, accepting her fate.

She tried. One last time.

Please, someone, help me...

.

.

.

The air fell ice-cold.

One by one, torches blew out.

Shadows and smoke danced at their feet like fog in the night.

A devastating force burst from around her, slamming the soldiers into the graystone walls surrounding them. Alora had no idea what had happened—*how* it had happened. Even if she could call on her magic, it had never done *that*.

None of them saw the blackened, moonlit figure stalking the shadows behind them.

Not until it was too late.

Three heads went flying, blood splattering into the backs of the others. Those who remained unsheathed their swords, but whatever the figure was had disappeared.

The only sound: their uneven breaths.

And then ... their bloodcurdling screams.

In tendrils of clouded smoke and shadows, the dark figure appeared with a sword drawn and dripping blood at its side.

Alora watched in frozen horror as the figure fisted the commander's hair. Its darkened gaze speared into his eyes until every last breath and shard of soul was sucked from his depths.

The male dropped limp onto the dirt, skin and eyes cast in gray like spoiled meat.

The shadow-covered figure slowly cocked its head to the second. The male who had stuck her with the needle. Without a moment for breath, the male's head detached with one perfect, effortless swing of a sword.

A faerie who had been attempting to grab Alora stumbled aside, hands shaking as he withdrew.

Like smoke on the wind, the shadow moved.

Blade met blade, piercing her ears as sparks rained. In the moonlight, the much smaller soldier crossed swords with it—him—the shadow—Death—whatever it was. The figure was too focused on the soldier that it seemed unaware of the approaching threat stalking behind. Meticulously prowling close, two others ready to sink their blades truly believed they would down Death.

One raised his sword, a perfect angle to plunge right into Death's back.

"Behind you!" she screamed.

Alora watched as, with one movement, a shadow-covered hand rose, freezing the two mid-step as the other hand granted the defending soldier their bloody end.

Death's attention carelessly turned from those frozen. Black legs stalked toward the remaining two, who cowered against the wall near Alora.

One drew a bow and nocked an arrow.

Then let it fly.

It was a perfect shot—on anyone other than Death himself.

The figure effortlessly and with unperceivable speed, slapped it away in an explosion of wooden shards, inches from its darkened face.

"That was a mistake," Death finally spoke. Its malicious voice echoed through the alley as it lifted a palm encased in smoke and shadows and jerked its hand forward in a sweeping motion.

A solid wall of wind rippled, barreling into the soldiers and forcing them to fly into the alley wall.

But they didn't fall to the ground.

Death held its hand steady in the air and prowled forward. Every inch of its body releasing tendrils of darkness. For a moment, they lingered—hovered—in against the graystone, like the two others who remained frozen in time.

That malicious voice growled as he willed the commander who had ripped Alora's shirt open to fall to his knees. "I have *enjoyed* this. Right about now, you should be regretting ever drawing your first breath."

Death cocked its head in her direction.

That familiar caress tingled against her mind. *Look away.* The voice raged with icy warning as the soldier on the ground became engulfed in shadows ... and split in two.

On perfectly placed feet, the figure twirled around with a mighty swing and shoved the sword into the center of the last's face.

It stood there, the uneven breaths a companion to the roaring silence. The moonlight enough to cast a white glow onto its blood-covered form, illuminating it from face to boots.

With the sword by its side, its hand raised one last time. The two remaining necks were entangled with smoke and shadows. An effortless twist of its wrist later, Death enclosed its shaking fist until no breath filled their lungs.

Gray-faced, they plummeted to the bloody dirt below.

It was over.

Or so she thought.

She could see it now, its face under a black hood.

His face was peppered in fiery rage, the shadows and smoke faded, making way for the view of bulging, blackened veins on his arms and neck. His eyes, pools of ink that devoured the moonlight in their intensity.

With a few menacing steps, he crossed the battlefield, clearing the distance between them. Before she could flinch, that dark voice rasped with such power—such force and intensity—that he could have summoned the sun to scorch the earth to its bitter end. *"Run."*

THE HIGH KING's soldiers rounded a corner of the alley moments before Alora escaped.

The air, spiked with an unnatural winter's chill for the season, stung her face as she foolishly peered over her shoulder, knowing Death was close behind. As she did, she tripped but didn't find herself flat on the ground.

Broad, icy hands wrapped around her upper arm and pulled her to her feet. Steadied her. And that grip didn't leave, not as he pulled her forward, and she failed to meet his pace, realizing her legs were giving out.

"Eyes forward," he sharply commanded.

Only ten steps would burst them into the next street, unaware of what dangers waited.

Alora wanted to call him to stop. When, suddenly, three riders adorned in battle-black armor and bright crimson cloaks filled the end of the alleyway, led by a white horse with an empty saddle.

Death's hand vanished from her arm, leaving whorling darkness where it had been.

Then, he vanished.

Panic tore through her, almost making her stop when a clatter of metal crashed behind her. This time, when Alora turned, Death was twenty feet behind her, appearing again within a storm of smoke and shadows. His sword collided against another, fighting off the soldiers in their pursuit. Just as she had witnessed before, cutting them down with ease and perfection.

His abyss for eyes found her as shadows replaced his figure, vanishing again.

Before she could blink, he was holding onto her arm once more.

"What did I say? *Move!*" Death guided her forward until they reached the riders waiting on anxious horses. Without hesitation, his muscled arms lifted her into an empty saddle and climbed behind her, toweling his arms around Alora's sides before grabbing the reins.

Sucking in breath after breath, Alora tried to center herself. Tried to rationalize what was happening.

With a swift kick, their white horse reared up, and Death thundered, "*Ride!*"

CHAPTER 6

Night air whipped Alora's face, stinging her tear-drenched cheeks. It was strange—the false sense of safety entangling her by hands that were covered in the remains of the once breathing. And as they rode toward the north of Telldaira and those bloodstained arms toweled around her waist, covering her with his cloak, gripping the reins ... a sickening unease struck her nerves.

She knew them.

Knew those bright crimson cloaks. Had seen them in the tavern leaving by the order of—

The stranger in the tavern ... it was *him* behind her.

Alora struggled to feel the breath in her lungs. *Where are they taking me?* Falling rigid when he shifted in the saddle and his fingers brushed across the front of her ripped tunic. One broad hand gently splayed across her middle, pulling her against him tighter in the saddle.

His hand ... like ice crystallizing over a winter lake, sending shivers waving across her skin.

It became crushingly clear that if she had any hope of jumping off the horse and running, that was now impossible.

"Stay calm." She felt his chilled, caressing murmur seep into the depths of her—as if he truly cared. But that was quickly rectified, because as their horse pushed through the darkness, they entered the main street of Telldaira. Straight into the path of awaiting soldiers.

Whatever plans of survival they had ... it seemed that self-preservation wasn't one of them. As far as her eyes could see—an ocean of silver and purple—were the High King's soldiers. Some carried chains latched onto grief-stricken faeries' shackled wrists, others stood in conversation, gripping the pommels of their sheathed swords. Torches were shoved into the dirt, horses tied to posts, the scents of blood and burned wood and bodies so strong it forced a sting in her eyes.

There was a choked scream—a wail of deafening heartbreak—laced with something final, and she shuddered. Some faerie was being ripped apart by the sound of the screams.

An unsettling heat raged through her veins, and she dared a pleading whisper. "We can't go this way." The fools would have them flogged at a post or burning on a pyre. Anywhere but there.

Anywhere, even—*The Manor*. The west side was certainly protected by Kaine's status and dealings with Castle Galdheir. Protected from attacks such as these. The High King's advisers and noblemen and appointed lords were housed in such places in every city in Zyllyryon.

"Get to the western gates inside the city. We'll be safe there. My"—Kaine's—"manor. We'll be safe there." Keeping the tremble from her voice took effort. At least for tonight, Kaine would be gone.

"It is not safe there."

And this is? she thought and moved to speak again, but he raised his hand in the air.

Their group slowed at his simple command.

Alora stiffened. *We're riding right for them. Stop. Stop. Stop!* She shifted in the saddle once more, her boots prepared to meet the ground and escape. Her thighs loosened, legs sliding down the saddle when his icy grasp enclosed her hip and shoved her upright, pulling her against his freezing body.

So much for running.

He shifted in the saddle, reaching down to pull a new cloak from his saddle bag. Before she could protest, dark fabric gently draped around her shoulders, and he closed it around her front, secured by a fire-spitting dragon clasp. The same one she had glimpsed in that meadow. A strong leather and metal scent covered her when the male positioned the hood over her cloud-colored hair, completely obscuring her view of the glowing amber night sky.

That icy grip stopped on her upper left arm, as if in emphasis, when he murmured again, "Keep this on. Do not remove it."

The realization hit her before he finished his words. Her tunic ... it had been torn. And that death mark she was cursed with would've been on full display. Along with her secret, her shoulders, upper arms, and chest were exposed to any wandering eyes.

Her chest tightened as she fought for each breath. Twisting around in vain, she strained to meet his gaze, desperate for some shred of reassurance. But all that stared back were cold, haunting eyes.

"*Eyes forward*. Do not turn around unless I say," he demanded. Something in his voice ... was enough of a warning to have her shaking hand clutch the clasp, not daring to meet his eyes again.

The air thickened the closer they moved forward. And by her rider's posture, it was as if they were strolling through a field of flowers. Something lazy in his bearing—almost pompous in the way he sat tall against her back. Unaffected by the vicious sights and the screams filling the street around them. And by some miracle, none of the buildings had been destroyed. Not yet. Though the glistening silver bodies adorned in their proud purple capes held torches, it was evident they were ravenous to shatter windows and set structures ablaze.

They were approaching the first blockade of soldiers, with plenty gathered and positioned behind them further down the street. Surrounded. And until that moment, there may have been a chance to fall inside the shadows of another alley, but when the head of a patched commander turned, that moment fled.

Their approach stirred a motion of signal commands and shouting, the clanging of metal and rushing footsteps the first warning to turn away.

Only, by no surprise, they didn't.

Facing capture and death, they moved forward, toward the commander with swords drawn and soldiers falling shoulder to shoulder in formation. Beyond the blockade, rising tall above the buildings and a mere fifty feet away, salvation—the red-stoned walls surrendering to the northern gates—danced with shadows from the city's flames.

Her rider stiffened as if an iron rod had been shoved down his spine, lifting his chin high. With a flick of his wrist, he motioned, and one rider moved alongside them.

Strength rolled off him in waves as he sat perched upon his ebony horse, towering over her rider by one hand length. He stiffened, and for a moment, it seemed as if there would be conflict. Visions of bloody bodies and blades, with her at the end of a sword, peppered her mind...

Until his smooth voice sliced the tension as if it were a sharpened knife. "You *dare?*"

The commander's face blanched. Almond eyes darted from the rider to her own, stumbling a step back. Whatever the meaning, those words had rippled across the street like a solid wall, and he rasped to the soldiers alongside him, "Stand aside."

The blockade, without hesitation, split, like the six of them were on fire, and they cared not for a searing burn as they passed by. Keeping a wary distance.

As her rider broke through the crowd, Alora glimpsed something unsettling. Unnatural. And if anything from tonight didn't send every bit of her consciousness into a fit of petrified worry, this certainly did.

For when they rode through, the soldiers didn't stand glaring at the riders, swords ready to run them through. They didn't attack in a fit of fury or pride.

Not one moved.

Their eyes were tormented with controlled panic.

Her rider tightened his grip as they passed the end of the blockade.

Alora loosened a breath. *Did ... did some of them ...*

No. She was struck by an illusion...

Surely they couldn't possibly have bowed.

CHAPTER 7

T he group rode in unnerving silence. Into the blackened abyss. Into whatever night horrors awaited them beyond the gates. Not a sound. Not a mere word—for miles.

Only shifting their hoods and exchanging glances at each other. And if their silence wasn't unnerving enough, the absence of all other sounds made Alora's skin crawl. No chirping of night-bugs, even the horses' steps were barely a whisper against the chilled breeze. The moonlit sky carried satiny clouds across the vast view. Stars gleamed brighter with each step away from the burning city behind. Thankfully, the smell of burning wood and blood was exchanged for fresh settling dew upon the grass.

It made breathing easier at the very least.

Still, nothing had been explained to her. *Why did they save her? Why did they force her out of Telldaira?* Who was the male behind her, and where were these faeries—High Fae—humans, *whoever they were,* taking her?

She had almost wished she was safely back at the manor with Kaine. Almost.

You were never safe there. You know that.

Alora shivered at the voice and turned in the saddle to gaze back, hoping to catch one last glimpse of the city. And as her eyes watched the flames disintegrate in the distance, the shadow behind her moved.

Her treasonous eyes flickered, meeting those night-dark eyes that reached oblivion, and a taut, snarling face.

'Eyes forward. Do not turn around unless I say.' She remembered his warning a little too late but willed the courage to speak to the face encompassed in a sea of black, and moonlight reflecting from his eyes. "Where are we going?"

Silence.

Tears coated her sore eyes. Not of panic, which had subsided the moment they crossed the northern gates, but of frustration.

"Please," she growled, the bite of her own tongue surprising her. But with each passing footstep, his gaze was unmoving—uncaring—surveying into the darkness beyond.

She turned and tightly gripped the cold clasp of her borrowed cloak to the point it threatened to slice her palm.

With Kaine, she knew him. Knew his movements, how he spent his days, his manipulations, and his tantrums. Knew how far to push and when.

But this stranger ... there was no way of knowing. He'd ridden into Telldaira outside the meadow. Had watched her—fought for her—in the tavern. Killed those soldiers in the alley. Took her out of Telldaira. He had plenty of opportunities to do ... whatever it was he planned to do now.

And she didn't care to find out what it was. She was outside the walls. That was enough.

Squinting her eyes, Alora searched for recognizable landmarks. Truthfully, hardly traveling north from Telldaira, there wasn't much hope, but surely something would become familiar. If she could find somewhere to hide, maybe she could call on her magic to—

My magic.

The thought hadn't dawned on her since the alley.

With only four riders, maybe she stood a chance. The cover of night would be far better than waiting to discover where they were taking her. Even with little knowledge of how to wield her powers, it was still better than nothing. And even though she had wielded her powers only a little in the past, she still had to try.

Closing her eyes, she willed the familiar burn to her palms.

It was useless.

The warmth inside her veins, the heat that pulsed across her being, was not there. And the flicker of embers didn't spark in her hand when she tightened it in her lap. The rage in her heartbeat pounded against her chest as the pinprick sting drew her attention to her arm. To where the soldier punctured her death mark, rendering her powers completely futile.

Instead of allowing her nerves to consume her, Alora simply drew in a determined breath.

She had prepared too long to escape the claws of Kaine to let her nulled powers be the breaking point. Powers or none, she would escape. She would finally be *free*.

So Alora waited. Continued for some time. Passing lush meadows swaying in the breeze, small groupings of trees that yielded little cover, and trickling streams that were only useful for watering horses.

Then, there it was.

Ahead, on the side of the road, a forest nestled atop an upcoming hill. Illuminated in the moonlight as far as she could see. Forests had always been her solace. She felt natural in them. Accepted and safe. She knew how to run over the covered forest floor without stumbling, which trees were best for climbing, and was somewhat skilled at concealing her tracks. If there was ever a better place to escape, this was it.

She shifted unnoticeably in the saddle. Hopefully, her rescuer—captor—whatever he was, wouldn't perceive her intentions.

Within the cover of the cloak and darkness, she cautiously readied her hand.

She was ready.

Ready to escape whatever this was.

Her thighs loosened on the saddle once more, slower, more calculated this time to conceal her intent.

Alora adjusted her balance enough that when the moment provided, she would easily slip from the horse and run toward the tree line. Her last hope relied on this specific moment; a moment only a few breaths away.

Any hesitation would render her plan useless, perhaps even get her killed.

It was worth the risk.

She would *not* be someone's prisoner again. Never again.

Her rider drew in a hardened, deep breath before Alora grabbed her fist and shoved an elbow into his solid torso.

With a menacing growl, his arms loosened his hold, his body barely falling off balance from the impact. She slid from the saddle, boots slamming into the dirt.

There was no time to adjust her balance. If she had any hope of escape, she had to keep running. And couldn't stop for anything.

Through the grass and to the tree line, she ran until the darkness swallowed her whole.

SOMETHING WAS WRONG.

No shouts of pursuit.

Not one footstep crackled the dried leaves and sticks on the forest floor.

With every step deep into the forest, nothing came for her. Despite the absence of pursuit, she had only paused for a moment to pull her dagger from her boot, and swerved through heavy-trunked trees, jumping over any barrier in her path. It didn't matter if they were three feet behind or three miles. She wouldn't give them an advantage of her resting. Any prey should know that. And she wasn't foolish enough to believe that this was over.

Something moved ahead—a shadow within the trees.

No. Not a shadow.

Alora's breath stopped along with her feet.

There, leaning against a significant ash tree, a few feet in front of her, smoke and shadow danced around Death himself as he cleaned a nail with the tip of a knife. By the laziness of his posture, he'd been waiting for quite some time.

Her lungs refused to cooperate.

Panic-filled bones refused to move.

How could she have been so foolish? How could she think she could outrun Death?

Alora desperately scanned the darkened forest. There had to be *somewhere* she could go, somewhere she could hide. Anywhere. There had to be. She hadn't endured the last twenty-six years of her life with Kaine, only to meet an end in this forest.

His voice cut like the dagger that was meant for her awaiting heart, freezing her to the ground she shook on. "Thought you would take a stroll?" He pushed from the tree by his bent leg; that darkened gaze roamed over her as he very slowly—silently—prowled closer, dagger at his side. "Careful, darling, the darkness"—fingers danced in the air, spreading the whorling shadows around them—"betrays you. They are servants to me. Did you truly believe you could escape the Lord of Darkness? You cannot run from me." Another step, swirls of darkness hovered around him.

Alora's grip tightened around her dagger and held it in front of her. Her shaking breaths so sharp they felt like broken glass. "Don't come any closer," she warned.

Eyes like the night flashed to the weapon as his grin widened in the moonlight.

Within a blink, he was *gone*.

Tendrils of shadow wisped where his body had stood.

The air drew colder. The forest silent in anticipation. She could feel every heartbeat, hear every strained breath leave her body, the vapor clouding in front of her face. Her wary eyes searched the area as her body stood frozen, the dagger positioned in front of her, ready to fight.

Ice-cold breath fanned across her neck.

A low snickering growl pierced the depths of her soul.

His body—his power—the smoke suddenly surrounded her. "Closer" —freezing breath bit her neck—"like here?"

Terror chills trickled down her spine. She smelled the leather and metal scent of him, the smoked dawnwood of the shadows now cascading over her body. His shadow-covered arm laid across her chest, icy to the touch as a dagger pressed against her throat.

Alora pivoted the dagger in her hand, angling its blade to sink into him, but a chilling, dark laugh escaped his lips.

"*I dare you*," he growled with bitter amusement.

She forced her hand back in one steady movement, expecting to meet soft flesh. Slicing the air between them, Alora met an invisible force inches from his cock.

No matter the force of her wavering strength, the knife embedded in a wall of nothingness. And if that was not warning enough, before she could wrench it back and retry, darkness engulfed the dagger, disappearing with it in the night.

His grip clamped around her forearm, and he leaned into her.

"*Please*... Just let me go. I'm nobody—just a barmaid." From the corner of her eye, she glimpsed his consideration.

"Oh, but you are much more than that, aren't you?"

The forest succumbed to darkness. Every tree around them began to fade into nothingness. Every nightsong, rustling of leaves, even the breaking of twigs beneath their boots, a distant memory as shadows turned them into cloud and ash and mist.

Her body felt light as if flying on a spring breeze. She was no longer standing in the forest. No longer looking into the moonlight.

A matter of seconds away from the forest passed before the shadows and smoke cleared. They were once again sitting atop the white horse.

She struggled against him, every bit of fear and panic and anger burst through every vein in her body. There was no use. Every futile movement she made was intricately counteracted with a strong force of his resistance.

Her arms broke free, scratching at his legs, arms, and any exposed skin within her reach.

Muffled laughs snickered from behind, and a pleasantly thin, cheerful male voice taunted. "Maybe we should help. Seems to be a bloody wicked little thing."

"Shut up, you fool," a raspy female hissed.

Given another opportunity, Alora would have happily ignored them, but their taunting was only heightened by the arms clamping across her chest and the shadows enclosing her legs, holding her motionless against him.

With no other option, Alora slammed her head back, with perfect accuracy and incredible force, into the male's nose. Resulting in a pleasing crack.

"*Fuck.*" His broad hand gripped her chin instantly, pulling her back against his shoulder to look up into his darkened eyes before he wiped a trickle of blood seeping down between his lips.

His nose. It looked broken. *Good.*

"Do that again, I will tie you up and slump you over my horse." His chilled breath breezed across her face as he bared his blood-covered teeth, threatening the little sanity she had left.

Close behind, the three riders amusedly waited in the darkness. She could feel the rage pulsing through his body, trembling inside every flexed muscle and threatening to ignite his surging power.

"Am I to be your prisoner, then?" Alora snarled through gritted teeth, matching the very rage in his visage.

Blackened abyss speared her eyes once more. His lips parted, breathing heavily as he gritted his bloody teeth as if he would speak. Such boldness wasn't well received.

Her captor forced her forearms down in her lap. Making one thing clear:

This was his game ... and she would play it.

CHAPTER 8

As they deviated from the road hours ago, moonlight guiding them, Alora had been able to track every turn and every landmark. They only stopped to allow the horses to drink and riders to stretch their legs.

Surrounded by silence, *he* had pulled her from the horse, steadying her when her knees buckled, and avoiding her cold glare when a waterskin was shoved at her hand.

She had refused to accept it, earning her an unamused expression and something she thought may be a disgruntled curse in a language she'd never learned. And when he wouldn't be rejected and forced it into her hand, Alora had leisurely opened the top, her eyes defiantly glaring into his, rotated her aching wrist, and emptied it at his feet.

The rod he had shoved so far up his ass, securing his back in a permanent, stiffened state, eased into his neck by the time they continued their seemingly endless journey.

Good. Let him be angry. He wouldn't win without a fight.

Under the limited glow of starlight, she was certain that they had long since crossed two calm streams, a tall, grassy meadow, and the north side of a thick forest. Beyond this, they eventually emerged into a clearing overlooking a valley.

Ten soldiers adorned in the same scaled, battle-black armor and dark cloaks were standing guard, to her surprise. Spread in units, wide across the cliff's edge, with swords strapped to their sides and various weapons, such as spears and bows in hand.

A rider trotted up from behind, a raspy female voice breaking the silence. "Your orders?"

"Ride ahead. Ready the tents." That deep voice had calmed. So had the tension pulsing through his muscles.

Alora swallowed in nervous anticipation.

So, this was it. Her captor's destination. And no inclination of what horrible fate lay ahead. She had been saved in the alley, then forced through a sea of the High King's army, only to be abducted once more when she tried to escape.

Alora watched as the female loped through sentries with no warnings or objections and disappeared, out of sight, over the cliff ahead.

Her rider—captor—the *prick* behind her, leaned forward, adjusting her darkened hood as another rider nudged his horse beside them. That iron grip remained solid around her waist as he, without turning, commanded, "Inform our sentries of tonight's events, then wait below."

Glowing golden eyes caught her curiosity.

Before she could take them in further, their *dick-tator* motioned to the last rider awaiting orders, nodded to the darkened eyes that no doubt burned through the moonlight behind her, and rode forward to greet the summoned male.

Against her body's every protest, they too closed the distance.

Both males climbed down from their horses and stood in conversation with the sentries, who bent at their waists when her rider passed them by.

Alora tried not to focus on the sentiment. Because what opened in her view was both breathtaking and gut-twisting.

The valley beyond opened to sounds of an encampment below. As if she hadn't seen enough stationed around the perimeter, more soldiers were settled within white tents, and the very same dragon that secured the cloak around her neck, embroidered into the canvases. The glow from the fires and torches lit up the entire vale. Sitting around and walking by those fires were more soldiers. They crawled the land like vermin.

She'd never seen anything like it. Thousands of tents scattered, most only large enough to host two bodies inside, but a few ran in long rectangles, like barracks.

Among the sea of tents stood one lavishing structure, fit for a king. Only its canvas was muddled onyx.

Those tents extended far beyond the base of the hill, stopping outside the banks of a glistening lake that she could barely see across. A forest surrounded the outskirts until it bordered the edge of the steep hill they now descended. Campfires released heavy tendrils of smoke far into the night sky. Their burning aroma falling heavier and heavier with every step.

As they approached the bottom, the world turned completely silent. A surge of static energy charged the air. An overwhelming taste of metal intruded her mouth as a thrumming, tingling sensation rushed through her entire body, prickling her fingertips like needles and standing her hair on end.

As swiftly as it came, it was gone, shrouding her in a wave of piercing dizziness.

What was that? Alora's mind surged, struggling to blink away the clouds covering her vision.

Fighting off the spinning and spotting dots, she knew that she had only managed to remain upright because that solid wall behind her interfered. When her body had fallen loose and limp toward the ground, his solid arms toweled around her, holding her steady. No doubt an act of pity, simply because he wouldn't want to drag her into camp.

Then he was speaking to her.

Alora understood a few words. 'Last.' 'Breathe.' 'Over.' 'Listen.' But she couldn't determine their meaning, nor did she care.

Their horse stepped onto flat ground and continued on, weaving through tents and small collections of soldiers who were preparing meals over roaring fires.

Slowly, her mind returned, and that uneasy feeling stealing her balance subsided just as they eased to a stop beside a row of tents.

Her captor jumped off and offered his hand.

Instead of accepting his aid, Alora managed to swing her leg over—rather clumsily—and jump down. The long hours of riding and whatever had attacked her body moments before had her knees buckling.

He caught her shoulders, again preventing her from falling. The feel of his fingers gripping her shoulders was a reminder of her position—of her weakness to stop what was surely coming.

She glared up at him, knowing that in any other circumstance, she'd be grateful. With that wicked fire she wished would scorch in her eyes, she imagined burning into the endless vision of darkness in his cold ones.

He turned his head, jawline tight, settling on where the last riders were tying their horses. One cloaked, petite figure prowled toward them. "Jade, take her to a tent," he said.

Alora wrenched her shoulders from his hands, stepping back. "What —not *yours*?" she spat, twisting her mouth in a snarl. "I'm not going anywhere until you tell me why I'm here." That, very well, may have been a mistake, she realized too late, triggering a predatory response.

He tightened his jaw, and that hooded head slowly cocked to the side. Brewing with malicious intent, his eyes raked over her until that growl, low and brutal, shook the earth below her feet. "You will do as I say."

Too many times had she heard those same words. Too many times had she submitted to the demands and cowered, allowing whatever punishment followed.

She'd had *enough*.

Alora lowered her chin, glaring through her top lashes. She dared to take a step closer, and a voice, as icy as his, growled, "*No.*" He had probably never heard that word in his entire life by the look in his eyes.

Every menacing step in her direction crunched the dirt and rocks beneath his boots.

This time, she closed the distance for him. Puffing her chest and lifting her chin in rebellion. Meeting his simmering gaze.

"Get"—his breathing uneven—"in the starsdamn tent ... before I throw you over my shoulder and take you in there myself." An unnerving wind breezed through the camp around them.

Icy hands gripped her shoulders, pulling her forward.

She stumbled to catch her footing before slamming into the arms of an awaiting female. Jade—the female in question—pushed her off with a hiss before removing her own hood and resting a hand on the hilt of her sword.

Jade grabbed Alora's forearm and hissed again. Only, this time, adding, "Move. Right now."

The male stormed away. And with the last riders walking beside him, they neared a large tent at the end of the row past a calm fire.

Alora could hear familiar male voices. One notably different from the deep growls and agitated orders of her escort. She recognized the cheerful tone from the road when he'd addressed her captor. "That was ... fun—"

The voices faded as they disappeared into the waiting tent.

Jade pushed her inside a small entrance.

To the left, a lantern and wash basin full of steaming water rested atop a humble wooden table. A small flower, crafted in a pearly sheen across its wave-like petals, laid in front of it.

Alora rolled her eyes at the sight of it. *Real welcoming.* And sought to rip the petals from the stem the moment she was alone. If she ever would be alone...

A one-person cot, covered in a charcoal and burgundy wool blanket, sat against the canvas wall and a pile of clothing was heaped on top. Black pants, a long-sleeved, dark, dusty-rose tunic, a black leather corset vest, and knee-high black boots. But if they thought she would accept whatever piss-poor attempt at niceties, they were sorely mistaken.

Alora ignored the accommodations and twisted her cresting rage toward the female. "Where am I?"

That rage simmered over when Jade simply ignored her.

"Wash. Change. I'll collect you when he demands it." Jade's raspy voice felt cold, like the night air. No remorse, no soothing tones of understanding, or any consideration for answers.

Jade turned, moving to leave, when Alora's resolve finally snapped. The water basin flew across the tent, aimed directly at the entrance in front of Jade, and collided with perfect accuracy.

Steaming-hot water soaked the opening, splashing beads onto Jade's cloak before the metal basin clanged outside.

"I demand to know where you've taken me and why!"

Jade swung around on her feet, drawing her sword. "Bitch!" she cursed and steadied the sword's edge against Alora's neck. Her enraged green eyes were like daggers into the soul. "You'd be wise to cull your emotions. If you wish to remain in the stench of tonight, then I don't give a shit. Try that with me again and I'll rip your fucking heart out."

The painful reminder that she was a prisoner wasn't nearly as bad as Jade's boot that speared Alora's gut, throwing her back onto the thin cot.

She grimaced in pain, clutching her stomach, then glared up at Jade, who hovered over her.

"There's a guard outside. Don't get any more ideas." Crimson twisted behind Jade's body as she stormed out. Her voice, muffled by the distance, hissed through the night as it trailed away, "Move that damn tree trunk away from the fucking fire."

And then only the crackling pops of bursting and flaming wood danced in Alora's ears.

Alone. She was finally alone.

But alone where? With whom? Alora looked around, one hand clenching her aching stomach. There wasn't much to defend herself with. Not even her powers, though amateur at best, could help her. The weight of the world pressed heavily on her chest as she looked down at her hands. Moving her fingers, the memory of what it felt like to have her powers blistering through her veins ensnared her.

"Why hasn't it returned?" Alora whispered as she gazed into her rotating palm. She twisted her hand and aimed for the tent wall. Closing her eyes, she called to the depths within her.

Nothing.

What is happening? Her hands began to shake. She grabbed her palm and squeezed as she pulled it into her sternum, shivering at the foreign chill of her skin. Never in her life had the warmth of her fire living on her skin abandoned her.

Eyes brimming with tears, she looked up as if to find the sky through the canvas, pleading to the stars. *Please. Please don't do this to me again.*

The heaviness crashed. Shoulders no longer strong enough to carry the weight. Her throat tightened with each labored breath, and the realization hit her like a fall from a cliff.

She had escaped one hell.

Only to be thrown into another.

Alora sat on the cot, rubbing her cold hands. Warm tears spilled down her cheeks. She pulled her feet onto the cot, bending her knees into her chest before her arms squeezed around her legs.

For the first time all night, she was alone. No one was touching her, hunting her, no one commanded anything of her.

Utterly alone.

Even the darkness offered little comfort as it—the voice inside her mind—whispered, *Everything will be alright. I have you now.*

EACH SOUND RIPPED her from slumber. Every boot scrape against dirt, smoke-induced coughs, the crackling of fire, even the chirping of night-bugs kicked her heart into a lurch, causing her mind to wildly hallucinate.

Was that the ocean she heard? Or a blazing wind that didn't shake the canvas?

At one point, she moved the bedside table in front of the entrance. It wouldn't prevent anyone from entering, but it would allow her time to prepare a defensive measure. She knew this diversion well. Many times, she had poised a piece of dawnwood furniture in front of Kaine's bedroom door. Especially on nights when he would return smelling of wine ... and Taryn.

It had been some time since she'd heard footsteps and movement outside her tent. If Jade was to be believed, there would've been guards watching all morning. Strangely enough, no footsteps had ever wandered close, and no one came to ascertain her status or pull her to inevitable doom.

Perhaps that's where the false sense of hope billowed from when her sore legs swung over the cot edge and planted softly on the dirt below.

Her boots glided to the entrance without a sound, just as she'd practiced numerous times throughout the night. Only this time, accompanied by shaking hands and a heartbeat that Telldaira most likely could hear, she gripped the canvas entrance.

Her breath slowed, for fear it would arouse attention.

Then she pulled back the canvas with two fingers, enough to steal a glimpse without alarm. Expecting to see dawn, instead, the camp appeared darker than when she arrived. Maybe she had slept much longer, sleeping through the entire day and waking to the night.

Embers from a fire glowed in a stone ring. Tents were darkened around her as if every soul in camp slept, and—

Her eyes widened; lips parted in disbelief.

No guards. No guards anywhere.

And he wasn't anywhere to be seen either.

She might not have an opportunity like that again. So, like a ghost in the wind, Alora silently moved the table and slipped through the canvas.

ALORA HAD ESCAPED FAR ENOUGH down the path that the fire's glow didn't reach her. Consumed by the darkness, her eyes could clearly decipher her surroundings.

Still, not a single sound stirred. An eerie feeling chilled her bones at the thought of it, but she pressed forward. *Keep moving. You can do this.*

In the darkness, feet away from a quiet tent, the glow of white hair moved and shimmered, glistening in the moonlight. The horse she had ridden into camp on. It was grazing, untied, like it was meant for her. If she didn't know better, it could be a scheme by her captors. But the lack of tack and ropes proved that to be unlikely. If a setup, wouldn't it have been tied up instead of walking about with its own free will?

It may not have been the perfect plan. A horse's footsteps would surely draw attention. Stirring the camp and ultimately sending anyone within hearing distance rushing after her.

But she had to try.

And this time, he wasn't around to hunt her.

Soundlessly, her boots moved across the trampled dirt. The horse barely cared as she crouched at its feet to scan the area.

No one had come. No sound of alarm.

Shaking knees pushed her up, and she placed her palms on the white horse's side. "Okay ... horse. Get me out of here," she said, voice shaking in a whisper. Alora gripped the horse's mane, ready to swing herself up, but darkness swarmed her feet, gradually drifting up her legs.

A menacing chuckle scraped every inch of her body like the claws of a beast, embedding ice in her veins. Every hair stood on end as she felt his body press against her. "Hello, clever girl."

Darkness unfurled up her abdomen. She swallowed the bile rising in her throat.

"What am I going to do with you?" A shadow hand, made entirely of darkness, gripped her shoulder.

"Please, don't—"

"Begging does not convince me. You will never beg me." An icy arm, also forged of shadows, wrapped around her chest, and he turned her to face him with them. "It would seem someone cannot stay in her tent. Perhaps mine would be more suitable." The darkness swirled around his body. Only it wasn't his body at all. More of a figure made of whorling ash and smoke in the shape of him.

And his eyes... She couldn't see them but knew they were locked onto hers. He—the darkness—stared, and the shadow head tilted as he lifted a finger to her chin. Somehow, she felt that too, like he'd fully manifested in faerie form.

That deep voice growled, "Jade, take her to my tent. Make sure she is *comfortable* for my return." A phantom hand gripped her arm and drew her from the shadows. Pulled by ... nothingness.

"I will see you soon," the darkness threatened as it misted away. And with it, the clouds in the sky drifted from the moon, casting a glow once again into the sleeping valley.

Or what she'd thought was a sleeping valley.

Nails dug into her forearm. Jade—where she wasn't before, she now was—pulled her along. Where an empty campsite was a moment before, now stood guards outside her tent. Even the fire blazed, no longer only embers.

Passing onlooking guards outside her tent, they snickered with amused smiles.

His game, she thought. It *had* been a setup.

Erected at the end of the row, facing the walkway, a larger tent than any of the others appeared. Two guards were positioned outside, spears in hand. Both proudly waited, one with night-dark, feathered wings tucked tight behind his battle-black armor. The other without wings, High Fae by his stunning face and pointed ears, narrowed his eyes, meticulously considering her and Jade's approach.

Jade neared the tent, and the two guards reached to their side, opening the entrance wide, and allowing them to enter.

Alora stopped.

His tent. She was going into *his* tent... To wait for him—to do what? She fisted her palms, desperately calling to her fire that still abandoned her.

Jade was nearly halfway inside before turning around, her nails drawing blood from Alora's forearm when she didn't release the punishing hold. "For fuck's sake, move."

Alora was forced through the entrance, eyes adjusting once more.

The tent was pitch-black inside. She didn't know what to expect. A chair made from the bones of his victims? Blood pooled in glasses and bowls for sacrifices, maybe even to drink? Perhaps tortured victims in shackles and chains to do his bidding?

A candle lit as Jade swiftly moved away from her, casting dancing amber shadows around the space, forcing Alora to squint.

No bones.

No blood.

The only chains were locked around a large leather chest in the back. Beside the lonely candle Jade had lit and the table it rested on, a large cot, fit for three of her size and full of furs, was positioned against the canvas wall. Decorated with hanging metal lanterns, an animal pelt rug beneath the cot, and the large chained trunk in the back, which held two large swords on top.

Against the right wall, a table prepared for two sat, with parchment spread out, a cask of wine, decanters of amber liquid, and two chairs with peaked backs and red cushions were pushed under it. A form stood in the far right corner, holding the armor she'd seen him wearing the night before.

"Sit," Jade commanded, pulled a chair from the table, and motioned to it.

Alora gritted her teeth and stepped toward her. "I don't know who you think I am, but I'm *done* being ordered around."

She could down her, Alora was sure of it. Jade's height was about half a foot shorter than her own, easily manipulatable. The long, fiery red ponytail would be easy to grab and wrench Jade's head back, then she could steal a sword and shove it into her muscular torso. After all, she did owe her for the blow earlier. If that didn't work, a fist to her high-cheek-boned face might render her unconscious.

Jade's clothing—knee-high, brown boots tucked into black pants, a black tunic stuffed into a chest-high corset belt, hidden under a light brown leather jacket—Alora could possibly change into and escape under disguise. No one would think twice if she looked like her. Even their skin color matched. Both pale. But her eyes certainly wouldn't fool anyone. Jade's greens; her bright blues. And their ears were both pointed too, but Jade's were much shorter than her own. Easily hidden with a cloak, though...

"You going to just stare at me all morning or get your ass in the chair? Perhaps my boot would be more comfortable shoved up your—"

"Perhaps she would be more comfortable on my bed."

Alora whipped her head around to find shadows diminishing around the chair in the middle of the tent.

With his cloak still shrouding him, he sat, one leather-covered ankle rested on his knee and a glass of amber liquid in his hand. Condensation gathered at his ... *bloody* fingertips as he lazily leaned back in the chair, his blood-covered forearm draped on the armrest.

Jade backed away a step. Carefully laying a hand on the chair's back.

"Leave us." His deep voice sounded dismissive as he flicked his hand, motioning to the exit with his attention fixed on Alora.

Nodding, Jade walked toward Alora. A sharp glare and a hard bump of her shoulder later, Jade walked out of the tent and into the dawn.

Alone. They were dreadfully, dangerously, alone.

Alora waited in silence, bones threatening to tremble. Her eyes couldn't decide if they would surrender to his burning gaze or find something else to consider. The dirt by his boots perhaps, or the tent wall behind him, the bedside table...

She willed herself not to swallow.

His bed... Perfectly made, not a wrinkle, thread of fabric, or piece of fur out of place. Ready for him to—

Her body stiffened. Vision narrowed at the thought.

"Relax. If I wanted you in my bed, you could have graced it hours ago." He tugged at the fabric against his abdomen.

She gritted her teeth, pressing her lips taut as scarlet flushed her cheeks. And their eyes finally clashed.

"You have not slept." He surveyed her, and the hood, casting shadows in his eyes, shifted slightly. Mouth twisting in displeasure when her filthy, dirt-covered arms dusted against her borrowed cloak. "Or washed." Agitation filled his posture. "The clothing I had prepared for you ... not suitable enough?"

Sapphires observed her attire. She nervously scraped a patch of dried blood from atop her fingernail. "I'm fine."

He tossed back the glass to his lips, emptying it with a grimace. "Try that again. The truth this time."

She paused for a moment, then balled her hands into fists, and stepped forward. Body tense, pleading for her magic to burst out of her and rip the tent apart—set it on fire—or do *anything*. But still, *nothing*.

"You steal me from my city, and you're only worried about what I'm wearing?" Alora glared.

A wicked smirk crossed his face. "Is that not the sort of thing females worry about?"

"I could give a shit about what I'm wearing. I want answers."

He leaned forward, resting his elbows on his knees as he had done in the tavern. With his arms outstretched in front of him, he looked down at his bloody fingers now steepled, and she noticed the candle's glow reflecting from four rings—three on his right, two black and one silver, one black on the other.

Ignoring her wandering gaze, he conceded, "Ask and I will answer."

The blood on his hands should have stopped her, but she didn't care. "Who are you? Why am I here?" She seethed.

Removing the hood, he kept his head lowered to the ground. The side of his mouth twisted into a grin as burned ash and smoke-colored hair fell in loose waves across his forehead. Blood that she *knew* wasn't his own speckled his face, accentuating the already healing wound across his nose.

"*Well?*" she barked, and his grin only widened, irritating her even more.

"*I* ... am High Prince Garrik of Elysian. These faeries are my personal soldiers—my Dragons Legion." Pausing, he lifted his head and stood. Then crossed the two steps to stop inches away from Alora. His shoulders were as high as her forehead. Freezing, bloodied, ringed fingers gripped her chin and lifted it, looking down into her eyes.

Her body froze.

"I was sent to find you for His Majesty, High King Magnelis."

CHAPTER 9

They stood in the quiet.

The only sounds around them, her racing heartbeat, the roaring in her ears, and the lonely candle crackling its flame as shadows flickered across the alluring face of Elysian's darkest nightmares.

The Savage Prince.

He'd found her.

Sheer horror chilled her bones. Never a believer in such stories, not until she was in this very one. Knowing that there was little point in running—her fate was sealed the moment he entered the West Gate— she eased into the surrounding stillness.

Some stories foretold he was worse than his father. That there was no other match in time to his brutality; her skin would be burned and flayed from broken bones, piece by piece. Her powers, ripped from her body by the High King's jealous hands. And when only pain and the memory of who she once was remained, her mind would irrevocably shatter until nothing remained but a shell to mold and manipulate.

It felt as if the stars had crashed down. And without her magic, still unreturned, she would be his—Magnelis's pretty little plaything—until he reached his fill of her pain and anguish.

Alora's eyes shot around the tent, searching for anything to cleave her fate from the High Prince's ruthless hands.

There.

To her right, propped against a leather chest, the salvation of two swords rested. Like a caged beast ready for slaughter, she tore her chin from his grasp.

And lunged.

Pale hands connected with the leathered hilts, and twisting, Alora positioned both swords in front of her, feet steadied on a darkened pelt.

"I have no interest in you or your father's orders," she warned.

Body tense, Alora maneuvered into a ready-attack position that she'd learned from Rowlen. Though she desperately tried to control it, her hands trembled.

The High Prince tilted his head, holding a predatory grin as he rolled up his tunic sleeves. "We have been here before—or do you forget so easily?" He settled his boot on the chair and leaned forward, one forearm resting across his knee. "It is treason—an act of war—to draw on the High Prince. Drop the swords." He cocked his head. "My patience draws thin."

The words hit her like a wall of solid stone. *'My patience draws thin.'*

Picturing a flooded Telldairan street. The reverberating crack of a spine. A heap of silver armor and purple fabric over a mound of warm, dead flesh.

Alora surveyed him now, finding his silver eyes lacking the endless oblivion she had glimpsed on that street. And the face that stared back at her was nothing of the monster that rattled the brickwork under her palms.

"You're not *him*," she hissed. Whatever this was ... whatever game he was playing. Her time hadn't run out yet. "I saw what *he* looked like in Telldaira. You're not him."

"Is that so?" A wolfish grin twisted up the side of his face. "If you wish to see the Savage Prince, allow me to indulge you."

The imposter's skin—his face—rippled. Before her eyes, facial bones reformed under tanned skin that had blanched, tightening and stretching to the point she thought it might split. His bones sharpened on his cheeks, and the eyes of a fiery beast took shape. When his smile widened, his lips curled back, revealing teeth as razor-edged as the swords she held. And his veins... They were branching like lightning strikes from his chest and up his neck, spiking from his fingertips as dark as the night sky.

"Tell me again who I am not, or perhaps you would care for a demonstration?" The candle on the bedside table dimmed. Shadows from every darkened corner surfaced like mist across the pelts on the floor.

By some miracle from Maker of the Skies, Alora held strong, feet planted firmly, though her blade quivered.

He reached out, tapping the blade's edge with his black, veined finger. The blade glided upward.

"Unsteady hold," he taunted, rasping in a dark chuckle through pointed teeth. "Do you truly believe someone such as you can champion one such as me? Careful who you threaten, darling, especially when you are so ... foolishly unprepared."

Before she could convince herself otherwise, Alora cleaved the air, drawing her trembling blade to his throat and holding the other on her outstretched arm.

The iron edge sliced into his chin, releasing a small trickle of blood across the cold metal, dripping to the pelts below.

Twice. She had drawn his blood *twice*. And blood still filled her veins. Breath still filled her lungs. Next time she might not be so lucky.

The High Prince snickered—*actually snickered*—seemingly unfazed by the hostility billowing from her darkened eyes and irradiating from her taut lips. "If you wish to leave here with your head intact"— amusement rippled across his features, and she pressed her blade to the blackened veins branching his neck—"drop the swords. I am sure you remember ... I do not ask twice." Garrik shifted once more, steadying his foot back on the ground before turning from the sword as if she wasn't holding his life at the end of it.

Using his thumb, he wiped the blood seeping from his chin, hovering it before his mouth, and licked it clean off with a sinister grin.

As in the tavern, Alora watched, disbelief settling in her eyes as he sauntered away like any other pompous noble she ever had the displeasure of conversing with. His arrogance led him to stop near the fur-covered cot, and even more brazenly, he offered his back to her like she was something inconsiderable. A mere gnat that was easily swatted away.

Dismissing her as such turned her blood molten. With him facing away, she could deliver a lethal strike. If killing the Savage Prince could bring some justice to their cruel world, it would be worth the inevitable death to follow.

In a single, swift movement, Alora vaulted onto the chair, toppling it as she launched herself through the air, swords aimed to sink into the skull festering behind gray hair.

It was a good plan—might have even worked.

On anyone other than *the* High Prince.

Muscles shifted and flexed under the movement. His body twisted downward, crouching on his knees.

She soared over him, slamming in a tangled mess of limbs on his cot only to realize she had merely succeeded in losing the swords. Alora's legs scrambled, clawing at the velvety furs, desperately warring for possession of the blades.

But the High Prince's broad hands claimed her waist, pinning her onto her stomach and knocking the wind out of her as she was reminded of Jade's earlier kick.

His swords, which had landed in the furs, were tossed to the ground behind them. They clanged against one another as they settled near the toppled chair.

"Sire, are you alright?" a guard called from outside. They would have heard everything.

But Alora continued to thrash. Spinning herself under his grip. Embodying a feral fury of sharp nails and vicious teeth.

Garrik climbed on the bed and straddled her in an attempt to stop her rage. Broad hands met with her fists. The icy chill bit into her skin as he pulled them across her chest. And her legs ... pinned to the cot by some force of nothingness.

"*Enough,*" the voice of the male in the alley thundered, shaking everything around them.

Even in such poor light, she could see his eyes turn dark—cold.

"Sire, are you well?" The entrance pulled open but was forced closed by tendrils of whorling shadows just as fast.

Garrik leaned close to her face, so close she could feel the feather-light tickle of his freezing breath. "Perfectly well. Do not disturb me unless I call."

"*Don't touch me.*" Alora growled, chest tightening. This was stupid. So dangerously foolish, the position she had allowed herself to become trapped in.

Kaine. He would force her like this weekly—almost daily.

Throat constricting, Alora fought off the tears threatening her eyes. From fear and anger and every single bit of humiliation burning through her veins. Despite it all, she surveyed him. Watched him.

That strong body had gone wholly rigid, every muscle solid as ice. Garrik's face... Not of the demon she had witnessed manifest shortly ago, but of the enchanting face of a High Fae male now returned.

He pulled away slightly, lips parted, but previously tanned skin remained pale. A black tunic hung loosely off his chest, tucked into dark pants, open to reveal carved swells and dips of muscles. The strong grip he maintained caused veins to bulge up his ... blood-covered arms. The black sleeves were rolled up to his elbows.

Alora squirmed under him.

The pants pulled tight across his legs as he straddled her waist, leaving his lower half every bit appalling and ... sinfully appealing. And though she'd never admit it, she found an attraction to his body. It was difficult not to. The way it moved above her. His strength and power ... the ice in his touch instead of warm hands.

A heat flushed her cheeks that quickly faded.

She knew his kind well. Because she had survived another monster. But this male wasn't Kaine. He was something much worse.

Silver eyes stared back into hers with ice as he clearly registered her greedy exploration of his body. Clenching his defined jaw, he breathed so heavily that she could feel his chest brush hers. And that gray hair— waving gracefully on top of his head like grass in a meadow. A few strands draped down in front of his eyes, masking the blood splatter on his flesh, which only heightened his devastating, gorgeous face even with the wounds she had delivered to him earlier.

"Enjoying the view?" he quipped with a wicked smirk.

Alora watched as his silver glow traveled from her face and down her body, just as she'd done to him. Painfully aware of what he found; his borrowed cloak pooled on the furs and her ripped, navy tunic, courtesy of the High King's soldiers. Revealing a perfect view of what she would never offer him willingly.

"Get"—Alora's voice shook—"off me."

He gave her a considering stare. "That would be unwise."

"The mighty prince is afraid of a female so ... *unprepared?*" Alora taunted with a pleasing grin.

Garrik scoffed. "Perhaps I am imagining the inconvenience of cleaning up your blood from another failed escape."

Perhaps I'm imagining your head on a pike. How pleasing that would be.

"Were you aware that your cheeks scarlet when you picture death? What a wicked, clever thing I have captured."

Had—had she said that out loud?

"Only ... that was not truly what you were imagining." For only a moment, a glistening softness flashed in his eye. She felt a slight tremble, a hesitation in his grip. "Was it?" that honeyed voice whispered, flowing over her in a wave of confusion and sharp intent.

And Alora relaxed her body in response, loosening her taut face, sinking into the plushness of the furs. That cunning mind began to race, parting her lips slightly as an abrupt breath escaped.

Garrik's eyes went lazy. Half-lidded as his strong neck loosened to drop his head lower. His cold breath trickled across her neck, and he took in a greedy inhale.

Their lips—they were entirely too close ... just as she had planned.

And he fell for it...

She touched her lips to his and fought away a heart thundering panic in her bones as cold lips brushed back. Quivering when they so softly pressed down.

Stars. The icy chill from them radiated down her spine, and his touch to her skin was unlike anything she expected. The carved muscles of his body pressed against her, and one strong hand loosened its hold with every tender kiss.

Slowly gliding the ringed fingers down her side until they rested at her waist, the other lifted her arms above them.

He kissed her like she was his to own—deeper—pressing her head into the pillows by the crash of his lips.

Everything in her body, even her scent, created the illusion that she was enjoying every moment. Illusioned desperation. Wanting more as his hand left her waist and brushed to her neck and chin, gripping there too. She inhaled a breath, sharp as shattered glass, at the touch of his calluses. The chilled trace sent deep shivers across her body.

She *hated* it.

Hated that she almost enjoyed what he was doing. What she was letting him do. This was nothing but an illusion. It wouldn't be more. Couldn't.

Panic deepened within her chest in thundering beats. *Focus.*

His tongue traced her lips.

Understanding his ask, Alora parted for him, allowing him to slide inside, claiming her mouth in lazy scrapes of his tongue. Garrik's kissing was ... intoxicating. Surely perfected by years of bedroom proclivities that a royal such as himself would lure females into. And so, she let him lose himself inside, let him focus on the movements of his mouth—on her.

Typical royal male. Easily distracted by a female to bed. Taking pleasure whenever he desired, simply because he was born with gold dripping from his privileged body and power in his tainted blood. It was easier than she imagined it would be to distract him.

Alora arched her back, pushing her chest into him, swallowing hard at the feeling of the contact. Not entirely sure if the small moans escaping her mouth were a part of her illusion or if she nearly enjoyed this.

A broad hand softly brushed down to her shoulders. He released a pure, primal male groan against her lips, pebbling her skin and sending a heat pulsating between her legs.

Alora found herself traitorously rolling her hips when he moaned again, feeling him hard as iron against her.

What am I doing? Alora protested, registering the shudder of his body before his lips pulled away. Then his gaze speared her with a stirring of darkness. He was the Savage Prince. She needed to find a way to—

He feverishly kissed her again.

—distract him, to—

A pleasured growl reverberated from deep in his throat. They were close enough that she could almost feel the vibrations.

—make him drop his guard enough to ...

Garrik's hand slid down her body, lower, lower, lower.

Her neck stretched, abandoning all reason and slipping to the edge of insanity when those incredible lips trailed kisses down it.

Garrik loosened his grip on her forearms that he'd pinned above them and rubbed down her side. The invisible pressure restraining her legs on the cot released as he adjusted his knees beside her.

The High Prince cursed inside a breath as if he'd forgotten who he was supposed to be.

She gently pulled her arms down, rubbing them along his chiseled sides and exploring to his belt. Inspecting, under the cover of desiring hands, under the cover of whorling darkness there, for what she hoped still remained.

No weapons. The dagger he'd used in the tavern was gone.

Alora guided her leg up, rubbing his calf with her boot, and bent her knee slightly. In perfect range to knee him between the legs.

An icy smile formed against her neck before her knee was thrust back down onto the furs by a phantom hand.

"Clever girl," he breathed. A menacing chuckle followed.

Her eyes shot open with his lips still pressed there.

Pulling away and planting his hands beside her head to hover above her, Garrik released a fever-kissed, breathy laugh. "Clever, clever girl." A wolfish grin climbed his face.

Smoke and shadow whorled around her hands at his belt, encircling her forearms as they—the darkness—pulled them over her head. The High Prince exchanged their hold for his own as he clamped around her again.

Her eyes lined with liquid as flashes of Kaine plagued her memory. If she had deigned these schemes on him, she would've awoken two—three—six days later.

Her heart threatened to explode. She had attempted twice to escape the High Prince, twice she injured him, and now she had invited him to kiss her, denying him pleasure.

Alora's words caught, almost choking. "I ... I'm sorry. Please," she whispered, suddenly all too aware of his body, of his leather and metal scent, a vanilla and oak sting burned against her lips. "Don't ... please, don't ... force me."

Garrik's face twisted into something vicious. That iron grip loosened, and his lower body lifted slightly. And she watched through the liquid brimming her eyes when his face paled and he gritted his teeth in utter disgust.

"I never intended to. I am not a fucking *serpent*."

Warm tears fell from the corners of her eyes, streaming down her neck and soaking the fabric of the cloak. "What are you going to do to me?" Her lips quivered.

Garrik swallowed, chest heaving. "I had not planned on doing anything to you. Not until"—he paused—"this." Garrik's thighs loosened their grip. "Unless you desire more, I am going to release you. You will calm yourself so we can have a discussion."

"You're ... going to let me go?"

His attention snapped to the entrance. "Speak," he growled.

Had she missed his guards stirring at the door?

"Apologies, sire. Riders were spotted in the forest... A Raven's crest."

Which only meant one thing. The High King's soldiers had arrived. And they were there to shackle her, carting her off to Castle Galdheir.

A sharp pain rippled through her heart. *They've come for me. I have to get out of here.*

The High Prince scanned her face. As if he could decipher what she was thinking, he spoke with a reassuring sternness. "They are not here for you. Believe me when I say this, you are safe here." He waited, allowing his words to settle. "I intend to release you. I need to know if you can be reasonable. Tell me, should I let you go?"

"Get off!" She squirmed, attempting to pull her arms down, but his grip was unwavering.

"As much as I *enjoy* having you on your back beneath me, I do not have all day. Will you try anything?"

Bastard. She'd cut his balls off if given the opportunity. But if she wanted any chance of escaping—of survival—she needed to appear willing to cooperate. With a deep sigh, her hostility faded—on the outside, at least.

Alora scoffed. The tension in her muscles relaxed, and she dropped her head into the pillow. "No. Now get off."

Garrik released her crossed forearms and cautiously lifted himself from her. He hovered for a moment, surely watching for another attempt at hostility. But what he didn't know was that she was determined to not fall into another position of vulnerability.

In the absence of any retaliation, he slipped his legs off her and planted himself on the pelt beside the cot.

A tap hit the canvas. "Sire? Your orders?"

Alora soothed down her forearms to her bruised wrists, the piece of her that remained untouched by the High Prince, and swung her exhausted legs off the cot before sitting up.

"Send riders. The Ravens can wait until my business is concluded." Garrik held his focus on her as he spoke, carrying the same stern look on his face.

Adjusting his tunic at his abdomen and rolling up a sleeve, the silver of his eyes still never left her. "Jade, bring my guest new clothes."

Guest. She could've laughed.

Jade called from outside, annoyance surging in her tone, "Yes, sire."

It was then Alora noticed the golden glow against the canvas.

Dawn was rising, offering its burst of warmth in shards of sunlight. Lined shadows were cast across the tent and illuminated the space around them. She could almost feel the heat of the sun emanating from the canvas, wishing that the very same heat was coursing through her veins and her magic returned.

He leaned over in front of her, reached toward a metal water basin on the bedside table, and pulled a dripping cloth from inside. The High Prince offered it to her, but she flinched, refusing it instead.

"Relax. I will not hurt you."

"I've heard those words before," the words spat viciously from her mouth, and he ignored her.

"Clean yourself up." This time, he dropped the cloth on the cot and prowled away. Righting the chair that had toppled over in the fight, he moved to the table on the far right of the tent, poured two crystal glasses of wine, and walked back to her, extending a glass.

The gesture had her flinching once more. She hadn't noticed sooner, likely out of the shock and adrenaline. Not only were his hands drenched and face specked in dried blood but the knuckles were split open to festering wounds. Blood splatters trailed up his entire arm until the crimson disappeared beneath rolled sleeves.

Garrik placed the glass on the side table and opened his mouth to speak, but it was her shaking voice that disturbed the silence. "Who—who's blood is that?"

"Not mine."

As if that was any bit of a relief.

He sat in his chair. Legs spread wide, sunken back, his bloody arms draped over the armrests. Condensation formed at his fingertips on the glass between them. Garrik twisted his wrist, forming a powerful fist.

"A pathetic piece of waste unworthy of the air breathed to mention them by name."

"Are they ... dead?"

"Death would be too merciful."

She rubbed her bruised wrist and followed the movement up her arm. "Why?" Her voice a shaking murmur.

"Because it was enjoyable to see them beg within an inch of the afterlife." He tightened his lips at the sight of her disapproval. "It was deserved for—" He relaxed his fist with a vicious sigh. "I am finished wasting words on Elysian's shit. You have questions, and I am growing tired. Speak."

He sat evaluating her, but it felt more like she was under trial. Glowing silver scanned from her dirty, white hair to the scuffed, black boots on her feet. With the damp cloth, Alora washed the dried blood from her wrist, wincing at the sharp pain it created, all too aware of his piercing gaze when he shifted in his chair.

Feeling the pressure of his eyes, Alora considered the alley. If he was the High Prince of Elysian, then shouldn't he have allowed those soldiers to capture her? Instead, he ruthlessly—horrifically—killed them.

And if he was the High King's son—

"Why did you kill your soldiers in the alley last night?"

A muscle ticked in his cheek.

"They were not my soldiers." Shadows covered his forming fist. "If not for the threat of discovery, it would have been much worse for them. Simply killing them was not enough."

Their gruesome deaths made her bones tremble. But he was right. They did deserve much more than the deaths they received. Her stomach twisted, feeling the ghosts of their touches, at their lips against her skin, at—

Without thinking, Alora gripped the cloak, adjusting the fabric to cover her.

"That is not all you wish to ask me."

Of course it wasn't. But along with her racing heartbeat, she struggled to keep her thoughts straight.

"You say I'm safe here? Hard to believe when you kidnapped me from my city and smuggled me in silence just to imprison me in your camp. How do I trust that you're not here on orders from your father?"

Something like indignation rippled across his face. "If I were following Magnelis's orders, you would find yourself in his dungeons as we speak. I would be more grateful if I were you." He leaned back in his chair, a quick tug at the fabric across his stomach before settling the glass on the armrest and crossing his bloody arms. "I know it is difficult to trust me when I brought you—"

"Stole." She gritted her teeth.

"—saved you from Telldaira. The truth is that if you remained there, you would have become imprisoned or worse. That was almost proven to you before I intervened on your behalf, acquiring wounds myself. You can thank me anytime." He smirked as he raised a brow and glass in her direction.

She twisted her mouth in disgust. *Thank him? The nerve.* Alora crossed her arms instead.

He breathed in deeply. Drawing the glass of wine to his lips, draining it whole.

"So, *oh-so-chivalrous-prince*, now that you have me, what do you plan to do with me?"

"I had hoped that you would join me."

"Join you? On a picnic? To the shores of Horatha? In the swamps of Lirazkendra or a nice lope through a meadow? Perhaps you'd venture to hunt me down in the forest again and do stars-knows-what to me. *Out with it.* Like you said, you haven't all day."

Garrik stood from his chair. Bulging arms crossed as he paced the ground. Stopping, he gripped the back of his chair, the wood flexing underneath.

"I once commanded Elysian's destruction, seated at the head of the High King's army. Most believe I still do." Those silver eyes dulled as his head dropped low. "When once I was forced to believe this was what Elysian deserved, I now know it to be disillusioned greed." He peered back up at her, gripping the wood so hard it began to crack.

"Nearly three years ago, I ... changed. Where once ruthless, bloodthirsty killers hunted in the name of the High King, now a hidden enemy marches. When you walk through this camp, you will not find loyalty for Magnelis, but instead, a combined hatred."

The High Prince paced to the table and poured a knuckle length of amber liquid into his glass. He downed it whole before pouring a second, tossing it back just as quickly.

"Elysian regards a mighty army marching, but concealed under my protection is something far worse. Under illusion, my Dragons seek Mystics—Marked Ones—not to thieve their powers, but to offer refuge inside this camp."

Alora shifted on the cot, closing her grip over the edge. Squinting her eyes and gritting her teeth, she glared at Garrik. "Why should you care about what happens to any of us with magic? You're the High King's son. Shouldn't you be basking in your glorious robes, females flocking to your bed, in your lavished royal comfort? Why care at all?"

Garrik took a measured step closer, pausing for a moment as if deep in thought. The shadows hovering like a fog darkened his eyes when he proceeded to unbutton his tunic.

A silver ring on his finger glistened in the dawning light as he pulled his collar over his shoulder, exposing his muscled left upper arm. Baring himself to her.

Alora's eyes narrowed on an all-familiar sight; a death mark—what was left of one.

Healed, singed skin and painful scars covered his flesh until the tunic concealed them away.

The High Prince's eyes turned cold.

"*Why do I care?*" he rasped through gritted teeth. "Because. I was hunted for my magic, too."

92

CHAPTER 10

A death mark? That didn't make him their equal. Didn't make her pity him. So, he was hunted, too? Not like she was—not like all the other Marked Ones—Mystics—*innocents* who had one foot forward and their heads turned over their shoulders.

He was royalty. How could he possibly know what that kind of pain was like? Was his mother murdered? Did he lose a beloved father? Was he forced to eat insects and chew on grass until he could earn enough coin to buy moldy bread?

Hunted for his magic. Alora held back the overwhelming urge to roll her eyes.

At least he still *possessed* his magic.

What pain did he suffer from his father because of it when it was still his to command?

None. He didn't know pain like everyone else. A royal, pardoned because of his bloodline. The only pain he'd probably ever known was exerting himself across a golden footpath instead of a male servant carrying him. How dare he compare himself to them—to her.

Lies, lies, lies. *It's all lies.*

She wouldn't believe it—not for a moment. Rescuing faeries and bringing them to his camp to do *what?* Rise up against the most powerful king—High King—in the history of Zyllyryon ... of all of Elysian?

You'd have to be raving mad to believe this. It was a death wish. And she already had one over her head simply for being born with magic. She didn't need another one. The moment she found an opportunity, she would run. It didn't matter where; it didn't matter how far. She'd been a slave to the service of one male, she wouldn't do it again.

Never again.

'You cannot run from me,' the High Prince's words echoed in her mind.

She blinked out of the forest in her daydream and looked reluctantly into his eyes.

Watch me.

"Enter." Garrik pulled his shirt over his death mark and buttoned it.

The guards positioned outside the tent pulled the entrance open as Jade walked through, carrying the same dark rose tunic, black pants, leather vest, and boots that had been in Alora's tent that morning. The clothing was mundane, almost similar to Jade's attire. Simple. Movable.

Easy to escape in.

Nothing like some of the luxurious ballgowns she'd been forced into before.

Jade stormed to her and threw the bundle of fabric and boots into Alora's chest. "Your guest's clothing." If Jade's voice was able to set the tent ablaze, they would all burn in the inferno. "Won't cover up the stench." She sniffed. "Unfortunately for us."

"That will be all, Jade." Garrik growled.

Jade's fiery red ponytail fell in long, loose strands and large braids down her back as she nodded with a scowl, and like a funnel cloud full of rage and destruction, stormed out.

Garrik stood with his arms crossed, jaw tight, looking at the tent entrance a moment too long. He turned to Alora, still displeased. "Apologies for her behavior. Jade's trust is not easily won. It took her a while to like me. Given time, I imagine you will become friends."

I doubt that. I won't be here long enough.

"So, am I to get dressed in front of you, mighty prince? Surely you have enough females around to tend to your fantasies. I won't be one of them."

The High Prince wickedly smirked. "As pleasing as that would be..." His traveling eyes glanced over her figure. "No." He turned away, picked up the swords, and leaned them against the table. "I will not watch, but I also will not leave. Can't have you fleeing or making a daring attempt at my life again." Garrik's back turned, pressing his fingers into the table, and he surveyed the maps that filled it.

Taking a moment to confirm his intentions, Alora, too, turned until their backs faced each other. She removed the cloak, pooling the night-dark fabric at her feet, and shuddered at the lick of air against her exposed skin. Her sapphires narrowed at the clasp before she pulled the ripped tunic over her head, then her lacey underthings, and exchanged them with the simple fashion Jade had thrown in her arms. Toeing the heels of her boots, she slipped them off, then undressed her lower half and exchanged the rest for the clothing left on the pile.

Surprisingly, the fabrics and boots were a perfect fit, almost as if they were created in her specific measurements. And much to her surprise, they were comfortable. She admitted that she would've worn this clothing at the manor if Kaine had ever allowed it instead of the extravagant gowns he kept her in.

"Mmhm," she coughed and watched the High Prince's attention stir. His chin rose from the maps but remained with his back turned. "Does this please His Highness?" The sarcasm flowed precisely as she had hoped, taunting him with a curtsy expected in the presence of royalty.

Garrik tore his glance from the canvas and gazed over his shoulder. Grinning, the powerful muscles in his back and shoulders flexed. He released his hands from the table and closed the distance between them in five steps. "And if I told you that it did?" he asked. She didn't mistake the gleam in his eye. "That I find that particular color, on you, to be ... especially appealing."

She held her ground as he stepped within a breath of her. "Then I'd say in your damned dreams."

Garrik darkly chuckled and returned that devilish grin.

Alora intended to threaten his proximity when a loud crash of iron and stone caused her heart to leap.

The muffled sounds of voices carried into the tent as they both turned to the entrance.

"For fuck's sake, Aiden. Must I constantly be surrounded by morons?" a gravelly female voice hissed.

"I'll have you know—" A sharp yelp and splash of liquid cut him off before he continued, "You. Have not had your dose of souls yet this morning, have you? Woke up on the wrong side of the cot?"

"I did not hear a word you just said. I was distracted by this pathetic —obnoxious—little noise that turned out to be your voice."

Another clash of iron was drowned out by Garrik's unamused, irritated voice. "I thought to invite you to breakfast, but I am beginning to think you should stay here until I attend to"—he glanced at the door—"a pest problem."

The bickering outside continued as he sighed. "Come out whenever you are ready. We will talk more after. I must warn you, do not wait long. Some in my Shadow Order have an appetite. Likely to be nothing but scraps should you delay." He grabbed his swords in one hand and exited the tent.

From the outside, Alora could hear Garrik's deep voice speaking to the guards, "You may retire for the morning. Go eat and take rest. I will call should I require you further."

Food. Right. She hadn't eaten since ...

When was the last time?

Alora scanned his space. Rather odd of a noble to have such simple accommodations. No gold statues, ornate rugs or curtains, no crown. The only piece of finery in there was the leathered chest on the floor, and even that didn't seem to fit the assumed belongings of royalty.

Quietly gliding across the room, Alora's curiosity peaked upon noticing the parchments on the table. Upon the maps routed with every trade route and passable dirt or stone path in the kingdom. To her disappointment, there was no mark, no inclination of where or which direction from Telldaira the camp sat. They could be anywhere north.

Though it was still quite foolish of the High Prince to leave out the very thing that she required to find herself as far away from him and his legion. Alora rifled through the parchment, finding not one but two maps of identical landscapes and terrain. Hopefully, he wouldn't miss one because, as Alora hesitated and decided, the map hidden at the bottom of the pile was rolled and shoved into her boot.

It could be foolish. Not only because the High King decreed that anyone found harboring a map would be sentenced to death for his own selfish reasoning. He'd deemed it necessary to keep Marked Ones from finding refuge within the realm. But by the time Garrik noticed one missing, she would be long gone.

Alora then looked to the table itself, bending down onto a knee and searching underneath. A map served only the purpose of a route and destination. But if she had any hope of succeeding, weapons would greater her chances. There had to be a weapon somewhere. One he'd forgotten, one easily obtainable, close and concealed. Perhaps even her weapon; the obsidian jeweled dagger that had vanished in a cloud of smoke and shadow in the forest. She ran her fingers under the table, under each chair. Shuffling her feet to the High Prince's chair, she searched there too.

Nothing.

His scaled armor waited, perfectly displayed on a form in the corner. She ran her hands through it, carefully pulling the battle-black leather pieces aside.

Nothing. *There is nothing here.*

It would've been easy to succumb to defeat. To accept that she was stars-knows-where in the kingdom. She could dwell on the fact that she was surrounded by soldiers who could possibly be nothing more than footmen for the High King. That the High Prince was lying and the moment she stepped from his tent, those Ravens waiting would bind her.

But she'd come too far in her suffering to surrender so easily.

And that's when she saw it.

Gleaming silver on the cot. On the black cloak she had worn all night ... the iron clasp. And as if the stars were on her side, on it would be a rounded flying dragon with sharp, pointed wings and a spiked tail.

Alora snatched the cloak from the furs, ripped the metal from the fabric, and stuffed it inside her corset.

A ridiculous laugh roared from outside, making her flinch.

Her stomach protested its hunger. Though she may not have wanted to risk it, she knew if she didn't eat soon, any escape attempt would be useless.

With a deep breath, Alora stiffened at the tent door, her eyes pressed tight and a silent prayer on her lips, opened it, and walked into the warm golden light of dawn.

CHAPTER 11

The heavy scent of fire, cooked meat, and coffee hovered in the breeze as the rising sun bathed the valley in warm light.

In every direction, an ocean of canvas as far as she could see marred the landscape. The High Prince's Dragons were ... a considerable force. Of remarkable size, almost unbelievable in its magnitude.

She hadn't taken in their particular firesite since her arrival. Being that she was struck by something like lightning and could barely remain on the horse. Her best conclusion was that the High Prince's personal soldiers' camp sat in the heart of the valley. Which made perfect sense; the High Prince would be positioned in the middle of his army. Not that he appeared to need protecting by it.

From his tent, she stared down a wide, trampled path, large enough to house two horse carts beside one another. To the left sat two canvases —one hers, the other no doubt one of his ... Shadow Order? Large enough to host three bodies comfortably, except hers, of course, which was the smallest. To the right, the same setup. Two more tents and horses tied to a long hitching post. Equal amounts of tents spread in every direction beyond there.

She fixed her hair, staring at the back of a tent with its entrance facing the steep hill in front of them.

At least the morning air was chilled. Normally, her burning skin would welcome the coolness of the outside air. But her fire was still gone, causing a soft chill to crawl across her skin instead.

Alora reluctantly walked forward. Straight for the fire filled with conversation and cheerful voices.

Toward them. Toward the laughter.

The raising of glasses, untroubled as they slay their hunger, disgusted her.

How can they be laughing after what happened last night? She balled her hand into a fist and shoved her arm around her torso, cheeks filling with heat.

Around the fire, the High Prince waited along with three of his soldiers. Garrik—the mere thought of his name had bile burning her throat—was sitting on a stump tall enough to sit comfortably for his height.

To his right, on a long since fallen tree, held the male who had nodded at her in the tavern, sharpening a monstrous, rune-covered sword. The words 'House of the Seventh N' engraved down the length of the golden blade jutting from the cross guard. It had a black, spiral leathered grip, and feathered wings with a golden pommel sat at its top.

To his right, Jade. Her end of the log a healthy distance from the flames of a roaring campfire. Alora didn't spend too long assessing her; she didn't deserve the attention.

To the High Prince's left, a new face that she hadn't been forced to meet yet. He was scruffy; disheveled, shaggy, black hair fell down to his chin. Wisps of it fell in front of light blue shale—somewhat mistakenly gray—colored eyes that created wrinkles as he laughed. The male stirred the contents of the iron pot, arm muscles outlined in his open-collared, long-sleeved, white tunic, and a bandolier strapped across his chest.

The male jumped from the ground onto his folded buckled boots. A red sash tied down by a thick leather belt around his waist swayed as he pointed at the fire upon her approach. "Welcome! Do hope you enjoy this morning's selections. We have a meager variety of last night's venison stew, courtesy of moi—best in the kingdom. Rock-solid morning bread is also on special, complete with a big cup of our finest roast." He sniffed a cup in his left hand. "Some sort of... Is that darkforest blend?" The male took a sip, twisting his face in disgust. "Oh, that is truly awful... Grog! Grog is always a favorite. Highly recommended. So many wonderful choices. How will you ever choose?"

What the hell—

"Aiden, sit down before you scare the poor girl off," a dark-skinned, High Fae male on the log joked. Clad with inked markings, symbols, and beasts over every inch of his arms, hands, and neck, he threw a piece of morning bread with perfect accuracy.

Aiden rubbed the back of his head where it had landed. "Scare? I think she rather likes me."

Garrik stood from the stump and walked to her, carrying a bowl full of stew. "Ignore him. We all do." He said, grinning as Aiden crossed his arms, "Allow me," and offered her the bowl.

With a crooked snarl, Alora replied, "I'm perfectly capable of getting my own." *It's likely poisoned.*

Garrik raised an eyebrow, and with his right hand, scooped the stew, and proceeded to eat as she watched him. "Have it your way." He returned to the stump, settling back down to eat from the bowl meant for her.

Scanning the firesite, she found an empty bowl beside Aiden. He caught her glance and lifted it to her with a reassuring smile.

The corners of her mouth twitched as she accepted it from him and spooned stew from the iron pot above the flames. Alora searched around for a spot to sit. The only option was beside Jade, who took notice of her and shifted her position enough that she covered the space left.

Alora didn't care to find herself in a territorial battle. Instead of standing awkwardly, she decided to walk past them, in the direction of her tent.

"Where do you think you are going?" Garrik still faced the campfire.

"I'll eat in my tent ... alone."

"You will stay here with us." He stood. The muscles in his forearms shifted as he beckoned her to the stump. Tanned skin had been washed clean. His voice roughened. "Sit."

Alora stifled a frustrated growl. *I'm not one of your soldiers. You can't order me around.*

She reluctantly walked back and sat.

Garrik waited for her to settle before he found a new position in the dirt alongside Aiden. And, before long, the group sat eating in silence.

The crisp morning breeze was yielding to warm air filled with the sounds of camp and the aroma of campfires cooking. Alora was careful to scan the area. Searching for any points of weakness to make her attempt at fleeing. But it was utterly useless. They were surrounded by thousands of tents and patrolling soldiers.

It was Aiden who broke the silence. "Garrik, I've been meaning to ask. How did you get that lovely scrape on your chin? Get in a scuffle with a water troll again?" Aiden motioned with his thumb and rubbed his own chin where Garrik's cut lay.

"I'm sure the story is much more interesting than the water troll. Wouldn't have anything to do with what happened to your nose?" The dark-skinned High Fae leaned in and grinned.

Aiden's shale eyes beamed. "Yes, do tell us, how is your lovely nose?"

Garrik simply stared at them with stern eyes. Alora thought a temper would rise, but he merely countered, "Most of my introductions with newcomers are not quite as eventful as this one, I will admit. Our ... *charming* guest decided to demonstrate some of her"—The High Prince paused and raked his eyes over her body, sending heat to her cheeks once more—"skills this morning."

"I'm sure you gave him a run for his coin!" the male roared, patting Alora's shin with a tattooed hand. "I'm Thalon. It's truly a pleasure."

Thalon was about the same size as Garrik, taller by one hand. He didn't dress like anyone else. In fact, everyone around the fire had traded their armor for normal wear. Adorned in a white shirt that was tied with a leather string from the chest up, Thalon's sleeves were ripped off, exposing the impressive swell of his inked biceps.

A black and brown leather vest hugged tightly to every muscle on his torso. His beautiful, unmarked, clean-cut bearded face, illuminated by the dawn, revealed golden eyes just as magnificent, and dark, half-shaved locks and braids carried rounded, golden beads at the ends.

But that wasn't what she dwelled on as she inspected him.

It was the markings. They covered him. Sleeves up his arms and chest extended to his neck halfway until they stopped. They consisted of magical creatures, plants, ancient languages, and various faerie marks that she couldn't read. And placed on his upper left arm, Thalon had a swirling, cracked circle, storm-like in appearance, like lightning strikes.

Her inspection ended on the mark. It seemed hidden by a fire-spitting dragon. The same she had seen on the clasp from her cloak.

Alora gripped her bowl, feeling the heat seep into her fingers. The High Prince mentioned that she had made an attempt on his life just moments ago. Not one harbored any expression of rage, not one pulled a sword or threatened to take her away. The two males only sat, gleaming like younglings on Winter Solstice morning.

"From the looks of it, your meeting went well!" Aiden raised his cup.

"You know he let you do that," Jade interrupted the laughter. "Garrik is a master swordsman. Your head wouldn't be intact if he didn't allow it. If you were anyone outside this camp, you would have lost it."

Aiden ignored her. "Ah, don't be scared. We've all taken a crack at the bastard at one point," he said and jammed his spoon into Garrik's side, who pushed it away with a low grunt.

Alora scrunched her eyebrows, pressing her lips tight.

"What of Eldacar this morning? He is missing breakfast." Garrik's focus shifted beyond their firesite to behind his tent.

"I heard a rumor that he was nose-deep in the Morgacca this morning. Some new discovery. I didn't want to bother him. He could get *short* with me." Aiden winked at Alora.

Thalon shook his head, threatening to throw another piece of bread.

"Who's Eldacar?" Not that she truly cared, but the benefit of information might aid her in escape.

Aiden leaned over to her and elbowed her leg. "You'll love him. Smart, chatty, dashingly good looks. Not as dashing as I, of course." He winked again, brushing his hands back through ebony hair.

Alora froze.

Unlike High Fae, Aiden had rounded ears.

Another myth. Monsters from far beyond their world. Dark creatures, evil beyond anything their world had ever seen or imagined. Demons who walked their lands and destroyed anything they put their hands on.

Her eyes widened in fear. She leaned away, voice shaking. "You're human?"

Aiden's face turned unreadable. His cheerful demeanor fell uneasy. "You can see my ears?"

The group was unnervingly silent.

"I ... um." Alora's breath caught.

Aiden's face twisted into a wicked laugh. "I'm messing with you. Half, actually. Father, High Fae. Mother, human. Made for interesting family reunions. Zero out of ten. Would not recommend. Stopped aging around twenty-eight human years thanks to one grumpy witch that we shall not speak of." Aiden shook off a disgusted shudder. "We age fast. Your one hundred years to our ten. I've been alive close to sixty, but just as devilishly handsome."

Alora pinched her eyebrows and shifted in her seat. She herself was three centuries old, and scanning the circle, most of them seemed to be around the same age. Thalon, perhaps, a little older. Aiden was no exception. His face didn't reveal sixty human years. He was as young as they were.

"So, you finally admit that you're a child." A pleasing, mocking grin covered Jade's face. By faerie years, Aiden would still be a youngling if his blood was like them.

"Now that one"—Aiden pointed with his spoon at Jade—"We don't know what the devil she is. Death herself? Mmm, possibly. Don't get on her bad side. She's been known to look a male straight in the eyes and his soul willingly left his body."

"Smartest thing a male could ever do." Jade leaned back on the log and propped her feet up, clutching the ivory pendant, set in melted iron, of a necklace.

Aiden motioned to Thalon. "Him. Nicest High Fae you'll ever meet. Has a ... higher calling. Golden personality. Saved my bloody ass a time or two. Thank the seas and stars for his portals or I'd be—"

"You're a Marked One?" Alora shifted toward Thalon.

"Indeed." Thalon gave her a reassuring, gentle smile.

"Thalon is a Mystic just as you, as I." The High Prince stared into his bowl and continued eating.

"You're all Marked Ones then?"

Aiden's eyes widened in shock. "Bloody hells, no! I'd be completely irresistible then. Can you imagine these looks and magic? The kingdom would simply crumble under jealousy."

She looked around the group, sapphires falling upon Garrik. "And what of the mighty prince? What's he like?"

"Ah, Garrik. Well, he's..." Aiden shifted his weight, turning to the High Prince.

Garrik leaned forward, rested his elbows on his knees, and glared.

"He's—"

Garrik arched a brow, still those silver irises burning with lethal warning.

"Better stop while you're ahead, or you'll be tending the horses tonight." Thalon laughed as he scraped his spoon around his bowl.

Aiden and Thalon continued talking. Unlike the two males, Garrik remained quiet. The silver of his eyes seemed worlds away, deep in thought, as if considering the mountains far in the distance.

All the stories ... everything she'd heard of this Savage Prince who claimed no prisoners, save for the Marked Ones he procured for his father, swirled in her mind. The High Fae sitting on the ground before her didn't offer the same image those tales rumored.

Perhaps he *could* be trusted.

Perhaps she was a damn fool for even considering it.

When the conversation slowed, Garrik stood and inhaled deeply. "Aiden, find Ghost. Thalon, Jade; Brennus summons us to his camp. Making him wait much longer would be an act of war."

"Shall I fix up a lovely breakfast basket for him? Might help turn his permanent frown upside down," Aiden joked, complete with hand motions.

Garrik crossed his arms. "And lead him to believe he was being poisoned? Are you trying to have me killed?"

The males laughed. Thalon and Aiden settled their bowls on the dirt and rose, adjusting the swords sheathed at their sides.

Before leaving, Thalon stopped and offered a hand to Alora. "It's nice to meet you." He paused. "I'm sorry, I didn't catch a name?"

She raked her eyes over him. Something on the ground behind him ... his shadow. Large and wing-like in the morning light; hidden to the eye unless searching for it. It seemed to connect to his body's shadow. But when she surveyed his considerable form, there was nothing. Sleep deprivation certainly caused this illusion, she reasoned. And he still waited with an outstretched hand.

Her name.

He'd asked, and she hadn't given it. Names were powerful. Names meant something. They could be manipulated to control the being who owned it.

"Nadeleine," she said. Her mother's name. She hadn't spoken it in years. The mere sound of it calmed her nerves as she clasped Thalon's hand and shook it.

"Her name is Alora." The three of them turned to Garrik, who stood with his arms crossed.

Shock and confusion covered her face. *How does he—*

"It's an honor to meet you, Alora." Thalon's voice was comforting, soft. Like smooth fur in the freezing weather. "From one Mystic to another, I'm glad you're here. You're safe with us." His tattooed palm gripped the top of hers before he let go completely.

Aiden dramatically bent at his torso and bowed, arms out at his sides. Then, the two walked off behind them toward the hitching posts.

She whipped her head to the High Prince, eyes widened. "How did you—"

"Come with me." He gave her little regard as he turned and walked toward his tent, as if he expected her to follow. Like any royal would.

But Alora stood firm on her feet, fists balled at her sides. "Not until you tell me how you know who I am."

Garrik stopped mid-stride.

His deep voice shook with frustration. "Come. Now."

CHAPTER 12

Garrik escorted her through a maze of tents and shadows with unsettling silence.

High Prince or not, no one held the power to know who someone was without a name being spoken to them.

And she would never grant him that kind of power over her. Never.

Their intended route brought them to the front of a massive tent, much larger than any other in camp. Not even Garrik's compared to its size. Seven steep peaks topped the long, draped, black canvas, and open windows fluttered in the morning breeze, allowing a glow of dim light to escape the inside.

It was dark—very dark. The image of such a blackened structure among the white sea was so out of place, Alora's feet protested the path ahead. Her heavy steps scuffed the dirt and grass, beholding it as they walked to the doors.

A strong scent of aged vanillin wood hovered in the air. The grass outside the door completely trampled from heavy traffic.

Garrik held open the tent entrance for her, gesturing for her to walk inside. "Go in."

"What is this, your traveling throne room? Your golden crown awaits." Alora pulled the opposite flap open, scowled at him as she passed, and ducked inside.

Not an ounce of sunlight touched the space, save for the small rays peeking through four open glass windows, one on each wall. It was like she'd stepped into a great hall.

How was that possible? Alora's eyes widened, raking them over an unbelievable room. Instead of canvas walls and an open breeze, she was greeted with glass lanterns spread across the ceiling, hanging from a two-story, open-concept—

No. Surely she was dreaming. There was no other explanation.

A library.

Even the libraries in Telldaira were nothing compared to the beauty and the ancient smell this place held. Tomes upon tomes and leather-bound texts of every color and shade were wedged tight. Thousands of books lined every corner of the shelves in the spectacular room.

On the floor level, hiding under the left mezzanine that stretched around the entire room, sat a small cot fit for one, and even that appeared layered with open texts, parchment, and quills.

In the center, atop wooden floorboards and a gold-lined crimson rug, a polished, long rectangular desk waited. It too overflowing with mounds of open texts and one lonely lantern dancing its soothing glow. Seven polished coffee-colored pillars jutted to a ceiling that beheld a dancing clouded sky, yet its light didn't touch the dim library. Wrapped around the center-most pole, a winding wooden staircase pierced through the top to where she believed she could see a rooftop terrace.

A pile of books toppled to the ground to her left.

"Well, actually, it's mine." A short, lean-built, brown-eyed High Fae male with curly, auburn hair poked his head around a book pile much taller than him. He leaned down and picked up the tomes that had fallen, wrinkling his nose to adjust round-rimmed glasses. "Not a throne room, but much better." He paused, fumbling with a book to reach his palm out to her. "Nice to finally meet you! I'm Eldacar."

Garrik speared him with a stern glare.

"How is this possible?" Alora questioned, eyes so wide the whites glowed.

"Forgive her manners, this is Alora." Shadows whirled in the High Prince's hand, disappearing on a phantom wind before revealing a small, red leather-bound book. He stretched out his arm and handed it down to the redhead, who graciously accepted it.

Brown eyes practically gleaming in excitement, Eldacar nodded a sheepish bow and mouthed a quiet, 'Thank you.'

Turning to her, Garrik explained, "Eldacar is one of my most trusted advisers and friends. He and his library accompany us wherever my legion moves."

His short size, and even the appearance of his high-collared, brown leather jacket, made Eldacar appear out of place. No armor, just as the rest. No weapons that she could see. The lack of muscles, not useful in a fight. Crunching her eyebrows in confusion, Alora questioned, "So you're a soldier, then?"

"Oh, skies above, no. I wouldn't know what to do with a sword. Books though." He opened his arms, pointing at everything around him while spinning slowly, red book still in hand. He hit a mound of books piled beside him, knocking a few down. "Books are my weapon."

Garrik knelt down and picked them up, placing them on the table.

"Thank you, sire." Eldacar grabbed one of the remaining books in Garrik's hands and settled it atop the one he still held.

"Eldacar is skilled in the knowledge of magical gifts from times past. The books here carry wisdom suited for our kind, to help us understand our powers, to train." Garrik leaned back against the table, one foot crossing his leg, and he folded his arms in front of him.

Walking around the space, careful to avoid stepping on any books, Alora turned and ran her hands over a leather-bound text falling apart on a nearby bookshelf. Next to the cot was a glass chest filled with what seemed to be ashes of a nearly destroyed book, save for a few rips of pages, and scraps of burned, discolored leather. The case held her attention for a moment longer as she considered it.

Until her head pivoted, and she scanned the lower level.

Her eyes traced up the winding staircase to the mezzanine, raking her sapphires over those overflowing surfaces too.

"You've read ... *all* of these?"

Eldacar smiled and adjusted his glasses by wrinkling his nose. "More than once. They're quite the page turners. And our most gracious High Prince has once again returned from another daring adventure with my next read." He patted the red book in hand as his smile stretched to his ears. "Now, if you're here to see me, that must mean you too have magic. Tell me, Alora, what can you do?" With an excited grin, he patted his upper arm where her mark would be.

From the shift in stance and stern stare from the High Prince, she couldn't hesitate long. Another moment of asking for critical information from her. Another piece that could be used against her.

After enduring her hesitation for some time, Garrik pushed off the table. He turned to one of the books he had set there and opened it. Glancing at the page, then turning to another, he spoke to no one but the page in front of him. "Alora can summon fire and bend objects at her will."

She stiffened.

Another piece of her that she had never offered him.

A look of shock covered Eldacar's face. "How interesting! I haven't crossed someone with more than one gift in ages. None other than Garrik, of course." He excitedly clapped his hands and ran around the bookshelves.

Then, Eldacar's feet padded up the winding staircase and exited to the right, bouncing along the shelves. With a hop, he plucked a green leather-bound book wedged within, toppling two to the ground before he turned, barely keeping his balance, before winding down the staircase back to them.

Beaming, he said, "Perhaps there's more. Tell me, have you ever held a dead rose and it came back to life?"

Her teeth gritted as she shook her head.

Why would she *ever* want to bring a rose back to life? Especially the blood-red, stars-awful ones that she doomed to wilt away after Kaine's half-assed apologies.

Though she had never attempted such a power, even if she had and discovered that she could, she still wouldn't have told them.

"No lifeline shifting then, what about controlling trees or vines?"

"No." Alora rubbed her bruised wrist and stared at the floor.

"Hmm." Eldacar flipped a few pages. "The ability to pick someone up and drop them flat on the head?"

She concealed her amusement. Although, she did find it rather enjoyable to picture the High Prince plummeting from the sky and landing on that smug face. Alora's cheeks scarleted at the mere thought. "Not that I'm aware of, but I'd be happy to try."

Alora flexed her palm in Garrik's direction.

He released an almost inaudible growl, causing her to snap her attention back to the redhead.

"That would have come in handy, I'm sure." He looked at Garrik, who folded his arms in front of his chest. "Tell me, can you see into minds around you?"

The High Prince went rigid, and she hesitated.

Honestly, she was uncertain. A time flooded back to her when Kaine cornered her, standing atop the grand staircase in their home. Nausea formed in her gut as she remembered his screams for disobeying one of his ridiculous commands. Those screams had filled the entire manor, like smoke from the roaring fireplaces and sconces on the walls. To the point her ears had rung. She'd only wanted the screaming to stop. Something inside her mind tingled in a calmed caress, desperately warring to rip away the splitting headache before she closed her eyes and her entire body froze.

Kaine had stopped screaming.

His face, body, and fingers grew relaxed. As if by some miracle, he had stopped.

But it only lasted for a few seconds until he twisted her arm. Blaming her for the moment of peace before he threw her down the staircase where she ended up laying for hours until her body mustered the pitiful strength to rise from the floor.

Garrik shifted in his position uncomfortably, clearing his throat, waiting for a response. His face had turned from curiosity to tight agitation as he dropped his arms and walked closer to her. In a subtle attempt to touch her arm, he reached for her.

"Are you alright?" Garrik's voice broke the heavy air around them.

Alora pulled away. Everything inside her screamed to say nothing. "Don't touch me. I'm fine." She turned away and banded her arms around her torso.

Garrik's face shifted as he walked close enough that she could smell the leather and metal of his scent.

Silver met sapphire.

His body dangerously close.

"Do not lie to me." The High Prince gritted his teeth. A small wisp of smoke and shadow rose from his shoulders, and the darkened tent added to the intensity cascading from him.

"You don't scare me." And she turned every bit of that panic, that fear, into embers ready to explode. If her magic ran through her veins, they would have ignited.

Alora stepped back. He mirrored her, closing the distance between. Then, another step, only to collide against the wooden frame of the cot with her calves.

"Then why is your heart racing so fast?" His hands. They were far too close to her. His breath. Ice.

Eldacar quickly made himself scarce within the library.

Alora willed herself not to swallow and straightened her neck upward until her sapphire gaze burned at him. Gritting her teeth, baring a quieted snarl.

"Why should I tell you? You think that just because you're the High Prince that I have to tell you anything? Shove your ego up your ass."

Shaking palms slammed into his broad chest, sending him backward toward the table.

Garrik was behind her in a heartbeat, gripping her forearms across her chest. "Careful, clever girl. I could kill you for that."

"So could another faerie. A cat. A dedicated pigeon. You aren't special. You think others haven't tried? Go ahead." Alora forced her arms out of his hold and twisted to face him. "Give it your best shot." She outstretched her arms at her sides. "At least I could go down fighting instead of the High King ripping every bit of magic from my body."

A low rumble vibrated across the floor as Garrik flashed his teeth.

Alora glared straight at his eyes. Not afraid. Not backing down.

The High Prince backed away first, controlling his rising anger with measured breaths. He closed his eyes as if counting to ten before he spoke again. "What must I do to make you trust me? Is it that hard to believe someone might wish to help you?"

"*Nothing* will ever make me trust you. And if I had any bit of my powers right now, I'd use them to burn that smug look off your face and get the hell out of here. I do not trust you. I don't want to be here in your fantasized heroic adventure. I don't wish to help you. I want to be free."

Face tight, Garrik balled a fist at his side. "Perhaps I should have left you to die in Telldaira."

"Maybe you should've. It would be better than spending another second waiting for someone else to determine my fate while I'm left here powerless."

The veins in his arms bulged the tighter his fists squeezed. Shadow and smoke tendrils began to engulf the surrounding space.

"Powerless," he scoffed, cutting himself off with a vicious growl. "If you wish to have your powers back—"

"*Back*," she snapped. "What do you mean, *back*? You've taken them?" Her voice rose. She advanced at the High Prince, ready to swing. All this time, she thought whatever the soldiers injected her with was the cause. Thought that its lasting effects were soon to wear off, only to find out it was ... *him*?

Garrik growled again. "Enough! When you can be trusted, like answering my starsdamned questions, they will be returned to you."

"Trusted. *I* can't be trusted? What about you?" She stepped closer to him. "You want answers? How about when we were riding from my city and I begged you ... *begged you* to tell me where you were taking me? You said nothing. Here's the same courtesy, mighty prince."

"Would you rather have had a picnic in the middle of the night with Magnelis's army present and acquaint ourselves a little better? Perhaps you would care for everyone in the starsdamned kingdom to know who you are and what you can do."

"You could've told me."

"I am under no obligation to explain myself to anyone. I am the High Prince." Garrik's voice raged as he slammed his fist into a pile and sent books tumbling.

"Sounds like something your dear father would say. I knew you were just like him."

Glass exploded from the windows, blasting across the library. The essence of death in the room could be sliced with a blade as the lanterns above their heads rained down the broken shards.

The High Prince's eyes turned into a sea of ink, vacant of any light. Smoke and shadows tore away at pages, flinging books open in a harsh wind. The stacks, every one of them, beveled and rattled. The wood swayed and buckled. Some toppled and flipped over the mezzanine railing to crash into the open space of the first floor. The whole library was about to burst.

"Sire—" Eldacar's voice cracked, calling from behind a pillar.

"*What?*" Garrik's eruption shook the wooden floor and remaining upright shelves as he snapped his head in Eldacar's direction.

Eldacar flinched, backing away into the shadow of the furthest mezzanine, eyes wide in fear.

Garrik's voice softened. His face relaxed with a deep sigh as his storm around them began to fade, leaving a disheveled mess of torn pages, toppled piles, and shelves in its wake. He scanned the carnage, then looked to his shaking friend and swallowed hard. "Apologies, Eldacar. Please, speak."

Eldacar hesitated. Hands trembling as he gripped a ruined book. "Might I make a suggestion?"

The High Prince nodded.

With a flick of his wrist, his shadows whorled and tendriled across the destruction. In a surge of darkened mist and clouds of ash, the library was returned to its previous state. Garrik moved with measured steps, leaning against the table as he did before. With a quick adjustment of his tunic across his abdomen, before he crossed his arms, Garrik lowered his head to stare at the gold stitching on the crimson rug, listening.

"Perhaps we can discuss dear Alora's powers after dinner? I would be happy to meet with you myself, in here, with all of my friends." He sheepishly grinned, handing her a book. "They know so much more than I do and are great listeners."

Alora rubbed her arm, then reached out and accepted the book. It beheld an image of a butterfly, its wings made of fire. She traced her fingers over the indentations and a language that she had never learned. *How will I get out of this? I don't trust them.* Burning tears brimmed her bottom lashes.

"We are trying to help you." Garrik's gaze lifted from the floor, and a softened gleam in his eyes met her. "I would not have risked my friends' lives otherwise."

She refused to meet the High Prince's stare but reluctantly nodded, glimpsing the redhead in the dim lantern light.

Eldacar gazed at her with an awkward smile. "We haven't had anyone like you join us yet. I can't wait to see what you can do." He tapped his fingers together in delight.

"You may never get to unless the mighty prince gives me back my powers."

Garrik shifted against the table. "In time, until then, prove to me you can be trusted without them. I will not allow a loose weapon in this camp before I know how it works."

"I'm not an 'it' and don't need my powers to be a weapon." Alora purposefully jerked her eyes to the sword sheathed at his side. "I think I've proven myself already."

That irritatingly annoying smirk crossed his face, and she balled her fist to prevent it from careening into his cheek.

"There will be opportunities for you to display what you can do. For now, stay and get acquainted with camp. When I return from my summons, we can find a place for you here that you are comfortable with."

"What, you don't wish to bring me along to keep an eye on me?" She crossed her arms.

Garrik's smirk deepened. "Are you eager to sit on my horse once more?"

"Not as eager as you are to have me riding it, I'm sure." Alora scoffed and rolled her eyes.

Desiring silver irises flicked down to her mouth, then slowly traveled up to burn into her sapphires. He cocked his head, eyes lowering in a squint as if he could see right through her.

Garrik held his wolfish grin for a moment longer. Alora warred off a sudden flutter low in her stomach from that stare when he turned to the librarian and said, "Thank you, Eldacar, for your knowledge. We will return later for training. Do not go wandering off."

Eldacar gaped. A puzzling look crossed his eyes as they widened. "Me? Wandering? Oh, sire, sometimes I wonder if you even know me at all."

Garrik motioned for Alora to walk in front of him to leave. This time, when he held the entrance open, she reluctantly passed through without a glare.

IT WAS EASIER to hate him.

To imagine him as the greatest enemy Elysian had ever known.

Not the High Fae male who greeted every soldier they passed when returning to the firesite. Not someone who actually cared enough for the well-being of those patrolling, those resting around crackling fires or tending to tack and armor. Questioning if the accommodations and food were up to his standards. If their cots were fitting enough, if they had enough lanterns or blankets.

A few mentioned minuscule things, to which he effortlessly waved his hand, and smoke and shadows whorled, dissipating around his palm or on the ground, revealing the very thing requested.

He almost seemed to care.

But no amount of warm greetings or charm would change her mind.

A shadow darkened the sun above them. Alora glimpsed the sky to see the black wings of five faeries, and one with pearly white feathers, flying in the sky. A clanging of metal echoed into the valley as they paired off, meeting metal on metal, raining sparks above the tents like trickling rain.

In the distance, near the lake, more sharpened metal rang.

"The Wingborne," Garrik interrupted the sparring sounds, noticing her curiosity.

One dark-haired faerie with glistening black wings swept through the sky to defend an incoming blade. She recognized him as the guard who was stationed outside the High Prince's tent.

"Their general." He nodded to the two. Wings of black and the other of white mixed in a blur as they wrestled, airborne, and their bodies pushed from one another in a fury. "Keeps them in constant operation. Soon, the entire sky will be filled. It is quite a magnificent sight."

Noticing a strange, subtle gleam in the High Prince's face as he observed them, Alora said nothing. Drowning out his voice to quiet a rippling fire still raging in her veins from Eldacar's tent.

And now ... not only did she have to worry about patrols on the ground but the threat from wings above, too.

He registered her silence and stepped in front of her, blocking the view of the sky. "I should not have said those things."

She stayed silent, tightening her lips, refusing to look at him, and instead watched a soldier pulling on his boots near a fire.

His chest rose with a deep breath. "I will ask you again. What must I do for you to trust me?"

You can die. Her eyes darted beside her, assessing the fluttering fabric of a tent, focusing on anything but him.

Garrik crossed his arms. His jaw tensed as he lifted an eyebrow. "I am waiting."

He could wait all day. She didn't care. Maybe she should say it. A true sacrifice for the realm, the only thing worthy enough for her to trust him. In truth, nothing she would ask of him would matter. Not when she would be gone soon and never see it through.

"You want to prove to me that you can be trusted after everything you've done?" Alora turned to him, digging her heels into the dirt, stretching her chin high in defiance. "Bring me a burning Blazebloom, mighty prince. Then I'll trust you."

The High Prince's skin paled. Tension rolled through his shoulders and neck.

A Blazebloom—a burning Blazebloom—the rarest, most impossibly difficult to locate, eternal flower of the southern kingdoms. And not just any kingdom—the Fire Kingdom. A sky-high wall of burning flames separated their lands and all others. Even High King Magnelis couldn't penetrate their borders.

And their flower—their most *sacred* flower—only mentioned in ancient tales of times past was said to contain eternal flames from the stars themselves. A magic unlike anything this world could contain. Full of danger, destruction, passion, desire. The power of life. In the wrong hands, they could level an entire world. In the right ones...

No one past the Fire Kingdom's borders had ever seen one. They didn't exist as far as anyone knew.

"You know not of what you ask." Smoke and shadows danced around Garrik's rigid shoulders.

"I do, in fact, know a thing or two about this world. You asked me what it would take to trust you. After everything you've done to me. To all those I've heard stories about. It would take a damn miracle for me to trust you."

She turned to walk away, but his strong grip found her forearm. "You would have me go as far as the southern shores of Fire Kingdom just to pick you a flower? Risking my life in Kiagan's lands to find some rumor in the wind? What you ask is impossible."

As long as it's as far away from me. "I'm sure the High Prince of Elysian will be just fine." Her brow arched. "What? Afraid are you?"

"Afraid? Never." He paused, veins bulging in his forearm. "Challenged." That wolfish smirk returned, irritating her wholly. "You wicked, clever thing. If you wanted me to get you flowers, all you had to do was ask."

Alora rolled her eyes so far that a wind could've been summoned. She laughed at the thought of it, though. At even requesting one of the very things she hated the most.

He chuckled. "Alright then. If I complete your task, you will trust me. But shall we sweeten the deal?" Garrik's shadows danced around his shoulders wildly now, and he fixed his eyes once more on the clanging of swords in the sky.

THEY RETURNED to find Aiden in the dirt, on his back, with his feet propped up against the fallen log. Sharpening a curved sword and humming a cheerful melody as his boots bounced midair to the beat.

Jade had traded her normal attire for her battle-black armor, lodging daggers, quite accurately, into a tree nearby. Alora wondered if Jade wished it was her face those daggers were embedding into instead.

"Ghost?" In no way of a greeting, Garrik stalked toward the fire.

"Attended to and saddled. Prepared to leave at your command." Thalon emerged from between two tents, also adorned in his armor. Rolling tension from his back and shoulders, he sheathed a golden sword behind his back and wiped a sheen of sweat from his forehead.

Aiden held up a longsword by the blade as Garrik passed him by.

In a smooth motion, Garrik gripped the hilt, pulling it from Aiden's hand. "Aiden, see to the training arena." Glancing at Alora, who sat on the stump by the fire, he added, "I expect to return within a few hours."

"Aye aye, Captain." Aiden pulled himself to his feet and sheathed his own sword.

Garrik turned to Alora. "Stay within camp until my return."

Those silver eyes flashed to her boot, the map concealed inside, and she warred off the flush of scarlet burning her cheeks. He couldn't know about it—he hadn't been inside his tent since he'd left her inside.

"Aiden will remain here should you require anything." And before she could say anything—do anything—shadows tendriled from Garrik's body, swirling around him in clouds of ash and smoke, engulfing him in a storm of darkness.

She watched him step from it, mesmerized.

His scaled battle leathers were now returned as he walked toward the hitching line. The tendrils of darkness swirling behind his back as he walked away.

Warmth brushed her skin before Aiden's voice murmured beside her, low and with just as much wonder as her examination. "Smokeshadows," was all he said, gesturing with a nod to the whorls dancing around Garrik's shoulders.

Alora couldn't take her eyes off them, off the power she could feel rippling from them. From *him*.

Thalon and Jade followed to where three horses were tied while a white one grazed, saddled and unhitched, and each mounted. Garrik patted his white horse on the neck and offered it a stroke before sheathing the sword to the saddle. In one effortless swing, his foot slipped into the stirrup and he mounted.

Her name fit well. Ghost, Alora heard him call her. Much like the shadows, they too were difficult to turn from. They looked almost majestic together. And as if the skies were in agreement, she could have sworn she saw a glistening twinkle of starlight on Ghost's forehead. Only for a moment. Perhaps a reflection of light from somewhere in camp.

Garrik caught her enchanted eyes, and she quickly tore them away. "I will return soon. Remember, you are safe here." He about nudged Ghost, then stopped. His eyes flashed to her boot once more before his careful warning laced in the air. "Do not do anything foolish." With a resolute nudge of his heel, he, Ghost, and the two others rode down the line of tents.

The sound of hooves faded as they climbed the hill, diminishing from view when they passed the sentries, leaving only a rising swirl of thick smoke and shadow dancing up into the sky.

He'd left her.

How foolish of him.

How foolish indeed.

CHAPTER 13

Alora paced the empty firesite. An occasional, crisp breeze, laced with smoke and the earthy taste of a nearby lake, echoed of clanging steel mixed with confident cheers and grunts across the valley. Far from the padding of maidservant footsteps turning over bedrooms and preparing for a new day at the manor.

And unlike the spread of warm, steaming pastries fresh from the ovens and lush fruits of ripe flavors, her breakfast settled like stones in her stomach, with the savory, smoked waft of stew lingering on the wind.

Camp teemed with life, unlike the early hours of darkness. Through a trampled path that lay between Garrik's tent and expanded out into smaller walkways, Alora could see flashes of blackened armor and the gleam of steel in the shards of sunlight. She only knew one path within the labyrinth, the one to Eldacar's tent. And given the amount of canvases she glimpsed in the moonlight, there really was no clear path out.

Even so, Alora ached to follow the scurrying of steps trailing between the rows.

If the High Prince expected her to stay in the confines of his secluded area in camp, he was highly mistaken.

Alora pivoted on her pacing feet, turning to the hill in which the High Prince rode off and thrust a highly satisfying middle finger in the air. She wondered if she would've had the courage to shove it in his face. Wondered enough to the point of wishing he would soon return so she could try.

Wherever this newfound courage had uprooted itself from, she relished it. After all, she'd been fanning her embered self, from the ashes of Kaine, for many years. Slowly, she was igniting back from a dark and lonely place. Back to who she knew she always was, and away from the parts of her that he stole. Or suffocated.

With the High Prince, it almost felt easy—effortless—to be herself. *As simple as with any stranger*, she supposed. Easy to be who she once was with people who hadn't seen the person Kaine had broken her into.

Alora didn't know how she held the courage to fight. In fact, it was even more dangerous to disobey the High King's son, especially amongst his army. Especially inches in front of him.

She didn't care.

Screw *him* and all the males who ever thought they could control a female.

Screw. Them. All.

Though the emptiness, and lack of watchful eyes, was a welcoming feeling.

She could return to her dreary, cramped tent. Sit and take pity for her situation, for getting herself into another game of beauty and beast. But stars be damned if she'd surrender now. And the longer she waited, the harder it would be to escape. There was no time to find comfort or let her guard down.

If I could just walk around this place, I'd find the best way out.

The trampled path beside the bastard's tent remained empty for some time. It seemed the best option to wander off.

Alora scoured the area once more. The hill would hold little cover for her to climb, and once she crested the top, she would have to slip unseen through ten sentries before reaching the swallowing darkness of the forest. Low odds of success. The only option would be to explore the maze of tents until she found an unguarded opening or blind spot before slipping into the forest on the valley level.

If she was captured again, she could use the excuse of falling lost on her way to relieve herself, perhaps even to secure food.

Alora was so lost in her scheming that as her boots brought her to the edge of the path, she didn't notice Aiden leaning against a tree, clouded in the shadow on the far side of a tent. Waiting at the edge of the path beside Garrik's lodgings.

"As enticing as it may be to find yourself on a morning stroll, entertain yourself within our firesite, love. Wouldn't want you getting yourself lost. Garrik would have my head for dinner. Which, in all honesty, might actually taste better than what's planned for tonight. Thalon's cooking." Aiden's mouth twisted into a disgusted grimace. "But I still wouldn't like my head to roll." He pushed himself off the tree, his frocked black coat, embellished with ornate brass buckles and buttons, danced in the wind as he walked toward her.

"You can't expect me to sit here and do nothing waiting for the High Prince to return." *I'm not his wife, and I certainly won't wait around for him to return.* Alora crossed her arms, visibly annoyed.

"How about a nice nap? Freshen up for this evening? Maybe a fun game of poker or Liar's Dice?" Aiden produced two marble cubes from his pocket and smiled.

The dice were ... oddly designed. Unlike others she'd seen, these both had skull faces on the side reserved for two blacked dots.

Alora surveyed them, and her expression warmed to fiery rebellion. "I'm going exploring. If you don't wish for me to get lost, then you can join me if you must."

Without waiting for any protest, Alora strutted past the High Prince's tent and began her path of weaving around canvases. Taking great care to memorize every turn, how many soldiers were stationed at each fire, where random trees grew, tables ... and weapons.

Eventually, she emerged in a large clearing where a wooden, oval-shaped wall was constructed only feet from the smooth, white stones lining the lake. The lake was silently present, mirroring the landscape of endless pines around its shores where water rippled and passed over the stones.

The oval structure—it was nothing glamorous. In fact, it was quite ordinary. Nothing but sun-faded wood, nearly waist height, large enough to fit a hundred bodies, with benches just as sun-soaked scattered around it.

An arena. A training or sparring arena based on the intricate maneuvers of swords, groaning battle leathers, and fists on flesh from within the walls. Horses were hitched to the left, some cargo wagons and carts stationed to their right in front of the forest.

The crunching footsteps on gravel and dirt disturbed her marveling.

Aiden jogged up beside her and slowed to match her pace. "If you want a good show, the ring is always busy. A great way to pass the time. Faeries practicing sword skills, Mystics practicing magic."

Alora went wide-eyed, as wide as the moon himself. "You practice magic *out in the open?*" She stopped on suddenly numb legs, heart thundering. "Isn't that just *begging* for someone to see and alert the High King?"

Aiden only smiled. "Garrik's powers protect us."

She pinched her brows. *His ... Smokeshadows, was it? They protect this place?* She crooked her neck, searching for any inclination of those powers manifested around them, but when her survey fell short, her confusion slid back to Aiden.

"He did tell you, didn't he?"

"No." *Of course not. Why would he tell me anything that is actually important?* "Tell me what?"

"Well. You see, Mister Tall, Gray, and Scary has a shield over this valley." Aiden cupped her upper back, swiping his other hand through the sky.

So not Smokeshadows but another *power?*

That must've been what Eldacar had referred to. How he'd never met anyone else with more than one power except the High Prince.

A shudder rippled through Alora's flesh. Almost as if his lingering power surged through her in nothing other than a gloating, confirming display.

Even so far away, the smug bastard stirred the irritation inside her.

Aiden continued, "You can't see it, but it's really bloody amazing. He can protect an individual by focusing on them, even shield an entire kingdom. Quite possibly all of Elysian at this point. You felt it as you entered camp last night. That rush through your body. It was his shield. Given time, it won't affect you as it did. We all get used to it. Garrik is a master of illusion. And his shield makes the eye see what is not there. Anyone who wouldn't know better sees a camp full of soldiers. From the inside, we are, well ... this."

A prickling ache bit her fingertips, pebbling her skin and reminding her of the moment she felt this so-called shield thrum through her bones. "So, the mighty prince is still keeping things from me—"

"Not keeping them from you, possibly just slipped his thoughts. He has a lot on his mind these days. Impending doom of Elysian and all." Aiden winked. "Be grateful. Without his shield, faeries like those two wouldn't be able to stand in the open and practice their talents."

Alora's eyes followed his pointing finger to the arena.

A lavender-skinned faerie with short iridescent wings held sunbursts of fire in his hands. To his right, a High Fae female hovered a few feet off the ground, clothing whirling in the wind around her as she lifted into the air.

Eldacar stood at a small table behind them, a book open in his hand. He had one raised high, waving it around, moving his palm like he was lifting something.

The High Fae hovering focused on him like student and master.

It was an *incredible* sight. Even bitter for being kept in the dark, she could admit that.

Besides Rowlen, she'd never witnessed anyone else using magic. Not ever. Captivated by the sight of them, Alora could only stare, as if the magic was a natural wonder.

The fire danced in the faerie's palm, bursting in shards of flame and swaying in such magnificence. It was almost a sin to watch such a spectacle.

Her body slouched in jealousy as she imagined her own white flame's heat in her palms, but it was promptly replaced with awe when the faerie's fire swirled around his body like a shooting star and disappeared into the clouds.

Her eyes burned from the liquid lining them.

This was ... beautiful. How magic *should* be.

Free. Flowing. Painting the sky, the earth, everything around with its brilliance—perfection.

Not used for evil or stolen for a single tyrant's selfish gain.

Alora had to turn away. If she stared a moment longer, she would've burst with grief over her loss. Over her powers stolen from her. Maybe if she knew when they would return, it would've made it easier to continue watching.

Aiden's eyes glistened like he was just as enchanted as she was. *Could he be jealous, too?*

But she found herself studying him. Studying his unusual clothing, the curved sword to his side. And she spoke before thinking. "How did you end up in Zyllyryon?"

"Ah, you noticed." Aiden half bowed. With his left hand, he lifted the tricorn hat from his head to his chest before straightening. "Captain Aiden of the Cursed Sails." He adjusted the red sash around his waist. "My, what an adventure that was. My father and I traveled through realms never heard of on a ship with no limits. I had no magic, but I didn't need any with her guiding the way. When Father"—he tilted his chin to the sky—"I became captain at a very young age. I had this unwavering desire for not only fresh coddlefish but for magical items. We pillaged and plundered realms unknown, collecting many along the way. Until I found a magic atlas. Anywhere I would point, the Cursed Sails would go. One day, I met a fiery redhead. She stowed away on my ship, and before I knew it, we ended up shipwrecked far off the coast of

Zyllyryon. Losing every bloody magical item I procured. Damn shame. That ship was my life."

Alora gaped. "You're a *pirate?*"

Aiden furrowed his brows, swaying his gaze to his right, and spoke to the air. "Out of all of that, she only heard pirate?" He laughed and turned back to her. "Any*waves*, eventually, my skill of item procurement came in handy one day in a tavern. Our dear 'Gray and Scary' thought I would be useful to him, and he offered me a position in the army. The rest is history." He shrugged.

"That was three years ago, when he formed this Dragons Legion?"

"No," he said, elongating the vowel as it rolled from his mouth. "It was long before that." A shudder wracked his body as visible pain danced in his eyes.

"What?"

It seemed as if he battled his own thoughts, unlikely to say anything else. But Aiden's face softened. "It's not my place to say. Garrik is ... different ... now." He spoke slowly, as if the words were cutting wounds into his tongue. "Sometimes the worst pasts can charter an even brighter future. You don't know him—yet. He's trying, Alora. He's been making up for his forced mistakes for almost three years now."

"Forced mistakes?" Alora scoffed, furrowing her eyebrows.

Aiden sighed and pulled his hat off his head, brushing the velvet clean, avoiding her critical expression. "I'm sure you've heard stories. Magnelis's Savage Prince. Ruthless, bloodthirsty, strikingly handsome." He grinned, but the attempt to make her smile failed. His hat dropped to his side, distressed, and his body was unable to remain still. "That wasn't the real Garrik. He didn't want to do any of it."

Her mouth twisted as his words boiled her blood molten. "There's a big difference between not wanting to do something and actually doing it. We all have choices. We must live with the consequences of what we choose. Murdering younglings and their families, burning down cities, imprisoning his own kind. It's not a matter of wanting to. He took pleasure in it, I'm sure."

Something like thunder must have shaken the entire valley, because it roared straight through Aiden. His shoulders tensed, chest puffed, and that once bright-and-shinny face exchanged for a lethal snarl. "You'd be wise to change your opinion about him. Garrik didn't *decide* to do a bloody thing—he carries the scars to prove that. Magnelis is a ruthless High King. Not even his own son can escape his wrath."

ALORA PACED the outer arena wall, observing small collections of soldiers sparring and Mystics performing unimaginable powers.

Aiden remained on the other side where she had left him, but those shale eyes still tracked her every step.

With the silent lake behind, Alora leaned her forearms on top of the faded wood, stopping to take in the expanse of the valley. She could view the entire camp from there. To her left, the forest was the thickest, allowing little hope of successfully escaping through it without drawing attention or slowing herself down. Her eyes scanned across the tree line until her view became blocked by large, long tents—barracks, she presumed. Next, she landed on three large, upright weapon racks on the other side of the arena. All brimming with various sizes of swords, war hammers, battle axes, throwing stars, knives, bows with arrows, and ... daggers.

Her dagger. The obsidian blade she had acquired from the green faerie in the markets was ... was it *gone?* The High Prince had swallowed it with his shadows. *What did that mean for it?* She wrinkled her nose as she gripped the top of the arena wall tightly, about to curse his name, when a familiar voice called to her.

"Alora!" Eldacar waved with a book as he stumbled to the wall. "So nice to see you again. Did you come to practice your skills?"

She lifted her hands, forming fists and unfurling them—repeatedly. "Nope. I still can't use my magic. Courtesy of your beloved High Prince." Her voice pierced with sarcasm.

Eldacar pushed his glasses up with a wrinkled nose. "Soon. I'm sure of it." And patted her hand.

Sure... Soon. She didn't believe him.

Alora gripped the wall and leaned over, scanning across it until her eyes found Aiden. "Could I borrow some books about my magic? I'd love to learn more." Maybe once she passed the High Prince's shield, her powers would return.

Eldacar paused.

"What?" Alora crossed her arms, tightening her face. "He won't allow that either, will he?"

"No! No." He smiled, cheeks swelling, pushing his glasses upwards. "Of course! I had hoped to see you again today. I brought one out for you in anticipation." He held up a finger and spun around, almost knocking into a soldier walking by. His short, red hair swayed as he nearly skipped over to the table full of books and rifled through them until he landed upon a blue leather-bound book wrapped with leather strings. Eldacar's grin widened. "There you are! If I remember correctly, you'll want to start on page ... twenty-three."

Alora pulled the book from his hands with a grateful smile. "Thank you, Eldacar." Her hands gliding over the engraved, burning butterfly on its cover when someone at the far end of the arena shouted in victory.

Short, golden hair reflected shards of sunlight, so pale it reminded her of Rowlen. She bit back a wave of heartache, watching as a female stood above the male, a sword edge dangerously close to his throat. The corners of her mouth twitched, almost smiling, before splashing from the lake drew her attention.

She turned around, along with Eldacar.

A faerie with prismed scales, covering her exposed skin, walked between two walls of waves. Offering a perfect view of the lake's bottom. And jumping between those walls, sea creatures formed only of water splashed and merged with the lake's water. That faerie and her magic allowed the walls to crash behind her every step, closing the tunnel as she crossed the white stones of its shore, teal hair, and battle-black armor completely dry, meeting Alora's enchanted eyes with a welcoming grin.

Alora was almost too awestruck to speak but managed, "There's so many of my kind here. I've never seen powers like these." Her eyes glistened, tracking the movements of the water faerie conjuring a helmet-sized flying dragon in the sky.

"Would you like to learn about them?" Eldacar sheepishly grinned, and Alora nodded. "Wonderful!" Clambering over the wall and using his hand to brace himself when his feet betrayed him, Eldacar led her to a nearby cluster of trees off the edge of the lake.

The stories poured from him soon after.

She was starry-eyed listening to his tales—his knowledge. Completely enthralled.

Eldacar was much different from the rest. Not stone-cold like Jade, rather warm and kind-hearted. Soft-spoken, much like Thalon, but more reserved with a shy demeanor. He was quite the opposite of Aiden. Not one for attention or dramatics, surely not one for jokes. But when he held his books, when he spoke of magic ... *that* was Eldacar. And she thought him to be much younger than the rest, sitting there, gleaming over his books. Like a faeling who loved stories—he was created for storytelling. Made for the books themselves. Their keeper. Their interpreter.

His brown eyes irradiated confidence as he spoke.

"... and then there are earth shifters. Now they are really quite something. Imagine commanding Elysian's tallest and strongest mountains to simply pick themselves up and move. Something as simple as a bowl of dirt turned into a marching army. Making grass into tiny daggers. They are really sublime!" Eldacar plucked a blade of grass and pretended that it was a weapon. "And healers. Mystics who can touch a festering wound and seal it to healthy skin. Can you imagine that?" He cupped a hand against his chest, utterly awestruck.

"I don't have to imagine. My closest friend had those abilities. He cared for me a great deal of times when..." *When Kaine would—*

Alora pushed the thought from her mind as tears lined her eyes. She sniffed and wiped one on her sleeve. Rowlen deserved the thought, and Kaine wouldn't ruin it—not this time, anyway.

But Eldacar's face still softened with troubled curiosity. A pitiful reminder.

He pushed up his glasses, shuffling in the dirt beside her with a tender lilt to his tone. "Is everything alright?" Before she said a word, he pulled a cloth from his jacket and handed it to her.

'Please, be careful.' Rowlen's voice brushed her like a whisper in the wind. Alora pictured him there, standing beside the trees. Even though it was devastatingly obvious that he wasn't truly there, she still felt something like calming flutters rest on her heart.

Why hadn't I just stayed?

'Please, be careful.' She saw herself walking away. Why did she walk away?

A choked whimper escaped her lips. "I ... I don't know if he's alive." Alora wiped another tear and pushed herself up onto her feet. That was enough weakness. Time to shove it away, bury it deep until she could find him again. She *would* find him again. "Thank you Eldacar. This was very nice. I'm going to take this book back to my tent and read for a while, if that's okay?" She smiled at him, a real smile, as tears still threatened to fall.

Eldacar's sheepish grin swelled his cheeks, pushing his glasses high. "Absolutely, my ... friend. I'll see you later for dinner, I'm sure. I'll bring you another book then."

Alora nodded and started walking around the sun-faded wooden wall toward the tents. Rowlen still haunted her mind no matter how ruthlessly she wished him away. Through the burning heartache, guilt, and unrelenting tears, everything within her wished that she had some way to learn if he was still alive.

In her fog, she didn't see the darkened figure stalking beside her. And when she least expected anything more, Aiden held out his hand in front of her, stopping her mid-step. "Off on another stroll on this fine afternoon?"

Blinking, realizing who had stopped her and where she was, Alora deeply inhaled, returning to her usual frustrated state. "I'm getting tired. I'm going back to my tent to rest. I can find my way."

"Oh, I don't doubt you can." Aiden waved his finger at her like she was a naughty faeling and beckoned her with his palm. "After you."

AIDEN ESCORTED her back to her tent. Before he left her, he was sure to alert her that he'd be right outside if she required anything. To which she was tempted to ask for a horse and supplies but wasn't deluded enough to think he'd actually oblige her ask.

Then again...

So she did exactly that. And he simply laughed, flicking her nose with a wry grin, and sauntered away.

It was worth a try.

Would the High Prince have reacted the same? *Surely not.* He'd only simmer and brood, likely freeze her to the bones with his cold glare until she physically pushed him away. The mighty bastard. Still, her suicidal tendencies again wished he had returned, only to spear him with her eyes and promise him fiery death upon her magic returned. Watching his pants light with fire as he ran around camp to put out the flames...

Alora chuckled, falling onto the plushness of her cot and staring at the canvas warming in the sun. She quite liked imagining him that way. Or with her dagger sinking into his most delicate male parts—that he was sure to use often, being a pompous royal.

It was only a quick thought; her dagger, his cock. Until that thought brushed across her mind to his tent. To how his body had pressed against hers. How cold his hands felt. His breath. Scent. How his thighs straddled her. Her hands on his belt... What—what she felt straining below.

Perhaps if she had found a dagger then—

Thinking of my cock again, clever girl?

A tingle caressed the inside of her mind. Alora shot straight up on the cot.

His voice—it sounded like he was directly beside her, whispering in her ear. She really needed rest if she was imagining his voice.

Alora shuddered away a flush of scarlet and decided to think of *anything* other than him. Deciding that her surroundings were a better subject, like the clasp from the cloak that was still hidden inside her corset or the treasonous map concealed safely in her boot.

And then, she peeked out of the tent entrance to determine Aiden's position. Always in the same place, her faithful watchman, lounging near the fire with his body facing her tent, reading a book. Surprising—pirates can read?

I'll never get past him if he sits there all day.

She paced the floor, thinking. Reviewing the path to Eldacar's tent and the maze to the arena. They were in opposite directions, but both could potentially lead to the forest. The forest by the arena *might* be passable, but further behind Garrik's line of tents would be best.

From the view of the trees, it didn't appear to be as thick with brush. She thought of the different tents and barracks she had passed both ways. If she took one wrong turn, she could end up face-to-face with soldiers.

Sapphires traveled across the dragon clasp now displayed on the cot. Her eyes widened, heart roaring when she noticed again that the tail was a sharpened edge. And as if her salvation smacked her across the face, Alora lifted it and cupped it in her palms.

That tail could cut through canvas.

Veins rippled with adrenaline as she fell to the cot, clutching the dragon clasp in one hand and the book Eldacar gave her in the other.

When the sun dips lower and casts shadows on these walls, I'm gone.

Until then, Alora laid back on the cot, opened the blue, leather-bound book, and began to read.

CHAPTER 14

I *'m ready*, Alora thought to herself, gripping the cold metal of the dragon's clasp so tightly it left reddened impressions in her palm.

The sun cast darkened shadows on the canvas; the moment she had waited for.

On the side table, Aiden had brought a generous slice of grained bread with soft, salted butter and honey, strong, crumbled cheese, and a motley of sweet berries and assorted nuts while she rested. She stuffed them inside her cloak pocket, knowing that it could be days until she would find her next meal.

That didn't worry her. She'd done it before.

The fact that she didn't possess any weapons *was* the issue.

Flipping the bedside table, Alora quietly kicked off a leg, splintering it around the nail. The only weapon she had was the dragon clasp. And that wouldn't get her very far if she needed to fight.

Creeping across the dirt to the tent entrance, Alora glimpsed between the thin crack. Aiden sat on the stump from breakfast, the fire slowly licking its flame against a black iron pot. Fumes of thick, hearty gravy, garlic, herb, and pepper-rubbed venison, boiled potatoes, and onions and carrots wafted her way, triggering an angry ache and growl from deep in her stomach. Aiden's hands scrubbed a saddle on the fallen log with a greased brush, lathering oil into the embellishments and tassels.

Completely unaware of her intruding gaze.

Unaware that in a matter of seconds, she'd be gone.

This is it.

Alora backed away from the gap now that she had her final confirmation. Careful to make no sound. *I must go now.*

She pivoted to the back canvas before pulling the dragon clasp in front, angling the tail. All that stood between her and freedom—real *freedom*—was a thin canopy of fabric. It could've been a twenty-foot stone wall, she'd still climb it.

Every nerve in her body pricked with energy when she lifted the clasp halfway up the wall. Flexing the fabric, the tail connected, popping and shredding as it poked through. Alora paused. Her breath stopped in anticipation, uncertain if anyone had heard.

Nothing. Nothing but the sounds of a harsh brush scraping against leather and the crackling of burning wood.

She guided the dragon down slowly, the shredding canvas threatening to give away her escape until the long cut reached the dirt below. She'd done it.

And now could breathe again.

No turning back now.

Alora toweled the cloak over her shoulders and buried the clasp in her corset. She carefully concealed the wooden leg inside her cloak, unseen, unnoticed, ready to strike if required.

When her shaking hands lifted the canvas apart and slowly pushed her head outside, dusk greeted her with cast shadows. She was surrounded by an alley of canvas.

If she could sneak through this, she would reach the back of Aiden's tent, slip across to the High Prince's, and then vanish through the maze until running into the safe arms of the forest behind.

Breathe, Alora. Just breathe. You can do this.

Garrik's tent was in front of her in mere heartbeats.

Directly ahead, a small path between his tent and a line of four more pathways that led to barracks, which would force her to make a choice in direction. With one more quick glance at Aiden, she dashed across the opening and crouched beside Garrik's tent, listening for footsteps.

When no one came, Alora swiftly moved to the barracks in front of her, forcing her to make that choice. She'd been both ways today. To the left, the arena and lake. To her right, somewhere, Eldacar's blackened tent stood.

Footsteps startled her thundering heart.

Not from behind. It wasn't Aiden.

A soldier emerged from a tent to her right, settling near a firesite where four other faeries lounged.

She could've sworn that they could hear her heartbeat from there.

Alora almost stepped out into the path when a soldier looked her way and stared. His gaze didn't falter for what seemed ages until he returned his attention to the fire.

Slipping around the barracks, she dashed down the long pathway, clutching her hands to her chest. Another firesite sat directly in front of her, this one too filled with soldiers. That was the problem with escaping at dusk. The army was retiring for the evening, all but sentries patrolling. She was exposed where she crouched. If one of them turned their head, they would see her, and by now, everyone in camp likely knew she was the High Prince's prisoner. There were no allies here. And she wouldn't be enough of a fool to believe she could sway any of them into helping her.

She fled to her left, down a new row of tents, crossing over another main walking path and into the next alley of canvases.

Another barracks tent sat before her as she leaned her head out. An entire area of logs and tables sat: the mess area. It was completely filled with faeries eating, talking, laughing. That would've been the best route if it was empty, but there was no choice now. She had to go right.

Within minutes, relief bubbled inside her chest at the sight of a familiar structure—Eldacar's black tent. The furthest she'd been on this side of the camp. An amber glow of lantern light seeped through the structure's open windows. She ran to it and crouched below, listening to Eldacar mutter to himself inside.

"... figure out how, we could reverse the washing." He sounded distraught, flipping book pages as he sighed. "Nothing. There's *nothing*."

A hand grabbed her shoulder, spinning her around to meet his crimson eyes. Along with battle leathers, a sword glistened, sheathed at his side. "Identify yourself *at once*." He pulled her bruised wrist, forcing her to stand.

She yelped at his embrace, and the sharp pain thrumming up her arm. But the pain was nothing compared to the panic raging inside. Her eyes widened. Lips shaking, unable to form any form of communication whatsoever.

"I—I—" Stuttering, horrified, Alora scanned his angular face. He turned his head and opened his mouth to sound an alarm, but she finally blurted out, "The High Prince"—lips trembling—"he ordered me to return this book to Eldacar. I was about to call out to him." Alora pulled the blue leather book from her corset.

The sentry took it and hastily flipped through the pages before slamming it shut with a hollow clap. Pausing for a moment, he searched her face before offering it back to her. "On your way then." He nodded, released his hold, and continued down the path.

That was too close. Releasing a deep breath to settle the rising bile in her throat.

"Hello! Did I hear you say that you've brought back the book?" Eldacar poked his head out the window, startling her so badly that her skin almost jumped off the bones.

Shit. "Eldacar!" She backed away slowly and faked a pleasing smile. "Yes..." Alora scratched her neck, concealed one arm behind her back, and then moved to the blackened window. "It was great. Thank you for letting me borrow it." And handed him the book.

"Wonderful! I do have another one for you. Shall I bring it to dinner, or would you like to take it back with you now?" He beamed.

The possibility of him watching her leave was overwhelmingly high. If she could send him away, she would be able to continue running, and the best chances of that were if he left before she did. "Why don't you go grab it, and I'll bring it back with me?" She smiled, hoping that would convince him.

"Splendid! Wait right there." He dashed back into his library. The sound of thumps and books falling echoed from inside.

Alora didn't hesitate. It was one straight shot from there through the grid of tents that lay ahead, and as long as she wasn't discovered by another patrol, she would make it.

But when she arrived at the end of the line, Alora was forced to a stop.

Sentries.

They were stationed forty feet apart, lining the forest's edge.

To her left, a hitching line teeming with horses was stationed. It stretched a hundred feet with no sentry patrolling between them.

Alora darted to her left and sprinted. Drifting between two horses as another patrol emerged from a pathway, a mere breath away from spotting her. The horse she stood beside startled, swishing its tail and rearing its head. The damn thing was going to betray her position, so Alora reached up and gently stroked its neck, waiting for the patrol to pass.

She hadn't even considered it after her first failed attempt. But as she stood, cocooned in the shadow of the hitching line and forest, one thing became evident just as before. Her chances of escape were greatly increased on horseback. And just because she was discovered the first time, didn't mean this time would be the same.

Untying a black mare, she slowly guided it forward by the reins, careful to discern the sentry's location, until she slipped into the forest unseen.

Freedom.

The thing she had fought viciously for the last few months. It was right within her grasp. All she had to do was run, with nothing to stop her. Not even him. Not Kaine. Not the walls of Telldaira. *Nothing.* She had made it. Made it out alive. Made it out of whatever Firekeeper-filled-*hell* would've swallowed her up if she stayed in the manor ... stayed there. Freedom. Agency. It all waited for her beyond.

With a swift hop, Alora threw her leg over the mare's back and steadied her balance. "Let's get out of here."

Static energy rippled through her body the moment they crossed the tree line. By Aiden's explanation alone, Alora recognized it as Garrik's shield. She fisted the horse's mane in one hand, the reins in the other, steadying her balance as her vision spotted and a wave of unease stole into her senses as the last reminder of the High Prince's control over her became a dark memory.

Disoriented, Alora allowed the horse to press forward, nudging its belly with the heel of her boot. It was the only way. She couldn't have led it herself, not until the shield's effects wore off.

Closing her eyes, Alora let the relief burn through her veins. Since leaving Rowlen in Rhidian, this was the first moment she felt a sense of true relief.

And when she thought the voice had left her, it haunted her in enough of a plea, shuddering in the depths of her soul, that she almost obeyed it:

Alora, stop. Go back.

But not this time. She was too close to freedom.

Too damn close.

Alora gripped the reins, the dizziness subsiding as she guided the horse over a fallen tree.

Maybe it was that death wish marked on her arm with dancing flames and sparks. Maybe it was pompous pride of her own, but Alora twisted on the horse's back and found her eyes searching for his tent. One last sign of him.

"You cannot run from me," Alora mocked, reiterating the words in his refined accent and tightening the reins with a scoff.

She stiffened in the saddle at the reminder, gritting her teeth. Picturing him standing at the edge of camp.

The mighty bastard would finally be the powerless one.

Chin dipped low, glaring through the slits in her eyes, Alora avowed in a lethal whisper, "Watch me."

SHE HELD no sense of direction. The map in her boot was useless until she found a town. And the forest was falling darker by the minute. The only things that could help were the stars, which were nearly blocked out by the heavy canopy above. Because, *of course*, this couldn't be easy.

Alora scanned trees as her eyes adjusted.

There had to be a way, had to be something.

Fighting off the urge to look back, Alora hallucinated every shadow as something more than a boulder or a tree. Half expecting the High Prince with his smug face, leaning against a tree, waiting for her. But he wouldn't be. He probably didn't even know she was gone yet.

And looking back would only slow her down, wasting time that she didn't have.

Sweat-soaked, her horse panted. They'd been running and leaping over foliage for what seemed like hours, so she decided to slow their escape, allowing the horse to catch its breath. Alora was grateful. After all, her feet wouldn't have carried her that far.

She patted its neck, praising it with a grateful whisper. "Thank you for getting me out of there."

They continued walking through the forest, spooking at every rustle of leaves or snap of a branch. Animals scurried up trees as starlight butterflies demonstrated their breathtaking light show of wings. The calming sounds of the breeze through the trees rested on her ears, causing her to close her eyes and smile.

Before long, they arrived at a trickling stream, and Alora dismounted.

She led her horse to the water and knelt down, cupping her hands together and bringing the sweet, cold liquid to her lips.

"We need to find our way out of here, my friend." Looking into the horse's eye as it drank. "If they haven't figured out by now that I've gone, they will soon."

As she stood up from her position at the stream, she noticed that the sounds of the forest grew silent. An eerie sensation chilled her bones as her eyes fell upon a dark figure prowling within the trees ahead of her.

Ten times larger than a High Fae, a bear, or anything she'd ever seen. The creature moved its way out of the tree's shadows, crushing brush as it passed, and stood in the thick grass thirty feet away.

The creature had skin shaped like black crystals, forming a skeletal physique. Six legs, two of which jutted out from its shoulders with three fingers on each, formed jagged razor claws oozing with hot inky liquid.

Everything it touched was engulfed in a sizzling vapor. The vision of nightmares, prowling in a forest much too small for it. Its jagged tail drug through the grass, flattening a path behind it. And if that sight of horror wasn't enough...

It stopped and flexed its spiked leathery wings.

Tripling its size.

Gamroara. Alora froze, holding onto the reins of her horse. *No sudden movements.* These beasts were cursed with terrible vision. On its spiked, skeletal head sat four sunken, empty eye sockets. But their hearing was impeccable. Her best chance was to remain still. Pray that the beast prowled away without noticing that they were there.

The creature stood for a few moments, flexing its wings.

Its giant head cut through the air, flaring its black crystallized nostrils. And by some miracle, it slowly turned itself around in the direction it came.

A crackling of branches and thundering hooves broke the silence.

The creature whipped its head around.

Stood up on its two back legs.

And with an earth-shattering shriek, stomped its feet to the ground, rattling the dirt.

There was no time to do anything ... because that beast of crystal and claws and teeth...

Ran straight toward her.

CHAPTER 15

Telldaira still burned in the distance. Smoke drifted on a phantom wind, disturbing the coral and crimson hues of the sun-kissed sky, were not the lasting remnants of a destroyed city.

Instead, the smell of destruction and the distant memory of strangled screams burned the air above a sea of deep, dark purple tents as Garrik crested an overlooking hill.

The High King's army waited in the valley like a sleeping beast. Magnelis's, in such loose terms, *exulted* Ravens were favored above all else. They acted as his ruthless iron hand, collecting misery as payment, and death as their right to execute on a mere whim.

Headsmen of Elysian, given authority above every living thing.

Except the one that dined with darkness ... who was its master.

Garrik rolled the tension from his neck and shoulders, gripping the reins until his knuckles turned white and threatened to split. Knowing what was to come—what was always to come. Of who he had to be. And if he was foolish enough to unleash his rippling power without the High King gaining knowledge of what his wrath had carried out...

The entire sea of canvases would be leveled.

Nothing left.

Not even a bloodstain in the dust.

One day...

Through whorls of creeping Smokeshadows, Jade and Thalon were engulfed in a storm of his incredible powers, turning them into shadows as he too became smoke and air and ash. And when that wave of nothingness enveloped his body, transcending them into such great forces, the entire world shifted, flying by as if they were floating in air. Like swimming through the coldest waters of Zyllyryon, crashing inside a billowing wave, and manifesting inside a roaring flame, they drifted on a twirling wind.

He called it 'dawning'—one of his treasured abilities only possible by Smokeshadows. To be transported through space and time, to become the darkness and appear at whatever destination he chose. This time, they arrived within the border of the High King's camp, extracting them like he had done to Alora in the woods. He could have simply dawned them there earlier, but he would rather enjoy the solitude and silence of the ride. Besides. There was no rush to endure the dealings of the Raven's camp. That would come soon enough.

And that time had now come.

Their bodies manifested back to their born forms as they each straightened in their saddles, like transforming into darkness was nothing more than a simple, meaningless thing, utterly unaffected by it.

Instead of the lush grasses from atop the hill, Ghost cracked loose pebbles of the road beneath her hooves.

They rode in unison onto the loose, pebbled path. Thalon sat rigid, his back straightened, and chin high to Garrik's right, hand on the hilt of his golden-runed sword sheathed at his side. Jade, to Garrik's left, burned her death glare forward with knives strapped to her thighs, one idly spinning between her fingers.

The smoke in the valley burned into Garrik's eyes as they neared two sleep-deprived sentries lazily guarding the border of the Ravens' camp. They looked young. Likely new recruits in training, given border duty because some commander was too indolent to leave the comfort of his bed to instill proper protocol after a siege.

Even so, their attention snapped from their very fingernails when the echoes of hooves rippled across the stones.

"*Halt.* Identify yourselves in the name of the High King," a young, six-winged, gray faerie commanded, unsheathing his sword and standing ready.

Pathetic. Garrik formed a wicked grin that was so starsdamned delicious when his silver eyes glimpsed a tremble in the sentries' knees. Lifting his head, face covered by the black cloak he wore, surging satisfaction thrummed inside his veins.

Without even blinking, he released Smokeshadows upon the ground —effortlessly. Allowing them to fog dauntingly around the sentries' boots.

It was pleasing to watch them squirm within an inch of their lives. To watch their faces as death stalked them. Purely exhilarating—even though there was *nothing* pure about him—not anymore.

Not since—

Lightning threatened to strike from Thalon's voice, like a brimstone fury. "Your *High Prince*. Garrik of Elysian. Stand the hell aside."

I love to see Ravens cower. Garrik's malicious grin widened. It was the one satisfaction he got from these summons.

Thalon was frightening enough, but nothing compared to the sinister look on their High Prince's face in that moment. From the stories of times past, Garrik could thieve the life from their lungs without uttering a single word or blinking a dismissive eye.

The Savage Prince—ruthless—bloodthirsty—an unrelenting executioner, prowling and malevolent before them.

He reveled in their cowering.

Enjoyed every bit of fear radiating from their bones.

The older of the two stood at attention, sword shaking in his hand. He almost dropped it to the dirt as they parted, allowing their High Prince and his Shadow Order to pass.

In doing so, Thalon's dark horse swatted its tail, cracking like a whip into the younger sentry as they passed by.

Jade amusingly grinned, murmuring, "Aren't animals lovely?" And patted her horse on its dark chestnut neck.

Garrik's smile half twitched at the corners, draping Smokeshadows from his shoulders and flowing them behind him like a cape as he pulled forward, leading them through the checkpoint, and leaving the sentries all but pissing in their armor behind.

To the right side of the dusty road, the Ravens that had summoned Garrik outside his camp that morning impatiently sulked by a small purple tent. And with little pleasantries, the Ravens escorted them through a labyrinth much like their own.

Ten guards greeted them first as they rounded a corner, standing alert outside a massive structure's entrance. Their spear ends cratered in the dirt as five more soldiers reclined by a fire, cooking what smelled to be decaying fish that had boiled in the blaring heat for a week on a blackstone. And they did it all under the blistering sun of a rainless desert.

Fucking repulsing.

This campsite sat in the middle of camp, and the canvas they were guided to was equal in size to Eldacar's library. Purple canvas was plastered with the High King's crest so large it could be determined from the sky. A red-eyed, black raven, outlined in flakes of gold.

Another pathetic display of *disillusioned* power.

Brennus can shove it up his—

A female figure parted the ten guards, walking their way, and stopping Garrik's thoughts like a fortress crafted of crystal. No one else would notice the pulse of his unusual heartbeat begin to thunder or the way his body stiffened, forgetting to breathe. Or the way his fist trembled, illusioned by something malicious in his twisted face.

She was dressed unlike the rest.

In the smoke-filled breeze, a floor-length, sleeveless, black gown accentuated the swells of her chest and curves, as the silken fabric fluttered with every slithering step. A slit rose up to the hip, revealing toned, pale legs that he wanted nothing more than to devastate and snap and break.

And where he imagined his hand around her throat, gripping and denying air to her lungs, a caged, black necklace, waving like a nest of serpents, wrapped the length of her defined neck and connected at the chest of the gown.

Garrik gritted his teeth, tightening his jaw at the sight of her. A vicious growl escaped his lips. He smelled her... Smelled the sickly sweet and venomous aroma carrying in the breeze from the long waves of raven-black hair cascading down shoulders that he never wanted to touch again.

And those eyes.

Serpent-like, wholly inked like an abyss, stalking his movements and every labored breath.

Jade loosened a vicious hiss as Thalon bounded off his horse, hand steady on his golden sword. Ready—waiting—with focused intensity.

The High Prince dismounted too, speaking softly for only Ghost to hear before her nose nuzzled against his hand, and he turned to Thalon.

"Wait here, tend to Ghost."

But Thalon's face burned with something lethal, taking a step to settle himself between the female and his High Prince, the grip on his hilt tightening enough that the leather groaned.

One brutal flash of Garrik's eyes was enough to convey a simple command, and Thalon pressed his boot a step back, nodding ever so unwillingly, and submitted.

Watching the female slither closer, Jade's face was much the same. Tension rolling in waves from her shoulders until it reached her toes, the contorted snarl from her lips perfectly displayed her virulent disapproval. Jade's palm fell to the hilt of her sword, half unsheathing it as the raven-haired female snaked closer, and the twirling dagger between her fingers sat motionless, perfectly positioned to glide through the air with brutal accuracy.

His Shadow Order's loyalty would not save him today. It never could. Not from—

Garrik pivoted, facing the serpent, who locked black eyes on his figure. A growl as deadly as the depths of Firekeeper's realm reverberated from his soul, slicing the thickening air between them.

If a name could freeze the flames of Firekeeper's realm ... hers was the one. But he would not give her the satisfaction of that poison from his tongue. Not *ever* again.

The female stopped at his side, displaying a wry, graceful wave. She scratched her nails, sharpened like the edge of a sword, and fingertips covered in ombré black until it faded at the knuckles, onto the chest of Garrik's armor. A slithering darkness snaked down her fingers like venom and then danced in the air around her hand.

"My pet." The voice, sensual and as deadly as poison, carried memories of dark rooms, endless screams, and bloodied skin. Oblivion for eyes, lust playfully flickered, following her outstretched nails tracing down the muscled planes of his body. "So nice to *feel* you again."

That touch...

The dagger-nailed hand instantly crushed in his unrelenting grip as a shivering growl seethed through the air.

Garrik's eyes turned cold as death. "*Do not fucking touch me.*" His threat lingered heavily in the air as he stared forward, refusing her the satisfaction of his attention. Not after all she had done. Not after she...

With a menacing side-glance, the combustible rage—because that is what it was now, only rage and pure undiluted hatred—detonated inside his heart and soul.

His mind powers, that shield, weaponized and exploded in a city-leveling airwave from his body.

In the wave of his destruction, it forced her back on impact, stumbling away on stiletto, silver snaked-covered heels, and tearing into that perfect black dress. Garrik's blackened gaze seethed as he willed that weapon to fade away before it demolished a single tent—it was not meant for them—not yet.

Her lips curled in a wicked, playful grin as if she had trapped him in a scheme, wiping blood that dripped from her nose and mouth.

"What?" That serpentine grin twisted. "You didn't miss me?" Arching her back, the female pressed the swell of her breasts toward him. Then she was close once more. A fingernail grazed his chin before its touch was too denied by a wave of his shield.

"*You seem to forget what I am.* Touch me again and you will find yourself missing your hands that you so dearly treasure." Black Smokeshadows cascaded from Garrik's body. Gritting his teeth, he thrust a smoky hand around the serpent's neck.

And squeezed.

She let out an amused moan. "You do not scare me. You *know* that." And slid her inky fingers along his wrist. Her lips widened, a snake unhinging its jaw, exposing sharp teeth that her tongue lustfully slid across.

"Come now..." Her *name.* Someone spoke venom into the air. "You can have your fun with your whore later," a smooth voice called from between the tent soldiers.

A lean-built High Fae with short, night-dark hair sauntered forward. Adorned in a dragon-scaled onyx coat, the back draped down behind him to his knees. With a jagged collar in the shape of dragon wing spikes that lifted to the back of his head, it perfectly hugged his figure. The male walked on knee-high boots, curved around his dark pants underneath. Needle-like spikes jutted from the coat's shoulders and wrists, stained with blood.

Garrik's attention snapped to the male. "The fuck did you call me?"

"You clearly heard me."

"And you clearly do not wish to take the risk of saying it again to find yourself suddenly breathless." Without blinking, Smokeshadows formed around the male's throat.

"Mmm." The female hummed, whipping her neck from Garrik's hand before slithering away. "I do love when you two fight over me. Malik, sweet thing. Since when have you known me to give up an opportunity to enjoy my plaything?" Onyx eyes flirted, hips swaying as she paced between them slowly. With her back to them, she waved a dismissive hand. "I look forward to seeing my handy work again ... and soon, Garrik." Pacing on stilettos, and with a bite on her bottom lip, she grinned at Thalon across the firesite. "I've always wanted to corrupt one of your kind. Tell me. Are you a good fuck like the High Prince? I want to hear that pretty, marked throat scream."

Thalon was a solid wall, unshakable—unbreakable—as he towered over her. He could snap her neck without breaking a sweat. They both could, but did not dare.

Not here. Not now. Not yet.

Garrik saw his world turn to darkness, but it was Thalon who thundered, "I'd rather lose every last one of my Earned than disgrace my Keep with the scum of you." His face remained unshaken as his tongue burned with holy fire. "Dishonor our High Prince again and it will not be my throat the screams will be wailing from. I'll send you to Firekeeper, where you belong."

The serpent cocked her head. "Before you die and I take them all from your ripped open scalp and bloody braids, you will be begging me for a ride." She outstretched a pointed nail to his tattooed chest. And before it could make contact, it snapped back on itself in an unnatural bend. Whorls of smoke and shadow seeped from the split skin.

Garrik's fisted into her hair, wrenching her neck back on itself, so inked orbs stared into the death of his. His hand closed around her throat. Digging his boots hard into the dirt, he leaned in close. Icy breath, he knew, chilled her ear as he whispered loud enough for only her to hear, "I could tear you apart if I desired. Make no mistake, if you *ever* touch what is mine"—he tightened his hold on her hair with a jerk that snapped her neck back further—"I will rip your bones apart, one by one, before I strangle you by your insides."

"Mmm? My pet is jeal—" Pleasing choked coughs escaped poisoned lips.

He squeezed tighter, still looking as if he would splinter the bones in her neck.

Silence roared. Everyone watched as Garrik's skin paled and pointed teeth formed through his gritted mouth.

Their Savage, High Prince returned with sharp cheekbones and a glassy, obsidian, spiked crown covered in shadows, rising through his gray hair. Only for a breath, a warning to who they all knew he was. Of who lurked deep inside his soul and shadows.

Garrik. Thalon's voice inside his head shook away the deathly intention.

The half-beast slowly faded back into a High Fae male with death still claiming his eyes.

"Get"—he growled so deep the dirt trembled—"out of my sight." With a snap of his wrist, Garrik released her, stumbling forward on snake-adorned heels.

Each breath struggled for air as she gripped her throat. The female wickedly laughed before turning on her heels, "You'll be mine again," she promised and slithered across the firesite, disappearing between the purple tents.

He fought the urge to adjust his battle leathers, now unnaturally snug against his body, feeling the beast caging itself inside. How many times had he imagined his hands around her throat? His Smokeshadows penetrating her to the core until they sucked all the air from her lungs. He would revel in it. Enjoy every second of tearing the life from her flesh. From her wretched hands. Her body.

One day.

Malik grinned as he scanned Garrik up and down, then turned his attention to the High Prince's Shadow Order, and smirked.

"Who let you out of your cage? Little. Dragon." He flippantly emphasized each word before his night-blue eyes flashed something crucial, locking onto the green of Jade's as the tips of his coat spikes ignited into navy flames.

"Malik. Never a fucking pleasure," Jade hissed, shifting her posture, intensely watching his flames dance.

Malik's gaze narrowed, A muscle feathered in his cheek as he folded his arms over his chest and smiled. "Oh, I *know* the pleasure would be all mine." He formed a blue flame on his finger poking out from his bicep, twirling it in the air, watching her just as intensely.

Jade drew her sword. "You're not worth the dirt it'd take to bury you in. Piss off, *flame* fucker."

Curling his lip, Malik moved to step forward.

Garrik palmed her shoulder, the iciness radiating through her armor. "*Enough.*" He had the fury of a thousand thunderstorms, but Jade could level kingdoms with her attitude alone.

With an amused smirk, Malik shifted his focus back to Garrik's darkened eyes. "You're not in command here. Watch your tone."

"You would be wise to stay within your piss-poor protection under the Ravens. If I see you outside these borders, your head will be mine. And I would enjoy every last bit of it until your embers are ash in my wind."

"Is that a threat?" A reptilian grin crossed Malik's face as navy flames rose from his hair and cascaded down his neck, shoulders, and as far as his fingertips.

"You would know when I am threatening you. That was a promise." Garrik glowered into Malik's eyes.

And I would not require such an embarrassing display of magic while doing so. Now run along, before I remind you what real magic can do, the High Prince's voice seared deep into Malik's mind.

Garrik lifted his chin, tilting his head slightly to the side with a menacing grin. How he *loved* this game. Every burst of his magic pricked his skin, pleading to fire. But he much preferred the invasiveness of haunting one in the comfort of their own thoughts. The intimacy of the attack.

His most treasured power—stealing thoughts.

Always being twenty steps ahead.

Malik gritted his teeth through the headache Garrik knew was forming behind his eyes, straightening the collar of his coat to lift his chin high. The look suited him. Like a conceited royal who never was worthy enough of the bloodline. "Brennus has been waiting for you. You know how he hates to wait." His voice slithered, more like a threat than a statement.

"Then why are you standing in my way?" Garrik knocked shoulders with Malik, storming the middle of the line of guards, before bursting through the tent entrance, with no consideration for permission.

Inside, the stench suited a brothel, but the finery was fit for a king. Brennus certainly thought himself one.

Golden banners with the High King's Raven crest decorated the walls, lavish, golden chairs filled with plush cushions, a four-post bed rested in the center. Numerous female High Fae peppered the space, lounging on plush, round cushions on the floor in the back, talking and laughing. Ancient vases, a red-stained wooden table teeming with glasses and liquors, weapon racks of swords that were ineffective in battle, golden armor, rugs of fine animal pelts covered the dirt. It was extravagant, almost blinding.

A table constructed for twelve waited to the side. Drawing his eye, a large map of the kingdom was laid out.

Brennus, much shorter than Garrik by three hands, leaned against it by his fingers, wearing a long, regal robe, decorated with gold filigrees, and spotted fur that covered his neglected, round figure. Dull, stringy red hair and beard were greased and disheveled as if he had just woken from a restless sleep.

"So, you finally decided that you wasted enough of my time today?" Brennus's eyes, one scarred and white, the other a sandy hue, glared enough that they could have stabbed holes through Garrik. His battle-worn face set in a permanent frown.

Garrik nodded—a small gesture—a forced bow. He hated that Magnelis ordained Brennus with the honor of authority over him. The heir to Zyllyryon's throne under the command of one such as Brennus. It was humiliating.

"Apologies," was all he muttered. The word burned like blazing coals in his throat.

Brennus turned without any regard and slumped onto a throne-like chair, holding a large goblet of wine between filthy fingers. One blonde, curvy female, scantily clad aside from the little scraps of red-laced underthings, sat mewling on his lap, tracing her fingers along the opening of his robe in an open display of seduction.

His mouth twisted in disgust at the sight of it. "Is it not early for a revelry, Brennus?" Garrik trailed to the table of liquors, scanned them with significant hesitation, and poured himself a knuckle's length of amber liquid, tossing the contents back before pouring a second. It would do little but was enough of a burn to calm the rising hostility fitting to explode. For now.

A tall, scarcely dressed, brunette toweled her leopard spot, tattooed arm around Garrik's icy neck, nearly knocking the glass from his hand, before rubbing down his chest. Before he could react, she forced a second around his waist, down the V of muscles, and pushed inside his waistline, where he grabbed her.

Garrik viciously growled and pushed her away before adjusting his armor at his abdomen. *"Do not touch me."*

Brennus called her to his lap. "I was subject to entertain myself while waiting for you to arrive. Bloodshed and sex, two of the most pleasing ventures. I delighted in that brunette this morning."

Inhaling a steadying breath, Garrik closed his eyes.

When they opened, the brunette had Brennus's robe open at the chest, tracing lazy circles around his flesh. Thin fingers running through wisps of hair.

"Undoubtedly, I was not summoned here to be informed of the latest activities inside your bedchamber." *Or to fucking witness them.*

Seething, Garrik pressed his hand onto the map strewn across the table, his throat working at the lingering memory and touch of hands. He squeezed his abdomen under the armor and focused on the trade routes of Zyllyryon until they reached the shores of Galdheir.

Soft purrs and pleased mewls tainted the air behind him. A never-ending reminder of...

Garrik bit back the nausea rising. If it were not for his own powers rendered null on Brennus, he could simply steal into that repulsive mind and obtain the reason for this summons. But Brennus was conniving. The High King, resourceful.

By Garrik's ... unwilling participation so many years ago, Magnelis discovered a foothold, a way to subdue and protect his own mind from his, in *incredibly* loose terms, son. A drug was formulated. One that left Garrik's powers of the mind wholly useless on those who were deemed vital enough to savor its effects. And Brennus, being the second-most powerful High Fae in Elysian, was one of them.

Without fail, Brennus never missed a dose.

When a strangled moan reverberated through the tent, Garrik slammed his fist on the table, rattling his glass. "What of Telldaira last night?"

Brennus's breathy chuckle was enough to send Garrik over the edge, but he stood from his chair, pushing his females aside, and circled the table while fastening the belt of his robe. "My Ravens seized one Marked One in the north. When questioned, his demeanor shifted, and we determined an attempt to protect someone." He collected the glass Garrik had not emptied and threw it to his lips, grimacing at the burn. "Telldaira was ripped apart until we were satisfied that she was gone."

Garrik forced himself not to smile. "She? Did he surrender a name?"

"No. Your snake and Malik administered the pre-washing on him. But it was determined he would be more compliant in Galdheir's dungeons. My Ravens departed with him for the castle a few hours ago and should arrive within two weeks. I require your abilities to locate her."

Gazing at the map as if it held every answer, Garrik traced his fingers along the shores of Castle Galdheir, across the trade routes to Telldaira, over mountain ranges, swirling vast rivers, and forests. The Kingdom of Zyllyryon —his mother's kingdom—his birthright—was the largest in the realm. Double to the three kingdoms that occupied this piece of land. No High Fae, save for himself and his dawning powers, could cross it in less than five months.

"I will require time. The moment my powers locate her, you will be informed." Garrik wrenched himself from the table, pivoting fast enough that his cloak caught the wind before storming toward the entrance.

"You were not dismissed, *boy*." Brennus adjusted his robe and slumped back on his throne.

Garrik bore his gaze into the furs on the ground, lifted his head, and sighed, which went unnoticed. "By all means, do go on." Annoyance filled his tone. He turned back, facing Brennus.

"I have a tent waiting for your quiet reflection. You will find the Marked One here within my camp and then you can leave. I am certain we can find something for your," he said, pausing, "gutter rats to do in the meantime." Brennus lifted his finger. "Guards!"

Four Ravens entered and stood at attention in the doorway.

"See that the *prince* is comfortable in his accommodations for the afternoon."

One guard outstretched his arm, gesturing for Garrik to walk through the exit. Jade and Thalon were waiting, arms crossed and faces taut. Upon seeing his return, they both walked toward him and met by his side.

"Sire? Are we returning to camp?" Jade questioned.

The guards flooded around Garrik, ushering him along until they stopped at a nearby tent. His new make-shift prison was fit for a servant.

"Brennus commands the use of my powers for a missing Marked One. Wait here. I will collect you once I find her."

Jade and Thalon exchanged knowing glances before nodding.

Garrik bent at his waist, entering the obvious display of blatant disregard for who he was. Inside, a small, rickety chair sat against the wall, and a table with a map waited.

He leaned back through the canvas, giving the order, "Do not disturb me." And ducked low, vanishing inside.

CHAPTER 16

Two hours passed. No one witnessed Garrik retire from the tent. And they would not have. Simply because he had not been there since he sealed the tent with his powers and dawned away in a cloud of Smokeshadows.

A tap outside rippled through his mind, calling across the kingdom from where he had stolen away to, alerting him to the unwanted intrusion.

A voice, muffled inside his mind, echoed, "Brennus grows impatient. He summons you."

Then another voice, one who knew of his absence. One who knew a diversion was needed until he transformed into his shadows and misted back inside the tent...

Thalon's voice cut in, "*Sire*. Show some starsdamned respect."

Garrik chuckled a breath through his nose, twisting the side of his mouth as he sheathed his bloody sword and stepped away from twelve motionless bodies. Thalon was ... his protector, ever since Garrik was a little shit-spoiled, royal faeling, training in the citadel of Galdheir. They had been brothers of different blood since Thalon's sacred duties placed him at the young prince's side. An unbreakable bond of brotherhood and loyalty.

"Wait here until I return," Garrik warned the only body left standing, not waiting for a reply before Smokeshadows dawned him away.

He flashed Thalon and Jade a smirk before he stepped back inside to find Brennus sprawled on his bed with the two females from earlier. Their clothing was nowhere to be found.

"Well, boy. Have you located her?" He grunted.

Garrik scowled, turning back to the table of liquors and pressing his fingers into the bridge of his nose and eyes. Desperately wishing to have that image burned from his mind forever. "I am inclined to believe that she has protection magic surrounding her as the last few. They are growing resourceful. I cannot break through it, yet." He set a glass of ale on the map and leaned on it. "However, I sense that she has fled east."

His fingers traced the map, running over the eastern cities. He knew exactly what he was doing. Sending the High King's army in the opposite direction, away from his legion. From her. He also schemed, for the sake of Zyllyryon, how little towns remained there for Brennus to destroy.

Brennus shuffled his robe on, sauntering to Garrik to loom over the map. His face twisted as if he considered Garrik's words. "There is vast territory that we have not searched in the east." He paused, chewing on his cheek. "I will send my Ravens to find her. Your little band of misfits will continue north as the High King commanded."

Garrik buried words of displeasure and only nodded. "If that will be all then"—he turned away to leave—"I will return to my camp and press forward—"

"*Sit. Down.* You may leave when I grant it." His tone lazy, expectant. A male who was not disobeyed.

You are lucky I am granting you the gift of breath. Garrik's shadows threatened to explode before he shoved his anger down.

The evening dredged on.

The females served them wine, careful to stay away from Garrik's death glares. He sat and was forced to reminisce about past raids, laughing at the bloodshed, basking in the glory of bringing Marked Ones to the High King and watching him enact disillusioned justice.

Garrik endured what he deemed as punishment for two more hours while Brennus drank his wine and boasted of his horrendous accomplishments.

When the general had his fill of misery and pain, he drunkenly rose, half stumbling from his throne. "Be off with you. I have had enough for today." Brennus leisurely waved his hand through the air.

Garrik stood in silence, face unreadable as he toweled his cloak over his shoulders. He knew they were there, the dark circles under his eyes, felt the blinding headache behind them, reminding him of how exhausted he was. Tired of the energy it took to fake the illusion that he actually was enjoying himself. The stories plagued his mind while his boots knew the way to the door and his mind, in a daze, simply allowed them to lead.

"To the High King." Garrik glimpsed Brennus raising a shaken glass and continued walking.

He would have said anything in return ... if it were not for his breath knocked from him as something tore through his magic at that very moment.

Someone had broken through his shield around camp.

He stopped.

Inches from the entrance.

His vision blurred as he focused on his camp.

And there ... white hair ... riding a night-dark horse...

Racing through the shield and into the woods.

No. Panic struck his heart and pulsed through him.

Alora, stop. Go back. He blinked rapidly, pulling himself out of that darkened forest and back to the tent, where he nodded at Brennus in acknowledgment and goodbye.

The tent flaps burst open, spitting out his armored form. Garrik stormed past the guards, motioning for Thalon and Jade, who had Ghost saddled and ready, to follow behind his quickened pace. Before his Shadow Order could jump onto their horses, Garrik had already taken off.

They caught up to him outside the camp.

"Garrik? What's wrong?" Jade called to him.

"Return to camp, *now.*" Ghost picked up her pace as he nudged with his heels.

When they found refuge in a meadow far beyond the Ravens' camp, certain that they were not followed, Garrik ordered, "*Thalon,*" and pointed in front of them.

Thalon immediately knew what was required of him. Clasping his hands together, in one practiced movement, he pushed his arms in front of him.

A burst of thunderclouds and striking lightning swirled in a hurricane portal, opening wide enough for a horse and rider to slip through.

Beyond the swirling, their firesite appeared as if they were on the opposite side of a door and simply needed to step through.

Garrik vanished inside, and Jade and Thalon followed.

The portal imploded, closing after their horses vanished through and leaving nothing but a crackle of electricity in the air.

CHAPTER 17

A flash of metal sliced through the air and sank deep into the beast's crystallized shoulder.

Before the weapon had pierced to its full depth, a high-pitched screech reverberated, tearing bark from the nearby trees by its vibrations. Shards of oozing, black crystal splintered to the ground, and it reared on its back legs.

The creature's eyeless head thrashed. Its claws desperate to pry the embedded sword from its skeleton arm. Each movement sprayed more steaming ink in the clearing, sizzling everything it touched. Its wings flexed, and another wail of agony followed, leveling trees a hundred feet apart.

Alora spun on her heel, not entirely sure whose shadow had burst through a thicket of bushes in the dimming light, but grateful all the same.

Aiden's coat caught the wind as he ripped it from his body. The black material was a battle cry on the breeze. His white shirt rippled in the wind as he unsheathed a sword from the saddle, holding it high as his horse thundered toward them.

"Don't let it touch you, it's poison! Get to the trees!" he shouted and closed the distance between Alora to challenge the beast.

Unable to do anything more, Alora leapt onto her horse's bare back, the mount amateurish as she fought to collect her balance, and fired off toward the tree line.

Ear-piercing shrieks and earth-shaking sizzling thumps prowled behind her as she vaulted over a boulder and landed in the stream. From her vantage point, she could see Aiden in the falling sunlight. Slashing at the giant's rock-solid legs, stabbing his sword everywhere within reach.

Crystal slivers sprayed. The blackened shrapnel pierced into the dirt with every blow. Toxic flesh and liquid inners permeated the floor in a monstrous soup of peril.

It was no use.

The beast wouldn't be downed.

Get out of there, Aiden. Run! Alora's hands gripped the reins, eyes desperately searching for *anything* that could seal that fatal blow.

Nothing. There was nothing.

The gamroara reared up and swung its front leg, colliding with Aiden's horse.

No.

A crunching stab of its crystallized fingers skewered Aiden's horse before it lifted its enormous wings and took flight. Aiden swung his leg over the saddle and vaulted to the ground. Landing on his leather boots beneath the creature.

It dove.

Daggered claws dripped with inked, steaming liquid.

Ready to send him to whatever hell he ran from.

Aiden rolled to the ground, nearly missing the swipe of claws, then jumped back to his feet, sword drawn alongside taunting eyes.

"Come on then, you scurvy dog!" he yelled and ran, sight set on the beast's belly before he jumped, sticking his blade between pieces of bone and crystal.

A hit. Finally, a hit.

The gamroara roared in pain. Lifting itself into the air by those monstrous wings, carrying Aiden, who hung by the sword.

Alora tightened the reins even further, her horse stomping its feet in a predictable itch to flee.

"Damn Suzy, who hurt you? Was it mother?"

It crashed its feet down onto the earth, shaking its body with violent twists to release the weapon protruding from the crystals. Aiden plummeted to the ground, landing on his back, his sword remained wedged in the creature's side.

Everything was happening too fast. One moment, Aiden had rolled backward, pushing to his feet, wholly unarmed and exposed in that clearing. The next, he was disappearing into the forest.

Emitting a terrifying shriek, the beast expelled its poisoned ink from the wound, causing it to sputter uncontrollably.

In the trees, her ebony-haired rescuer crouched low, patting down his body. Aiden was searching for weapons, she realized. But those shale-colored eyes were so focused, frantically seeking anything to use, that he didn't notice the razored tail slicing through the air.

Didn't notice it maneuvering around the trees...

In one swift movement, it didn't only find bark and empty air.

But sliced into flesh and bone.

No! Alora gasped, eyes wide, utterly frozen as the beast's tail speared through Aiden's torso.

Blood crawled like lava out of sliced holes in his once-white shirt. Strangled groans and even more blood trickled from his mouth, eyes half-lidded, bobbing as his skin turned ashen. The only reason he remained standing was because that tail that had stabbed through him now lifted him off his feet.

It finally retracted.

With a fierce swing, Aiden careened from it, slamming the entire weight of his body into a tree with a sharp grunt. His body slid down the bark and landed at the base, unmoving.

Glistening by fading sunlight, a crimson trail streaked down the trunk from where he had impacted, down to where he lay motionless.

His eyes were open, staring off into the dim light. His body still.

Those eyes ... utterly soulless, staring at her.

Freedom. It drove her. Drove her to this terrible, horrible thing ... drove Aiden to—

A strangled cry fell from her lips. She may have wanted to escape, but this... Even if she hated them, Aiden didn't deserve to die like this. Even if every aching and dying piece of her bruised and bleeding life wished to be free, *this* wasn't what she wanted.

And sitting there, as soulless eyes burned into her, she realized her freedom was once again paid with someone else's life.

That chance at a new life—it was so close—right there. All she had to do was turn and run—

A gurgle.

Then a breath from Aiden's mouth.

Aiden. He's alive...

Alora clenched the reins until her knuckles blanched, head swiveling from the tree line to Aiden. From freedom to who had aided in stealing her from one prison and throwing her into another. A life, a living, breathing life, bleeding and dying on that clearing floor.

Alora slammed her eyes shut, inhaling deeply. *Stars be damned...* Freedom would have to wait.

Shoving every ounce of bitterness and fear and heartache deep inside her bones, she kicked her heels and spurred her horse around the stone. With lethal intent, those sapphire eyes burned, searing into the beast that had heard Aiden's choked breath, too.

"Don't you dare," she snarled at it.

Blood slowly trickled from his mouth as he coughed again, pebbling beads of crimson down his shirt, drawing attention to himself. The color had drained from his body.

His hands slowly inched toward the gaping holes in his torso. Shaking. Desperate.

Aiden looked up, only half aware.

A streak of black barreled across the clearing like a raging storm. The horse's breaths matched her own, heavy and uneven. And as they approached the beast, a damning notion gripped her; the only weapon she carried was the clasp of her cloak and the wooden leg from the bedside table.

What the hell would they do to crystal?

If anything, maybe a distraction. To turn the beast's trajectory. Stop it from ripping Aiden apart. Disappear into the trees while it chased her. Find shelter in a cave... It was *something*.

The sharpened edges of the wood dug into her palm, gripping it like it was the last tether to life. This time when the beast turned, she refused to run, but instead, javelined that wood straight for the beast's back.

"Over here, you ugly beast!" she shouted.

The gamroara, feet from Aiden, whipped its head and shrieked once more.

"That's right, look at me," she murmured to herself as her horse anticipated an incoming blow, leaping over the swing of the beast's spiked tail. *Not today, Death.*

The beast reared up once more, crashing its feet down beside Alora as she raced past. Spinning her horse around, they charged once again, only this time when she neared, Alora balanced her feet on her horse's back, gripping black hair and reins.

Her eyes focused on Aiden's sword still plunged deep into its flesh. *I need that sword.*

They charged for each other. Her horse lunged to the side, driving enough force into her boots to thrust her high into the air. Every muscle in Alora's body seeped in adrenaline while she flew. The sword connected with her outstretched hand. *Yes!*

She heaved it from crystallized flesh, avoiding the splintering shards raining around it.

And then it was free.

Sword and warrior fell, landing on the ground beneath the beast.

But the gamroara was too swift. It clamped its feet around her, moving its considerable head between its front legs, blaring eyeless sockets into the darkness.

She was *trapped.*

Every option of escape was blocked and caged beneath its dripping underbelly. Alora knew something about cages. But this ... this wasn't one she could escape.

The tail wrapped around her body, squeezing and squeezing and squeezing until choked gasps tore from her lungs. And yet, the pain still wasn't anything worse than what Kaine had done to her.

Pricks of stinging needles spiked her clothing, and threatened to pierce skin, before a lack of air forced her palm to open. And for the sword to drop.

The gamroara ripped her from underneath it. Guttural clicking and snorting sent vibrations through its chest as she slid by it.

Her boots scraped and dug into the steaming, rotting grass. It was seemingly impossible to breathe. The creature's tail was relentless in its hold, pulling her to its face. Dangling her before empty eyes.

But it didn't matter if there were eyes there, Alora couldn't see them anyway. She couldn't breathe. The clearing began to fade into stars and darkness.

The gamroara flexed its leathery wings with one hard flap, and they shot into the sky.

At least she'd get to glimpse the sun one last time. The trees ... and the forest below... She deserved it, after all. After leading Aiden to his agonizing death. Being burned from the inside, holes plagued his body, blood weeping, draining his life drop by drop.

If she would've stayed in camp. If she could've listened. If she wasn't so damn stubborn...

If you weren't so fucking stupid. It wasn't her voice that snickered. Like a chiseled memory, this—another—voice haunted her. The voice she had run from; the voice that filled her daily, never-ending nightmare.

Kaine.

From the depths of her mind, he taunted again. *If you wouldn't have left me like the* pathetic *weakling you are, you wouldn't be dying right now. Was life with me really that terrible?*

Yes. And she'd prefer this death over his hands any day. He wouldn't be the last thing she heard. He wouldn't be the last thing she thought of before the beast stole all the life from her body.

His scalding hands wouldn't be her final touch.

The biting wind grew cruel the higher they flew.

Alora winced, squeezing her eyes shut in agony, forcing all the energy left inside to obliterate Kaine from tormenting her mind.

But his snickering remained, just as it did when she would hopelessly fight him back at the manor. That same snickering wrapped her mind with barbs and thorns as it did before her flesh would tear from broken mirrors or her bones would shatter down *that* marble staircase.

Terrifying, high-pitched shrieks surged across the dusk sky as the voice invaded again. *You'll die like the worthless trash you know you are.*

What was left of the fading dusk was blackened out by whirling mist. The shape of a flying creature blocked out the sun as its wings unfurled from its back and flexed at a length equal to the beast.

No. *Not real wings.*

Smoke and shadow wings ...

And not a creature but ...

A voice—catastrophic as an atomic explosion—unleashed across the sky. Tendrils of Smokeshadows carried the High Prince on a hurricane wind above the beast. A glint of flashing metal caught the sun's golden rays as he plummeted toward them.

Crystal, rock, and bone cracked.

Cracked with so much power, the creature's arm shattered from its body. Crashing to the forest with enough force, it leveled the trees below.

The tail of the gamroara released Alora, writhing in pain as steaming black liquid poured from its wound and sprayed the air.

And then ... she was falling down that damn staircase again. Only this time ... it would be the last.

Her limp body plummeted dangerously fast—too fast—toward the ground. Through blurry eyes, she saw emerald, rug-covered wooden floors as she desperately fought to refocus on where she was.

Dense trees spinning.

Portraits hanging at an odd angle.

Back and forward, her mind splintered.

Then, the dirt of the clearing spotted into her view, feet from her face when Smokeshadow-covered, icy arms wrapped around her, folding her against a solid chest.

Garrik slammed into the dirt beneath her with a distinctive crack and pained grunt, knocking the air from his lungs. His shadows exploded into smoke on the wind before dissipating into the soil. Thalon and Jade burst through the tree line. Their voices now familiar. And neither horse stopped as an odd swirling circle of thunderclouds and lightning appeared in their path. Swallowing them entirely and spitting them out beside the High Prince.

Jade slid from her saddle, ripped throwing daggers from her thigh straps, and positioned herself between them and the flying beast.

"It's a gamroara," Thalon called out. "It's only killed by shattering the neck from its head." Ripping his golden sword from the sheath, Thalon positioned himself as a shield beside Jade.

Something frigid was pressed against her cheek. Hard and scaled indentations pulsing with an unusual beating rhythm. She heard the voices, barely able to decipher the exchange. Heard the rumbling groan from the hardened surface beneath her as it moved.

Garrik ... he was telling them that he was alright. Then his cold hands cupped her shoulder and back. The deep, honeyed voice of the High Prince chilled her ear ... he was whispering.

"You are alive, darling. Try to breathe."

Breathe.

Alora sucked in deep, greedily inhaling the refreshing air of dusk and the scent of leather and metal as Garrik's body twisted, gently lowering her to the dirt.

He brushed sweat-soaked hair from her face, hovering over her, scanning for injuries she knew were likely to be there. When he found none other than the burned flesh from the gamroara, he turned to his Shadow Order. "Thalon, attend Alora. Jade—Aiden. Go, now," Garrik growled as he vaulted into the air, and she felt a static energy ripple through her body, leaving her head in a wave of unease.

Smokeshadows once again formed into those impressive wings, hurling him faster into the sky. Those wings curled around Garrik's body. Like an iron fist, he blasted through the sky and collided directly into the beast's neck. Breaking through it with an eruption of shattering glass.

The creature's head exploded into a downpour of crystal, shimmering star-like in the sky as it embedded into the surrounding earth. Failing to penetrate through an invisible shield that formed over their heads. Not even the dust of a stray crystal infiltrated it.

The gamroara struck the ground like a meteor. Spraying dirt, rock, and grass out of the crater of rising debris. Rattling the ground so brutally that those standing lost their footing and braced themselves on the dirt.

Garrik slammed into its back with wings flared and unfurled. Demolishing every last shard of the beast into a pile of shattered rock, black crystal, and steaming, rotting bone.

The very air stilled.

Until...

"He's not breathing!" Jade panicked, pumping Aiden's chest. "Come on, dammit. *Breathe!*" She lifted her fist, harshly pounding it down. "I *swear* if you die, I'll find you in Firekeeper's realm, bring you back, just to kill you myself."

She pounded again. *"Open your damn eyes!"*

CHAPTER 18

A iden's face filled with life, choking on air between his half-blue, blood-covered lips.

"Come on, that's it," Thalon cried, frantically rushing to cover one of the burning puncture wounds. "Aren't captains supposed to go down with their ships? You're not dying today. Not on dirt."

In Jade's relief, she loosened a shaking breath. "You fool! Don't you know better than to take on a gamroara by yourself?" And ripped off a scrap of her shirt, balling it to pack the other wound.

Aiden moaned in agony, blood slipping slowly between his teeth.

Behind them, Alora could only focus on the uncontrollable shake of her hands. She couldn't acknowledge it when the High Prince slammed to the dirt below the pile of remains and ran to her.

"Are you injured?" He cupped her upper arms. Pitch-black abyss scanned her body.

But she could barely speak, surrendering to a slow, dazed shake of her head. "N—no. I'm ... I'm fine." She hardly convinced herself through the hoarse whisper.

The smooth metal of his rings brushed her ripped tunic, tracing until it met the clammy flesh of her shoulder, and his calloused hand gently squeezed. "Wait here," he murmured.

But her eyes flickered ... to the tree line.

And his darkened orbs tracked the movement, determining what that hesitation meant. "Please, Alora." Voice raw.

Fading black eyes pleaded into hers, and she nodded, knowing that her legs were unable to run even if she willed them to.

Garrik jerked to look behind when Aiden groaned again. One last brush of his hand against hers, and he twisted away. He stepped, and she didn't miss the slight stumble as Smokeshadows engulfed him, ripping him from space and time.

Reappearing in a cloud of shadow and ash, he roughly landed on his knees beside Aiden. "Still with us, brother?"

Aiden buried his fingers in the dirt, choking through a painful breath. His eyes fluttered, forcing a smile. "Garrik, if I die—"

"Shut the hell up!" Jade pressed the bandage tighter, pulling a strangled cough from him.

Breaths later, Aiden winced. "If I die ... whatever's left of me, give it to someone who needs it. But my middle finger ... gift that to the High King for his birthday." Aiden's voice shook.

Garrik grabbed Aiden's balled fist and squeezed, leaning close to Aiden's bleak face. "Give it to him yourself. Stay with us, that is an order." The words were rushed. Firm.

Aiden's eyes fluttered. "Bloody hells, guess I can't die then, can I?"

The corners of Garrik's mouth twitched, and he lifted his head, scanning the wounds before turning to Jade.

"This is very bad. We need to get him to a healer." Jade's hands were soaked in blood. The bandages appeared soaked entirely through.

"Ozrin was sent to Brennus's camp last night to care for the wounded. He was there as we were leaving. He wouldn't have returned tonight." Thalon's distraught eyes had lost their golden glow, and he pressed more cloth to the wound, but it wasn't enough; blood spurted too quickly.

Garrik's face turned wholly rigid. "Thalon, take him."

Thalon's matched with brutal hesitation. "You mean—"

"Yes," Garrik snapped. "Get to the trees, out of sight, and ride like hell until you have reached Ozrin."

Aiden violently coughed blood, spraying it down his chest before falling back to the dirt. His eyes traveled backward, his body fell limp as the last bit of color faded from his skin.

160

"Go!" Garrik jumped up and heaved Aiden over his shoulder, running to Thalon's horse.

Thalon mounted beats later as Garrik lifted Aiden, settling him in front of Thalon. Steadying him between his arms, Aiden's body lay lifeless against him, head falling back onto Thalon's shoulder. Clasping his hands together, Thalon thrust them forward.

Thunderstorm clouds of striking lightning swirled into a spiral before him, leading to the hill outside camp where two sentries sat, guarding on horseback. They all watched as Thalon ran through, barking orders to the sentries to follow him.

And what Alora now knew was a portal closed behind them.

Then, it was unnervingly silent.

So silent that even a whisper was too loud.

Heavy breaths escaped Garrik as he dropped his chin to his chest. His shoulders rhythmically rose and fell. The creatures and night-bugs tentatively resumed their sounds as the forest returned to its peaceful self.

It was peaceful.

Only for a moment.

Only until the sliding of metal against leather disturbed the silence.

Garrik turned.

Jade maliciously stalked toward Alora, twenty feet from where he stood.

"This ... is *your* fault!" Jade's rage rippled across the clearing. A flash of metal in the moonlight revealed her sword trained high, aiming for the soft flesh of Alora's chest.

Alora backed away, hands trembling in front of her in terror.

She'd survived it all to die at the hands of fury. And if Aiden died, she wouldn't blame her for it.

Jade swung her sword, but a hand enclosed around her wrist, catching the blade's edge in the other.

Crimson oozed from Garrik's grip. His face tight, eyes fading to black. The High Prince leaned his weight into the blade, cutting deeper, forcing it away until it rested a hair's length from Jade's throat.

His face ... the same face as that in the alley of Telldaira.

Jade's contempt pushed back.

It was as if two explosions detonated and warred to be the victor of the deadliest destruction.

Garrik sunk the blade against flesh and growled, low and vicious and all-ending. *"You dare to defy me?"*

His power drove a humbling wall of air against her.

Jade stumbled backward, releasing her weapon. The muscles under

Garrik's battle leathers rippled as he threw the sword away and prowled forward, fists balled while crimson dripped from his palm.

"Get ... the horses," he snarled, the thunder in his voice barely restrained.

But Jade didn't move. Not an inch.

Tilting his head like a beast stalking its prey, Garrik again stepped forward. "*Now.*"

Jade's lips curled, quivering as if she would speak. Still, she didn't move.

Garrik pulled a dagger from his belt. "By the laws of—"

"I'm sorry," Alora whispered in the darkness. "I'm so sorry." She covered her mouth with her palms as tears flowed down her cheeks.

Garrik's oblivion for eyes remained on Jade's and loosened his tongue. The words, crackling like a raging wildfire, were far from the common tongue but wholly natural like a treasured melody on his lips. And he spoke a language that Alora had never learned. He lingered there, body shaking in unrelenting rage.

Whatever he was saying, Jade's face burned as red as her hair. She balled her fists, face twisted in repulsion as that same language spewed like venom from her lips. Not as graceful and melodious as the High Prince's, more malicious with a stinging bite. The muscles in her arms tightened as she pointed a stiff finger at Alora.

"*Her?*" Jade hissed as she considered her from head to boots.

He spoke again, the language dripping from his mouth as if he had been born of its tongue. And when the words stopped, the common tongue filled his voice. "*Do not think I won't.*"

Those words alone ... they speared something wholly terrible in Jade's eyes. Turning them from uncontrollable rage to ... pure unadulterated terror. Was that even possible? Could Jade even possess a bone in her body that could be convinced to cower from spoken words?

Relentlessly gripping her necklace, Jade stormed away without another word, the darkness silhouetting her out of sight.

They were alone.

Garrik peered over his shoulder, eyes tracking Alora as she lifted Jade's sword from the grass. Tears still streamed down her face, but she raised it, hand quaking uncontrollably. "Don't come any closer," she commanded with fear plaguing her eyes. "Don't," she repeated. *As if pleading with him would matter.*

Garrik stalked closer. "I told you to stay in camp." He swung his forearm, hitting the sword with such force it tore from her hand and landed in the darkness.

Alora stumbled a step backward. She lifted her arms in front of her face, expecting a heavy blow to follow the High Prince's advance, but only his words struck.

"Did you not consider the consequences? *You could have been killed.* When you leave camp, you are not only risking your life but everyone around you. Do you have any idea what I would have—" He choked back his rage and grabbed her forearms, pulling them away from her face.

"I ... I'm sorry." And suddenly, it wasn't the face of the High Prince staring down at her. That horrible, enchanting face was merging into a creature so vile and so awful. Her body began to cower. No matter how strong she was. No matter how many times she fought back. Kaine was there, and he always carried the power. Even now, when he was stars-knows-where, he still controlled her body.

Garrik's face softened, and she felt her veins fill with sharpened glass. He released her, turning away with tension thrumming across his shoulders.

Leading the horses to their side, Jade returned and stood in silence. Still scowling at Alora.

"Get the hell back to camp." Garrik didn't so much as turn to them—to her.

Alora, fearful of repercussions, grabbed the reins of her dark horse from Jade and began pulling herself up by the mane. Her limbs, with little strength, shaken and empty, struggled to mount. The sounds of footsteps wracked her heart in a fury, hammering against its cage when freezing hands reached her, and she flinched.

"I can do it." Voice cracking in a whisper as she inched back from him. Alora attempted to mount again; she nearly succeeded this time, but ultimately failed when her foot slipped and her body slumped breathlessly.

"Allow me." Garrik remained agitated. Interlacing his fingers and cupping his hands together, he lowered to a knee, gesturing for her to place a foothold.

Refusing him again would most likely end in a death sentence. Alora swallowed, emotion still infesting her body. She was angry, fearful, humiliated, worried. Wishing her body could focus on just one, she placed her boot on his hands, and he lifted her onto the horse.

Before she could do so, Garrik stole the reins and prepared to mount behind her.

He could have easily done so ... if it were not for the movement of the mare.

Garrik's palm flattened against its croup in time for it to step sideways, causing him to stumble forward and brace against its flank.

The horse side-eyed him, as if the beast knew what she'd done, and Alora dared to grin. Only a little, until she glimpsed Garrik's irritation.

His mouth twisted, tightening the reins as cold eyes bore into the mare's, and he mounted without interference, pressing his icy body flush against Alora's.

"You two are perfect for each other," he muttered, squeezing his thighs to balance without a saddle and stiffening his spine. Feeling the contact and tension between his hands and the bit, Garrik lightly nudged his heels back, and they left behind the battlefield...

Along with Alora's last shred of hope ... and freedom.

CHAPTER 19

The forest had fallen completely dark. As they rode, the only things they encountered were shadows and outlines of the foliage that lay in their path. The moon crept through the tree canopy, shedding minimal light to guide the path. Ahead, torch lights peaked in between the silhouettes of trees, dancing the amber glow from the distance between swaying branches in the breeze.

She would be a prisoner once more. Surely worse than before after tonight's events.

And the punishment to come...

Alora shuddered at the thought. At all the horrible things her mind pictured.

There was no mistaking the looming pressure of Jade's eyes stabbing her back. She imagined a blade plunging deep into her own spine and shivered.

None of them had spoken since they left the clearing. Which was no surprise. She'd rather it be that way anyway. There was nothing to say.

Not until camp became clearer and clearer and the High Prince finally spoke in a soft yet demanding tone. "Alert the sentries of our return, and stand post until I grant you leave."

Jade's shoulders tightened, and Alora unnoticeably grinned.

"Yes ... sire."

Apparently, Jade didn't appreciate border duty. Her dark outline feathered into the blackness until she too became a silhouette against the torchlight.

A heaviness cascaded off Alora soon after. The pressure of Jade's death glare was no more, yet it still sat uneasy. How couldn't she? With muscled arms of Death toweled around her, it was inevitable. And even if she wanted to, she couldn't stop feeling his armor brush against her back with his every breath. Entirely aware of his every heartbeat, the ice not only in his veins but seeping from his skin.

She hated it—hated him. Hated his touch, like all others.

Knowing that his touch would never do anything more than send embers threatening to burst and ignite flames on her skin.

Garrik remained quiet. One arm draped across her stomach, steadying her without a saddle. His hand gripping the reins still dripped with blood from Jade's sword, soaking a dark patch on the horse's black hair. He clutched the reins tight regardless of suffering and pain.

He must've felt her observing the wound. The subtle shifts in his posture were enough that she cautiously turned her gaze to him. There she found pain—disappointment—irritation in his eyes, forcing her heart to skip a beat.

Tears welled, spurred by the events caused by her actions. She knew he saw it, but didn't care. *Let him see.* Let him see what's become of her since he brought her to this place. Since being with him. Being forced to flee. This was his fault—not hers. She wouldn't have needed to escape if he hadn't taken her. Taken her magic.

The air felt heavy again. It was suddenly harder to breathe.

Too hard to breathe...

She couldn't breathe—

Easy. You will be alright. It was the voice again. There when she needed it.

Garrik's arm tightened around her waist, and she almost leaned against him in her panic.

"I understand how it feels to be trapped," he started. "Feeling hopeless, stuck in a cage without a key." His deep voice almost soothed her emotional heart. "I allowed you no way of freedom. You acted as I would have."

Alora's throat tightened; she swallowed her emotion.

"You have been running and hiding your entire life. Why would

166

today be any different?" He pulled back on the reins and they stopped. As if the words were foreign to him, Garrik deeply sighed, and said, "Forgive me. Today was my doing."

Her blood seemed to hollow out.

"You must understand, Magnelis's power grows stronger with every passing moon. I know you have heard the stories about me. I understand your reluctance and fear, your hesitation and refusal to trust me." His breathing became shallow. "Out of everything I have done since our eyes met on the road into Telldaira, I have protected you. I will continue to do so. When you are with me, no one will harm you. Not even the High King... I will not harm you, Alora."

She looked at his bleeding hand, feeling the vibrations of his words rumble from his chest into her back, still unable to speak.

"Stay with me—us. Allow me to honor that. Help fight, protect our kind. Elysian. Or keep running for the rest of your life, in terror, watching the world burn behind you in Magnelis's pursuit"—his voice was full of warning—"I only ask that you offer me the chance. Ride with us to the edge of the northern kingdom. Allow me to escort you there at the very least. When we reach Dellisaerin, if you wish to go, I will not stop you."

She looked back at him. The stiffened back of the High Prince had bent, sitting him lower as if the weight of Elysian was forcing him down. It was then she noticed dark circles under his eyes, illuminated by flickering torches in the distance.

Garrik closed his eyes, those weighted shoulders slouched with a tired breath.

Then she felt a pulsing sensation creep across her skin.

An exhilaration of energy prickling every nerve.

Warmth. Incredible, overwhelming, familiar warmth formed in her palms.

My magic.

Alora looked into his slowly opening eyes.

"I will never control you again." Garrik released his arm around her waist and lifted her hand, twisting its palm up. With little Smokeshadows, a black-bladed dagger with one star-shaped, crystal gemstone appeared within the tendrils, and he closed her fingers around it before pulling his hand away. "If you could grant me one request, do not make me regret this."

For a brief moment, she pictured how it would look shoved into his neck. The black hilt covered in freezing blood as he fell from the horse. How his muscled body would lay in the moss only to be found by some miracle after she finally escaped through the trees. After she found true, unconditional freedom.

An icy chill breezed through the leaves, and movement caught her attention as, stiff-bodied, the High Prince nudged their horse forward.

Reluctantly, she secured the dagger to her waist, allowing his arm to drape across her once more. He'd returned her magic—and the dagger. He sat behind her, exposed and weaponless as far as she knew.

He was trusting her.

"I'm not promising to stay until Dellisaerin, but I will ride with you. Can you agree to that?"

The High Prince stiffened, considering her words for what seemed ages when he finally spoke. "You do not disappear. I wish to know the moment you decide to leave, and I will not interfere unless it is unsafe. Until then, you will be treated as a Dragon. And trained as one. Bound by law and expected to uphold our purpose, following my every order and those of your generals. When you cross beyond the shield, you are ... mine. Under my command.

"In return, I offer you protection to my fullest powers, shelter, anything you desire ... within reason. Those are my terms. Will you agree to them?"

Though distrust hovered in the depths of her heart, she witnessed the High Prince's protection, not once, but many times since Telldaira. And today, he'd saved her life when he could've allowed her to be crushed to death, let her fall to the earth without the cushion of his body to cradle the impact, even ended her life for escaping. He could've allowed Jade to run her through with a sword.

But he hadn't...

He didn't have to give her back control of her powers, but he had.

Alora leaned into him, feeling that same weight that he must've felt, and breathed, "Yes."

CHAPTER 20

For two centuries, hope was this depraved, fleeting thing. Cruel and lost in whispers and sung to shadows from the ashes of her tortured life. A flicker dying in an ember. A song forgotten, stolen in the wind. It was this thing that she cupped in her hand, like water, spilling away one moment at a time until hope was nothing but droplets remaining.

But tonight ... where hope had been a spark fading too quickly, it now reignited, ready to burst—to flame.

The High Prince's promise of freedom was enough.

Her choice ... it would be her choice. Not someone's iron fist collecting the ties of her life and tethering them tight to a sinking ship. Not Destiny forcing her hand. She would decide and be free.

But at what cost? What would her time in his army take from her? What was left?

The air was unsettling. The future, unnervingly unclear as the High Prince approached Eldacar, who was settled near the fire.

Garrik's eyes were glazed, focusing on the amber glow of the flames.

"I want to hear nothing of tonight's events. Eat. Rest," he decided, then motioned for Alora to sit before he turned and disappeared inside the darkness beside his tent.

Alora's attention rested on the dancing heat, her vision going blurry as she narrowed on the flickering, too nervous to lift her eyes anywhere else. She considered retiring to her tent. At least there she could be alone. Comfortable to a point. Safe inside the walls of ... fabric.

Scoffing silently to herself, *Not safe at all.*

At least she had her dagger.

Eldacar exhaled his grief in a long, steady breath. He leaned forward, drawing up the iron pot of food that Aiden tended earlier, to hang above the fire. "Shall I make us something to eat, then?" Muttering in a whisper, his voice cracked.

Alora watched his hands when a wave of guilt rushed over her. Had she caused him problems for his unknowing part in her escape? By now, it was evident that he knew the meeting at his tent was a diversion. She used him. Lied to him. But when she trailed over his hand that stirred the food, his expression was soft. Almost smiling as he glanced her way.

Was that forgiveness in his stare?

She half-smiled back and returned her gaze to the flames.

After some time, the aroma of gravied meat, green vegetables, and potato stew revived her hunger. And with flawless timing, Eldacar lifted the spoon from inside the pot and ladled a generous serving into a wooden bowl.

Alora folded her hands in her lap, squeezing them tightly, uncertain if she should remain or wander back to her tent empty-handed. But as her legs intended to rise, Eldacar smiled and offered her a bowl.

"I brought you another book to read." His voice was gentle as he pulled a red, leather-bound tome from beside him. Handing it to her before he poured himself his own portion. "I had hoped to give it to you earlier, but—" Brown, sheepish eyes drifted away, his head angled down to look at the dirt.

"I'm sorry, Eldacar." Guilt lined Alora's tone. "I'm so sorry."

But Eldacar only grinned, wrinkling his nose to push his glasses up. "Tomorrow will be a new day. What's wrong will be made right, I know it." He scooped himself a spoonful and shoved it into his mouth.

Between the crackling of fire and scrapes of spoons on wood, heavy, rushed footsteps trailed their way. Emerging from the path beside Garrik's tent, six soldiers clad in Dragon's battle leathers marched from the darkness. But the sight of the force wasn't what shoved an iron rod deep into Alora's spine.

It was that of the High Prince whom they trailed.

Adorned in his armor, Garrik's face was taut as the visage of Elysian's deadliest warrior spurred toward the fire. A storm raged in his bones and death stalked his presence.

It terrified her.

Because that very real fact was like an ocean crushing her under its waves. She was now one of his Dragons. A soldier under his command. 'Mine,' he'd said.

And she was a Dragon who had disobeyed his orders.

Bile burned her throat with each of his steps.

This was it. The time had come to punish her for escaping. And not only that, but her rebellion had resulted in one of his soldiers—his revered Shadow Order—injured gravely. There was no escaping this.

Her eyes met his as the distance between them closed, expecting him to stop. To wrench her to her feet. To—

Alora braced herself, digging her nails into the fallen log beneath her until the splinters bit her flesh.

Only, the High Prince and his soldiers didn't stop and shackle her in chains. She wasn't carried in Smokeshadows to a dungeon. They didn't consider her at all. Their footsteps continued on, past the firesite, and marched down the clearing of tents until they were engulfed by the darkness once more.

Alora's focus was glued to the shadows, feeling her taut muscles relax as confusion engulfed her unsettled nerves. *What's happening?*

Heavy stomps of horses faded in the distance as silhouettes of the soldiers climbed the hill, guided by moonlight. Alora half-expected the High Prince to accompany them when he appeared inside the glow of the fire once more. Casting shadows across his handsome face. His battle-black armor lit up from the light with each determined step.

Garrik didn't turn to them as he passed. He continued walking until he reached his tent entrance, then, forcefully pulling the flaps aside, slipped inside.

Alora glanced at the fabric swaying in the wind. Candles lit the inside and cast shadows onto the canvas. The High Prince's towering shadow paced the tent, and her eyes tracked the movement. Wondering where he had gone and what his soldiers were commanded to do.

Eldacar noticed her stare and sighed. "It will be a long night for him, I'm sure." Then he was silent. Nothing but the crackling fire disturbed the air around them. But his soft expression made way for a face twisted and wholly troubled. "Our healer is away, tending to Aiden. Thalon is in danger, being inside the Raven's camp as a Mystic. Garrik won't sleep until they're back. Not like he'd find any sleep even if all was well—" He stopped himself. As if he'd said too much, dropping his eyes to the ground.

"The High Prince has trouble sleeping?" Alora raised an eyebrow, turning back to watch the High Prince's silhouette near the table she stole a map from.

Eldacar considered carefully his next words, his mouth twisting in hesitation. "It's likely been ... weeks since he last rested."

It's been five hundred years since those cursed with magic rested. Who cares if a spoiled royal loses some sleep?

Alora continued watching his shadow pace against the flickering of candlelight. If he were anyone else, perhaps she'd find it in her heart to care. But watching as he sat in his chair, as shadows stirred around his chiseled form like the very smoke drifting into the sky before her, Alora couldn't summon an ounce of compassion.

Let him suffer sleep. It was none of her concern.

Rising to her feet, Alora clutched the book in her hand. "Goodnight, Eldacar. Thank you ... for everything," she said and turned to her tent, leaving Eldacar alone by the fire.

Garrik sat rigid in the candlelight, holding a glass of strong, amber liquid between his fingers, condensation forming around the tips. It was the perfect remedy for his tortured mind and aching back. Each stretch of an arm or elongation of his back became a reminder of the impact in the clearing.

He had endured many battles. Suffered countless wounds. Still, he would prefer the slice of a blade over the cracking of bones.

Cuts healed faster.

His elbow dug into the armrest as he pushed his thumb into his cheek. Two ringed fingers rubbed his aching forehead. If it were not for camp, he would release a roar so devastating, the entire valley would level. Enough to demolish a starsdamned mountain. But not now. Not here.

He closed his eyes, plucked the fabric of his tunic away from his abdomen, and exhaled a long, liquored breath.

Thalon, he called—pleaded—commanded to the stronghold deep within his mind, and sealed by magic.

Instantly, the weightlessness of clouds caressed his skin, releasing pressure from his bones. Much like floating on a calm lake or fading carelessly from consciousness, his awareness of the tent and everything around floated away, entering a state that no normal faerie, High Fae, or even Mystic could go. Not to the extent that he could.

Mind magic.

The curse from the stars gifted at his birth. Powers of illusions. Of thieving thoughts. The curse of location and an ability to mask an entire world in a seal of protection—or use it as an invisible weapon.

His magic surged. Bursting and rearranging what was reality and what lurked inside the intermedial. Unlike imagination, this *was* real. By powers of location, his power hurled him into a picture-play of Zyllyryon's landscape, deep in his subconscious.

Garrik transcended through it all, as if flying on the wings of a thousand sky creatures. Sweeping over the route from his camp to Brennus's, in pursuit of answers.

On a vivid, grassy hilltop, his sentries' faces appeared as if they were standing directly next to him, without the knowledge of his presence. Magic pushed him forward through the forest beyond. Ash trees, woodland creatures, coarse moss, tall grass, and stones flooded his mind as he persisted forward. The stinging scent of sage burned his senses on the breeze.

Something outside the tent disturbed his focus. His body trembled in reality, rattling his exploration across time. Garrik balled his hand into a fist and clamped his eyes with more force.

An impenetrable shield encompassed the room, freeing him of distraction beyond its walls.

Then, he was flying again, over a loose pebbled road, passing the sentries that guard the Raven's encampment. He weaved through the grid of dark purple tents, passing the structure that was Brennus's, knowing Thalon and Aiden would not be there.

Thalon. His focus deepened, leaning forward in his chair, ignoring how the fabric of his tunic uncomfortably shifted on his skin.

Garrik's mind raced through the tents of the High King's army until he landed on one tent among the thousands. Thalon's magic ... not only could Garrik feel it, but like every Mystic, it carried its own marker. Thalon's cast a golden hue around the tent, much like the hues of a city with its fires burning through the night, casting a glow into the sky.

Thalon was in there. So, Aiden would be too.

Inside.

Garrik gripped his glass with such intensity, that it shattered to the ground.

He saw Aiden. Bleeding and bandaged. Unmoving on a cot.

Ozrin's scarlet robe was an intelligent choice for a healer. Blood did little to stain it; it was already that color. The extent of Aiden's blood loss was unknown as those wrinkled hands worked tirelessly to close wounds and scrape out burning, steaming flesh from the oozing poison of the gamroara. Weary brown eyes were meticulously attentive to the hole in Aiden's right side, administering a vial of milky liquid over ashen flesh as gray as Ozrin's long hair.

The High Fae elder male was calm-faced, which allowed Garrik some reassurance. Ozrin's tells had never failed him in all the years those withered hands had tended to him. And even if the healer's face wasn't enough, Aiden's chest slowly—steadily—rose and fell.

Breathing... He was breathing, but *barely*.

With blood-covered arms crossed, Thalon stood stone-faced above Aiden's head toward the back. It was evident that he had assisted their healer in surgery. Blood soaked into every inch of his tattoos and clothing. So much so that he had discarded the white tunic and only the leather vest remained.

Garrik pictured a wall of blaring sunlight inside, so bright that an ache formed behind his eyes. Thalon's mind would soon fill with tendrils of his shadows, and they were dancing along the rays as he sought out permission.

A burst of swirling sunstorms receded, opening a door that Garrik's shadows drifted through before the wall was resurrected.

Shifting in his stance, Thalon closed his golden eyes and met Garrik there.

Aiden?

Thalon's voice was clear as if they were shoulder to shoulder. *Holding on. He's lost a lot of blood, but the gamroara missed major organs. Ozrin was able to stop the spread of poison. If Aiden survives the night, Ozrin is optimistic for a full recovery, but it won't be easy. Aiden has a long road ahead. Weeks, maybe months. Shit, Garrik, he'll need to return to Galdheir.*

Fuck.

Garrik forced a swallow, gripping the armrest of his chair. *I have sent six guardsmen. Inform them to escort Aiden and remain until he is recovered or they are relieved. Return to camp. Find me when you arrive.*

Yes, sire. Thalon paused, adjusting nervously on his feet. *Are you ... alright, brother?* The words were carefully offered, delicately handled as if at any moment, an explosion would detonate.

A slithering, phantom touch trailed across his shoulder and down the swell and dips of his muscled chest, knowing the meaning behind

Thalon's words. Knowing his Guardian's intentions, but also knowing himself. But if he let *that* touch affect him, if he let it settle into his mind like it did his body...

Garrik shuddered it away, Smokeshadows whorled around his palm, producing another knuckle's worth of amber liquid in crystal. He lifted it to his lips, anticipating the welcome burn to sting his throat. *I will see you soon, until then...*

Every icy vein thrummed with static energy, pulsing in waves as a shield cascaded across Zyllyryon, toweling around that very tent. Around Ozrin, Aiden, Thalon, and the soldiers that Thalon had brought with them.

No one can enter without my allowance. Hurry back, Realmpiercer.

Like a hand reaching, Thalon began, *Garr—*

The connection broke.

Dull silver eyes struggled to open.

Garrik collapsed back in the chair. A throbbing pulse threatened the sanity behind his eyes. Unable to form one structured thought or any amount of ambition to move. Even lacking the motivation to breathe. The one thing that was supposed to be easy, he had to *choose* to continue doing. He was exhausted. In more ways than one.

So starsdamned tired...

But his eyes, they could not stay closed. For the moment he began to slip into the darkness, the moment he would drift away—

This time, Smokeshadows brought him an entire bottle.

It would not be enough. No matter how much. It was never enough.

A tap at the entrance had him setting the bottle beside his chair as a hushed, bleary voice drifted through the canvas. "Sire? Might I come and bring you something to eat?"

Garrik stood from his chair at Eldacar's voice. He opened the entrance, allowing him to come inside. "Thank you, Eldacar."

Eldacar stepped inside, the scent of the steaming bowl of stew proceeding his arrival.

Garrik had moved to the table and pulled a chair to the center of the room, sitting it angled to the side but facing his own. The High Prince waited for Eldacar to sit before taking the bowl and finding his own. They sat in silence. Garrik ate slowly, blinking away the exhaustion with every savory spoonful as Eldacar twirled his thumbs in enclosed hands.

When the silence was too much, Eldacar leaned forward in his chair. His mouth opened and lingered there before he retracted to twirl his thumbs.

"Out with it." Garrik spooned another bite.

From the expression on his face, Eldacar was quite hesitant. He peered down at his boots and twisted one in the pelt covering the dirt. "How many days has it been since you've slept?" Eldacar's eye held the reflection of Garrik's untouched cot.

He continued to eat.

"You mustn't push yourself this far, sire."

Garrik swallowed a hearty bite. "I am fine." And scraped the last of the stew inside.

"You're not fine. You look like you will collapse at any moment. How many shields are you holding? Not to mention the amount of darkness you've been using. I'm surprised you're still conscious. You need rest, sire... *Real sleep.*" Eldacar opened his bag and began to shuffle around inside. Glass clanged together in his search.

Real sleep? Garrik held back a scoff and instead exhaled an easy sigh, watching as Eldacar produced a familiar jar.

Lifting his palm in a pointed gesture, Garrik refused to use it. "I will sleep when I am dead." He grinned, placing the empty bowl on the ground before walking to the table and shuffled through the parchments lying there.

But Eldacar continued. "That may very well be soon if you don't rest. The books warn that if you push too far—"

"I know what the books say. I will not hear this again." Garrik glanced over his shoulder to see Eldacar surveying the ground with a blush heating his freckled cheeks. It was not lost on him that Eldacar simply cared. They all did—*too much.* But their concern was ill-placed. Misguided. Unaccepted.

He was ... fine.

"I have news of Aiden," Garrik redirected. "Thalon confirmed that if he should continue breathing by morning, recovery is strongly expected."

Those flushed cheeks swelled Eldacar's glasses up his face. Relief bubbled with a long exhale. "Thank Maker of the Skies. Never thought I'd see the day when Aiden would be brought down over a female." Eldacar shook his head, meeting Garrik's quiet smirk.

Garrik turned his eyes to the unicorn insignia crested on the correspondence crackling in his grip, but the ink lettering was a blur. The subject of discussion lost to his sight behind flooding memories.

In the simplest and kindest terms ... Aiden belonged in a brothel. His ventures were wholly relentless over pursuing females. Not only of his own kind but in any form of High Fae or faerie. Relentless and unabashed.

In the past, even quite recently, Garrik unwillingly interrupted his captain in the throes of his night's latest consensual conquest. One in particular sent a repulsed shiver down his spine recollecting an opened door and a pale ass pounding into a creature that smelled of stagnant sea on a blistering day.

Many times, Garrik had rescued Aiden from threatening fathers over their daughter's honor or paying the dues of parlor house visits. Even so, Garrik would never admit it, but he would not wish Aiden differently.

The daydream faded. Garrik placed the parchment on the pile, splaying his fingers to shuffle pages across the table. Grinning over the obvious tampering—and not from his own hand—and poured himself another glass of bourbon before returning to his chair beside Eldacar.

Lips trembled and Garrik wondered if it was from a memory spurred by Aiden's condition. When finally Eldacar spoke, his voice cracked and hands quaked even though they had folded together atop his lap. "My apologies, sire."

Garrik arched a brow.

"If I would've realized what Alora had planned—"

"You are not to blame, Eldacar." Garrik tossed the crystal against his lips, downing the contents whole. "You are needed tomorrow at the arena. I intend to see what Alora can do." Then Garrik stood. "It has been a long day. Get some rest. I will meet you in the arena in the morning." He walked to the door and held it open.

"Yes, sire." But before leaving, Eldacar turned, and his face furrowed with something akin to concern. "Take care of yourself." He paused, sheepishly lowering to an unnoticeable bow. "Do try to get some rest, too."

Garrik forced a smile. "Go on. I will see you in the morning."

Eldacar shifted on his feet, adjusting his jacket before walking through the open door.

Returning to his chair, Garrik slumped against his sore back before drawing his fingers to his temple once more. The dim candlelight danced shadows around the canvas; the heavy smell of smoke burned his nose. He inhaled, extending his lungs to release a substantial amount of burden weighing on his shoulders.

His fingers flexed, and shadows gently cascaded around them. Strength faltering the longer the night drudged on. He waved them until a bottle of amber liquid appeared in his palm. The night was too long to even care about finding a glass before he threw back the bottle and swallowed the smooth vanilla and oak burn of his usual escape.

He pulled it from his lips and rested it on his knee, watching bourbon slosh inside. The liquor the only music he needed.

With one last heavy sigh, the High Prince turned his head and stared at his swords leaning against his untouched bed.

Now then. Shall we visit an old friend?

Garrik laid his head back against the chair and closed his eyes.

With little effort, his chair and swords were engulfed in swirling tendrils of darkness, thickened smoke, and deathly shadows. The small candle dimly lighting the room fought to stay aflame.

His swords disappeared.

Smoke and shadow lifted to the ceiling.

And The High Prince's chair was empty, leaving an overturned bottle rolling on the dirt below and a dying candle sending spirals of smoke into the air.

CHAPTER
21

F ive flickering candles illuminated the High Prince. Yet, darkness
still snuffed out the light enough that his face was cast in
dancing shadows, making him all the more menacing.

He stood, armor traded for his tunic, waiting in the middle of his
quarters. Back turned and sword drawn to his side as Jade and Alora
entered. The blade's edge was embedded into the ground beside him.
Smokeshadows created a veil of power around him, gently lifting from
his body to the ceiling as dust swirled around his boots.

He breathed heavily, evident by the harsh rise and fall of his
shoulders, and tossed a satchel onto his side table. Still, he kept his back
turned as they stood square-shouldered in front of the tent entrance.

Alora knew. *Of course* she knew. Out of everything that happened,
this moment was inevitable. The moment she dreaded all night. The
time to have her punishment delivered.

The High Prince squeezed the hilt of his sword with a second
bandaged hand.

That was new.

He turned, dragging the sword across dirt and animal pelts until he faced them.

Alora's lungs refused to cooperate, anticipating something truly terrible when, at last, the High Prince broke the roaring silence.

"I have half the mind to wield this sword after your insolence today." His hoarse voice exuded disappointment and wrath all the same, and she willed herself not to meet his cold, bloodthirsty eyes. "You disregarded those around you, disobeyed my orders. Your selfishness caused affliction and endangered this entire camp."

Alora's bones started to run away; her skin wanted to follow.

Squeezing the hilt until his veins bulged in his forearms, Garrik's lips curled in silence. Smokeshadows whorled from his arms, the tendrils swirling down around the blade like they enticed him to pull it up and use it. His focus turned to the tendrils. With a deep breath, they retreated into his skin.

The High Prince stopped in front of Jade. Chest pushed out, an edge in his eyes as he looked down at his other bandaged hand and squeezed. "Your actions against one of our own will not go unpunished."

Jade simply blinked as if it was all she could do. As if the source of her High Prince's anger, her own doing, caught her by surprise.

Long, agonizing minutes passed before he spoke again, and when at last that hardened voice thundered, it rattled everything in the tent. "Law in my camp dictates a painful death if you turn your sword on my Dragons. When you joined my legion, you swore to it on your life." Garrik stabbed his sword into the ground as something sharpened in his voice, and he bared his teeth.

Alora didn't dare move for fear his wrath would be unleashed on her.

"You betrayed my fucking trust today."

Jade's breath escaped her. "Sire—"

"*Silence,*" Garrik growled. Smokeshadows exploded around him. "If it were not for *my flesh, my blood,* Alora would be dead, and you along with her."

Jade scowled. Her body tensed as she retorted, "If it were not for *her,* Aiden would be sleeping in his—"

Garrik kicked his blade in such a way that it lifted from the dirt and traveled into his awaiting palm. With an incredible twist of his wrist, the cold of the sharpened edge met flesh. One smooth motion. That's all it took. And his other clasped around the back of Jade's neck, drawing her into the blade until crimson appeared, and those furious, silver eyes turned into endless oblivion.

"*One more word,*" he dared.

She lowered her head until her chin kissed cold steel, reverent against his sovereignty.

Garrik carefully pulled away, tossing the blade onto the soft furs of his cot, and released his grip. He stood for a moment glaring at her, considering his next words, when a silent whimper traitorously escaped Alora's mouth.

Shit. Her body uncontrollably trembled as he turned his darkened eyes to her.

"Alora," was all he said, his attention shifting as that anger seemed to subside slightly. "I ordered you not to leave camp. You disobeyed my command, causing harm to one of my Shadow Order and endangering everyone in this valley." And like a king on his dais—on his golden throne—Garrik twisted and sat rigid in his chair, measuring them until his ticking jaw stiffened.

Fury couldn't even come close to describing the brutality on his face.

And in that moment, Alora wished that the gamroara would've killed her instead.

Blaring, hot anger simmered into cold indifference and disdain. Garrik's Smokeshadows tendriled around his limbs, making him appear more ruthless and powerful and eternally deadly.

"I cannot allow rogue action to endanger my legion. Because of the disobedience you have both displayed, my ruling is this." He angled his head, critically surveying them as he rested his elbows on the armrests, steepling his fingers in front of his face.

"Alora, you cannot be trusted to flee from camp. Jade, your malevolence, causing harm to your sovereign, and endangering the life of a Dragon calls into question your loyalty." He turned his contempt to Jade. "Your duties as my Shadow Order are withdrawn until I am satisfied by your fealty. And as you know, I am not easily convinced. You will not attend my war tent, your opinions are dismissed. You will personally stand guard ... to Alora. If she flees, there will be consequences."

Jade's face tightened as his gaze snapped to Alora.

"Barring our arrangement, you do not possess the freedom to do as you wish. Not until I can trust you. You will not go anywhere without Jade's escort."

"And what am I to do when she sleeps? Camp outside her chambers?" Jade scowled and crossed her arms.

"You will share lodgings."

"I'd rather sleep in pig shit." Jade pressed her lips tight and burned her glare into the High Prince's face.

"That can be arranged," Garrik snarled. "Regardless, you will not leave each other's side. Have I made myself clear?"

Jade trembled her own snarl. "Yes, sire." And nodded before ripping her glare to the table of parchments.

Garrik shot Alora an impatient, pointed look. "*I am waiting.*"

And she barely heard her own voice over the quaking of her bones. "Yes."

His face tightened, rising from the chair as if he were in a throne room of golden tapestries and marbled floors. Finding his boots inches from her own.

Her head as high as his sculpted chest, she could feel how angry he was by his breathing alone. Then, freezing fingers gently gripped her chin, lifting her face. Her eyes trailed over the black tunic, glimpsing a raised, rigid scar on his neck, his defined, gritted jaw until she met his darkened eyes.

That touch so demanding, she couldn't prevent the ruthless shudder burning down her spine as he growled, "*Sire.*"

And she realized her seemingly lethal mistake.

Alora's mouth went dry. "Yes ... sire." The words were like ash in her mouth as he released her chin.

She now understood why he was coined the Savage Prince. The sheer sight of him, when he was enraged, could topple the indestructible Blackstone Mountains of Kadamar. She feared the day when every bit of his wrath would be poured out.

He turned to Jade. "Prepare your tent. *Get out.*" A low growl escaped his chest as he waved his hand in the air. It appeared as if he couldn't care at all, motioning for her to leave.

Jade stormed out.

Garrik flattened his palms on the table, tension flexing his shoulders as he leaned heavily on his corded arms. Surrounded by silence again, nothing but her heartbeat thrumming as she watched him. Watched his head drop incredibly low, chin to his chest, almost as if he had forgotten that she was there. From the way he stood, he looked like a frontline soldier returned from merciless war. She saw the way his arms trembled. The way his breathing fell in uneven waves.

Then, his head lifted slowly. An unearthly strength rippled across his flesh and bore into the canvas above the table like it had that morning.

"I need a fucking drink," Garrik murmured, his voice unlike it had been before, almost ... pained, haunted. No trace of the High Prince who delivered punishments to his soldiers. That male that she had glimpsed in the tavern returned—for only a moment. Those powerful back muscles shifted as he pushed off, found a bottle, and poured himself two knuckles worth of amber liquid.

Garrik moved on heavy feet, dragging a chair across the pelts and settling it to face his own. "Sit." That too sounded strange. Almost as if he was asking. Only she knew better; it wasn't a suggestion.

Maybe it was his softened voice, or the drained, tormented dullness in his eyes, but whatever compelled her to do so, Alora willingly obliged him. The wooden chair creaked when her trembling knees bent.

Noticing with the first long sip of his drink, whatever Garrik had been warring inside settled as he wandered back to the table. There, he grabbed a thick bottle along with another glass.

She hadn't expected it, but as he held out the crystal and nodded to it, this time, she didn't refuse.

Garrik poured an amount worthy of her boiling nerves and reclined in his chair while she welcomed the burn over her quivering lips.

That critical gaze returned.

Alora sat uncomfortably, nervously tapping the glass with a fingernail. Watching as Garrik widened his knees and rested his arm across his thigh. She began to explore, observing the bandage on his hand that Jade's assault caused, and the other with a strange scent like ... burned flesh.

"How often have you trained with a sword?" Garrik took another sip.

Her eyes shifted to where Garrik had thrown his blade across the cot. Though she agreed to Garrik's terms, she still didn't want to be there. And, knowing enough, he wouldn't grant her leave just yet.

Alora's cheeks flushed scarlet. Despite everything, even the return of her dagger and powers, that dark part of her that remained distrusting, wickedly whispered to take that sword and plunge it into his neck.

Submitting *again* ... to someone—a male—to him.

It sickened her.

Calling him 'sire' was enough to feel her embers threatening to ignite in her palms, sending an ache to her twisted gut. He may have rescued her from the gamroara and even from Jade, but she vowed—*vowed* a long time ago—no faerie, High Fae, or male alive would force her to submit.

Never again.

Alora half considered moving for the weapon. Like she had upon first meeting with him. This time, he was sitting—drinking. It was possible that he could be subdued in this state. With her powers returned, they could assist her. What could shadows do to fire, anyway?

She stared into the liquid in her glass like it held the answers. Feeling that beautiful, safe net of power heating her palm.

Don't, her mind coldly growled. Only the voice seemed ... different.

She recognized it—mostly. But that voice had ... had shifted to something dark.

Something like ...

Sapphire eyes darted to him, wondering.

It ... it sounded like ...

Whatever was inside her glass was affecting her too quickly. The thought was outrageous. Or perhaps, he'd simply spoken but she was too distracted by scheming that she missed his mouth moving.

As if in response to her wondering, like smoke on a phantom wind, a gentle irritation, the one when she heard that voice, waved across the space inside her mind. Bouncing from the walls, rushing like the waves—searching, invading.

And she wondered again. *Did he ... No. That's not possible.*

"It is," that voice manifested from his lips. Arching a brow, Garrik's enchanting, silver eyes locked onto hers, and she lost all sense.

"You—"

"Heard your thoughts." Garrik wolfishly grinned in the candlelight. Smokeshadows whorled around his form, dancing around his boots and drifting across the pelts on the floor.

Indeed, I did. And what a delicious mind you have.

Warmth rushed to her cheeks as burning embers formed in her hands. This whole time. Every thought. Every fleeting moment, each move she schemed before she followed through. The constant voice in her head of warnings, of guidance... In the market. The alley.

Alora gritted her teeth, hearing his voice echo.

'I dare you.'

'Clever girl.'

'Do not do anything foolish.'

He knew. He *knew* it all before it happened. *Everything.*

The chair slid back, toppling backward to the ground. Glass shattered beneath white flames.

"You *knew,*" Alora snapped, her voice burning like her flames.

Smokeshadows hurled the chair upright behind her. "Sit down," he growled, but she was only seeing red.

"Is that the command of the *mighty prince* or the *prick* in the tavern?" she asked, growling back.

Garrik's gaze simply shifted to his sword, then, it flickered back to her, freezing her with an incline of his head. He stood, towering over her as shadows danced around his shoulders.

Do not make me ask twice, clever girl.

He stepped forward, the challenge set. But she remembered that

184

very posture, the way he moved toward Jade in the moonlight. She remembered that very look on his face. It was enough.

Alora slumped down into her seat.

Garrik watched her for a moment, watched as her blood boiled and those embers calmed in her palms. "You agreed only a few hours passed to obey my command. Yet, you still entertain visions of ending my life?" The High Prince relaxed back in his chair. A curious expression rippled across his features.

"It will take more than fighting beasts and proclaiming half-hearted remorse for my trust. Especially knowing my mind isn't safe from you." She stiffened, fingernails digging into the armrests until a waft of smoke rose, scorching the wood beneath her grasp. At least in here, with the High Prince, she could release her anger through her powers. A new form of release that, before now, she was never allowed to attempt.

Silver eyes descended, critical, raking from the white glow under her fingertips scorching his chair, across her body, and settling on her eyes.

She felt that gentle caress again and snapped, "Stay *out* of my mind."

Garrik wickedly grinned as if he had won the final piece to a game. "I would. But when you are offering every piece for anyone to see... How can one resist?"

Slouching back in her seat, Alora shot him a smile just as sarcastic. *See this, prick.* And graciously produced a middle finger from the confines of her mind.

Garrik's resolve broke. A deep laugh rumbled from his chest.

It sounded foreign, and if she wasn't so mad, maybe she would have enjoyed it but instead rolled her eyes and snapped her gaze away.

He sighed, his shadows producing a new glass, and poured some from his bottle, handing it to her. "Your mind is safe. I rarely invade my Shadow Order's thoughts. I mainly utilize my power for concealed communication... And the occasional fucking with my enemies when they piss me off."

The mind-shattering. She'd heard the stories—back when they were *just stories.* In all those tales, he was merciless. Ruthless. Sadistic. Bloodthirsty. Taking pleasure in ripping the minds from souls kneeling in front of his sword. And he certainly wasn't known for the slightest amount of clemency. The High Prince who relaxed in the chair before her didn't appear to be the same gray-haired demon those stories detailed. Not in his bedchamber, anyway.

She gripped the new glass and focused on the liquid inside with a question burning her mind. Perhaps it was foolish, but the words escaped her lips before she could convince herself otherwise. "Why did you let me off so easy?"

There was that critical gaze again, like he was studying her. "Do you wish for me to punish you more severely? Perhaps for my barbarous side to inflict harm upon you? Cut off your hands for attempting to steal Ghost. Break your legs for running. Tie you to a tree, lash you a hundred times for Aiden's injuries."

The blood in her body drained.

"I am not *him* anymore," Garrik continued, deepening a long, slow breath, and lifted the bottle to his lips. "Your punishment fits. But if you wish to be punished more—" Setting the bottle on the ground beside him, Garrik moved to stand.

"*No* ... *No!*" Alora repeated, her panic making him pause. Her voice breathy and words a jumbled mess of incomplete thoughts. "It's only ... I caused this—Aiden to be ... I just expected something ... more."

The High Prince's mouth twisted into a grin, amused. "Then my orders stand."

THERE WERE days that Alora would enter Kaine's bedchamber, only to find his back turned as he removed the finery from his jacket sleeves.

His cold face would turn to hers. As if he'd been expecting her to attend to his perversions much sooner than her arrival. And when she wasn't quick enough to please him. When his desires exceeded even his own awareness of them. When her feet had begged not to climb the staircase and go to him, those were the worst, most brutal days.

Alora dragged her feet until they stopped inches from Jade's tent.

She imagined that standing outside this thin wall of fabric would feel much the same. A wooden door or canvas, it didn't matter. Behind, a terrible storm was dawning.

Inside, Jade stiffened on a cot that was mounded with plush pillows to the right, and she continued sharpening her sword. The room was nearly a perfect reflection of how she expected it to be. Besides the clothing trunks, a cot-side table with a lantern held dancing, glowing orbs of light instead of flames—that was unexpected. Pelt rugs left not one inch of the dirt below, peppering the floor in her kills. And by no surprise, a weapons rack, filled with blades of all shapes and sizes, covered the length of the back wall. A wooden pillar in the middle held two nails; one supported a mirror and on the other hung a leather corded necklace with an ivory ... bone? Alora couldn't be sure. Whatever it was, Jade took notice of her stare and snarled, baring her teeth.

"Garrik said I couldn't kill you. That doesn't mean I won't thrust my daggers into your hands for touching anything in this tent." Jade slid a sharpening stone along the edge of her blade. "And don't even think about bringing fire in here."

Alora's lips tightened, entertaining the idea to light her palms in flames just for the sake of pissing Jade off. But it wasn't worth it. Not tonight. Not when she was exhausted and only wanted to crash her head into a pillow instead of starting a war—because that is exactly what it would be—a battle to the death.

She scanned the room. Pushed off to the left corner, in a wrinkled heap, laid Alora's cot. Unassembled. *Of course.* Instead of breaking her resolve, she strode to a large trunk that sat in the way, glanced at Jade with a sarcastic baiting grin, and pushed it to the side. New spot chosen, Alora began setting up the cot.

Jade hissed, but she didn't care.

When she had almost completed the setup, the lantern light darkened entirely, and Jade laid back on her cot. By the rustling of furs and blankets, Jade had settled. And to no surprise, her sword draped across her stomach, hand tightened around the hilt.

Alora lifted her eyes and shook her head as if she could see the night-dark sky. *Maker of the Skies, give me the strength not to kill her.*

Before long, the cot was shoved against the tent wall and her obsidian dagger was pulled from her waist and nestled between the frame and mattress. The leather hilt jutted just enough that the crystal gemstone would gleam in the light—if there was any—and was easily accessible if she needed to counter an attack.

With warm hands, Alora tapped around for a blanket. Her eyes focused enough that she could see there was none there.

Fighting the urge to remove the dagger and embed it into her new tent mate, she twisted to her feet. *She must have left it back in my old tent.*

With a frustrated sigh, Alora moved to exit but hesitated.

The only thing that calmed the bite on her tongue was the fact that Jade, comfortably settled on her cot, would have to get out to follow. "I need my blanket."

"And, so?"

"You're to accompany me everywhere I go. Too bad you *forgot* my blanket." That felt good. So. Damn. Good.

Jade twisted onto her side, facing away. "I'm in bed. I'm not getting back up for you."

"Suit yourself." Alora pushed through the opening and was greeted by the smoky night.

The fire had died down and that lonely candle cast silhouettes against the High Prince's tent. As she walked out around the fire toward her old resting place, two hardened and sharp male voices were arguing inside.

"*Look at you.* You can barely stand now..." Thalon returned with a sharpened bite of something final in his tone, and the sound rattled down her spine. "*No,* Garrik, I won't do it." That ... *that* was panic in his voice.

"You must. You are the only one I trust to do so."

"Garrik, don't make me do this."

Jade's hand grabbed Alora's shoulder and spun her around. "Spying on the High Prince? *Cursed Flames,*" she swore. "I should run you through this instant." She scowled and pushed Alora forward. "Get the starsdamn blanket before we're both in shit again."

Thalon burst from Garrik's tent, almost colliding into them, visibly conflicted and clutching the pommel of his golden sword with a tattooed hand. He nodded, locks and braids with beads shifting with the movement, before continuing to the tent past Jade's and retreating inside.

A shadow shifted beside them. Garrik's hollow eyes stared into the darkness as he leaned, rigid, arms and ankles crossed, and broad shoulder digging into the post that held the tent up. Shadow tendrils lifted from his shoulders and around the veins bulging in his forearms. And that same tormented dullness covered his eyes.

Alora quickly retrieved her blanket and was roughly shoved back inside by Jade. She didn't care to say goodnight. Didn't care that Jade threw her boots and jacket on the floor near her bed. What did matter was an unusual glow dancing on top of her pillow that hadn't been there before.

Her feet cautiously tread to the side of her cot, and on growing closer, Alora's face lit with the white glow of flames.

A Blazebloom.

It couldn't be...

Wide-eyed in disbelief, Alora outstretched her hand to touch it, only to be met with Smokeshadows enveloping her hand as her fingers settled upon the burning flower.

That gentle caress tingled the walls of her mind. *Careful.*

Shadows tendriled in her other hand, misting away to reveal a small, ashy-edged parchment.

Alora lifted the Blazebloom, the barrier of shadows still protecting her skin. She pulled the flames close to the page, illuminating the well-postured handwriting, and read:

Time to trust me, darling. Sleep well. I will find you in the morning.

—G

CHAPTER 22

A lora considered ignoring it. That distant, muffled bellow of a boned horn, and the hustling of soldiers' boots. Although she was half-awake, every inch of her body became utterly aware that she wasn't lazing in silken sheets. Nor was that cooled, lush pillow captured by her arms actually Kaine's warm body imprisoning her in his blistering-hot bed.

She burrowed into the pillow further.

And that horn wasn't a cheery breakfast bell or the paddling of soft-slippered maidservants carrying platters of decadent pastries into the dining room.

Jade shifted at the far end of the tent as the horn blew again. Alora heard leather groaning and metal clinking before something heavy and cold thumped across the blanket covering her bare legs.

"Put those on," Jade barked before moving toward the tent entrance. Careless to avoid kicking Alora's boots out of the way. "Some of us don't get the luxury of sleeping all day."

Heat blared into Alora's cheeks.

Perhaps the High Prince was right. Her cheeks *did* scarlet when she pictured death.

Before she could do so, Jade tossed a night-dark cloak on the bed, piling on top of unfolded leathers much the same as the Dragon's armor she wore. But that cloak ... it smelled familiar, not new. A leather and metal scent had mixed with her own, and a new clasp fastened it.

Another horn blew, and Jade's taut face turned as bright as her hair. "*Move*, princess. That horn means Garrik wants camp to report, and I won't be late because of your slow ass," she snarled and stomped to the door. "Be out in two minutes, or I swear, I'll drag you out by that pretty white hair." Her sword clanged as she thrust the tent entrance aside and disappeared.

Aching legs swung out from underneath the blanket, and she dressed in the worn-out battle leathers. Fumbled with the three straps and buckle closures below her right shoulder. Wiggled into the leather pants that were far too warm for her skin—which was utterly *perfect* because chafing from sweat on her first day of training would be absolutely *wonderful*.

A black leather hilt scraped against her leg as she buckled the thigh straps closed. Twisting, Alora grabbed her dagger from between the mattress and sheathed it before tucking her feet into knee-high training boots.

None of it fit right. The jacket was too loose around her hollow waist, the sleeves were too long, and the pants needed to be held by a belt, which, *of course*, she didn't have. It wasn't made for her, would perhaps even hinder her movements and any countermeasures to defend herself in the training arena. If Jade wanted her to fail, this was a good start.

The scent of fresh dew was heavy when she ducked from the canvas. Jade waited by Aiden's tent and a pain stabbed from inside Alora's chest at the thought of the empty cot inside.

Basking in the warmth of the rising sunlight and scraping dirt from beneath her nails, Jade leaned against the tree with the look of something rapturous crossing her face. She appeared to consider Alora with a slow, scornful examination before pushing from the tree.

Jade twirled the dagger between her fingers before sheathing it, then she twisted away, the action reminiscent of a lord—or lady—dismissing those beneath them. Regarding Alora as nothing more than a servant might've been preferable to a dagger aimed at her head, but the indifference chilled her.

You seem to forget that we're one and the same, Alora thought, offering Jade that same critical assessment before crossing her arms and squaring her shoulders.

The game that Alora anticipated had started when Jade threw a baiting grin over her shoulder. "Don't fall behind."

THE TRAINING ARENA had been dismantled and transformed into a dais.

Alora silently scoffed. So, the High Prince did have a traveling throne. And his charmed subjects were all gathered below it.

A sea of soldiers congregated, clad in scaled armor—mostly—save for a few donned in common wear. Awaiting some grand speech of duty and honor and whatever other bullshit the High Prince marveled to stir. Perhaps a desire to watch them fight to the death while he stood in his perfect glory.

Unlike the wide-smiled, beaming High Fae she met at the firesite the morning before, Thalon was a tower of strength and beacon of authority with ink-covered arms tucked behind his back. Standing at attention, commanding a brutal presence with a face taut and golden eyes lacking their glowing luster. Not a trace of the carefree High Fae who taunted and teased his friends. She imagined this same look to be how the Royal High Guards in Galdheir appeared, standing at the base of Magnelis's throne.

No. Thalon embodied everything she thought a commander of armies to be.

Damning and unyielding and stringent.

To his right, Garrik stood stone-faced and stared as coldly as the dead of winter. A bloodthirsty blade drawn, and its end embedded into the dais floorboards as he crushed the pommel inside his grip with one hand atop the other.

The High Prince murmured not a single word or order. His visage alone was enough to command unearthly authority. By his presence, he needed no silver tongue. Every one of them felt who he was. *What* he was. He didn't resemble a mere prince. No. Garrik was born a Celestial —the very stars, Moon, and Darkness they all worshiped. And he ruled with a simple breath. An unstoppable force. Immovable. Unshakable. Endless in his sovereignty and perfection in his existence. He was *made* for power, for authority, to deserve all of faemanity bending to his whim.

Screw that.

Garrik's enchanting silver eyes searched the crowd until they fell upon Alora. Tracking her like a wolf stalking its prey before she and Jade arrived in the foreground of the dais, settling beside Eldacar.

When the crowd filled, Garrik lifted his head. It was all the movement he required before the sea of soldiers instantly fell silent.

Alora surveyed the crowd, observing the ones who took to their knees.

Garrik's voice, as loud and thrumming as thunder, blanketed over them. "Rise."

Then he waited, emotionless and exuding total control.

"This world," Garrik began, "is cruel and dark and merciless. Enduring vicious nightmares, many of you forced to wander the realm, searching for a home while grieving your losses in the shadow of Magnelis's barbarity and malevolence. And now you stand, of one accord, the same purpose, defiant toward the throne of iniquity."

"*Death to the usurper High King!*" someone shouted, and the crowd boiled in a mighty uproar. Their voices ruthless. A continuous repetition of curses, bubbling in searing waves through the valley until it echoed from the trees and surged across the lake.

Garrik's eyes darkened in the chaos. Alora watched as his chin lifted, drawing his shoulders back as the pommel of his sword groaned inside his grip. "In time, brothers and sisters." By the sound of his voice, the crowd cascaded to nothing more than whispers. "We do not strive for revenge. Revenge will not return those we have lost. Elysian looks to us —to fight. To give power back to whom it belongs. Soon, Magnelis will face the swords of thousands upon ten thousands. The wrath of powers he will never behold... But that day is not today.

"Today we need reminding of our unparalleled duty to brother, sister, kingdom, and realm. To remember why we brandish these leathers, train until our backs threaten to break. Not for valor or the histories to recite our names.

"We fight to free the souls who remain. For a future that is brighter than anything we have ever imagined. And we cannot do that with disregard toward our fellow soldier."

Hushed whispers burned through the crowd. Heads warily twisted, searching for the subject to whom the High Prince spoke.

Alora felt the ground slipping from beneath her. The blood drained from her face.

Because that 'disregard' he spoke of wasn't disregard at all.

It was blatant contempt—she willingly *chose* to defy his orders. That 'selfishness' was planned, not neglect or blissful ignorance. Acting on her own will, for her own well-being, ultimately resulting in unintentional and almost fatal consequences.

And now ... he must have rescinded her previous punishment. Her real and true suffering was to be conducted before his Dragons as a lesson of rebellion.

She waited for his darkened eyes to find her, to outstretch a damning finger and to be hauled onto the dais. Waited for that head of gray hair to morph into ebony and for Kaine to stand before her. Her bones rattled, her breathing falling shallow when Jade glared at her.

She needed to run ... needed air ... needed—

Something cold gripped her chin.

A ... shadow. Formed in the likeness of a hand that lifted her head to find Garrik's cold eyes now half-lidded, looking straight at her.

Easy, darling. It was his voice inside her mind before he spoke again.

"I stand before you because I cannot allow a grave injustice to go unpunished. Two nights ago, Brennus raided Telldaira. Our Shadow Order successfully extracted a Mystic and secured them within our shield. Like many of you, I discussed their purpose but failed to explain why their presence needed to remain within the shield. As a result of my selfishness, this camp was endangered and our captain severely wounded. Regardless of the intention, the rule of law commands a punishment to be executed. By my oath, as the same for you, so shall it be for I."

Murmurs flooded the crowd.

Alora blinked. Too stunned to breathe. Too stunned to think.

This was about ... *him?*

The High Prince nodded to Thalon, who stood with his head lowered and that same unusual shadow stretching across the wooden boards below him.

Thalon shifted, lifted his head, and pulled a multi-fringed leather whip from behind his back, dropping it at his side.

Gasps rippled through the valley when he stepped forward, addressing the crowd. "I, General Realmpiercer, and Guardian born to House of the Seventh N, charge High Prince Garrik of Elysian with negligence. By our laws, you are hereby sentenced to fifty lashes. Let this be a reminder of how high a duty we hold to Elysian."

Fifty.

Garrik outstretched his hand, and Smokeshadows whorled in a small cloud upon his palm. Dancing away to reveal a syringe of glowing white liquid.

Thalon's face remained a stone wall of displeasure as he tightened his lips and hesitated. But the High Prince gritted his teeth and pushed his hand closer with a demanding expression, forcing Thalon, with something *final* flashing in his eyes, to collect it.

With a palm flattened over Garrik's heart, Thalon suffered a long, pleading, critical glare before he reluctantly plunged the needle into Garrik's tunic over his death mark.

Smokeshadows raged from the area, attacking and crawling up the syringe until Thalon emptied the contents.

Then they promptly disappeared.

The High Prince never flinched. Instead, he slowly unbuttoned his tunic, rolled his shoulders backward, and peeled the sleeves from his incredible arms.

Alora wasn't the only one who gasped. The crowd flooded with them.

Garrik's flesh ... his sculpted torso...

Bile burned her throat.

Horrendous ... *unbelievably barbaric*, raised, rigid scars.

They *covered* him. Torn into his skin and down from his chest as if a beast had taken considerable pleasure in mauling him. Stab and slash wounds were strewn over his abdomen. Barely a piece of skin left unmarked. And the worst ... traveled below the V of muscles at his waistline. Gashes stretched around his ribs and stomach, extending behind him. On the side of his neck laid a single, long scar.

Alora slammed her eyes closed, hoping that she was imagining it. That her mind was playing cruel games of guilt for being the cause of this show. But that horror cascaded to reality as her vision returned and the scars still remained. *With fifty more to come.*

Garrik tossed his tunic aside, turning to settle himself in front of his sword. His incredibly defined muscles rippled as he dropped his arms to grip the pommel once more.

Nausea rose up from her stomach. The sight of his back ... apart from recent, dark purple and crimson bruises, was much the same, yet somehow different.

A High Prince—a face of beauty and perfection—with the body of a despised prisoner.

But it was Aiden's words that filtered into her racing mind. *'Garrik didn't decide to do a bloody thing—he carries the scars to prove that. Magnelis is a ruthless High King. Not even his own son can escape his wrath.'*

Alora's eyes scanned the horrific scars. *Did Magnelis do this?*

She didn't understand. Not the scars, not why he was allowing his body to be stripped in front of his Dragons when the events from last night were entirely her doing.

Why are you doing this? Despite all the times she despised him observing her mind, she hoped he was listening. *This should be me.*

Garrik tilted his head slightly, and she glimpsed murky silver looking over his shoulder.

Back at her.

But he said nothing.

Alora's stomach twisted, wondering how he would feel—how she even felt—about being willing to take his place. To admit such a thing to him.

There was no warning. Thalon's whip cracked across Garrik's back, laying reddened welts.

Garrik's shoulders tensed but stood otherwise motionless, like a stone. The skin on his back quivered. He breathed in heavily, gripping his sword pommel with crushing force. With a graceful glance, Garrik found his general, who hesitated to lift the whip into the air.

Garrik nodded at him, a command to strike again.

Thalon still hesitated.

"*Again,*" Garrik commanded. His voice controlled but rough. The only inclination of how the first stripes must have felt.

No sooner did his word roar, the whip collided again. Leather striped across his scarred skin, scourging the High Prince's back. Over and over, Thalon laid the thick fringes across splitting flesh.

Blood sprayed to the dirt when he pulled back. And wet thuds echoed in the air when the punishment connected across raw wounds.

Crack. Jade flinched.

Crack. Eldacar breathed a distressed whimper.

Crack. Alora's limbs felt empty of blood.

Shouldn't she be pleased that he was suffering what he deserved? Shouldn't she be smiling, elated that the demon prince was punished so horribly? Her eyes should be delightedly drinking in the scene with a wicked smile peppering her face.

Instead, she felt the opposite—wracked with uncontrollable guilt that bordered on self-loathing.

Crack.

The lashes continued. With every swing, Thalon released grunts of protest, but Garrik still had barely moved. Not even a sound.

The sea of Dragons stood silent in reverence and recognition of what their High Prince endured. Their faces didn't turn as lash after lash was laid upon his back. More than a few flinched with each crack of the whip. Perhaps they felt sickened by it, too. But it had to be done. It was a lesson, a bloody one.

Crack.

Long streams of crimson dripped as Thalon concluded his last lash. He hurled the whip to the side of the dais; the fringes' watery slap hit the wood as they pooled in a heap of leather and blood. Thalon cursed under his labored breath before placing his hands on his hips, bowing his head low in regret. Broken in spirit and heart.

Then Thalon moved, speaking to Garrik privately as his hand hovered near the High Prince's quivering shoulder.

Garrik lifted his hand in a sharp wave, dismissing him. Not one sound was made as he rounded on his feet and wrenched the sword from the floorboards. Not one whisper when he straightened and dragged the tip of his sword across the floor before reaching the edge of the dais.

Everyone stood deathly still. Eyes locked on the blood pooled on the dais.

At their High Prince, whose face remained unyielding of any pain as he sheathed his sword to his side and jumped to the ground below.

It was impossible how he carried himself. The lashings should have reduced him to unconsciousness. No faerie could withstand a beating so gruesome and walk away.

Instead, he breezed along with perfect posture as if he'd simply been brushed by a feather. And Alora watched—searched—for signs of pain or discomfort or *anything*. They simply didn't exist.

The High Prince rasped as he parted the crowd and left, "Report to your generals for orders."

CHAPTER
23

It had taken every ounce of strength not to collapse before his tent closed behind him.

Through the haze, Garrik stumbled. Double vision impaired him enough that his hand lurched in slow motion for the chair only to topple it and slam his shoulder into the center wooden pillar.

He panted—choking on agonizing, skin-splitting breaths. Weathering ruthless spikes of pain that were pulsing down his spine and pebbling his skin. Stretching the festering flesh to yield more and more and more of his blood until he could taste the iron in the air.

He deserved it—all of it—not just *this* pain.

Garrik forced his eyes closed.

He had to feel it. Had to endure it for everything—*everything* he had done.

With wave after wave of searing, rippling agony, Garrik strained to keep himself upright. Somehow he managed to push himself from the pillar, clutching his chest over the normal heartbeat unworthy of pulsing, as step by staggering step, he cursed the High King's name...

Cursed his own.

Garrik's trembling palms flattened against the bedside table. His arms nearly buckled the instant his clammy hands and rings scratched the wooden surface, scraping against the galvanized steel of a water basin that had fallen frigid in the night.

Walls of thick canvas began to swallow him. Suffocating like he was drowning underwater, starving for air.

The borders of his vision darkened. The threat: an endless abyss of terror.

His world sunk deeper ... into a dark dream—a memory—the horrific place he wished was long forgotten by time instead of the slow, terrible death he had been forced to endure.

That blood dripping from his back did not soak into the soft furs beneath his feet but on graystones stained by endless years of throat-tearing screams and unimaginable suffering. And those breaths ripping the lashes open with each excruciating inhale were cries for mercy under ceaseless pleas bound by shackles and chains and ...

Garrik's legs buckled as he forced his eyes open, almost dropping to his knees.

Part of him wondered how he could be such a starsdamned fool. How he had not anticipated what they planned so long ago in Magnelis's war room when they—

Another wave of agony pulsed across his flesh, and he realized that his complexion had blanched.

These visions were prone to getting painfully physical. Having power over him until he inevitably was thrown into the depths of his personal hell. Preying on him with something as simple as a brush of the wind.

Like a sharpened blade, they cut deep and slow. And the scars on his back ... they were nothing compared to the ones lurking under the surface.

Even so, he deserved the consequences he had willingly suffered today.

Every last stripe.

Feel it, starsdamnit. Feel what you have done.

Thalon could have cleaved him in two. It still would not be enough to cover his sins. To purge even the outer layers of his immorality.

Garrik gnashed his teeth together, willing himself to remain upright.

After some time—which would *never* be enough—Garrik braced himself on the table with a trembling arm and dunked a washcloth into the clean, cold water. He nearly groaned at the relief when he lifted it over his shoulder and squeezed. Allowing it to flow down his flesh, forming rapid streams of crimson that poured from the wounds. Over and over he repeated, feeling the water cool his boiling flesh and soak his pants.

He did not turn when the sound of fury-filled footsteps burst through the door. There was no point in turning. He already sensed who entered as he stiffened into an illusion of strength, because anyone seeing him with such weakness was wholly unbearable and unacceptable.

"You bastard!"

Garrik forced his eyes closed and unamusingly sighed. *"Try that again,"* he growled, tensing at what his voice and breaths felt like.

"No, *bastard* is exactly what I meant."

A low growl reverberated through his chest, and he splashed the washcloth down, returning that hand to grip the table. Garrik managed to tilt his head over his shoulder, spearing her with his unfocused stare.

"What is on your mind, Alora?" he asked. But what he really meant was, *I am* not *in the fucking mood.*

"What in Firekeeper-filled-hell was that? You tell me last night that my punishment was a loss of my freedom and today do *this?*"

His grip tightened, deepening a nerve-settling breath. Otherwise, he would snap. "You are angry ... because you stood in the comfort of your own unharmed body ... while I was ripped to shreds in front of my Dragons by my brother's hand? Bold of you." Garrik's vision returned to the water, almost emptied, housing a revolting crimson hue.

Behind him, Alora fumed. Only by the small use of his powers did he see those sapphires blaring to whitened embers, staring at his bleeding back.

"You did this to punish me!" she accused, and it took every last shred of his sanity not to bite back.

Garrik slammed his fist on the tabletop, thankful his Smokeshadows were subdued by the drug Thalon administered, causing Alora to flinch.

"Punish *you?*" He scoffed, twisting to her and ignoring the sharp pain. "Forgive me. I did not realize that these lashes fell upon your back."

With the last bit of his strength, Garrik swung an open palm, barreling into the water basin, sending it whirling across the room with a metal clang.

"Take your punishment and *get out.*" The words, the pain, they were too much. He stumbled onto the pillar as it collided with his chest and shoulder.

Alora lunged forward. Catching—stopping—his feverish body from plummeting to the ground.

"Do not touch me," he grunted as the fiery heat of her hands tore into his skin. Unable to continue the façade that the pain did not affect him, the motion of falling forward must have changed the pressure in his head enough that the entire tent began to whirl and saw six—seven, he couldn't determine how many—forms of Alora stood there.

Garrik felt his heart miss a beat and gripped his chest.

"Help!"

He barely heard her through the drifting darkness swirling his senses, threatening to carry him into the torment of unrest and oblivion. Then, there were so many hands gripping him. Pulling him, dragging him away. His bones trembled, fevered veins churning with burning shards of shattered glass.

They were back ... it was too soon. *It was always too soon.*

They were dragging him down...

Down and down and down.

Back to—

Thalon and Jade carefully banded their arms around his waist, slinging his arms over their shoulders.

But it wasn't their hands forcing him across the floor but another's.

"Stop," Garrik spit between heaving, unsteady breaths as they lowered him to the chair, and panic boiled in his body.

He knew what was coming. What *always* followed.

Garrik braced himself. Forgetting the pain in his back, he wrenched backward, attempting to lean back against the chair, but strong, tattooed hands pulled him forward and steadied him.

"No, don't lean back." That ... that was Thalon's voice. Thalon was there? "Garrik, can you hear me?"

Yes, he wanted to say, but his mind was warring with itself to see reason. Thalon could not have been there. Magnelis would never allow it.

Whispers swirled around him, then the gentle voice of his Guardian spoke again. "Brother, open your eyes. Look at me. It's not real."

He did so. The murky silver struggled to focus, but there was no mistaking who held him there. And as he centered his attention on the darkened ink on Thalon's skin, the walls of his mind cleared, taking in the sun-kissed canvas, bright red hair, and wide, troubled sapphire eyes.

Thalon was right. It was not real. He was not back there with—

It was Jade who spoke next with urgency, and he remembered the pain slowly returning to his body.

"I'll get Eldacar." She rushed out the door; her footsteps vanished behind the tent.

Thalon steadied Garrik on his forearms, so they pressed into his knees before turning. There was something like panic in his features as he collected the water basin, and his voice trembled, flashing his eyes between Garrik and Alora. "I need to get more water. Stay with him."

Alora did not have time to respond. Thalon was gone too quickly. And Garrik almost wanted to order her to leave with him.

A pulse of energy rippled through their bodies.

His magic tore through the veil of dizziness overcoming his head.

Garrik grabbed the armrest, the color draining from his lips as he recognized his body falling limp. Abruptly, he shook his head, blinking rapidly to snap away from unconsciousness with heavy breaths, but he was fading too fast to stop it.

Alora cried out, dropping to her knees in front of him like a weight had forced her down. "What is that?" Then that energy thrummed through them again, and she cupped his knees to stabilize herself.

"You are ... alright ... *breathe*." He paused, glimpsing her shaking the dizziness from her head. "My ... shield. If my consciousness falls, they will all collapse. I must remain awake, Alora. Do not let me fall. That cannot happen." And then it was his palm cupping her shoulder.

Thalon and Jade must have felt it too, as they were back within a breath, rushing Eldacar behind them, who was carrying a stuffed leather satchel.

"Your Highness, we need to move you to the bed." Eldacar started emptying the contents of his bag. Bottles filled with shimmering liquids, odorous herbs, and cloth spilled onto the table behind them.

Terror flashed in Garrik's eyes. "No. Do it here."

Thalon knelt in front of him and braced Garrik's body by his collar bones.

One moment, Garrik was snarling up at golden eyes blazing in heated fury and concern and the next ... Eldacar had uncorked a bottle containing a black, airy substance, and started to pour it over his back.

He knew this serum well, Ozrin had concocted it especially for him; it was ink-like. Flowing like liquid and clouds. Light caught its reflection, making it shimmer in hues of violet, emerald, and gold. It sizzled across Garrik's back, producing a choked cry from between his gritted teeth. Like a hand to an open flame, a fierce burning crept down his back as the onyx rainbow seeped into his wounds.

Garrik's shield pulsed around them again, his muscles twitching and screaming out.

Thalon cupped Garrik's paling face when he could not contain the agonized cry escaping his lips. "A few more moments, brother. It's working. *Stay with us.*"

White-hot steam elevated off Garrik's skin as the black potion, that was once sizzling, disappeared, revealing his wounds sealed and back half restored, scars intact.

Thalon loosened his grip, steadied his hand above Garrik's glistening, sweat-soaked chest, and quickly let go.

Garrik's chest heaved in rapid breaths, falling forward to rest his forehead on Thalon's shoulder.

"What were you thinking?" Thalon breathed low enough that only he could hear, but there was so much more unspoken, hidden behind the words.

That care, hinted with reprehension, was not ill-placed. In fact, Garrik should have listened the night before because this show of humility was indeed completely reckless, no matter the intention. If the shield had fallen—

This isn't about the damn shield, and you know it, Thalon's mind barked.

Garrik ignored it. Ignored it because pale, trembling hands had reached out, intended for his back, but they were met with his firm grip around their wrist.

Registering Garrik's firm objection, brown eyes turned wary and Eldacar whispered in a quiet plea. "Sire, I know ... but please, allow me to check. I have to ... touch you."

A muscle flexed in Garrik's cheek, but he nodded in agonized approval.

Eldacar ran his gentle fingers over the pinkened scars and restored skin, inspecting the half-healed lashes. Tender fingers turned to iron pokers that left phantom brands in their wake.

They had fussed enough over him. "Begin training. We have wasted enough time that we cannot get back." Garrik started to push himself from the chair, but his legs buckled.

"You can't go anywhere until you've rested," Eldacar cautioned.

"I will do as I see fit," he growled as the face of the High Prince returned.

"You may be my High Prince, but I am one of the only ones left in camp who carries some knowledge of healing. I only know what the books say. I'm not skilled like Ozrin. But I do know that if you don't get into that bed this instant and rest, you'll put this camp in danger again. And you can't afford another fifty lashes. Now, go!"

A layer of shock blanketed the room.

No one spoke, no one dared to.

Eldacar blushed and sunk his head slightly. But Garrik was ... *impressed.*

"One hour," Garrik compromised. "Then I want to hear clashing blades and taste magic in the air. Understood?"

They all nodded and moved to leave, but Alora hesitated. She met his wavering stare over her shoulder. "What you did out there ... it was—"

"*By the Flames, you stupid girl,*" Jade hissed and grabbed her arm, brow vexed as she twisted hard.

Garrik lifted his hand. "It is fine, Jade. You may go." He gestured for her to leave, waiting until the door swung closed before turning his attention back to Alora. "Well? Go on. Start calling me a bastard again," he said and stood, steadying himself behind the chair.

She looked at the ground covered in blood and water and rolled her lip between her teeth, not noticing Garrik's careful assessment. "I'm ... sorry. This was my fault."

Silent frustration filled his low sigh. He could explain it to her, but at that moment, he did not possess the stability or patience. "One could say that this is Magnelis's doing. None of us would be here if it were not for him." He shook his head. "This is done. Now, go prepare to train. I wish to see what you are capable of."

She remained, watching Garrik unbuckle his belt and pull it through the loops with a crack as beads of water pebbled off and dripped to the furs below. His hands stilled at his blood-soaked pants, ready to unbutton them too, but stopped, realizing that she was still there.

He raised an eyebrow, meeting her gaze, forming that smirk that irritated her wholly as he watched her breath catch. And how pleasing *that* was—to watch her cheeks scarlet before she turned away, and without a word, rushed out.

Garrik chuckled, undressing entirely, before he pulled a glass vial from the bedside table. He sunk into his cot, uncorked the vial, and drew it to his nose.

The scent enveloped his senses.

Inhaling deep as a calming rush filtered through his nerves.

And before he laid back, he returned it to the table as he refused a memory threatening to form.

'That's it, son. It's over. It's all over.'

No, Garrik thought. *It is not.* Warring off the male's voice, he focused on the smooth blankets of his cot.

It was warm from the sun blaring against the canvas, and his fur-covered pillows welcomed his spinning head. The pain of his back was not sufficient enough to suffer the unbearable touch against his abdomen, he could never do that, so he laid on the half-healed lashes and placed one arm beneath his head.

Closing his hollow eyes, Garrik surrendered to the merciless oblivion. Allowing the screaming darkness of a torturous nightmare to capture him and imprison him inside.

CHAPTER
24

In an incredible surge of tendrils, Garrik, forged of darkness, parted the swarm of swirling ash and whorling smoke before materializing in his High Fae form.

"Why haven't I seen the High Prince training?" Alora tracked the movement of shadows far off to her right, inside the arena.

His overt displays of power were of little surprise at this point; she'd been at camp for two weeks now. The High Prince seemed to manifest himself inside his powers more often than not—and simply dawn from darkness without warning.

Dawn, she played with the word in her mind. Another new piece of the High Prince being stored away.

Only this time, he ushered someone behind him; an elder High Fae male with long, tattered, gray hair and a scarlet robe.

Thankfully, Garrik didn't seem to notice her careful evaluation when he dropped to his knee beside a wounded faerie. The young male wolf shifter was bleeding from a head wound sustained in a sparring session. Not with the High Prince, though. Garrik was never seen conducting in sport. In fact, she rarely witnessed him carrying a blade in camp at all. And when he did, she thought it looked more like a prop than a weapon.

In the short moments that followed, Garrik banded his arm around the faerie's waist and threw the male's arm around his shoulders, avoiding the claws that were slowly retracting. The movement was effortless. Lifting him before staggered footsteps trailed to the wooden wall to meet with the elder male who made quick work of bandaging the head wound.

Alora remembered how only a week ago, two others had their arms banded around Garrik's waist, settling him into a chair while he struggled to remain conscious. And now watching him move as if nothing had happened ... as if he hadn't been lashed and humiliated at all.

Silver eyes flashed in her direction.

Her head whipped away. Denying completely her stare, she lifted her hands in front of her, focusing on a large chunk of iron within a pile of various stones just as she practiced countless times that week.

"Focus now. Lift only the iron, nothing else." Eldacar's gaze met hers from over his round-rimmed glasses. A pencil scribbled a note in the book he held before using it to point at her belt. "Try to replicate the shape of your dagger, without fire this time. See it in your mind." In the air, he traced with his pencil, outlining the dagger at her side and marveling at the ordinary shape for effect. "The shape, the edge. The way the leather curves around the handle."

Eldacar had stared at the dagger for days before he made the suggestion. Something about it had sparked his interest, but he could never quite identify why.

Alora had asked about his curiosity, then, when he blushed and fumbled with his pencil and notepad, he simply said, "Please forgive me. I believed I had seen something similar in a book, perhaps ages past. I regret I couldn't locate which text." Those brown eyes pleaded for forgiveness above stumbling lips as if he'd struck her a damning blow. He had turned away, distraught, and shuffled to the sanctuary of his tent mere seconds after, but his curious spark remained.

Alora dropped her palm to the hilt of the dagger, narrowing on the chunk of glistening iron among the stones on the table.

Practice had been the same in most of her training thus far. Her task, like each day that week, was to lift the iron without her fire igniting from her palms—or the object itself—leaving the stones where they lay. Then mold the metal into something other than its original form, though the strain of every muscle and thought made that part near impossible.

If she couldn't mold it into anything more than a rounded glob, bursting with flames, all week, how did he expect her to create a dagger like her own?

Regardless, the stones on the wooden table began vibrating as if the ground beneath them quaked. Some slid to the dirt as her fingers curled, trembling into fiery fists. Wrinkling her forehead, Alora squinted her eyes, teaming with focused determination to be able to do this—*just once.*

The table too began to shake, and as before, the iron chunk drifted upward in a white, flaming ball. As if it had been heated over fire, its form began to ripple. Liquefied metal was a prize, and hers to win.

It's working! Sort of. She gritted harder. *Come on...*

With little surprise, the metal exploded into hundreds of molten shards, and everyone in the arena dropped from the incoming impact.

Garrik whipped his head in their direction in time to throw out his palm and conjure an invisible wall. The shrapnel pelted into it without passing through and simply fell at the impalpable base.

A wicked fury emerged from Alora's throat as she pushed herself back up. "I'm better with just my fire, Eldacar." She squeezed her hand until an ember formed.

"That was better than yesterday. Progress!" Eldacar wiped off the lens of his glasses as they had fallen to the ground. "You've rarely practiced this power before. Your fire comes naturally; this will take some time." He smiled, always kind, always patient.

Alora exhaled frustration. *How much time?* How much more embarrassment must she endure in front of such skilled Mystics and fighters? Every day, a crowd formed to watch. Making it much harder to focus. Especially when this power—raw and untested—was incredibly dangerous and so unpredictable.

"Come on. Let's try again." He gestured toward the table.

"No. I will hurt someone else." She raked her eyes around, noting every new, smoldering hole in the arena walls, and soldiers relocating themselves closer to the tent line.

"No one got hurt today. You're doing well!"

"Today," a gravelly female voice snickered from the trees near the lake.

Alora glared over at Jade, who leaned against a pine with arms crossed. The urge was there, but she mustered enough self-control to not produce a healthy, middle finger in Jade's direction.

Though she truly didn't want to admit it, Jade was right, which boiled her blood even more. *Today*, no one had yet been carted to the infirmary from injuries her magic caused.

"I don't understand. How can I summon fire or even use my magic to wield a sword, but I can't do this without it exploding?" Alora picked up a piece of jasper and threw it over the wall into the lake.

Eldacar smiled again, swelling his cheeks to lift his glasses. "It takes great concentration to do all things. You're not only lifting one object among the many, you're changing its entire being while keeping your fire at bay. Everything it has ever been. Everything it wants to remain as." He paused. "Water runs when poured. You can't expect it to flow up to the stars. That is against its nature. This iron has been its true form for its entire existence. It won't be easy to form something from what it *was* into something you want it to *be* just because you wish it."

That doesn't help. She lifted the stones from the ground and placed them back on the table. "If it's *my* magic, why can't it just do what I command?" she asked and turned to Eldacar, frustration winning the war inside her veins.

A presence moved close.

His deep, calming voice rushed over her body, whether she wished him to be there or not. "Power is not simply given. It is earned." Garrik moved by her side. Smokeshadows whirled in his palm before cascading away to reveal a new piece of iron. "Kick, shout, and curse as much as you wish, but power will not permit you to use more than it will allow." He placed the iron in the center of the table. "It needs to know we are worthy enough to unleash it. To even protect it. We must strive for its blessing—to trust us. Practice, make it and us stronger, together. Stand with reverence. Humble yourself before it. And thank it every time magic works in our favor."

Garrik crouched and swept his hand in a smooth, gliding motion in front of him as a rippling wave of air crossed through the grass. "It can give you as little..." He paused, swiftly twisting his toned body around and toward the lake, simultaneously thrusting his palm in its direction.

Power erupted, causing a massive force of air across the water, rippling waves in its wake that almost crashed against the trees on the other side. Garrik wrenched his hand back, forming a fist as the waves stopped like they hit a wall, climbing it until they eventually lost momentum and died into calm waters.

"Or as much as it allows," Garrik finished. The sun caught silver as he stood and faced her, sending glistening sparks in his eyes. And he seemed to be captivated by the release of magic—as much as she was. "Power earned is much more pleasurable. You cannot command it. *Ask* for its help."

It was hard to deny—his magic was beautiful. Deadly. And she wondered: how many years must it have taken him to perfect it? For his magic to grant such power, for it to allow him to use it, ceaselessly, to shield his camp, his people. To invade and manipulate minds. And not even that power. But his Smokeshadows seemed to be able to do *anything.*

She shuddered.

Will mine ever allow me the same strength?

Eldacar dropped his pencil in the book and closed it. "Go on, let's try again." His auburn curly locks danced in the gentle breeze.

Alora hesitated, but Garrik stepped forward. "You promised to trust me, remember?"

She frowned, squeezing her hands into fists. *That damn flower...* "I'll just end up hurting one of you."

Garrik grinned. "Luckily for you, my magic possesses the power to protect. Try again. You will not hurt us. I am here. I will contain it for you."

With her eyes closed, her heart hammered against its cage. *I don't want to hurt anyone again.*

You won't, I promise. Just breathe. Ask your magic.

Alora reluctantly nodded, turning her gaze to the table.

Jade pushed off the pine and stationed herself behind. "Here we go again."

Garrik shot her a deathly glare before turning back to Alora. "Ask."

Alora sighed and lifted her palm once more in front of her. *Okay magic. If you would allow it...*

Good. Garrik lifted an eyebrow.

The same feeling as when her fire pricked her skin rose through her veins in that moment. For the first time all week, her power felt relaxed. Calm. It was unified with her being, rather than railing against it. Her body loosened, heart slowing, as the iron, engulfed in flames, lifted from the table, and glided into her awaiting palm.

Alora blinked, doubting what had just happened.

The High Prince walked slowly until he was between her and the table and relaxed back against it, folding his arms. "Now, take the dagger from your belt. Imagine the iron as such."

Alora backed away. "You're too close. What if I—"

"You will not hurt me." He said it so calmly that she believed him.

Pulling the blackened dagger from her belt, Alora studied the empty settings where jewels once sat. Completely focusing on the night-dark, waved blade covered in matte onyx whorls that weaved from both ends of the metal. The white stone glistened in the sun. Beautifully crafted despite the damage on the leather handle. In all honesty, she'd never owned something quite as exquisite. Something that was just hers.

A perfect reflection of her own self.

A deadly weapon with missing pieces.

The chunk of iron felt warm and steamed in her other palm as she gripped the hilt of the dagger. Her eyes flowed from one to the other, noting the details of the blade as she squinted her eyes, and the noises of camp quieted around her.

But it wasn't her doing. She side-eyed the High Prince, knowing his magic was to thank.

Deepening a breath, she thought, *If you would allow it, magic. Form this iron into the dagger.*

Like warm honey flowing from a bucket, the steaming iron melted in white flames across her palm. Tendrils of silver streamed and pooled until it began to take on the form of a weapon. Its shape melded into a wave amongst the white glow. Swirls of molten vines crawled across the smooth surface. The metal itself changed properties until a leather-covered hilt and glistening white gem sparkled inside it.

A perfect replica.

Eldacar erupted in joyous clapping with a grin that covered his face and once again pushed his glasses up.

Shock wracked her body as she lifted the blades in front of her.

This ... this wasn't *possible.*

Garrik's grin was nothing short of wicked. "See what happens when you trust me?"

CHAPTER 25

"You're looking down at your feet again." Thalon tapped Alora's boot with the edge of a rune-covered golden sword and flicked it up with his wrist. "Your body follows your head. Eyes on me when you advance," he instructed.

True. She was watching her feet. But more looking at the large shadow cascading from Thalon's body in the sunlight. Barely noticeable, but enough to pull her focus and leave her falling flat on her ass a few times. Thalon always noticed. How could he not? And he took advantage of her slip of concentration every time.

Alora repositioned her feet to where Thalon had told her to at least twenty times in the last thirty minutes.

The smell of the lake and pine around them covered up the stench of sweat she desperately wanted to deny under her leather armor. The heat from her skin made them nearly unbearable to wear. But it was either sweat from the heat or wind up dead in battle. She chose the former.

Along with trembling knees and stiff fingers, her shoulders and upper back burned something fierce. But nothing compared to the unwavering heaviness of humiliation when the skills she thought she possessed were little in comparison to his. Apparently, her time with Rowlen offered little to aid her training now.

Thalon may have been a soft-spoken swords-master, with shining smiles and bulging muscles, but there in the arena ...

She quivered.

The High Prince may be Death itself, but Thalon ...

He executed justice, carrying an ancient wrath onto battlefields.

The kind of warrior who would slaughter ten thousand and then grieve their souls after. A solid killer of strength and ruin on the outside and a kind-hearted, protective soul within.

Alora rotated her neck until cracks released pressure on her spine. As it turned out, her strikes were sloppy and easily anticipated by her enemy. Her calculated movements and foot positions were amateur at best. Compared to Thalon, anyway. She could certainly win a fight against skilled fighters, but against him? The chance of survival was less than nil.

Still, he offered reassuring words of praise, encouraged movements and actions that could be used to overpower and eliminate an enemy. Plus, he corrected learned mistakes that could render her killed.

"Again," Thalon said with a single nod.

Alora lifted her sword in front of her and prepped her combat stance. She wiped dripping sweat from her hairline and cleared it on her hip before forming a fist steadied by her side. Why was this so difficult now? She was a skilled fighter. She brought down Rowlen many times. And he was trained by some of the best swordsmen in Telldaira's guard.

But Thalon was the swords-master of the Dragon's Legion.

Compared to him, she had as much grace and capability as a flailing fish out of water.

Sapphire eyes locked onto Thalon's bustling figure with intensity and sharp focus. He towered over her as she advanced with hostile speed. If she couldn't bring him down by force or out master him by skill, then speed would be her next option.

She dug her feet into the dirt and launched before he'd returned to a defensive position.

Thalon swung with little effort. His blade collided with hers in a burst of sparks. The vibration and force pushed her off balance enough that she stumbled backward off her feet and landed back first in the dirt.

Jade howled from the arena wall. Her feet dangled over the edge as she jabbed a dagger into the wood and twisted it between her thumb and finger.

Failing at her magic with a crowd of onlookers felt like nothing next to the humiliation of Jade's gleeful jeers every time Alora's ass hit the ground. Again and again. And training would be much easier if she didn't have an audience. Especially one who wanted nothing more than to see her fail. She wanted to pummel that sneering face until Jade's skin matched her hair.

Bending aching knees, Alora silenced words of war brimming in her throat and scuffed her boots back. Heat marred her cheeks.

"Your focus was much better that time. Well done. Now, refuse the temptation to be the faster fighter. Chasing after speed is like chasing after Garrik's Smokeshadows. If you pursue speed, all you will achieve is an urgency in movement. Timing. Control. Fluidity. That is what you want." Thalon held out his hand with a reassuring grin and pulled her to her feet. "Let's try again. This time, control the movements. Strike when the time is right with a flow like molten metal. Understood?"

Alora nodded. *Easier said than done.*

They continued. Practicing defensive blocking maneuvers, disarming her opponent, and handling two swords at once, attack sequences, and hand-to-hand combat when her fingers were too numb to grip the sword. A likely scenario in battle.

"Lose your blade, lose your life. Your steel is an extension of your arm. Wield it as such. But if you're ever found without it, let your other instincts take over. Elbows and knees first, then fists"—strong fingers tapped her knuckles—"use them."

White cloth wrapped around her hands with ease. Good timing for her aching knuckles. His hands, though gentle, made her red burning skin sting. She began to wonder if she'd ever be able to fully open her hands again.

Genuine curiosity crossed her face as Thalon finished fastening the cloth. "Why fight with swords and fists when we have magic?"

Most of the warmth from her body drained away into a cascading prickle across her skin.

Alora rolled her eyes and clenched a fist. Knowing that the all-familiar invasion and stripping of her magic could only come from one source.

Thalon noticed her change of expression and smiled. He tilted his head to the side of the arena where the High Prince stood, arms crossed with one ankle over the other, boot tip digging in the dirt.

The High Prince's face was, of course, covered in a wolfish smirk.

Prick. She sarcastically smiled, showing him her middle finger.

Garrik chuckled. *Thank me later, clever girl.*

Thalon patted her shoulder, drawing her attention. "Your magic will not always be there to help you." He grabbed her wrists and pulled her arms up in front of her. "Arms up, fists ready. I want to see your punch."

"Powerful punches require space. If you're being attacked, get in their safe zone. Do *not* give them an inch. It will be difficult to land a hard blow." Thalon motioned for her to turn around and carefully came up behind her. "Cross your arms up in front of you."

Alora hesitated a moment, fighting off a sharp twinge of panic before she reluctantly turned.

Through a heavy, sharp breath, Alora closed her eyes as Thalon wrapped his tattooed arms around her. Something hot and wet ran down her cheek before she realized that she had begun to cry. Her bones felt the unearthly shake as Thalon's arms loosened. When she looked down at the arms caging her, she didn't see ink and beautiful, glowing brown skin.

Those arms were white, slightly tanned, lined with red scratched lines from her nails. From the last time Kaine had put her in a choke-hold.

Not now. Please. It was going to happen again, just like on that cliff. *Not now. Not now. Not now.*

Thalon must've felt it. His arms dropped from her. He backed away. "Whoa. Alora? What is it?"

And then, she heard Kaine, like he was standing directly beside her. The monster of her walking nightmares. *You're letting another male put his hands on you? You're mine. And when I find you—*

"I'm fine," she breathed a sharp whisper and stiffened her spine, blinking away Kaine's voice. "Show me again." Alora didn't turn. Didn't as much as peer over her shoulder to watch the Guardian's tentative approach.

She felt his warmth near her arms again, but he didn't touch her.

"May I?" Thalon murmured.

Alora felt her breath catch and eyes brim with tears. She nodded through the panic, and his tattoo-covered hands settled around her healed wrists before he positioned them to cross her chest.

Sapphires sealed shut, feeling Thalon's warm hands—as warm as Kaine's—feeling his light grip around her wrists, the hold nothing in comparison to the treatment she was used to. *It's not Kaine. It's Thalon. And he doesn't want to hurt you.*

You know that's not true. They'll all hurt you. Use you. Once your usefulness has run out, you'll be back on the streets begging, crawling back to me.

But Thalon's voice shattered through Kaine's. Calm and tender as his arms held strong. "If you're ever in this position, the knees and elbows are the hardest parts of the body. Use them to your advantage. The knee gives more power, but the elbow has versatility. I want you to force your arms down with all your strength. Elbows back into my ribs. You'll wind me enough to escape."

Alora heard him—barely. She was still focused on the feeling of his arms and the evil voice that haunted her. "You want me to—"

"Hit my ribs, yes."

She danced her feet in preparation and ripped her arms free, jamming elbows into rock-solid abs that barely knocked his breath loose.

Kaine's voice viciously laughed. *Weak. Like you'll always be.*

Thalon positioned her arms back in front of her and reassured, "I know you can do better than that. Try again."

Snickering hissed from the wall as Jade picked off a piece of splintering wood. "Please put her out of her misery. For the love of stars above. This is *pathetic.*"

Kaine laughed inside her mind again.

Alora whispered under her breath, "*Shut up.*" Teeth gritted as she scanned to Jade, spitting her words at her too. "*Shut the hell up.*" And Kaine's voice faded away, leaving a brush of fire burning her throat as she repositioned.

A wooden board bowed from behind them. Garrik's heavy footsteps trailed their way. "Jade," he called and something cold in his voice stirred her nerves to ignite, "replace Thalon. If you are going to provoke, you will do it dodging blades."

Alora's eyes widened. She'd successfully avoided any sort of physical contact with Jade since the gamroara. A hard lump formed in her throat as her lips went taut. And now she would face her after an already tiring day.

With a pleased grin, Jade jumped down from the wall and sheathed her dagger into thigh straps. "Dodging?" She scoffed and unsheathed her sword, twisting her wrist to spin it by her side. "She'll be kissing the dirt from beneath my boot within a minute." Jade snickered at Alora with a hungry smile, like she'd been staring all day at a perfectly roasted turkey covered in herbs and butter. A crunchy seasoned skin just waiting to be devoured. And now she could finally eat it.

Garrik wasn't quite as amused. Glancing at Alora, Smokeshadows whorled in his hand until a sword appeared, and he handed it to her.

"*Anything* is fair in battle. Show me what you have learned." Garrik tapped the palms of her hands, and she understood his subtle inclination before he walked to the arena wall where Thalon waited.

Thalon shifted with arms crossed with a look that read, '*They're likely to kill each other.*'

Adjusting his tunic, Garrik leaned back against the wall and crossed an ankle over the other, folding his arms inside themselves. Relaxed, cocky even. He smiled at Thalon, and with a nod, turned to the awaiting fighters. "You two act as if we are not anticipating war. Get your heads out of your asses and those swords ready. I do not care if you leave bruised and bloody. You will fight until those attitudes are gone. Make no mistake, if you do not convince me, you will remain out here until you cannot even crawl to your beds."

Placing his hand on his hip before lowering his head, Thalon uncomfortably rubbed the back of his neck, knocking a few gold beaded braids together. The sound danced on the breeze and echoed in Alora's ears like a war cry.

Jade slowly took a semi-circle step. "Best to surrender now. Wouldn't want that pretty hair matching mine or messing up your armor."

Two more steps.

Alora countered, moved her feet, and positioned the sword in front of her. Her eyes saw nothing but red hair circling. Not the arena walls nor the glassy lake, the trees, not even the camp beyond them.

"I'm not naïve enough to think I will beat you, Jade. Not yet. But know this, if you cross blades with me, I won't stop until I'm commanded to—or dead." Alora dug her heel into the ground and tightened her grip until the leather groaned.

"Good." Her words carried a tone of whispered disdain.

Metal clanged as Jade took the first swing.

Alora dropped a knee to the dirt and thrust her sword long sided into the air, colliding with Jade's blade above her head. With a strong spin of her arms, Alora swung the sword down at Jade's feet. Licking her boots before she bounded back.

This would be more than a training session.

This was a battle.

Against someone who might actually kill her.

And because of that fact ...

All bets were off.

CHAPTER
26

Jade's blade pierced Alora's leathers at the heart, leaving a hole straight through to her undershirt.

She flinched back with a hiss, expecting to feel the steel sink deep into her chest. Alora's eyes turned to smoldering embers with pinched brows.

Jade had tried to kill her.

"What the hell is your problem?" Alora growled, circling Jade with a death glare more murderous than her red-headed opponent.

"*You*, pretty princess." Jade stormed across the disheveled ground. With intense force, she kicked Alora in the gut so forcefully that Jade had to stab her sword into the dirt to remain upright.

Alora flew backward, knocking her head on the cold dirt.

For a moment, her vision spotted. The air escaped her lungs. Jade's footsteps drew closer, but with her head spinning, her mind struggled to comprehend the danger. Soon what was left of the sun was drowned out by dancing fire in the sky.

No. Not fire.

Long, bright crimson hair in a half-braided ponytail flowed around Jade's irate face. The bone and metal necklace dangled from her neck. She stood, straddling Alora, sword drawn high that caused her battle leathers to creep up her abdomen, revealing a hidden bandolier of knives.

"Any last words before I run you through?" Triumph glistened in Jade's eyes.

Alora pivoted her head, searching for the High Prince.

He just stood there, face unreadable. *Unmoving* like he couldn't be bothered.

Rippling anger boiled inside her veins. *He's going to let me die.*

She frantically patted her hand on the ground, hoping to connect with her sword, only to be met with Jade's boot as she twisted it down on her wrist.

"How does it feel knowing that is the last thing you'll ever do?"

A tingle caressed the inside of her mind. She heard the High Prince's words again. *Anything is fair in battle.*

Sapphire eyes flashed to him again on the wall. His head was turned, speaking with Thalon.

A prickling sensation glided down her neck and into her arms.

"Anything is fair in battle," she muttered.

"What was that?" Jade taunted, pressing her boot harder, leaning into it with a hand on her knee. "Don't let your final words go unheard by at least one, not that I'll tell the world of your existence. Come on, how does it feel?"

Alora threw her glare at Jade with a baiting grin. "You tell me."

White flames burst from her hand. Dancing sparks blasted from her palm and stopped inches from Jade's face, not by her own will.

Jade shrieked and stumbled to the dirt, cowering down to shield herself with her arm and sword.

And if Alora didn't know better, that was unadulterated terror in her eyes while she trembled.

"Fuck you, damn witch! Can't win with a blade, so the perfect little *princess* has to use her powers. Nothing has ever been hard for you, *has it?*" Still vicious, Jade's tone sliced like the very blade she held.

Alora jumped to her feet. Heat blushed her cheeks as she held her palms down at her sides. White fire danced in glowing spheres inside them. Her head tilted in search of her sword. *There.* With an outstretched arm, fire engulfed it as it flew into her hand, and she gripped it until the leather stretched impossibly between her fingers.

"Can't stand to train and get strong like the rest of us," Jade persisted. "I bet your entire life was fluffy pillows and dinner parties."

She stood and adjusted her armor, terror-ridden eyes locked onto the growing flames.

Fire slowly rose up Alora's sword. "Stop talking, or stars be damned, I will make you eat your words." And slowly, she prowled a step toward Jade. Leaving white flames shaped like burning footprints in her wake.

Thalon stepped toward them.

Garrik's hand swung, hovering before Thalon's chest and flashed him a critical glare.

A menacing laugh tore from Jade. She'd found the spot to push Alora now, and she'd whittle it down and make sure it scathed with every word. "Being waited on hand and foot." Jade spun, sword colliding into Alora's, producing a shower of sparks from the impact. "Getting anything she wants, anytime she wants. The perfect little princess. Bed never cold, worshiped by males, servants left and right. Just look at you. Perfectly kept hair, pretty dresses and jewels, no doubt. You won't last one day on the battlefield. Your easy days are *over*." Jade relentlessly swung. One. Two. Three.

But each ruthless attack was perfectly defended by Alora's flaming sword.

Their blades caught. Alora relentlessly pressed against Jade's strength, flashing her clenched teeth inches from her face.

"*Easy?*" Alora's throat began to constrict. "You think my life was *easy?*"

A ring of fire surrounded them on the ground. Like following a path across the dirt, it flowed in two directions until the flames connected at both ends. With painstakingly slow speed, the flames climbed higher into the air.

Panic filled Jade's eyes as her breathing picked up pace, scanning the growing inferno. "I bet you've never had one hard day in your life. Never had anything to fight for. It's not surprising with the way you fight. Someone should've taught you a long time ago how it feels to fight for your life." Jade's hand traveled down to her leg and pulled out a dagger before launching it into Alora's armor at her stomach.

Flames burst around the impact as Alora shrieked.

Jade flinched back, catching her breath as the flames faded.

Somewhere outside the flames, Garrik growled, pushing off the wall, "That is *enough*, Jade."

But neither of them listened. Jade inched closer until Alora could see flecks of bronze in her green eyes.

"Perfect little princess. No one has given you a reason to fight, have they?" Patronizing and cruel and—

"*Shut up.*" Alora's vision lined with red. She couldn't stop it anymore. Couldn't hold it back.

"I said *enough.*" Garrik took another step.

Fire burst in front of the High Prince.

Alora looked at him. All the life left her eyes. Only glowing white embers surfaced in its place.

Alora—

Shut up, shut up, shut up!

The flames in front of the High Prince flared higher. Garrik started yelling, but she could only hear Jade's piercing words wounding her deeper than any sword ever could.

"Face me, coward. You think the High King's army is going to just walk away from you because you're scared? You won't last a minute on the battlefield. We should have left you to die in Telldaira, we'd be better off for it."

She was burning. Everything felt too hot.

Way too hot.

Too—

White flames detonated into a castle-high explosion.

Thalon flew into a swirling storm of lightning. His body appeared and crashed into Jade's on the other side before they were swallowed by thunderclouds and striking branches of light in hurricane winds. Then they disappeared from the arena.

Smokeshadows whorled to every faerie within range of the fiery destruction, dawning them away before a wave of flames crashed into the arena walls. Railing against anything that dared keep them from expanding, the fire fed on the surrounding air. Starved and finally taking its fill.

Inside the flames, Alora couldn't get enough air. Her voice ripped through the veil of sound and space as her inferno climbed higher and spread beyond the walls.

She hit her knees, screaming from the depths of her core. Her white hair glowed in the fire's intense light; her eyes burned beneath streaming tears.

The last time this happened, Rowlen came to save her, came to pull her out.

Rowlen, she cried out for him.

But he wouldn't come this time. Because she'd left him there—*left him to die.*

She pounded her fist into the dirt and screamed again. Screamed for Rowlen, screamed for herself.

And her shrieks grew louder as Kaine's ghost burst through the flames and grabbed her by the throat. His fist raised, then slammed down into her back.

She fell forward onto her hands. Each phantom collision of Kaine's made the fire rage hotter with explosions like a dying star.

She couldn't snap out of it.

She felt everything as if Kaine were there.

Help me. Please. Rowlen. Somebody. Help me!

Smoke and shadow wrapped around her. And what once was an empty space between her and her white flames now appeared a tall figure in black clothing. Waving wisps of silver hair rustled around worried, colorless eyes. Garrik's ringed hands reached out, and he dropped to his knees with her.

"Open your eyes!" Icy hands pulled her face from the dirt and molded to her burning, wet cheeks. Fire and glimmering sparks licked at his skin, but he held strong. "You need to open your eyes!"

His shouts were nothing but a whisper in the depths of her mind.

She was trapped. Trapped in Kaine's bed, letting him do what he wanted to her. Distant screams from outside her bedroom door rocked the surrounding walls. She began to see darkness as Kaine's hand squeezed her throat.

Life faded from her eyes.

The bedroom door burst into thousands of splinters as tendrils of darkness invaded in a murderous sweep. Kaine's body became engulfed in tenebrous ash, ripped from her by hundreds of Smokeshadow hands.

His eyes were pierced by tendrils, mouth gaping open as they tugged and carried him out of the open door into the blackened abyss.

Then it was Garrik's arms lifting her from the bed.

"Open your eyes, Alora. This is not real." Was that ... *panic* in his voice?

He pushed himself closer to her, inside the flames, until a knee wedged between hers. Magic sent a burst of flames against his arm in warning, but he didn't flinch. Didn't leave her. Icy hands cupped her cheeks and leaned closer. "Come back to me."

The chilled grip on her fevered face sent shivers down her spine, and a white glow kissed her burning eyelids as she opened and saw a wall of Smokeshadows fighting back the inferno.

His lips were moving. She focused on them until there was nothing else but his voice and his eyes and his touch.

"Breathe," Garrik whispered. His chest rose heavy and fell, lips pale and trembling. "Please, breathe." He pulled her balled fist up and placed the palm over her racing heart. "Feel the breath entering your lungs. The kiss of the wind." The silver of his eyes went muddy. "Hear me. Listen to my voice. You are safe. I am not leaving. Focus on me." He inhaled deeply like he was showing her what to do. "Listen. Breathe."

Finally, her lungs extended in a greedy inhale, mirroring his. She felt the pleasant sting of a cold hand softly gripping hers. Then another trailed her burning cheek, thumb swiveling in a gentle circle.

The air felt heavy with ash and dancing flames. Still, Alora breathed, watching his chest draw in its own life, and her fortress of flames began to die.

"See those trees?" Garrik gestured with his eyes. "What kind of trees are they?"

She sucked in a breath, following the path to evergreens above the valley.

"Come on, darling, you know what they are."

Another deep breath. "Ev—evergreens," she choked out.

"Good." He brushed her cheek, and his gaze returned to the dying flames. "And what kingdom are we in?"

Alora closed her eyes and leaned into that frigid touch. "Zyllyryon."

Ember by ember, their cage diminished before Smokeshadows swallowed them entirely, blocking out the rest of the world until it was just him and her and their syncing breaths.

Garrik didn't remove his hands. "That is right," he praised on a murmur. "Keep breathing."

"Did I"—her lips trembled between the whisper—"h—hurt"—her balance went unsteady—"k—kill—"

"No. We are all still alive." Garrik brushed a strand of hair from her face. "Sorry, you did not kill me this time," he joked with a trembling grin. "Let's get you out of here."

Garrik lifted her by the waist as he stood and pulled her to her feet. Steadying her on shaking knees, he scanned down her body.

"I'm fine." Alora's words slurred, and she pushed away from the High Prince with what little energy she had left. The movement caused her head to spin as if all the blood was draining—rapidly.

Only it was not her head that was bleeding.

Droplets fell onto her boot in a rhythmic cadence.

Within one step, the darkness circled her vision. Leaving nothing but the sound of her name on the High Prince's lips before she collapsed into his arms.

Alora.

CHAPTER 27

It's said that a battle is easier to fight on the outside. Slashing blades against flesh and fighting to the bitter end across a bloodied battlefield piled with corpses. An honorable way to die. But when you're at war with your own mind, your own heart ... the demons haunt with the pain of the past. Nipping at your heels. Slowly chipping away at your broken pieces and leaving permanent scars. Unapologetically, ruthlessly, eating away everything you once were until you've broken so far down that the only place to go is the dirt below your feet.

That is worse than death.

That is what she felt.

Living death.

Alora was certain her eyes would never open again as she lay in a cloud of nothingness. Her mind suspended outside of her body. The will to convince her limbs to move a far-off whisper.

It was all a dream, right? The training. Jade. Her fire ...

Stars above, burn me.

Her fire ...

Everyone had seen her. What had she done?

Underneath the heaviness of the blackened abyss, Alora breathed out a quiet groan as consciousness crept in. The feeling in her hands and feet flowed from the faintest of sensation to a warmth covering her like dust on an abandoned redwood chest.

Her aching head rested on clouds, her body, too.

She knew one thing for certain at that moment; she wasn't dead. And it wasn't the glow of moonlight and starflames in the Stars Eternal kissing her eyelids.

Again a whimper escaped her dried lips when her aching fingers flinched against soft furs of ... of a bed.

Alora stiffened, but at least her heart beat once again, unlike those long moments in the arena where she was unsure whether she was dead or alive.

Metallic thumps on wood startled her. The rushing of what sounded like water streamed into a dense pool shortly after.

The bed sank by her side; the wooden frame creaked from the weight.

She drew a sharp breath when a pleasantly cold, wet cloth was draped across her fevered forehead.

"Welcome back." A cold thumb brushed her cheek, the High Prince's calm voice breaking through the darkness. It was nearly soothing, if not for the small hint of unease that lay within the words.

His darkened silhouette was outlined in her spotting vision. Then, the soft glow of the sun against white canvas. The rays shining through the entrance in a smoky breeze. Her upper armor, sword, and dagger had been shed. Discarded in the shadows beside the door.

She was in his tent.

His bed.

Alora shakily lifted a heavy arm and rubbed across her face. "How did I get here?"

"I carried you," that deep, honeyed voice answered.

Alora blinked her burning eyes. Through shards of darkness, she recalled the faint memory. She'd fallen. Blood had drained from her head as she fought to stay awake. Strong arms caught her mid-collapse and lifted her against his tense body. Her vision had darkened soon after. Then flashes of sunlight. The High Prince's face, weaving through tents, a clouded sky around ashy hair. Until she had completely given into the darkness.

He carried her.

Water trickled down Garrik's broad hands, along his corded veins to his elbows, as he rang out a white cloth in the water basin. He turned to her, focusing on her head and removing the warm cloth, before replacing it with the new, cooled one.

Alora's eyebrows pinched as she flinched back.

"Easy." Garrik held his hand up near her. "It is only cloth. I am not asking you to marry me." His face was close enough to smell a strong scent of vanilla and oak.

She nodded and closed her eyes as he carefully draped the cloth on her burning forehead.

The touch of cold metal brushed against her lips. "Drink this."

Normally, she would refuse his chivalry, but given how dry her mouth was, Alora opened to icy, sweet spring water.

"I heard you calling for ... Rowlen. I have heard you for days ... wondering, the guilt of leaving him behind." Garrik fell silent as he gradually poured another sip into her mouth. "He is alive—safe. Now living in a ... city south of Telldaira."

Had the sun always been so bright? Especially through thick canvas. The furs wrinkled as she pushed herself up on her elbows and sank back against the piled pillows in the corner of his bed. All the feeling had returned to her body. Every sensitive touch against her skin from the soft furs, the scratch of the cloth on her aching forehead.

With raw eyes, Alora pleaded into the silver of his. "Rowlen's alive?" Her voice cracked, and she fought back burning tears.

"And well." Pivoting on his feet, Garrik leaned for the water basin. He rang out another cloth and wiped a bead of sweat from her forehead before glancing up to where the sky waited beyond the canvas. "The Ravens have moved east. He is safe there. I wanted you to know that. So you can have some peace."

Alora's lip quivered. Warm tears spilled out over her lashes. "Thank you." She wrenched in a breath, fighting the urge to sob in front of the High Prince.

Rowlen was alive. He didn't suffer a terrible fate in the raid. And now she knew. After wondering, after pleading with the stars to give her a sign. Now she knew.

"Thank you," she repeated. But her eyes widened. Rowlen was a Mystic, just like them. "He doesn't belong here. Please, don't bring him here."

"Rowlen is a healer—"

"*Leave him out of this.*" Embers lit inside her eyes.

Garrik fell silent, his jaw clenched at the sharp edge of her tongue. Observing the sapphires threatening to ignite, he gritted his teeth. "Very well."

226

Instead of a white, fiery glow, Alora's eyes welled with tears, and she nodded. She refused to subject Rowlen to this.

"I need to tell him what happened. He needs to know I'm okay. He'll come looking for me."

Garrik dropped the cloth in the basin with a splash, beads specking the bedside table. "He knows that you are safe. Thalon sent word. He believes you have made your way north. Once settled, he expects correspondence from you. I had planned, in the case of your disapproval, to keep him updated, if that is what you wish."

"Yes." Without question, at least he would know. At least neither of them had to wonder.

Alora bent her knees to her chest at the thought, excited to communicate with Rowlen for the first time since the cliff, but that excitement was short-lived. Wincing, she whimpered when a brutal sting burned up her leg from where freezing Smokeshadows whorled over a wound. Pulling a knee to her stomach, her fingers picked at the edge of a blood-soaked bandage covering her training leathers.

Garrik's shadows receded, leaving the cruel warmth of the tent to settle on her wound. "I need to clean that."

She lifted the bandage to reveal a gash the size of her hand to the inside of her right knee. "Why didn't you?"

He nodded at her pants. "You will need to remove those for me to do so. It is not serious enough for me to make that decision for you."

Alora's cheeks heated at the thought. Close to bare in the High Prince's tent. In his bed...

In his dreams. "No. I'm fine."

"Do not be stubborn. If you wish, I will find Jade and she can—"

"No!" Alora sighed so pointedly her nostrils flared. "Fine. But if your hands go anywhere but my knee..." she hissed and pressed her lips tight. In one ungraceful movement, Alora lifted her hips, wiggling her leather pants down to her boots before ripping her black undershirt down and over her thighs.

Garrik took on a wolfish nature and stood, stalking to the edge of the bed.

"*Tempting*, certainly," he said and placed his hand on the tip of her boot, pulling slowly on the heel until it was off, then repeated with the other. "But I think you are in no condition for where that may lead, no matter how *pleasurable* you would find it to be. Would you not agree?"

Instead of lunging at him, she settled for hurling a large pillow at his smug face.

Smokeshadows cascaded from his shoulders, intercepting it before whisking it away into thin air as he smirked.

She snatched another from behind and placed it across her thighs before he gripped the ends of her pants and slid them off.

"Taking your clothes off for me already? You have not even taken me on a date yet." Mischief swirled in his stare before he turned away toward the entrance.

Another pillow went soaring through the space between them. This time, successfully landing a soft blow to the back of his head.

He spun back around and glared; fists balled to his sides.

Smokeshadows whirled above her like rain clouds.

With one quick glance up, her head was met with the weight of the missing pillow falling flat into her unsuspecting face. If her forehead wasn't already piping hot, it would've been steaming from the look she bore into mischievous, silver eyes.

Garrik released a deep laugh as he turned, pulling at the tunic fabric against his abdomen, avoiding the middle finger proudly raised in his direction. A sound she'd rarely heard since her arrival at camp.

She almost ... liked it.

He walked to the table at the far side of his tent and removed the papers from the top.

A nervous rush filtered through her nerves. Remembering the map that remained hidden, rolled inside a hollowed-out leg of her bedframe.

His corded arms lifted the table with ease and placed it within arm's reach of Alora. "Can you stand, or shall I lift you?"

Alora crossed her arms and glared at him.

Before she could say a word, one of the High Prince's arms wrapped around her back, the other under both knees, effortlessly lifting her from the bed to the tabletop.

The pillow toppled before she could capture it, so she quickly readjusted her shirt to cover her thighs and pressed her knees as close to each other as she could handle.

Garrik gathered a leather bag from his chair and placed it beside her before rifling through the contents. Through glass clunks, he found what he needed and set clear liquid bottles and clean cloth on the table.

Eldacar's medical bag.

Maybe she should've asked for him instead.

Garrik poured clear liquid on a clean cloth and hesitated. "If I am to clean this." He cleared his throat. "You will need to spread your legs for me."

Alora bit her bottom lip. *Stars above, burn me now.* She gripped the edge of the wooden table and tried to steady her twitching arms.

His eyebrow lifted. *I promise I will be gentle.*

Her grip went clammy as a flush climbed up her face. "Can you

WHAT LIES WITHIN MASKS & SHADOWS

make this any more awkward?" She swallowed and looked away. Through the corner of her evaded vision, the High Prince's broad shadow stalked closer.

I can make this many things, clever girl. Garrik's solid body pressed against her trembling knees as he leaned into her, causing her grip to release from the table's edge and avoid his incoming proximity.

A black sleeve entered her vision as his silver and black rings scuffed forward beside her thighs. She was failing the fight to remain calm when his calloused hand rubbed against her cheek, grazing her chin before it turned her to face the silver of his predatory eyes.

Alora's heart skipped a nervous beat. His leather and metal scent, mixed with a warm hint of vanilla and oak, was inviting.

He leaned close.

The corner of Garrik's mouth twisted up, his fingers gliding against the warm skin of her thigh. Traveling up until he gently squeezed above her knee. His thumb traced idle circles against her skin. The other moved under her white hair until it settled on the back of her neck.

A warm pulse radiated between her legs. How this sinfully beautiful stranger could make her feel things she could never admit to herself was a mystery for another time. Her mind was lost within the silver of his eyes and the pulsing desire to feel his hand moving against her skin that carried a memory from not long ago—a memory of his tent. In his bed.

She pleaded to every Celestial that he couldn't discern how her aching body was reacting to his touch as he pressed his against the crease between her closed knees.

Garrik leaned forward, eyes locking onto hers as if nothing else in the world mattered until his lips brushed against her jawline. Gracefully descending along the curve. Icy breath traveled across her, and the pressure at her knees pushed a little harder.

Alora parted her lips with a sharp breath. Then angled her head, causing his lips to brush her chin as her traitorous legs drifted apart until his body was poised between. She felt the hand against her neck trace down her spine to the table, brushing against her outer thigh.

Until it steadily backed away.

Garrik's lips ... they were inches away.

Those sinful lips feathered across hers, driving her to the edge of insanity.

"Good girl," Garrik breathed.

The sound of his voice could have sent her into the next realm if it wasn't for the shriek of pain from her lips as Garrik tightly pressed the wet cloth against her wound. She leaned back on her palms until her nails scratched rivets into the wooden tabletop and curled her toes.

His palm clasped her shoulder, careful to keep her from writhing in pain. "Consider us even, clever girl." With a smirk, he pulled the bloodied cloth away and tossed it to the dirt.

"*Bastard!*" Alora shoved his chest hard and backed it up with a swift kick to his thigh.

He stumbled out between her legs and adjusted his tunic.

"I hate you." She hissed with gritted teeth and a sharp breath.

"I know." The smirk on his face was more menacing than usual and accompanied by an amused laugh.

Alora pressed her lips tight as he prepared another cloth and reached to her wound. His wrist was instantly caught in a scorching, embered hold.

"I'd say you made things even when you had Jade nearly kill me today," she accused.

Garrik's hand enveloped hers and pulled it away.

She sucked in a swift breath as he wiped bubbling blood from the wound. Its sting significantly lessened this time. "She'll never forgive me, you know. I'm at the top of her hate list."

The High Prince wetted another cloth from a green bottle. Its contents ran yellow on the fabric. "I assure you, there are others much more worthy of her hatred than you. Her father being one. And the entire male race is a close second."

Alora looked away anticipating the incoming sting. "Excluding you and the others, of course?" Her voice rasped as he rubbed the cloth again over the gash. A numbing sensation crawled across it and irritated the skin.

"I am irresistible. Nobody could hate me."

Alora rolled her eyes. "*Okay*, Your Royal Highn-*ass*."

Garrik chuckled once more. "The five of us have bonds only family hold. Jade and I share similarities with our childhood. Her father and Magnelis are..." He paused. "He would be dead if I found myself in her realm. He and all the rest of the males on that starsdamned piece of dirt."

"Why?" Alora pinched her eyebrows.

"It is not my story to tell. Be patient with her. Just as you would wish me to be patient with you. In time, she will defend you as one of her own, as one of us."

"Defend me? Yeah. Right. I'll fly on wings of fire the day that happens. Jade wants to kill me. Why did you give her that chance?"

"I have seen you attack when angry and scared. You needed to be reminded of that. You are powerful, Alora, once you get out of your head. Jade needs to release her rage or she will become reckless. She is so loyal that it is her greatest weakness. If I am there, I can stop her before her anger escalates. You were never in any real danger." He pointed to the hole in her leather armor behind them. "That would have gone through you."

"And why didn't it?"

His hands shuffled through Eldacar's medical bag until he pulled out a needle and thread.

Needles. Out of all the sharp and pointed killing objects she was used to being around ... a needle sent a spike of nausea to her throat. Her skin turned a dying grass shade of green.

Smokeshadows danced around her wound. *Look away.*

Alora did as told and felt the blood in her arms and legs draining.

The High Prince's shadows whirled behind her, creating something for her to lean back on. "I shielded you both. And she knew that. So, she fought harder and released her pent-up rage."

Thanks for telling me, bastard.

Garrik smiled. "If you would have known, you would not have fought like you did. Training with Thalon is incredibly valuable. But nothing compares to someone trying to shove a blade through your heart." His hands threaded the needle through her numbed skin.

Alora leaned back onto her palms, not daring to watch. "I got my ass kicked. Horribly."

"Yet, you did not yield." He dropped to one knee and grabbed bandages from the satchel. "The courage to fight in the face of death is rare."

Her lips twitched into a smile as she peered down at him. Enjoying the view of him on his knees.

"I am proud of you." A cold hand began wrapping the wound with rolled cloth.

Alora's heart dropped. *Proud?*

Who could be proud of someone cowering in fear before their enemy? Jade had found a weakness and pushed on it until she eventually burst. Just as she no doubt had been trained to do. Find the enemy's weakness, exploit it, use it to bring them to their knees. And it worked. Alora had played right into Jade's taunts until that ember lit and eventually burned uncontrollably.

He called her a weapon once. He was right. She was a dangerous weapon. One that should be locked away to protect the camp. Only to be unleashed in the face of the High King.

She bit her bottom lip and dropped her gaze. "Proud of the way I lost control of my magic and panicked on my knees?" She sighed and leaned back on the table.

The High Prince continued to roll the bandage around her leg.

Jade was right. Pathetic indeed. Kaine should've killed me a long time ago.

A low growl reverberated from Garrik's chest. He finished with the bandage and stood. His icy hands planted onto the table beside her thighs before leaning in close, and those muscular legs pushed between hers once again. All the way. Until he touched the table.

Swirls of ink formed in the glistening of his silver eyes as he leaned in close to hers.

The air changed.

And before her eyes stared the look of a killer.

The Savage Prince's voice was quiet and tense. The sheer rage behind his visage could level a kingdom as his anger rippled in waves. "Do not *ever* think or say that bullshit again."

Every bone in her body rattled. She looked away at anything other than him.

His grip enclosed around her chin and guided her back to look into oblivion. "Never again, Alora." His eyes lingered, locked onto hers before his fingers brushed down her skin and let her free.

She was unable to speak but managed a nod.

"Crying is not a weakness. It makes you stronger. Sometimes, you need to be beaten lower than you have ever been to stand taller than you ever were." Garrik looked over at his tunic covering his death mark. "The pain of the past is everlasting, yet it can eventually mend. Until then"— the black in his eyes slowly retreated to reveal his silver once more—"I may be the last person you would want, but I am here should you need to talk about that which torments you."

The sides of his hands lightly brushed against her thighs as he pulled away.

She shook her head, eyes spearing the canvas bunched at the top of the tent as warm tears lined her eyes. And there it was. That all-familiar feeling. Deep inside her aching chest and fingertips. The pulsing and ripping tension that hindered any desire to speak or to even try to move. Every bone in her body seized up, her blood felt heavier. All she could do was close her eyes and let the tears stream down. Because being broken like this, being silent about her past and letting Kaine beat not only her body, but allowing him to linger in her mind, was incredibly exhausting.

Alora filled her lungs and lowered her head, voice shaking in a whisper. "I'm not a princess." As strange as it was, Jade's taunting was the only thing her mind had repeated since the fight. A princess. Draped in lavish clothing and jewels, a kingdom of adoring subjects. An easy life

—happy life. Not one locked in a tower and waiting for a knight to come save her. Rather, the princess who was stolen away and locked in a molding, stinking cellar.

Garrik retreated and pulled her pants from the bed before walking back to her. He held out his palm, and she recognized the silent ask to place her ankle in it before he slipped it through a pant leg and repeated with the other.

He grinned. "Of course not. You are far too beautiful to just be a princess."

Alora scoffed and wiped a warm tear from her cheek. "I'm serious." She shuffled on the wood until her pants rested around her waist. "I wasn't born into royalty. I didn't have servants waiting on my every desire. My fluffy pillows were a hard wooden table covered in my blood. My bed was warmed with endless nights of shaking bones and teeth until the darkness caressed me to sleep." She rubbed her wrist where bruises had once been painted. "My betrothed." Her throat choked on air, chest tightening. "Kaine." She squeezed her eyes shut. "H—he—"

Smokeshadows lightly wrapped her skin in a cool, calming touch.

Her lips trembled, unable to continue as she gripped the edge of the table. Her fingertips ached from deep inside. "I don't know if I'll ever be who I was before."

Garrik stood there with tormented eyes fading into an endless abyss as they had been moments before. His voice broke as he tenderly whispered, "No. You will never get her back. Trust me when I say you do not want to. You are far braver than you think. Stronger than you yet know because of what you have endured. Never wish for those broken pieces returned. They will only cut holes into who you have fought to be now."

"Who I am now?" She breathed a laugh. "I gave up. That's who I am now."

"There is a difference between giving up and knowing when you have had enough. You, darling," Garrik said and paused, "did not give up. You fought with every shard of the broken pieces you had left. You are still fighting. I saw it today in the arena. I see it now. Still fighting the demons that plague you, the memories that sneak out of your eyes and roll down your cheeks." He stepped toward her and lifted her chin, a thumb gently brushed a tear from her cheek. "You are one of the strongest I have ever met. If you could see what I see—"

Alora shoved him again in the chest, but he remained solid in his foothold. "You have no idea what you're talking about."

Garrik heavily sighed and stepped back. A hand rested on his hip as the other pulled at the fabric disturbed against his chest. "Do not be quick to assume I have not been or have not endured such as you have. Even monsters have nightmares. If you would allow me, I may help you with yours."

"I don't need you or anyone to help me. I've been taking care of myself my entire life."

A taut line formed on Garrik's mouth. "Very well. I shall leave you alone in peace. Take as long as you need here. I will see you for dinner." Smokeshadows danced across his form, the tendrils slowly whirled around his body until he began to fade.

She watched as his figure was engulfed in darkness. Until only she stared into fading cloud and smoke. For the first time since she arrived, she didn't want to be alone. But couldn't believe the admission to herself. That she wished he had stayed and that she hadn't pushed him away. But it was too late now. She *had* pushed.

And he had left.

Was that not what she wanted?

No. In fact, every part of her stubborn mind screamed for a bone-crushing embrace.

Even if it was from him.

Alora looked at the door, wishing he would burst through the entrance and see himself back in front of her.

Then she found herself admitting an unsettling truth.

I need you. Her eyes glistened as seemingly relentless tears streamed down her cheek. *Please don't leave.* Her throat tightened as her heart jerked in stabbing pain.

The tent shook with a soft, chilled wind. Darkness seeped from every shadow and darkened place within the fabric walls. Such beautiful Smokeshadows crept along the dirt from every corner until they reached the table and climbed up.

His silhouette appeared before her like rolling thunderclouds in the night. The High Prince stepped out and strong arms lifted her from the table. Shadows danced around them as he pulled her against him. And, wrapping his arms around her, his core trembled.

Never. Garrik's voice caressed her mind. *Wherever there are shadows, I will always be.*

Alora buried her face in his icy chest.

Garrik placed his hand on the back of her neck as she began to open her mind to him. Through a heaving chest, she replayed the deepest scars of her past, the pieces of her tortured heart shattered by cruel hands, ebony hair, and betrayal behind mahogany eyes.

CHAPTER
28

Once the words inside her mind had begun vividly flowing, Alora had no hope of stopping them. They rolled like waves in the middle of a severe sea storm, crashing from one dreadful memory to the next until she was certain she would drown.

Only, she didn't.

There was an unsinkable ship amongst the deadly waters, and the High Prince's ice-cold arms kept her above the waves. And he held her there, listening to her like one might listen to the rain.

Alora hadn't the slightest idea of how she would look him in the eyes again. Not after everything he'd seen. Not after her humiliation was cleaved open and scattered into thousands of pieces.

So, she simply lingered in the silence outside of the firesite's glow, stroking her midnight mare's neck, feeling the strong muscles flex with a subtle turn. And when its ears twisted to the gentle sounds of footsteps approaching, her heart quickened, and she began to fumble on words forming in her mind that had no hope of collecting into intelligible sentences.

"You two look exquisite together," Garrik said in way of greeting, and she continued stroking night-dark hair, avoiding his attention. "Storm seems quite comfortable with you. She's never flattered anyone's hand." As if to emphasize his meaning, Garrik's lifted to scratch between Storm's ears, but the mare sharply lurched away, swatting her tail like a whip against his side.

A flash of white appeared in the darkness. Storm lowered her head and began to turn as Ghost emerged, head high and neck stretched with her ears flattened. The encounter lasted only seconds. The intensity of Ghost's posture was enough to warn Storm to step away and graze.

Garrik subtly shook his head. That hand intended for Storm's ears gently stroked Ghost's nose. "Like squabbling younglings," he scoffed and turned glistening silver orbs to Alora. Garrik regarded her evasive eyes, speaking quietly among the crackling of the fire behind him. "You look exhausted."

"Not as tired as you." She didn't know why she said it, but at least they weren't talking about Kaine.

The corner of his mouth twisted. "I am so tired that if I were at the castle and it were on fire, I would die because I slept through it. It would seem we both could use a day off."

She breathed a laugh at that understatement.

Then Garrik's smile faltered, and his expression turned gentle—the same way as in his tent earlier. "I am not going to ask if you are alright, because I despise being lied to," Garrik said, glancing around at the stars. "If you do not wish to talk about your past any further, I am someone who understands that more than most and will honor your decision."

She found Garrik's eyes then; they glowed inside a darkness so crisp; she could feel it brushing her skin.

"I want you to know, though," he said, gently enough that she almost felt the words caressing the bleeding wound in her heart, "that with me, you do not ever have to pretend."

Pretending was easier, though. To act as if nothing happened was better than the alternative. Better than ripping off the armor and leaving a soft spot—perfectly placed—for the enemy to strike. Why should she willingly hand herself over to that kind of bitter end?

But she wasn't there to dwell on the past. Especially not one that seemed to possess a desire to haunt her every waking breath.

There was something in the High Prince's voice though. A truth and honesty she was unable to deny.

Something she had rarely experienced after her parents died.

With no retort to his kind reassurance, Alora may have, for only a moment, felt a stirring of trust bubble. And she wondered if maybe he saw it too, because when those silver eyes flickered to her again, he stepped forward, reaching out a hand as if to take hers.

Perhaps more out of reflex than anything, Alora flinched, brushing her hand over her death mark, when, instead of Garrik's hand, she remembered a warmer one. One deadly and vicious, one that was adorned in the finery of painful sins.

Garrik dropped his hand, which she didn't expect, and whispered, "What can I do to help you?"

Kill him for me? She deepened a brutal, damning breath, surprising herself at the thought laced with venom. Through all the beatings ... every hand laid upon her ... not once had she wished for Kaine's death. Her heart hadn't been able to bear the thought, no matter how truly cruel and despicable and black-hearted he was.

Her eyes burned, brimming with liquid as she surveyed the male who had stolen her from her city and now was offering her a caring hand. To trust that. To trust him. The shield around her heart had barricaded itself in another solid layer, warning of the dangers of loosening her tongue.

But even so, it didn't stop her from saying, "I feel like even though Kaine isn't here, he still controls me. That I'll never be able to move on. That I'll never be healed or able to breathe again." *That I'll never feel whole.*

"Alora," Garrik breathed with a smile so bright it could have been mistaken for the stars. "You will not always feel this way." But his eyes ... they seemed to war between pain and hope.

"How do you know?" The words were strangled enough that they collected as whispers.

Something frigid as winter tickled inside her palm. Alora twisted her wrist and opened her fingers before a pearl-petal flower appeared inside tendrils of Smokeshadows.

"Flowers still grow after forest fires. How could I not believe that we can, too?"

She gripped that flower as if the act of opening her fingers would have it misting away.

"Your fight was not fair, and the path ahead will not be easy. Look forward with hope, even if you never forget the pain of the past. You are a survivor. You are not the pain you have suffered."

Alora felt the stirring of hope.

"You are sunstorms and starfire. Refuse to surrender."

CHAPTER 29

Slowly, her nerves returned to their normal state of functioning anxiety as Eldacar served mouth-watering, fire-roasted sirloin tips complete with garlic-buttered asparagus and honey-drizzled carrots. The garlic and butter aroma spurred her empty stomach to growl stridently; it could surely be heard in Telldaira.

Thalon was the first to offer her a tankard, unusually cheerful after a near inferno destroyed the arena that afternoon. "How are you feeling? It's been a long couple of weeks of training for you."

She forced a grin from her seat in the dirt. By reflex alone, Alora rubbed the gash in her leg. "I feel like I've been chewed up, spat out, and trampled over ... repeatedly. Then rolled off a cliff, only to have it all happen again once I've landed." She tipped her head. "And again."

A mighty laugh echoed from his lips. "That's normal for your first weeks of training. You've lasted longer than most. I usually order new fighters in an ice bath within their first midweek." Thalon palmed her shoulder and toasted her. "Well done. Impressive."

It was becoming easier to converse, even laugh at Thalon and

Eldacar's banter. But Garrik was … much different around the fire. When he did speak, it was in short returns. Always listening, always watching. Offering brief discourse and retorts if the conversation seemed to please him. But never seeming to allow himself to truly connect.

"… and then Garrik flung the chicken out the window after his instructor chased him down the hall. I don't think I've ever seen someone punished to train that many hours in my life." Thalon roared so viciously he grabbed his stomach and clenched his eyes.

Eldacar cut in, "Remember when Aiden took a Hiyrythean to bed? He woke, covered in slime, screaming back to camp *'what the hell happened last night?'* The stench didn't leave him for an entire week." He removed his glasses and wiped them with a cloth between chuckles, not forgetting to dab the corners of his eyes too.

"Garrik made him ride ahead of the legion all week to ward off incoming danger." Thalon was practically convulsing.

Alora watched the males chatter as Jade relaxed with ankles crossed on the fallen tree and Garrik grinned at the dirt. The guilt slowly crept up her limbs when Jade unnoticeably turned her eyes and glared at Alora.

She ripped her gaze away, focusing on the dancing flames between them. "Is Aiden to return soon?"

It was Garrik who answered. "I have visited daily. He will be back within a month, maybe a little more. The reports are good. He is recovering well. Slow, but well. He has never been away from us long. The moment he is able to stand, his stubborn ass will find us."

Alora turned her gaze south when Thalon countered, "Aiden's like a cat, nine lives and all. He's sure to make a fine entrance when he returns."

And that caused something like a smile to twitch on her face.

In the distance toward the lake, a loud cheer erupted, cutting through the heaviness like a sharpened blade.

"Bout that time." A feline grin covered Thalon's face. "I'm sure the torches are being lit as we speak." He twisted his body and looked over the tents toward the lake.

"Time for what?" Alora asked.

"For some fun!" Thalon jumped up and stretched his arms over his head before pointing to Eldacar. "What says you? You going to give a blade a go this evening?"

"Oh, stars above, no! The pen is my sword. And considerably easier to write with." He elbowed Alora and smiled.

Excitement glistened in Alora's eyes. "You're sparring tonight?"

"We're *competing* tonight!" Thalon drew his sword and maneuvered it in front of him. "Two nights before we move out, Garrik allows us to compete. The entire camp. No rules. It's the perfect way to blow off the heat of the journey and, of course, earn bragging rights until the next one. I have championed all I've fought in."

"You've never lost? Not even against the mighty prince?"

"No, he's never competed before. He's too deadly." With a wink, Thalon swung his sword once more.

She looked over at Garrik, remembering how she'd never seen him sparring—not once.

Garrik simply shrugged. "They cannot handle me."

"I bet I could." Alora goaded and flicked her thumb on her chin as if to remind him of the cut she'd given him in his tent.

"I would pay good coin to see that!" Thalon stabbed his sword into the dirt and started patting his pockets.

Garrik rubbed his chin, amusingly looking at Alora. "Is that so?" And she flashed him a cocky grin back before he shook his head. "Not this time, clever girl."

She almost said something when Thalon abandoned his search and spun his golden sword in an effortless twist of his wrist, pointing the sharpened tip at Jade. "I get a go with you tonight. I want to see that red hair get pummeled into the dirt."

"More like your sorry ass ending up in the lake." Jade threw back as she jumped to her feet. "I'll be taking one of those Earned tonight, mark my words."

The two of them squared off, offering friendly fire in the way of their words, but Alora furrowed her eyebrows. "Earned?"

Garrik leaned forward; his forearm draped over a bent knee beside her. "The golden beads braided into Thalon's hair," he started, low enough that only she could hear him, "are a holy symbol from Tarrent-Garren Keep—Thalon's home—settled in the mountains of their own territory and governed by no king. Not even Magnelis can break the exalted bindings.

"Worldly known as 'Earned,' they are only worn by those who are honored to be titled as 'Guardians.' Each bead is an opportunity; lose a battle, lose a piece of honor, displayed by the loss of a bead—which is what will happen if Thalon loses tonight. And if a Guardian loses all of their Earned," Garrik continued, reflecting flames in his eyes, "they are no longer worthy to be titled and excommunicated forever, along with their family."

Alora watched as the beads reflected the amber glow of the flames. Her eyes drifting over every perfect one, too many to count, weaving throughout his locks, save for one strand that collected in a long row of ten.

Then the roar from the crowd thundered once more.

Thalon lifted his sword into the air with a mischievous smile. "Let the games begin!"

THE CROWD THRUMMED WITH EXHILARATION, anxious and hungry for an entertaining fight.

Stretching beyond the tent-lined border, a vast expanse opened up, leading to the arena—marked by the cessation of tents. Alora couldn't yet see inside the arena, but with each step closer, she caught glimpses of what waited inside. The night was dark, but a hundred torches—bound to the wooden walls—illuminated the inside as fifteen fighters prepared their battle-ready positions.

Garrik walked through the crowd with an air of pride, parting the sea with his sheer presence, and was escorted to an erected platform on the side by the lake. And before she could find her place amongst the shouts and roars, Garrik hauled her up to stand beside him.

The boards beneath her feet were vibrating—shaking so intensely she thought the platform may fall. But Garrik seemed unfazed by it and scanned the crowd with a devilish grin.

She did too. There was no stopping it.

It was *electrifying*.

Before her, as far as the tree line and mere feet from the tents, the crowd moved in waves of unbridled excitement. Billowing with riotous roars of speculation and predictions as to the competition's outcome. The sounds of their screams were so loud she couldn't hear her own calls to Thalon, who stationed himself beside her, beaming like a youngling waiting for their favorite dessert.

Alora had learned, through the maze of tents, that this tradition was a fight to the last. Seven rounds of extraordinary magic, sharpened blades, and cunning minds until a victor emerged. Nothing would be off limits. Mystic versus soldier—just like war. Then, each victor of their round would battle in the last until one remained. When questioned, Thalon had explained that most choose an ally, fighting side by side until their only choice was to abandon the alliance and turn on the other. Others fought in packs, while a few relied on their own abilities.

Forsaking the command by his hand, Garrik instead raised his voice, booming like two mountains colliding together. "Weapons ready?"

The roar that followed was momentous, clanging weapons and beating fists into the arena walls and air.

The elegant mask of the High Prince was ripped away. No trace of a royal High Fae of impeccable, distinguished bloodlines. It was replaced by something wholly roguish and irrepressible.

Without any need for horns or convincing speeches, every muscle rippled in Garrik's body as he tensed forward. Enthralled in the intensity of the moment, those darkened eyes morphed into something utterly devilish, spearing into the crowd as he growled, *"Rot an li vencath!"*

Fight to the last!

As the last word escaped his lips, the fighters *lunged*.

Like rabid beasts, an outright brawl of steel, fists, and entertainment erupted.

Immediately, six fighters were conquered and yielded to various strikes while the others wrestled and bombarded their opponents with skill and agility.

Duck! To your left! Keep that sword up!

Watch your feet! Do you even know how to fight?

Come on, get up!

You call that a punch?

The crowd's energy engulfed Alora to the point that her throat threatened to raw from her own shrieking. Ignoring Jade's scowls and hisses as she dug her boots deep into the platform's edge. Being outside the ring wasn't close enough. She craved more.

Thalon beat his chest with a fist as he screamed at a young High Fae, "Get up! I've taught you better!"

Three fighters remained.

They prowled around each other with swords drawn and clenched fists. Searching for weakness to exploit. One pulsed magic through the air—a mighty lightning strike fell through the dark, scorching the ground between them—and sent two fighters onto their backs.

One fighter crawled his way across the charred, cracked dirt to the wall, collecting panting breaths before hands pulled him over. He stood with a nod and a heaving chest.

Out, but uninjured.

Two fighters remained—the Mystic and a soldier who fell on her back. Each positioned themselves apart from one another.

Talenciya, as the crowd screamed, held out her hand once more just as the soldier leapt into the air. The pommel of her sword cracked into the chest of the Mystic, rendering her immobile and breathless for a moment. The fight was a spectacle. Lightning and metal crashing together as the two gave their best performance.

"Let's go Talenciya! Show us what you got!" someone screamed from the crowd.

Being a light and energy manipulator, Talenciya raised her palms once more. Energy thrummed around her fingers in small branches of lightning, and her smile crackled across her face, baring teeth as the soldier bounded forward.

Power *exploded*. Vaulting the armored female ten feet backward.

She moved, thank Maker of the Skies, on buckling arms, but the female could now only yell and exit the arena. *Out.*

"Are you fighting tonight?" Alora screamed, barely loud enough for Thalon to hear even inches between them.

"Yes! But not until the fight gets more interesting!" he shouted back, throwing his fist high into the air as Garrik called the next round to begin.

ONLY ONE ROUND remained until the victors would fight. Thalon had won with minimal effort. It's no wonder he was a general in the High Prince's Shadow Order with his incredible sword skills and flawless magic. He portaled effortlessly through the arena, grabbing his opponents from behind, forcing them to yield at the end of his blade while warding off impressive attacks until he was the last.

Jade had jumped in the round after. Her fiery red hair swung in the wind as she exemplified impeccable maneuvers of her blade, befalling every opponent in her path. Her impressive attacks and defenses led her to a striking victory against three males double her size. She seamlessly knocked them on their asses before sticking a blade to the last one's throat. They might as well have been trees ready for her axe.

In all the excitement of the victory, Alora's eyes turned feisty as she pulled her sword from her sheath. "It's my turn."

"You think you can handle it?" Thalon's eyes glistened with intrigue.

"I know I can!" Alora leapt from the platform and landed in the arena with dust clouding around her boots. In the madness, she could have sworn she heard a deep voice call out. But it was too late.

She was in the ring. *No turning back.*

The crowd roared around her as the next set of fighters entered.

Sparring against Thalon and even Jade was one thing. But, there, she may actually have a chance of winning her round.

The last of the fighters jumped down beside her, trembling the earth.

Ready to stare them down with an intimidating grin and wrist rotation of her sword, Alora turned.

And her face instantly paled.

Familiar silver eyes glowered behind wisps of magnificent gray hair. Blustering arms half-covered by a black button-up tunic tucked into his pants clung against his sculpted torso and biceps.

He didn't have a weapon.

He *was* the weapon.

The dirt beneath their feet vibrated as the sea of faces erupted louder than ever before.

And then ... the thirteen faces around them panicked.

Nobody moved.

Nobody *dared.*

Nobody wanted to be the first. Glistening metal and trembling fists stood staring each other down, contemplating their first move.

Garrik didn't look at Alora, but she assessed him. That same menacing and bloodthirsty face that she saw against the High King's soldiers in the alley—and the gamroara—plagued his face.

His eyes ...

Went ... *black.*

Someone flinched.

Six fighters sprinted toward Garrik as Alora tucked and rolled under a faerie twice her size with his sword drawn. She twirled around on her knee in time to slam the pommel of her sword into his muscled back. The perfect positioning of the impact forced him forward onto his face.

On scrambling feet, and a slide across the dirt later, Alora jammed her knee into his back. The cold metal of her blade pricked the back of his neck.

"Yield," she ordered with a victorious grin.

The male's tense body relaxed with a nod of his head in defeat.

Dilating pupils and electricity surging through her heart, Alora sprang to her feet. The chants of the crowd charged the air in prickling intensity. Deep roars and shrill screams of victory rang from all directions of the ring.

Torches in the clear night danced their amber glow into the fighter's path, illuminating sweat, blood, and metal.

One calculated scan of the ring revealed three fighters down. A leopard shifter struggled to catch her breath from the comfort of her back, another fighter leaned heavily against the wooden walls with the crowd's hands patting his shoulders. The third made a quickened escape over the wall and joined the spectators with fists held high, cheering on a blond-haired female dressed in red with earth-melding power. Two High Fae males fought with bursts of their own magic and steel against her.

Alora grinned wickedly.

The female was overpowering them. Easily.

A rush of footsteps and boot scuffs against hardened dirt tore her gaze from the fight. She scanned over the grounds once more until an icy chill bit at her cheek. Flaming torches violently fluttered as she turned to her right.

Carnage.

The High Prince viciously dropped four warriors on their backs within an instant of charging at him. Luckily for them, only minor injuries covered their bodies but enough to leave them writhing in pain at their High Prince's boots. His bloodthirsty orbs of night stalked two more in his path. Their swords were drawn in quaking anticipation. He tracked them as he stood deathly still; only his eyes glided across the space between.

Every muscle in his body rippled as they circled close.

Then, they lunged.

Malice twisted up the side of Garrik's face.

With a sharp squeeze of his fist at his side, Alora watched with widened eyes as the two fighters were wrenched back on a phantom wind. Their bodies, as if in slow motion, hovered in the night air like feathers on a soft breath.

A flick of his palm and they were released from their slow-moving hold and hurtled through the air. Dolls to be thrown aside by bored hands. Their bodies pummeled into wooden walls as the crowd behind was swept back by his rock-solid shield.

The impact of the blast silenced the crowd. A hushed aura Alora suspected had never graced such a tournament before.

Garrik took a step, his lip curled, revealing sharpened teeth as he growled. Heavy footsteps crunched the dirt and rocks beneath. He reached an unconscious body, towering over the faerie before he grabbed the sword still enclosed in their fist.

The Savage Prince turned.

Smokeshadow tendrils escaped his monstrous form while he began to fix the darkness in his eyes on two of the three remaining—the female Mystic and her last opponent.

Garrik's chin dropped low; eyes sharp on his path. The sword tip scratched the dirt as he stalked forward.

Then ... he was *gone.*

Only the diminishing cloud of ash and smoke lingered there.

The crowd screamed in electric anticipation once more.

Feet from the two fighters, Smokeshadows exploded as he stepped out, sword drawn in front of him.

Alora forced a swallow and twisted her boot into the ground. The High Prince's back was toward her. The perfect opportunity for a surprise attack. With every bit of energy she could muster, her feet bolted across the dirt before she vaulted into the air.

A flash of metal and a sea of sparks met her blade.

She was instantly on her back.

Air refused to fill her lungs. She couldn't move, held down by shadows, when the icy kiss of a blade touched her neck.

A muscle flexed in Garrik's jaw as he gritted his teeth and wrath poured out from his voice. "It is hard for me to keep my fucking *promise* to you when you do stupid shit your first weeks here." Kneeling on one knee beside her, his blackened eyes burned into hers. An enraged face was half-hidden behind the smoke dancing off his shoulders.

Alora's eyes snapped behind his head in time to see the female Mystic become swallowed in Smokeshadows with a shrill scream. The High Prince never flinched. Never took his eyes from hers.

Garrik gripped the hilt, leather groaning under his grip. "Get the fuck out of the arena." His deep voice was laced with the burning intensity of the stars themselves. Almost unrecognizable.

The sword retreated from her throat. Blackened eyes flickered to the last fighter with unfathomable rage.

Alora rushed to her feet. She raised her palm, begging her magic to pull the sword from his grasp before striking down the last opponent.

The sword did nothing more than flinch.

He whirled around and growled inside her mind, *What the fuck did I say?*

Refuse to surrender, remember? Alora snapped back.

But a wall of shadow and smoke blasted toward her. Tendrils licked at her boots and crawled up her legs until she was completely engulfed. Swirling silver clouds and ash began to turn her into shadows, into nothingness.

No. Alora's body felt light, the High Prince's power tearing at her being, dawning her from the arena.

With a fisted hand, Alora opened her arms. Shadows shook in an unnatural movement, slowing their intense surge around her.

Embers warmed in her palms as she opened clenched fists and burned with glowing intensity.

Smokeshadows burst from her body in an explosion of fiery power.

Sapphire eyes blazed into a winter sky's glow.

"Hey!" she screamed to draw his attention, white flames dancing in her palms.

Darkened abyss glared back over his shoulder.

I warned you. Garrik turned toward her and lifted his hand with a murderous smile. *Yield.*

Never.

Before his Smokeshadows could enclose around her neck, Alora unleashed a blast of fire, and glistening sparks barreled toward the High Prince. The inferno circled him—and his shadows. A cage for a beast.

She panted with the pulse of flames, his shadows never relenting in their unpredictable destruction of her fire.

The final fighter took his chance. With Alora's help, a small window in the flames opened. Enough room for him to maneuver his way inside.

Victory in his eyes. He swung his sword high.

Garrik's head turned in time to counteract with his weapon, knocking the warrior down. His blade touched the flesh of the male's throat, ending the last round of the competition.

The Savage Prince won.

Six of the seven victors entered the arena. Garrik stood, arms crossed, on the platform, and nodded. The final round continued without him.

One by one, they each fell and surrendered. By the end, Thalon and Jade remained.

Their swords clanged in a shower of sparks and screaming iron. Alora watched in nervous curiosity as to whose threat would become denouement; Jade with her fiery red hair in the dirt or Thalon thrown into the lake.

Hopefully Jade. What she would give to see Jade at the end of Thalon's sword, in front of everyone. The thought tasted like a sweet, juicy apple, perfect and entirely satiating.

Jade danced. Her feet were rhythmic—calculated—precise.

Though Alora hated to admit it—beautiful.

Her fighting was art. Painted by an awful creature of hate and the worst death glare anyone had ever seen. Jade appeared as if she could

247

dance on air. Spinning, twirling, contorting her body in graceful ways that worked to her advantage as she fought off Thalon.

Thalon knew her moves and knew them well. He successfully blocked every damning blow. But Jade knew his, too.

When Thalon would portal, she perfectly predicted where he would appear. If her back was turned, he'd portal directly behind her, giving her time to swing around and meet his blade before it hovered at the back of her neck. Even as he portaled above her, she miraculously rolled out from under him.

With one last incredible maneuver, Thalon opened a portal. Much to his surprise, Jade jumped through it before he leapt in.

Alora gasped, tracking the air for the crackle of an opening.

The two spiraled out, landing outside of the arena in a tumble of limbs, spinning into the lake until Jade landed on top, dagger drawn to his neck.

Everyone echoed their cheers as the competition had come to its conclusion and their victor stood tall. Jade's sweat-ridden face was taut in victory. The fiery adrenaline in her bones hadn't settled as she sheathed her sword, ignoring the crowd behind them.

Laughing in amusement, Thalon roared from his back as Jade offered her hand. His smile burst off his face as they locked arms, and he jumped to his feet, splashing the water around them.

With one quick slice, Thalon removed a braid from his hair, slipped off a golden bead, and paced it into Jade's awaiting hand.

Jade snapped her head to the platform, glaring where Garrik was standing cross-armed, surrounded by cheering Dragons.

The High Prince lifted his hand.

The crowd's cheers died.

Eyes gleaming, Garrik stared down at Jade. "You have made me proud." He paced the platform before silver scanned the crowd. "Dragons ... *your victor*."

With a nod of his head, the roaring of the crowd lit up the valley once again.

The rest of the evening was filled with laughter, celebration, and drinking—*lots* of drinking. Alora hadn't yet felt excitement such as that since she was forced into camp. The air sparked with energy. Fighters who had faced each other in the arena—bloodied, bruised, and bandaged —served one another tankards, shook cut hands, patted shoulders, even hugged with laughter.

Alora buzzed around, interacting with faeries she hadn't met. Shaking hands as they congratulated her on her courage to join the competition, even though she'd lost.

She thoroughly enjoyed herself in those moments.

Until ...

Until her eyes met the High Prince's unamused gaze.

"WELL ... aren't you going to yell at me or something? Or are you just going to smolder until you explode?" Alora's feet wobbled. The ground beneath her seemed to shift with each step back to their firesite.

His lips created a thin line and brows angled. "Do not do that again." Frustrated, he kept his eyes forward on the path.

"Do what? Enjoy myself? Am I not one of your soldiers? Do I not get the same privileges as everyone else?"

"You have been training for only a few weeks. My army has been training most of their lives. One wrong move and you could have caused them to kill you."

She grabbed his forearm and pulled him to meet the embers in her eyes. "*Them?* Caused *them* to kill me?" she fumed. "You think so little of me that their actions are what's on your mind? Them! I could have handled *them* just fine." With shaking force, she shoved hard against his chest, barely making him flinch.

Garrik grunted, pulled himself away with a pluck of his tunic, and swerved around a barracks tent, ushering her beside him. "You think that if I cared so little that I would have gone against my better judgment and jumped in the ring to protect you?"

"Why do you care?" Alora stumbled a step, swatting his hand away when he reached to steady her. "I don't need you or anyone else protecting me. Or have you forgotten that so easily? I've been doing that my entire life, mighty prince. So, shove your chivalry right up your ass." Surging at him, two strong fists slammed against his chest before his solid grip wrapped around them.

A sigh filled his lungs as he tried to be reasonable. "You are drunk."

"And you're a prick." She almost spat in his face before pulling away and storming ahead.

He grabbed her arm, spinning her to face him mid-step. "Why can you not see that the things I have done are for your own good?"

"You? The monster I saw tonight? My gallant protector! Thank you so much for saving my life. Pffft." Maybe if she wasn't completely wasted, she wouldn't have said that, but even so, was glad she did.

"You need sleep. Get your ass to bed and in the morning when you have returned to your ... *charming* self, we can discuss this further." Garrik held onto her upper arm, leading her as she staggered through the grid of tents until they found their firesite.

Thalon was removing his armor and weapons by the fire when they barreled in, readying himself for a well-earned night's rest. "Jumping into the ring so soon? You've got Guardian blood in you. Truly impressive."

"Not according to the mighty prince." She pointed to Garrik as he let go of her arm.

Garrik gritted his teeth. "Bed. Now," he commanded before turning to Thalon. "See to it she stays there. I have business south."

Thalon merely nodded and before anyone could say anything, in a storm of Smokeshadows, Garrik dawned away into the night.

"See to it she stays there," Alora mocked into the empty night air, noticing the dark chuckle from the Guardian steps away. "I hope you stay there," she grumbled and folded her arms, hoping sound traveled through whatever void he dawned through before she tore her tent open and slipped inside.

CHAPTER 30

Blood rained. Dripping from the borders of her mind. A steady cadence, laced with the guttural screams of something vicious, longing to break free. The darkness called, a sound unlike the screams.

Alora felt it ... trying to lure her, pulling her like a silver rope, coarse and demanding, wrapping around her flesh. Relentlessly, it coiled around her skin until she felt uneven ground, forcing her to ignite a ball of spark and flames in her palm. White flames illuminated a familiar corridor. She could see the graystone tiles beneath her feet through the dancing light.

And the door.

The blackwood door that haunted her. Closed. Sealed off. With nothing but darkness crowding the cracks of the threshold, imprisoning the screams inside.

Alora felt her hand drop. The cold leather of her sword hilt groaned in her unrelenting grip. Then she was reaching. Reaching for the door, daring to clasp the doorknob, refusing the heart-shuddering panic that rippled down her spine as she turned it.

Stop. *She tried to turn from the voice but couldn't.* Please.

The screams stopped.

A bloodied hand pierced through the unending darkness inside, reaching for her light, reaching for salvation. It gripped her wrist, pulling her into the darkness as it desperately called to her.

Help me.

It continued to pull her, luring her into the darkness, through the threshold. The desperate cries grew louder as the abyss inside the room fell darker. A true oblivion, endless and terrifying. Unending horror covered it, surrounded it, choked it enough that even she couldn't breathe.

Alora raised her sword to the hand, knowing it wouldn't stop pulling her in until she succumbed to whatever hell awaited deep inside. She felt the sword slowly plummeting in the air, ready to cut the hand away, ready to—

Thunder cracked, shaking the ground beneath her boots.

Slowly, in a daze, Alora blinked. Surveying through the small spots of vision returning, a darkened tent appeared cast in the moon's amethyst glow. Rain droplets tapped a rhythmic cadence across the canvas from the aftermath of what had been a raging thunderstorm.

And amongst the gentle calm, she felt a burning in her arm.

It was raised, she realized. Hovering in the air, slowly sinking down toward ...

Jade. Sleeping soundly in her cot.

A quiet gasp, sharp as glass, scratched down her throat, and she lowered the sword to her side. Blinking rapidly until her body began to feel the blood in her veins and her mind could focus.

It was *the* dream.

A recurring, occasional nightmare that haunted her sleep for the past three years. And when it did come, her tense muscles and shot nerves would force her out of bed, usually to peer out Kaine's bedroom window as rain pelted the glass under a moon's glow—like tonight's.

Alora carefully dropped her sword on her cot and brushed through the canvas door, rubbing her trembling palms down her face, picturing Jade's. Picturing blood dripping from the cot and her sword shoved through Jade's chest as she listened to the squelch of mud beneath her boots. Imagined the sound of Jade's blood being the liquid she tread through.

If she hadn't woken—*no.* She wouldn't think about that.

The water of a nearby barrel splashed against her burning skin. Over and over, Alora drenched her face, allowing the crisp flow to spur her mind fully awake and settle her nerves. Allowing it to wash away the screams still echoing inside.

Her fingers curled around the barrel edge, breathing deep, feeling her knees quaking when something rustled to her left. A rustling of fabric and small tinging of metal stirred her heightened attention. Alora slowly turned her head to see that Garrik's tent was dimly lit when it hadn't been before.

A shadow drifted across his canvas walls. By the muscled silhouette, he was toweling off before dressing. Her traitorous eyes traced that shadow, following how his muscles were perfectly displayed until the candlelight diminished.

Alora frowned, frozen in place. It had been an entire day since she'd last seen him. Since he dawned away after the competition. And she didn't mind, because that festering resentment would've turned to boiling fury the moment she laid eyes on him.

It didn't matter where he'd been...

As long as it was far away from her.

Moments passed. She still didn't move, didn't dare make a sound. Likely, the mud beneath her boots would betray her, ultimately alerting Garrik that she was outside her tent without a guard. And the last thing she desired to do tonight was to explain why she dared defy his orders, again.

Feeling as if she'd escaped discovery when his tent remained dark and quiet, she stepped forward, sliding in the wet mud, only to come to an abrupt stop.

Garrik emerged from his tent. Pausing outside the entrance, he stood with his arms at his side, face lifted toward the clouded night sky with his eyes closed. Breathing deep the strong, musty aroma of the thunderstorm's aftermath. A breeze fluttered his hair across his forehead, the appearance messy but ... charming.

Even with the warning coursing through her bones, she couldn't turn away. Imagining him as a warrior preparing for battle. His monstrous sword was sheathed at his side, another settled in a scabbard down the straight of his back. A black leather bandolier of throwing daggers hung across his broad chest.

More ruthless and deadly than she'd seen him in the alley of Telldaira. More... She couldn't place it. Just ... something *more*.

Much to Alora's surprise, his gaze didn't roam her way. His vicious figure simply turned and disappeared down the moonlit path.

And she foolishly decided to follow him.

Ahead, torchlight appeared.

One by one until an annulus of light formed.

Alora slipped quietly behind a thick tree at the edge of a small clearing. Mere feet from a torch that emerged from the ground before her. Careful to stay hidden, she braced her hands against it and slowly inched out enough to see the High Prince standing in the illuminated center.

He'd almost evaded her in the forest. With nothing, not a broken branch or a disturbance of raindrops on leaves. Not a boot print or rustling of trees. Nothing was out of place. The High Prince was skilled —stealthy—no doubt years of training were to thank for that. By luck alone, she saw the small glow and followed.

Fire light danced on his rippling figure. He was death and stolen dreams filled with mystery and hope. She couldn't help the hard swallow at the sight of his sinful form. Her breaths drew short. Careful not to make a sound. Knowing, with his magic, he would likely hear the faintest whisper on a wind.

Garrik unsheathed his sword at his right side. Rotating his wrist to swing the weapon in a circle with his dominant hand. He began maneuvering his feet in perfectly paced footsteps, not one out of place. Strategic. Calculated.

Like frozen ice on a winter lake, he stilled. Head tilted. And a lethal grin appeared.

With the scoop of a hand, Smokeshadows billowed in tendrils across the annulus. Mist and darkness swirled and raged until three large clouds molded into the shapes of—

Alora's eyes widened, scratching the bark into her fingertips as her grip tightened.

Faeries.

They looked like faeries. Two males and a female by their shapes.

He created his own sparring opponents. Each had their own shadow swords. Each slowly circled him as if they possessed their own minds. As if they were living, breathing beings.

Garrik dug in his heels. Muscular legs launched him high into the air toward them. Carried by a cloud of shadows, his sword cut through the air, crossing the shadowed blade of a male.

Puffs of shadow tendriled around each stab and slash over the figures. Each advancing on him as if in real battle. And surrounding him, they attacked from all angles.

Not one came close to grazing him with their sword. She was certain that they would have if given the chance. But his strikes were brutal—

barbaric—yet intricately magnificent with each ruthless and horrifying kill of the shadows. When the last, the female, fell to her knees before him, Garrik's sword sunk deep into the shadow's skull until he cleaved her in two. The tendrils misted away, leaving its split body to fade into the dirt too.

The sight mesmerized Alora. Her hand clung to the bark of the tree to steady herself.

Garrik's intoxicating figure rippled with every movement, pushing against the sleeves of his tunic. Perfectly carved leg muscles strained against his pants until the clothing restricted him enough that he tore his tunic off.

It had to be a sin to watch something so breathtaking.

Even with his terrible scars, he was the most beautiful male she had seen. In fact, the scars made him even more spectacular. The way his skin pulled tight across them, the swells and dips of his muscles ... the darkness that followed him.

High Fae were incredibly beautiful, even the less pleasing ones. Differing from most faeries in mismatched and sometimes horrifying forms, High Fae were of a human-like appearance. They walked with gentle, almost perfectly quiet grace, with eyes that glowed even on a cloudy day, and elegantly pointed ears ranging from linear outer ears to a dramatic curve like the moon himself.

He was like a wild dream; she hated to admit, but she would be happy to sleep within it. No wonder there were myths of humans desiring to find themselves sleeping with a High Fae—a High Fae Prince especially—and steal them away into their fantasies.

And Garrik was a perfect fantasy.

From the way his body moved ... his seemingly perfect physique ... and that V of muscles she couldn't tear her eyes from...

He could bring any female to her knees.

Alora swallowed hard as blood rushed to her cheeks, ruthlessly pushing the thought away.

ALORA WATCHED him for almost two hours. Lunging, jumping, rolling in the dirt, only to use his massive legs to jolt him into the air and land back on his feet.

Garrik eventually sheathed both swords before scooping up his tunic.

He paused a moment to breathe, hand on his thigh as he closed his eyes and tilted silky gray hair to the stars.

Not long after, slowly, the torches were engulfed in Smokeshadows and snuffed out one by one as he slipped through the trees and thick brush. She paused a moment longer, not daring to make even the slightest sound—to not even breathe—cursing her own hammering heartbeat in fear that he might hear it and turn back.

She scanned, unable to see him anywhere by the light of the few remaining torches...

When a snap of a branch pierced the air behind her.

The sound of death in the form of metal slid across leather.

Alora turned...

Meeting the kiss of a blade pinching her neck.

"Thought you would go for another stroll, clever girl?"

She froze, working her throat against the bite of the blade.

That cut of Garrik's dark voice brushed her like a damning blow. Ruthlessly pebbling uncontrollable tremors and shivers down her body as his head glided from the darkness into the torch light. The alluring face of Elysian's gray-haired demon, completely covered by Smokeshadows cascading off his shoulders as if a mocking warning from the stars, was so close.

Too close.

Garrik's mouth twisted, brightening the amused hunger in his eyes like a predator who had caught his prey in a game that only he could win. She could smell the scent of vanilla and oak from his lips and the alluring aroma of lemon, rose, and lavender breezing from his hair.

"Maybe I should double your guard. But then again, it would not make for such." He paused, biting his bottom lip. "*Pleasurable* interruptions to my night." Ravenous eyes raked over her pressed against the tree, looking as if he would revel in finishing his kill.

She met his stare, unafraid—unyielding—and with a sharp wince, pushed against the blade; the pinch of the sharpened steel produced a slow trickle of blood down her neck.

"Prick." Her eyes lit with embers.

Garrik breathed a haunting chuckle and leaned in until his lips almost touched hers. "Hiding in the shadows." He paused to let out a low grumble that she could *feel* against her flesh. "Careful. You should know by now that you cannot hide from me. Especially with them watching." Shadows swirled around him in whorls. They cascaded from his shoulders, tendriled down around his torso and arms. They were *made* to belong to him.

Then he stared at her. Not with eyes that promised painful death, but the silver glow glistened in feral excitement as he held the blade there.

He was absolutely sinful to look at.

And she hated herself for admitting it.

Had she truly forgotten what it felt like to have a male so close? To have Death so close and it not wrack her in a panic to run? It was hard to deny, after years of loneliness, years of mistreatment and manipulation, there were days where she entertained thoughts that somewhere, maybe someday, someone would desire her the way she wished.

This isn't desire though ... right? She pushed the thought away. Flirtation at best. How could desire be a blade and darkness mixed with gray hair and silver eyes in an amber glow? He could snap her neck in an instant for disobeying his orders. Instead, he stood with silver eyes glowing and searching hers.

Though she tried not to tremble, the sapphire in her traitorous eyes couldn't fight against it and raked down his body.

She became painfully aware of every breath. Every vein and muscle on his exposed skin. His powerful arms and sharp jawline. How the flickering amber glow of the remaining torches created dancing shadows across the raised ridges of his scars and fell upon the mystifying, V-cut muscles that extended below his waistline. How that muscle in his cheek feathered the more he gritted his teeth when she pushed back against his blade.

Why does he have to look so starsdamned beautiful?

Garrik's lips parted with a slow breath. The side of his mouth curved up into a playful grin. "If you want me, darling." Garrik placed a hand beside her head. The cold of the blade lifted her chin to meet his eyes. "All you need to do is ask."

Her heart jumped at the thought. And from the bloodthirsty desire that crossed his silver eyes, he knew exactly what her mind was warring with.

It had been too long since anyone had looked at her that way.

Why did staring into the face of death and darkness cause a sudden, unrecognizable shock to ripple inside her? She'd never felt *that* with Kaine. Not with anyone. Almost as if his shadows chilled her veins yet set a fire burning from every nerve. Like the two mixed together was a new kind of magic.

She quivered from it, unsure if she should break free from the blade and pull a dagger from his belt or if she wanted to indulge in the *Lord of Darkness* and pull him near.

The Lord of Darkness? his voice groaned, musical and breathy and far too dangerous, infiltrating her in teasing waves. *Be careful how you* think, *clever girl. You might lure a starving beast. Every female needs her own villain, and I promise you, you do not want me as yours.*

She swallowed, lungs stretching to breathe in his threat. Managing the thought, just as breathy as his, *Stay out of my head.* Only, it didn't sound as demanding as she hoped it would be.

Garrik grinned. Flashing sharp canines that she wanted to be devoured by. The very predator she wanted to be at the mercy of.

Alora bit sharply on her bottom lip as her desire stirred.

Garrik tracked the movement with predatory, lethal focus.

To be wanted. Even a little ...

Even if by him ...

Fueled by the sound of her sudden breath, Garrik pressed his own neck against the blade, cutting into his icy skin until streams of crimson pooled with hers.

For a moment, the hardened face of a killer softened, as if he forgot for only a moment who he was. Cold breath whispered, "Forgive me."

She had no time to protest. Admittedly, not that she even would have.

The High Prince's lips brushed against hers, claiming them as his. Alora fell lost to the taste of him, the bite of warm vanilla and oak that coated his lips.

Garrik's ringed hand cupped her cheek, its size large enough that it rested under her jaw, against her trembling neck. Strong fingers weaved through the hair on the back of her head, gripping—pulling—her to him with desperation. His lips moved, molded against hers like they were sculpted for one another.

The kiss was deep—*intoxicating*—almost painful in its longing. Like it would be the very last kiss either of them would have. That they would have all the time in the world to enjoy it and hate it after.

Iron twisted between their necks and fell. Fell with an unnoticeable clang against the forest floor. His icy hand found her other cheek and cupped it, too, pulling her even closer as his kisses' intensity built. There was perfection in his lips, and they demanded her every breath, to which she drunkenly gave.

That must be what the stars themselves felt like in all their glowing magnificence. When mates say they flew on top of the clouds or could get high off just one touch, even a mere thought.

A touch exactly in comparison to his.

If Kaine would have ever even kissed her with even an inkling of what this felt like...

His mouth pulled away, shuddering a breath as if to speak.

But Alora's hand, against her better judgment and control, extended and brushed against the rigid scars on his abdomen. Her body ached for his to push against hers. Ice and fire could never survive together, but the way his chill felt against her burning skin, against her lips, made her realize that she could very much enjoy this type of attention once again.

The press of his hips pinned her to the tree, and she felt him hard as steel against her. That hand on her cheek traced down her jawline, brushing the flesh of her neck and over the curves of her body until he found her thigh.

Garrik groaned against her lips. His hand squeezed there, hungrily pulling her leg to wrap around him as his body trembled with a quick press of his hips.

Alora was a tinder box fit to burst. She curled her fingers in the intensity, nails digging into the scars of his abdomen, edging on the verge of insanity from his kiss, his hips, his touch.

Garrik's body shuddered, falling utterly rigid, and tore away without a word. He stumbled back onto his heel. Dropped her leg from around him. Silver eyes so wide—so primal—the whites even glowed, yielded his alarmed expression.

Releasing her face, black boots then twisted and paced to the side of the tree. With a flex of both hands at his thighs, he lifted the tunic from where he had dropped it.

The High Prince, Lord of Darkness, returned on a smokeless wind.

"Why were you following me?" Fabric tore off his shirt. He reached out to her, offering a silent gesture toward the cut on her neck, now smeared and dried against her fiery skin.

Panting, Alora could only stare, leaning against the oak. The presence of his icy lips still hovered. Still *tasted* his vanilla and oak on her tongue, still felt his fingers through her hair and hands against her cheeks and thigh.

His hand remained extended, waiting, before she accepted the scrap and pressed it tight against the wound.

Coherent thoughts struggled to form even a sentence, wrestling with whatever *that* just was.

"You are going to make me ask twice?" He arched a brow.

Drunk. She felt utterly drunk as she pleaded with her mind to focus. "I ... I don't know." Her voice shook. "You were gone all day. I saw you leaving your tent, armed. I hadn't seen you like that since Telldaira." She rolled her lips in on themselves and rubbed her death mark nervously.

Garrik's face paled for a flash before a wolfish grin climbed up the side of his face. "So, you missed me then?"

"I didn't say that," she snapped.

Garrik chuckled. "I went to see Aiden in Galdheir. Now that I know you cannot live a day without me, I will invite you next time." He pulled a sleeve over his arm, then the other.

She kicked at the loose dirt under the tree to hit him with it.

Dirt bounced off his pants. Garrik amusingly breathed a laugh.

Alora scanned his scars in the torchlight. A small breeze tickled the open sides of his tunic as the flickering glow of the annulus danced over the raised ridges.

He registered her curiosity and his grin straightened. "Go ahead and ask about them. Most want to. They are too damn scared to."

She wondered how many he had allowed to see them? Of what the result was when they did? How many, outside of his legion, still carried breath that dared to call on him about them? How many did he share his past with, if any at all?

But she hesitated, much like everyone else likely did. Did she truly want to know the answer? "Who..." Failing, fumbling over the words. "Who did this to you?"

Garrik's face was unreadable. "The High King." He swallowed hard, and Alora fought off a wave of bile rising in her throat.

His ... father ... did this?

"And a few others. He allowed them to conduct their desires and steal pleasures from me—many years ago." Deep pain flashed in those enchanting eyes. Garrik's face dropped as he gently rubbed down his abdomen, over the display of brutality that expanded past his pant line.

Alora's heart sank into her stomach. Throat constricting until her breaths felt painful at the thought, at how deep the scars went. "Your father—"

"*He was never a father to me,*" Garrik growled. "I was never treated as his son. He is High King, nothing more." Picking up his sword before slamming it so brutally into the sheath that it threatened to cleave through, Garrik released a second growl, and she felt the air thicken in his burning rage.

Why did he do this to you? Alora felt as if she would vomit as the question she wasn't even sure she wanted the answer to surfaced.

"I refused something that he commanded." Garrik stepped closer to her. "So he ordered his ilk to"—he rolled his eyes to the sky before breathing deep—"convince me otherwise."

Alora rubbed her upper arm, relentless tears dropped down her skin. "I'm so sorry." She wanted to reach out, to offer a soothing touch like the one she desperately needed on so many nights with Kaine.

"Don't be. The scars remind me of who I once was. Before I was made into the monster that the stories tell of." Garrik slowly walked away and sat on a fallen tree outside the ring of torches. "You saw some of it at the games, in the alley. You could have seen it in the bar if that pompous asshole would have continued with you and challenged me."

Alora settled beside him. "That's why you won't spar with anyone in camp?" Her tone warm, understanding.

Garrik was silent for a few moments as if scouring the entire realm for the words to say. When he did speak, his voice was caged, almost leery to offer a vital piece of weakness. "When I am fighting, I see ... black. Even in training. Something inside me changes—I cannot control it for long until I am completely lost inside my mind. I will not train with my Dragons. I will hurt, even kill, anyone. I ... cannot stop myself"—Garrik closed his eyes and shook his head—"even if I wanted to."

"You jumped in the ring with me at the games. You weren't afraid of what could happen? Why didn't you just let me fight?"

He sighed. "I have barely seen you fight with a sword and your magic is adolescent at best."

Alora crossed her arms and speared him with an unimpressed glare.

He frustratingly frowned back. A quiet apology. "Most fighters wait months before joining the games. They allow time to train until their skills are perfected. I was." He sighed again. "*Worried* about you falling injured. And against my reasonable judgment, I knew if I could force you to yield quick enough, no one could harm you. *I* would not hurt you."

"You almost ripped them to shreds just to protect me?" Alora's arms loosened around herself.

He was silent before plucking a small white flower growing through the bark. "For that reason, I have never joined the games." With his thumb, he popped the head from its stem. "So I do not rip anyone's head off. Training at night is safe. No one to try and invite themselves to cross my blade." Garrik's voice dropped to something like a whisper as if he never intended to say it out loud. "Plus, it passes the time when nightmares threaten my sleep."

"How often do you have nightmares?"

Silver found the stars again, and she was unsure if he would even answer, but, instead, Garrik's cautioned voice painfully admitted, "Every time I close my eyes." Then silence, all but the night-bugs sang through the forest. "Any more burning questions? Seems I am an open book tonight." He relaxed against the tree behind him and interlaced his fingers behind his head, closing his eyes again.

"Why are you telling me all of this?"

"Perhaps I enjoy the company, for once. No one watching my every move or waiting for an order. No one calling me 'Your Highness' or 'sire.'

Even if I do get called a *bastard* or *prick*." His eyes shifted to her, smirking before they closed once more.

Alora grinned slightly. She really did enjoy calling him those names. But a question lingered like an unquenchable thirst. She'd been wanting to ask him for days. "What are they? Your ... Smokeshadows?"

A chuckle released from his lips as he opened his palm and shadows whirled inside. They blew away, leaving the same white flower, now fully restored, lying inside. He tenderly dawned it onto her lap, Smokeshadows fading on a phantom breeze once it'd settled.

"Darkness and shadows are guardians." Tendrils danced around his fingers. "You should not be afraid of the shadows, but hear me when I say, be mindful of the light. *That* is where real monsters hide."

The flower was in her hand, twirling between her fingers while examining the stem. "And you command them? *All of them?*"

Garrik closed his palm as Smokeshadows diminished inside his fist. "The darkness lives inside me. Makes me cold to the touch—among other things." He leaned back against the tree and rested a hand on his chest. "One day, maybe I will be able to explain it to even myself."

They sat in silence for a while, listening to the creatures of the night, the soft chilling breeze rustling the leaves in the canopy above.

"I am glad you decided to stay, for now. Even if you still do not trust me completely, I hope you do soon." He stood and extended his hand.

Alora observed it, rolling her bottom lip between her teeth but didn't take it.

Garrik's eyes darkened and flickered to the flower still dangling in her hand. He said, "Let's head back to camp. You need sleep," and paused as a baiting smile crossed his face. Alora grabbed his outstretched hand before he countered, "Unless you want to stay and kiss me again?"

She would have scoffed if not for the minor tug from his powerful arms to pull her to her feet. She went tumbling close to his chest, steadying herself against the hardened muscles there.

With cool breath fanning against her cheek so impossibly close, he added, "I take that as a yes."

Alora scowled, slipped from his lax hands, shoved his shoulder to step behind him, and sent a withering glare over her retreating shoulder. "You're *astoundingly* impossible."

Garrik's elated expression lit up the dark forest. His head tilted to the opposite of her path. "Camp is *that* way."

CHAPTER 31

Golden shards of sunlight basked the valley in warm light. Camp teemed with the stirring of wooden carts moving through firesites, horses stomping in the cold dirt, and soldiers' feet prowling the grounds, preparing to move out. Their shouts of orders filled the valley, echoing across the lake. The symphony of sounds indicated the deconstruction of camp, which, luckily enough for her, the Shadow Order was the last to be torn down and the first to be constructed when settled at a new location. And thanks to Jade's loose position, Alora was able to enjoy such luxuries.

She awoke to the luscious smell of pork fat and eggs sieging the canvas. Jade was gone that morning. Either she hadn't attempted to wake Alora, or by some unlikely miracle, allowed her to sleep longer.

But after the events of the night before, Alora happily rested in elated gratitude at the small mercy.

The phantom touch of Garrik's icy kiss against her lips still remained as she brushed her warm finger across, shuddering—smiling—

at the memory as morning light washed away the cool darkness of the night before. To Alora's shock, Garrik hadn't chastised her. There were no words of punishment, no scolding, or the swift slap of a hand. Only a delicate, short goodnight as she'd entered and crawled into a mound of woolen blankets and lush pillows.

It felt like breaking through a water's surface. Coming up for fresh air.

Easing from underneath the blankets and brushing her feet across the soft furs on the floor, Alora noticed something new sat folded on her bedside table, beside her Blazebloom, and illuminated in its dancing starlight glow.

Scaled, perfectly flawless, Dragon armor and a white flower rested on top.

Unlike her training leathers, the thick, night-dark battle leathers were adorned with silver flourishes, metal clasps, and buckles. Black pants sat folded beside it, with leather leg guards and thigh straps for daggers.

She would appear as one of them by midday.

The thought stirred her heart into a jolting panic.

One of them.

'*One of us.*' The High Prince's voice echoed from a few hours before.

Adorned in nothing but a long, crimson night-tunic and underthings, Alora stood, scanning her trunk full of clothing. She wouldn't need to become a soldier of war just yet. Breakfast first, then the colors of the Dragons could cover her.

Legs aching, Alora moved toward the trunk when she glimpsed her reflection in the mirror hanging from a wooden post holding the tent upright.

Alora's eyes widened, stumbling across the tent until she was inches from her reflection.

Her neck...

A fresh, reddened cut in the center.

And a blade hadn't wounded her while training with Thalon.

The bastard.

An icy chill ruthlessly scratched down her spine. As much as she wished to keep last night a distant memory, the evidence remained on her pale skin.

Perfect! A frustrated groan vibrated from her throat as she ran her fingers over the mark. How would she explain this?

Alora knelt at the trunk, throwing the lid open with agitated force to her awaiting garments. Clothing given to her by numerous females in camp when she first arrived, since she had nothing but what she rode in with.

Desperately looking for something that could cover her well enough to deter troublesome conversation, her eyes fell upon a red button-up tunic with a raised collar that rested halfway up the neck. Faded gold stitching on the fabric ran down the two sides of the collar to the abdomen, with longer sleeves that were sheer, exposing her arms and death mark. Not her usual wear for camp, but it would have to do. She didn't have much of a choice.

Alora quickly swapped her night shirt for the tunic and buttoned up the shirt as far as it would go and braided her voluminous hair to that side, leaving wisps hanging out on the other. Semi-covering the lingering mark from the High Prince's challenge last night.

Stars burn me. Alora inhaled a long, deep breath as she shook her head and emerged from the tent, allowing warmth from the sun to sink into her trembling skin.

A scan of the roaring fire revealed Garrik sat in his usual position, relaxed on the dirt beside Thalon, who preferred the stump. Eldacar and Jade sat shoulder to shoulder on the fallen log. None of them wore battle leathers, maybe just as inclined to enjoy one last normal morning as she was.

It had taken her a slightly longer time to reach the fire. Carefully considering how her collar moved against her neck, mindful of the fabric concealing her wound. And when she leaned over to grab her awaiting plate beside Eldacar, his usual timid smile peeked up at her as she filled it with steaming bacon, pan fried potatoes in garlic butter, and perfectly cooked eggs—soft enough in the yolk to dip toast into.

"Good morning." Garrik's voice was quiet as enchanting silver beamed in the morning light, looking up at her.

Alora quietly cleared her throat, trying not to draw attention. Her eyes shifted to everyone around the fire, but meticulously avoided him. "Good morning."

Garrik scooted away from Thalon, providing an opening for Alora to sit between them. Gesturing to her with a nod, Alora reluctantly maneuvered around him and carefully settled down, ensuring to adjust her collar before beginning to eat.

You are trying too hard. Painfully obvious. Relax.

She almost dropped her plate as the High Prince's luring voice invaded her thoughts.

Casually shifting her eyes, Alora unnoticeably turned to him as her cheeks filled with fiery warmth. *Stop.*

Silver traveled to where his blade had been, hidden by silken white hair and the red collar of her tunic. Garrik's devilish side smirk lifted before he met the burning intensity in her sapphire's.

Alora scowled. No, not just a scowl—a death glare—one comparable to Jade on her best day.

"What's up with you two this morning?" Thalon's interrogative voice cut like a knife through the heavy air. His suspicion squinted in their direction, spurring Eldacar and Jade to shift their focus too.

"Nothing," they spoke simultaneously, capturing each other's gazes once more. Garrik's coy and playful. Hers took on a more lethal intent.

"Mhmm. Alright. Nothing." Thalon shoved another bite of food into his mouth. He leaned forward with a tattooed hand gripping his plate and rested it on his knee, golden eyes shifting between them rather skeptically.

"I believe Alora to be nervous about breaking camp." Garrik sarcastically smiled at her.

Alora rolled her eyes. "I believe the mighty prince to be incorrect... I'm fine." Alora took a long drink of coffee.

The High Prince stretched one leg in front of him, keeping his other bent. Placing his empty plate on the ground beside him, he propped his forearm across his knee and leaned back on the other. "I should think that after the woods last night, you would call me Garrik." *Or maybe your* lips *prefer Lord of Darkness?*

Coffee and air entered her lungs as she choked, almost spitting some out. Alora's glare was as sharp as daggers. Searching for razor-edged words as the liquid in her cup began to boil, debating to chuck it at him.

"I think I'll stick with mighty *bastard* instead. Seems to roll right off the tongue."

Garrik's face twisted into a grin as he lifted his own cup, draining it whole, and chuckled. "As you wish, clever girl."

"What happened in the woods last night?" No cheer, no laughing, a tone filled with a sense of unease and confusion. Jade's face rippled with shock as the green in her eyes bounced nervously from Garrik to Alora. Obviously unaware that her charge escaped while she slept.

Alora sat rigid. "*Nothing*," she snapped, glaring at Garrik once more. *Don't.*

He ignored her warning. "It was more than nothing." Looking to the sky, grinning. "I showed her some of my ... skills. She was a fantastic student." He tapped the sword sheathed to his side that dug into the dirt behind him. Which was strange because Garrik never bore his weapons in camp.

266

Alora rubbed the wound slowly in humiliation, feeling her cheeks scarlet again while Garrik's face softened. She almost mistook it for regret but knew better.

Thalon noticed and gestured toward the wound. "If that's the only battle injury you received last night, you're a lucky one. He used to leave my ass pummeled in the dirt or lodged in a tree. Was it absolutely dreadful?" He was *laughing*.

Alora's heart beat faster as she pictured the cold blade to her throat and his calloused hands, those ... incredibly chilling lips. Passionate kisses. The way he pushed against her. Broad shoulders she could be crushed under. And that ... solid chest of muscles. Glistening, silver, enchanting eyes. His hard c—

Garrik cleared his throat, brushing his corded forearm to cover his lap, startling her out of her lustful daydream.

Pacing seemed to be the only option to settle her nerves.

An hour later, the armor still waited, taunting her with the very real fact that once she put it on, she would become one of them.

Her fingertips began to ache.

No longer would she be training in the valley. No longer a mere soldier under instruction within the protection of camp, the familiar mornings, cool breezes that carried the scent of fresh pines would be gone.

Was she ready for this? Ready to leave her new familiar? All along, she wanted nothing more than to leave this place. Though she would've preferred, still, to be leaving on her own. But a new, unsteady feeling covered her bones, wondering if it was excitement as she surveyed the armor.

Until a sharp pain jolted in her heart.

That wasn't excitement. The embers threatening to ignite in her palms were proof enough.

New boots hugged her well over pants that were a perfect fit, even the black undershirt sat on her comfortably. Small growth of muscles that hadn't been so present weeks—even months—before outlined her arms.

Was she ready to put it on? Ready to accept everything it stood for? *Who* it was commanded by? To become *his*?

267

Today was the day she would become one of them.

A Dragon in the High Prince's legion.

The thought brought an understandable flush of nausea.

It was just leathers on a body, nothing more. But the meaning behind it was so much more than she ever imagined. *A Dragon to the High Prince of Elysian.* She'd soon be fighting against the enemies that swore an oath to rid the realm of Marked Ones, allowing nothing in their path to hinder that vow.

She'd soon try to convince others, others just like her, of their purpose and great duty to save the land. Would they take great convincing and tactics like her? Would she have to force them into camp as she was? Could she do that to someone?

Tears lined her eyes. It felt too heavy. The weight on her heart, the aching in her fingers. Her legs trembled as the blood thinned within. Alora settled on the cot with so much to think about. She'd put her trust in so many strangers these weeks. Trained with them, practiced her magic, which was progressing faster than Eldacar imagined. Her sword skills had greatly improved with Thalon's teachings too, though she still had much to learn.

Tapping at the tent entrance drew her attention. With subtle permission, Garrik pulled back the entrance and walked inside. Like the day he rode into Telldaira, his sculpted body was perfectly outlined by his armor, making him appear almost too big to be inside the small tent.

With a petrified expression, Alora's head dropped low to stare at her prickling fingers draped in her lap.

Garrik walked closer to the foot of her cot and started, "When I was a faeling, Magnelis dispatched me to train in the art of weaponry and battle strategy. I was to learn how to kill my enemy, win a battle, mount and control a horse before my feet could settle in stirrups." He knelt down on one knee, picked up the leg guards and dagger straps, and motioned for her leg.

Gently, those calloused hands rubbed down her calf, and she tried not to recall how those hands had held her the night before.

Removing her boot, he slid the straps on with her hesitant nod. "I would escape and run home crying from fear, only to be met by Magnelis's iron hand dragging me to Brennus to cart my ass off once more."

Alora shifted on the cot as his calming icy hands pulled dagger straps up her leg, clasping the buckles on her thigh.

"An inevitable beating to come, my dear mother, without fail, would catch me before I would return. Her tender voice would soothe my young nerves. She told me that our path is not written in stone, but in the ever-changing skies above. And in those skies—"

His hands traveled down to pull on her boots before lacing them tight.

"—the Celestials would move just as they were always destined to. The sun brings hope of a new day. The stars shine in the darkest of nights. And the darkness covers us, protecting us. We need not be afraid of what is before us, as it is already lingering in the skies." Garrik stood and leaned to grab her black upper armor, offering his hand to pull her up.

Next, he guided the scale-like armor onto her arm and toweled it around her torso. Latching three metal clasps and straps near her right shoulder above her chest. A dragon spitting fire, surrounded by matte smoke embellishments, lay engraved above her left breast.

It felt lighter, airy, the gentle breeze streaming through the open entrance of the tent licked at her warmed skin.

"She told me"—his hands fastened straps on her upper arms—"your path ahead is not a matter of chance. It is choice. And yours alone. The sun and stars will find you along the way, just as they were always meant to." Garrik finished with her gear and pulled daggers from his own belt, placing them in her thigh straps. He leaned, reached around her, grabbed her obsidian dagger from the cot, and sheathed it at her side.

"I know you are scared of what lies ahead. I know it is hard to trust me. You have chosen to stay and become one of us until you deem that time as concluded. Ever since that moment, Maker of the Skies aligned with you. Fear not the path ahead, for you are not alone. The sun brings you a new day, and He and His stars are with you on your worst. And if by Destiny, the stars fail you, shadow will follow. *I* will follow. Even in the end of days, you will never be truly alone, Alora. You are safe. You are protected."

But I am afraid. Alora dropped her chin, knowing he could hear her.

The High Prince shifted his weight. He gently lifted her chin to meet her worried sapphires with reassurance. "Fear is in here." Garrik tapped on the dragon over her heart. "No one can make you feel fear. Danger is real, but fear is a choice. Never trust it. Do not let it consume you. It does not know your incredible strength. Feel it. Every part of it. Then let it push you to your greatest victory over yourself and above all else."

Alora's troubled heart calmed listening to his quiet voice so full of certainty and belief. In her.

With a soft brush of his hand, shadows stirred in his palms in a gentle movement toward her head. A budding pearlsea flower shadowed between his fingers before he brushed her hair back and steadied it on her ear. Garrik traced his ringed hand to the soft spot between her neck and shoulder, thumb brushing against the cut on her neck.

"I am sorry for what this and my kiss caused you today. This was not your doing, but my selfishness alone."

Alora's breath stopped at his touch. At his words.

"I should not have taunted you about this. I am sorry. It will *not* happen again." The taunt or the kiss? Garrik examined the mark, softly brushing it once more before looking down at her evaded eyes.

Her warm skin prickled with a chill at his touch. *Strange.* Her training armor overheated within minutes of simply putting it on. But this ...

Garrik noticed her confusion. "I had one of our armor smith's and Eliya's ice powers craft yours specially. It should allow you cooler comfort against your skin but still protect you the same. There is only one thing missing."

With swirling shadows, a crimson cloak appeared in hand.

Garrik draped the fabric around her neck as he had done once before. He pulled the silver dragon clasp to the left of her neck—where it sat on each of his Dragon's—and tightened the straps before trailing his hand across the fabric under her collarbones.

A *red* cloak.

Not black, worn by his entire Dragon's Legion.

Red.

The color respected and adorned only by those in his trusted Shadow Order.

Through the glow of the sun's rays on the canvas, the High Prince's brightened, and silver eyes stared into her glistening sapphires. Then his voice, like an ethereal melody once longed to hear but forgotten by time, drifted around them. A language she never spoke, but so simple and beautiful and something incredibly ancient in his voice.

Alora's eyes burned, threatening to burst at the emotions surfacing.

Like a sacred blessing. He spoke. In alluring swirls of his tongue, bending the air around them, the inflections of every word raw and damning and consuming but every part cocooned with demanding hope and overpowering conviction.

The words trickled like a sweet mountain stream. Like a morning song, calling the sun to rise. Something of protection and power and grace.

Something lethal.

An oath. A promise.

Mine. Maybe she imagined it. *You. Are. Mine.*

She allowed the words to flutter over her. Simply basking in his incredible voice, in his presence, until Garrik squeezed her shoulders and brushed the chill of his hands down her arms and stepped away.

The words stopped. She desperately wished for them to continue as her heart thundered. And by the stars, gratitude swelled inside her chest as his warm voice returned.

"Are you ready, Ara darling?"

CHAPTER 32

There were nine successful rescues of Mystics on their way north. Welcoming in a total of seventeen to their growing forces in the past two months.

Along with the arrival of new Mystics, reports arrived frequently to the Shadow Order in forms of missives carried and delivered by Thalon after he would return in his impressive swirl of thunderstorms and lightning. On each arrival, his shining smile beamed as he strutted into camp with news from other allied courts and kingdoms; their numbers were growing strong and preparing for the inevitable battle to come.

Jade, Alora decided as she walked to the arena walls, had diluted her prickly personality some. Slowly softening that permanent scowl and occasionally allowing them to have a moment of strained yet endurable conversation—other than the usual snide comments. Not often, but it was enough that waking up in the morning wasn't met with harsh threats or burning glares every moment their eyes clashed.

In fact, as Alora walked across the open field teeming with soldiers sparring outside camp, Jade may have unsuccessfully attempted to hide a twitch at the corner of her mouth when she saw Alora walking her way.

Or perhaps it was due to the awaiting death trap below the arena walls.

With the wind behind her disturbing loose strands of white hair that had fallen from her crown of braids, Alora glanced down into a training

...

Coliseum.

Before he and Thalon dawned from camp, Garrik had effortlessly delivered Jade's vision in a storm of Smokeshadows early that morning. The walls of the training arena opened to a long, spiraling stairway into the depths of what surely would be a new form of torture. Jade its curator.

Unlike rumors of such structures used for entertainment, Jade had more useful purposes. And when her voice quieted to whispers with the High Prince, when Garrik's face twisted into something clever and pleased and somewhat wicked, he simply patted Jade between her shoulder blades, and with the flick of his wrist, constructed a pit of *doom.*

A collection of stone structures, obstacles, trapdoors, and tunnels expanded across a surface so vast it could've been the foundation of a castle laid to ruin.

Intended for a ruthless day of training to the testament of skills and abilities not even a Raven could withstand, mock battles would be performed at Jade's every whim until perfected and instilled for the unthinkable in war. And much to Alora's reprehension, Jade's battalion would be the first to test the trials below. More than three hundred females were soon to be striking blades and bursting with magic, the only all-female battalion in the camp—to which Jade honorably led.

Alora bit back her pride and admitted to finding some pleasure in being a part of it. Of the strength it took to train and earn her place.

The males could train with brawn and brutish strength. Females with quite more of a ... bloodthirsty grace.

Jade crossed her arms, scanning the multitude below. Searching for weakness, her green side-eye glanced at her when Smokeshadows whorled near the edge of camp and neither one of them could contain the slight smiles growing on their faces.

The tendrils began misting away. But something like disappointment flashed across Jade's face the instant two High Fae males and a female with massive, leathery white wings stepped from the storm.

Then Jade turned to Alora, who stiffened, frowning. "Every time they dawn home, I expect to see him returning with them."

Alora knew exactly who she meant. That guilt always returning upon each arrival.

Gently, she dared to bump her shoulder against Jade's, attempting to turn that heavy, uncomfortable burst of emotion away from what viciously scratched Jade's mind. But when Jade said nothing, Alora countered. "Are you going with the High Prince to see Aiden next time?"

Jade chewed on the inside of her cheek. "The last time I visited, he couldn't open his eyes... I can't see him like that."

That was a month ago.

There had been complications by Ozrin's reports. He had permanently set up in a small but well-equipped and comfortable lodging in the city to care for Aiden. Garrik would dawn there a few times a week to check on his healing, rotate soldiers, and tend to any necessities Ozrin would require. Only bringing Ozrin back to camp if an injury needed tended to.

Aiden was progressing well for some time, but the long effects of gamroara poison were tricky. His improvements were stable some days and tumultuous others. If Aiden had been full High Fae, his recovery would've been much easier, quicker. Though Ozrin remained firm and hopeful Aiden would return. It was just a matter of when.

Gesturing with a nod to Jade's sword, Alora asked, "Want to spar?" Hoping it would distract Jade from Garrik and Thalon conversing with the female they brought into camp, closing the distance between them.

For a moment, Jade considered it. As in those green eyes that had dulled, a gleam of gratefulness flashed back. But niceties were never in Jade's temperament. Alora knew better than to hope for anything more. Jade blinked, and that softening appreciation melted into taut lips and a harsh line between her eyebrows.

"You've wasted enough time watching today. Get your ass down in the pit." But where Alora expected the graveled fire to spit from her voice, there was something less than expected. More casual than demanding, almost a suggestion, not a command.

Alora smiled and didn't care if Jade saw it.

That smile quickly faded when her eyes once again met the stairs, and her legs began to tremble. Trembling because not twenty feet down, it wasn't only wooden boards that waited for her ... but that death she often pictured behind mahogany eyes and ebony hair.

Coward. Kaine's illusion snickered, his lips just as evil as she remembered them.

Darkness swirled in her vision as he began climbing those stairs. Each step, her heart pounded in unison, hearing the thumps of his boots.

And she knew she couldn't take that step, knowing too soon the wooden boards would morph into marble, knowing the pit's floor would soon be redwood instead of dirt. That the splattering of the other warrior's blood across the ground would become piles of red petals.

Alora slammed her hand down on the handrail, catching her balance when it began to sway.

Coward. Kaine spit again, drawing closer to the top, and she began to see the manor. Began to feel his hands on her back, ready to push her down and down and—

"Hey, clever girl."

The calming cold of an icy palm clasped around the top of her hand. She almost burst into tears, the darkness clouding her eyes. Taking a step back, she hadn't realized how close Garrik was until she bumped into his body, a solid wall of stone.

It steadied her at the very least.

She thought she heard him curse, but when she turned to meet his gaze, there was a flash of concern in his eyes. "Have you eaten today?" His eyebrows crunched, and she felt his hand on her upper arm, then the other lifted, grasping her near buckling body from collapsing.

Had she been that unsteady that he thought her weakened by a lack of food?

"No, I—" Alora swallowed, blinking away the vision of Kaine waiting on the coliseum stairs. "I'm ... hot." It wasn't entirely a lie.

Garrik smirked, moving to speak, but she snapped, *"Don't."*

Her attention focused to the new female standing beside Thalon, ignoring the gentle caress against her mind. Ignoring Garrik silently asking to allow him inside to speak.

"I'm Alora. It's a pleasure to meet you."

Before her eyes, the female who arrived in nothing but a long, white robe, tilted her head as if in critical examination. Before their eyes, the female's skin rippled—rippled like Garrik's when he transformed into the face of the Savage Prince so long ago. The female's tall body shrunk, wings vanishing, and short onyx hair lengthened and lightened into luscious white braids, twisting into a crown on her head.

And where lavender eyes had been, now gleamed a hue of sapphire. And on her body, now rested battle-black Dragon's training armor.

Alora was speechless, almost breathless, scanning the female.

Scanning ... *herself.*

Thalon stepped forward with captivated eyes. "Isleen is a shapeshifter."

"I gathered that." Still scanning, still marveling. And as if in

275

emphasis, the perfect likeness of Alora quickly shifted into a near-perfect likeness of Thalon.

Isleen's form rippled again, back into her true form before she outstretched a hand. "It's a pleasure to be here. Our High Prince told me much about you." Lavender eyes flickered to Jade as well.

Turning to her, Alora noticed Garrik's slow rake across her training leathers—tight against her legs and ass —and up her body, appearing uncomfortable before he addressed her. "Escort Isleen to Deimon's company, and then you and Jade report to the war tent."

But Jade was speaking with Thalon, who bounced like a faeling playing in mud to the edge of the pit. Entirely vibrating with anticipation when Jade pushed his chiseled side and snorted when he almost fell over the edge.

"Gonna get your old ass down there and spar with me?"

Thalon barked a laugh. "*Old ass?* I'm only sixteen years older than you, *sis.*"

"Then prove it, *Grandsire,*" she taunted back.

Garrik's smile lifted as a High Prince would, and Alora couldn't stop herself from wondering just how high that smile could go if he weren't in the company of a recruit.

Then Thalon whipped his head to Garrik, forgetting entirely their company and forsaking proper formalities to a High Prince. "You going to get your ass down there, too?"

Breathing a laugh, Garrik insisted, "I am far too old for that," and smiled again, this time a little higher.

"*Unleash Michael!* You're only a decade younger than me! Now who's the grandsire?"

"Still you." Jade stood with crossed arms and winked, reminiscent of Aiden's and just as taunting.

Thalon twisted back to her before murmuring something, and they both sprinted over the edge onto the staircase, disappearing below.

The sound of rushed footsteps crunched the drying grass of the meadow behind them before an urgent voice called out, "Your Highness!" Deimon, an amber-eyed faerie with night-dark feathered wings called, "A raven flew in this morning," and held out his tanned hand, presenting rolled parchment, sealed by a fading fox insignia Alora didn't recognize.

Garrik's expression fell to a neutral, princely disposition before he opened it.

Shouts of frustration and pleased snickers resounded from the depths, covering the silence of the High Prince and the cold expression now hardening his face. And perhaps she was mistaken, but for a moment, she glanced at a sheen of sweat forming on Garrik's brow before he rolled it up and transferred it inside his armor.

"Deimon, this is Isleen." Garrik gestured to the faerie whose lavender eyes were widened, staring into the pit Jade and Thalon sprinted down.

Upon hearing her name, she turned and offered a sharp nod, flickering her attention between Garrik and Deimon.

He continued, "She is to join the Wingborne and report to Alora once settled."

Wary eyes flickered to Alora.

Alora recognized that look because she herself had carried it her first weeks in camp. So, she stepped forward and quieted her voice to something soothing. "Deimon is one of the best here. You're in trustworthy hands." She gestured to the coliseum, still bound by punishment, and explained, "Once Jade is finished below, I'll come help you settle in. Shouldn't be long."

Her smile seemed to do it. Isleen nodded and turned away, exchanging quick greetings before wandering toward camp. Leaving them alone.

Terribly alone.

On the edge of a damning pit, shoulder to shoulder with the High Prince and his alluring scent of metal and leather dancing on the northern breeze.

She didn't know how long had passed. Didn't know much else other than the slow quickening of her heart when she heard Garrik's breathing become slightly uneven.

"Is everything okay in Galdheir?"

"Want to go down with me?"

Their voices combined.

Garrik ran his hand down the back of his neck as Alora cleared her throat, adjusting her balance. She rarely saw him so undone.

Rolling her lips between her teeth, she'd forgotten what she asked, peering into the darkness now bursting with explosions of glowing magic. One scan of the hundreds of spiraling steps and felt her blood iced over—

"We can dawn down. I am too tired to walk," Garrik imparted as Smokeshadows began tendriling from his shoulders, and she turned to meet his glowing silver irises, forgetting the lightning in her veins the moment they speared into hers. Forgetting everything but him.

Crossing her arms, Alora pursed her lips and glared through critical, slitted eyes. "I thought you didn't train with anyone?"

He smirked and stepped closer, his back to the pit's edge mere feet away.

Alora dared to remain, stiffening her back to raise her chin to him.

Garrik closed the distance. "No, but I would not mind chasing you," he teased, stepping so close she couldn't help but survey the movement of his chest and curse the thrum of her now boiling blood.

This time, Alora drew closer, brushing her hand to his chest in a slow, daunting trace upward.

Garrik stiffened, appearing to falter in breaths under a tremble from her touch. Then his hand twitched, and a tendril of Smokeshadows whirled around her hand, responding to her but quickly misting away.

The shadowy touch was like velvet. Like the gentle caress of Garrik's hands.

Thrilling.

Dangerous.

Alora stepped, forcing Garrik to step backward. His gaze was as piercing as a sharpened blade.

She stepped again.

He did too. Boots connecting with the edge, crumbling dirt down into the pit.

A devilish smirk grew up his face when he glanced over his shoulder.

Alora stretched up onto her toes, leaning into him. "Then I guess I better start running," she whispered and pushed him over the edge.

A CIRCULAR TABLE stood in the center of the war tent. Twelve generals sat, discussing their next route as the High Prince leaned back in his chair between them.

Shadows swirled around his hands, around the parchment that Deimon had delivered before the discussions. Parchment that wild tendrils of smoke appeared tempted to eviscerate.

Garrik reclined in his chair, eyes slowly scanning the ink again before finally misting it away in a cloud of smoke and shadow. He stiffened in his seat, steepling fingertips in front of his face while dulled muddy-gray orbs burned into the maps strewn across the table.

In the back of the tent, against the canvas and away from the table, the growing heat of her skin made Alora's cheeks flush. She sat tentatively listening to the elevated voices of the generals and Shadow Order. Discussing and planning a route to Alynthia, a guarded town of the richest sweet water and lush forests. Almost a paradise. Protected—hidden—by treacherous trails in the mountain and avenged by a beast that lurked within its shadows, Alynthia was a town of myth, merely rumored by a small etching on the maps of its existence.

No faerie outside the mountain could—with any certainty—prove it existed.

And the Dragons would be marching to it in a few days' time.

The plan, always the same. Garrik and Thalon would extract the target while the army camped ten miles south.

Along with ongoing orders of training new Mystics, both with weaponry and powers, Alora herself had grown stronger in the two months on the road. Every stop for the evening was filled with sparring sessions with not only Thalon but Jade, too. Her temper made for great practice. Alora had even eventually perfected skills that outwitted Thalon during one stormy training session, which brought him to his knees in the mud.

She was growing stronger.

Faster.

Her magic more controlled with each passing week.

Alora rubbed her death mark under training leathers and her mouth curved into a smile at the strength she could feel. It had been quite some time since she thought of herself as strong.

She had been Alora, child of Nadeleine and a beloved father whose name had never been spoken to her. Alora the orphaned faeling in the markets of Telldaira. Alora, the young, beautiful female, working and singing in a tavern just to stay alive.

Alora the betrothed of Lord Kaine Dralkin, Lord of Telldaira. Only that title still remained—*betrothed*.

The word threatened to ignite embers in her palms.

Betrothed.

Still owned by him. Still haunted by him. Still *his*.

Her palm tightened until it trembled, feeling power, feeling the strength in her grasp.

She couldn't remember a time when she looked this way—*felt* this way. Kaine would never have approved. He preserved his females in a state of destitution and submission, wearing ornate gowns and pseudo smiles only when it suited his pristine image of trickery. A pretty ornament for his mantel, shining and quiet, a trophy to be admired, his great victory of wealth, status, and power.

There was a time she went running once. Feeling her body grow tired day by day from lack of movement. The stones of the street had crunched beneath her boots as fresh morning air whipped her face, and her ankles had ached at the unfamiliar impact. If she hadn't been so malnourished, perhaps she could've run farther, maybe never to return at all. But when she arrived home with a painful ache in her side and half breathless, Kaine had taught her why she would never go running again.

Can't have one's punching bag able to punch back.

Blackened abyss met her eyes covered by daydreams. Alora hadn't realized her face had twisted at the memory. She loosened her mouth into a half-hearted grin.

Just another thing you can kill him for. Garrik's voice brushed away the remaining poison left behind by Kaine. He leaned back in his chair and crossed his arms, face turned up in a snarl.

Shouldn't you be more focused on them than what I'm thinking? Alora rolled her eyes.

You are far more interesting. Next time, try not to feel yourself up in my presence and I will not desire to know what you are thinking.

I wasn't feel— Her eyes forced a glare capable of burning a hole through him. White embers heated her palm. Alora subtly lifted a middle finger in his direction, the tip dancing with a controlled flame. *I hate you.*

He quietly chuckled. *I know.*

"Perhaps we should leave these Mystics be. Alynthia is protected by the mountain. There is no simple way around it. Many a traveler has been assumed to have disappeared once they entered the trails. Not even Magnelis or Ravens have been able to cross the wards. The forest is said to be protected by powers far older than Zyllyryon itself. The legends say—"

"The legends are shit," Jade interrupted the female faerie—Deiyanira, one of the generals. "Made-up stories from cowards who can't even fill their own bath water." Slumping back in her chair, Jade draped both legs over the armrest and picked dirt from beneath her nails with a dagger. "If you believe this shit, then stay behind. The rest of us won't cower on trembling knees."

A low growl escaped the High Prince's mouth that had Jade nervously clutching her melted coin and bone necklace.

Alora breathed an inaudible laugh as she shook her head for Jade to see. *Always so cocky.*

Jade shot a look that translated to Alora being doomed for a brutal training session in the evening hours. Either that or she would be humbled by carrying back whatever downed prey they would hunt later.

The hum of the generals drummed on in a steady cadence. Old tales of deathly creatures devouring small children who found themselves wandering the forests beyond, to myths and legends of river wraiths who lured unfaithful husbands to their doom in its waters.

One thing was certain, the legion would be moving into those mountains in a few days' time—regardless of what lay ahead.

With a cock of his brow, Garrik pressed, *What? You would not agree?*

Alora leaned forward, elbows resting on her knees. *Legends are legends for a reason. We'd be fools to ignore them.* She peered up through her eyelashes at him, face taut with silent warning. A small flame sparked on the tip of her finger. Her eyes glistened, watching it slowly dance until it bounced across each finger and faded away within her palm.

Are we boring you?

The tip of her boot twisted in the dirt. *I think there's a better way to do this.*

Oh? Garrik titled his head. Amusement flickered in his eyes.

Can't you and Thalon dawn inside?

Not with the wards. Unless they are down, even my magic cannot penetrate them.

Alora frowned. *You've been looking at these maps for weeks. Besides the obvious fact that no one is certain if Alynthia exists—*

Garrik crossed his arms.

—besides you, mighty prince, she sarcastically jabbed, *the obvious route is straight up the mountain to the main gate. No turns, no blockades. Legend or not, if you're trying to seem easy to reach, somewhere that you don't want anyone to get to, that is where I'd place an attack. Make intruders drop their guard, attack when they're unsuspecting.*

Garrik grinned, a cunning expression crossed his features. *What route would you take, then?* Smokeshadows tendriled across the maps, outlining each trail seen and unseen.

I'm not one of your generals. She sank back in her chair and placed her palms under her thighs.

Humor me.

Alora nervously bit at her bottom lip.

You are going to make me beg? And when she didn't oblige him, he implored with an amused plea, *Please?*

Garrik begging was ...

She warred of the sudden ripple of pleasure in her blood. Deciding whether to remain silent or indulge the Lord of Darkness's curiosity, Alora pushed forward on her chair and looked across to the table.

With the map a distant view in front of her, she squinted, determining her position in the back of the tent as impossible to scan the routes from. But her vision began to shift and instead of glancing from across the room, she now appeared to be looking down over the maps, picturing herself as if she were staring into a mirrored reflection.

It was Garrik's eyes she was staring through. Projecting the images into her mind.

And for a moment, she couldn't help but survey herself.

The near-perfect radiance of her wavy, white hair that created an aura around her entire body. How her eyes irradiated with a captivating sapphire glow. Filled cheeks and muscles that were hugged by battle-black armor that she could *feel* a strange, desiring need to strip away and touch perfect porcelain skin.

And not just her physical body ... but Alora could sense something vital—something consuming and awestruck and mesmerizing at the mere thought of her voice. At the mere thought of the smile that crept up her face.

In every reflection she'd seen, she hadn't looked quite like ... like *this*.

Was this how *everyone* saw her?

Was this how *he* saw her?

Alora scanned the room from his position. Everyone else looked ... so muted. Jade's fiery hair lacked its intensity, Thalon's Earned lost their shine. Even the room was cast in a darkness she hadn't seen in her own vision.

Ignoring those strange feelings, Alora blinked, realizing that Garrik had too with a nervous inhale. There would be time to decipher what it meant later.

Their eyes scanned over the routes together, like she was controlling his movements. Carefully following the Smokeshadow trails that cleaved unmarked paths through the mountain and followed ones routed in ink. Over streams of rich sweet water, down lush valleys, over rockscapes, and trees taller than the forests of Telldaira.

And hidden within the mountain, mere miles from the vibrant town on the map, a small cave system that unveiled entrances to both sides of the mountain. To a place she doubted sunlight had ever touched or boots had ever exited once entering—if the stories were to be believed.

The legend's lair.

Their eyes burned into the caves and swirls of darkness there.

Interesting. Garrik lifted his head, eyes scanning the map with a devilish grin as her eyesight returned to her own view. *You would go to the beast in the mountain?*

If you're trying to keep someone out, what better place to make your entrance? Make it appear as the last place you'd go.

You are not afraid of what lies within the darkness?

I've lived my entire life in darkness. It doesn't scare me anymore.

Garrik pushed his chair back, the legs scraping against the dirt drawing the room's attention. *Then it is settled.*

To Alora's horror and rapidly blushing cheeks, he stood, silver irises locked onto hers before he spoke.

"We go through the caves."

CHAPTER 33

The thought of entering Alynthia, and even the surrounding mountains, was cocooned with a heavy pressure of unease, making Alora's fingers ache as they rode north.

To make matters worse, the shifting eyes of the generals and Jade added to an uneasy fact. That in a few days, they would execute a route conjured by someone below their honored and ruthlessly earned ranks.

Alora. The High Prince sought strategy from *her* over his trusted council.

And when he revealed that small detail, the tent had erupted in bursts of protest from not a few, but almost all. Thalon had been a steady rock, beaming ear to ear in whatever amusing notion of heroic scenarios he pictured at the thought of entering the caves. His ecstatic smile forced the edges of her mouth to twist up before his palm had patted her shoulder in pride. And before he exited the tent, he was sure to show Alora precisely where on his arm he'd ink whatever beast they might encounter.

Apparently, those markings inlaid in grave detail were all the horrific monsters he'd slain. Like trophies, the mere mention of new ink had him vibrating out into the sunlight.

There was no gamroara though, she'd noted. And when questioned about it, Thalon had simply explained that it wasn't him that had felled the beast. That honor, if Garrik would ever allow him to mark his skin, belonged to the High Prince. And Thalon was convinced that Garrik would collect ink one day. He just needed a little more convincing.

Two. That made two who approved.

The churning in her gut didn't pair well with Storm's steps across the loose dirt and stones when they moved out the next morning. She had little training in battle strategy from the few nights of schooling by Thalon and short, restless lessons from Garrik. And now the Dragons would follow a path routed by her, a common Mystic compared to the rest. Almost an outsider by the years of trust that bonded many of the others.

A Mystic that hadn't accompanied any extractions as of yet.

She hadn't been ready to—not yet. Though the High Prince had given her a choice, declining to persuade faeries to fight had been easy. Her experience hadn't been of her own choice, and she wasn't sure she could be the one to convince another to potentially give their life to a cause she hadn't joined willingly. And she'd certainly never put herself in a position that might force someone from their home ... even if saving their life.

Alora shifted in the saddle uncomfortably, clenching the reins.

To that point, her own situation was an incident that required a rescue. Luckily, the multitude of the High King's Ravens were sent east. Sometimes she wondered if she could see smoke cascading into the sky from burned towns in their wake. Just like Telldaira. Just like countless others before.

The only threat they displayed in their travels was the High Prince arriving at the city gates, under the cover of those terrifying stories foretold of the ruthless gray-haired demon of Elysian. An illusion. And despite the nerves threatening to unsettle her, she knew it had to be done. Garrik had no other option. He had to play the part.

Even when the legion crossed through towns with no path around, they all had to appear just as unyielding as their commander. If anyone outside the legion learned of their treason, Magnelis would unleash his wrath upon their shield's border.

No one could be trusted.

So that's who they were forced to be.

Murderers conducting the evil biddings of the High King.

It had been a long, harrowing day, sitting in a saddle, treading a rocky trail that offered breathtaking views and colors that Alora never knew existed. Most of the world she'd seen was Telldaira, full of crippling stone homes outside of her gated community, small shops, the grungy tavern she worked in. The bustling market where city folk gathered supplies of fresh produce, newly crafted attire, furniture, and jewelry that was far too expensive for most of the common folk.

But this world, this ... *this* was extraordinary.

Vast, steep mountain ranges cascaded in colors of rich navy blues, purples that would make a simple lavender bush jealous, and ashen rockscapes that spanned the entire length of the horizon. Many peaks were so high, they disappeared into the clouds completely. Lakes and rivers peacefully rested below with the most unbelievably clear teal water safely harboring marine life and plants easily seen in their depths.

Forests of vibrant colors surrounded the trail, swallowing them with the peaceful songs of winged creatures and lurking beasts. Waterfalls of magnificent power and strength called to them as they passed by. Skies so beautiful it seemed as if they were painted by Maker of the Skies Himself.

But amongst the beauty, an ugliness had formed in a shroud of battle-black armor and scowling faces.

Beside her, Alora side-eyed the grumblings of two males. One in particular had been shouting inside the war tent the day before.

That same glower cursed his face now, making the black horns spiraling from his red hair look ever more so devilish. And it didn't help that his skin was set in a crimson glow.

Haiden, General of the Bloodbane, murmured something to a male wolf shifter she recognized as one of Garrik's commanders. Draven, was it?

They must have noticed her evaluation because Haiden stiffened and dismissed the male, who, in turn, gave Alora a wink and a cocky nod, before he strode forward and collected himself by the High Prince's side.

But Haiden, *The Destroyer,* as she'd heard him coined, never lifted his blazing sunset eyes from her.

That was *enough.*

Alora turned to him fully, embers lighting in her eyes as her threat poisoned the air. "You wield your sword well, Haiden. Perhaps you should refine your tongue as diligently. If you have something to say—"

"I wish I could return the compliment," was all he snapped back, stiffening his back and tightening the reins in his hands as if he were the High Prince himself.

Alora scoffed as soldiers around them started turning their heads.

The usual low murmur that rolled through the throng of Dragons was forsaken to shift their attention between them.

Haiden continued, "You doom this entire army by your lack of discipline and ignorance of powers you shouldn't own. Almost getting yourself and others killed. And you have the *nerve* to believe *you*"—a dark laugh—"can advise in the war tent."

There it was.

She never wanted the attention. Never wanted to sit at the High Prince's war table or to even be considered in discussions she had no business being in. All she ever wanted was freedom. But now that Haiden had finally dared to speak directly to her, attempting to use his voice as a boot to wrench her further into the ground, she started to feel rather attached to the idea that her voice belonged at the High Prince's table.

"If I needed a lecture, I would approach the High Prince, not the one who failed him in council." Her words heated Haiden's face, so she pressed the dagger disguised as her tongue further. "Are you *questioning* your High Prince?" Alora glanced around at their growing spectators. "Among his soldiers, you deny his leadership? I don't think he'd take too kindly to being *doubted* in such a way."

A noticeable growl later, Haiden's face brightened to an even lovelier shade of dark crimson. Clearly, 'The *destroyer*' was only skilled with weapons and not at keeping his wits when insulted.

"That's what I thought," Alora sneered, pride budding as she raised her head and leaned back in her saddle.

The others around them murmured in shocked whispers.

Haiden kicked his horse, and the poor thing startled, disturbing loose stones and dusting the dirt as he drove forward. His tight expression formed an embarrassing amount of rage on his lips as he knocked his horse into Storm and spoke so only she could hear. "The only reason you're still alive is because our High Prince humiliated himself and took the lashings you deserved. Nothing is more pathetic than a coward letting another take their blame, and if I were the High Prince—"

"*What a shame.*"

It was as if a mountain had exploded.

A ruthless, lethal growl devastated the air, thickening it, almost as if soundless destruction had leveled a city and its dust constricted their lungs.

Alora hadn't realized that Storm had simply stopped moving.

Everyone's horses stopped moving.

The magnitude of the force was so immense that it couldn't even be fully observed from a cliff. An entire army, at an effortless, silent command, didn't dare to move.

Ghost inched forward in a graceful, slow movement, almost menacing in the sheer magnificence of it. Her head dropped low, ears back, while the face of the Savage Prince rippled until his skin stretched. Revealing bones that seemed to be carved from marble and teeth as sharp as his unavailing sword.

Almost like a dragon passing for a faerie, ravenous hunger flickered in Garrik's gaze. A promise of endless torment in the afterlife. "We were all getting along so civilly." The beast underneath his skin rippled again, clawing to break free as he cocked his head with an animalistic perfection, and Alora wondered if he could truly transform into something ... *more*.

"Your Highness." Haiden trembled.

Behind Garrik, Thalon beamed in elation, every mark of ink glistening in the sunlight with his arms crossed. An eager smirk settled on his face. And she must have been dreaming it, but Jade's disposition mirrored his all the same.

"Tell me who the High Prince is, *general*?" Garrik mused with a hint of toying barbarity in his tone.

The general took on the very picture he deemed as *pathetic*, and Alora stifled the amusement boiling in her chest. He cowered, dropped his head low, and said nothing.

"I did not realize that the decisions of your sovereign had ailed you so. Perhaps I can remedy that. If you wish to lead the army..." Through Garrik's locks, an obsidian spiked crown manifested as if it were plucked from the air, reflecting the sunlight as he pulled it from his head, hovering it in the air by shadow. "Here is my crown."

The challenge set.

But Haiden still didn't dare move. Didn't dare speak. His eyes cast down to the dirt below the closest soldier's feet, and even his lids refrained from fluttering.

Alora didn't blame him. If she were the subject at the High Prince's bidding, she would have sunken too.

"No?" Garrik hummed. A coy twist of his lips, much like a cat playing with vermin, contorted his face. "I suggest you hold your tongue and remember that not so long ago, you were not welcome in my war tent. Or have you forgotten so easily?"

Still. Silence.

"*I cannot hear you.*" That toying calm shattered against Garrik's razor-tipped teeth.

At last, Haiden wisely said, "No, Your Highness."

The obsidian crown returned to Garrik's head. He raked his eyes over Alora, that ravenous hunger razed into something like primal need when she lifted her chin and met his. Entirely unafraid of the beast who stared back at her.

Alora imagined the event was over now—hoped for it—as every eye turned to her, the subject causing their High Prince's scolding.

But Garrik's attention flickered back to his general before he offered another threat in one simple, cold word. "*Beg.*"

Every soldier, in one towering wave, *flinched* at the word. At the cold death emanating from it.

Haiden's complexion couldn't deteriorate any greyer; a disgusting comparison to the phlegm those in Outcastle Alley coughed up in the deadest of winter. "Sire?"

Garrik said nothing. His eyes only darkened more, void of all light.

It was enough to have a sheen of sweat collect on the general's forehead as he turned to Alora. "Forgive me." The apology was nothing sincere—vindictive at best.

The fool.

Hardly anyone moved as Smokeshadows haunted the dirt, weaving between horse's legs, and spiraling around Haiden's until they brutally squeezed and squeezed and squeezed.

Haiden surged forward in the saddle, tearing his fingers into the relentless shadows. He tried fleeing from his mount, but Garrik's endless —bloodthirsty—power imprisoned him there.

Until he screamed, "Your Highness, *please.* I'm begging you—"

"*Are you?*" Garrik snarled. His voice *nothing* of this world. Like *Darkness himself* transcended the bounds of realms, the Celestial sovereign ruler of night emerging. "If you were truly begging, then you would be on your knees."

Smokeshadows ripped the general from his mount, slamming him into the dirt in a burst of dust and darkness. Wisps of smoke settled on Haiden's horse at the same time, a soothing hand that calmed it as its rider was dragged off. Tendrils shackled his wrists, forcing his hands to the ground until his back bent, head wrenched backward until he stared up at Alora.

She couldn't decide if the fire in her nerves was complete satisfaction or from humiliation. Stopping an army ... for *this*? For *her*? Over something as mundane as spoken word—

Haiden choked on his breath, a worthless heap on the ground, when his lips finally opened, eyes tightly shut, and groveled, "I'm sorry! I spoke out of turn. I shouldn't have questioned you, Alora."

"*And?*" A thrum of something all-ending—something powerful—laid inside that voice. Its viciousness trembled the earth until she felt certain Garrik would cleave the ground open and send Haiden to Firekeeper.

"For calling you pathetic ... a coward," he wailed, wrists lightening to a shade of pink as the cruel hold of Garrik's Smokeshadows denied them circulation.

Lowering his head, a flicker of his power swept over the crowd. A reminder of who he was—of what he could do on a whim.

Garrik's voice rumbled as he said to them all, "Remember who wears the crimson cloak." A ruthless breeze tore through the masses, collecting the fabric of Alora's cloak and snapping it in the wind. "And it is not you."

Not Haiden.

Not another general.

Not any mere soldier there.

Not even the High Prince himself.

Perhaps a threat to all else, but never to Alora.

She met Garrik's stare, and her blood went molten as something fluttered low in her stomach. To admit it would be to betray herself. But there was something about those simple words. Something that made her insides quiver.

And after months of travel. Of her inner thighs and tailbone aching something fierce as her body adjusted to hours in the saddle. An ache that had her wincing the first night and hobbling to her bed the second...

That ache—once a source of her pain—now rubbed just right against the spot his words had chosen to settle on. Pulsing a heated desire between her legs.

No one had ever defended her like that.

Alora forced herself not to swallow. To not allow anything to take that feeling from her when Garrik's voice, even in his anger, brushed her like the gentle rake of a knuckle down her cheek.

"Insult what is mine again and find that my knowledge of pain far exceeds the control of shadow. *They* will grant you mercy. I will not."

Garrik tightened his fist in his lap. Smokeshadows squeezed again, drawing out another wail.

"*Get out of my sight.*" With a loosened grip of his power, Garrik twisted his wrist, and Haiden and his horse disappeared in a storm of wrath.

Then Garrik turned to the multitude. Most sat rigid in their saddles as if anticipating his fury to be turned on them. Only a few, like Thalon and Jade—and even Eldacar—sat poised and composed.

Icy death remained in his abyss for eyes. The High Prince's voice soared; the tone that of a fiery winged creature transcending realms.

And it was still every bit as damning as that male she had watched in Telldaira's alley when he spoke to no one in particular. "Anyone else care to question my decisions?"

Nobody said a word.

SHE'D BARELY BEEN able to keep her focus off Garik in the hours after. Suppressing the uneasy pining that constricted her chest, at what exactly that ache meant.

Luckily, Eldacar rode beside her. The perfect distraction to what had settled over her mind and body every step along the way. He held a red leather tome, opened and balanced in one hand, while the other wildly tapped a pencil on the pages. Completely lost in thought.

Tap, tap, tap.

The same heightened rhythm that her heart had hammered. Hammered at the first call—at Garrik's cruel and malicious and irritating voice. But her mind wasn't easily convinced. Not now. She had to battle with herself. To persuade herself that it *was* irritating and smug and ...

Beautiful. Lovely and—

She was losing the battle, fast.

Feel with your head and not your emotions, for star's sake, she scolded herself. *He would've defended Jade like that, too.*

So, she turned to Eldacar and studied the engraving on his tome. The lettering appeared to be outside of her knowledge and recollection of any tongue she'd spoken. Her brows pinched with curiosity, tracing each curve and sharp line, every dot and twist of lettering, and finally asked, "What language is that?"

Eldacar startled as if he'd forgotten she was there, almost losing his pencil to the soil. Adjusting his glasses along his freckled cheeks, he rattled off something that she had no hope of repeating—not with the same inflection and certainly not with the accent of its culture.

She opened her mouth, mindlessly gathering her tongue along her teeth to maybe attempt to repeat the word.

"One of the ancient languages of Elysian. I had hoped I could find something about that dagger of yours," he explained, pointing with his pencil to her sheath, "in here but, alas, still nothing." Eldacar slapped the bookends shut with a hollow thump and pocketed it in his leather satchel.

Noticing the frustration, just as before, Alora sought to distract him.

"How many can you speak?" she questioned, honestly curious, not just to turn his attention.

"Oh, my. I'm afraid there isn't enough distance left in the day to name them all."

Her eyes widened. "That's ... *impressive.*"

Eldacar's shoulders lowered, his chin dipped in that humbled look he often gathered, and he gestured ahead of them with a slow nod. "Not as impressive as the number Garrik can speak."

Now she was thinking about Garrik again. *Perfect.*

Alora swallowed, avoiding any more mention of the High Prince she desperately wanted to—*for the moment*—distance herself from and made a quick nod of her own at Eldacar's bag. "Could you teach me one?" Maybe not exactly *that* one, as even the name seemed impossible to accomplish.

His smile brightened, gleaming like endless starlight. "Which one? I would be happy to." Adjusting his dark cloak and patting his armor, which seemed so out of place on him, he pulled a notebook from a side pocket, fumbling with his pencil once again.

And though she desperately didn't want to, her traitorous sapphires found Garrik again and grinned.

"Rot an li vencath." Her words not nearly as perfect; not easily as pronounced and filled with that roguish intent as Garrik's had been on competition night.

"Fight to the last," Eldacar repeated with an air of excitement as a calm breeze ruffled his curly auburn hair.

"Yes. I heard those same words in a tongue he spoke in my tent before we left camp outside Telldaira. Would you teach it to me?"

Eldacar scribbled something in his notebook. Sequences of numbers and clusters of letters bunched together and separated by dashes and decimals. All listed in at least nine groupings. Almost code-like. "When my library is returned, I know just the books to start with." He tapped the list, and she realized it was a sorting system for his stacks. "We will add it to your training."

Something like nervous determination pricked through her nerves as Eldacar pulled another book from his bag and began leafing through it. Alora turned her attention back to the High Prince, sharpening her smirk as she watched his body sway atop Ghost.

In the hours that followed, at one point, she found herself and Storm mindlessly walking alongside Garrik. To keep her attention from any unwanted emotions or desires, she began questioning, to herself, just how many of the stories she'd heard about him could be true. After the months they'd spent together, she'd only glimpsed in short bursts the once savage warrior that so many feared.

Sometimes she wondered if he'd been reading her thoughts. Because his eyes would shift and look at her, followed by either a scowl, soft grin, or mindless conversation.

Alora's eyes brazenly explored him, painfully aware of his rousing figure, and remembering how it went rigid laying out the general's lashing by his tongue. The tall black boots ran up monstrous calves; the leather pants tucked inside hugged every bulging muscle *exquisitely* as he lounged perfectly balanced in the saddle.

Battle leather sleeves were bunched up, revealing a rippling, veined forearm that rested down at his side, and she couldn't help but trace those lines. And *that hand*—she failed at not imagining how it had once felt resting on her neck and jawline—now draped on his upper thigh as his other gripped the reins.

Losing the battle, fast, her mind repeated, and she scolded herself. *Stop it.*

But her gaze remained locked on every body movement caused by Ghost's steps. Watched his abs pulse and the force of his incredible thighs gripping the saddle. Explored lower, landing on his belt swarmed with blades.

The ... buttons and ties of his pants.

How the mere glance made her heart jolt and blood scarlet her cheeks. Thinking about his ... *sword.* How skilled he most likely was at— she gulped—using ... it.

"See something you like?" That irritating, wolfish grin climbed up the side of his face before he fully tilted his head. Silvers had discovered her prurient assessment.

Alora forced herself not to swallow, exhaling a scoff of disgust. Then tried to convince herself he hadn't listened to her thoughts. Because knowing him, he had.

"As much as I would desire to indulge your curiosity ... again." He chuckled. "I think it inappropriate to do so in front of so many spectators." Garrik scanned the Dragons, then looked back at her.

She straightened in her saddle, visions of the annulus flooding back. "In your dreams," she said, tearing her gaze away.

That wolfish grin didn't falter. "You do much more than those slow, long looks at me in my dreams."

Slow...

Long...

She hadn't missed his arousing implication.

Alora refused to allow him to see the slight scarlet warming her cheeks, no matter how much it irritated and—if she were honest—excited her.

In an effort to appear dispassionate, she pressed her heels into the stirrups, straightened her back, and forced a flippant smile, trying all the while to disregard the sudden jolt in her chest. "Treasure those, mighty prince, as they'll be the *only* times I'll do anything with you ever again."

Storm drove forward, leaving behind his sharp, *irresistible* laugh.

CHAPTER 34

F or now, Alora could see a faint hint of the sun's rays exploding into dusk's falling sky. The navy and lavender peeking through impressive, menacing rainclouds, soon to be traded for deep, comforting darkness and glistening stars under the incoming storm.

Another cold night dawned, but she welcomed the treachery of darkness and uncertainty of storms over the golden sun, any day. Maybe that was why, as she dangled her feet near the clear lake water, resting comfortably on the sun-faded boards of a dock, she couldn't help but smile, staring at the departing evening sky.

Or maybe it was the fact that soon she'd be in Alynthia—or outside of it, anyway. A place with impenetrable, ancient wards that prevented them from discovery and protected the mountain and city within.

Somewhere untouched by the High King's control. Shrouded from his cruelty by a labyrinth of protection.

If places like that even existed...

Hell, she'd live in the swamp waters of Lirazkendra if it meant she would be safe.

Garrik and the others—the entire legion—had their purpose. And she'd never once forgotten hers. That dream of finding her true freedom still caressed her mind like a beast's claws. Scratching and ripping relentlessly until the legion moved on without her. With Alynthia's mountain resting a few days away, easily spotted in the distance, that very moment may be closer than she imagined.

But that still left one issue.

Alora's eyes drifted to camp, passed Jade cleaning her sword on the shore, and to a gray head of hair. She watched Garrik conversing with a small group of Mystics who were sitting around a fire and tending to their armor after a long ride. Their High Prince sat in the dirt below them, tending to his own with a quiet expression.

She'd sworn to tell Garrik when she decided to leave. And with his word that he wouldn't interfere, she didn't believe him. Would he truly allow her to leave? After knowing so much. After witnessing meetings in the war tent. Hearing strategies. Reading correspondence. Training.

Perhaps the reasoning was that he would steal into the depths of her mind and shatter those memories. After all, it's what she'd do if she harbored his impressive powers.

Parchment crumpled as she drew it from her armor.

Rowlen had written another letter.

One of many that she'd nestle away in the growing stack inside her trunk. She hadn't realized the weight that settled deep into her shoulders, now easing, as she opened it fold by fold and hungrily devoured each line of ink. Experiencing for the first time the giddy excitement of those a century younger. The first swell of a heart or rush of fingers to tear open the latest correspondence. Smiling foolishly like a love-struck faeling at each curve and line of the words. At Rowlen's excitement for an upcoming ball for some lord's wedding ceremonies. And she knew better when he asked if she could join him. In fact, they both did because instead of scratching out his ask, Rowlen merely mentioned that he didn't want to see her in danger.

That letter felt more like home than anything she could hope to experience in reality. And though it ripped her heart into a thousand pieces, she carefully brushed her thumb over his final words until his next letter would arrive, likely in another week's time.

And remember ... the only limit exists beyond the stars. You are fire with the heart of a lioness. Yield to no one, not even him.

Rowlen.

With a crooked grin, Alora pocketed it, scanning her eyes to that very *him* Rowlen referred to before she flattened her palms on the splintered edges, curling her fingers around the board to lean forward, and closed her eyes.

Muted voices wisped within the northern breeze before near-silent footsteps creaked across the boards of the dock. She felt his icy chill before opening her eyes. Felt how the wooden boards flexed as he came to stand beside her.

Then, that voice, warm as honey, breathed an airy chuckle. "If you wish to escape the army so badly, there are far easier and less painful ways than drowning, clever girl."

Alora groaned, keeping her eyes closed. "How perfect, it's you," she scoffed and heard another chuckle, half tempted to splash him as she opened her eyes, glimpsing his face.

His troubled eyes.

Staring into the same sky. At the incoming storm that carried a calm breeze across his hair, strands tickled over his forehead that seemed to glisten against the falling sun.

She wondered for a moment what those silver irises saw. The laggard sweep across the horizon, drifting along the clouds as if they were speaking to him. As if at any moment, something would fall from them. But Garrik deepened a heavy sigh and tore his focus away, something critical flashing inside his eyes. And as quickly as it was there, it disappeared.

If she didn't know better, that could've been misery in his eyes.

Garrik's gaze turned down to her, and she quickly found the lake more interesting, hoping he didn't see her regarding him. Instead of his voice, she felt his stare and saw a shadow move. When Alora turned toward it, she saw his hand stretched down to her, and a knowing smile inched up his face.

"Come with me," he insisted in a serene voice that was so unlike him.

But Alora didn't move. Her gaze fell on a darkened ring under the fading sunlight instead. Tracing from that ring across his broad hand that simply hovered there, waiting for her to take it.

Still, she didn't move.

If the High Prince was impatient, he didn't show it. Garrik's face softened as he watched her exploration and urged with a reassuring grin, "Trust me."

That hesitation fed into her hammering heartbeat.

Alora scoffed quietly and pushed herself up, refusing his hand, earning her another amused chuckle.

Then, in an explosion of Smokeshadows, unfurling from Garrik's back in whorls, the night itself transcended. Incredible, daunting wings of darkness extended wide across the dock.

The shadows reflected off the water, snuffing out the sunlight that was soon to be engulfed by the darkened night. And as much as she wanted to admit it, there was something enchanting about seeing Garrik adorned in a mighty manifestation of his magic. An extension of his unearthly power, rippling in tendrils and whorls, submitting to his every command—every whim.

The true Lord of Darkness. Wielding the shadows at his simple breath. Using them for everything from the creation of a smooth, perfect petal to the destruction and leveling of an entire village.

An unnatural shudder shot lightning down Alora's spine as she stumbled backward a step, her heel pressing the edge of the dock.

Off balanced, she slipped enough that she began to fall toward the water when Garrik's palm gripped her wrist and the other flattened against the small of her back. Pulling her close to him, close enough that she flattened her palm to the dip of his solid chest.

Garrik's wings tucked in tight behind him and the silver of his eyes glistened, reflecting the lake like flawless crystal.

"Easy," he breathed, and she felt it like a feather across her cheek. Cold and ... far too dangerous to be this close to him. "Am I truly that terrifying that you would fall into the lake just to be away from me?"

She blinked, feeling the absence of his hand. An icy chill resonated in its place. Unable to feel her heartbeat as he steadied her on the dock and stepped away.

Garrik stretched his wings wide. Rolling the tension from his neck and shoulders before he again stretched out his hand and peered at the sky.

Her eyes widened until the whites glowed, and she was certain her face had blanched just as white. *"You're joking."*

Darkness whorled around his hand and danced toward her. Garrik side-eyed it, smirking when it escaped his hand completely and swirled around hers before it misted away. "Is there anything about me that ever suggests that I am joking?"

Rolling her bottom lip between her teeth, noting Garrik's critical stare, Alora's eyes flashed to the sky, then back to his hand. Sapphires bright as they took in his wings of darkness, then the glowing, beaming silver of his.

This is stupid. Irrevocably foolish and dumb and—

—exhilarating.

Heart in her throat, Alora blurted, "Don't you dare drop me."

Rolling her eyes at her own loss of sanity and the death wish beyond the one marked on her arm.

Again, silver beamed impossibly bright. "I would not dream of it."

And before she could react, Garrik effortlessly scooped her into his arms, lifting around her shoulders and under her knees.

Instinctively, she buried her face in his chest, feeling the unusual rhythm of his heart before the ground dropped from beneath them. One magnificent beat of his wings was all it took before he lifted her as though she were nothing more than air and soared into the sky like a strike of lightning.

She had no time to feel the bite of the cold wind. No time to watch as they joined the sky. Alora cried out, tightening her arms around his frigid neck. And then it was his voice, not the wind that had her hair whirling around, that danced across her ears.

Garrik's voice reverberated from his chest to her cheek as he whispered, "Apologies." There was something sincere there, but she was too busy worrying about falling to focus.

Cold hands gripped her a little tighter, thumb lazily brushing a reassuring circle over her shoulder. He truly sounded as if he meant it. Like their ascent had even surprised him.

"You did that on purpose," Alora whimpered, sinking her fingers into the muscles of his shoulders enough that she hoped it hurt.

"Not entirely," he retorted with an uncomfortable grunt, and his smile could be heard lifting in the words, "but I will say, the results are quite enjoyable." Corded arms emphasized his *pleasure* with a tight squeeze, pulling her even closer.

Please—please don't drop me. Something warm dripped down her cheek, soaking into his tunic.

How could she have thought she could do this? Flying was this unobtainable—unimaginable—thing, only available to those with wings. To those who were born with the desire to hurl themselves thousands of feet into the sky and not give plummeting to death a second thought.

By the absence of that invading caress inside her mind, Alora knew he wasn't listening. Which was why when wings of the night incarnate flared wide, slowing their ascent to a careful glide, she was pleasantly relieved. As if he knew ... as if he sensed that cresting, detonating panic.

"Take a look, darling," Garrik softly murmured in her ear.

She gambled the very real possibility of passing out and slowly, unsteadily lifted her face from his chest. Feeling a delighted hum leave his throat as her eyes warily opened, she released the tears imprisoned inside. A twist over her shoulder was all it would take. A minute shift of her neck. And so she did it.

Alora glanced down, warring off a wave of nausea threatening to drain the blood from her head.

Garrik must've sensed that too because he breathed, "I have you."

The words misted away from her tongue before they could form. *I know.*

Unable to speak because the view was so unbelievable, it didn't seem real. Because that sea of tents that she lost her way within more times than she would admit were now like grains of sand on a beach. And that lake was nothing but a mere pebble in the ocean of trees that expanded beyond kingdoms.

The world ... was rearranged into brushwork. Strokes of dark emerald and the blue of the lake appeared so deep it was almost black.

It all faded into the distance, and Alora couldn't stop herself from gawking. Of all the paintings in grand halls she'd seen, none compared to this. Not a single one captured the startling beauty.

After some time, Alora realized that her grip had loosened around his neck. And that gentle stroking on her shoulder had moved to her arm.

Garrik's eyes seemed to be just as captivated by the view as Smokeshadows carried them across the sky.

"Where are we going?" she asked.

That peace that had settled in his face shifted. Garrik's eyes flickered higher to the dark above before he met hers. And something had changed. The way he held her closer again, as if to shield her from the wind. And the way his voice cracked almost unnoticeably as he said, "I need a drink."

Alora drew back slightly, furrowing her eyebrows. "We have drinks in camp."

"Not the kind I need."

"Why?"

Garrik's face was unreadable before she felt his body tremble. "The next few days will be"—dulled silver scanned the clouds like he did from the dock—"I just need a drink."

She understood the look. She herself had been plagued by that very same look many times. Often when Kaine was drunk and storming through the manor. When she'd hide, locking herself in her music room, anticipating him breaking down the door and—

Alora felt her palms warming, cupping Garrik's neck.

He made a low humming sound. Did he ... did he *enjoy* it?

So she did it again and watched as his hollow eyes half-lidded, feeling the deep, soothing breath extend his chest into her.

Whatever it was that was bothering him, perhaps she could do the

same as he'd done for her not too long ago. "If you need to talk about it..."
She watched his shoulders relax under the warmth of her palms. But his
eyes. They conveyed the message. Another that she was familiar with—
he didn't feel like talking.

So, instead, Alora pulled her hand from his shoulder as a thought
surfaced. And even if it was utterly ridiculous, she still wanted to try.

Alora's palm lit with embers, sparking around them like stagnate
raindrops, lighting the darkness like—

Like a night sky. Teaming of glistening stars.

For a moment, those incredible Smokeshadow wings slowed.
Garrik's mouth drifted open slightly as his eyes scanned the thousands
of sparks around them. Illuminating his hair in a white glow so bright it
too seemed to glisten.

And that was very dangerous indeed. Because as she watched his
mouth close in wonder ... as she watched that tormented face...

All she imagined was him smiling.

Alora couldn't turn away—she didn't want to.

"I—I've never," Garrik stuttered.

He was smiling, then. Almost a real smile, one that she'd rarely seen.
One that made him appear to be ... something other than the perfect
royal blood that flowed through his veins. So un-High-Prince-like.
Carefree and utterly peaceful as the white-hot glow of her sparks
streamed into the air.

And then, his shadows were dancing. Her magic almost singing to
them. Whorling around each spark. Like how she imagined the darkness
kissed every star in the sky. His power flowed. Caressing hers and, as
unlikely as it was, something fluttered in her heart, feeling him through
her sparks. Feeling a deep, unsettling, ancient longing inside the
shadows. Something unmasked, honest, and real; something so
tormented that only a spark of light could strip away the suffering.

Alora couldn't drag her eyes from his. The echo of her sparks
became a mirror, another piece of Garrik that had somehow also given
Alora a piece of herself. They reflected her magic, wholly awestruck as if
it were the most beautiful thing he had ever seen.

ALORA'S FINGERS grazed the scar on his neck sometime later. Raised
and rigid—haunting. Feeling his pulse so close there, the place lifeblood
could spill from in an instant. Stroking across it as if it would speak to

301

her of how it happened. Staring at it as if her heart knew something terrible had created it.

Then she felt the chill of his hand, gently stopping the stroking. Felt his neck tremble.

Alora's cheeks scarleted, eyes flickering to the surrounding sparks. "I'm sorry."

His voice, so warm, so patient and gentle, brought her back. "No. It is alright. It is just that." Pausing, he exhaled a short breath, unsure of the words. "I am not sure what peace feels like anymore ... but I imagine it to feel a lot like this." Garrik squeezed her hand, nearly unknowingly, as he followed one of her sparks dancing with his shadows.

He smiled.

And she found herself smiling, too.

This ... this did feel like peace.

In the glistening starlight, in the magnificence of her sparks caressed by his shadows, they stared at each other, close enough to share breath.

Something was different about him. The way he looked at her through the bursts of dancing white light. Garrik's eyes half-lidded. His breathing, uneven. The tightness in his shoulders, in his muscles and neck, had recoiled. And that tormented look in his eyes had fallen. She felt his heartbeat—quicker than its unusually slow beat. And maybe it was that small, uncertain flutter inside her, but she couldn't stop her hand from brushing the back of his neck. From feeling his silken hair tickling her fingertips.

Still, he stared at her through those slitted eyes, almost closing them when her fingers slowly trailed higher, tracing through his hair.

Chin lifting, his lips parted, and an almost unnoticeable groan released from his mouth.

"Do you like this?" she whispered, feeling that groan vibrate in her chest, watching his eyes close when her hand brushed higher. And for a moment, she didn't think he was breathing.

He said nothing for far too long as she stroked his hair.

Finally, when his eyes did open, and the entire expanse of stars flashed inside them, did he breathe, "More than I can say."

So she stroked again, in gentle swirls of her fingertips, watching the glow of starlight gleam along strands of hair.

Garrik's voice was quiet when he said to the sparks, "I think I had forgotten what ... gentleness feels like." He shuddered. "That feels ... really nice." Almost seeming afraid to speak the words.

Alora snorted in a hushed breath, beaming a smile across her face. "Really nice?" She giggled, feeling her shoulders bounce. "You've lost your silver tongue, mighty prince ... *really nice*." And giggled again.

A real smile widened across his lovely face, and his eyes softened. "Better to lose my *silver tongue* than my grip." Those icy arms folded her tighter against him, blanketing her in a safety that for so long she hadn't quite felt. Not for a long time.

And she wondered if it was the same for him. After years of fighting against the High King, marching under illusion, scheming.

The words, like an anchor underwater, Alora pulled away slightly. Until she thought she wasn't brave enough to ask. But did anyway. "Do you mind if we stay like this a little longer?"

"Of course not," Garrik said, his voice carefully delighted. "We can stay until dawn if you wish." The words felt like delicate, silent snowflakes as Smokeshadows flared wide, easing them to a slower glide.

"What about that drink?"

"This is far better than any drink."

"Yes." Voice breathy, Alora continued weaving her fingers through his hair as the rest of the world around them faded.

Garrik's eyes fluttered closed, and, again, she couldn't look away. Couldn't help herself from watching her hand brush around to the side of his head. Couldn't help staring as he tilted his head to the side, allowing her more purchase. She reveled in the feeling of it. Of everything. Not just the silken touch. But his hands that had gently continued to brush her arm. His scent. The breeze from his magnificent Smokeshadow wings.

The sound of his groan when she brushed the tip of his ear.

His chin dropped low, nudging closer to the soft spot between her neck and shoulder. Sending vicious shivers down her spine, feeling his frigid breaths.

It had been a long time since she touched a male like this. Kaine would never—

Garrik's breathing surely stopped this time.

Alora's finger followed the linear line from the tip of his ear, twirling around to the soft skin and nerves behind. She felt his body tremble. Saw the way his chest struggled to rise with air.

He looked completely undone—or was close to becoming so—when he groaned again. But this wasn't like before. This was primal. Hungry. Edging on something ... utterly desiring.

A low, deep curse rumbled from his throat.

His pulse quickened.

Alora felt his body tense before his hand snapped to grasp hers.

Eyes widened, Garrik panted and rasped, "Stop." That broad hand was so careful, pulling her away, but she didn't understand what she had done to make him want to end her finger's chosen path.

"Sorry. I..." Shaking her head, Alora withdrew.

It was some time before his breathing had evened. Before that tension rolling in waves across his body had relaxed. "You don't know much about High Fae males, do you?"

Alora shook her head. The only males she'd truly known were Rowlen and Kaine. And she never touched either one of them like *this*.

And something ever-so-bizarre happened then.

Garrik's cheeks scarleted.

Furrowing her brows, Alora pulled back entirely. "What?"

Garrik cleared his throat and cracked his neck with a stretched twist. "Our ears are ... rather sensitive."

"Ticklish?" Alora's shoulders bounced, giggling.

The blush on his cheeks grew a shade brighter. "Something like that."

"Oh, come on, the High Prince of Elysian has ticklish ears? It didn't look like I was tickling you." It almost looked like...

Garrik's brow arched as he chose his words carefully. "I do not wish to embarrass you. But if you would have continued ... I would have." He paused and cleared his throat again, flickering his eyes anywhere but on her. "It is a form of pleasure. Of ... sexual release."

Oh. Stars. Horrified, heat instantly flushed her cheeks as red as his.

"Do not feel embarrassed. It is alright. It is just..." His head bowed. "No one has ever touched me this way. Not like that." Garrik's eyes flickered into the night. "I cannot say that I did not enjoy it. But I thought you should know. I would not want to subject you to something so vile, so personal, without your consent and knowledge."

Is that why Kaine never let her touch his ears? "I'm so sorry for touching you like that. If I would've known..." She shook her head, unsure of what else to say.

But Garrik's breath hitched, his head swayed back slightly, enough to notice the warm sort of relieved satisfaction, of comfort and perhaps deliverance, of careful forgiveness, that flickered across his features. And she thought she imagined it, but Garrik's eyes went glassy ... until he blinked and smiled at her. "There is nothing to forgive."

Then, those enchanting eyes scanned the landscape below, falling on an amber glow in the distance.

Before long, they both had forgotten her touch and the way his body reacted, and those incredible wings of shadow soberly glided them closer and closer to the dirt. The heights she'd first been terrified to soar at were left behind with a feeling of disappointment, for it had all ended too fast.

Garrik effortlessly dropped his feet into the tall grasses atop a hill just beyond a swaying meadow. In the short distance behind them, that amber glow had brightened and the scents of breweries, tanneries, animals, and the heavy aroma of salt and straw carried on the breeze.

Garrik had settled her in the grass, his hands stabilizing her until she found her balance after the long flight.

He was standing on the edge, overlooking the night strewn across the meadow. Listening to the cold northern breeze tickling the stocks of grass and wildflowers, waving like the surf of a sea when a cold wind ruffled his hair, stirring dark-gray hues and revealing softer tones in the moonlight. Garrik inhaled a deep, long breath. Tilting his chin to the sky as if he were enjoying the scent carried across the hills.

She wanted to know what captivated his senses. So, Alora deepened a breath, too.

That northern breeze offered an alluring scent of leather and metal. A promise of something cold and inviting and utterly perfect in the way, to her, how rain from a freezing thunderstorm would feel.

That smell was too dangerous because as she watched him in that peace that was so rare, she wanted to get nearer to it. To envelop herself in that smell and allow her own heart to feel that peace. To know that if only for a moment, standing on that hill, there was nothing around them that would require a sword. That neither of them had to remember war awaited. Garrik's scent and that meadow and the stars glistening in the sky was ... everything she needed.

And that was *terrifying*.

Alora's eyes flickered to his shoulders. They had dropped low. His hand rested on his hip near a sheathed sword, the other kneaded long and hard circles into the back of his neck. Entirely enthralled by the beauty of the hills rolling before him.

Then Garrik turned to fully face her, extending his hand. "Come. Let's have that drink."

CHAPTER 35

Apparently, that 'drink' was nothing more than his usual glass of bourbon, perhaps a little less expensive, the glass a little less crystal, and it slid across a shadowed table near the back of a bawdy tavern. One reminiscent of her recent past—and their first meeting.

They sat out of the path of wandering eyes. Scantily dressed barmaids, who were searching for a lap and generous pockets, they were also keen to avoid. Garrik swirled the bottom curve of his glass on the sticky wooden tabletop, fingertips lightly tapping on his knee. The dark cloak covering his hair sunk over his brows, clouding his face in even more shadow.

It was wise to have dawned them their cloaks before entering inside. As far as she imagined, no one in Elysian looked quite like him. The fabled savage warrior, the only gray-haired royal... Even without the obsidian crown, he would be difficult to dismiss—and her armor just the same.

Out there, and perhaps anywhere else, Garrik was breathtakingly

306

handsome. More beautiful than most royals and their bloodlines. Usually, he walked with sophisticated posture and embellished grace. With measured steps, exquisitely precise, like a practiced dance that observers couldn't help but stare with silenced tongues because the sheer sight of him was nothing more than something out-worldly. But here, in this town. In a tavern so lowly that no one but a commoner would visit ... anyone would recognize the difference even with that darkened cloak over his shoulders.

Perhaps that's why, as he walked around the tables of faeries and High Fae, his steps faltered slightly. By calculated purpose. The master of illusion held his chin low, and those incredible shoulders slouched forward as those enchanting silver eyes lacked their luster. The gleam entirely extinguished as if a day in fields or hammering iron into blades demanded price on his body.

A flawless disguise.

As he sat there, reclined back in the chair, scanning across the patrons whose voices were filled with pleasured groans and drunken chatter, he appeared no less dangerous and alluring as he did on the night of the High Queen's Candlelighting.

But something was ... different about him in the low light. Something dangerous.

The flickering from a candle on their table danced shadows across what perfect planes she could see of his face. And even though that illusion was nothing more than a male drained and exhausted at a table, she could see *him*. Could see the tension rising in his shoulders, the taut line of his lips, the way he positioned himself on the chair, back always to the wall, as if anticipating the unpredictable.

Always watching. Always ready.

She broke the silence with a goading smile. "If you wanted to take me on a date, all you needed to do was ask."

Garrik scoffed, stopping his glass halfway to his lips, then smirked. "Doubtful." The cloak shifted somewhat as he tilted his gaze to her. "You would not have accepted my invitation."

A small grin tugged up her face. "You're right."

He brought the glass to his lips. She tracked the movement as if it were the only thing shifting in the room. Knowing he scanned the crowd, was prepared for even the smallest of threats, Alora relaxed enough to focus her attentions on something more important. Him.

"Where are we?" she asked.

"Planning to settle here, clever girl?" His brow arched. The glass tapped against the table, and his gaze flickered behind her, spearing the door before finding her again. "I do not recommend it. Besides an inn and a few supply stores, this place is a shit-hole." Garrik's gaze fell to her boot, hovering there. "Give it to me."

Alora narrowed her eyes at him, furrowing her eyebrows. "What?"

The cloak shifted again, enough that silver reflected her confusion as they bore into her. When those eyes didn't move, Alora reluctantly lifted her boot to the edge of her seat, sunk her hand inside, and pulled out a crumbled piece of folded parchment.

Garrik outstretched his palm, gesturing her to place it in his hand before he flattened it on the table and planted a finger on the terrain, saying nothing more than, "Maraz."

Alora's mouth slightly gaped.

Garrik smirked.

"How long did you know?" Her eyes flickered from him to the map, knowing the very treason surrounding it. Of what could happen now that she had been discovered with it.

"Since the very moment you took it from my tent." He silently chuckled.

She pushed the cool back of her hand against her warming cheeks. "Why didn't you say anything?" He could have at any moment revealed her treason. At any moment demanded it back.

"You might need it someday. Wouldn't want you getting lost." Then he slowly traced his finger west to a small, nearby lake, tapping twice with his middle finger. There wasn't anything but guidance in his voice. "Camp is here." Then, from there, a silver ring glistened in the candlelight as those strong fingers trailed to a mountain range no more than a few days north. "Alynthia is here in these mountains ... Galdheir to the south." The veins in his forearm constricted. "The border at Kadamar is here, but never go there. *Never.*"

His words echoed with every brush of his finger. *'You might need it someday.'*

Echoing until her words echoed, too. *'I'm not promising to stay until Dellisaerin.'*

'You do not disappear. I wish to know the moment you decide to leave, and I will not interfere unless it is unsafe.'

And she knew ... with every trace of his finger, every scan of the routes ... she knew.

He wasn't simply showing her their kingdom. Each one of the unmarked towns he pointed out was a possible place of refuge. Maybe that was why he steadily brushed his fingers across the parchment, holding them there, explaining roads not visible and towns unmarked. Knowing as well as she did that she would never stay until the northern border. And instead of allowing her to make brash decisions, he was helping her. Making sure she knew safety and ease in her flight from him.

Alora followed everywhere Garrik's fingers drifted with her eyes. The scratch of his skin sounded like a quill drawing on parchment, sending small, needless shivers down her spine. She moved her finger, trailing from Maraz, following his guide, over the swamplands of Lirazkendra, over mountains and flatlands.

Until his finger stopped. And she was too mesmerized by the movement to realize they had landed on the northern border of Dellisaerin.

Their fingers touched, hovering over the ice wall marked there. Something like freezing lightning shot through her finger as it made contact with his skin.

Alora gasped in a sharp breath, flinching away from the shock.

Garrik's eyes flickered to hers. He felt it and flinched, too.

They were quiet for a few breaths, the only sounds being patrons and barmaids around them. A silent question on both their tongues that neither were able to speak.

Then Garrik blinked. Instantly returning to that stone-cold face of an Elysian warrior as he drew the contents of his glass to his lips and downed it whole, slamming the dirty glass onto the table, making her flinch again.

With a sharp flick of his wrist, he gestured to the barmaid attending the counter and, without any warning, whipped his piercing gaze to the door.

A CHESTNUT-HAIRED BARMAID placed a glass of bourbon in front of Garrik with fast, yet timid, shaking hands as Alora fought for anything to take her mind off that touch.

It was nothing. Nothing but the storm that finally crested over the town. Static energy from the sky, perfect timing, nothing more.

Alora curled her lip at the taste of her ale, missing the burn of whiskey, when something she considered close to water washed across her tongue instead. The ale here was worse than Telldaira.

At least it was a distraction. Garrik seemed to be just as interested in his drink, too.

That disgust lingered. Her eyes traveled back to the barmaid weaving around tables, adorned in a flowing dress of cheap fabrics. Most of the males in the room watched her. Even those who held their arms around another who whispered in their ears and tickled their legs. The way she moved. It was as if she had practiced footwork like those on a dance floor. Precise and calculated, light and airy.

Someone like her would be the center of attention at gatherings—she would know. Kaine held too many for her to count. And at each one, she was adorned in obscene amounts of layers of frilly fluff and mounds of finery that could've fed an entire town. It was ... disgusting.

Garrik chuckled a breath from his nose. "What is that look for, clever girl?" he inquired, lifting his glass to his lips.

She hadn't realized that her stare had turned critical, watching the female, succumbing to a memory. "I hate ball-gowns." Alora took a large gulp of ale, twisting her mouth at the horrible taste.

"Noted. No ball-gown leathers. I shall alert our armorer."

Alora scoffed and rolled her eyes. "Kaine would host these stars-awful parties, and I'd trip over my skirts all night trying to impress his guests. I hated those parties. Well, except for—" She nibbled on the inside of her cheek.

"Except for?" Garrik arched a brow, leaning forward on his forearms.

With a heavy sigh, she continued, "The music ... I loved the music. I loved dancing to it, but he'd never dance with me. I was to be a trophy. Poised and proper. To be seen as ... as a wall ... flower ... and not..." her words trailed off.

Then Alora's senses perked to a faint stirring of lovely notes drifting from somewhere in the bar. Perhaps outside.

A pressure built inside her head, feeling a burn tickle inside her nose as her eyes lined with liquid.

It was a melody.

One that kissed her like a northern wind. Carrying the gentle caress of something so familiar, something loving and peaceful and safe. Wrapping around her like a long-lost parent's embrace. Like the touch of winter and ice and the night sky against her blazing flesh. Softly tracing her skin; a healing brush against a broken heart.

She listened to it, her vision narrowed, seeing the notes as if she were sitting at ivory keys again—wanting to play them.

For a moment, the familiar melody trickled through her veins, like a call home. She hadn't realized what she was doing until her fingers forgot her tankard and hovered above the edge of the table.

Tilting her head, Alora closed her eyes to the strumming of strings. Those fingers arched and swayed over the wood like they were dancing. By muscle memory and exquisite skill, her fingers lightly tapped the table as if there were ivory beneath her fingertips. Softly pressing into the wooden top as if they were producing the notes.

"Where"—her voice, it mixed with the notes like her tone belonged with them—"where is that coming from?"

The music flowed louder, like a leaf drifting across calm waters.

Like gliding through the night sky on shadowed wings.

Alora scanned around the room. No one else seemed affected by its breathtaking sound. No one but Garrik, whose eyes had softened staring at her, his mouth parted slightly.

"Dance with me," he whispered. His voice was just as beautiful as the melody.

She swallowed hard, meeting his gaze and curling her fingers into her palms before dropping them to her lap, unsure she'd heard him correctly.

But Garrik whispered again. "Dance with me."

Alora scanned the bar. No one was looking. No one seemed to notice. Her heart pounded in her chest as her eyes darted back and forth between his outstretched hand and the bustling tavern. And for a moment, she considered it—taking his hand that slipped across the table. Considered staring into his eyes as his hand would grab hers and the cold of his rings tickled her fingers, the other falling to the small of her back as he led her slowly twirling around the room.

For a moment. She wanted to.

"I—"

"Sorry for the intrusion."

The music stopped.

That softness in Garrik's eyes fell. "I would prefer for you not to interrupt us at all," he dryly rasped, not bothering to so much as glance at the barmaid.

The female flickered her gaze between Garrik and Alora.

Garrik stiffened, still glowering. "You can leave now—"

"Where is the washroom?" Alora blurted, pulling at her fingertips under the table.

The female pointed behind Garrik and turned in time for Alora to slip from her seat and rush away.

ALORA ROUNDED the corner of the hallway and stopped. Sinking her shoulder into the wall when a barmaid caught her eye.

311

She was adorned in a revealing dress that matched her night-dark hair, cut low enough that if she leaned forward, her swelled breasts would likely fall out. Her hair spilled around creamy shoulders in long waves as she walked across the tavern.

The barmaid was beautiful—save for the black, dirty nails from washing dishes all evening. Carrying a simple glass of amber liquid with only one patron in her eyes.

Garrik didn't seem to take notice of her. Surveying the door again, his hand rested motionless on his knee while the other held an iron grip on the empty glass in his hand.

The barmaid didn't say anything as she approached him. Her gaze carried a lustful gleam and widened smirk, raking across his form with ravenous eyes. A night-bug willingly flying into the jaws of the beast.

Honestly, she couldn't blame the female. Even in his illusioned form, Garrik was—

Alora shifted uncomfortably, blinking with a sharp shake of her head.

She wondered if Garrik would enjoy this female's company over her. How his hands might touch the barmaid, caressing her thighs like he did to her when she was on his table, injured in his tent, bleeding from the arena. How his lips might brush along the barmaid's jawline, whispering in her ear before capturing her lips.

Perhaps that's why he really came here ... to drink *her*.

Alora couldn't resist it ... the mere thought of his body pressed against the female, crushing her under his shoulders, or his hands brushing through raven-colored hair. Unbuckling his belt to offer himself to her. Allowing her to enjoy the pleasure of his thrusts. Being *inside* her.

A sharp pain in Alora's palm drew her steaming attention. She realized that her nails had sunk into her skin from a trembling, iron-tight fist.

What Garrik did with his body was none of her concern or business.

But even so ... she couldn't tear her eyes from the female's intention. Not when she planted the bourbon on the table. Not when she pressed a cocked hip against it.

Not when Garrik's breathing went unnaturally uneven because a pale hand had fallen to his and slowly, disarmingly, inched up his arm.

An iron rod shoved into Alora's spine, feeling the air heat around her.

Garrik wasn't moving. He was barely breathing.

Something tormented flashed in his eyes as his skin blanched.

That exploring hand turned into two. Both were on his shoulders, massaging gently while the female's lips moved.

Then, she sat on his lap, leaned close to his ear, whispered.

Alora felt her skin tighten, rippling with heat. Uncontrollable—strange—dangerous heat.

It felt as if the entire tavern would ignite.

Her feet were moving before she could stop them. Every table in the bar a blur. Alora didn't know what she was going to do, but that female was touching him, and all she knew was that she didn't like it.

Feet before she was going to thread her fingers into the barmaid's hair, Garrik's deep, menacing voice growled, "*Do not touch me.*" In a pointed thrust of his hands, the barmaid slipped from his lap, her arm knocking over his glass in the process,

She stumbled away with confused, widened eyes.

"Fetch me another," was all he said, staring at the bourbon dripping from the table.

The female quickly peddled away.

Alora watched as a small tendril of shadow overtook his toppled glass. When it misted away, the glass had been nearly half-filled, and in an instant, the High Prince downed it. Another shadow whorled, repeating the same until his glass was half-filled again.

Then again.

"You have to fly us back tonight," she warned, her critical gaze drifting over him as she stepped around his chair, dropping back into hers.

He was lifting it again, so she outstretched her hand to stop him, but he pulled away.

"I will be fine," Garrik retorted and emptied the glass.

She frowned. "Are you okay?" Her eyes flickered to the barmaid preparing him a new glass behind the counter.

At last, the glass settled on the table, and this time it didn't refill. His mouth opened, seeming as if he would speak, but instead it morphed into a forged smile. "Never better."

Alora furrowed her brows, reclining back in the chair. Scanning his body, his face, she knew he was lying. But even if she asked again, she knew he wouldn't tell her the truth. Instead, she merely raised her tankard to her lips, swallowing down the less-than-satisfying liquid when footsteps scraped across the wooden floor.

The female had returned and settled Garrik's new glass in front of him. Her shifting movements betrayed her discomfort, her eyes desperate for the solace of the bar. "Apologies, sir, but there's a male requesting your attention."

Garrik's head tilted, following the female's gaze, grinding his teeth as irritation rippled across his features. "Requests my attention," he repeated. This time, hostile amusement brightened his face. "Have him come to me. I require a moment." And he dismissed her with a sharp flick of his wrist before deeply inhaling, facing Alora.

Alora stiffened, pivoted to the bar, and regarded a cloaked figure lifting a tankard with his back toward them. As his arm lifted, his cloak slid down somewhat, pulling away from his skin and revealing unfamiliar inked patterns lining his porcelain wrist and hand.

"Who is he?" she asked, watching as the female gently cupped the male's shoulder and whispered in his ear.

Glowing bloody crimson eyes turned toward their table, and she ripped her glance away.

Garrik's voice dropped to a concealed murmur. "One of our spymasters."

The sound of footsteps drew near as wooden legs scraped across the floor, and Garrik stood. The icy chill of his palm brushed Alora's chin, drawing her attention up at him. "Wait here. I will return shortly."

She reluctantly nodded as those cold fingers lightly brushed from her skin, warring off the sudden ache of missing that cold touch as he turned and greeted the cloaked male with nothing but his own nod.

Garrik gestured a hand, beckoning the male to walk ahead before a quiet, broken whisper flowed back to her.

"... news ... lon ... razkend—"

Broken pieces. It was all she could hear before Smokeshadows whirled in Garrik's palm, producing a stack of parchments, tied by a strap of leather, all sealed with the mark of his Dragons. Before their bodies were consumed by the cover of thunder, he handed it to the male he towered over, their figures fading into the pouring rain.

CHAPTER 36

Sitting there alone was about as dreadfully boring as one of Kaine's parties. Though, at least when she stifled a yawn, she didn't have to worry about the fists that would meet her later in the night—for daring to show anything but polite zeal in front of company.

The tavern was so simple that there wasn't much to keep her occupied besides flicking crumbs across the table from whoever had sat there before. And once the last crumb of something that could've been either stale bread or a cracker flew across the wood and landed somewhere on Garrik's chair, did she shift her hips slightly in the seat, reclining back with a bored huff.

He was taking his time out there doing ... whatever it was he was doing.

Instead of memorizing every sequence of grain in the wood beneath her palm, Alora rose. Carrying her tankard across the floor, she settled herself on a tall stool at the bar, kicking her legs against the hem of her cloak while a barmaid refilled drinks with her back turned.

Scanning the room, Alora's mind wandered into a corner of darkness near the back hallway. Half imagining the silhouette of a piano, remembering that song—her favorite song—that she heard earlier. One that she hadn't heard since she was a faeling. The one her mother ethereally hummed her to sleep by. And only years later, when Alora had taught herself how to play on keys of ivory, did she try to master its haunting beauty and divine expression with notes that could touch beyond mortal comprehension. A sound that transcended realms.

"Where was that music coming from earlier?"

The barmaid swiftly raked her eyes over Alora, assessing her as if she'd gone mad. "There is no music here," she clipped out and twisted toward a door that smelled like a kitchen, disappearing inside.

Alora frowned. There was no mistaking it. There had been music.

And Garrik had asked her to dance.

No one had ever asked her to dan—

"*Alora.*" Her name brushed down her spine, hauntingly cold, like someone had breathed in her ear.

She shuddered, turning to scan the tavern. But when doing so, there was no one close enough to whisper like that.

Not until she twisted around.

Not until mahogany eyes stared back.

Behind her, the tavern door opened, heavy with footsteps and clanks of metal, but her entire world had frozen too completely to care about who walked in.

"Alora."

Something crackled deep inside her veins. Prickling every nerve ending, threatening to explode with embers as she sat rigid, her hands trembling to keep her grip on the edge of the counter, to keep her steady as her world crumbled down.

Terror. Pure, unadulterated terror crackled inside her veins. Alora tried to breathe—*couldn't breathe.*

Every ounce of Thalon's training ebbed from her body, disappearing into the night, only to be stolen and safeguarded behind those sinister eyes that trapped her inside of ruthless memories.

No one in the bar was looking—not one. None of them knew who he was or what he would do.

None of them knew...

"Kaine," she choked but barely heard her own voice over the ringing in her ears.

Somehow, a glass of scarlet liquid had settled in front of him. She could barely see that, either, nor the single red rose draped across the wooden surface.

"Didn't I tell you that I would find you?" That glass lifted to his lips, but she could only focus on his broad hand squeezing it. "Imagine my surprise when I returned home yet again and found not only my bed empty but my manor, too."

Alora opened her mouth to speak. Nothing but strangled breaths came out.

"You've been whoring yourself, haven't you? I smell *him* on you."

Him. Her mind echoed with the word, and suddenly the stiffness in her body loosened slightly.

Garrik. He was outside. Somewhere. And at any moment, could walk through the doors and—

"He's not coming for you." The crackling in her veins turned into shards of molten metal. "I made sure of that. You're *mine*—you will *always* be mine." Kaine lifted the glass as if the entire world burned at his feet and he lived on the ashes.

"No," she barely breathed. The word struck some crucial part deep inside her. She wanted to turn to the door, to run out, to find Garrik—wherever he was—not believing that Kaine had done something terrible when she knew that he could. But settling inside her bones, covering them with a film of hopelessness, knowing the male he was...

There was nothing she could do.

She almost heard Garrik's voice then. *Run.* Just like in the alley.

Kaine arched a brow and snickered. "No?" Then snickered again, turning his body to fully face her, draping an arm across the bar while the barmaid simply wiped the counter around him. "I should drag your worthless ass to the back room and remind you who you belong to." Kaine's hand brushed along the snaps and ties of his pants.

His perfect little trophy on display for all to see.

His canvas to paint and mold and manipulate.

His little, doting *wife.* Made to simply warm his bed and suck his—

"You're coming home with me." Clanging noises shattered through her every bone as Kaine pulled shackles, which were far too large for his pockets, from behind him. Chains so short, she wouldn't be able to walk in them. "And when we get there, these will never leave your body ag—"

Her chair toppled before he finished his last word. Alora stumbled back, heat flaring, her palms outstretched—aimed in front of her, aimed at him.

"Don't," she quivered, the sound unlike the strong female she'd ruthlessly fought to become.

Chairs scraped along the wooden floor behind her, but she didn't care to turn and see, not while Kaine had dropped a shackle to dangle and sway, holding the other with one cruel finger curled around it.

317

He stepped forward with a wicked grin.

She staggered back.

"*Get on your knees before your lord,*" he decreed, his voice as raging as the scorching heat boiling inside her. "You know what happens when you run from me. And I know I trained you better than that."

Heat. Terrible, blazing heat rippled through her. Enough that she thought she was on fire.

She couldn't breathe.

It was too hot.

She couldn't breathe.

Swirling sunstorms ignited in her palms before she could stop them, casting dancing white light over every surface and blinding his wickedly handsome face. If ever the moment came that she would encounter him again, she had hoped for more strength than this ... this pathetic trembling in her knees. Than the terror that gripped her and had her frozen to the floor, unable to control her flames.

Kaine stepped forward, so hauntingly it was as if he weren't real at all.

And she couldn't do *anything*. Nothing but cry out from the depths of her mind as those flames in her hands sparked and created a circlet of fire around her on the wooden floorboards.

Please, someone, help me.

Kaine's boot stepped through her toppled chair as if he were made of illusions.

Somewhere in her mind, she registered the strange movement. Even saw the faint wave of his body as if he were a fire and she was staring into the heat that manipulated the view above it. Kaine wasn't a Mystic. She'd seen his body enough to know as much.

But it was too late. Far too late.

Kaine's body misted away into dust and air and white light.

Alora held her palms out, embers exploding in her eyes.

And stared at the empty space Kaine's ghost had just been...

As the entire room ignited into flames.

No one had walked down the sludge and mud of the alley

concealing them. No one would want to venture out into the burst of storm clouds damning the ground with its relentless, frigid rain.

Lightning was their only source of light as Garrik leaned against the wooden wall of the tavern, arms crossed in disbelief as the sharp chill of rain sunk deep under his cloak and into his tunic.

"You are certain?"

Crimson eyes like blood blinked underneath the cloak. Even in the darkness, they glowed. "Yes."

Garrik's chin dropped low, staring at the puddles forming around his boots, half in shock while the rest bubbled in relief. "And you know a way in?"

The male nodded enough to shift his cloak. A lock of pin-straight black hair spilled out. "The wards—"

Thunder rattled the ground, loud enough to drown him out.

Garrik's attention drifted upward, scowling at the untimely crack of the skies when the stars seemed to pulse brighter. He tilted his head, narrowing his eyes on the stars seen through the thunderstorm clouds.

They pulsed again, as if drawing energy from Elysian.

"High Prince?"

Garrik snapped his attention back to the male. "Yes, I—" The stars pulsed again. Brighter this time. "The wards. Yes." His eyes flickered to a rolled parchment with a fading fox seal in the male's hand. "Assuming it is detailed inside, have Thalon read the missive."

Shifting from the wall, Garrik slid three rings from his fingers, leaving only one behind, and handed them to him.

The male simply nodded before pocketing them, along with the rolled parchment and a stack of letters.

"Wait a week's time unless I come to you."

The male nodded again. "If that is all?"

Garrik returned the gesture, dismissing him.

As crimson eyes retreated into the darkness until he faded, morphing as if the air itself, not even a lingering of his scent was left behind to tell a tale of his presence there tonight.

Garrik's gaze fell to the mud below, his throat tightening as the rain soaked into his cloak. His gaze did not move, listening to the relentless pour of the rain. Not until something like a dagger stabbed into his chest, pulling the air from his lungs as the stars flared again.

Something tore through his magic—straight into his mind.

Please, someone, help me.

Garrik's arms unfolded, dropping to the hilt of his sword.

Alora. That was pure terror in her voice, rippling deep into his heart.

His feet were moving before reason caught him, barely keeping his footing in the sliding mud as he rounded the corner of the tavern and reached for the door.

And before he could open it, the glass shattered around him in an explosion as bright as starlight.

CHAPTER 37

Something blunt and hard hit the back of Alora's head the instant her flames exploded, knocking her to the ground.

In clouds of ash and smoke and flames, she lifted away her arms that were shielding her face.

Through the smoke, glistening silver armor and purple fabric hovered above her until the hardened faces of Ravens baring their teeth stood over her. Each shape blurring until she couldn't count how many were truly there. Only then did she realize...

Those footsteps she'd heard coming inside the tavern. They weren't other patrons.

They weren't Garrik.

She had laid ruination to the room, but not a speck of dust touched Kaine. He wasn't there to feel it.

He was never there.

In her deadly eruption, the entire tavern had been reconstructed into a mess of embers, ash-covered flesh, and screams.

Chaos.

Then they were pulling her.

Ripping her along the floorboards by her hair, pulling so tight, her vision spotted believing at any moment they would rip it from her scalp.

The hard wood of a wall smacked into her back, knocking the air from her lungs as a warm hand clamped around her throat. They were speaking—screaming—at her, but she couldn't determine what language.

Her head slammed into the wall, rattling what remained of her vision. Sending the borders of her mind dancing with darkness when she felt a whimper choke from her mouth.

Hands raided her body. Inside her cloak. Brushing along her belt and down her legs with brutal urgency. She lifted her arm to swat the hand away but was only met with a crushing grip. Her wrist enveloped and slammed into the wall beside her as the other hand continued its exploration.

Alora's eyes shot open the moment the male's hand pulled her sword from the sheath, disarming her as far as he could determine. But they didn't search her back. Didn't find where she'd hidden her obsidian dagger.

If she could only get to it. If she could collect her senses enough, stabilize her mind and breathing enough to wield it...

She tried to deepen a breath, but that hand around her throat squeezed tighter. So tight, she was sure the darkness would claim her.

"*Get your hands off me,*" choked out, but it was more a gurgle of words than anything.

They were snickering then. At least five voices echoed off the walls of the hallway. "I didn't think Marked Ones were so stupid." She didn't recognize that voice, didn't recognize the cold face of the male as her hand inside her cloak drifted behind her—slowly.

She had one chance. One swift swing to sink into soft flesh and flee. And maybe it was a fool's hope. Maybe she could only take down one before the rest swarmed her. She still had to try. One less Raven in the world was better than nothing.

One ripple in time could stir an unending wave, and she would be its curator.

"Are you alone?" The stench of his breath waved over her senses, stirring her focus to sharpen on the shine of silver on his chest and the menacing scratch of purple hanging from his shoulders.

"It wouldn't matter if she was. From the way the inside of the tavern looks, I would say they are all dead, including Hawke and Twinn," another voice growled from behind.

Alora could just barely see over her captor's shoulder, glimpsing four more Ravens casting shadows from the blazing, glowing white gleam of her fire still burning inside.

Taking a quick glance over his shoulder, the Raven gave Alora just enough time to wrench her knee up, slamming it into his groin before dropping him to his knees.

Pushing from the wall and choking on smoke-filled air entering her lungs, Alora began backing away—toward the door at the end of the hall —toward all the doors. Any one of them a potential escape.

"Stay back," she rasped and held it in front of her.

The four Ravens standing stalked closer, their focus entirely on her, on the gleam of the crystal on the handle, on the edge of her blade. Metal slid against leather, and she felt her heartbeat race as, one by one, their swords were unsheathed. All trained on her. On the very small blade in her hand.

"What you going to do with that, *princess?*" The one closest to her stepped forward, taunting, gesturing with the tip of his sword at her blade.

Clutching his balls, the male on the floor rose, digging the edge of his blade into the floorboards, lip curled to bare his teeth.

"Stab it through your ugly eye," Alora avowed through gritted teeth, taking another step back as the floorboards shuddered.

They all felt it. Like something plummeted to the earth, rattling the tavern ... rattling all of Zyllyryon. A tremor that cracked deep into the core, haunting every living thing clear down to Firekeeper's realm.

Alora's blood went molten. Knowing that ancient power ... knowing the only thing capable of such ominous force.

The white-hot glow from the tavern suddenly dimmed as if the thunderclouds outside had roared along the ceiling. Darkness swirled around their heads and tendriled around their boots before a voice, low and vicious, and carrying with it the sound of damning nightmares, wickedly snarled from behind.

"It is unwise to touch what is not yours."

Her legs trembled at the sound, like cold, bitter, endless death.

And she found herself wanting to be wrapped in it.

Their faces hardened as the Raven who once tightened his grip around her neck whipped his gaze over his shoulder. "This is none of your business."

Every shard of light behind them had muddled to nothing but a memory, leaving the hallway as dark as the night as the voice of *promised* death—the voice of a beast damned to the depths of the darkest abyss— spoke again. "You made it my business the moment you so much as thought about touching her. She is *mine.*"

Something cracked, shifted, rumbled.

She felt the mist before she realized what had happened.

Blood sprayed her face and dripped into her leathers. The taste so strong it sent bile burning her throat.

Through the darkness ... somehow, she knew ... somehow, she could see.

Four males were gone.

Just ... *gone.*

Misted into bone dust and blood and shadow in the air.

And when her eyes lifted, adjusting to the darkness, the form of the Savage Prince parted those shadows, the white glow of the tavern a radiance of firelight outlining him.

The male in front of her wrenched his sword from beside him, twisting away from the beast who prowled, the beast with pure, primal, predatory eyes and malicious hunger. Wholly ravenous. A monster to everyone in Elysian—but her.

The male dove for her. Metal careened through the air.

But shadow moved without fatigue or fae limitation.

Transforming into a cold, frigid body inches in front of her, Garrik threw her behind him so fast she didn't have time to brace for the impact of the wall.

But she didn't need to. Pillowed by whorling shadows, her body didn't feel the wooden boards against her as the Raven's sword barely missed her and barreled toward Garrik instead.

She thought she heard someone cry out, a grunt of pain.

Then, with a thundering roar, the gleam of Garrik's incredible blade cleaved through the air...

And embedded into the male's face.

Alora watched the whorls of shadows. They receded down the hallway as a warm, white glow spilled out from the tavern, illuminating the once dark passage. The fire inside, ablaze with radiant light, now chased away the darkness that had previously consumed the corridor. In the very same spot, he had ripped the Ravens who were attacking her from time itself.

Garrik's shoulders rose and fell with heavy tension. She listened to his uneven breaths as he towered over the body in the hallway. She was tempted to step back, run through the door, and vanish into the night within the town.

But he had brought her there on Smokeshadow wings. Returning to camp wouldn't be easy, if even possible. She *needed* him.

Then his voice, like endless death, scratched like a beast's claws down the bloodstained walls. "What were you thinking?"

It was enough of a chilling threat to have her draw back a step for fear of becoming his next victim. He wasn't himself when he was angry —he'd told her as much once before—and the blackness in his eyes reminded her of that. Even if he wanted to stop himself, she wasn't sure he could.

Garrik's cold gaze peered over his shoulder, finding her hesitation. But she wouldn't give him the satisfaction ... wouldn't tell him about Kaine constantly haunting her. Not here. Not ever.

Alora's fists balled, ready for another fight.

"*Are you out of your starsdamned mind?*"

"Oh yes, because we can't all be like you, oh-so-great-and-mighty-prince." The deliciousness of her venom settled sweetly against her tongue. She was fully aware that she had reduced his title, proudly grinning at the fact. He deserved it, after all.

Turning to walk away, an icy hand caged around her forearm, and Alora found herself unwillingly within inches from his face, so close, they almost shared breath.

The High Prince's lip curled, baring his teeth. "You think after training for a few months that you are ready to challenge the High King's elite?" He breathed a dark laugh against her cheek. "If you wanted to flaunt your new ... *skills*, choosing Ravens as your first opponents was utterly foolish. Do not provoke fights with those you are not evenly matched with. Especially those wanting to take you for your magic. Have you learned *nothing?*" he roared the last word. "Have I failed so extraordinarily in your teachings?"

Alora ripped her forearm from his hold and shoved her palms into his chest with a heated fury.

He remained a stone wall against a tidal wave.

"I did nothing." *Bastard.* "They dragged me in here. I was protecting myself!"

"After you lit the tavern on fire," he snarled through his teeth.

"I don't have to explain myself to you." *Don't have to tell you why my flames exploded ... who I was trying to defeat ...*

Alora wanted to heave her fist through his face. She nearly did it, too, if it wasn't for the fact that, in this state, he could kill her with little effort—most likely none at all. One breath and she would be gone. And he'd probably relish it, too. After all, he had taken great pleasure in ripping the males apart.

Garrik's chest vibrated in a low, continuous growl as he prowled a step forward.

His power—rippling like a solid barrier—slammed against her.

She stumbled back, pressing against a blood-splattered wall, trapped, with nowhere to go.

Stepping again, Garrik's eyes speared her to that spot, flattening his palms on either side of her head as he leaned over her. Imprisoning her in the walls of his arms, leaving no means of evasion or escape.

Alora's heart thundered against its cage, desperately attempting to conceal her trembling fists. She wanted to flee or fight—or scream. But in fear of his predatory nature, the choice was removed, robbed from her consciousness by a primal instinct not to offer him the chance to give chase.

For several beats, he remained there. Chest heaving in heavy breaths. Until the slow rake of his darkened abyss burned ice shards into hers. His mouth hovered entirely too close, growling like a night besieged by a deadly storm.

"I am going to say this only once." A muscle ticked in his jaw. His eyes reflected her enraged expression, like polished glass. "I would take no pleasure in your death. I believe I have made that perfectly clear. But make no mistake, clever girl, this is no fairytale. Do not expect me to be a hero. I am the villain, and you won't like who I was *made* to be.

"I do not care. Elysian will not be compromised by foolish action. If you continue to do stupid shit like this, then this blood will not only be on my hands, but yours too. I will not allow anyone to touch you.

"Or have you forgotten my promise so soon? Decide right now if you cannot handle this, because if not, walk away. Find some pathetic coward's life, which you so desperately wish for."

His words ... they turned her blood molten, as hot as the embers igniting in her eyes.

Without thinking, without breathing, she barely saw through the red swirling her vision. Barely felt her palm barreling toward the High Prince's infuriating and smug and irritating face.

In a cloak of shadows, one of his hands effortlessly caught her act of treason. Caging her hand before it collided with his icy cheek, Garrik's lip curled. That blackened oblivion in his eyes grew darker—impossibly void of anything.

"*Try that again,*" he dared.

Garrik leaned in so close she could see his pulse erratically beating under the scar of his neck. The scar she had so longingly trailed fingertips over only tonight was now a target she wished to pierce with her dagger.

His hold on her hand felt brutal yet controlled; the tender violence in his seizing caused her to pause and examine him closely.

And she must have possessed some kind of death wish. Because, as his eyes met hers and promised the very same, Alora dared to raise her other palm and slap him.

Sapphire eyes widened; she hadn't expected to land the blow. Not on him. Not on the Lord of Minds.

Mere seconds after the sting burst through her fingers and down her arm, the Savage Prince stole that one too.

He raised both above her head, pinning her to the wall with the chill of his skin. Hands curving around palms like shackles made of ice. His chest heaved, lips quivering as if he were about to erupt in a fit of temper that she knew too well from Kaine.

And perhaps it was cowardly to do so, but Alora slammed her eyes shut, whipped her cheek against the cold wood, and drew her shoulders up tight. Each cluster of nerve endings primed themselves, anticipating the incoming blow, fortifying against the pain.

Her body fell cold despite its permanent heat. As cold as the ice running through his veins.

But nothing came.

Garrik only held her there. Teeth gritted as his inked eyes surveyed her panicked body.

Then his grip loosened, and he stepped away, dropping her arms. "I may be a villain, but I am *not* Elysian trash. I am trying to protect you, not hurt you." Somehow, the rage in his voice softened.

She almost believed him. *Almost.*

"I can take care of myself," Alora spat, liquid forming in her eyes for reasons she felt incapable of deciphering.

Crossing her arms, she quickly wiped a traitorous tear escaping over her eyelashes. Crying because of a male—how *ridiculous.* She could've laughed—might have even wanted to—but the tears seemed to keep falling. Each droplet felt more like a wave of despair; a pathetic and ugly weakness splayed out for him to see.

Garrik lowered his head, shoulders dropping in a deep sigh as his hands found his hips.

Alora slumped back against the wood and waited for him to say something. Listening to a cadence of something dripping. She counted them, deliberately, allowing her heartbeat to slow as well as the tears burning her eyes to fade away. Had the steady drips been there the whole time?

Her senses snapped, attuning to Garrik when he shifted, and she watched him run his hand through his blood-crusted hair. The cadence quickened with his stretch. It didn't take long before she noticed the crimson droplets splattering on the floorboards near his boot.

Furrowing her eyebrows as he glanced at his side, Alora followed suit with her own assessment. "Are you injured?"

"It is nothing," he censored, sounding callous and dismissive.

Mouth tightening, she noticed the slight wet stain darkening his tunic. The slice in the fabric and the red, festering, slice beneath should have reduced him to suffering at least somewhat. Pushing from the wall, Alora extended her hand, moving to examine the wound.

"It's not 'nothing.'"

But Garrik backed away, his lips forming a thin line. "I do not care to repeat myself." He turned toward the door at the end of the hall. "Come. We need to move—"

Muffled shouts tore from inside the tavern behind them. *"Fan out,"* a female voice ordered as footsteps thumped against wooden floorboards around the corner. *"Find whoever did this and bring me their head!"*

Garrik lurched forward, enclosing his hand around her forearm. "Move."

CHAPTER 38

Hiding in the shadows and leaving a blood trail of droplets every few steps, she expected a storm of darkness to overtake them. Instead, Garrik led her down an alleyway.

Why wasn't he just dawning them back to camp? Why physically run from the horde of Ravens scouring Maraz for the murderers of their comrades? She had to admit. Going back to camp—to Jade and her tent and her punishment—was the last thing she wanted to do. But running? When he had the power to take them anywhere? It didn't make sense.

Barely wincing in pain, Garrik braced himself against the alley wall, hand clutching his side, as he warily scanned the street stretching out before him.

"Where are we going?" Not daring to speak above a whisper, Alora followed his gaze.

He simply pushed off the wall before stepping out under a fire-lit street torch. "This way."

Another twenty blood-dripping steps and he led her to a three-story stone building with dark wooden beams. It was half falling apart and cracked stones crumbled on the front near a rickety wooden door that the doorknob jiggled when turned.

Garrik held the door open for her and let it quietly close behind him.

Six steps inside and across a slick bricked floor, a short gray-haired High Fae elder stood behind a long counter. Dried herbs hung from above as well as a wall of keys behind. His round-rimmed glasses nearly tumbled off his nose when he looked up from a steaming mug he was stirring, and he smiled wide, rounding his cheeks.

Garrik nodded in a way of greeting.

The elder nodded back, never once missing a stir of the mug.

Odd.

But Alora said nothing as she followed him. And rounding a corner, she noticed his shoulder brushing against the dirty, cream-colored wall as if his balance was unsteady.

Then he stopped, and her gaze landed upon the rickety staircase instead. Its boards warped, uneven—and nails jutted out at odd angles. She tensed her shoulders as if bracing for impact. Fingernails dug into her palms, and her breath quickened ever-so-slightly, eyes widening at the unstable incline.

Her boots almost stopped, hands trembling as the borders of her vision cascaded with darkness. But Garrik stopped below the first step, clutching his side, and deeply inhaled, scanning up the darkened corridor.

"I can hardly walk," was all he said before she felt tendrils of shadow dancing around her body.

Like in that forest on her first night with him, Garrik's Smokeshadows dawned them away. Her body was enveloped by swirling darkness. A velvety touch caressed her skin as she breezed into a void of nothingness, into something as light as air. Misting away on ash clouds and the unimaginable comfort of shadows.

Who knew darkness could ever feel like ... *this?*

Smokeshadows misted away.

Alora materialized as her born form. She should've been angry, but as she stared at a wooden door instead of the boards of a staircase, somehow, she found it in herself to be a little grateful.

They had dawned to a door a few levels up. A tendril was whorling in Garrik's hand, producing a brass key as simple as the building they were standing in. He sunk it into the lock and twisted it. The movement created grinding sounds like rusted, old metal groaning against metal before the hinges squealed, allowing the door to drift open.

"Where are we?" She stopped a few feet away, unable to see inside.

"Not camp." Gripping his side, the muscles in his forearm bulged as he held the door open for her to pass.

"Why?"

"Because neither you nor I wish to return tonight. Plus, I like it here."

"*Here?*" Alora frowned, turning her mouth up in disgust. "Why?"

Garrik sighed. "No one bothers me here. Now, are you going to go inside, or will you be staying out here tonight?" He motioned with his head to go inside the room.

And she did. Hesitantly, but she did.

The room was nothing special. In fact, it wasn't anything she would expect a commoner to reside in, let alone a prince. *Especially* not a High Prince. The wooden floor creaked with every step, scuffed and dirty, caked with dust that left boot prints on its surface.

Sparse, basic furniture filled in the room. A dresser, with a mirror, covered in dust along the wall to her left. A crumbling fireplace with no wood, only ash, laid cold and empty beside it. A filthy green chair with a large rip down its back sat near a half-fogged window. A door to their right that seemed to be a bathroom.

No artwork of any kind on the peeling cream walls and an old, fraying rug sat near—

Her cheeks heated.

A bed. Barely large enough to hold Garrik, waited near the window.

"Mighty presumptuous of you, High Prince." Alora frowned, her eyes settling on the sheets as she crossed her arms.

"I am not fucking you, so do not ask." A muscle flexed in Garrik's cheek as he bolted the door behind him, walking straight to the bathroom without a second glance at her.

"I wasn't going to," she murmured, willing the burning temper rising in her head to calm. Tempted to throw anything within arm's reach at him.

Instead, she stomped forward to the dresser. Pointing her finger against a candle until her flames sparked and lit it before tossing herself onto the bed, coughing from the incredible cloud of dust misting off it.

At least it wasn't camp.

And the only sounds were the water splashing in the bathroom and the whistling of the wind against the window.

"No one knows of this place. I would like to keep it that way," he called.

She ignored him. Dancing her feet over the edge of the bed, Alora pulled her obsidian dagger from its sheath. Laying the tip into her finger as she swirled it. The soft candlelight created matted white light against its blade and sent glistening flares off the crystal gem on the handle.

Curses and grunts hissed from the bathroom. Enough that she swung herself up to sit and lean, scanning the open door of the bathroom. Garrik was shirtless. The dancing glow from the candle cast shadows across his skin. Long streams of blood extended from a deep wound across his scarred ribs, down the V of muscles, and drenched his pant line as he held a needle between his fingers.

Alora felt her cheeks tingle and her head spin.

Garrik's eyes jerked her way.

Placing the needle between full lips and maintaining one hand on his wound, he leaned back and closed the door with his free hand.

Fine. She didn't want to see him anyway.

Laying back on the bed once more, the mattress dipping and croaking from her weight, Alora examined the dagger as she had a thousand times before.

Rolling the hilt between her palms, newly formed—thanks to training—calluses scraped against the empty settings. Her fingertips traced the barren indentations where she could only guess gems once called home, where now only grains of dirt and flecks of dried blood remained. Picking at the opalescent gemstone near the pommel, she chipped away the grime and traced her blood-splattered fingertips over the embellishments.

Taking in the unknown symbols and swirls across the blade, Alora considered the questions Eldacar had yet to find answers to.

It was a beautiful weapon. Likely with a story behind the missing stones. Maybe they were pawned off to earn coin for traveling or to buy land. She wondered if all the empty settings held gemstones the same as the one that remained. Over and over, she twisted it in her palm. Conjuring stories of where it was from and who once owned it and what the blade must've done. Until her eyes grew heavy and it rested on her armor.

Soft rustling stirred her mind awake sometime later. Her eyes opened to see Garrik in front of the dust-covered dresser, in nothing but a white towel draped flawlessly around his waist. The candle had burned down by an inch at least, and its white flame was hardly flickering, nearly snuffed out by whorling shadows.

His back was to her. The scars on full display in the glow of the amethyst moonlight.

Alora tried not to look at them. To not lay there and wonder what sort of brutality he had endured to suffer such horrific marks.

It appeared as if the scars were layered. How there may have been multiple moments, separated by time, when each scar was laid. How some appeared lost to time but others were somehow recent.

A vicious shiver scratched down her spine like talons at the sight of him, but she couldn't turn away. Every mark seemed to be worse than the next. Most were bumpy, thickened in some areas, while others were drawn tight and discolored. She knew those types of scars well.

Burns.

And mixed throughout, most across the expanse of his shoulders and below his neck, were horrendous slash marks like ...

Those were *tallies* ...

Alora saw something move in the dresser mirror. Garrik's hand was tracing down his chest, down to his abdomen. His eyes were closed. The muscles in his back expanded with long, deep breaths as the hand brushed across the overwhelming amount of scars on his front, which were entirely different.

With these scars, somehow, her entire body *felt* the difference.

Somehow knowing that they were caused by a more terrible monster than those on his back. Not burns, but something wholly evil. A creature that existed outside of darkness; a void so empty light had never touched it long enough to bask in the shade. She couldn't find the words to describe the scars themselves.

Alora watched as his hand trembled, his face taut and lips quivering with each raised ridge his fingers found. Too many to count. Far too many.

Then that towel loosened around his waist, drawing her attention away.

The temptation was there—to continue watching.

Garrik's muscled back rippled as he opened the towel.

And her throat went dry, imagining what those muscles would feel like under her hands—

"There is a hot bath if you wish to wash."

Heat flushed her cheeks, tearing her eyes away with only the sound of his towel dropping to the floorboards below.

The dresser closed moments later before she felt him moving, heard his footsteps peddle to the edge of the bed. Then silence until she was brave enough to turn her gaze—oh-so-slowly—to find him standing over her feet at the foot of the bed. Fully clothed in black night pants and a soft tunic with no buttons, perfectly hugging every swell and dip of his muscles. The blood was cleaned from his hair, face, and hands.

Luckily, Garrik didn't comment on her exploration. Maybe just as inclined to pretend it didn't happen as she was.

"I would say to hurry if you wish to bathe in the heat, but I am sure your fire can remedy that."

She blinked, wondering if she'd heard him correctly.

A bath? It was nearly impossible to contain her excitement or the embers that sparked in her eyes. The thought alone sounded glorious after weeks of washing herself in rivers or a water basin. And even if it was nothing in comparison to the luxury of the manor, it was still a tub, soap, and a *real door.*

Alora's eyes flickered from the very thin door that a small faeling could probably kick through, then back to the High Prince, who settled his shoulder against the wall beside the window. Crossed-armed, his biceps nearly split the sleeves of his shirt. The ratty brown curtains drawn back in his fingers allowed the moon to cast its purple glow across his handsome face.

"There is a lock on the door." His deep voice was low, reassuring in a way.

Even so. What's stopping him from dawning inside? she thought as her heart dropped, and she felt like a faeling having a trinket taken away. The thought of being bare and exposed and vulnerable when he could effortlessly make his way inside and—

"Your honor is safe with me, Alora. I will not bother you. I think I have proven that you can trust me." Without as much as a twitch, those silver eyes remained locked on something outside the window. "Unless you would rather find a dirty stream nearby—"

It was enough.

Alora fired off the bed before she could hear the rest of his words. An amused chuckle echoed behind her, and she locked herself inside a bathroom that seemed too large to be attached to the room they rented. But it didn't matter. There was a tub large enough for two of her, steaming with clean water and a mound of crackling bubbles. Vials of soaps, shampoos, and washcloths that looked like they'd never been used a day in their life sat on its ledge. Plump towels had been left by the tub, and a rug at its base offered comfort as if it had been waiting for only her.

Her battle-black armor peeled from her body. She tried not to gag at the flaking dried blood and stars-knows-what else dusting down onto the wooden floorboards. Catching a glimpse of herself in the mirror, the amber glow of the candles danced off her porcelain skin, causing her to appear a few shades darker. The bags that plagued under her eyes for so many years had mostly faded. And where hollow cheeks once sunk in, they were now more filled, even lifted. And if it wasn't for the specks of blood, her white hair would have completely glowed.

A smile twitched the corners of her mouth.

For once, she didn't mind who stared back as she turned away and stepped a foot into the steaming water. Thanking the stars as the glorious heat washed over her screaming feet, she lowered herself until the water swept over horrendously sore shoulders. And for the first time in years, Alora closed her eyes, relaxing into the bliss of a bath.

She hadn't *felt* like this in years.

Not worrying about Kaine barging in to rip her out by her hair and drag her across cold marble floors. Not listening to his screams from down the hall, before she would panic and jump out, covering herself. Waiting for whatever rage induced fury was to come or what piece of furniture he'd break with her body.

No. Right then—everything seemed peaceful—felt peaceful. It shouldn't have. Not with Elysian's Savage Prince on the other side of the thin wooden door. Not with the threat of Ravens wandering the town.

Alora sunk under the water, her hair fanning around her head in a white halo as she allowed it to wash over her memories.

CLOTHING RESTED FOLDED in a pile in front of the door; soft, silk night pants and a crimson tunic that was just as smooth. She'd dreaded sliding the fighting leathers back on and over clean skin the moment she stepped from the bath. Alora didn't have to guess where they came from. And though she didn't want anything from Garrik, still, she tugged them on. Even stifling the smile that threatened to climb up her face when the silk brushed so delightfully against her skin.

But that disdain instantly misted away the moment she walked through the threshold.

Garrik...

He sat hunched in the chair next to the window, elbows resting on his knees and chin tucked to chest, lost to the darkness that swirled around him like gathering storm clouds. A silver gleam of a ring reflected against the amethyst moonlight, drawing her attention to the rhythmic swirls of his fingers rolling tension out of the back of his neck.

Noiselessly, she watched him as if he were unaware of her presence, then slipped through the threshold and peddled across the dusty floor until his low, weary voice surrendered.

"You here to chastise me again?" he murmured, not lifting his head. Those strong fingers stopped kneading and sunk craters into his muscles.

"I am not sure I would survive it right now. So if you wish to deliver my end, now would be the perfect time."

Part of her searched for the words, the ones that cut as sharp as shattered glass and sent her poisoned tongue to sizzle anger and bitterness into his skin, but the other half remembered the male who had been wholly awestruck by her sparks in the night sky. The male who was tender and warm and so peaceful that he was seemingly incapable of breathing.

Alora cautiously extended a step, said, "Not tonight. I still need a way back to camp," and dared to ask when he didn't smile or even so much as lift his head, "what's bothering you?" Trying to mask that slight worry in her voice, coaxing him into talking about what she'd seen bubbling inside him since they flew from the dock.

Garrik dropped his head lower, fingers splaying through his hair until his nails curled brutally into his scalp. "I think it would be far easier to tell you what is not." His words were flat, tormented.

She dared another step. The worry only built as she stopped inches from his boots. Still, he didn't look at her. He said nothing more at all, which only fed her concern. "You don't have to go through whatever this is alone." She hoped he could hear the sincerity in her tone.

But he darkly laughed. A sound that sent vicious shivers through her bones. "I *have* to."

Alora held her gaze on the slow curl of his fingers, imagining for a moment a tint of crimson. "Why?"

He didn't respond for some time.

At last, he deepened a breath. "To keep everyone safe."

Everyone—she knew he meant so much more than his friends, his Shadow Order, his Dragons. He meant he'd shoulder the burden of Elysian's safety, too. And far beyond that, if given the chance. She'd come to know him as the selfless male who would battle a beast on wings of shadows for someone who wanted nothing more than his death. Garrik, the Savage Prince, who would quite possibly save the most ruthless heart if he could find a way.

But *this*. This wasn't the High Prince she knew. This wasn't the male who taunted and irritated her until her cheeks would scarlet and her blood would boil, threatening to launch a fist at his smug face or tease back. The lovely, smooth-talking High Fae she met in a tavern or the stone wall High Prince of sophisticated grace who led armies. Who flashed her the most honest smiles when no one was around or spoke of strength and comfort in sun-kissed tents.

There was no trace of him there.

And Alora couldn't bear it. Couldn't bear the thought—the question
—*who kept him safe?*

Garrik went still when her fingers lightly brushed his chin.

Look at me. Come on, just look at me, she thought, needing to see his
eyes.

For a moment, the softness of her fingertips brushed his skin. Then,
she lifted his chin, expecting to see silver.

Instead, black, branch-like veins staggered from his tightly closed
eyes. And only when Alora gently dropped to her knees, did he only
half-open them, shuddering a breath before those veins receded to reveal
incredibly pale skin.

She'd never seen that look on his face.

It terrified her more than anything Kaine could've ever done.
Rattling a place deep inside she didn't know, until now, existed.

Alora dropped her hand to his knee before she recognized her own
touch. Garrik's eyes widened and swirled with cascading oblivion.

Whatever was tormenting him, it was wholly evil. Somehow—she
could *feel* it.

She couldn't let him sit there like that any longer. No matter what
happened in the tavern. No matter what that racing heartbeat inside her
chest meant or the breath in her lungs that seemed to catch and refuse to
break.

Standing, Alora leaned closer, drawing Garrik's stare to follow her
movement as he pushed from his elbows and fell back in the chair.
Cautiously, she brushed a hand to his cheek, reveling in the incredible
feeling of his cold skin against her warm hand, swirling her thumb idly
when his hollow eyes half-lidded. The eyes that she'd do anything to see
glowing and teeming with life again.

Then the warmth of her lips pressed against his silken hair. And
stars ... his scent.

Garrik leaned into that gentle kiss, swallowing hard as his eyes
closed again.

And she may have felt or heard or sensed something in the veil
tearing. The veil that clouded over his being and left him holding it all
inside. For a moment, she felt him. The strong shoulders of Elysian's
strongest warrior dropping as tension rolled out in one damning ripple.
Like the weight of an entire world had simply dripped off him.

So Alora lifted her other hand and spread her fingers through his
hair in one gentle stroke.

Something like a strangled groan vibrated from Garrik's throat.

Stroke by gentle stroke, Garrik's body loosened, and he groaned
again. "Alora."

The sound of him sent spikes of molten metal through her veins.

Alora. His voice echoed like a prayer. Like it was the most beautiful thing he'd ever spoken. A name to be worshiped on humble knees and whispered on tongues ready to serve.

Garrik's head fell against the headrest, a quiet curse fell from his lips when his thighs flexed.

She wanted to know what her name *felt* like ... breathing and groaning from his lips. So Alora braced the hand from his cheek on the headrest, brushing her quivering lips to the cold skin below his ear, feeling Garrik's pulse sharply quicken. She didn't stop, not when his breathing fell uneven, almost entirely null, and brushed her lips down his neck.

"Alora," Garrik groaned in a desperate whimper.

Her knees threatened to buckle at the sound. And she swore she could've shattered just from his voice, knowing she would do anything—*anything* to hear her name like *that* again.

"You"—his breath shattered—"don't need to do this for me." Garrik's hand gripped into the armrest so tight, his knuckles whitened.

But I want too. If *this* is what he needed, a distraction from whatever in Firekeeper-filled-hell was bothering him, she was willing. Because that devastated look in his eyes ... she *never* wanted to see it again.

Alora took that hand braced on the headrest, cupped the back of his neck, and dared to trace her tongue in soft, teasing swirls on his skin. Licking up the taste of him.

"Why are you doing"—Garrik's breath stilled when she grazed her teeth under his jaw—"this?"

She bit down. Enough to pull a hiss from his teeth. Enough to have him stretching his neck, begging for more.

And she said the only thing she could think before pressing a kiss to the brutal scar there, feeling his cold pulse as rapid as her own. "To show you that you're not alone."

Garrik shuddered, not from her lips but from the words.

His thighs flexed and her traitorous gaze raked down the fabric of his dark shirt, settling on the massive bulge straining against his pants. Her mouth went dry when he tightened his abdomen, watching that bulge twitch when his hand gripped her waist, almost ... almost as if he were holding her back. Holding himself back.

"Alora." His voice sounded more like a question, more of a plea than anything.

"Yes," she answered, breathing hot, soothing air against his icy skin. Trailing lower, finding the hardened muscle between his neck and shoulder, and bit there too. Trying but ruthlessly failing to distance the thoughts of Garrik's hard cock feet from her hands. From her body.

Her mouth.

Garrik's throat worked before he released a deep groan, and Alora filled with hot need. Her thoughts collecting around what that sound would feel like. She wanted to kiss that, too.

"You are—mmm," he groaned when she kissed that hardened lump ... when her hand planted on his chest and curled into the fabric to refrain from touching his hardened length.

Garrik's hand enveloped hers, trembling as if he were bound to pull her away.

But didn't.

"You are so warm."

With his hand on hers, she stretched the fabric, lowering Garrik's collar to kiss a long line down the column of his throat.

"I did not bring you here because I wanted something from you."

Feeling the whispered words as he grunted, her lips brushed down, passed the hollow dip below his throat, kissing the muscle swelled at his chest. "I know," she breathed. "Do you want me to stop?"

Garrik's legs widened slightly. His trembling hand stilled her movement in a claiming grip, denying her exploration beneath his chest. He was still holding her back, she realized. Permitting her no closer than just inside his knees. Only, she couldn't decide who he held back for—himself? Or her?

"No," Garrik groaned.

Alora's hand splayed up into his hair, pulling the fabric of his shirt to draw him near. And when the warmth of her lips grazed against the ice of his, he didn't pull away.

He met her with a slow—soul-crushing—kiss. The taste of him, warm vanilla and oak, enveloped her every sense. Garrik's lips met her stroke for stroke. Unrushed. Unhurried. Kissing her as if the world was ending in ice-storms and starflames and the only salvation was her lips.

Kissing her like he'd never want to forget.

And then it was her body against his and those incredible, powerful hands wrinkling the fabric of her shirt as he roamed her back. His other fell from her hand and gripped her thigh, and drifting over his leg to rest a knee on the chair, she offered him access to it.

Garrik moaned against her lips. "You have no idea how badly I want to take you to that bed and fuck you till dawn."

Alora could hardly think past his words.

Sex. Sex with the High Prince of Elysian. *With Garrik.*

His powerful, sinful body on her. Feeling every inch of hardened muscle moving as he thrust *inside* her. Long. Deep strokes. Drawing out every strangled cry and pleasured scream from her lips—so loud the stars would rattle. To feel a pleasure she hadn't known and knew Garrik could fulfill beyond what the world could imagine.

Stars. The overwhelming need spurred by lust alone surged through her veins like an unstoppable inferno.

Garrik opened his mouth to speak, but it was far too late. Alora's lips crashed into his, diving her tongue inside his mouth, which he accepted. Sucking her inside to tangle hers with his own.

He jerked against the headrest the moment she stroked the curve of his ear and the sensitive nerves there. Eyes so wide, the whites glowed. Garrik's body stiffened entirely, gaping at her as if too stunned to speak.

And she stroked again.

Garrik's chin lifted. His hips did too.

And again.

She knew he had lost all sense of his own control.

Kaine never allowed her to touch his ears—she never knew why. And feeling Garrik's reaction, it was evident. Kaine would never have allowed his dominance to be manipulated like this. Not like how Garrik surrendered himself to her will.

Every stroke of her finger seemed to shatter him more and more. Playing with that sensitive spot that had his body quivering and his breath shuddering.

Another stroke had his hands sinking into the armrests, almost piercing the leather with his nails.

"Alora?" he called, seemingly unsure of where he was from the pleasure.

She answered with a taste of her lips.

"I'm going to—" The breath stole out of him; she knew he was close to shattering.

"Please." The word ... his voice ... it was broken, almost debilitating.

It was then she noticed. Those icy fingers had pierced through the leather. Knuckles whitened to the point his skin threatened to split.

"Please," he begged again. But he wasn't begging for pleasure. This ... *this* was pain.

Pulling her fingers away, Alora whipped her gaze to his face. It had gone ghostly pale. His *entire* body was pale. In his eyes, the blackened abyss overcame every inch, snuffing out his enchanting silver.

And there was terror there. Unadulterated terror.

The hand on his chest suddenly recognized his thunderous heartbeat.

Panic flooded his features. His body *convulsed* in shivers. "Forgive me ... Alora." Saying her name as if he were trying to convince himself of who he was with. It didn't seem possible, but his skin fell another shade lighter. "I can't—I thought I could—" he stuttered in a voice utterly unsettling.

Those hands hadn't stopped their relentless hold.

The racing heart inside her chest cracked. Not for failing to bring him to completion, but for the humiliation in his expression. Warm palms fell to his cheeks, rubbing her thumbs in soft lines, shaking her head in concern and confusion as liquid lined his eyes.

"You deserve so much more than me." She felt him shudder, the words like a blade through his heart. "I am nothing but *her* wh—"

And before she could say anything, before he finished speaking, Smokeshadows whorled around them, turning her body into nothingness for a split second before she felt the chill of sheets toweling over her legs and her body returning to her born form.

A shadow stirred in the corner of her eye.

Not a shadow. Garrik. He had dawned to the door.

Raking his hand across his abdomen, plucking the fabric away, Smokeshadows slowly cascaded from his shoulders. Swirling around his neck and face when his eyes closed again, and he flattened a quivering palm to the wood.

Panic and confusion and a deep ache that she didn't understand rippled through her body when he twisted the doorknob. Alora rushed to her knees and blurted, "Please, stay. You don't have to leave. We can forget it all. Like nothing happened."

Garrik's chin lifted, and she watched him suffer a tortured breath. "That is just it, Ara..."

The door opened. He stepped into the hallway.

Peering over his shoulder, oblivion found her as he said, "I never want to forget this. But you *must*."

And the door closed behind him.

CHAPTER 39

Rain pelted against the window, and a low rumble shook the bed. The pleasant aroma of the damp earth fluttered through the walls, stirring her awake. In a rising crescendo, the thunder grew. In the absence of lightning, she listened to it, felt the bed gently quaking with each roll.

It took her a few moments to collect her focus. To realize that Jade wasn't sleeping feet away on a cot. And that wasn't canvas her eyes were adjusting to but dreary walls. Limbs weightless, like the blood was waking and flowing back through her veins, Alora traced the reflection of raindrops from the window as the moon's amethyst glow beamed onto the ceiling.

An icy chill trembled beside her.

Garrik.

He had returned sometime in the night, so quietly he didn't wake her.

She lay still, ears strained to the crashing thunder that railed against the darkness. Tilting her head on the pillow, she settled intently on his face, every fiber of her being focused solely on him. The rise and fall of his chest. His unnatural heartbeat. The breathing a little too erratic to ever find rest or peace.

His eyes were closed—pressed tightly together—face twisted and teeth gritted, jaw set tight. A glimmer of sweat pebbled across his forehead. Garrik's skin ... utterly pale in the moonlight.

He trembled again. Harder this time.

And she felt his hand beside her move. An iron grip on the blanket he laid on top of.

Thunder cracked, violently spearing the rain into the window.

Garrik's body tensed through the tremors. "*Stop.*" She barely heard his choked whisper. Voice so hollow and raw that the room filled with deep, dark pain.

And darkness reacted. Now stirring, dancing from the walls, the ceiling, the floor. Crawling up the sheets, pulling at his legs and arms, hovering and circulating.

His abdomen became the source of vortices, where tendrils sprouted in an attempt to escape across other parts of his body before being forced to the join the gathering cyclonic turmoil.

Alora lurched upright, twisting onto her knees. On instinct, her hands dared to touch him. In the darkness, they glowed with embers, lighting up his body as it shook again. She laid those hands, one on his chest, the other on his shoulder.

The room ... it began to darken.

Another crack of thunder. Louder. Closer.

"*Don't.*" This time, a strangled whimper. "*No.*" Garrik's voice rose. Violent and brutal, almost wrathful in its tone as his face, the skin, seemed to ripple in the clouded moonlight.

"*Wake up!*" she cried, shaking his shoulder, stabilizing her hand on his chest.

His heart; it was dangerously slow.

She shook him again.

He only released a pained groan as his knees bent upwards. Arching his back against the blankets, Garrik clawed into the sheets as his face contorted into something terrifying. Something tormented and excruciating and terrible.

Sweat poured down his face, soaking his hair and skin, following the black veins bulging—crawling—from deep inside his tunic, from his heart and up his neck.

Garrik cried out again, the sound more than something terrible. It was infernally torturous. Like he was being ripped apart piece by piece.

Smokeshadows tendriled around her wrists as she fisted his tunic. Shaking him so violently that he *had* to wake from it.

"*It's a dream!*" It *wasn't* a dream but a starsdamned *nightmare.* "*Wake up,*" she screamed, the intent viciously ripping her throat raw in her desperation.

A voice laughed beside them. Someone in the hallway. A female voice. Far away and calling to her pet.

Then a wave of air burst from his body, slamming into her, the walls, the furniture, and shattering the window.

Alora screamed, flying from the bed, feeling the air forced from her lungs when her back rammed into the wall.

Garrik hurled off the bed, his back slammed into the door, cracking the wood as darkness furiously raged around him.

Eyes as black as the night widened, staring at the bed, chest heaving as he blinked. Hands were drawn out to defend an attack, and those same hands began shaking, lifting in front of the darkness receding in eyes as his palms twisted, observing as if it were the first time he had laid eyes on them.

His hands...

They brushed down his body, wrinkling his tunic until his fingers dug into his abdomen.

Slowly those hands traveled to his waistline, tracing over the top of his night pants, hovering there while his eyes squeezed closed, and he choked on a breath.

Then, his head whipped to the window she trembled under. Blinking as he surveyed the room—at what he had done. The dresser, fireplace, chair. All reduced to splinters and rubble and dust.

With the iron taste of her blood filling the room, Alora felt warmth trickle down her arm. Felt the sharp sting and hissed. Only because of the moon's glow could she see a shard of wood embedded in her arm.

He saw it too.

In an instant, Garrik was by her side. The darkness swirling in the room, returning every broken thing to the way it had been before. In his hand, a towel appeared. Without a word, Garrik pulled her to her feet, settling her on the edge of the bed. Even when he carefully pulled out the shard and pressed the towel to her wound, the silence blanketed them.

His hands ... they trembled. His pale face was cascading to a sickly shade of green. "Forgive me," he exhaled.

But Alora saw his muddy, silver eyes. That enchanting glow snuffed out. Saw the pain that covered them. Shaking her head, she lifted her palm, attempting to touch his cheek as liquid settled low in his eyes.

He was ... *devastating*. The High Prince of Elysian, kneeling in front of her.

"You were dreaming. You didn't mean—"

Garrik was gone.

Misted into smoke and shadow and clouds of darkness before the bathroom door slammed behind her.

She ripped herself from the sheets, moving as quickly as her legs could carry before she met that door. Pressing her shaking hands to the wood and laying her ear against it. She could have sworn she had heard him retching moments before. But only silence danced from the other side to the point she wondered if he was in there at all.

Should she knock? He did, after all, close himself inside.

Perhaps he didn't want to speak.

Alora palmed the door and laid her forehead against the cold wood. Closing her eyes to picture him in that bed. The way his body tensed. The way he screamed. She steadied a shaken breath, feeling her heart thrumming as her hand slid down the door, her mind calling to the other side.

Breathe. It's all she could think of to send to him. *Listen to my voice.*

Something tingled against the walls of her mind.

Alora loosened an intense breath when she felt it—felt him, and sent those words again. *Listen. Breathe.*

She stayed like that. Her forehead resting against the door, easing herself to her knees as her hands scratched down the barrier between them. Kneeling. Waiting ... as long as he was in there, she would stay.

How many nights had she wished someone would be waiting on the other side of a door for her? How many times had she needed someone to come to her aid when Kaine was erupting on a rampage? And when she had woken in the middle of the night with nothing but the darkness to comfort her, that was enough.

Would it be enough for him?

Alora heard something slide down the door, ending with a thump against the bathroom floor. Stirring to silence once again as she felt a heavy weight flex and press against the wood that had cooled like a winter's lake.

She couldn't see him, but knew he was there.

If you can hear me ... I'm right here.

CHAPTER 40

Garrik hadn't spoken a word since it happened—she'd decided against the suicidal impulse that would either have her plummeting from the sky or a lengthy training session with Jade—and determined questioning him about the night before would be best suited for another time. Maybe never at all.

They landed mere steps outside the shield. The static pulse thrumming against her flesh as the hairs on her arms began to stand on end. She had traveled through it enough times that the effects were only just a nuisance, like the quick flick of a finger on skin.

If only Garrik's piercing gaze was the same. Those silver eyes were darkened and distant. Sending a deep shudder down her spine when he finally spoke his first words that morning. And they were every bit as cold and dismissive as in his tent the evening he poured out her and Jade's punishment.

"I have business elsewhere. You can see yourself back to our Shadow Order."

Fine. He could act that way. Treat her only as another Dragon under his command. Act as if nothing had happened. As if his lips hadn't been on her and she hadn't heard his horrific screams. Hell, he could even forget they had flown away from the lake, forget that they'd watched their magic dance like ... like it belonged together. Act as if they never left camp at all.

This was fine ... Because the alternative of actually caring might have been more than she could withstand. He would never be anything more than the gray-haired High Prince, too pompous to allow anyone to actually see inside. Never anything more.

"Alone? Don't think I'll decide to leave forever?" Alora admitted to herself that the jibe wasn't only to lighten the air around them; baiting him seemed to always be somewhat of a game. Even so, perhaps right now, in that moment, it wasn't the best time because his eyes only darkened more, drifted down to hers, and a harsh line formed on his lips.

"Will you?" It appeared that he wished to say more, but by the sound of his voice, he wasn't in the mood. When she said nothing but instead shook her head, catching a cold northern breeze that soothed her prickling nerves, Garrik simply turned toward his sentries and called back to her. "Dress for riding." Then, the measured steps of a High Prince preparing for battle trailed away.

She heard his deep voice like a whisper—urgently giving orders to Deimon, the tan-skinned faerie with pitch-black feathered wings and amber eyes—before she crossed the shield. Alora had learned that Deimon was in command of the Wingborne and oftentimes spotted around Thalon.

Garrik's quiet voice brushed across her ears like a feather. "—over the next few days of travel."

Deimon's wings tucked tight into his body, and he crossed his muscled arms as the wind disturbed his short night-dark hair and battle-black armor. "And Alynthia?"

"Possibly the same as Maraz. Keep a perimeter and report to General Realmpiercer. If Ravens were in Maraz, then we can predict that their movements will settle in the mountains."

THE SUN SHIFTED across the sky, indicating that they had come close to their stop for the evening. A few short miles laid between them and the much-needed rest from today's journey.

Thalon settled beside Garrik as his second in command, looking onward in the distance to a lush meadow already dotting with white canvas. Alora had discovered throughout the past months that Thalon was Garrik's immediate general, in charge of the army in Garrik's absence. Jade, his third, and in command of her own battalion. And Aiden ... well, the entire army would be doomed with him in command, but apparently, he held a special skill set of his own that she had yet to learn.

Keeping her gaze forward, Alora couldn't stop herself from wandering back to the flight, the Ravens ... and what happened in the inn.

A gentle caress against the walls of her mind tingled. And she debated a moment, wondering if she should let him in—but did so anyway.

I am sorry for the way I spoke to you in the hallway. I spoke out of anger and ... Garrik's voice, almost hoarse—almost choked—heavily sighed. *I was worried, Alora. I should not have left you alone.*

She chewed on the inside of her cheek. *It's okay—*

No, it is not. And you do not have to forgive me. I just ... wanted you to know how truly sorry I am.

That caress lifted, and she suddenly felt empty.

Hours later, Garrik was still affected by it—it manifested through his taut shoulders. Appearing tense, he was quiet as usual, with only the soothing voice of Thalon corresponding with him. His own voice hadn't spoken in hours. Simply watching. Listening. Few times she caught his chin lifting. As if he followed the sun's position or watched a cloud drift across the sky. His gaze would linger there as Thalon spoke, absentmindedly stroking Ghost's mane.

At one point, Thalon drew back, allowing Garrik to ride without interruption, and found himself riding beside her with a gleam in his golden eyes and a foolish, beaming, faeling grin.

"You went flying." Even his voice was playful.

Alora gazed at him, attempting to adjust to seeing him adorned in Dragon's armor and red cloak. Despite his faeling excitement, Thalon, in fact, appeared more deadly than most in their leathers. Even so, she tore her thoughts away and shrugged as if her soaring in the skies, near the stars, wasn't anything more than brushing her hair. "I wasn't flying."

Thalon's grin widened. "Was it your first time in the sky?"

That terror ... the trembling hands and draining blood from her veins when the ground fell from beneath them ... Garrik's arms wrapped around her while tears burned her eyes ... it flooded back.

Alora gripped the reins tighter, forcing a swallow. "Yes."

Golden eyes were entirely awestruck before they closed. Thalon's chest rose with a deep breath, and he smiled. Smiled like he was wholly sated, basking in a sunlight that warmed him to the bones as if he were made to enjoy its company.

Like he was kissed by the sky.

Then, those golden eyes opened, entirely glowing in a magnificence she didn't often glimpse. "It was absolutely wonderful, wasn't it? Flying with Garrik." His shoulders rose in another satisfied breath, utterly speechless as his eyes glanced up at the sky.

"I can't imagine it being any sort of pleasure flying with the High Prince." That was a lie, but it didn't mean Thalon needed to know it.

Thalon barked a laugh. Rubbing his hand through his locks until his Earned clacked together, he turned back to her. "Next time, ask Garrik for Smokeshadow wings of your own. He enjoys flying with company."

She shook her head. "Right. So I can leap off a cliff and plummet to my death? Why trouble attempting to run me through in the arena when you can be rid of me that way?" Straightening her spine, she adjusted her seat in the saddle.

"Garrik was trained by..." Golden eyes shifted to Garrik then back to her like he was searching for words. "The general of the Wingborne. Garrik would train you too if you asked him."

Training with the High Prince? "Now you really are trying to have me killed. Tell me, have you ever flown with him?"

Thalon opened his mouth to speak, but an ear-piercing shriek filled the air.

A pitch-black storm turned the peaceful sky into something menacing and treacherous. Crimson lightning surged from a portal high above them. An unusually large, half-skeleton raven bearing inked, dagger-like feathers burst from it before it imploded behind. Its lethal talons were outstretched and blood-red eyes glowed in the swarm of magic cascading from its wings and body.

The creature lunged down, straight for Garrik.

Static energy thrummed through Alora, through every Dragon, encompassing them all in Garrik's shield.

Thrashing its massive wings, the raven hovered feet in front of Garrik and released an ear-piercing shriek again. Its wingspan mirrored the size of a horse; its wings splayed out to complete the aggressive display.

Garrik's face hardened into something brutal and all-consuming, wholly menacing as he controlled Ghost's stomping halt. "*What do you want, Nevilier?*" Growling as his eyes faded to oblivion.

The raven screeched, revealing its serpentine tongue, and lurched forward, causing Ghost to rear up in an effort to kick the flying beast.

Garrik, seemingly unfazed, calmed Ghost and returned to a halt, his army deathly still around him.

"*He* wants an update," Nevilier hissed, eyes glowing crimson as tendrils of blackened magic swirled around its wings and body.

Garrik stiffened as if an iron rod had shoved down his spine, His hand gripped the hilt of his sword until the leather groaned and metal threatened to burst. "Tell him—"

The beast screeched again as it rushed forward, piercing a crimson talon into Garrik's armor at his shoulder.

Alora watched as hundreds of Dragons drew their swords but stood down with one swift, raised hand from their High Prince. Surprised, she felt leather in her palm and realized she'd drawn, too.

"I won't be telling him. You will return with me. Now," Nevilier threatened as it spun around, spreading its wings enough that he pushed soldiers back, creating a wide clearing.

"*Now*, dog!" it screeched.

Garrik growled low and terrible and pierced his abyss for eyes at Nevilier with the promise of tortured afterlife. "Thalon!" his voice roared. "Should I not return before morning, continue without me. I will find you."

In one effortless movement, Garrik swung his leg over the saddle and slammed into the dirt below, shaking the ground. A whinny and snort of protest from Ghost followed.

"Easy, girl. Not this time." With a quick wave of his hand, Smokeshadows whorled and enclosed around Ghost's bridal and saddle until they misted away, leaving her bare. Garrik scratched her nose before turning to Thalon and spoke quiet enough that Alora could barely hear him. "If I do not return. Seek out Lirazkendra."

Thalon's eyes widened, mouth slowly gaping as Garrik simply nodded.

Garrik twisted a silver ring from his finger and offered it to Thalon who reluctantly took it in his palm, gripping it tight as if the act of uncurling his fist would have it crippling to dust.

"You don't think—"

"Take care of them, Thalon."

With an unsettling glance back at Alora, Garrik's eyes marveled at her like he had in the inn. Captivated, raking over her armor until he captured her sapphires and, for a moment, eyes as black as the raven's feathers specked with silver.

She felt her heart hammering then. Felt the surge of confusing emotions constricting her body. The wrath building from deep within as she surveyed Nevilier. How breath refused to enter her lungs, looking at Garrik with worry and uncomfortable anticipation.

You are safe, darling. Alora almost shattered at the devastation in his voice. But then he smiled. And she heard that smile in his next words. *Wherever there are shadows, I will always be.*

Garrik didn't turn his gaze from her. The enchanting planes of his face rippled into something sharp when he snarled to the beast, "*Get on with it, then.*"

Nevilier swung its wretched body into a whirlwind, causing a spine-chilling storm of crimson lightning and magic to surge and create an ominous portal inches from the ground.

"After you," it screeched.

With one final look at her, the world seemed to freeze. And before she could say a word, Garrik stepped forward into the storm of tendrils, engulfing his body until he was no more.

The sky returned to the cloudless horizon as the storm vanished. Blaring sunlight, like a beacon, displaying an empty space where Garrik had stood seconds before.

And along with it ... a shadow of fear took possession of thousands of Dragon's eyes.

"THE BASTARD!" Thalon raged as he threw his rune-covered sword into the dirt at their new firesite. Pacing the grass with hands resting on his hips, his chest heaved from the anger bursting from him.

Alora only got as far as the first tent of the Shadow Order before she leapt off Storm, demanding in a shaken voice, "Who was that?"

The taste of pure, all-consuming, fury clouded the air.

Jade's dark chestnut mare stormed into camp, sliding to a stop before she too swung from her saddle with a hand ruthlessly gripping her sword so hard her knuckles blanched. "The fucking prick himself, Magnelis's messenger." Her voice cracked. "He spawns unannounced and forces Garrik to the castle to submit to the High King's sadistic will." If at all possible, Jade's face turned ashen, almost choking on the words.

"What's going to happen to him?" Alora panicked, noticing Thalon and Jade's harrowing stares.

"It's always different." Tattooed hands ran down Thalon's face and Earned swayed on his braids as he looked to the skies as if to say a prayer.

"Magnelis doesn't have family. He doesn't have friends. Only those who do his bidding, and his favorite slave is Garrik. He could send him to Brennus to follow whatever heinous orders he chooses; he could hold him there for weeks until he's satisfied with Garrik's reports on our progress—"

"Magnelis could fucking imprison and torture him if he's discovered our treason." Jade's usual stone-cold expression shattered into uncontrollable terror.

Eldacar stood in the shadow of Garrik's tent. His lips quivered as he was trying—and failing—to form words. "We ... we mustn't worry. He always returns," he breathed, nudging his glasses up with his nose.

Alora didn't appear so convinced. Eldacar's words weren't enough. "What do we do?" She rushed toward Thalon, hand falling to the sword sheathed on her side.

"There's nothing we can do. The last time Nevilier showed up, a third of our army burned into ash the second Garrik returned. Because Magnelis poisoned his powers, Garrik couldn't do anything to stop it. It took him *months* to get over that summons, all because Garrik spared a youngling." Thalon's hands turned into tight-knuckled fists. "A babe whose mother was a Mystic."

The words were unspoken, but she understood them just the same; a cruel punishment for an act that was deemed a weakness.

Jade let out a furious screech as she threw her sword into the dirt, perfectly impaling it to stand upright. "What are our orders?" Her eyes almost turned as fiery as her hair as she panted in Thalon's direction.

"As long as Garrik's shield remains, we're to do the same as always." *To train and press forward.*

Thalon sighed before adding, "I'm informed of towns and Mystics along the way until Dellisaerin. We continue on."

Alora knew he didn't only mean on the road.

He meant without Garrik, too.

CHAPTER 41

One day. Two days. Three ... Garrik still hadn't returned as his Dragons moved forward. Each passing day, the distance between where he was last seen stretched further and further until he was nothing but a memory.

Had the High King uncovered their plans?

Was he northbound at that very moment to kill them all?

They wouldn't allow themselves to think of it. Until that time came, until they knew their beloved High Prince was dead and the battle for Elysian was waged at their frontlines, they wouldn't allow any delay.

Yet, when she wasn't training or hunting, even riding north, Alora couldn't help but stare at Garrik's unlit tent—set up every day just like Aiden's—and waiting for his return. Picturing his silhouette cast across the canvas, breathing in his scent ... wishing he'd burst from the tent entrance and sit in the dirt by the fire.

Missing me, clever girl? She imagined him saying it in that voice she would crawl for. But it wasn't him. It was never him. No matter how many times she called out to him, pleading for him to be listening.

It was never him.

Where are you? Are you okay? Jade, Thalon, and Eldacar, they ... we are very worried about you.

But he never answered.

One thing kept them hopeful—Garrik's shield remained strong.

He was still alive, at least breathing. But how painful were those breaths?

For three days, only gut-wrenching silence surrounded by an awful, unsettling feeling that something was horribly—*horribly* wrong, wracked through her bones. And in the silence of his voice, she hallucinated strangled screams among wicked snickering. The slithering voice poisoned with venom scratched like talons across her mind and shred gashes into her heart until she could no longer sit in the torment and had to do *something*.

"Hunting this evening?" Thalon questioned in the silence, turning to where Alora burst from her tent, geared up for a distraction, bow in hand, a quiver of arrows on her back.

But it was Jade who answered, "As soon as Alora gets off her ass, we'll set out." Green eyes turned unamused as she glanced at Alora sheathing her obsidian dagger, glowering at Jade who was the one 'sitting on her ass.' "Hurry up, I actually want to get back at a decent time tonight."

Alora gritted her teeth, declining to snap back, knowing—with Jade—it was utterly pointless. "Ready if you are."

"Pay attention!" Jade quietly snarled as Alora bumped into the back of her.

Beside a bush, Jade crouched low and examined broken twigs. A few steps ahead, a large animal print—likely a wolf of great size—sunk deep into fresh, slimy mud caused by an early afternoon downpour.

They continued trudging through, deeper and deeper into the forest outside camp's borders, guided by near-perfect tracks. Ferns scraped against their legs, soaking the rain drops deep into their pants as they weaved around towering spruce and oak trees. Somewhere in the distance, a heavy smell of pine rustled between the canopy of leaves, carrying the earthy scent of moss and dirt on a gentle breeze.

"Jade," Alora whispered, scanning the tracks ahead of them.

"Quiet," Jade snapped, her eyes narrowed on a sweetberry bush to their right.

Alora crunched her eyebrows, tilting her head to listen. "There are no bugs."

Jade didn't so much as twitch.

"There are no other sounds other than the wind." And their footfalls. But she followed as Jade kept on. Following until the tracks disappeared at a mountainous granite wall.

Something wasn't right. The trail was too perfect.

So Alora spoke up again. "These tracks are flawless." Crouching down, Alora ran her fingers across the indented muddy print and glanced to the next. Perfectly mirrored as if the print was simply flipped and inlaid.

Jade's eyes shifted from displeasure to doubt. "As much as I hate to admit it." She grumbled. "You're right."

Alora flashed her an amused smile and straightened upright.

"Don't get used to it." Whipping a small throwing dagger from her belt. "Turn back. We'll find another trail. Maybe—"

Deep in the shadows behind them, a creature stirred.

A terrifying growl rumbled like thunder before glowing blood-red eyes split the darkness, shining like sun rays on a ruby.

Every instinct screamed at her to run, but by the time her mind could convince her legs, a monstrous black body broke through a thicket of spruces.

And as they both pivoted their eyes to one another, they realized:

The wolf had laid its trap.

Cunningly leading them to the stone barrier. Ambushing them, ensnaring them inside a stone cage with nowhere to run except back to its awaiting drooling—dripping—razor-sharp teeth.

A hiss of metal cried out as Jade unsheathed her sword. Throwing dagger in the other hand, she trained her focus on the beast prowling toward them.

Alora gripped her bow and nocked an arrow, pulling back the bowstring to take aim. "Get to the trees. If you can climb high enough, I can lure it to you. Once it's in range, jump down and plunge the sword into its skull," Alora sharply commanded.

"Are you insane?" Jade snapped. "The moment I run, it'll lunge."

"I can shoot arrows faster than it can reach you. Just trust me."

Jade bent lower, her sword in front of her. "You're going to get me killed." Her eyes still tracked the menacingly slow prowl of the wolf.

"I'm the one staying in its path, if anything, it'll kill me first. Should make you happy. Now ... *go!*"

Alora let loose an arrow before Jade could object. It flew through the space between them and struck into the wolf's muscled shoulder, causing a roar so fierce it echoed off the stone.

Jade sprinted for the trees to the left.

Alora dropped to a knee with razor-sharp focus.

The wolf leapt. Gnashing its dripping teeth. Ready to clamp down on the soft flesh of their necks.

Four arrows flew with rapid speed and accuracy, peppering the wolf across its body.

The beast howled viciously in pain, wrenching itself back.

Then ...

It stopped.

With a scrape of its monstrous front paw, it pounded the dirt. Through an earth-shaking howl, its black figure began to ...

Alora's eyes widened as she caught her breath, releasing another arrow.

An earth-shattering scream rippled beside her. "*Stop!* It's a reike!" Jade threw her dagger at the incoming arrow, missing it by an inch as it embedded into the beast's torso. "Each wound only makes it grow stronger!"

"*No.*" Alora panicked under her breath.

Arrows burst from its body in streams of crimson as the reike grew higher and higher and higher, three times its size. It reared up on its back legs, slamming its front paws so hard on the ground that Jade and Alora fell to the dirt.

Jade shrieked in pain, grabbing her ankle.

No, no, no! Alora screamed as the wolf thundered toward Jade.

Alora reeled her arm out, fire bursting from her palms as her magic seized the scattered, bloodied arrows on the ground. They flew through the air in a firestorm as she moved her hands, commanding anything around to form a barrier between them and the beast.

Thousands of pounds of bone, fur, and teeth slammed through a wall of arrows, rock, and deadwood as fire raged around the heap. Alora's eyes glowed white with embers in Jade's direction, hand outstretched as her power ripped Jade's sword from her, transforming it into a second wall of flame and metal wall between.

She held strong, hands clenched into fists as flames raged from her palms.

The reike thrashed against it. Its razor-sharp claws punctured through, creating large grooves but unable to cleave a path of any real use.

Blood still dripping from its wounds, the beast turned its attention to her. It stood, breath heaving, when a menacing growl tore from its curled lips.

It dropped its head low.

The hunted and hunter met each other's murderous eyes.

With everything left in her, Alora brought the entire force of the wall down onto the reike's body, crushing it to the earth under a burning force.

The surrounding air filled with sounds of bones cracking, snapping, and whimpering as the beast began to once again grow.

Metal bent until edges burst into sharpened shards between gnashing claws.

And as if borrowed from the stars themselves, Alora sent an explosion of white flames across the pile, engulfing its body in a storm of flames and sunbursts until the reike's shrieks died and the only movements were flames licking up every last bit of wood, metal, and fur.

Then the calming, cool silence rushed on a gentle wind.

"Alora?" Jade's pained whisper echoed from behind the massive heap between them.

"I owe you a sword," Alora muttered so quietly she wasn't sure it'd been said aloud and stared in shock at the molten pile she'd forged.

"Alora."

Jade's voice shook her from the scene.

And without a moment to breathe, Alora rushed around the chaos and slid to a stop on her knees beside Jade. "Are you okay?" Frantically, she ran her hands over Jade's bruising ankle.

Jade's body lurched; pain shot through her. "*Starsdamnit!*"

"It's sprained." Alora ripped off her jacket, gathered two sticks to lock it in place, and began wrapping. "I need to get you back before anything else from these woods wants to try to make us into their next meal."

Banding her arm around Jade's waist, Alora slung her arm over her shoulder as Jade did the same before they stood. But the pain in Jade's ankle radiated through her leg, buckling her at the knees.

She slumped back down to the dirt. "No. Go get help. I'll be fine here," she insisted, wincing.

Alora shook her head and offered her hand. "I'm not leaving you here. Either get up or I'll carry you. But I'm not leaving you behind. There may be more of them."

Jade scowled but reluctantly grasped Alora's extended hand and was pulled to her feet.

"Let's get out of here," Alora breathed.

CAMP WAS FAR.

They managed to wander the forest for nearly an hour before they discovered the reike tracks. And with Jade's injury, it would take longer to return, even with Alora's help.

Distant howls prowled their every labored step. But when they finally died down and seemingly disappeared, Alora slowed the pace and stopped by a fallen tree to allow Jade to rest.

Pulling her ankle up with a wince, she readjusted the sticks and jacket. "Fuck." Jade cursed under her breath and frustratingly leaned back against the log. She shook her head, irritation covering her features. "I've been through countless battles, grueling training, slayed so many horrendous beasts that their pelts could fill all of Galdheir, but tonight. *Tonight*"—she darkly laughed—"I get taken down by a starsdamn earthquake running away."

Alora shot her a reassuring smile. "You didn't run away. We had a plan. You just didn't get there in time."

"You could've let the reike kill me."

"Why would I do that?"

"I tried to kill you—more than once. You could've done the same. Blamed it on the beast when you returned alone, got your freedom back."

Alora pulled a waterskin from the pack and handed it to her. "I could've also slit your throat as you've slept these last few months, but I didn't."

A resistant smile formed on Jade's face. Her fingers nervously clasped around the small bone and melted metal necklace around her neck as she drank.

They sat in the quiet of darkness for a few moments. Shadows stirred around them, gentle snaps of twigs from stags foraging, birds settling in their nests. The trickle of a nearby stream flowed off to the right.

Jade rolled her necklace between her fingers, her eyes as far off as the moon himself. "Can't see a starsdamned thing out here."

Heat pooled in Alora's palm as she held out her hand. Embers sparked—

"No! No more fire." Those embers instantly died out. Jade shuddered and squeezed her necklace nervously, scuffing her boot against the dirt to push herself back.

That look in Jade's eyes ... Alora had glimpsed it many times over the last few months. A flame would come too close in the arena, Jade would flinch. Never to hold a torch or stir food over the campfire. Forbidding candles inside their tent. One of the few times Alora had ever seen even the smallest amount of fear in her eyes was around a flame.

"You want to tell me about it?" Careful to ask casually, to coax Jade to talk.

Green eyes glazed over in the darkness. "No," was all Jade said before she dropped her necklace inside her tunic and tightened her jaw.

Alora tried not to frown. "You know, I would've never thought monsters like these existed only a few months ago."

Jade's face was unreadable.

"I thought monsters only existed in stories for the longest time. Well, until I lived with one." Even the mention of Kaine had her skin crawling. Alora pictured him standing there in the darkness, ready to come for her. But she quickly turned away, refusing to let his snickering grin steal her mind. *Not now.*

Alora pulled the waterskin to her lips and drank deep, closing her eyes with a hard squeeze. Moments passed by.

When her eyes slowly drifted open, Kaine's visage misted away as if he'd never been there at all. "I wish this was whiskey." She breathed a laugh and handed it to Jade.

"Me too." Jade tossed it against her lips. "Garrik told me very little about the monster you lived with." She paused and tightened her lips. "That ... my treatment against you that first night may have been a small example of what you went through and, by his vagueness, I can only assume it was quite often." Jade's stare flashed to Alora's stomach. Perhaps remembering that brutal kick. "Males are truly horrific creatures. I am sorry." The words seemed sincere, believable.

Alora slipped down to the dirt and reclined against the log. With a calming sigh, she asked, "And the monsters you lived with?" And nodded to the bulge in Jade's tunic, hiding her necklace.

It took a few heartbeats before Jade reached in and grabbed the leather around her neck, pulling the pendant back out. She held it between her fingers, examining the melted paths of iron seeped deep into ivory bone.

"It's the last coin my master made off of me ... and a bone from his spine when I ripped his neck out."

An icy chill ran down Alora's.

Master. She shuddered at the word.

"The Fighting Pits of Torgal. Where my sisters-in-kind died for the pleasure of the males who deemed themselves superior to our sex. My

359

father sold me to make his house—him and my brothers in blood—coin for their coffers and to build their castle high on my back. On my mother's back. Females were nothing more than for breeding males and entertainment in the pits. My realm, doomed if you didn't carry a worthless sack of balls between your legs.

"Fire was Kieran's." She cursed the name. "Favorite form of punishment. His flame—*king* as we call them in Elysian—Killian, bought me and allowed him to do as he wished.

"In my cell, underneath the coliseum and battleground, Kieran would light unending flames, bursting them on my skin until I yielded. I fucking hate fire." Jade shuddered and tensed. "Which is utterly pathetic seeing as I'm the daughter of the most powerful dragon shifter in Torgal," she added.

"Even so, I wouldn't let Kieran or his flame breed me, never let them bed me, which made the punishments with fire worse. I wouldn't produce either a son, and I wouldn't bear a daughter into this cruel world. I wouldn't let them control me—the daughter of a flame would win them enough wealth and power to last centuries with one kill after the other. And when my usefulness ran out, when I could no longer stand to slaughter my sisters-in-kind just to live, I was to die in those pits." Jade's eyes turned glassy in the moonlight.

"The last night in my cell, Kieran burned his property. Three of my sisters-in-kind died in front of me until their screaming faded and the steaming piles of charred flesh peppered my senses. All because they tried to help heal my wounds from my last fight. It was the last night he ever fucking breathed again. I took his coin and ripped out his throat before escaping on Aiden's ship in the night. He found me stowing away below and agreed to sail away with me on board."

For the first time, Alora saw liquid lining Jade's eyes. Despair, anguish, hatred, and rage burned within the tear that slowly dropped down her cheek and sunk into the ivory of the bone held in her hand.

"Garrik told me I was mistaken to say those things to you in the arena. That in time, you may tell me why. And though I will deny it if you ever speak of it outside these trees..." Jade sighed heavily before rolling her eyes to the sky and shaking her head. "I'm shit at apologies. So, unfuck you or whatever."

Alora couldn't help the choked laugh and nodded.

Jade was trying. As best as Jade could.

"I was giving you a compliment when I called you a princess."

Alora scrunched her eyebrows. Confusion covered her face.

"You fight like a princess because you fight like me. And I didn't like it. Not when you fought the gamroara, against me... *We*"—she looked away—"don't fall easily. You wouldn't be an easy fight. And I didn't want to stare my kind in the face and fight my own feelings. If I could break you, then I wouldn't have to watch you die, just as my sisters-in-kind in our fighting pits. You didn't belong here."

"So, it was never about Aiden?"

Jade worked her jaw. "Not all of it. But if you ever lead any of my *family* to be injured again—"

"I know. And at this point, if anyone hurt them, I too would do the same." She shocked herself at her own admission. "And if you ever speak a word of *this* to anyone outside of these trees..." Alora looked up to the stars and shook her head, picturing Eldacar, Thalon, Jade, Aiden, and even the High Prince.

Family. Jade had called them family.

What she wouldn't give to feel that someday again. She glanced over at Jade. The stars cast a glowing white light across her exhausted, freckled face and red hair. Seeing her in a new light, brighter in some way. And she felt that new bond stirring between them as a simple, real smile grew on Jade.

"Jade?"

"What?"

With a smile, Alora ventured, "We all need therapy."

"Indeed."

Amused laughs echoed through the trees.

THE PULSE of energy irradiated through them as they reached the boundary of camp. A deep wave of gratefulness shuddered down Alora's spine. Not simply for the fact that they had returned, but that thrumming energy, that taste of metal that had her arm hair standing on end, meant one thing.

Garrik's shield still held.

Alive. Garrik was still alive.

A sentry spotted them as they crossed the tree line, and soon three Dragons wearing battle leathers rushed to them. Two lifted Jade and carried her back to the Shadow Order's firesite. The third assessed Alora and escorted her to Eldacar, who was examining Jade's ankle.

"Unleash Michael, what happened to you two?" Thalon stood cross-armed. Alora could have sworn he took on the High Prince's unamused pose.

"It was a reike. Damn beast almost killed us." Jade winced as Eldacar wrapped her ankle with healing hands and white cloth.

"How in Firekeeper-filled-hell did you get away?" Thalon's expression was something a little more than shocked.

"Alora—*ah!*" She winced as Eldacar moved her ankle into its correct position and finished wrapping, before turning to Thalon to speak—

A pulse of static energy rippled through their bodies.

"*Shit.*" Thalon barely breathed as another pulse only seconds in-between shot through them.

Paralyzing fright flooded Eldacar's eyes as he looked up. The stars wavered, throbbed with otherworldly purpose. A shuddering gasp escaped him.

The hairs on Alora's neck bristled. And they all watched the disturbing oscillation distorting the night sky. Pulse after pulse after—

Only this time...

It didn't return.

The group remained unmoved. Camp was completely silent save for the crackling of wood within fires.

Alora stared—horrified—at Thalon, who dropped to his knees and rested his head in his hands.

The shield had fallen.

CHAPTER 42

Seconds after Garrik's shield fell, Thalon unleashed a magic so bold Alora wondered how he could wield such unearthly power. Static energy surged through the air before the bitter taste of metal invaded her mouth. And if that wasn't enough to recognize what was falling over camp, the sudden thrumming and tingling sensation that rushed through her body was.

Another shield.

How was that possible?

Fingertips still prickling, Alora massaged them, turning to Thalon.

He twisted the silver ring that Garrik had given him on his finger, then whipped his head to Jade and Eldacar, then to Alora, with agonizing distress and harsh decisions crowding his golden eyes.

"Alert the generals. No one leaves the border. We are protected from the outside." Those troubled, golden eyes scanned each one of them. Still, he twisted that ring. "Prepare to portal in two nightfalls. Garrik's ring will protect us mere days, no longer."

Jade shakingly rose to her feet, aided by Eldacar. "The High King. You think he's coming?"

Thalon nodded, slow and precise.

A brutal curse burst from Jade's lips.

Alora's body suddenly felt cold and about to buckle, like a massive wall of ice had collapsed around her. Not for fear of the hell-storm that would be unleashed from the High King, but something deep inside had shaken so viciously, she was unsure if it could ever be restored.

Before she knew what she was saying, Alora blurted, "We have to get him."

Three sets of eyes stared at her in silence.

Why weren't they grabbing weapons and storming camp, preparing to lay siege to Galdheir? She didn't understand. Couldn't leave him. Couldn't pretend he was simply lost.

So, she said it again in fear that she may have spoken too softly, "*We have to save him.*"

Thalon was the one to speak, stepping toward her deliberately. "He's forbidden it."

"*He's not here,*" she snapped, feeling her palms threaten to ignite. "You're in command." Alora flashed her piercing glare from Thalon to Jade to Eldacar. "*We can't just leave him there to die!*"

Warm, tattooed hands cupped her shoulders as she felt scorching, daunting tears begin to fall.

Thalon's eyes seemed to be replaying a terrible memory, as if he were hearing screams and seeing living nightmares surrounding them. He blinked, shaking his head with a heavy, final sigh. "I know how you're feeling. But our High Prince has given an order, and we must follow it. Garrik knows far more than we ever will. To go against him could prove catastrophic to the future of Elysian."

"And what of his future? *Who's going to protect him?*" The words sounded like someone else shrieking them, not her.

Thalon tilted his head at Jade and Eldacar, giving them the gentle, breathy order. "Go. Alert camp." They left and Thalon continued to grasp Alora's shoulders. "We have to trust he knows what's best."

"That's bullshit," she growled, wiping a tear from her cheek with a violent swipe.

Warm arms pulled her into a gentle, benevolent embrace, and her legs almost buckled at the overwhelming surge of protection within it. "I know. And just as you hate him for it ... I do, too."

THERE WAS a high possibility their High Prince wouldn't return.

That fact covered every general's face in crippling anguish seated around the war tent. Since dusk the previous night, they gathered for a series of briefings, barely resting a minute to eat, to sleep. Discussing— arguing—preparing. Continuing, no matter the circumstance. No matter the cost. A free Elysian required their sacrifice until their dying breaths. Until Magnelis was in a grave.

Only then could they collapse and shatter and break.

To mourn those lost.

To rebuild a new life without them.

Without ... *him.*

Alora sank back in her chair as every distraught face molded into a sophisticated illusion of strength.

One by one, they left the tent. Haiden not even giving her one glance as he was the last to leave only her and Thalon behind. Smoke gently whorled from candles littering the table. She followed the swirls of tendrils—of mist—into the cold evening air, silently wishing it was Smokeshadows dawning Garrik back when Thalon wordlessly collapsed into a chair, massaging his temples in deep, slow circles.

Usually a strong and unbreakable force, he was now reduced to total devastation. The magnificent warrior and legendary Guardian trembled as he swallowed. His shoulders sinking low as if deep in thought. And she wondered if he was desperately trying to reach Garrik's mind with his own pleas, just as she'd done all day.

Thalon's eyes closed, and his mouth began to move silently for some time. He was praying, she realized. Then, his sorrow spilled into the room as he looked to the ceiling.

"I failed him again," he murmured, shaking his head.

Alora was tempted to stand from her chair—the one across from Garrik's, which sat empty as a cruel reminder. She'd never seen Thalon so defeated ... so ... so fallen. "You didn't fail him." She did it anyway— stand—and moved to his side of the table, settling a hand on his shoulder. "Thalon, you cannot fault yourself for this."

"I can fault myself. Because we've been here before."

His meaning escaped her.

"Before the Blood Years," he started, and Alora's mind drifted to stories of seventeen years of death and horrific destruction. Of when Garrik—the Savage Prince who clouded the land in fear, violence, and corruption—eliminated anyone opposing Magnelis's rule. Even kings fell. Executing raids on cities and towns, searching for Marked Ones without one single act of mercy. When younglings were burned alive in front of their mothers, fathers were flayed on pikes, homes destroyed to dust in a single blink of an eye. Generations of Mystics reduced to ash, magic lost—stolen from them.

Alora felt herself shudder as Thalon continued, "I should've disobeyed him, should've protected him. I'm his starsdamned Guardian. I—"

Somewhere in the distance, a horn resounded. Camp exploded with shouts.

Thalon was on his feet, bursting through the tent doors with Alora mere inches from his heels.

The sky was feathered with blackness, snuffing out dusk until the camp was engulfed in an early night sky. Raging shadows from a localized storm and lightning shot through the sky. Alora knew this magic. She'd seen it four days ago when the same storm whirled, producing a portal as it did now, floating down beyond their obstructed view of tents.

And then they were running.

With imperceivable speed, the edge of camp blurred around them until they crossed Garrik's shield.

The stormy portal hissed and shrieked as it hovered above the ground in the open field outside camp.

"Nevilier!" Thalon ripped his golden, runed sword from his side. "Get to your positions, weapons ready! Everyone else, get inside the shield!" he thundered to soldiers crowding around the tents, drawing their weapons.

The portal raged. Lightning struck out in every direction, preparing to yield whatever threat was coming.

Nobody moved.

With a flash of light, a mass plummeted from the portal and slammed to the ground. The portal imploded as it disappeared, hauling the ice-cold wind and darkened skies along with it.

The mass laid unmoving, covered by the tall grass.

And they were running again.

Alora's eyes widened as she came closer.

Because that *mass* wasn't just an object ...

Black pants, dragon-scaled armor, gray hair ...

"*Garrik!*" Thalon slid to his knees, dirt spraying at the impact, scooping Garrik's limp body into his arms. He placed his ear to Garrik's chest. "He's breathing!" he screamed to the soldiers running through the field before turning back to Garrik.

"Brother, listen to me, you're alive. You're home." An inked hand frantically cupped the back of Garrik's head and pulled him to his chest. "You hear me? *You're safe.*" The hand that held Garrik's shoulder began to tremble as Thalon cried, "I'm so sorry"—a tear streamed down his cheek—"I'm so damn sorry."

Alora dropped beside them, scanning Garrik for injury. Alarmingly, his body, from what she could see, was unharmed, his clothes impeccably flawless, his weapons remained sheathed on his back, side, and belt.

"No wounds. How is this possible?"

"You never know with Magnelis."

GARRIK HADN'T awoken in the hours after his traumatizing return. No one knew why.

Limp and pale, Garrik laid atop the plush pillows and furs on his cot. His breathing shallow—too shallow—and uneven. Small injuries like cuts on his hands and little bruises on his neck could be easily healed, but they didn't dare search elsewhere. And Alora recalled her own injuries, how he'd left her clothing untouched until she regained consciousness.

Thalon vaguely explained that Garrik would never allow it. Never let them know what happened while he visited Galdheir.

They always knew, though. He tried to hide it, but friends always know.

"What if..." Eldacar choked on his words, sitting at the table between Thalon and Jade. "What if Magnelis stole his mind ... his power?"

A sharp breath wrenched out of Thalon. "He's tried before, never succeeded. The deal that he and Kerimkhar struck doesn't allow him to steal the powers of his blood or name. It's impossible to take power from him."

"He could use them, though." Jade rubbed her temples in agony. "The fucker has done that before."

Alora stared at Garrik's chest that barely moved. Thalon, Jade, and Eldacar's conversation faded as she focused on his face.

Please, wake up.

367

Nothing.

Through a heavy sigh, she pulled a chair closer to the side of his cot while the others ruffled through books from Eldacar's library.

A worrisome yet playful grin climbed her face. *I'll let you pin me against a tree again, but only if you wake up, right now.* She stared at his expressionless face, hoping that her attempt to arouse him would work.

But again. Nothing.

Come on. I'll let you do— She couldn't believe what she was about to think. But if it worked... *I'll let you do anything. Just ... wake up.*

Alora leaned forward, dropping her face into her hands. Something burned on her palms, and she realized that she had started crying.

Anything?

Her head snapped up and eyes narrowed as that familiar, deep voice caressed her mind. She straightened in her chair, doubting the voice was real. Had her mind conjured it?

Alora looked at his face and expected to see that nothing had changed.

Instead, those usual beautiful, enchanting silver eyes were weak, dull, muddy-gray orbs, peeking through slitted, trembling eyelids. Garrik's chest moved at a slightly quicker pace, but not much more than before, and the High Prince's hand softly twitched on the blanket as he struggled to fully open his eyes.

Thank Maker of the Skies. He was awake.

Alora leaned forward and clasped the top of his hand before she started to turn. Ready to tell his friends that he was awake. But his voice stopped her.

I need a moment. Breathless and exhausted, Garrik's voice strained in her mind. *Please. Just a moment before you call to them.*

She understood. A few more minutes to pass by in peace before his friends would berate him with questions and heartfelt relief.

Embers lit in her palm, cupping her hand to a metal washbasin on the bedside table until steam rose. Water silently dripped as she pulled a warm washcloth from it and placed it on his chilled forehead.

His eyes widened, opened, and met hers, head trembling at the touch. Something unsettling crossed his face but fell relaxed as his breathless voice brushed her mind. *Thank you.*

Garrik's eyes fluttered closed.

What? No clever girl or darling?

Hmm. A calm groan of comfort as a faint grin climbed up the side of his face before collapsing just as fast. He sunk his head back into the pillows before she noticed he fell perfectly still.

A few minutes passed. Alora began to wonder if he would wake again soon. The softness of the back of her hand touched his forehead. His temperature was back to the normal icy chill his shadows kept him in.

The gentle touch stirred him, and he brushed her hand resting on the cot beside him as he gazed up at her with that intoxicating side grin she admittedly missed.

Garrik pushed himself up on his elbows with a sharp wince and slumped back against the mountain of pillows stacked against the wall of the tent. Silver eyes looked rested, lovely, and bright once more. The color of his face had returned to its tanned glow.

With a swinging motion, he threw the warmed blankets off his body and planted his feet on the furs beneath.

Thank you. Garrik squeezed her hand before standing.

When he let go, Alora's eyes fell onto her palm where a small pearlsea rested around swirling Smokeshadows.

Garrik cleared his throat, adjusting his leathers at his abdomen, and proceeded to his chair in the middle of the tent, grabbing his swords that rested against it.

The group instantly jumped up from their seats and turned.

And Garrik closed his eyes. A pulse of energy thrummed through them all. Through everyone in camp.

Sighs of relief and cheering rattled the camp. A victory cry by its intensity. Their High Prince had returned to them.

Eyes opened and arms crossed, Garrik grinned. "What did I miss?"

GARRIK DIDN'T BOTHER DISCUSSING details of his absence.

He slouched in his armchair, fingers loosely clasping a sweating bottle of amber liquid. Beads of moisture gathered on the glass, catching the dim light as he swirled the contents.

Their concern was appreciated. He thanked them for it, for their obedience to their duties.

With a quick wave and a burst of Smokeshadows in the corner of his tent, a tall box-like structure with a mix of earthy colored stones, replaced the table.

Upon quick examination, Alora recognized small details like a ledge with vials and a steel fixture that mimics rainfall. Such details reminded her of those in Kaine's manor. He had many washrooms with the same symbol of luxury. The stones formed a shower fit for thrice

Garrik's size, and a crystal door was propped open, waiting to be occupied.

Garrik shifted in his chair, grimacing as the bourbon burned down his throat before the soothing sound of water began pelting onto the stone floor and steam billowed from beyond the crystal threshold. A heavy aroma of lemon, rose, and lavender accompanied the steam.

They all registered the gentle request to leave him to the peace and quiet.

After his days at the castle, he was sure to deserve it.

On his way to the entrance, Thalon paused and palmed Garrik's shoulder, and Garrik shuddered at the touch. "Welcome home, brother. You know I'm here *when* you decide to talk." Tone filled with relief, he flashed Garrik a stern look, as if he knew there was so much more to be disclosed. But instead of pushing, Thalon twisted from his finger the ring Garrik gave him and returned it to his nightstand before walking out.

The sun had vanished by then. And through the crackling of fires, camp had quieted. A cloudless night sky proudly displayed a breathtaking view of glistening stars across the horizon. With it, a peaceful, cool breeze.

Mostly everyone had retired to their tents, but Alora's nerves shot lightning through her limbs as she tossed and turned. Sleep was utterly pointless.

So she stirred herself up and threw on onyx pants, leather boots, and a red leather jacket given to her by Calla, a rose-gold-haired faerie with bright yellow eyes skilled in phytotherapy. Calla insisted that Alora would look lovely in it and gladly gifted it by a river they were doing their wash at.

Grabbing her obsidian dagger and its twin from between the cot and frame, Alora quietly slipped to the door, deciding on target practice. Two more steps and she would've been outside in the refreshingly crisp air.

If it wasn't for the rustling beside her.

Armed with weapons set for battle, Garrik, tense shouldered, stormed out of his tent.

This time, she didn't question herself. She knew exactly what was coming, and even with the brutal warning, she followed him anyway.

CHAPTER 43

An annulus of torches appeared beyond the tree she leaned against. Surrounded by thick forest, Garrik began training with fine sword mastery in each movement of twin blades. A style much like Thalon's, she noticed at some point, but crafted in his own magnificently lethal perfection.

By his expression ... by the brutal warning of his rippling power, she knew.

This was a bad night.

Maybe tonight wasn't the best time to disturb him. Stars-knows how many times she'd rather be left in darkness to battle her own haunting day-terrors. How many times she'd rather fight in silence while trapped in her screaming mind.

A double-sworded swing cleaved through the air.

Garrik cried out—a sound so excruciating that her own body rippled in phantom pain. Grabbing his right side covered by a dark tunic, his swords clanged to the dirt.

Wisps of breath panted from Alora's lips in the cool air. Garrik panted alongside her, wedging his right knee mercilessly into the dirt, but his breath matched the air's temperature, and nothing but wind left him.

"You should know by now that I am aware of when you follow me." Garrik lifted one of the swords, face deathly, and thrust it into the ground. He held onto the hilt, still clutching his ribs with the other hand. "Show yourself!" he demanded.

Alora slowly walked into the annulus, palms raised in peaceful surrender. "I know. I wasn't sure if you wanted the company," she admitted and rubbed the back of her neck. "You're wounded. Why didn't you say anything?"

Garrik's eyes shifted to hers, agitation burned in his cold voice, "I am fine."

"Yeah, you look *fine*," she stabbed, matching his agitation as she stepped forward, reaching to his side. "Let me look."

"*Do not touch me.*" Grimacing, he pushed off his knee and stood. Swirling ink began to fill his eyes.

"What? Are you afraid I'll see your rippling body and instantly climb on top of you?" The attempt to make him smile failed.

"I am not in the mood." Garrik growled through uneven breaths, clutching his side as he walked away and leaned against a tree.

A bad night, she reminded herself. A very bad night.

"Fine. I thought I'd come out here to be a distraction, but I can see that my presence is unwanted." Alora started walking to the edge of the annulus. "*Goodnight...*" *Mighty bastard.*

"*Stop.*"

The command sent a shiver deep into her core.

"You know, you really are a prick!" Alora whipped her head around to glower at him. "We spent four days out of our minds, pleading to Maker of the Skies for you to return alive, only for you to completely shut us out. Not offering any explanation as to why you were thrown from a portal unconscious, and now *this*." Gesturing with a finger to his side, arms tense, she balled her hand into an embered fist and stomped toward him.

"Shake off the façade of 'I can never show weakness.' Show you give a damn that your friends care about you and love you so much, they'd die for you. Let them into your darkened world for just a moment.

"Everyone breaks, mighty prince. Including you! And if you weren't so arrogant, you'd come to realize that those around you want nothing more than to help you through whatever horrors you face." She was steaming mad as she marched inches from him, daring to shove him back into the oak.

Before her hands could, Garrik grabbed her forearms. His face turned pale as snow. *"You want to know what happened?"* Viciously growling, he pushed off the tree, releasing her before his voice rose in rage. Silver succumbed to the deep, darkened abyss as if she were attacking him with sharpened iron.

Garrik ripped open his shirt.

Horrendous hues of deep amethyst, dark emerald, and onyx-navy painted his scarred skin. Across the right side of his body, the artwork, a barbarous masterpiece of searing pain, extended around his ribs, down into his pants line.

"Go ahead," he growled, wincing at the movement, *"take a long, starsdamned look."*

That was a crack in his voice.

Alora's heart sank.

Words came out in choked breaths. "Magnelis forced me to slaughter in front of his entire court and throne. When it was not bloody enough, when I instead stole deep into the cores of their tortured minds and melted everything they once were"—nostrils flared, he became a hint of a sharp toothed beast—"Magnelis ordered his soldiers to drag me down to my dungeon and remind me what a merciful hand would result."

Breathing unevenly, Garrik prowled to a tree and slammed his fist into it, cracking his knuckles.

"That was night one."

Alora shook, tears burning her eyes.

"I allowed them to imprison me in my cell, knowing if I resisted, Magnelis would do much more. If I shielded against the punishment, he would inflict pain on my Dragons instead. Another one of his tactics, giving me a fucking choice. And if I choose wrong..." Garrik shook his head. "Their war hammers collided against my side until my ribs cracked, and even after, they continued. And she..." His hand glided over his bruises and clamped his eyes shut.

"Night three, I was forced amongst the snickering and pathetic ilk of Magnelis's court. He waited on his golden throne, expecting my obedience when his worthless hand gripped my throat, demanding proof I understood my current position. Otherwise, Nevilier would be tasked with killing half my *entire* legion... Yet my reverence was not enough for his satisfaction." Tormented eyes glanced up at the stars.

"A young, wailing male convulsed at my boots. Barely clothed, his flesh had been ... flayed from his bones. The death mark ripped from his arm." His breath sharpened with a quick shake of his head. "And *she* was there, watching, after she ... in my cell." Garrik lost his breath as his body trembled, brushing a hand against the scars on his abdomen and balled a fist. "*Fuck.*"

It collided with the tree, splitting knuckles open.

Alora dared to touch his back, to comfort him, but he pushed away.

"She surrendered my swords before Magnelis ordered a slow and painful death. It was the Mystic or my Dragons. I ... couldn't save him." Garrik's lips trembled as his eyes went glassy. "I conducted a flawless performance. Slow. Painful. Bloody. The animal I used to revel as for the pleasure of the High King. Every scream, an illusion to the court. The fools unaware that his pain was imaginary. I would not suffer him to feel the torture. Magnelis mocked every drop of blood on the marble. Hungry for more every time I glared my own delusive amusement at the throne.

"After hours at the High King's pleasure, when my arm ached and ice scorched inside my weakened arms, I relieved his head to the bloodstained stone." Garrik fell to the ground on his knees, so hard it shook the dirt. "And yet, it was not enough," he lamented, his chin dropping to his chest.

"I do not remember what happened after. I heard your voice pleading so far away. Every word louder and clearer until you sat next to me, and I was able to open my eyes."

Silence followed for uncountable heartbeats.

"You question why I do not reveal what transpires against me? I bear it so no one else has to. I am the monster, prowling at the door, so those most important to me stay alive. I shoulder the horrors, allowing Elysian to press onward without the burdens I bear."

Alora dropped in front of him and grabbed his tormented face, her knees touching his as she lifted his head. "These burdens are far too heavy to carry on your own."

His eyes scrunched closed once more, head twisting, as if fighting awful memories from Galdheir.

"You can't do this alone," she pleaded. "This is too much for one to shoulder."

"The stars were cruel enough to curse me with the strength to do so. I have to."

'*I have to.*' She remembered those words. Remembered another one, too.

'*Tomorrow.*' The memory of Garrik's voice echoed in her mind. '*The next few days will be—I just need a drink.*'

Alora stiffened. "Did you know?"

Garrik simply blinked, facing her fully with a slow nod.

Alora gaped, her gut twisting. The ice of his cheeks was all she could focus on. How pale he was under her touch. The slow tremor echoing from his legs until it thrashed up his spine and tensed his shoulders.

The tavern ... and after when she tried to distract him from ... from the torment stealing his eyes in the inn.

Words echoed again. *'What's bothering you?'*

Garrik swallowed hard as if he were replaying it all, too.

Her eyes widened, hands shaking so much that she could barely brush her thumb against the muscle that flecked in his cheek. "You didn't think you would return," Alora murmured as another tremble rippled through him.

"No," he breathed. A sound so fractured she felt her heart split.

"You could have died." The tears began falling over her lashes, picturing him in a dungeon. Being beaten by weapons, hanging from chains while they sat in comfort around fires and continued without him.

'I think it would be far easier to tell you what is not.' His words echoed again.

"Yes," was all he said before his eyes closed.

He knew. He knew what was going to happen to him and yet said nothing. Allowing this horrible, terrible thing to torment him—alone. He endured it, Magnelis's wrath, physical, brutal pain and humiliation, like he deserved it all. For Elysian, for his Dragons, his Shadow Order...

For her.

Tracing his palm up his abdomen, it trembled under his touch.

"Why did you do it?" she asked.

Garrik's eyebrows furrowed.

"Why did you fly us from camp that night?"

He breathed sharply as he leaned back against the tree, pulling from her palms and resting his head on the bark. "Magnelis's mind is protected against my powers. I cannot anticipate his intentions. Knowing Nevilier would retrieve me and not knowing my fate ... I preferred a night away from camp if it were to be my last outside the walls of Galdheir."

"You thought Magnelis knew of our treason?"

"I have been meticulously ruthless in securing our secret in ways I cannot share. But with my powers null against him, I did not know what to think. If I would never see the sky again ... I wanted to fly amongst the stars. I wanted to take you there because ... perhaps you needed it, too." His gaze fell to the dirt, and he roughly said, "A memory I could hold on to if ... if they had me again. Something I could remember when the pain became too much."

She remembered what Thalon said about the Mystic whose baby he was merciful toward, and what Magnelis did to him after.

Tears brimmed her burning eyes. It was unimaginable what Garrik had thought might happen to him. Of what kind of suffering Magnelis would inflict on him in the discovery of high treason. But Garrik was willing to allow his capture—to go *quietly*—for the sake of one last night of peace. One last night of freedom that he spent with her.

"I could not speak to you that morning because I knew if you smiled at me like you did the night before ... if you touched me like that again ... I would have found a way to stay. And Magnelis would have unleashed his wrath on my Dragons, and I could not allow that to happen."

Alora's heart was breaking for him. The stranger she met a few short months ago, the Savage Prince she'd heard so much about. Her enemy in Telldaira. Her friend after the explosion in the arena. The male who flew her in his arms when he thought he was going to suffer by the High King's hand.

Garrik ... this powerful, *beautiful*, selfless male who would sacrifice himself just to make certain the world didn't fall to ruin.

An entire world.

An entire world.

"When you're out saving Elysian," she started, "remember to save yourself, too."

"Maybe I am not worth saving."

"Yes ... mighty prince, you are." She pulled herself beside him, leaning against the tree in silence. Taking in the scent of his washed hair —lavender and rose, lemon mixed with a hint of vanilla and oak on his breath.

Garrik exhaled deeply, and she thought it was more beautiful than an enchanting melody listening to him breathe. Listening to that precious, lovely sound.

They sat in that peace for what seemed like an hour of slow, healing breaths.

Then Garrik's hand lightly brushed hers on the dirt between them. "I recall you promising to do *anything* should I wake."

She stiffened, unprepared to hear his request. But Garrik's voice was so soft, she imagined it like a feathered touch. And before he spoke, she swore she could glimpse stars gleaming in his silver eyes.

"Tell me about your days while I was gone. What made you smile? I want to know everything."

Alora loosened a breath and began to grin.

He did, too.

"I killed a reike yesterday."

CHAPTER 44

"Alora! Come inside for dinner. Your father will be home any moment."

A bouncy, white curly-haired faeling stumbled barefoot across a dirt lane in one of Telldaira's northern communities. Adorned in a white summer dress with silver stitching and a delicate lace of snowflakes her father had bought for her. Shrubbery and bushes lined the street and yielded exquisite shades of fuchsia, violet, and pearl flowers as she followed the call of her mother.

Arms stretched out wide, Nadeleine whispered, "Come here, my precious lion cub." She knelt low as Alora jumped into them, clutching her white lion trinket.

A tear dropped down Alora's cheek when her eyes opened. Her mother's voice still caressed her mind.

Sleep. She didn't remember when it had come. Through the glistening stars and burning out torches, Garrik's warm voice had whispered long into the night. The soothing sounds and melodies from their distant camp quieted at one point, as if they had calmly faded away into a whisper on a cool wind.

When the warm morning sun kissed her face and an unusually pleasant chill against her head stirred her, she realized that she was still in the annulus. Covered by a green, woolen blanket that Garrik must have dawned and draped around her, her head comfortably rested against his shoulder.

Alora pressed her cheek further against his chest. The scent of him was soothing. Warm lemon, a calm invitation of lavender and rose, and laced within, his usual leather and metal scent offered a flutter of safety.

Garrik's arm was toweled around her upper arm, tracing lazy circles against the blanket where her death mark was hidden. The sensation only added to the protection she felt.

His silver gaze stretched out into the evergreen trees ahead. As if in loose thought, his head relaxed against the bark and a tender smile rested on his face, which mirrored the calmness of the morning. The grass gently swayed in the imperceptible breeze, the trickling of a nearby stream against pebbles, soft steps of mother animals and their young treading through the fields beyond. Glowing silver glistened against the shards of sunlight, and perhaps they pretended the past few days were nothing but a distant echo.

She'd only seen him like this once before, in the skies.

Peaceful.

Despite everything that had happened to him while he was gone.

He was utterly peaceful.

An aching neck begged her to move. Desiring a few more moments in peace, she stubbornly allowed it to throb. It was worth it—Garrik needed it—those moments. She did too.

For as soon as she would stir, their reality would flood back.

Basking in its rareness, the calm of the morning and soothing delight of her dream waved over her. Nothing in the world felt like this. Not for a long time, anyway.

Alora's eyes shifted to his and glowing silver irises peered down at her sapphires. With a deep, long inhale, that High Prince mask returned. Not entirely, but enough to realize that they had been out there too long and should be heading back to camp.

She shifted in his embrace, her boots scuffed against the dirt when she bent her outstretched knees. The blanket dropped down her shoulder under his touch before she lightly rubbed the back of her aching neck and yawned.

"We were out here all night?" Slightly embarrassed, she looked to where her head had happily rested on him.

"Indeed." He side-glanced at her. "Someone decided she wanted to sleep with a High Prince last night." That wolfish grin climbed his face.

Alora scoffed before crossing her arms. "In—"

"My dreams?" He grinned and pivoted his head against the bark to gaze at the evergreens. Silver eyes closed, and a breathy chuckle escaped his nose.

And there was that smile again. The one so rare, the one that made her question the monster inside that he was insistent dwelled there.

"I did not wish to wake you. You slept so soundly." Garrik's soft and gentle eyes looked over at her. "You smiled in your sleep. You were dreaming."

Fabrics of white and silver stitching flashed in her mind as her mother's voice called. Memories such as this one hadn't visited her in quite some time. Though a pleasant memory, her parents were gone. The faeling she was, gone. That memory would only bring heartache if she sat with it any longer.

Instead, she asked him, "Did you sleep?"

Garrik clenched his ribs and pushed himself from the ground, using the tree for stability. He let out a sharp grunt when his right side bent against itself. "They will be wondering where we are. Come." A palm reached out to her.

Of course he wouldn't tell her. He said so last night.

His burdens.

His to bear.

As they made their way back to camp, Alora couldn't shake the dream, couldn't shake the thoughts of the annulus the night before.

He hadn't answered her, leaving a burning, aching hole in her heart. Her problems were always her own, too. Anything that happened in the manor were hers to endure, alone. She'd rarely said much to Emeline. Rowlen knew some, mostly toward the end, but silence had always been her friend. Darkness alone heard her cries at night.

Shadows had licked the memories that fell down her cheeks for as long as she could remember. Understandably, the High Prince's retreat with such questions made sense; it mirrored her own ways of coping. Unhealthy ways, she admitted. But if she expected others to respect her silence, how could she not respect his?

So, she didn't press.

They reached their firesite, welcomed by an overwhelmingly loaded table in front of Garrik's tent. Breakfast meats grilled to absolute perfection, fried potatoes dripping with butter, herbs, and garlic, a pallet of assorted cheeses, and the most mouth-watering display of fruits and sweet pastries covered it.

Thalon was loading his plate. A grin that resembled a small faeling on Winter Solstice morning awaiting the new treasures he'd play with peppered his face. "Aiden will go mad that he's missed this." A red berry popped in his mouth as he spoke to no one in particular, eying a sizzling piece of pig fat on a platter.

Alora eyed it, too. "What's going on?"

The smell alone could've made her believe she was still in a dream. She brushed her hand along the wooden table, eyes glistening at the spread of food while her stomach growled something awful.

"Nothing." Garrik offered a plate to her.

Thalon whipped his head to look at them. "*Nothing?*" His own plate shoved into Garrik's chest, and he grabbed the empty one out of Garrik's hand. "Happy Birthday, brother!" he shouted and slapped Garrik on the shoulder. "Camp sends their blessings." Palm stretched wide, Thalon gestured across the table.

Beaming, Alora turned to Garrik. "Why didn't you say anything?"

Fire crackled behind where Jade and Eldacar sat eating, covering up the low growl reverberating from their High Prince. Garrik placed the plate on the wooden table and reached for a tankard on the edge. Something had changed in him. His eyes, a bit duller, his visage not of anyone who would be celebrating—but of some distant pain.

He stared into the bottom of his drink. That gaze didn't shift, like the contents were revealing a secret he couldn't turn away from.

"I tell them every year this is of no importance, and every year they decide to disobey me."

Garrik threw the tankard to his lips, emptied it, and settled it on the table. He shifted on his feet, headed toward his tent entrance, and stopped at the threshold, peering over his shoulder.

"Eat. We move out in two hours. Thalon, find me when you are finished," he commanded before letting the darkness of his tent swallow him inside.

CHAPTER 45

"Males." Jade rolled her eyes and continued sharpening a jagged sword in her lap, its twin laying at her feet. She rested at a safe distance from the fire, and Alora doubted she could even feel the warmth.

Face taunt and sporting a new blackening eye, Thalon's heavy steps thumped across the dirt and grass after exiting Garrik's tent. His golden sword stiff by his side, purple knuckles fisted the pommel. Without a single glance toward Alora and Jade, he stepped to the fire, angrily throwing a large bundle of parchments into the flames before summoning a portal, his odd shadow trailing behind in the sunlight, and disappeared inside.

Garrik stood, pushing three rings on his fingers before his arms crossed. He too had somehow obtained injuries on his face. With a busted lip, toweled by the darkness inside his tent entrance, he watched Thalon storm away. He wasn't the same male she'd awoken to in the annulus that morning. Instead, he was twenty shades of 'do not disturb me or face the fucking consequences.'

What happened in his tent? Alora threw a withered look at Jade, who merely shrugged as if she could read her thoughts.

The High Prince's death glare found her sapphires before he too began to storm away, around the side of his tent. With a quick stop, he turned. That deep voice carried a lethal edge. "The war tent, five minutes." Shadows whirled, and he was instantly gone.

Within an hour, word spread through camp. They would leave at dawn the following morning. Today, all training was optional; blades, magic, do as desired within the shield borders. Celebrations would be enjoyed throughout camp well into the night, according to Thalon. Dance, songs, displays of frivolous magic, and well wishes to their High Prince for another year of blessings would fill the day.

Alora decided that her day would be best spent amongst books. With the permission from Garrik, Jade was granted leave of her duties for the day as Alora's shadow and would spend her time elsewhere.

The air was electrified, even inside Eldacar's library. Through the towering shelves of books, pillars, and mounds piled on the wooden floor, she could feel it.

"You wish to do *what?*" Eldacar's bewilderment forced him to push his glasses up with a finger.

"Yes," was all she said, eyes gleaming at an ember in her palm, making Eldacar nervous around the aged books. "Is it possible?"

Eldacar shifted on his feet, tapping his chin in thought as he rounded a tower of piled books.

Many had been unshelved. The library grew with each town they passed through. And with every new Mystic arrival, Garrik would somehow always find his way to Eldacar with a new book or stack in hand.

Eldacar's pointed finger traced down the bounds of leather, scraping delicately against the spines. Reading hundreds of titles on the shelves with scanning brown eyes as he walked along the lower level. They weren't simply piles of pages and leather and ink; they were knowledge and discovery.

"I think I have just the one." He gestured with a finger, beckoning her to wait a moment as he stumbled up the winding staircase and ran to the left on the mezzanine.

She'd spent many hours inside Eldacar's tent, learning of her powers over the last months, and soon, she'd start to learn a new language. All her life, books had been there for her. The aging vanillin smell of parchment and leather was so pleasant she wished she could bottle it up. The perfect escape for restless nights and wondering minds after long, strenuous days of training.

One afternoon that she was given off from training to rest her sore muscles, she had escaped in here. Escaped the clanging of iron and barking orders of generals in the ring. Even escaped the crackling of fires and feet pounding into the dirt maze between canvases. And in her escape, she had questioned Eldacar, carefully roaming her enchanted eyes over the texts before plucking out an amethyst colored tome in the entertainment section. Fairytales. An odd choice for this library.

When she flipped through the pages, recognizing a familiar metal and leather scent, she'd asked about the library. How it was at all possible that, from the outside, a mere tent. But inside, three times larger than the canvas outside, a library sat. Eldacar had only sheepishly grinned, and his shoulders rose and head dropped low before he smiled and said, '*Garrik and his Smokeshadows graciously made it for me.*'

Alora smiled at the memory as she found the winding staircase in her grasp. Winding up, up, up into the cloudy sky that cast none of its light inside to a rooftop terrace. She glimpsed Eldacar many nights sitting up with the stars, reading among them. There, he could sit at night and read not just books of magic but stories from faraway worlds. Plus, the height excited him, oddly enough. As if he could soar with owls and dragons, feeling the wind between his curly locks.

"Ah! There you are!"

"You found it?" Alora almost squealed watching Eldacar rush down the staircase.

"Now if I could only find that book on that dagger of yours." He paused, glass-covered eyes scanning the shelves both up top and below. "But I think this one would be particularly useful to you. She's got many secrets just for what you need." Eldacar held the book tenderly as he tapped the red cover. "This one should be precisely what you require," he said.

Alora's eyes gleamed as her smile widened. Antsy hands lifted the book from him, and she began flipping through the pages.

"Would you help me?" she asked, white embers twinkled in her awestruck eyes.

"I'd be nothing but delighted to! Shall we open her up and take a peek, then?"

Fire inside the library was determined to be a fool's game. With the book in hand, and a few others that Eldacar deemed necessary for their task, they found a safe spot near the western border, inside the shield. And just as she'd done with the replica of her obsidian dagger, she began to ask her powers to mold a piece of silver. Though she'd not yet learned how to object bend without her fiery embers and flames, it didn't deter her from molding the silver in the shape she intended.

With the spark of white flames, what she envisioned began to take form. Until those flames slowly burned out, and the object laid steaming on the wood.

Yet, a small piece of her fire and dancing sparks remained within it. The essence captured. Without the help of Eldacar's book, the object would be merely a decoration, nothing more.

Only, this piece was meant for something greater, something much *more*. Her white flame danced within a small crystal—inside its new case. It would burn until her own light would be snuffed out and she called all her powers home to her.

They were both silent for a moment.

Awestruck. Speechless.

"It's absolutely splendid, Alora. Perfection." Eldacar's gentle voice cracked in an excited whisper. "An exquisite gift. One to be truly treasured."

Pure amazement flashed in Alora's eyes as she beheld it there on the table. Months ago, she would've never thought something such as this would be possible. And with a grin, she turned to Eldacar. It was satisfying. Seeing her power and what it let her do—what she asked it to do. Trusting each other to create such a magnificent item that beheld even greater power. A symbol of great importance and strength. A symbol of the High Prince's legion.

Placing the item in her bag, "You know what this needs?"

Eldacar shifted his glasses and shook his head.

"Wrapping. All gifts need wrapping."

He had that look in his eyes. The one that replaced the silver gleam and traded it for muddy-gray dullness. The one that she'd seen occasionally that he'd try to hide. More often escaping when they were alone. In the annulus. In the inn. Heard the tone of his voice when he would speak— or try not to.

Arms crossed and face tight, Garrik leaned against a tree, hidden in the shadows of a vast forest behind him that concealed an obstacle course Thalon was participating in. Alongside him, soldiers climbed tall towers, leaping onto platforms from various heights, attempting rope ladders and bridges, and performing incredible maneuvers to knock fellow opponents off.

From high above, the sunlight was disturbed by flying silhouettes.

She spotted Deimon flying beside Isleen, avoiding incoming faeries with wings, swerving and weaving; an incredible smile spread across his face as he held a ball in his arms. Sports. A flying tackle ball game.

Wings collided with wings, limbs tangled as he was hit. The ball bounced between arms until finally swooped inside a ring of fire controlled by one of the Mystics in the Wingborne. Though she didn't know the rules of the game, from the shouts of victory, one team gained a point.

Alora couldn't help but smile.

But Garrik vaguely stared into the sky, his eyes clouded. The shouts and clanging of metal far above didn't seem to break his attention. He was far off in a distant world.

Alora looked across the field at him as she walked. *Why don't you join them?* Remembering his shadow wings.

Silence.

Hey? A burst of cobalt magic wasn't even enough to stir his focus to her. *You okay?*

Thalon's demanding voice scolded some soldiers who lost their footing ... and foolishly, almost their heads atop a raised platform. The wooden boards beveled when he jumped and landed, tearing a sword from one of their hands before tossing it to the ground far below. "Go get your blade. The climb should get your head back on straight."

With a swift kick from their swords-master and immediate obedience, the soldier jumped to a lower platform before climbing the long rope down to his weapon.

Garrik shifted his feet, and a muscle flexed in his cheek when his eyes rapidly blinked. Then, she finally felt that gentle caress in her mind. *Apologies. Did you need something?*

Alora half-smiled walking beside Eldacar, whose eyes were watching the flying tackle game before he veered off in the direction of the bursting magic. *No, I'm fine. Are you okay?* Frowning, her attention stirred to Thalon, not daring to mention the way they both emerged from Garrik's tent with obvious signs of a fist fight.

He hesitated. *No. But I will be. Did you enjoy your time with Eldacar?*

By that time, she'd closed the distance, passing an incredible pit of doom—Jade's newly hewn coliseum—and stopped under one seemingly sky-high tower. "Very much so." Alora patted the leather bag by her side. "Come with me. I want to show you something." And offered her hand.

Garrik uncrossed his arms and half-grinned, taking it before she pulled him out to the coliseum edge.

Alora crouched down, swinging her legs over the side to sit, scanning the ruins below when Garrik did, too.

Jade was defending the attack of a group of five females. They had her circled, back against a crippled pillar. Sparks illuminated the darkness as harsh and brutal clangs of metal resounded up the dirt-hewn walls.

A gentle breeze brushed through the air, carrying Garrik's scent to Alora. She tried to ignore it when Jade cried out below.

Through the darkness, Jade stood, hovering above a female with her blade near her neck. The other four were collecting their weapons from the dirt. It was evident. Jade had disarmed each one before forcing the last to yield at the end of her blade.

Beside her, Garrik's pride beamed. His tormented eyes returned to somewhat of a glow.

Alora tried to ignore that too as she called down into the pit, voice echoing, "Jade."

Jade snapped her head up, brushing off dirt from her training leathers and looked at Garrik.

"She wishes to know what you need," he imparted.

"Tell her I need her to come up."

Garrik nodded and turned his gaze back down into the pit and sighed. "Here." Gesturing with his palm back and forth, he said, "You two can talk."

He turned to Alora and reclined back on his palms. That gentle caress brushed against her mind. But it wasn't Garrik's voice that she heard.

I'm not ready to go back to camp, so don't ask. Jade twisted her wrist, swinging her sword beside her. Angling her head and body to defend against another attack.

Neither am I. Can you come up here for a moment?

Jade sighed. *Fine.* And flickered her green eyes to Garrik expectantly.

Smokeshadows whorled around Jade's body, turning her into a darkness as deep as the pit. In swirls and tendrils behind them, Jade stepped out of the shadows, leaving them to mist away as Garrik and Alora stood and walked from the edge.

Alora pulled a small emerald cloth pouch from her bag and tossed it at Jade. "Open it."

"What is it?" Jade curled her lip in a scowl.

Alora rolled her eyes. "Just open it."

Jade held up a hollowed silver ring, crafted to resemble a coiled dragon clenching a blazing gemstone in its talons. Burnished metal curved into vicious claws, gripping a marquise-cut white stone. Within the colorless crystal depths, sparks danced and brilliant white flames glimmered as though a tiny cosmos churned hidden behind the smooth façade.

Alora smiled, watching Jade twist it in the sunlight. "It's to protect you from fire. As long as you wear it, flames can't burn you, and no one can remove it, only the wearer."

For once, Jade didn't glower, didn't grimace or frown, or threaten to cut Alora's hair off. For a moment, she didn't resemble herself at all. The stone-cold, solid look of unshakable steel was gone. Her face went unreadable as she beheld it in her fingers.

"How do you know it will work?" A small bead of sweat formed on her brow as her voice desperately tried not to tremble. "Did you test it?"

"Well no, but Eldacar and I—"

Jade hissed and shoved it back to her, turning back to the pit without a word.

"Test it now." Garrik stepped forward; hand outstretched. Smokeshadows whirled and misted away, leaving a flaming torch in his grip. For a moment, his eyes were captivated by the flame, but he blinked and shifted his gaze to Alora. "Give it to me."

Instead, she gestured to him, motioning for the torch. "It should be me." And moved to place the ring on her own finger when Garrik's fingers enveloped hers, pulling the ring away before she placed it fully on.

"No." Garrik enclosed it in his fist, inserting the tip of his finger inside the ring. In one quick motion, the torch lowered to his arm, and the flames licked his skin.

Incredible white light flared inside the crystal.

Garrik's lips parted as they all watched the amber flames from the torch lick his skin. Where there should've been burning, bubbling flesh, his tanned skin remained whole. Untouched by the flames.

Then, the torch lifted away. And there were no burns, as if fire never touched him.

Alora's hands were on him before she knew what she was doing. Expecting an icy chill, instead, she found his arm as hot as she normally was. She carefully twisted it, inspecting for any burns, and gaped when there were none.

Worried about me, clever girl?

Rolling her lips between her teeth, Alora backed away with a warmth of scarlet on her cheeks. *Not in the slightest. Just couldn't burn the mighty prince on his birthday.*

Garrik scoffed inside her mind before tossing the ring to Jade, who caught it one-handed, still staring at his arm. "Satisfied?" He raised an eyebrow as his shadows swallowed the torch.

Jade cocked her hip, gritting her teeth. The ring slipped across her finger, and she held it in front of her, frowning. "It isn't at all my color."

Alora shook her head and chuckled. "You're welcome, Jade."

CHAPTER
46

G arrik extended the shield far beyond camp, and dancing deep into the night sky was a glow of raging bonfires kissing starlight.

Alora tried not to gape as bursts of bright colors guided her with every step. Teeming with displays of loud, crackling and booming magic, over and over, the horizon ignited with exploding stars, shapes, and patterns. Expanding in prisms of color until they would rain down into dying embers on the faeries who were utterly awestruck by the sight.

Alora was captivated, reaching the crest of the hill above the valley. Even as she descended, it was difficult to keep her eyes off the spectacle that waited below.

Faeries with fire magic had ignited the bonfires in their special color. The brightest blues, purples, greens—every color imaginable burned the pyres. And around them ... she'd seen the army as a whole. Their battle-black armor was one considerable force marching through the kingdom like an unrelenting river seen from a cliff. Had seen the tents flooding the terrain until they looked like clouds in the sky. But never like this.

Never so many dancing inside the alluring melodies of music and drinking without a single care within their High Prince's protection.

Together, they would wash the land of impurities, a relentless force of *possibility*. Because this kind of joy didn't sprout under boots of tyranny. It was forged in the footprints of destruction left behind.

Not one scrap of armor in sight, Alora took in the celebration. Every Dragon was decorated in finery fit for a royal banquet. Panels of extravagant, flowing and loose fabrics hung from females twirling barefoot. Males in embellished tunics and pants, no swords at their side. And where grand marble and golden ballrooms should be, incredible bonfires were strewn along the landscape, and silhouettes of different shapes and forms danced across the trampled grass.

It seemed the entire camp had congregated. The sea before her settled a slow, anxious ache inside her fingers when she scanned, looking for any familiar face.

Before long, she joined in with a few females from Jade's battalion.

Alora danced wildly around the bonfire born of her white flames. Sparking embers swirled her like blazebugs—or snow. She spun and leapt with complete abandon. One with the glittering sparks that flurried on the air currents. Minutes—hours—went by as she lost herself to the magnetic blaze, her body moving freely in fiery harmony until fatigue gripped her muscles and her mouth cried out with thirst.

Giggling, almost blissfully drunk from song and dance, Alora weaved through the celebration, her eyes set on one of the many tables overflowing with refreshments.

Then she spotted him.

Like a timid beast caged, Garrik stood surrounded by chattering faces, each pining for his attention.

Alora was twenty feet away when Calla, the rose-gold skinned faerie, threw her arms around his neck. And she watched as Garrik flashed her his High Prince smile and respectfully pulled an arms-length away, tugging at his tunic before accepting a small rose-petal wrapped gift. Soon after, the male who she was sure alerted Garrik about Haiden's outburst, Draven, led the Nightfall pack of wolf shifters rolling barrels of ale to his boots. Garrik flashed the same grin and flicked his wrist, engulfing the barrels in Smokeshadows before they misted away and reappeared by the drinks.

A gravelly female voice stole her attention.

"Stars above, is that what I think it is?" Over by tables brimming with food and crowded by Dragons, Jade shrieked and ran to one covered in desserts and sweets. One particularly delectable round cake sat high on a stand, its brown icing glistened in the bonfire's warm light.

"Chocolate! Every single one of you will have to fight me for this. I'm not sharing."

Though weapons were far and few between, Jade managed to pull a concealed dagger from her boot, jam it into the cake in a few messy slices, and skewer a piece to bring up to her mouth. All before anyone around could say a word in challenge.

A soft grin lifted on Alora's face as she scanned back to where Garrik had been. In such a short time, he had vanished. Something like a silver tether drew her eyes to the tree line.

In the darkness, Garrik strolled in the opposite direction of camp.

It didn't take long until she had weaved through the crowds and fires and caught up to him. "Trying to sneak away?" she called out, chuckling as she bounded up to his back.

Garrik glanced over his shoulder, and a small smirk twisted up his face, a darkened bottle in his hand. "How could I sneak away? It would seem that you always find me." His voice was soft, inviting.

Alora panted in a breath, wiping a small line of sweat from her hairline. "What are you doing out here? Shouldn't the male of honor be down there?" she asked and dropped down to the grass to sit, draping her forearm over a bent knee to catch her breath.

Flames reflecting in his eyes, Garrik scanned to the trees behind them. His ring clanked against the bottle, drawing her attention. He opened his mouth to speak, and flicked his head from the trees to the bottle before Smokeshadows tendriled around his hand, swallowing up the bottle and leaving his palm empty.

Then his footsteps drew near, wandering beside her before dropping to the cool grass, wincing at the bend of his ribs, and reclined, just as she was. "It is much quieter here."

Incredible laughter echoed from the celebration. Jade was dancing. Spinning and twirling and bellowing with pure exhilaration as Thalon locked his palms around her wrists, spinning her in fast circles inside a circlet of bonfires, sparking their embers and smoke into the night sky.

Sparks and ash and smoke touched her skin, and Jade spun without a single care. Without a single flinch.

Alora grinned, marveling at the sight, and caught a gentle gleam in Garrik's eye as he watched her, too.

"What you did for Jade..." His voice was a tender caress. "Thank you. She would normally be standing in the shadows, so far ash could not touch her, on nights such as this." Silver eyes glistened in the starlight, turning to her. "Do not take this lightly, though. Giving your magic away is very dangerous. That part of you, your magic, will always feel the missing piece. It will weaken you."

Alora couldn't stop watching as Jade threw her head back, mouth wide, swelling her cheeks in a smile. "She's worth it."

"Indeed." Garrik watched Thalon lift and hold Jade in the air. Then he fell back in the grass, folded his arms under his head, and closed his eyes.

A sly smile crept up Alora's face. Maybe from that quick gentleness or merely because she occasionally wondered. "You and Jade. Was that ever a thing?"

Garrik's eyes opened, side-eying her, his grin twisted. "Never."

"Calla?" Alora smirked back.

Garrik's head rotated on his bicep, furrowing his eyebrows with intrigue. "Calla?"

"I saw the way she hugged you. Maybe you should visit her tonight, would certainly make a pleasurable end to your birthday." Alora gently elbowed him with a wink.

He scoffed, shaking his head. "I do not desire Calla. And from what I have seen in her mind, she would sooner visit Aiden. I am not entirely sure they have not ... I do not want to know."

Alora fell back on the grass and folded her arms underneath her head. "Has there ever been anyone?"

The echoes of music and frivolous laughing filled the silence for a moment.

"None that I truly desired."

Alora pivoted her head when she heard him shuffle, meeting his glowing silver irises.

"Not until you came, of course. You kissed me in my bed that first night and I knew I was forever yours."

The sarcasm was enough to irritate her wholly. "Mighty bastard." She gently kicked his leg, making him chuckle. "Seriously, though. There really hasn't been anyone?"

Garrik turned his head to the stars. The exploding bursts of shapes and patterns illuminated his face in hues of crimson, navy, and emerald. He was silent much longer than she expected when the gleam in his eyes dulled, rippling some brutal ache inside her chest.

"I have never willingly shared a bed with anyone." His voice so low, she could barely hear him.

Alora's eyes raked down his abdomen, watching the steady rise and fall of his breaths as the black tunic covered his rigid scars below. She should've realized, after all, she knew a small amount of his past. And from the change in his eyes, she knew she went too far.

"I'm sorry, I shouldn't have asked you this."

Garrik still stared into the stars. "You can ask me anything."

But she knew that 'anything' didn't mean *anything*.

Alora rolled onto her side, propping her head in her palm. Magic exploded in the sky, its detonation far louder than the rest. Garrik winced as if the sound had injured him. And she wondered, "Can you hear them all at once? Their minds, conversations. Does it ever stop?"

"Not always. Only if I am actively searching for something. Imagine it as water in a river. Winding from rock to rock until it finds its final destination. Most of the time, everything is quiet."

Alora twirled a cold blade of grass. "Did you have a good birthday?"

"It was just another day, but ... far louder."

Alora chuckled. "Does 'just another day' usually come with gifts?" Sitting up, she dove inside her pocket, pulling out folded parchment. A thin, silver ribbon that she'd scavenged from her chest of gifted clothes was tied, slack, around it. "It's not much, but ... it's your birthday. Everybody deserves a gift on their birthday."

"I do not celebrate my birthday. A gift is not necessary."

"Why not?"

Garrik went silent. Shadows swirled around his face, neck, pulling at his hands. "I did not enjoy the way it was celebrated ... who it was celebrated with." A muscle twitched in his jaw, illuminated by bursting light, as his eyes returned to that far-off, distant world.

"Do you want to talk about it?"

There was heavy silence. His breathing fell uneven, and she saw a spark of his eyes go dull and start to cascade into the blackened abyss

"Hey?" Touching his hand, Garrik flinched, the darkness faded. "Whatever it is, you can talk to me about it. Or don't talk about it. We can just lay here and I'll talk. I never cared for my birthday either. Kaine always made it a point to be away. I spent them alone."

"I wasn't." Garrik shook his head, blinking, and turned to the folded parchment in her hand. "What is it?"

She excitedly grinned, crossing her legs like a giddy faeling. "It wouldn't be a gift if I told you." Holding out her hand once more, Alora pulled Garrik's hand from his abdomen and placed it in his palm. "Open it."

Silver ribbon fell away. Black ink flowed across the parchment. Melodic sequences ended in rhymes under the burst of light in the sky.

Garrik rolled onto his side. "You wrote me—"

"A song. Well ... just words for now. Maybe one day I'll put music to it, if I ever see a piano again."

Garrik's eyes scanned the words solicitously.

The silence was unbearable. Why would she think that something as little as ink on a page would be a gift? With the silence, her nerves battled her heartbeat. Hands became heated and clammy. *Stupid gift.* What would the High Prince of Elysian do with a poem, at best?

"It's not a great gift. The lyrics are sloppy. The rhyming is—"

"Perfect," he breathed. A seemingly small amount of liquid lined his softened eyes. "It is perfect."

She saw the silver glow return as her own sapphires stared in disbelief.

His hand quivered. "Thank you, Alora." Voice cracking, Garrik folded the parchment and gripped it tightly. "This is ... this means ... more than you know."

COME ON, *darling. You need to sleep in an actual bed tonight,* Garrik's warm voice broke through a dreamless sleep.

She'd fallen asleep sometime after tracing shapes in the stars, laughing at Garrik's poor attempt to imagine a unicorn in the constellations, giggling over Garrik's stories of Aiden, and reminiscing of tales of her and Rowlen.

Garrik's arms were delectably cold, lifting her to her feet, steadying her on the dirt while she rubbed her eyes and yawned. When she blinked them open, they were no longer on that hill, and the heavy aroma of fires wasn't as strong.

She blinked again, feeling his calluses scrape against her arms as he pulled away only to see canvases around them.

He must have dawned them back to camp.

"Off to bed, clever girl." Garrik cupped her lower back and gestured.

But his hand wasn't guiding her to Jade's tent. Instead, he purposefully guided her forward. And when he noticed her confusion, Garrik simply swallowed. "You will not be sleeping in Jade's tent."

Eyes wide, Alora pushed herself from his hand, fully awake now. "And where *will* I be sleeping? If you think I'll be coming in your tent tonight just because it's your birthday—"

"I would not dream of it"—an edacious grin grew up the side of his face—"unless you are offering."

She produced a healthy middle finger and turned back to Jade's tent, but his voice stopped her.

"You two will not be tenting together any longer ... because your punishments are over."

Before she could consider speaking, Garrik faced Aiden's tent, and

Smokeshadows rippled from his shoulders, down his arms, and out his palms in the empty space beside it. In a storm of shadows, a canvas of similar size to his Shadow Order's individual tents appeared.

As the shadows cascaded away, Garrik turned to her. "Try not to cut a hole in this one."

With a wink, he held open the entrance.

It was empty, save for the canvas walls and chandelier-like faelight hanging, casting a comfortable, cozy glow.

A gentle breeze blew through the cracks in the tent's entrance, rustling his gray hair. "This is yours to make your own." Garrik paced, scanning the empty space. "Is there anything you desire? Perhaps something from Telldaira that was left behind?"

It was all too much. Happening so fast that she couldn't think. Rather than keep him waiting, Alora murmured, "A cot is all I need." And rolled her lips between her teeth.

Garrik tracked the movement. "That is not what I asked. You can ask to turn the inside into a castle full of rooms if you so wish. Anything. You should see Aiden's. It would put Galdheir to shame. He lives inside a ship. Sometimes, I can hear the ocean outside his canvas." He stood there and waited, watching her move around the tent.

The truth was, she didn't know.

Apart from the coin bag she earned to buy her way onto a ship to another kingdom, nothing in the manor was ever hers. Even her clothing wasn't of her own possession. She simply occupied space there. Anything she used to desire was crumbled away piece by piece. The smallest things she wanted were rejected by Kaine or if she brought something new in, he would find out, and it would be gone anyway.

The truth was, there was nothing she'd left behind that she'd want from the manor. Not the coins. Not the clothing. Not even a single notebook. All that was hers was lost.

Even herself.

You didn't deserve such luxuries. You didn't deserve anything at all.

No. Please no. Alora's eyes shifted around the room at Kaine's voice until they fell upon Garrik, who had walked to the other side of the canvas, still inspecting. Only, when she looked, she didn't see lush hair in gray hues; she didn't see his black clothing, or tanned, icy skin. The eyes that turned as he pivoted his head weren't those of glowing silver that drew her in like a blissful daydream. No. What stared back was her monster.

Her version of nightmares.

Kaine wickedly smiled in Garrik's place. Watching her freeze. Watching as her eyes narrowed and her vision blurred. She couldn't find her breath fast enough, couldn't calm the panic that gutted her heart and sent it into a racing pain.

You still think you can hide from me? You're still mine. *I will find you. And when I do—*

That gentle caress brushed against her mind.

Alora blinked. realizing that she'd frozen, blaring embered orbs into Garrik—into Kaine.

Kaine's mouth opened, but it was Garrik's voice that cut through like warm honey, soothing to her nerves. "Where did you go?" His voice ruptured Kaine's visage, shaking from one person to another as she continued to stare. Continued to fight and bring herself back to reality. "Alora, what is wrong?" That gentle caress was now a reassuring finger drawing down her forearm.

Shivers encased her spine from that touch. From his small surge of his power that made her nerves calm and settle. She couldn't tell him. Not that Kaine still haunted her, walking in and ruining every ray of light that brightened her day, hiding around every corner. Appearing in illusions at the smallest twinge of her heart.

She couldn't tell him that in the smallest moments of kindness, Kaine would invade her thoughts. Persuade her that everything around her, every conversation, every simple act—as little as handing her a dinner plate—every touch in the arena ... that it was all a lie.

She couldn't tell Garrik that oftentimes, even when she stared into his silver, Kaine's mahogany stared back.

Garrik closed the short distance between them, his figure passing through Kaine's, leaving only Garrik standing there. "Talk to me." Silver dulled in worry as he forced a swallow.

"Nothing," she breathed. "Nothing. It's only," Alora paused. What were they talking about before? Her eyes trailed around the tent. Empty. It still was empty. "I ... don't know ... what I want." Stuttering, nervously rubbing her thumb on her death mark.

Garrik stepped closer, extending a hand near her death mark, but stopped. "It is alright. You do not have to figure it out now. Enjoy the time to explore what you want, who you are now." His smile softened. "When you want something, it does not matter when, where I am, or what I am doing. Please come ask." Smokeshadows swirled in the corner behind her. A black, wooden framed bed, triple her size, adorned in a mound of plush pillows and soft, thin blankets rested on top. "What is your favorite color?"

That was an ... odd question. "What?"

"Your favorite color. What is it?"

"I—" It used to be green, was it now? She despised the color in the manor. It was suffocating. But out here, the evergreens they passed along the road and trails caught her eye. The green of emeralds or a delicious apple she enjoyed. Or maybe ... was it blue? Like the sky on a clear day. A sapphire like her eyes, encased in a fine blade.

"Green," she blurted, surprised. "I suppose it's green. Like dark emeralds."

Garrik's face lit up, and without a word, Smokeshadows swirled again. Across the bed, a new blanket, covered in swirls like smoke in emerald hues, laid across it. "Excellent choice. Anything else?"

She rolled her bottom lip nervously as her eyes avoided his.

"In time. You will come to know who you are. For now, dream and be not afraid to learn who you have become. Rest, darling." He stepped forward and leaned down. Pressing a tender, icy kiss to her forehead.

She took in a sharp breath, a blush heating her cheeks.

If he noticed her face scarleting, he didn't mention it. Garrik turned on his boots for the door and began to walk out.

And before she could stop the words, Alora blurted, "Can I have—" and stopped herself.

Garrik's boots twisted in the dirt, meeting her eyes. "Go on." There was no irritation there. Only a gentleness, lightly caressing her like a soothing kiss from a winter breeze.

"No, it's stupid. This is fine." With the bed to her back, Alora nervously sat on the edge and gripped the blankets, tracing the soft stitching with her thumb.

"Nothing about you is stupid." He stepped forward.

With a deep sigh and a shake of her head, she eventually added, "A window... At the manor, before it was boarded up, I would sit beside a north-facing window. It was the only one I felt comfortable by. I'd read, write songs, gaze at the stars. I'd like to do that again."

Delight filled his eyes as he smiled once more. "Of course." Garrik slowly waved his hand across the canvas near the door. A trail of Smokeshadows crawled along the wall, dancing as they carved out a floor-length, blackened, twisting frame fit for a royal bedchamber. Swirls of black wood entwined as if they were waves. As the Smokeshadows faded away, Garrik stepped back to observe it. "No one can see inside. Touch the window and my shadows can change the view to whatever you wish. They are yours to command."

Speechless was an understatement.

After warning her about giving powers away ...

He ... is giving me Smokeshadows?

Much to her surprise, shadows again escaped his hands, only this time, the tendrils settled beside the window and faded away to reveal a large emerald reading chair, plump with buttons and a black frame swirled with the same waves as the window. Gold accents like the night sky were laced within, its width large enough to fit twice her size.

Shadows misted away from either side of the window next, revealing a wall of black swirling bookshelves stocked full of tomes and texts. To the left of the chair, a notepad and pencil sat on a small black side table.

But he wasn't finished. Garrik outstretched his arms to his sides, fingers spread wide as he glanced over his shoulder at her, and she swore she could see the night sky in his eyes.

The tent erupted in a funnel storm. Ash and clouds and shadow swirled on a hurricane wind. The High Prince glided his hands through the air as tendrils of Smokeshadows escaped the swarm.

Alora's eyes widened in marvel.

Her simple bed transformed before her eyes. Two black wood posts jutted from either side to the ceiling, where long panels of amethyst, emerald, teal, and onyx curtains draped down the headboard. Gold specs resembling stars glistened across the panels, shimmering glitter-like specs across the cream canvas walls.

Smokeshadows misted away from the ceiling and left behind hanging stars, white flames dancing inside each.

The floor beneath them shifted, and she was no longer standing on dirt. A fine rug of deep teal and golden sky accents expanded across wooden floorboards of stained oak. Much like her bookshelves, dressers and chests lined the shimmering, curtained walls.

And at the bedside, a matching set to the dressers and bookshelves appeared. A small bedside table held her Blazebloom and an emerald vase filled with a dozen waved pearl-petal flowers—pearlseas.

The entire space was as enchanting as the night sky. She couldn't stop gaping at the bookshelves, though.

Alora stood to her feet and, like a faeling on Winter Solstice morning, skipped to the shelf full of books that carried a familiar scent —leather and metal. Gently tracing her hands over the shelves, reading the spines. The corner of her eye caught Garrik's smile, as if the act of giving her this gift meant more to him than receiving one himself.

"These were all mine."

She twirled to him as he spoke.

"Now, they are yours. Being High Prince does not allow me the time I wish to read. Perhaps one day when this is all over."

"Would you like to stay and read one with me?" She meant it, hoping he'd accept her invitation. "It's your birthday. I'm sure one night can be spared to do something you used to love?"

Garrik paced beside the shelf, plucking out a red book from within a series. He flipped it over and read the back before pulling out the green.

"Humans write such ... fascinating books about our kind. Start with these two. Try not to fall in love with the main character. He is a fool. But in this one"—lifting the green, he flipped through its pages—"another Lord of Darkness ... well, once you reach chapter forty-eight ... I think you would find it rather enjoyable to recreate that chapter, and I would be more than happy to assist." He smirked.

Alora surveyed the covers, slowly tracing her finger over the black embellishments.

"Try not to stay up too late reading. We leave for Alynthia in the morning."

Alora scoffed—he should have just told her to breathe underwater—but smiled and said, "Thank you."

Garrik brushed a finger down her wrist, hovering his eyes on the book in her hand. And for a moment, she almost asked him again to stay, but Garrik stepped back. "I will be unreachable tonight but will find you in the morning. Goodnight, Alora."

She stepped forward, not entirely sure why. "Wait!"

He was ducking out the door but pivoted back, hand on his sore ribs.

"I know you don't enjoy celebrating your birthday. But I hope this one was different. Even just a little... Happy Birthday, Your Highness." Alora pushed up on her toes, and, with warm lips, kissed his cheek, noticing how he leaned into it ever-so-slightly. How his eyes trembled closed. "I hope you sleep well tonight."

"Unlikely, but I do appreciate the sentiment."

"Don't forget. You've survived every nightmare so far, real and those that torment you. Don't let them win."

He squeezed her hand and forced a smile before vanishing into the night.

"HAS ANYONE SEEN GARRIK?" Thalon let the High Prince's tent sway closed as he scanned the open area of their firesite.

"He told me he would be unreachable tonight. That he'd see us in the morning."

Golden eyes glowed in the amber light. Thalon shifted uncomfortably. "Shit," he whispered through a cracked breath.

Alora noticed Thalon's face ripple with panic. "Is everything okay?"

"No." He was frozen on his feet, eyes scanning across the tents as if he could see through them. To no one sitting in particular, Thalon muttered, "Where are you?"

SWIRLING WINDS, a burst of thunderclouds, and striking lightning swirled, illuminating the path between Aiden's tent and Garrik's. Casting hues of blue and white strikes, and a cascading glow bright enough to think a star had exploded. With a bright flash, two silhouettes emerged, then it imploded, leaving the firesite illuminated only by the dying amber glow of the fire.

Jade and Alora still sat, Alora reading a red book. Jade happily laid on the dirt by the fire, one hand playing with a flame licking at her fingers.

With heavy steps and strained muscles, Thalon pulled their High Prince across the dirt, one arm banded around his waist while Garrik's arm hung over Thalon's shoulders, feet dragging and head dropping low against his chest. Passed out, drunk.

Alora's vivid hallucinating snapped out of the book she'd been wholly enthralled in and dropped it beside her. Sapphires assessed them as Thalon pulled Garrik close to the tent entrance. She stood, but one look from Thalon made her second guess taking a step. "Is ... he okay?"

Thalon only nodded before pulling the tent open and disappearing into the darkness without a word.

A gemstoned, ring-wrapped finger still played with a flame. Jade pushed up on bent knees and pulled her hand away. Face taut, her green eyes locked onto the burning wood beside her and cautiously explained, "He gets like this after visiting the castle."

The silence was only filled by crackling embers and far-off dying melodies.

Jade inhaled a long, labored breath. "Thalon's one of the best Guardians I've ever met. Always watching out for him. He'll stay up all night to make sure Garrik doesn't drink himself to death."

The illuminating glow of a single candle lit inside Garrik's tent, drawing Alora's attention to Thalon's silhouette removing Garrik's boots on the bed. "Why?"

"Bourbon is easier to swallow than old nightmares ... and new." Jade breathed deep again.

"Why doesn't anyone help him?"

"We try. Thalon was the only one who could get through to him for some months after he..." Her hand found her ivory and coin necklace, gripping it tight. "Came back to us. Garrik doesn't allow us to help anymore. There's no use. The nightmares will never leave him. Not while her magic's still inside him."

Neither heard the silent footsteps nor saw Thalon's considerable figure kneel down before the dying flames.

Thalon brushed his face with ink-covered hands then massaged the muscles on the back of his neck, relieving pressure and stress that also plastered his face. "They'll plague him for some time after this visit."

Looking to Jade, Alora nervously rubbed her death mark. "She. Whoever *she* is ... was there with him." Alora didn't dare repeat anything more—or break Garrik's trust. If he wouldn't speak to anyone else, if he'd only been speaking to her, she didn't want to ruin that form of release.

Jade swore under her breath and glanced at Garrik's tent.

"It's going to be a long while then." Thalon dropped his head low.

Stabbing the stump beside her with a dagger, Jade hissed and gritted her teeth. "I'll fucking kill her. One day. I'll fucking kill her."

CHAPTER 47

J ade rode to Garrik's left as the legion started their ascent up the mountain, Alynthia lying somewhere hidden within its peaks. Thalon wasn't with them. In the early hours, he had stepped through his portal of thunderstorms and vanished before camp broke.

Though Eldacar was speaking to another soldier beside them, Alora couldn't keep her attention off Garrik, watching him sit rigid, attempting to mask any inclination of his painful injury. Ghost's steps caused his body to sway and bounce in the saddle. His right elbow wedged into his side, harder than usual.

Does it hurt? Alora hoped he could hear her.

Ghost's steps are ... unpleasant. Nothing I cannot endure. Calla's gift, a healing balm, aids the pain. His voice paused as he shifted in his saddle. *Have you decided on your involvement today?*

She required a moment, unsure of what to think back. Up until now, she hadn't accompanied any extractions. Unwilling to be a part of taking

Mystics from their homes to join in what could be their last months on Elysian.

It ... didn't feel right, still. Her own fate was determined for her. Only after she had vowed to ride by the High Prince's side willingly did she stay. But how could she ask others to do the same?

Garrik glanced over his shoulder, arching his brow. A silent gesture asking for an answer.

Her breath sharpened. Still unsure of how to respond when he leaned back in his saddle, pulling lightly on Ghost's reins until she, Storm, and Eldacar walked beside him.

Garrik met her eyes, his inviting. "Today will be different. If I had more time, if there was any other way." He paused, silver growing dull. "I should not have tormented you in that forest so long ago. And what I did in my tent that morning." He deepened a long, regretful breath. "I thought ... that if I was your villain, that I could settle you safely in camp, away from me, until I could locate somewhere suitable. Somewhere safe. I ... should have allowed you the choice."

Alora frowned, dropping her chin in a stiff nod before fixing her attention on the leather of the reins in her hand, picturing that very same moment. The first time he dawned her away. She looked forward to the fast approaching forested trail ahead, knowing the entirety of the legion would break camp soon.

"Will you give them a choice?"

"Yes," was all he said, voice stern, and she believed him. "Most join us simply because they possess no other alternative. Between hiding in fear or a chance for freedom, it is hard to say no to liberation. A chance to change their life from looking over their shoulder every day, wondering if that will be the day the High King captures them. You know how that feels."

Eldacar heavily sighed beside them.

Garrik flashed him a knowing glance and offered a reassuring grin. "Besides, Eldacar is very convincing. If I cannot persuade them, he will."

Eldacar shuffled in his saddle and rubbed the back of his neck sheepishly, exhaling a sharp laugh. "You're too kind, sire. Indeed, too, too kind."

The three continued to ride beside each other, lightly talking, keeping their eyes on the forest.

The front of the legion was only moments away from reaching the splitting point when a thick smell of charred wood accompanied a thunderous roar and sonic hissing. Even the air seemed to retreat as a blazing heat rushed over them.

And then ...

Screams.

Screams of hundreds of faeries. Screams that echoed from deep in the mountain and bounced off of every surface. Agony. Pain. Loss. Fear. Screams of retaliation. Courage, anger, and rage.

The thunderous roar traveled closer, shaking anything that could move.

And *it* was moving. Coming closer to the legion.

Almost as if ...

Garrik's eyes darted to the air as a silhouette flew over the canopy of trees. Monstrous, membraned wings, countless horns on its incredibly pointed head, and a substantial body that covered the sun itself. Its entire being was glowing—not from sunlight—not from the shine of a precious jewel. Its skin was *moving*. Breathing. Living. Dancing with ...

Fire.

The legion looked to Garrik as he gripped Ghost's reins and unsheathed his sword. His hard eyes fixed on the creature soaring away.

Ghost reared as he kicked forward, darting a nod to Jade. "What is it you were saying about legends?"

This was not the plan.

Alora was not supposed to be there. He did not want her to be.

The screams of the injured and dying grew louder, but the beast had not been sighted since.

Instead, what guided their path was the stench of billowing smoke deep within the mountain. The legion moved as one, proceeding until they crossed an invisible wall, an illusion on the path, as if the ancient wards of Alynthia called to their aid and let them pass.

They would not make it to the caves. The battle was here.

And it should not have been that *easy*.

But it was not cries of joy that gathered at the gates. Nor gratitude in the eyes of those fleeing their homes as charred skeletons and ashes of once was laid in the dragon's wake. No.

When the front of the legion broke into formations at the wooden wall and front gate as high as redwood trees, Alynthian guardsmen waited. Arrows notched, aiming at the sea of Dragons in battle-black leathers and darkened cloaks.

Stay here. Garrik's eyes shifted to Alora.

No. I'm coming with you.

Alora—

I'm coming. I won't say it again. Alora nudged Storm, riding past him by a few feet.

Garrik restrained his frustration and trotted beside her, glaring in warning. Against his better judgment, he said nothing, and pulled in front.

Ahead, muffled shouts mixed with carnage, and shrieks rose over the fortifications. He pushed to see through the eyes of one of his captains at the front gates, just as he had with Thalon for Aiden, and Dragons parted at each of Ghost's steps.

Draven, commander of the Nightfall wolves, was shouting up the wall when Garrik arrived at the front.

A male stood in the middle of the crowd atop their towering wall. All eyes looked to him, waiting. A leader, perhaps.

Shouting at soot and blood-covered faces, Draven lazily waited. His horse stomped the dirt in anticipation. "What happened here?"

"Alynthia doesn't help outsiders. Leave." It was a burly, brown-eyed male, standing behind younglings of various species, all with weapons fixed to the murderous multitude below.

"Clearly you didn't hear me. I said, *what happened here?*"

Garrik's focus shifted to the younglings, some not even tall enough to climb a saddle. Something stirred inside him. Ice shards peppered his veins as sheer rage built and threatened to explode at the sight. His anger, barely restrained, covered his face, and he had to squeeze his fist on his thigh to keep it contained.

It did not help that he was still on edge from his drunken nightmares the night before. He felt like he could level a mountain and might actually do so. Especially if the prick-in-charge continued with this shit.

Brown-eyes stood behind the young, using them as a shield. Perhaps a poor tactic—younglings burned soft spots into hearts, preventing attacks or out of sheer stupidity. But against all delusion, he was still the Savage Prince.

In what realm would rumor of his merciless brutality not have traveled there?

Knowing exactly who he was ... what he did, despite the ages of those in his wake. Sometimes because of. To drive fear. He was coined the name for reasons far more barbarous than burning down cities and imprisoning his own kind.

They were not known as the Blood Years for his charming smirk.

Garrik's insides churned at the memories. He had killed younglings before. When he was not himself, the mind of who he was made to be. The mind of another. When he could not control it. And because he was to be who he once was, this placed him in a rather difficult position. It infuriated him enough that shadows threatened to burst and kill the older males for their lack of balls and sheer incompetence. His own father had not even sent him off to the training camps until stirrups reached his chest.

But this city was not Ravens or his enemy. He must remember that. They were not trained to be warriors. These were his subjects. Living their lives in whatever delusional form of peace they could conjure. Living on borrowed time, hidden by wards, protected by legends.

What would he have to do to keep up the ruse? To keep them protected. If they would not cooperate, if they would not heed his warnings and obey his orders, he would be forced to show them what the Savage Prince would do without hesitation. *Kill a few to save the many.*

Garrik curled his lip, flashing his teeth.

Could his Dragons see the slight tremble in his hand? How his boots pushed harder in the stirrups? He quickly glanced at Alora, who appeared as sick as he felt. Even with the exquisite, otherworldly radiance that always settled on her porcelain skin and hair, he could see the distress. Her enchanting, pleading eyes seemed to interpret every one of his thoughts.

Her quivering smile brought him a sense of peace, only for a moment. Would she still smile after what she would witness today?

Would any of them?

Garrik faintly smiled back before facing Alynthia's walls. Ghost stomped heavily into the dirt and shook her neck, mane slapping against her as a shimmer gleamed from her head in the sunlight.

Garrik nudged his heels, patting her neck, whispering 'good girl' as she advanced forward through the parting crowd of Dragons. Their weapons drawn; coy grins on their faces when he passed. They reveled in the excitement, despite what these types of encounters could come to. Everyone had to play the part.

Time for him to play, too.

Facial bones ached as they transformed under his tanned skin, pulling it tight to a somewhat painful stretch. Shifting into pointed lines on his cheeks, sharp eyes took shape. Smooth teeth sharpened, the edges knife-like to the touch as he scraped his tongue along them.

Garrik gripped Ghost's reins, watching his skin blanch through cascading inked eyes. Though his armor covered him, he knew his veins turned dark like the night sky, bulging across his arms and chest.

Through a swirl of Smokeshadows, a glassy, obsidian, spiked crown rose atop his head.

Becoming the monster was easy. Acting as one was an art he wished he had never mastered.

Draven's horse stomped aside as the last of the Dragon's front line parted. Adorned in a haunting Smokeshadow cape flowing down Ghost's hindquarters as she walked, Garrik stalked to the wall. Each calculated step more daunting than the last. Even Ghost played the part —and played it very well. The warhorse of a demon.

Garrik gritted his sharpened teeth. Eyes—predatorial—locked onto Brown-eyes as Alora and Jade fell in behind, flanking him.

There was no denying it. The pure fear in each one of their faces on the wall was exhilarating, feeding into his horrifically barbarous visage. It was wrong to love it entirely, to enjoy how their faces made him feel. A side effect of her lingering magic-hold on him. Yet, he reveled in it, knowing that his image alone made their knees buckle. Some had even pissed themselves in his presence. A reminder of how prey cannot help but turn from such a predator, the body their greatest enemy when instincts take over.

Perhaps if they were not young-using-cowards, he would not feel this way. But today, he fed on that fear, basked in it, as it fueled the beast inside even more so.

Garrik's face shifted to that of death and endless nightmares as he spoke in a monstrous growl. "What do we have here, Draven? Are we late to a barbecue?"

The Dragon's battalion commander wickedly smiled. One hand squeezed the pommel of his sheathed sword as a swift breeze disturbed short almond hair. "We seemed to not have attained an invitation, Your Highness."

"Pity. I do quite enjoy burning cities." With a click of his tongue, Garrik's beastly grin widened as his murderous eyes flicked to the drifting smoke in the sky beyond the gates. "There is not much left for me to play with. Quite disappointing."

Wide-eyed, Brown-eyes' voice cracked, shouting, "We don't want trouble. Leave or you'll die today." He slapped the shoulders of two younglings, motioning them to lift their bows.

Garrik and Draven wolfishly grinned at one another. A deep rumble bellowed from the Savage Prince's chest, roaring. "*Petty* threats do not work on me. I will be using your city for my legion. Choose your next words wisely or find your heads *spiked* and *displayed* in the square to remind you of who the fuck *I* am."

Brown-eyes pivoted his head, turning to the others around him. "Who do you think you are, the High King?"

"No. *I am his son.*"

The air pressure instantly shifted as cold, dark wind blew.

Disgusted by his own words, Garrik tilted his head and held the illusioned wicked stare on the male, who took a trembling step back behind the younglings.

Coward. Garrik's vision turned dark. He gnashed his teeth together until it hurt and bared them with a growl. That male would be the first to die.

Whispers filled the forest. The young held up arrows from the wooden walls. Bows shaking in arms too small to pull the bowstring to where their mouth met fleshy cheeks. The lack of training made him vigilant, though he knew his Dragons watched each twitch of their young hands. Too unpredictable in their age to foresee when they would let an arrow fly.

But even the older males—in ripped and charred clothing—held their weapons unsteadily beside them, some quivering with the same name on their lips. Chanting as if to pray to Maker of the Skies to receive mercy.

They were fearful, and a fearful faerie could always be trusted to do something foolish.

Garrik shifted his beastly eyes back to his Shadow Order and Dragons.

It took immense power to speak to the multitude as one. And he did it without taking a single breath. Effortlessly. *The young remain unharmed.*

As a whole, the legion pounded a fisted forearm over their chests and drew their blades. The sound echoed through the mountain. His eyes fell on Alora, whose throat worked, eyes scanning the wall before meeting his. Her glowing sapphires began to turn away.

You do not turn away. He called to her mind, seeing her fear there, *See the battle in their eyes. Promise them war inside yours until their eyes burn and they turn away. Demand their fealty. Make their backs break as they bow to you.*

She nodded and straightened in her saddle, replacing her spine with an iron rod. Glaring white-embered eyes into his.

He almost felt the scorch of that gaze when her face went taut and merciless. Almost ... wrathful. Gripping the reins on Storm, Alora's chin tilted high, and he imagined a shimmering, golden crown on her white hair.

Starsdamn. Garrik's thighs flexed. He needed to adjust his armor.

She looked like she belonged there, like royal blood ran through her veins and commanded an entire kingdom—realm—to bow. Stronger than she knew, almost deadly. He shoved that image to her mind, heart jerking as he watched her breathe deep, accepting who she was coached to be. *Stars damn them. Just like that. Even I have to look away.*

Stop. She raised her chin a little higher with an amused grin.

Yes, Your Majesty.

And suddenly it was her pushing an image to him.

A deep chuckle echoed in their minds at the strong middle finger. His armor groaned as he pivoted, turning back to the wall.

Shadows crept along the ground around the legion's boots. The sky shifted into dark clouds of shadows, snuffing out sunlight and the fiery glow from the city, transforming the mountain into a moonless night.

Terrified, echoed whispers filled the air:

"*The Savage Prince.*"

"Clearly my reputation precedes me. If you wish to remain existing, open the gates and stand aside. I do not ask twice, and my patience wears thin."

Garrik, archers are moving in the trees. Jade's horse swung around and paced the front line, motioning with her hand. Instantly, riders fanned out, nocking arrows and aiming at the shadows in the forest.

They were surrounded.

And yet, he mercilessly smiled.

The front gates burst open.

Rushing from the burning city, twenty armed males with swords drawn stood. "We're prepared to defend our own. Turn away, or the first arrow will be through your heart, Savage Prince."

Garrik leaned forward, resting a forearm on the saddle horn. "It is *amusing* how you believe you can threaten me. My legion will slaughter you all before you cower a breath. You will accomplish nothing but find yourselves killed, and then I will take pleasure in ripping apart your families simply for wasting my time."

But the brown-eyed prick did not stand down. "Kill him!" At the last word, the male thrust his fist high. Arrows flew, pointed at the Savage Prince. From the trees, hundreds of arrows cleaved through the air, aimed at awaiting Dragons ... at his Shadow Order.

Alora wrenched a breath behind him. His heart leapt at the sound.

Nobody blinked. Nobody moved.

Only Garrik's face melted into Death Incarnate.

Arrows from the trees shattered against an invisible barrier. Thirty arrows instantly misted into dust among Smokeshadows and littered the dirt inches before embedding into his face. Into Alora and Jade's.

Garrik sat, seemingly unphased by the treasonous act. He straightened in his saddle, face stiff, brushing dust and metal fragments from his lap.

By the cover of a stone-cold face, his malicious, unrecognizable voice growled like thunder, rattling everyone's bones. "It is an act of war to attack Elysian royalty." With the swing of his leg, Garrik slammed into the dirt, trembling the ground, and wrenched his sword from his side. "You have exhausted my patience." Smokeshadows swirled around him in a frenzy, turning him into an abyss of night. "My mercy ends here."

From his shoulders, down the rippling planes of his muscled, armored arms, and out from black veined hands, a storm of Smokeshadows surged.

Then he was gone.

Along with a hundred of his Dragons.

In pillars of whirling smoke and clouds of ash, fifty scattered shadows appeared. Arms wrapped around every chest and shoulder, the sharp edges of Dragon's blades laid across the necks of each Alynthian guardsmen—even the younglings.

Metal clanged with each drop of a weapon in surrender atop the wall and outside the gates. Male and females dressed in the same ilk were shoved from the trees by Dragon shadows, forced to their knees in surrender.

A squealing scream pierced the air before Brown-eyes shrieked in a dooming fall. His body thudded to the ground in a cloud of dust below the wall. Another shadow stepped from the wall's edge and plunged down.

Shadows exploded across the dirt as Garrik's boots slammed beside the male, shaking the ground. He crouched, arms resting on bent knees as he scanned the male's face.

"Please." Terror-filled eyes. Tone of horror. Blood trickled from the corner of his mouth. "Don't kill me."

How he loved to watch cowards beg.

"I fucking warned you." With a relentless grip, Garrik pulled Brown-eyes by the back of his tunic collar, dragging him out into the space between the gates and his front line. "It would seem you need made an example of." The male struggled on his hands and feet as the Savage Prince's voice roared, "Each one of you will see exactly what disobeying me results in."

Black veins bulging at his anger, Garrik whipped his arm with full strength, hurling Brown-eyes down onto his face.

Think about what you're doing. This isn't you! There was an intensity in Alora's concentration, fists balled on her thighs as she sat.

You are wrong. Garrik was electrified. Even her reasoning could not break through the rage he felt. The mask he had donned was affixed to his face now, immovable as it had melded to his flesh. Her words would not release the darkness that held it there.

An impenetrable wall of Smokeshadows burst into her mind, shutting her out completely. Metal slid from his leather sheath. The Savage Prince would have killed for much less in the Blood Years. If he was anything but today, if news reached Galdheir...

The male's throat pinched against the blade's edge. Garrik rattled a snarl, almost tasting the iron in the air.

The male would suffer ... but not before he would make him beg.

"Please! Please don't! I—"

Pleasing, gurgling sounds bubbled from the male as Smokeshadows constricted around his throat.

"*Silence.*" Garrik narrowed his eyes and felt a ripple of his power branch out in an invisible wave, extending over the captive masses, over his Dragons. "I did not grant permission to beg. There will be time for that ... *soon.*" His eyesight shifted into a haze as he spoke to his powers, raking his eyes over each Alynthian...

Embedding a delicious lie.

If he was to conduct himself as executioner for the pleasure of the High King, his manipulation would be illusioned lies of brutality.

"Bring her out!" Garrik's thunderous voice rippled, stirring the Smokeshadows that whorled around him.

To the horror and shock of the Alynthians, a young female, slender, pale, with long raven-colored hair and black clothing, was dragged on her feet from the gate by two soldiers. Garrik stiffened at the illusion he created, heart thundering as he raked his eyes over her and felt bile surfacing to the back of his tongue. A face he pictured countless times. A face he imagined flaying slowly—painfully—until every last drop of her was spilled. But this was not her. This was the lie. His powers made them believe they knew her, that she was one of them, someone important, someone they all cared for.

Garrik stifled a tremble in his grip. His Dragons would know she was an illusion. But Alora ...

He pivoted back to her. Jade had settled her horse only feet away. They were exchanging whispers. He focused, his mind drawing on their words.

It's not real, but you mustn't look away, no matter what he does. They will see.

Alora nodded and turned worried eyes to him, catching his uneasy stare.

But he said nothing and turned to the female likeness of one he truly hated. She would die today. And every time he needed an illusion such as this. Garrik ran his tongue along sharpened teeth and spots of blood surfaced as he allowed them to cut into it, plastering his teeth in crimson hues.

Tightening his blade against the male's neck, who was sobbing, fearfully pleading at his newest family member, Garrik manifested the male's personalized torture. A sister would do.

Garrik crouched lower, his leather armor groaning as he growled in the shell of his ear, "*Beg.*"

It did not matter what the male said. Garrik could not care to listen. He only imagined running his sword through her heart, over and over, until his body would give out. And when the male's voice was hoarse with unrelenting sobs, Garrik stood. His expression dismissive and uncaring as the male's shrieks chased his every bloodthirsty step.

The female's legs lost all function as iron ripped into her body, sagging down onto the sharp edge of the blade, splitting her open slowly. With little effort, Garrik carelessly wrenched his sword from her body, cursing her name under his breath as she slammed knees first to the dirt.

Wide-eyed, tears dripped from her black, serpent-like eyes, and raven-colored hair fanned around her face when it slammed into the dirt, where she remained lifeless. Dead.

"You are next."

"No! I have faelings! Please!"

"Do you now?" But he already knew that. Another illusion by his own trickery. Smokeshadows burst in a funnel cloud in front of them before coasting away. Three faelings stood, the illusioned likeness of their father, gripped on their shoulders and held into place by one Dragon each. It was the perfect lesson. If they wished to use younglings as a line of defense, then what came next should stop them from using them as soldiers.

Garrik's face was a thing of nightmares as he snarled, "You should have thought of that before you threatened me."

"I'm begging you! Not my family!" Snot and tears flooded his face.

Something tore in Garrik's chest. How bittersweet to hear a father who cared so much. To care about the faelings he only met today. Not even real, and this male loved them more than his own father ever loved him.

Garrik instantly twisted his wrist, bending stiffened fingers into a fist in the air. Neck bones twisted at odd angles. A distinctive snap resounded like the popping of firewood.

Crack. The first male faeling dropped.

"*No!*" the male's voice viciously wailed in agony while nails gashed lines down his face.

Garrik coldly stepped over the dead one, uncaring as he prowled beside the next and held up his hand again. "Beg harder."

A throat shredding scream. "Please, Your Highness, please have mercy. I'll do anything. *ANYTHING!*"

Crack.

"*No!*"

Garrik considered for a moment, watching the male shatter, crawling across the bloody dirt to his sons whose lives flashed before his eyes in an instant. Watched as he extended his mangled arms to his brown-eyed daughter whose fate was not yet determined. Considered as the male worsened his pain in the act of *reaching* for his faelings against all warnings from his body to remain still.

But Garrik still needed to play the part. Magnelis would never be satisfied if his son—an heir—showed an inch of mercy. Magnelis never showed him any, either.

He looked at the male with nightmares in his own and released the last tether of his mercy. "I am not convinced."

His wrist twisted.

Crack.

CHAPTER 48

I t *wasn't real. It wasn't real.* Alora's mind chanted, over and over. Blazing palms scratched against tree bark as she stumbled, knocking her shoulders into trunks before bouncing to the next, keeping herself upright.

Most of the fires had burned down, leaving heavy smoke choking the air and burning inside her lungs, but it didn't matter. She couldn't breathe anyway.

Alora's eyes watered with each resistant breath. Charred pine and burning flesh tore inside her nose as she finally heaved against a tree. Better to vomit there than wait until she returned to camp.

It wasn't real.

It looked real, *felt* real.

The cracking of bones. The twisting of younglings' necks. The iron taste heavy in the air. The deep agony and loss as each one fell to the dirt. How could she be expected to go to war when this sent her hurling through the forest, secretly emptying her stomach just to calm her fiery nerves and nearly molten legs?

She saw them again. Their faces as Death twisted their necks.

It wasn't real.

Alora held back the churning in her gut, afraid she'd vomit again.

She couldn't stay there anymore.

The forest floor spun as she pushed off the tree and ran.

Ran, hurdling over fallen logs and ducking under branches until the sun's rays illuminated the road to Alynthia. She ran past soldiers on their way to the front gates, on leave for the evening. Ran past sentries who parted in time for her wind to catch their hair. Ran until the camp's white tents appeared and she crossed through the shield.

Swerving—stumbling—through the maze, her feet carrying her to the middle until her tent came into view.

Someone called her name. Someone's rushed footsteps followed her, but she didn't care.

Black boots stormed across the inside of her tent, and she leapt face-first into the soft pillows. Gripping one to her face, Alora wailed, uncaring if anyone could hear.

The guardsmen, the younglings, the female ... *Him.* That distant and cold look in his eyes like he wasn't there anymore. Her friend was not there.

Friend? Oh Alora, how stupid can you be? Kaine's voice snickered like a dagger to the heart.

He'd been there at the wall, too. Mocking her as she lifted her head high atop Storm. Mocking how she could entertain the idea of ever being strong enough. Intimidating and ever present. Laughing at how she could foolishly believe she could ride by royalty's side. How she could believe herself to be one of his—a revered and feared Dragon.

Kaine's voice twisted the dagger. *You're weak. Pathetic. Look at you.*

The tent grew blistering-hot. A prickling, burning intensity flushed through her body. Flames threatening to burst from a metal container. She was too hot; it cascaded across her skin like a blazing wildfire.

Heart beating faster, Alora felt the tent spinning as scorching tears flooded onto the furs and hissed as their heat impacted something cooler.

A sharp gasp pulled inside her lungs, sharp as shattered glass. Her entire body tensed, every muscle taut as if ready to detonate.

He isn't real. He isn't here. It wasn't real. It wasn't—

An icy hand cradled her shoulder, and she flinched at the touch.

Icy hands. Not warm. It *wasn't* Kaine. He wasn't here.

A screaming release shuddered down in her chest as that deep voice, smooth, warm, and refreshing as a colorful sunrise, whispered, "Ara."

He isn't Kaine. But if she turned, would the pointed eyes of the

Savage Prince be staring back? Would Kaine's? Garrik's voice had returned to normal, but she didn't dare turn to see his face.

"Please, look at me." Was that a crack in his voice?

Could she even lift her head? The immense weight of what she felt mocked her mind and what she witnessed at the wall was too heavy.

"I never wanted you there. I did not want you to see … *me*."

The bed shifted against his weight. An icy hand pulled her hair away from the pillow, brushing against her neck as he exposed her skin there, too.

She shuddered at the touch, a reminder of who had once wrapped warm hands around her and squeezed, but also a reminder of what the High Prince's hands had forced his magic to do. Despite her every nerves protest, she allowed the coolness of his presence to touch her burning skin.

"Forgive me," he breathed a shivering whisper, gently placing a hand on her back. "This is … a mess." His hand shook against her leathers, cursing under his breath. "Alora, please."

Her tense muscles heaved in her shoulders against relentless sobs. A mess. This was a mess; *she* was a mess. "I'm sorry. I'm not the brave soldier everyone else is. I'm not sure I can do this."

"Brave? You were pretty damn brave today for your first time. You have nothing to be sorry for. It is I that holds this responsibility, I alone." His hand soothed her back. "Come here, come to me," he whispered with such a gentleness, a complete contrast to the beast outside Alynthia's walls.

Almost steaming, Alora's skin felt on fire. She wasn't entirely sure she wasn't ablaze. "I'll burn you."

"I do not care." And without warning, he was pulling, twisting her around to look into his eyes.

Not on fire. No white flames anywhere.

The overwhelming pressure glided her straight into his awaiting arms. She melted into his body, throwing her arms around his torso before burying her face in his icy chest.

And then, his solid arms locked around her shoulders, a hand brushed through her hair, pulling her against him. His abdomen tightened. Each breath he took, her heart slowed, and he didn't feel like the monster who could carelessly kill younglings in front of their father.

The burning in her skin subsided, listening to his unusual heartbeat. "I was afraid."

Garrik's body fell with a labored breath. "I was too."

Alora pulled from his chest, gazing at him. He was … pale. Dark circles laid under his eyes. His armor was dirty, covered in scrapes of dirt, a smear of blood on his wrist guard. She tried to hold it back, the look of disgust at the blood, the heart pounding in her chest from the memory of what he'd done.

He noticed, though. His chin sunk low before releasing his arms around her and pulling away. "Do you hate me for it?"

There was pain in his eyes as she sat back against the pillows, guiding her knees to her chest.

Before she could say a word, a flash of light lit up the canvas and heavy boots crushed the dirt outside. "Garrik?" Thalon's voice was urgent, trailing away as the sound of footsteps trailed off.

"Will you be alright?"

She nodded.

"I will be right outside." With a gentle squeeze on her knee, Garrik stood and walked to the door, peering over his shoulder before exiting.

After some minutes passed, Alora unsteadily rose. She exited her tent to find Garrik and Thalon holding a map. Strong fingers glided over streets and communities across an Alynthian mountain range, beveling the paper at Thalon's exploration.

"The ... *item* ... you requested is waiting at a tavern here." Thalon's tattooed finger pressed an indent into the map as Garrik glowered. Shrugging, he added, "He insisted."

Garrik growled, "He will pay for this."

Thalon's grin swelled his cheeks.

"Go, I will meet you there in four hours." Pivoting on his heel, Garrik walked toward his tent.

Thalon rolled the map and smiled across the firesite at her. She hadn't seen him since the night before at the bonfires and at their tents after.

But her eyes drifted to Garrik, who was almost entirely consumed by Smokeshadows, dawning to somewhere unknown. His head pivoted over his shoulder before his glowing eyes half-lidded. His mouth turned upward, flashing that irritating yet intoxicating smirk that let her know her friend was still there.

Smokeshadows tendriled around his body, fully fading into complete shadow.

And then he was gone.

CHAPTER
49

Alynthia wasn't a town ... it was a damn city. And Thalon led the long hike up the cobblestone street towered by the mountain. Passing storefronts with potted plants, patios with tables to sit and eat, and businesses with their doors darkened and closed. *Strange.* An odd hour to close shops.

It wasn't late, yet the gossip of the High Prince's soldiers in the city had spread. Fear-ridden business owners had closed early and ran to the safety of their homes and shuttered doors. This section of the city, untouched by the fiery beast, was mostly quiet, save for a few roamers on the street. They took one look at Thalon's towering, muscled figure and golden sword strapped to his back, and quickly made themselves scarce in the shadows of nearby alleys.

A darkened figure bounded on heavy steps down the sloped street toward them.

Thalon stiffened at the strangers' rushed footfalls. Cautious. Ready.

Creating their own wind as they advanced, the pearly white and golden threaded cloak around the figure's shoulders drifted open, revealing marked arms with beasts and runes.

Marks much like Thalon's.

They didn't slow. Not when Thalon's marked arm tore out in front, ripping the hood from their face. Not when a heavy crack resounded as he pinned them against a wall with unearthly strength in his bulging forearm.

In the golden sun's glow, perfectly resting between mountain peaks and over rooftops across the street, his unusual shadow flickered darker against the painted blue walls of a weapons shop.

For a moment ... Alora's eyes hallucinated.

Thalon's shadow. It *grew*. Outstretching wide like a flying creature's wings.

The strangers did too.

Jade ripped a dagger from its sheath. Pivoting her head, she scanned the street, rooftops, the alleys. Green eyes darkened with lethal focus as she shot Alora a commanding glare to draw her weapons.

She did as Jade asked.

Thalon's tongue erupted with brimstone fury. Unsettling in its power yet forgiving in its rush. A sound much like spoken word inside the back of her mind laced with melodic ticks and stops, crossing his tongue with graceful wrath. It was unnerving, rattling Alora's bones as she listened to its many layers of sound, wondering if Eldacar could teach her this, too. And as unsteady as her nerves felt at the foreign language crossing her ears, the female stranger remained unfazed, gritting her teeth but holding silent.

"*Answer me.* Did you earn these marks or are you playing a pretender? Dishonoring a Guardian in such fraud is grounds for *death* by the hands of Tarrent-Garren Keep." He pressed his sword against her gut, poking through the fabric. "*Speak.*" Holy fire ... *actual fire* ... glowed in his golden eyes.

Instead of turning into a loosened heap of cowering bones, this time, the female lunged back with a vain bite in the same tongue. A deep brown hand stretched out, and she flicked one golden bead on Thalon's hair with a baiting smile before he crushed her wrist in his palm.

"I like a male with intensity. Surely one of the later houses with a golden spirit such as yours. I'm Blythe, one of four Guardians of Alynthia. And you are?" She nodded and pulled the pearl hood over her thick, twisted ebony locks adorned in the same golden beads as his.

Thalon released the sword from her abdomen and sheathed it between his rippling shoulder blades, then retracted his forearm, still reeling before he nodded, bowing his head in honor. "Thalon, House of the Seventh N. Tell me, who is your family?"

"Buy me a drink first, Seventh N, then I'll share all my secrets." The Guardian shot him an enticing wink before she turned and walked up the street toward the tavern. Turned as if he hadn't just had her pinned to the wall. As if giving them her back didn't offer any risk to her life.

Not one of them moved, shifting eyes to each other in utter shock.

"You coming, Seventh N? Or has that High Prince's army slowed you? Surely not, seeing as you're dripping with Earned." Blythe's white cloak swayed through the swinging off-center door.

Jade crossed her arms, leathers groaning as she grinned. "I like her."

"I've never heard you say that about anyone. Not even me."

Alora snorted at Thalon's remark while Jade shrugged in smug satisfaction.

"Seventh N," Blythe's voice trailed in a taunting melody at the threshold before she disappeared within.

Thalon growled, "Come on, get inside." And he shook his head before wrenching the half-broken door open courteously for Jade and Alora.

The tavern was as expected. Grimy, green leathered booths lined two liquid splatter-stained wooden walls to the left and right. Round tables filled the center of the room. Directly inside the front door, one long bar waited with few empty round seats.

Two exits. One in the front and one atop the staircase to where she could only assume was an alley. No Dragon would enter a building without scoping out all obstacles and exits. Jade had pounded that into her so often that it was the first thought when she entered. And by the shuffling of feet of males leaving tables and the vicious whispers at others, a quick escape might be a rising possibility.

The air was heavy with the sweet aroma of tobacco, spices, wood, and leather, set in a seemingly permanent haze of smoke from a blistering fireplace.

Alora was suddenly thankful for her unique armor.

A smoke cloud rose from one table in the center toward the melting candle iron chandeliers. Four males played a hand of cards and sloshed tankards of ale to their mouths. One couple, with cold faces that showed a recent argument, sat in the shadow of a tall staircase resting against the far back wall. Leading up to a mezzanine that overlooked the tavern, a hallway broke off in the middle, full of doors lining both sides. Since Alynthia wasn't a tourist town, it was unlikely these were lodgings for travelers. And from the loud moans escaping the closed doors above and raised voices at the tables, it was obvious the rooms were for rent—most likely by the hour.

Through the lull, Thalon scanned each chair. When Alora saw that his eyes didn't find whatever he was looking for, they settled on Blythe sitting at a booth against the left wall. From the invitation of a quick flick of her wrist, Thalon turned and nodded to her and Jade before he settled at a two tankard table, sword resting on the leather seat beside him.

"Should we sit with Thalon?"

Jade was halfway to the bar, uncaring about the male's foot she *accidentally* stepped on as he left the tavern. "Leave him," she dismissed and plopped herself down on a stool within earshot of the Guardians, digging her hand into a bowl of salted nuts without a single care.

Alora claimed the stool beside her. It wasn't long before two tankards slammed in front of them, ale spilling over the tops as the contents settled inside. From the corner of her eye, she glimpsed Thalon. His back straightened and thick, muscled arms crossed when Blythe began to speak.

"So, Seventh N." Blythe paused, the glow of her cobalt eyes raked over him. She leaned forward, resting gold cuffed wrists on the wooden table.

"Thalon," he offered. "And hearing how little you reveal, I'd say you're not from the Third. Seeing as communication falls short with you." Thalon raised his chin higher, distaste burned in his glowing golden eyes.

Blythe grinned like she'd been found out. "Such peace-keepers, you House Sevens." The corners of her eyes crinkled. "Mother was Ninaj, once House of the Fifth J. Now Ninaje, the Protected of Dondreste, House of the First E. The *favorite* house," she supplied, her lip curled in a coy taunt, "original warriors. And you"—she set her blue eyes on a small marking inked near Thalon's heart. Three braids, woven into a circlet, a sword cut down through the center as they twisted around the hilt and sharpened edge—"Guardian and Protector. Are you still tied?" Thick twisted locks fell behind her shoulders as she reclined, Earned glistening in the tavern light.

Within his crossed stiff arms, Thalon involuntarily brushed his thumb across the mark. "No."

Brows crunched, Blythe's face twisted. "How did your Protected die?"

Thalon's face mirrored hers, yet he didn't move. "Not that it concerns you in your sacred duties or is in any way your burden, she was murdered—an accident," he quickly corrected.

A ruby-crested, golden dagger slammed into the table, cracking the wood under it. The tavern seemed unaffected by the sudden outburst and seething Guardian against the wall. *"Unleash Michael ... one of our Guardians was murdered. How would that not be a concern to me? She was avenged?"*

"She wouldn't have wanted me to."

"Peace-keepers," Blythe hissed a curse and dug the dagger further into the table. "And your child? Training at Tarrent-Garren?"

Uncrossing his arms, scraping against his leather vest, Thalon pulled the white fabric to cover the markings on his chest.

The bonded mark held one small golden bead inked into his skin.

"Fallen. With his mother." He swiftly raised the tankard in front of Blythe, not his which sat closest to him, and threw it back against his lips. The table cracked as he slammed it down, emptied. "Enough. Why did you call me in here?"

CHAPTER 50

Alora couldn't focus. Not after what she'd heard.

It had been several minutes since she watched Blythe cut a bead from her hair and offer it to Thalon.

After, he stood with relaxed shoulders, leaving the tavern with a sadness in his eyes as Blythe tugged his hand. Through the windows and under the dropping sun outside, Alora watched them stride up the street and fade around a corner.

Jade was sitting with her usual scowling face, peering into her second tankard as if it was speaking to her. She swirled the ale until small waves crashed against the wooden inside.

They would be expecting Garrik soon. Whatever—whoever—they were waiting for wasn't inside. Thalon would've made it known if so.

"He's never spoken about having a family. I didn't know." Alora rolled the velvet ties of Jade's coin bag between two fingers, staring at the shimmer of crimson.

"None of us speak about it. He and Garrik—"

The smell hit her before he did.

One clammy, solid elbow jammed into Alora's ribs before she was knocked from the barstool. It toppled over with a loud thump, and a few tables shot their gaze to the crash.

Correcting her footing and clenching her ribs, Alora whipped her dagger from its sheath, which was dripping with spilled ale down her armor.

"What's two beautiful females such as yourselves not fucking me in a place like this tonight?" Along with a hiccup, large sweaty arms pushed a tankard toward Jade, spilling half the contents on the counter.

A death glare Alora had seen many times covered Jade's usually cold face. Her tone could eat his soul alive. "It would be wise for you to recognize that some things are better left the fuck alone. For example." Jade twirled a throwing dagger around her pointer finger with perfect balance. "Us."

In one easy swing, the tip of the dagger embedded between the male's greasy fingers.

The putrid smell of his intoxicated breath hovered as he opened his mouth, exposing rotting teeth through a drunken smile. "Feisty. I like it." His head pivoted to Alora, and his pinned eyes grew larger than the moon himself. "My. You are the most beautiful female I have ever seen in here."

Alora finished wiping a cloth from the bartender on her leathers. "Well, I guess that means I better go find the best looking male then." Instead of indulging the stranger any longer, she roamed her eyes around the tavern, expecting to see Garrik walking through the doors.

She found herself frowning when the door didn't open but twisted back into a smile when a swift thump of Jade's palm knocked into the drunks' chest. He fell back from the bar on stumbling feet.

"Piss off," Jade hissed, narrowing her eyes.

"No, I don't think I will."

Alora pulled the dagger from the bar. "You really should." Her nervous eyes shifted to Jade, who turned away and preceded to toss her tankard to her lips.

He smiled and looked back at Jade. "Come on, princess—"

"*Oh no,*" Alora murmured, cringed, and on instinct, stepped back.

Jade's eyes went delightfully hungry. Tapping her fingers on the counter with a ravenous smile and a hum, her tankard connected with the male's jaw, producing a satisfying cracking noise.

He reeled back, landed, spine against a table, and fell to the floor. Unmoving, under the dirty boots of three males who took one look at him and stood.

Chairs in the center of the room scraped against the floorboards, toppling over as the card table fell to its side, spilling gambling chips and cards. The three males, twice their size in height and build, stood with fists clenched and vexed eyes.

One in the middle, tan-skinned and golden hair that reminded her of Rowlen, broke a leg from the table and clenched until his knuckles whitened.

Shit. Clasping the hilt of her sword, Alora pivoted on nervous feet.

Jade sat, seemingly unfazed by the situation unfolding, before she wiped her sleeve across her mouth and dug her black boots into the floorboards. Turning, she gave them a taunting wave of her fingers before turning to Alora. "Too easy." Green eyes glided back to the approaching males and gestured with a nod. "The two on the left are mine."

Jade took two hard steps forward and balled her fists tight in hungry anticipation. Tapping her fingers against her thigh, inches above her throwing daggers, Jade squared her shoulders to them. Ready. Waiting. Taunting.

One wicked smile and the red-headed killing machine came alive.

Alora found herself painfully aware of every minute sound—the rasp of inhaled breath, the screech of wooden chairs dragged backward. Shadows mounted and swayed as the candle chandeliers guttered low. All around, patrons shifted, hands dipping to hidden pockets or closing around forks. An atmosphere of tension roiled through the room as the occupants—mostly male—arose, postures radiating challenge and competition and a readiness to brawl.

"*Alora!*" Jade screeched from somewhere in the crowd.

Metal hinges groaned from behind. Corded arms latched around her shoulders.

Jade was fists of fury and daggers, feet in front of her, her boot slammed down into the face of the golden-haired male.

From the corner of Alora's eye, a fist barreled into her face. The arms around her held strong before another fist pounded into her cheek, this time sending her stumbling down on a bent knee.

"*Demon's whore!*"

Alora's eyes clenched with tears as she clutched her throbbing face, warring off a cruel memory of Kaine's fists. She refused to let it set in. Refused to allow that haunting voice of pure evil and hatred and lies to invade and render her weak.

Not here. Not now. Not again.

Her head spun, picturing two—three—four of everything in the room. She heard Jade grunting through flying fists somewhere. Dots spotted in her vision, and she steadied herself with a hand on the wooden floor.

Sweaty palms and large fingers dug into her shoulders, forcing her other knee to the floorboards.

With gritted teeth, Alora whipped her head over her shoulder just as the male straddled her back. She'd let her hesitation put her into this position. *Stupid.* But his stance over her only made her next move much sweeter.

His face lowered to hers. In the shell of her ear, he bitterly whispered, "You're mine now."

Embers lit in her eyes.

I. Am. No ones.

The back of her skull collided into the male's face with a crunch. His unrelenting grip released her shoulders and stumbled back into the mess of tables. She wickedly smiled at his pleasingly broken nose, now oozing bright as a ruby.

Taking the opportunity of him crying with eyes closed from the pain, Alora swung her elbow into his broken face. Her body seethed. Smiling in rich satisfaction over his motionless body under the table.

It felt exhilarating. So damn good. Every nerve in her body burned. Every muscle flexed with raging blood. Body spinning, rapturous for more, she needed to hit something, needed to feed on the adrenaline that sent electric shocks through her fiery veins.

The brawl must have attracted the attention of the rooms upstairs. Faeries ripped open their doors, hobbling to pull on boots and fastening their pants around their waists. Few lined the rickety railing. Most ran down the stairs to join.

Alora fought her way to Jade, who had been cornered. Still, she smiled like it was a game and led them into a trap.

"Bout fucking time!" Jade threw a table leg to her, and she caught it effortlessly.

A table leg, not a sword.

Alora understood the message: *Don't kill them.*

She hissed, no time to answer her as two males came up behind. With squared shoulders, raking the approaching male's hair to boots, Alora prepared her stance just as Thalon had drilled into her a thousand times.

"Come on, boys, at least give us a challenge!" Jade's boot collided with a face.

The room quickly surrounded them. Hard bloodthirsty faces snickered curses. Fists and weapons were ready to end them. They were trapped. Boxed in with far too many opponents.

"You're outnumbered, bitch." Ebony hair and hazel eyes stepped forward, staring at Alora. "Two of you against all of us." He snickered.

The crowd responded with laughter.

A whistle carried from the mezzanine.

All eyes shifted upward before black folded buckled boots slammed into the only upright table at the center of the circle. The crowd stepped back from the impact, dust clouding around where a male landed.

"*You* ... are horrible, really, at counting. Mother never schooled you?" He paused. "There's three."

I know that voice.

The room erupted into an all-out frenzy with colliding limbs, fists, and boots. The male wearing a long, frocked black coat, embellished with ornate brass buckles and buttons, pulled a curved sword with his left hand from his red-sashed belt and slashed it deep into the guts of two faeries.

"Bastard!" someone yelled, hands gripped around his ankles.

"That's Captain Bastard, you mangy dog!" Black buckled boots tore from the grip and pounded down onto the faerie's fingers.

"You're still alive?" Jade jumped on the table, seemingly annoyed.

"Well, don't sound so disappointed." The male picked her up and tossed her over the crowd. "I might think you actually don't like me!" The pommel of his sword smashed into another face when he jumped to the floor beside Alora.

Alora swung around.

The wooden leg she held barreled toward his face while her sword was fisted tight in her other.

He caught it with the edge of his curved sword and winked shale-colored eyes that, in the dim tavern's light, seemed completely colorless.

Eyes wide and foolishly forgetting the scene unfolding around her, fighting leathers groaned as Alora threw her arms around the male's neck, knocking his triangle hat to the bloody floor. "*Aiden!*"

Warm arms eagerly pulled her close in a tight embrace, and Aiden sarcastically shoved at Jade. "See? Now *that* is a proper welcome home!" Just as he let go, hands forced Alora to the ground and pulled Aiden into the crowd. "Do you mind? We're trying to have a reunion here!"

A heavy boot slammed into her gut, choking the air from her lungs as Aiden's face disappeared, running into the crowd. A glint of metal flashed high above her face.

With horror, she realized it was her own sword. Lost like a child on their first day of training. And then, like a cruel joke, it was Thalon's voice scolding her as the metal—in slow motion—inched closer to the hard spot between her eyes.

'*Lose your sword, lose your life.*'

How could she have been so incredibly careless?

427

'Anything is fair in battle. Show me what you have learned.'
Garrik's voice...

She wouldn't die there. *Not like this.* With no other option, Alora lifted her hand as a heavy whirl of black smoke whisked around it. The fireplace flames grew, and candles flickered as embers formed in her palm.

Sparks gathered and lit in her outstretched hand. Ready to defend her life.

But a shadow-covered ringed hand bent her fingers inward.

A rock-solid airwave barreled through the room, turning everything to ruin.

The room fell deathly quiet. All except for the harsh panting of the three left standing.

An endless abyss for eyes glared down at her. With sharp, gritted teeth and pale skin pulled tight across pointed facial bones, the Savage Prince growled in a thunderous breath, "I leave ... for four hours ... and you determine it suitable to demonstrate your powers to loose-lipped rabble. *Have you gone mad?*"

Alora could barely think past her panting and thundering pulse but managed to snarl back. *"You'd rather me die?"*

"Knowledge is currency. If anyone would have abandoned this tavern without our knowing, our efforts would be for *nothing*. Magnelis would be enlightened within hours and unleash himself. We would be dead, *you would be fucking dead.*" Garrik's lips and teeth quivered. "You think that display at the wall was for my own sick entertainment? We all have a part to play, you are no exception."

She attempted to pull her fist from his but he held true. Alora seethed, bracing her boots against the wooden floorboards warm against her leathers. "What was I supposed to do, then?"

But he didn't answer her, reigning his own anger through his tense shoulders and cold face as if he was counting to ten before speaking. Garrik scanned his eyes to Jade and Aiden, who waited, panting. *"Explain, now."* His growl shook the floor, and shadows from every darkened part of the tavern retreated at his voice.

Not one said a word. Not even a breath.

Alora whipped her fist out of his and rolled away, standing up with sore knees.

Foolish girl. You'll pay for what you did.

Shut up, she snapped at Kaine's voice running talons down her mind. *Shut the hell up!*

Remember what happened last time you put his army in danger?

Stop. Alora's bones began to tremble. *He won't.* Though she didn't

428

want to admit it, Garrik was right. Wandering eyes made for great enemies. One moment. One watchful, greedy eye could be their downfall—and she'd be to blame. *Again.*

Garrik stepped toward Jade and Aiden when the tavern door swung open and Thalon stopped mid-step inside the threshold. *"Where the hell have you been?"*

Widened golden eyes scanned the tavern, mouth gaping. Thalon forced a swallow and rolled his shoulders back, standing rigid. "I was ... out."

Garrik's power rumbled through the room. "I am waiting for a starsdamn explanation as to why those held in the highest regard of my ranks saw it fit to act like drunken fools. *Speak. Or I swear—*"

He's coming for you. Better run, foolish girl. Back to me. I'll protect you.

Shut up!

Aiden took a hesitant step toward him. "Well—"

"Not another word. I will deal with your bullshit later." Garrik whipped his head to Jade, then Alora. The ink in his eyes danced in alluring swirls, swallowing up any light shining into them.

Jade cocked her hip and cleaned a nail with a throwing dagger. "Males. What else? They wanted a fight."

"You know better." Garrik's eyes shifted to the bartender cowering behind a pillar. He stalked up to him, Smokeshadows pooling into his hand and revealing a coin bag. "For the damages." Garrik leaned in close to his eyes and added, "You will not remember who it is from or what happened here in the morning."

The bartender's eyes turned cold before he fell to the floor, motionless.

"We have somewhere to be." Garrik gritted his teeth and began to storm past them when his darkened eyes fell to the bruise forming on Alora's cheek. Murderous—ravenous—eyes drank in the rest of her body as if he was looking at her for the first time since entering. Veins in his arms bulged as he clenched his fists and took a bloodthirsty step toward her.

Garrik's wrath was barely contained. *"Which one?"*

Alora pinched her eyebrows, body subtly shaking. "Wh—what?"

"Who put their *fucking hands* on you?" His voice rumbled, an intensity of ten thousand thunderstorms, enough to level the mountain.

Sapphire eyes scanned every lifeless body. The simple fact dawned on her. She didn't know, didn't remember whose hands had struck the awful blows.

"Anyone could have—" Her words fell short as a gentle tingle brushed against her mind. Alora took a heavy step back and speared him with her eyes. Afraid he'd see. Afraid he'd hear—

"*Stay out* of my head," she hissed with fists heating.

And as quickly as the mild irritation was waving through her mind, it wasn't.

Garrik twisted around with murderous intent.

Thalon stepped forward, shoulder to shoulder with Alora. "Garrik." No longer the voice of their friend. The Dragon's swords-master stood square-shouldered and rigid. Thalon positioned himself in the stance he taught her, anticipating an enemy's advance.

Garrik whipped his head to them, shadow-covered fists balled.

You caused this. You're going to get Thalon killed. Then he'll come for you for that death, too.

And suddenly, like so many moments before, Kaine's figure began to manifest. Began to dissolve Garrik's enraged form, replacing his blackened eyes with mahogany. Replacing gray hair with the ebony she wished she could rip—*burn*—from his scalp.

Kaine was there. And he was coming for her. *Look at what you've done.*

No. I didn't mean to. Liquid lined her eyes as Kaine—Garrik— stepped toward them.

You're worthless.

Alora's vision spotted. The room began to spin.

You fuck everything up.

It was too hot in there. Everything was too hot.

You're pathetic. Weak. Weak. W—

"*Enough!*" White flames bursting with dancing sparks filled her palms. Every bit of shame and rage and all the terrible things Kaine had said fueled the inferno raging across the scars of her mind. His ceaseless taunting. Every mocking word. Every truth about what she'd done—and what was to come.

Alora screamed with the impact of her blazing skin to Garrik's battle leathers. A burning hole scorched into the solid wall of muscles of his chest, over his heart.

"*Fuck.*" Garrik cried out and stumbled back, clenching his chest. Glowing ash burned around the holes and singed skin.

Thalon prowled forward, a tattooed hand curled with static energy, sizzling lightning strikes in his palm, ready to use his portals as a weapon against the Savage Prince.

Without even a whisper in the room, they all could feel it. A fire threatening to ignite. The air promising to detonate in a shattering explosion that would level the entire mountain to ruins.

Hearing both Kaine and Garrik speak, two voices merged in twists of tongues. "Get. Out." Speaking to no one in particular, their murderous growl reverberated through every floorboard beneath their feet before he locked eyes onto a male outstretched and lifeless by the staircase. His blackened eyes raked over his shoulder to her. "Him?"

Her head felt it again, the invasion, searching for the memory.

He was going to see...

Thalon placed his hand on Alora's shoulder, staring into Kaine's—Garrik's—abyss for eyes. "*Garrik.*"

She shuddered at the touch, wrenching her shoulder away with white embers crackling in her eyes, swallowing her sapphires whole until not even a trace remained. One step forward, inches from the bloodthirsty beast that was holding his eyes. Her lips pressed taut, she hissed, "It was a bar fight. It could have been *you* who struck me."

Garrik's face turned cold, and he stumbled a foot back like she had taken her sword and shoved it through his heart. His voice was like death and unending nightmares. "*You think I could ever lay a fucking hand on you?*"

Kaine.

He'd said that to her more than once and proved that he could.

And right now. Before her...

She hitched a breath as Kaine stood there, ready to wrap his hand around her neck for ... *everything.* Every stupid little thing she'd done. For running. For hiding. For attempting to use her magic, like she once did with him, and jeopardized them—*him*—because of it. For her laughter. For friendship. For her clothes. For daring to touch a weapon. For her...

"Alora, I did not mean—" Brows lowered as an edge set in his eyes, and Garrik's voice softened.

But she didn't hear him. She only saw Kaine. Only Kaine.

Alora couldn't hold it in anymore. Her fingertips ached so badly she thought they'd burst.

Months. For *months*, he'd haunted her every step. Every corner she'd turn and see ebony hair. Every pivot of her head or the figure in the corner of her eye. She had enough.

Enough.

Enough.

Enough!

"*You're* the reason I'm like this! You did this to me!" Burning tears plummeted. Her palms heated, and she drew every ounce of fear, every ache of shame, and roaring anger into each piercing word. Unrelenting. Wicked. Masking every feeling, every bit of bottled up emotion that she refused to give in to these past months, convincing herself that she had moved on.

But it wasn't enough.

Kaine wickedly smiled at his victory, ready to strike and throw her down a staircase, shove her against a wall, cut her skin with knives. She wouldn't let him, not this time.

Never again.

"Burn in hell, you bastard! For everything you've done. Making everyone believe you're one thing when your hands are so stained with blood that it's a wonder you can wash it off at all."

Garrik took a step, eyes fading to silver orbs as he reached for her.

She felt a gentle caress against her mind. But instead of letting him in, she slammed her foot back and stiffened. "Never touch me *again!*"

Kaine's palm misted away from her, disappearing on a phantom wind before she heard his wicked voice laugh. *He'll hurt you too. You know he will. Everyone you have ever felt safe with. Everyone who has ever cared about you. They all lied. He is the gray-haired demon of Elysian.*

It was her own voice now as her eyes widened. *The gray-haired demon of Elysian.*

Yes. And he's coming for you, too.

Alora blinked, heart threatening to explode.

Before her, she only saw the blackened eyes of the savage beast that had ruled her nightmares, the gray-haired demon who stood beside Magnelis, who had ruined her life by taking away her *choice.* Her blood boiled at the sight of him. All reason snapped as Kaine twisted his lies into her long enough that she believed him.

She took her words and twisted them into his flesh like a sharpened knife. "*You.* Savage fucking High Prince, the thing of Elysian nightmares, you're a killer. Just like your father. My parents are *gone.* Cities burned to the ground led by *you.* Faeries tortured in front of your father's throne because you're too weak to pierce his heart. And I'm still supposed to believe that you won't hurt me because you say so? Because you had a change of ... what exactly? *Heart?* Do you even have one?"

No one breathed.

Garrik ... *flinched.* The boiling expression on his face numbed and eyes settled wide as he drew a sharp, strangled breath.

Some part of her knew she'd gone too far. Some part caged deep inside and surrounded by Kaine's wicked words knew that she struck him too deep. But she was trapped in the in-between of knowing who was real and who wasn't. Couldn't make out deception from truth.

She'd let Kaine control her once again. Spewing venom that was never truly meant for Garrik, mercilessly attacking the selfless being who sought to help her, repeatedly, without expecting anything in return.

Now, my love. Kaine's wicked voice caressed her like it did so many years ago. *Take the knife, sink it deep, and come back to where you belong. Come home to me.*

The Savage Prince had asked her two unanswered questions. One in her tent earlier. One now. Striking the final, deadly blow, Alora shot at his heart with impeccable aim.

"*Yes* ... and I do *hate* you for it."

Garrik froze.

The entire realm froze.

Something fractured in his face.

Alora saw it—felt it—not entirely sure if she imagined it. Imagined the distinctive crack in her chest and the unmistakable shudder of the floorboards beneath them.

And before he could say another word, she wrenched open the tavern door, disappearing onto the street. Leaving only the steaming amber glow of the iron doorknob and unbearable *silence* behind.

CHAPTER 51

Shadows leapt across gilt-edged cobblestones, dancing from the street torches that lined Alynthia's lavish, upper-class avenues.

No one followed her from the tavern. Nothing but her cruel shadow stalking her every step. Alora pulled at her aching fingertips, rippling with anxiety with only one thing on her mind.

Kaine.

He'd wedged his way in. Only this time, he won ... and she'd come pathetically undone.

Oh, stars ... Garrik's face. His ... chest.

It wasn't Kaine that she'd thrown her fiery palms into. It was Garrik.

Starsdamnit. It was Garrik. Alora's eyes welled with tears, and her throat constricted. "What did I do?" She breathed a pained whisper. An ache sank deep in her heart, and she pulled at her painful fingertips. *What did I do?*

Throwing her arms around her torso and hugging tight, she wasn't certain that her legs could continue. The blood had suddenly fled from them. Each step on the cobblestones was unsteadier than the last. With every unworthy breath she counted, she begged herself to turn back and find him. To apologize. Make him understand. While he would hesitate to speak to her about his demons, she isolated hers. Bottled them up and let it fester into a wound so deep that it allowed Kaine to tear yet another hole in her heart and fill it until she ignited.

Burning Garrik...

A soft whimper cracked her throat. Cracked just like her heart.

Kaine *ruined* her. He ruined her a long time ago.

Would she ever be free of him?

A splitting headache had her stopping to lean against the railing of a long staircase that she didn't dare look up for fear that Kaine would be standing there. Across the street, a flower shop with wooden barrels of lush reds and hues of pink flowers sat on either side of a crystal and iron door. The crystal sparkled from the iron lanterns outside, hanging on the whitewashed wooden storefront.

Flowers. A shudder tore through her body.

If she apologized to Garrik now, would he see it like she saw red roses? A mundane, lifeless apology that meant nothing, knowing this could happen again. If she looked him in the eyes, would she see her hateful eyes staring back, just as Kaine did?

She didn't deserve to look at him ... or the flowers. Not something so beautiful.

Alora tore her eyes away from the building and hugged her torso tighter before she forced herself to continue. As she passed each storefront—as she looked into the crystal glass—every reflection mirrored how she felt.

Weak. Broken. Worthless.

Before long, the crystal windows, whitewashed fronts, and weaving ivy had transformed. Neglected and rotting wooden buildings lined the streets instead.

She'd been lost in her own mind for so long that she'd mindlessly wandered, heedless of her meandering course. The buildings around her were unfamiliar, no landmarks in sight to orient herself. How on Elysian did she get there? How long had she been walking?

Long enough that her hands, despite her permanent state of heated skin, shook in the chilled mountain wind. It didn't faze her though, perhaps even thought that she deserved the biting crawl of pain that stiffened her fingers.

She allowed her mind to empty again, zoning out to the echoes of her boots when she felt a gentle brush against her mind. Her body froze. Her neck convulsed uncomfortably in a shiver, feeling the brush of his magic again.

Soft. Calm. Asking. Waiting.

Alora scanned the crumbling cobblestones and almost vomited.

She felt it again. He wasn't going to stop. Not this time. With a silent curse on her lips, Alora sealed her eyes shut, willed any ounce of strength she had left into her nerves, and let him in.

Garrik's voice was broken, and she could've shattered from it right there. *Are you alright?*

"I'm fine." Lies.

Like hell you are. Where are you?

As if he didn't know. As if he couldn't locate her ... but perhaps he was allowing her the choice to wander. Swirling smoke and shadow danced around her feet and began to climb up her legs. Was he going to dawn her back?

"I can take care of myself." She blurted and stepped from the Smokeshadows. "I don't need your help."

In the corner of her eye, a shadow stirred, and she went rigid. Was he already there? Or was it her shadow that haunted her every step? The thought only fueled her panicked nerves as she kept moving toward a sloping street full of red, wooden roofed buildings stretching up the mountain.

But his voice chased her again. *Turn around and return to camp.*

"No. Leave me alone." She charged ahead and steadied her breathing. Left. Right. Left. Focusing on each step as a distraction.

The shadow in the corner of her view slowly followed.

Alora, I am not asking. You need to come home—

A shadowed hand reached for her.

"I said *LEAVE. ME. ALONE!*" Fists balled in heated determination, she was ready to strike, to save herself from whatever was to come—what Kaine had taught her would always come. Thalon had taught her how to punch effectively. It was starsdamn time to practice on something other than that punching bag she'd burned more than enough holes into.

Alora spun around on her heels, expecting the High Prince to be inches away, unknowing and unprepared. She'd get one good strike in before he'd stop her. But she didn't care. She pictured him. Heard the crack of his jaw when the punch would land and hopefully send him stumbling away before she'd run.

But when she took that step, instead of gray hair and the deep abyss for eyes, amethyst eyes stared back. His lean body towered over her, causing her fist to stop abruptly and step back enough that when she swung her arm down, it caught her dagger, sending it tumbling to the street with a piercing clang.

"Sorry, I—" Stopping. Gaping. *Stars be damned.* The sight of him made her bones freeze over. Garrik's beauty was unmatchable, but this male ... was a close second.

His head was held high, demanding authority and carrying confidence in the step he took toward her frozen body. Pupils as wide as the moon. His shimmering hand wrapped around her upper arm ... and squeezed. Almost as if in warning, her magic barreled a white-hot surge, tingling through her to the contact point of his grasp against her skin.

"How did you get out?" The tips of his mouth turned up almost unnoticeably as he spoke. His face—a mix of shock, intrigue, and anger. But something twinkled in his amethyst eyes before his expression melted into stone and straightened his back, letting her loose to pull his jacket down tight. Adjusting the collar around his neck, he said, "Apologies," and chuckled in a tight breath, *"Lady..."*

Alora stepped back at his melodious voice as if he were singing her a Celestial song. She reached for her dagger by habit.

Only, it wasn't there.

"D—do I know you?"

The male's eyes ... he drew her in as if he was someone familiar, like something she'd seen a million times but couldn't place.

She scanned his face for a moment with a tilt of her head.

Dark cobalt skin—like the night sky—shimmered with emerald and dark amethyst when he moved. Silken strands of straight white hair cascaded over his lean shoulders with striking perfection. Not one piece out of place. Sections of thick braids were woven in locks, flowing down his back. He wore an immaculate night-dark jacket lined with glimmering silver threading that caught the light, and celestial designs glinted on the fastenings crossing the right of his chest. An ethereal radiance emanated from the tall, striking male. He could've been mistaken as the source of light that railed against the surrounding gloom.

He didn't belong in Alynthia. She knew that for certain.

Like the moon himself, those amethyst eyes glowed as he leaned down and collected her dagger. Rotating his palm with it before it laid open, he offered the weapon back to her.

"Do mind where you're shooting, Evening Star." He paused. "Wouldn't want to crash into the wrong hands." As soon as her hand wrapped around the dagger, he was gone. Disappearing like a burning star across the night sky.

Alora whipped her head around, searching for him.

Nothing. Nothing at all.

But his presence remained in the air, and it alone sent a shudder down her spine.

Childish laughter echoed behind her, catching the attention of a few street roamers who turned their noses up, as if it was nothing, like ignoring the sounds of an inconvenient wind. But she was drawn to it like a beautiful melody that once played from her fingertips across ivory keys. She couldn't stop her boots from turning, listening for their laughter's echo.

There in the street, littered with spoiled food, broken crates, and quickly fleeing rodents, three thin younglings played on their knees. The sight of them was enough to make her heart completely break. In the youngest's eyes, deep brown orbs so big as they beheld the wooden unicorn in her hand, Alora pictured her own face. Inside their filthy clothing and kneeling on exposed knees through ripped, decaying fabric, she saw a young white-haired faeling. Herself.

Memories of her harsh and cruel childhood flooded into her eyes and escaped through the tears dripping down her cheek. That deep longing, an ache she'd forced so far into the depths, crawled back in. And before she realized what happened, she'd taken six more steps and stood behind a gray-haired faeling with green eyes, playing with his own wooden wolf.

"Do you want to play with us?" the adorably thin, brown-eyed female squeaked.

Alora's heart melted again.

Before her, Brown-eyes held up another wooden animal.

A white lion.

Was she even breathing anymore?

The third, holding a wooden dragon, was a male youngling with membranous wings and night-dark hair. He giggled. "It looks like your hair! Roar!" Little hands mimicked claws. Gritting his teeth in a growl, he thrashed his head around, roaring another giggle before swiping his dragon and flying it through the air.

Alora knelt, too stunned to speak as she held the white lion in her hands. Too stunned to speak even when Brown-eyes giggled, wiggling her white unicorn up Alora's leg.

Alora snorted. It could've been Ghost without the horn.

They played for what seemed like hours. The moon hadn't changed positions. Everything inside her pleaded to stay. Wanted to bring them with her so they wouldn't need to live a life of hardship and cruelty such as she did. Orphans rarely survived to half a century old. She'd seen it enough. Watched as her friends had drifted away in their sleep from malnourishment. From the smallest of injury or illness. From imprisonment of simply stealing a bite of rotten apple or molding bread.

With the stars' blessings, she was lucky to have survived. Her mind replayed one blistering-hot day in Telldaira. She'd worn her shoes so completely thin that the cracked holes blistered the soft skin of her young feet. And even worse, the hunger pains had grown unbearable over three weeks, which inevitably led her to that decrepit booth of spoiled foods in the forbidden markets. She was dirty—so disgusting that her matted hair was a shade of charcoal. A loaf of bread, though stale, sat on the edge of a table as if begging her to thieve it. Smelling of mold and settled in a graying color in the golden sunlight, it still looked and smelled like a royal banquet to her starving belly. Her grimy hands had snatched it and ran, but she didn't make it far enough when the back of her heel was caught in boots, and she planted face-first into the stones of the street.

She didn't eat that day. Or the rest of the week.

Shuddering at the memory, Alora pulled out the red velvet coin purse she had snatched from Jade in the tavern. Maybe it was foolish. These younglings might not understand how to stretch the money, what to use it on or how to find themselves what they needed to survive, but she couldn't simply leave them there. *Not like this.*

Little Wings' face perked up at the jingling of the coins. His pretty navy eyes glimmered as he scooted on thin knees close to her. They all did.

"Listen to me." Not one eye shifted from her as she divided the coins up in her palm. "You are to use this first to eat. Slowly. Start with broth and small bites of bread. Don't eat meat until you've eaten this for a few days. Your bellies will want to eat more, but it won't hold as much as you think it will."

Alora handed Little Gray coins. "Buy two pairs of clothing. Wash one set each day, as well as yourself. Being clean will help keep you from falling ill." Little Wings shuffled closer, and she handed him his coins. "Find work. You're little, but not for long. You're valuable. Deliver correspondence, carry stones for buildings, collect hops for the tavern. Make coin until you can find a place to live—together. You are each other's strength."

Brown-eyes never took her eyes off Alora. She gently flipped Brown-eyes's palm and curled her little fingers around them.

"You are"—tears lined Alora's eyes—"braver than you think. Stronger than you yet know"—her lips quivered—"because of what you've endured. *Fight. Live.*"

Tiny arms wrapped across her chest and back as Little Wings hugged into her shoulder. Brown-eyes and Little Gray crowded into her just as tight as their voices squeaked a 'thank you.'

She embraced them, long and tight, tears streaming down her face.

Refusing to let go as if this was the only love they ever felt since they were abandoned or introduced too soon to the cruelties of life.

SHE WAS LOST. Of course she was, because *what else* could she mess up that evening? Somehow, she managed to wander out of the upscale shops and restaurants and found herself amongst dreary busted windows, dry cracking wooden walls, and the smell of something putridly burning. Her traitorous body longed for her tent. Burning legs screamed for her bed. A bath.

Anything but this.

You have passed those buildings three times.

Anything but him.

Alora froze and inhaled a steadying breath, shaking her head at the sky. She pictured Garrik leaning against a building, a torch post, perched on a roof, ready to dawn down and pull her back to camp. To inflict whatever brand of punishment that was waiting for her at her return.

There was nothing that could shelter her from the inevitable storm coming.

Alora willed all of her strength into her words, hoping—praying—he wouldn't come for her. "I don't need your help." What she really meant was, *I don't want to look into your eyes and explain why I said those awful things.*

Alora stared at a darkened, broken door of an abandoned building. The darkness, the shadows, had been unusually motionless but still watchful as she walked.

Suit yourself. Enjoy walking in circles. I am sure you will pass those buildings again in ... twenty minutes.

And she did. The same starsdamned, black-bricked, three-story building with the broken door and darkness eerily motionless in the broken windows. She passed it for the fourth time—just as he said—and exhaled a frustrated sigh, running her hands down her aching, throbbing face.

Exhausted and defeated, she considered that staying in one of the abandoned buildings would be far better than admitting that, maybe this time, she couldn't do it on her own.

Alora took a step toward a broken door.

This would be better.

Her boot nudged against the door. It fell open with a cloud of dust at her feet.

This would be far better.

He wouldn't be in there. She wouldn't have to face his eyes. Face the words she'd spit at him. Face the betrayal in his voice as he bit back. Wouldn't have to admit a truth that she'd known and felt for some time.

Alora surveyed the inside. The darkness felt ... *wrong.* As if even its comfort wasn't offered as she stood there. As if it knew and decided she was no longer worthy of its relief. She was wrong to have said those things to him, and they knew.

They all knew.

The darkness could swallow her whole tonight and she wouldn't care.

Alora took a step inside. Something stirred within. Something crashed.

She shrieked, stumbling out as her limbs emptied of blood, leaving her nerves shaken. The message was clear. She wasn't staying there tonight. And as her legs carried her around the street once more, not one building offered up a haven to hide and fall apart.

With no one around to find her way back to camp, Alora deepened a breath as sharp as glass, accepting her fate, and called out, "Fine." Looking to the sky through her eyelashes, she pivoted them around the street.

Silence.

"I said, *FINE.*"

Her mind was an endless abyss of her own echoing.

Of course, he wouldn't come now. Only prying when she desired solitude. With a deep-throated growl of frustration, she yelled loud enough for her voice to bounce off the walls, "*Bastard!*"

"Wherever there are shadows, I will always be," she mocked under her breath.

"You call for help yet insult me in the same breath." Swirls of Smokeshadows danced around a torch post directly to her left and blew away on a phantom wind. Garrik leaned, straight-backed and rigid, arms and ankles crossed, broad shoulder digging into the post. His hollow eyes were low, focused on the deep red lines marking his forearm. Another just as deep laid half-hidden under a slash in the upper arm of his tunic. And if he were in pain, if the blistering from her embered palms sunk deep into his skin, he didn't show it.

She almost called on him about it, but he arched a brow and spoke as if he couldn't be bothered to care at all. "Enjoy your stroll?" Face taut, undoubtedly restraining countless other words.

Alora crossed her arms, her leathers groaning in the movement, fighting off every ounce of fear and trembling bones, not bothering to mention his wounds. "Up until now."

He still hadn't looked at her. "The feeling is mutual. Next time, do not go wandering off and I will not have to come get you."

"I can—"

"Then do it. Take fucking care of yourself." He pushed off the post and turned up the street. "You do not need a monster's help. You have made that perfectly clear." Garrik cursed and brushed his hand back through his hair. He raised a palm, flicking his wrist in a rough command.

Smokeshadows whirled in front of her on a chilling wind, pulling at her palm. She uncrossed her arms and, with a rotation of her wrist, flipped it over, letting the shadows dance across.

Silken touches gently brushed her skin. When they drifted away, a rolled parchment remained, almost tumbling from her fingertips before her warm grip closed around it.

On closer inspection of it, a perfectly marked route on an Alynthian map sat, marked in red strokes. From her location and her rough determination, the end of the route was, perhaps, a fifteen-minute walk, near the outskirts of the city.

Her fingers brushed the parchment. Their camp was at the main gate, and she was walking in the wrong direction. In fact, she had crossed through the mountain range and found herself on the other side, in the Sunless Valley. Another half an hour walk and she would've been at the city wall opposite the legion.

Alora looked up from the map to find Garrik leaning against a building twenty feet away. Smokeshadows danced around his shoulders and hands before he quickly adjusted his tunic over his chest.

"Start walking." His words were distant, cold.

Alora stepped toward him, hitting an invisible wall, unable to get close to him. Physically feeling the barriers she had helped him erect to keep her out.

In a vicious, outstretched cloud of shadow and ash, Garrik shot into the air on Smokeshadow wings and disappeared into the night sky.

CHAPTER 52

T halon leaned against the crumbling foundation of a half burned-out two-story hovel—what was left of one. In fact, not a single structure still stood whole amidst the churned rubble. Smoldering ruins sent up smoke, reeking of charred timber and sizzling flesh. Collapsed rooftops spilled in on themselves, yet their foundations clung to a semblance of shape and bore gaping wounds where flames had licked their walls.

All around her, flakes of ash swirled through the weary air, dusting the blackened bones half-buried in the debris. Destruction and devastation inescapable to the eye. An amber glow lit the sky as the few remaining structures burned to the ground.

The attack from earlier was contained to this area alone, as if the dragon had continually—ruthlessly—relentlessly attacked this portion of the mountain. Until it had done enough damage to satisfy whatever brought it there and carried itself away with death and destruction below its wings.

"You look horrible."

"Not as bad as this place." Thalon was right, though. Her face hadn't stopped throbbing since the punch. The bruise under her eye had swollen horrifically.

Alora avoided eye contact, and silence fell between them. The occasional groan of splintering architecture yielding to gravity haunted the silence with moans of further obliteration.

She glanced at him. Thalon had taught her how to defend herself. She had watched soldiers in the ring get their asses reamed by their swords-master when they suffered careless blows enough times to know that she'd suffer the same fate. Even through the swollen and purple bruise, she felt blood scarlet her cheeks and nervously shifted in front of him.

Thalon registered her apprehension, tapping an inked finger to his cheek. "How did it feel?"

Alora rolled her lower lip between her teeth. "Being punched in the face? Like all the other times, I suppose. This one just..." White hair glowed in the moonlight as she paced, shaking her head. "I was careless. I messed up." Shame settled in her voice before she slammed her back into the wall beside him and crossed her arms.

"Hurts enough to remember what not to do next time?"

She pinched her eyebrows, pivoting her head to look at him, and replayed everything from the moment Jade threw the first punch. And somehow ... she couldn't help but think he meant her words to Garrik, too.

Eventually, Alora nodded.

"Good. Tomorrow, you'll show me precisely what you should've done until it becomes as simple as blinking." Thalon rolled his head in her direction, his Earned clacking together before he smiled.

Alora took in a heavy breath. Not as bad as she'd expected. She could handle sparring in the ring. Preferred it over talking with ...

She hadn't realized until now. Garrik wasn't there. Sapphires to the sky, she gazed around the stars clouded by rising smoke as if he would swoop down on Smokeshadow wings at any moment. When his muscled body didn't fall from the sky, she scanned the ruined street around them. Not even the shadows danced in their usual unsettledness when he was near.

"He's upstairs with our recruit. Garrik preferred to do this introduction alone."

The located Mystic. Her eyes shifted to the burned door. "Then why are we here? He can't handle himself?" Even talking about him made her blood boil. Her own stubbornness caused her long walk there, yet she still blamed him for not offering to bring her. And she knew it was foolish to think that way but didn't care. For now, she'd let herself be selfishly mad. It felt better.

Glowing golden eyes watched a small flame burn down to its last flicker across the street. Once puffed out, the gray smoke danced into the air to join the rest.

"He's asked a lot of his magic today, seen and unseen, and after what happened to him in Galdheir ... his powers are greatly diminished. They haven't returned to full strength. Though we like to believe he's all-powerful like heroes in books, he's still bone that can break, flesh that can be cut, a mind that can fall to exhaustion. He'll never admit it, but he's tired. Angry. Not at you nor I. Just ... angry."

The unseen. The four hours that he was gone. And then, the deep wounds on his arms. What had he been doing in the time she'd been wandering the city?

"What you said in the tavern. You know it's not true."

Alora's heart skipped, imagining how his eyes went bloodthirsty at the sight of her face. How he scanned the tavern to find the male who laid the bruise on her face.

"I know," she breathed and lowered her head as all of it came flooring back.

"It doesn't help when those he's closest to see him as the villain. Garrik does very bad things, so we don't have to. He has to remember who he is while playing the part of someone he's not. And when we cause him to pit himself against us because of our own damn foolishness, like running off to bed the first female Guardian I've seen since my Protected died instead of stopping Jade's temper, it's worse." Thalon's eyes hollowed out for a moment, scanning the ruble around them. Shame set in his face, and his thumb nervously rubbed his marked chest.

"Do you"—she hesitated—"want to talk about it?"

"The sex? Stars no." He forced a smile yet went stiff-necked. Through the clean-cut beard, she could see his jaw flex and his chest rise in a deep breath. "They died in a place a lot like this. Ev—Everlyn was traveling back to visit our families at the Keep for a sacred holiday, celebrating Maker's passing from life to life. She was a Protected—married. My wife. Her Guardian duties were discharged once she became with child." Thalon smiled. "Koen. We had so many dreams for him." The golden spheres in his eyes glistened.

Alora's heart fluttered at his smile but faded ... as it was only fueled by a memory. One he was lost in. One that, for a moment, was so real that it froze him solid to the ash-covered wall. She let him bask in it, let him feel the hope that once filled his heart. Until his eyes blinked and his glowing orbs dulled.

"I hadn't seen her in weeks and assumed that she'd arrived at Tarrent-Garren. She wanted to endure the journey instead of taking my portal home. Magic worried her. She was uneasy about transporting through space being with child.

"I don't know why she was there. Why she was in that place. Maybe she fell ill or was resting from the journey. But when I arrived, leading the second battalion of the Ravens through a freezing thunderstorm, as was my sacred duty to do as my High King commanded ... and saw that entire town was leveled to thick rubble and mud without a single scorch mark ... like a solid wave of air slammed into everything at once." He paused and shuddered a breath. "And saw the entire population laid in rows, bones crushed, their bodies so mangled it was hard to recognize them as once living beings."

Burning hot tears relentlessly streamed down Alora's face.

"Her wings were the first thing I saw. Broken. Shattered. At odd angles and snapped. The pearl white smeared with blood. And I saw ... *him*, standing in the rubble. Saw his black eyes scanning the sea of bodies while Ravens loaded one faerie into a prisoner cart. A child screaming for its mother who laid beside Ev.

"He watched me as I lifted her, as I took her Earned from her braids. And, like usual, he briefed me. Showing me in my mind what had happened. He slaughtered them all at once ... killed her. My son."

Alora's stomach threatened to empty at the insinuation. "Wh—who killed them?" But her heart already knew.

The hard lump of Thalon's throat bobbed as liquid lined his eyes. His hands shook enough that his fingers dug into his bursting biceps with enough strength to bruise thinner skin.

"The Savage Prince," Thalon's voice cracked in a painful whisper.

The air ripped from her lungs.

Thalon's knees shook. "Garrik wasn't Garrik. He was my brother held captive. And now, he lives with the pain of his past every day. Staring at the reminder every time he looks at me, looks at Ev's line of Earned in my braids. The"—he shook his head—"villain in everyone's story," Thalon whispered as if to keep Garrik from hearing him. "Only, he's not in mine. And she wouldn't have wanted him to be. We were both fighting to get him back, to find a way. Garrik would've never done that if he could've stopped himself ... if he wasn't..." Thalon brushed his hands over his face and squeezed the back of his neck with a curse.

"If he wasn't what?"

Thalon moved to speak, but Alora looked away for only a moment to cull the vomit rising in her throat. Her attention drew to a flare up of a flame four houses down, burning the dried kindling inside. A perfect distraction.

When she turned back, eyes still burning with tears, Thalon was no longer leaning against the building. Shoulders squared to her, his face was turned down in confusion as he brought his fingers to his ears and snapped twice.

Odd. She didn't hear the snaps.

He took two heavy steps, stopping inches in front of her, and mouthed, "Can you hear me?"

Barely. All the sounds around them stilled to less than whispers. The loud pops of smoldering wood were gone. Grass blades twisting in the wind were only movements, even the chilled wind across their faces was silent.

Thalon's voice was muffled like he was underwater. "Alora? Can you hear me?" he was screaming. She knew he was, yet she heard not even a whisper.

And then.

Everything detonated in an ear-piercing explosion.

They threw their hands to their ears and buckled under the intense pain. It was head-splitting. Deafening. Reverberating through her entire body as she twisted, hunching inward, begging for the sound to stop. Unearthly volume shattered through her eardrums. Her hands couldn't hold it back, though they remained sealed against her bleeding ears. All sound—sounds she hadn't heard in ages—attacked. Crying, laughing, high-pitched screams, shrieks of dragons, roaring of waterfalls, thunder, rocks tumbling from mountains, blazing infernos, the crashing of waves.

So many—*too many*—sounds. Her mind couldn't focus on one alone.

A tattooed hand gripped around her wrist, pulling her attention, and Thalon mouthed, "Stay here."

Before she could protest, a swirling cloud of thunderstorms and lightning appeared, showing a darkened, decrepit bedroom on the other side.

A blaring array of lights burst from the upstairs window, and she knew where his portal was taking him as he stepped through.

It closed behind him a breath later, swallowing him whole.

Ears screaming, Alora stood at the bottom of a burned-up staircase inside the front door, staring directly up into the face of a true demon—Kaine.

He waited. Fists balled and face taunting her from above.

Her legs viciously shook, unable to take the first step, preferring the deafening sounds over what she was fearing to do. How long had she been standing there, eyes fighting back tears as she looked up into the dark staircase? As she looked at Kaine, who she knew wasn't truly there. She'd never stepped a foot on it. It wasn't marble. It had no emerald rugs. The walls weren't decorative spindles connected to redwood handrails.

Yet she couldn't move.

Not until she heard Garrik's raging, guttural scream.

He was fighting something. And by the pain carrying in his voice, it was winning.

Then Thalon yelled, his voice as throat-ripping and pained as the High Prince's. Bursts of light exploded into the hallway. Flashes of light like those in Thalon's portals struck across the walls as small amounts of Smokeshadows exploded along with them, misting around Kaine's illusion and down the first few steps of the staircase before they retreated on tethered fury.

They could be dying. Right there. And she was cowering over a burned wooden step. Cowering over a damn memory.

Garrik cried out again, voice a thunderous roar, like his lungs had pushed past their capacity just to allow it to tear from him.

She had to move.

The staircase—Kaine—be *damned.*

Shaking legs refused to take an inch, but she forced them. One. Two. Three steps. Then five. Her legs burned and mind replayed memories of bloodstained steps. Seven steps. The sound. The memories. It was enough that she could collapse.

But she couldn't. Not when Thalon's voice cracked in pain.

Not when Garrik's screams had stopped.

Racing against her raging heartbeat and the sounds of her friends dying, her boots slammed through Kaine's illusion before her guts decided to empty. But she didn't dare look up for fear Kaine was still there. She had to keep moving. *She had to.*

Alora shakingly stepped onto the final step, gripping the crumbling threshold, unable to steady her panicked breath. Blood dripped from her ears, yet she couldn't feel it. In the bedroom across the hallway, half burned with the far wall and ceiling scorched out, Smokeshadows—in half their usual force—raged in a swirling funnel as portals flared, striking lightning into the winds.

Garrik was down on a knee, steadying himself against the blaring sound. With one hand outstretched to Thalon, the other shook in front of him as darkness exploded from his palm. His own trail of blood poured from his ears. He was going down, slowly, as if what was left of his spent powers could do nothing to whoever—whatever—was caged inside Smokeshadows.

Alora tried to scream, feeling her throat vibrate, knowing the sound should be carrying, but she couldn't hear it anymore.

Then she saw the shift in blackened eyes. Saw as Garrik noticed her standing at the threshold. Noticed Thalon slamming his hands to his own chest mouthing, 'take it from me,' with a shake of his head.

Garrik's face tightened, glaring at Thalon before he dropped his hand, exploding with darkness, and shoved a palm out to her.

The pulse of energy slammed into her. The ear-piercing sound diminished by half within a heartbeat. But when she returned her gaze to Garrik, he'd fallen to both knees, struggling to keep his arms pointed at them. Protecting them with his shield.

Get out of here! Garrik's voice rippled in agony.

Alora panicked. *What do I do? What do I do?* She scanned her hands that had burst with white embers. *How the hell can fire do anything to sound?*

Garrik dropped to his hands and gnashed his teeth together, fighting off a painful scream. *Alora, go!* Glowing silver eyes speared her where she stood and didn't move. Locked onto hers, viciously fighting to stay open. He breathed deep as if it could be his last breath.

He breathed deep.

Breathed ... deep.

Air. Sound needs air to carry! And fire ... oh, Maker of the Skies, if you allow this to work ...

Alora's hands burst into white flames.

The more air, the bigger the burn.

Garrik had once told her that her emotions carried her outburst in the arena. Fueled her magic to be greater, stronger. When usually emotions were a weakness, hers were an accelerant. And every time she trained with Eldacar, the more emotion she threw at her magic, the more she could do.

So, she threw every ounce of hatred of her words, every bit of embarrassment, every tingle of fear and panic at her flames.

And let it all burn.

Higher, higher, higher.

Until flames burst from the open ceiling.

Until they exploded around the room, hitting every rotting piece of furniture, every cracked floorboard, every thread of the bedspread. Her fire grew molten, burning everything except each of them.

And with every flicker of white flames, it grew harder to breathe.

Alora intensified her focus, screaming—pleading—to her magic. The white inferno irradiated in an ethereal glow, dancing sparks burst in the flames, sucking the air from the room.

The ear-shattering sound died down, more and more. Through the remaining swirling cloud of Smokeshadows, someone burst through with palms and knuckles whitening around their neck.

Alora, Garrik choked, his body convulsing on the floor. *Alora, stop. You ... will kill us.*

Thalon was down on his back, squirming, clawing at his throat, lips blue.

Alora, you can— Garrik's hand scratched at the wood, failing to crawl toward her. *You c—can stop.* He choked, only this time, when his mouth opened, his lungs didn't fill. His eyes widened, mouth gaping before his hand spasmed and fell.

White embers covered her sapphires, and Alora fisted her palms tight, calling her fire back inside.

The inferno ripped from every threshold and floorboard. Tore away from every open space and hole back into clenched fists. Shooting through her veins until flames returned to embers and died inside, leaving only a heavy surge of oxygen bursting back into the smothered space.

She stood, eyes fading back into jewels, ears bleeding, breathing, scanning.

Garrik's chest rose and fell, panting, gasping for the air.

He tried to speak, but his eyes closed instead, gasping continuously before Thalon's choked voice called out, "Yes, I'm alive."

Coughing stirred their attention.

In the corner, by what remained of a bedframe, whoever it was that unleashed the Firekeeper-filled-hell upon their ears was still alive, too. Footsteps made the floorboards groan. They were advancing. But Thalon and Garrik were still collecting their breaths and regaining strength.

Alora squared her shoulders and willed her emotions back into her palms. "Take another step and I'll turn your insides into barbecue." She extended her palms. Dancing flames formed into fiery spheres within them.

The figure stepped forward, out into the moonlight.

"Come on, I dare you!" she hissed as a semi-circle of white flames formed in front of them, licking at their bare feet.

Through the glow of the moon, a younger face, much younger than the three of them, twisted in anger. "We're not leaving." His voice was hoarse. Broken. Angry. "We won't be killed for our magic, not like our parents, not like our grandsire. Not by *that* demon." He prowled toward Garrik, who had barely pushed himself against the wall. "Burn in hell."

Garrik's eyes flashed with pain, not physical pain, but pain nonetheless.

'Burn in hell'—the same words she had spoken to Kaine ... to Garrik.

The villain in everyone's story.

Alora's hands remained raised with swirling spheres like the stars, anticipating another attack as the young male stepped again toward Garrik.

"My parents died too," she blurted. "Nearly three centuries ago at the hands of the High King's army."

It stopped his advance. Locking his eyes onto hers, brows drawn together as his mouth gaped, he sucked in a sharp breath.

Good. Look at me. "And now I fight ... with *him*." She nodded to the side, pointing at Garrik. "To bring Magnelis to his deserved end. Though it seems difficult to find that trust within yourself, we aren't the enemy, as I'm sure His Highness explained. We need your help."

Tears shimmered in his eyes. "*He* killed them! My sister, Grandmother, and I watched as *he*..." His young voice cracked, too pained to continue. "And I couldn't even give them a proper burial after what he did. Not after—"

"You never got to say goodbye, did you?" Alora cut in, stopping his spiral.

The male shook his head, mouth set in a hard line.

She lowered her palms, her fire dying inside. "Neither did I."

"Neither did he." It was Thalon's voice. His inked finger lifted from the floor and pointed to Garrik, eyes pleading for forgiveness as Garrik swallowed hard.

Nobody said a word as Garrik's head dropped against the wall, face taut, defeated. "You are not alone in your pain. None of you." Garrik's eyes shifted to the burned threshold beside the bed. A mirrored female likeness of the young male stepped out. Long wavy locks of blond fell from her head.

"I cannot alter the past, but I can fight to change the future. I cannot bring your parents back, but I make a vow to you that I will do everything within my power to help you avenge them in whatever recompense that means for you once it is all over." Garrik's hollow eyes shifted to Alora, squinting before he released a deep sigh and pivoted his head back to the young male.

The twin female stepped forward, motioning with her fingers in movements much like a dance.

Her brother watched and stiffened. Turning to the High Prince, he grabbed his sister's hand and snarled, "You want us to join you, *demon*? Then you'll need to save someone from a soulless death. Then, we'll join you."

Garrik lifted an eyebrow, silent for what seemed forever, straining and closing, then opening his hollow eyes.

And when he finally spoke, his voice was laced with unease, body stiffening unbearably. "You have a deal."

"It was coming for her."

Alora learned that the young male with short blond hair was named Zanayr. His sister, Nalani, spoke with her hands and not her voice. She was born without sound, not in her ears and no spoken words. Instead, her brother was her mouthpiece; she was his peace.

Twins who were both born with power.

The power of sound.

The power of silence.

Garrik knelt by the bedside, his icy hand wrapped around another—weathered and wrinkled.

"She's dying, and the dragon was coming for its debt to be paid."

Thalon leaned against the wall, pulling at his earlobe and extending his jaw. "Debt to be paid? Explain."

The chest of a frail faerie rose and fell dangerously slow. Her gray skin, like both her grandlings showed nearly a millennium of hardship as she lay under a stained quilt. Zanayr sat opposite of Garrik, squeezing her other hand tight as he brushed a thumb there.

"She sold herself to the legend of this mountain. For Nalani and I. Once she passes, her soul will be caged. We live because she will suffer after death, forever tormented as it uses her face, her voice, walking Elysian in her likeness whenever it sees fit."

Garrik's face paled at the words, and he cursed.

Thalon did too.

"You agreed to save her from this fate."

"Yes. And I will."

Their Guardian uncrossed his arms and tensed. "Sire, *no*—"

"I have made my deal." He turned to Nalani, then back to Zanayr.

"One of us will return to collect you once the debt is paid." Twisting up, he loosened his hold on their grandmother's hand, but she gently squeezed, almost unnoticeably. Garrik bent and sat on the bed, the wooden frame groaning beneath his weight.

Her pale lips moved, too silent to hear her voice.

"She wants to speak to you." Zanayr's lips curled.

Garrik bent low, his ear inches from her mouth as she spoke.

Silver eyes glowed when he bent up, then clasped her hand in his. His words were soft, unlike the wrathful male she saw in the tavern. And sweet, no semblance of the disdain he had carried in the street.

Like a beautiful melody, he whispered, "It is a high privilege ... the deepest honor to care for those who have long-suffered and cared for us young." Garrik wiped a tear from the corner of her hooded, heavy eyes. "Your grandlings will be safe with my Dragons. And they will live remembering your great sacrifice, knowing you drifted peacefully into the Stars Eternal upon your final breath." His icy lips placed a kiss on her forehead before a language Alora hoped to learn crossed his practiced tongue.

The grandmother squeezed his hand softly.

Garrik laid his hand on her head. It trembled as he closed his eyes— and continued trembling the longer it held there.

In one small breath, she slowly drifted into an easy sleep.

"What did you do?" Zanayr hissed in a panic.

"She dreams peacefully now."

CHAPTER 53

There was no shield that night as they stepped from Thalon's portal. Cobblestones to dirt, their boots fell heavy across the road. Garrik had walked slowly down the steps, leaving Zanayr and Nalani to spend what might be their final night with their grandmother. And after Alora's shaking knees almost caused her to fall down the stairs in the hovel they called home, Garrik's palm slammed into the wall, cracking the burned wood. Her aching fingers curled around his corded forearm, catching her fall before she plummeted. Without as much as a glance back, he slowly continued to the bottom, without a word.

Outside, it was like they had strode out of one realm into another. The ashes ended in a crisp line where clean streets began.

She may have saved their lives, but her words still echoed.

Likely, still echoed for him, too.

And instead of falling in line beside them, Alora decided to hang back. She didn't want to be close to Garrik.

Exchanging strained voices, Thalon and Garrik spoke, mostly

Thalon, but she couldn't focus enough to listen. Their low voices reverberated into her bones, but only the comfort of that shudder kept her walking and not completely breaking down behind them. Her hands were warm, threatening embers when she pictured the bedroom, pictured their dying faces. Pictured Garrik's face, again, yet this time in physical pain.

Pictured her flames and what she'd done.

Air. Her fire *stole air*. How was that possible?

Her boot scraped the back of Thalon's heel before she realized she had zoned out entirely. With a quick smile back at her, Thalon turned to Garrik, stopping beside an alley between two brick buildings full of living quarters. The glow of candles flickered out through a few windows and the street torches were still dancing their light when Thalon spoke. "You're not going to make it across this city like this." He was looking at Garrik, who had begun to slow in steps, his face drained of color. "Time to go home."

Garrik's eyes were glazed, and dark circles rested under his eyes as he nodded.

In dancing movements of his palms, Thalon commanded his portal to appear.

Alora almost squealed when she saw camp on the other side. Almost ran full speed into it when Garrik shifted on his feet and beckoned her to go first with his palm.

Still, he didn't look at her.

She never thought she'd be so happy to see this place. But something wasn't right. With every step she made closer to their tents, she didn't feel that familiar pulse of static energy. Didn't feel it surge through her body, the taste of metal, as they crossed through the protection of the shield.

When Garrik stopped at the line of sentries, she slowly—carefully—paced her steps, wondering if she should pass or stay behind him. He hadn't granted her permission to leave, even though she could do what she wanted. But after tonight, could she still?

"Have there been any more reports of Ravens?" His voice was incredibly hoarse. It rasped with a hard bite, but even with it mostly gone, it still carried his authority.

"No, sire. So far, only the few you encountered. Patrols are still searching the mountain."

Alora's eyes shifted to Garrik's arms. The painful looking dark red slashes carved in them had dried across his corded skin. Ravens. It all made sense. He'd encountered the High King's Ravens.

"I want patrols rounding every hour. Set up a perimeter twenty miles around the mountain. Find Deimon and Draven. Have the Wingborne transfer the rotations while the Nightfall wolves scout the trails. No Raven will enter the city while the wards are down. Understood?"

"Yes, sire." The sentry snapped his fingers, motioning to two others with wings who immediately took to the sky toward camp.

"Jade and Aiden?"

"They have not returned."

Garrik shifted, turning his head to the forest to their west. Murky, silver eyes closed, his eyes quivered underneath. Trembling for a moment as if in deep concentration, Garrik's body tensed and relaxed with a frustrated sigh.

A scowl pulled at his brows and lips when his eyes opened, and head dropped low. With a shake of his head, a curse left his lips. "Inform them that I require a briefing when they return."

IF SHE COULD SIMPLY MAKE it to her tent and escape inside without a single word, that would be enough for her. The entrance was dark, and even if the darkness inside wouldn't welcome her, it would be better than ... *this*. Walking behind him, watching him in silence, hearing every word he was not saying to her. It was agony. Worse than any blow of Kaine's hands.

Please, look at me.

She pleaded—*pleaded* with burning eyes to the stars that he was listening. That it would be enough.

Please. Alora's throat constricted, viciously fighting back an invading sob. Her neck tensed—her entire body tensed—with each step, with each moment of silence, and her own voice echoed in her head.

The gentle caress was nowhere. He wasn't listening. He wasn't there.

Would he ever be there again?

The air felt heavy. She forced herself to breathe, but with every bit of air entering her lungs, the molten tears built up around her lashes until one spilled out. Then another. Until they streamed down her face.

Please, please, look at me.

Garrik's disheveled hair was disturbed by a cold breeze. She watched each strand gently flutter in the moonlight and imagined what it would feel like in her fingers before closing her eyes and shaking the thought. His shoulders were heavy, low, as if an impossible weight was pulling him down. The same weight cascaded down his body into his slow and unsure steps. She'd never seen him walk in such a manner. So ... distracted. So ... unlike him. He usually carried himself in graces of unbreakable stone. The picture of perfect agility, strong minded, and unwavering strength. But *this*.

She caused *this*.

Garrik had veered to their right, toward his tent. A fire was stoked and blazing, ready for their return with a pot of roasted meat, boiled potatoes in butter and herbs, and mixed greens simmering as if someone had only been there moments before tending it.

A hungry growl rippled through her stomach, and she realized she hadn't eaten since morning. But the pain in her heart and mind ached more than the hunger ever could now. She'd rather starve.

Garrik stopped feet from her tent.

Still. He hadn't looked at her.

That darkened pit in her empty stomach caved in on itself, gutting it wide open.

I need you to look at me. I need to know if ... if I've lost you completely.

With a quick tug at his tunic, Garrik turned and those usually glowing, beautiful silver eyes were snuffed out completely. No luster, no shine. Like cracked dried mud or dead, spoiled meat. Lifeless, as he slowly set his eyes in her direction, focusing on her bruise.

It was like she was underwater, trying to swim, but her kicking only kept herself thrashing in that place. Her heart pounded when he lifted his hand, reaching to her cheek without a word.

And she knew by his movement, by the expressionless face and vacant eyes, that he wasn't reaching to grip her throat. He wasn't conspiring to meet her with a wrathful fist or leave her with the sting of a vicious slap. But on instinct, on nerves and habit alone, Alora lost her ability to breathe.

Trembling, she flinched back.

Garrik froze. As slowly as his hand was reaching for her, it retreated.

No. She saw that same look in his eyes as in the tavern. *No!*

Muscles shifting in his forearm, Garrik rotated his hand in front of him. Her eyes dropped to the movement, expecting Smokeshadows to appear. They didn't. The last few days at the castle, his drunken night away, everything he used at the wall, the tavern, the street, the hovel ... all of his powers had faded like the night with the gamroara.

Not a drop remained.

On blood-splattered battlefields littered with the dead, when everything had quieted and those once living were taking their final breaths, only the crumbling ash, the smell of wet iron, and burning smoke remained. The hoarse voices of warriors would whisper in their heart-wrenching victory. Only there are no winners in war. Only survivors. And his voice carried the anguish and gutted rasps all the same. "Go inside." Garrik turned and began to walk away. "Expect Calla with healing balm tonight."

"Please..." Alora's voice cracked. "Don't make me wait until tomorrow. Punish me ... get it over with." Willing every bit of that hate for Kaine into her eyes, she clenched a hand by her side, squeezing intensely until that shake disappeared. Until she was brave enough to look at him and find that he had stopped and remained a pillar of stone there.

Garrik didn't turn back. His hands trembled before they flexed. That hoarseness in his voice tore through the crack in her heart, for it was cold and distant yet again. "I'm far too tired for this. Go to bed."

"You're not going to punish me?"

The High Prince's hand rested on his hip as he shook his head low, shoulders tense as they rose. "You punished yourself enough tonight. I will honor that penance. Now, go to bed before you pass out."

The ice from his words stabbed every last bit of hope she desperately held on to. She said nothing in return because she simply couldn't form anything but her quickened breaths.

He began moving toward his tent again.

But she couldn't leave the night this way. Not like this. He had to know that she didn't mean any of what she'd said. And before her better judgment stopped her, Alora took a hard step forward, boot sliding in the dirt and gravel before her traitorous lips blurted, "I'm sorry."

A muscle flexed in his jaw, and voice like shards of ice, he said, "Don't bother."

THUNDER RATTLED HER TENT. Its mighty power not nearly as violent as the throat-tearing screaming before it. The horrific nightmare. It had returned. Causing her to wake in a blazing sweat as rumbling roared outside.

One thing was certain—she wouldn't find any more sleep tonight. Not after the screaming, not after the bloody hand reached for her and cried out her name through the darkness.

She was blistering-hot even in the chilled night air. Her entire body shook while her heart had taken off with itself.

Lightning illuminated her tent with each strike. She watched, hoping her heavy eyes would return and drift into a calm dream, but after some time, determined it wouldn't happen. Instead of laying in bed, Alora decided it was the perfect weather to read.

The amethyst glow of the moon shone through the rain that tapped a soothing rhythm on the canvas. It was unnerving in a way. Usually winds of such storms shook the canvas, but this time, it barely moved.

A certain magic in the air, Alora swung her legs over the side before lighting a lantern with a flame on her finger. Feet gently sliding into soft furs, she walked barefoot to her bookshelf. Twirling one toe against the wooden floor, she raked her eyes over the books smelling of leather and metal—Garrik's scent—until a green book laid in her hand.

Deciding on her bed and massive mounds of pillows instead of her emerald reading chair, she plopped onto the blankets, legs stretched out and ankles crossed, expecting her world to transform in her mind.

But tonight. Her thoughts raced. Rereading the same lines over and over and over.

She'd grown fond of these characters. They were easy to love, and normally when her eyes would glide across the text, she'd follow their story well. An enchanting, winged lover in disguise, found families, and a healing journey. The story had picked up its pace, a heart-pounding, incredible escape from the grasp of an old friend. But tonight, instead of picturing their incredible magic and standoff, she pictured Garrik's broken face. The betrayal wholly in his eyes.

Alora turned the page absentmindedly, out of habit. Her eyes scanned, wildly hallucinating about the tavern instead. In that page turn, her hand grazed across something coarse.

A small piece of parchment was wedged in the seam. A whorl of shadow misted away from it.

She recognized the scent right away. Metal and leather with the bite of vanilla and oak.

Was it a forgotten place holder from a time when he enjoyed reading?

The paper scratched against her fingers as she marveled at the way the penmanship gracefully flowed across the paper. Although still crafted in artistic curves, lines, and dots, it lacked the luster she'd seen on correspondences, maps, and a once goodnight wish that accompanied her burning Blazebloom.

Her thumb brushed the words, eyes scanning each spot the ink pooled heavily at, as if he'd stopped his quill, waiting to find the words to follow.

You saved my life today. Why?

Alora ran her fingers across the ink. The burned-out hovel narrowed in her vision. The way Garrik's ears had bled. The way his body burst with veins as he screamed and unleashed his power.

The way his face turned blue as she sucked the air from the room.

The question struck her like a damning blow in the arena. One she could've anticipated but was too distracted to counteract as it slammed into her chest.

"How could I not try? I couldn't lose ... the both of you." Alora closed the book with a thump and set it beside her on a pillow. Pulling her excruciatingly sore muscles, her knees bent to her chest, and she wrapped her arms around them. Tears welled in her eyes, threatening to stream down her cheeks.

At least he was speaking to her—sort of.

Another note drifted from Smokeshadows above her head. Weaving through the air like a feather falling.

You are right. You do not require my aid. I was

—the ink on the page pooled heavily again—

afraid of

—the words scribbled out—

You were breathtaking today.

She almost snorted, heart fluttering for the first time since before the wall. Alora rolled her eyes and whispered to the parchment, "Are you drunk?" Then another fell.

Not nearly enough. I unfortunately am thinking.

Thinking about what venom she spewed in the tavern? Alora lowered her head and picked at the hem of her oversized, crimson sleeping tunic.

"Did I hurt you badly?"

Her flaming fist. The burn. His heart. What part of him did she do irrevocable damage to? Which part of him had lost his trust in her and would never return? She almost couldn't stand the ache pounding in her chest and fingertips, waiting for another note.

Waiting.

And waiting.

Until she was certain another wouldn't come.

Alora brushed her hand through her hair after what seemed ages of nothing. When she set her arm back on her knees, a page crumpled underneath.

Is that why you are awake? You are worried about me?

Thunder rumbled outside, shaking the bed as if in answer to his question. The nightmare had woken her, but it was the tavern that rendered sleep impossible. Likely brought on by the events of the day, the nightmare that visited her often, always the same screaming. Always the same bloody hand reaching for her. She wanted to tell him about her nightmares. Yet the burden was too crippling to be shared.

It was a stupid nightmare. It meant nothing.

Smokeshadows nudged another note into her hand.

What is bothering you?

She could dance around it. Lie. Conjure a story that would fit better and convince him she was fine. She could ignore the question, ask him why he was awake. Even stay silent and hope that his notes would eventually change the conversation.

A Smokeshadow brushed her arm as if asking her the same question.

What's bothering me? Alora inhaled deeply through her nose and pulled her arms tighter around her knees. Everything from the tavern slammed into her at once. A load so heavy that she was thankful she was on the bed by the sudden change of pressure in her head. The room felt smaller, closing in. The air felt heavier, harder to breathe.

"I hurt you." Her voice cracked and released the dam, holding the liquid in her eyes. Alora's throat constricted as she whimpered out a cry. "I hurt you. Oh stars. *I hurt you.*"

Smokeshadows roared around her, their icy chill hugging against her skin.

"*I hurt you.*" Over and over and over, she repeated it. Thinking countless words that only her heart could say but her mouth couldn't. Heat rushed through her body, just as it had at Kaine's taunting in that tavern. Just as it did every moment he stood before her—real or not.

A note fell again. But she didn't see it. Didn't feel the next one fall, or the next.

Her eyes were lighting with enough embers to boil her tears.

Fists balling too tight, caging sparks inside that needed to burst.

Desperately holding everything in. Silently suffering for moments—for months.

The deepest scars in her mind split open. She thought of every horrible thing Kaine had ever said. Every lie and every scheme of his memory convincing her to turn on Garrik. Every stupid and evil and ruthless word he'd say before convincing her that he was the only one who could ever care for her. How his hands weren't stained with her own blood. That Garrik was her enemy, the enemy, the enemy, the—

Five more notes fell in rapid succession before she was engulfed in a white rage of flames.

The doors of her tent burst open.

Lightning crackled behind him and lit up his frame with natural brilliance before leaving him cast in the shadows of the opening. Rasping breaths drew his chest-high, and he panted alongside the raging storm.

Stepping into the glow of the tent, Garrik was soaked head to muddy boots. Still, the same dark circles laid under his eyes. If at all worse than before. His gray hair laid flat against his head, dripping water beads onto his skin. His tight soaked tunic hugged every swell and dip of hard muscle as he, with imperceivable speed, dawned to her.

And then, she heard him. Not beside her, but in her mind.

Alora, listen to my voice. You need to breathe.

White, burning flames exploded, throwing him from the bed.

She couldn't breathe. She could only see her hand burning a hole in his chest.

Garrik coughed on impact, choking on the wind that jutted from his lungs as he threw out his arms, consuming the entire tent in a storm of funneling clouds of ash and smoke and wind. *Alora! Please, listen to me! I will not hurt you. You need to breathe—*

My, how pathetic you are. Look how you fall apart so easily. You're weak!

No, I'm not, Kaine. I'm not!

Talons of vicious wicked laughs scraped every inch of her skin.

Worthless. Pathetic. Weak.

Alora felt flames roaring higher and higher and higher. Threatening to detonate and obliterate the entire camp. She had to do something, had to stop him from seeding himself and growing his wicked lies until she would hurt someone again.

Hurt *Garrik* again.

"*Get out of my head, Kaine!*" She ripped her throat to shreds, screaming, hands shaking with sunbursts and spitting stars as they fisted into her hair. "*Get out!*"

Her voice. It erupted into a blaze. Ripping through the veil of Smokeshadows until it lit the canvas beyond.

Ara! Garrik's hands commanded the shadows to the burning walls before they pulled the raging inferno—pulled her—to his chest. He heaved her from the bed before corded arms wrapped around her, embracing in a hold so tight, nothing would escape.

Alora's knees buckled.

Then she was falling—*they* were falling. Falling to the furs beside her bed when she landed in his lap. And before her body could drop to the ground, Garrik's arms laid her into the hard muscles of his heaving chest. His frantic, ringed fingers cupped her limp face when her sapphires rolled back.

Afterward, she was floating. Bursting across the night sky like a shooting star.

Her heart felt like it was cleaving in two—painfully. *Stars*, it hurt so badly. Perhaps not a shooting star, but a dying one.

Stay with me, Ara.

His voice was trailing kingdoms away.

Do not go. Hold on to me. Stay with me.

The night sky. It danced in her eyes, welcoming her home to the darkness that consumed her entirely.

CHAPTER 54

"Alora," Garrik hoarsely rasped. His entire body trembled, holding her balled up against him, rigid atop the furs on the floor. Pulsing every ounce of icy chill his body could possibly offer.

A pressure weighed heavy on her chest. His palm rested over her slowly beating heart.

Something frigid and wet dropped on her cheek.

"I ... thought I *lost* you."

The charge pulsed through her heart. It stung, but not as much as the pain before.

Alora's eyes slowly opened as another droplet tapped her cheek.

Garrik's eyes shined like smooth ice on a winter lake. Every rapid blink moved liquid over them as he took in shuddering—steadying—breaths.

Her mind was covered in clouds and heavy fog, unable to form audible noises, let alone sentences. But she looked into his eyes that had begun to glow once more while his hand held her cheek and the back of her neck. She looked into them as his thumb softly brushed the soft swell under her eyes, smearing the liquid across her skin.

Smokeshadows slowly hovered under his icy palm at her chest, lingering there as he rasped, "You are alright. F—*fuck*. Just ... breathe. Please."

His hair was still wet. Through the spinning swirl of clouds in her mind, she could determine that much. Blood moved into her arms, flowing down into limp fingers until they twitched against his leg. That was still soaked too.

How long had she been out? Alora's eyes drifted, fighting off the heaviness that still sat there and pulled them down, down, down until she forced them up again. Her vision blurred—in and out.

She could barely focus on the buttons of his tunic ... and the bubbled, oozing flesh underneath.

Garrik's eyes followed hers. "It is nothing." Brushing her cheek again. "I have had worse."

She opened her mouth to speak, but only air whooshed out.

Another soft stroke of his thumb glided against her cheek, and he bent his knees up, pulling her impossibly closer. "Do not try to speak. Close your eyes, rest. I have you."

Alora's eyes were slowly drifting back to that place. *No. Please ... I want to stay.*

There in his arms ...

With the Dragons ...

With ... her High Prince.

Please, let me stay. I want to stay.

Icy lips pressed against her sweat-ridden forehead. "I know, my darling." Garrik shuddered a breath before sleep found her again.

She told him *EVERYTHING.*

As he held her in his trembling arms, building with wrath and rage, she released every last secret. Every ounce of shame and hurt and vicious lies that held her at ransom.

When her sobs became too much, her mind opened. And once a tightly wound bud, her past and present bloomed, baring itself to him. Allowing him to weave through Kaine who had built such high walls that Garrik willed himself the strength and climbed. Higher and higher, until every piece on that surface, in that chamber of her consciousness, was ruthlessly explored. Until he knew *everything* and she was laid bare before him.

"I should have realized." He slumped his head back against her bedside table, dried gray hair scratched against the wood.

"I see him *everywhere*. With every turn, stalking me in the corner outside my vision. In your eyes. In Thalon's instruction. I thought I was strong enough when I schemed to leave him. When I did everything to escape. I thought I had let him go—I did let him go. But he won't leave me." Alora's lips quivered.

Garrik pulled away from her, his calloused hand cupped her cheek as glowing silver burned into her eyes. "Come with me."

Alora pinched her eyebrows, pressing her head deeper into his shoulder.

"I need you to trust me. Can you do that?"

"I never stopped. He"—she sobbed—"he convinced me otherwise. I didn't mean anything I said. I didn't mean any of it."

Garrik banded his arm around her back and lifted under her knees, effortlessly standing, cradling her in his arms. Her strength had returned, though she hadn't moved from the comfort of his embrace while she revealed her darkest secrets.

"Hold onto me," he whispered with a reassuring squeeze, cupping a knee.

The tent fell to creeping darkness. Engulfed in swirling tendrils of shadows and misting ash clouds, they turned into nothingness. Like floating, again, Alora raised her hand inches from her eyes and rotated her wrist. It was there—she knew it was there—but it also wasn't. Her shadow merged with the darkness, sweeping in like a calm dream. Weightless—airless—empty, yet teeming with life. Garrik's body still pressed against her. She knew he was there only by the pressure touching her skin.

Smokeshadows breezed around them until they misted away in puffs of swirling smoke. They had dawned—but where?

Alora's eyes adjusted. Her senses locked on to rhythmic drops into puddles and the heavy taste of wet iron mixed with rotting mold and something else so awful she was certain she would vomit. But just as the smell rushed her senses, it was gone, and only the dancing torch lights and stones remained.

It looked like a dungeon cell.

Horrible, rusted iron chains and clasps, terrifying torture weapons, and hundreds of torches hung from the blood-splattered walls. Far off in the corner, a long set of graystone stairs dripping with pools of crimson led up to an iron door sealed shut. Darkness danced behind it.

Alora hitched a breath and backed into a solid icy wall—into Garrik.

He was in his armor, a bloodthirsty sword sheathed in the scabbard strapped to his broad back.

"Where are we?"

Garrik's hand rested on her shoulder, calming her instantly. "I call this the Dawnspace. Where my shadows can erect any memory or simply a place to be surrounded by darkness. To simply just ... be." His footsteps echoed as he stepped from behind her and crossed puddles atop bloodstained graystones.

"You travel through here when you dawn?"

"Yes. Most of the time, it is empty. A blackened night sky. No moon, no stars. Nothingness."

But they weren't in nothingness now.

Alora looked down her body, her night clothing had been traded for battle leathers, black boots rippled a darkened puddle beneath her feet.

Garrik's eyes darkened. Swirling smoke cascaded across his pupils when he dragged a finger down the hanging iron chains fastened high up the wall beside them. "I understand why you said the things you did in the tavern, as I, too, have seen visions of those that haunt me. I will not say that it is acceptable to have said them, as I have spoken many regrettable words myself and must bear the shame of them. I made mistakes, and you will also. And we will learn from them. We can only move forward and strive to be better than who we were before."

Alora narrowed her eyes on the chain swinging from Garrik's touch. "Will you ever be able to look at me the same again?"

"If you are asking for forgiveness, *that* I will give you. Just as I plead for those I have wronged to grant me the same." His darkened eyes drifted to her, raking up her form, slowly, cautiously. His mouth tightened in a line. "But, I will not let *him* consume you any longer. That is why I brought you to this terrible place." Garrik raised his arm over his shoulder. Metal slid against leather and glistened in the dancing light of the torches. In a simple, precise movement, Garrik's sword twisted before the blade's edge was gripped tight in his hand. The muscles in his forearms shifted as he outstretched the pommel to her.

"Take my sword."

Her eyes widened as she beheld it. A sword so mighty and magnificent. Its size twice the size of the sword she had learned to wield. Alora gripped the hilt with both hands, and whereas Garrik's hand perfectly engulfed the entire leather grip, hers left plenty of space. He let the blade fall and the immense weight of it had her almost dropping its point to the stones.

Struggling, Alora lifted it. "The sword is heavy."

"As is our worst fears and battles. Given to the strongest of warriors. Those worthy to fight."

She willed herself not to swallow, stiffened her spine, and lifted her chin.

Garrik inhaled a deep breath, filling his entire body before he turned away and prowled along the blood-splattered walls. His steps were measured, careful, precise as they touched each stone like he was counting each laid in the floor. Amber light danced across his leathers, casting shadows in the swells and dips and scales cladding his body. Until he stood in the center of another open chamber. A massive circle had been carved deep into the stone and a lonely wooden chair waited.

With one lazy wave of his hand, three figures appeared in front of him.

A long red-haired older High Fae male stood. A gruesome scar went from above his eyebrow down over one whited-out eye, stopping just above his cheek. His red beard drifted straight to a point above silver armor and a purple cape.

Beside him stood a lean High Fae male with short night-dark hair and a dragon-scaled, onyx coat that fell low behind his knees. Needle-like spikes jutted from his wrists and shoulders, dripping with crimson, as searing blue flames tricked across his fingers.

And the last, a devastatingly beautiful female with long, raven-colored hair, adorned in a black gown of lace and silk that hugged every curve and swelled her breasts. Long black ombré fingernails extended up to her knuckles, accentuating fully black, serpentine eyes and onyx lips.

Alora found herself stepping forward, eyes narrowed on Garrik as she closed the distance, watching as he pivoted from one to the other.

"Kill the memory," was all he said before Smokeshadows wrapped around each of their throats. "You do what you have to do to the memory—"

The first male, in Raven's armor, gurgled as he choked. Garrik dropped his open palm to his side, curling his fingers inward until his fist shook. The tighter his fist squeezed, the more Smokeshadows constricted around the male's throat until he dropped to the stones blue-faced.

"—until they no longer grip you in fear."

When Garrik opened his palm, shadows whirled around a torch raging with flames. With one idle flick of his arm, the torch collided into the dark-haired male's black boots, consuming him entirely.

Fire viciously crawled up his form until blackened ash dusted across the bloodstained stones.

Garrik's steps shook the floor. He stopped without a single glance at the female before him. His entirely consumed silver eyes were lost to the blackened abyss when he turned back to Alora. "Until every last part of their worthless existence no longer lives in your mind and plagues you."

It was then, Alora realized. The same female standing before her was the female at the wall.

The female, with vacant eyes, extended her hand.

Alora watched as that hand dug its nails around Garrik's shoulder, and he slowly glanced down at it. Garrik spoke, but not in the common tongue. His voice was cold, uncaring, rapturous in its intent. Then, his hand wrapped around the female's throat, squeezing and squeezing and squeezing as he continued to speak that melodic language she desperately wanted to learn. With a swift recoil of his arm, his hand shoved deep into her chest before it mercilessly ripped out her heart.

The female grabbed her chest before stumbling forward.

Garrik stepped aside, allowing her to fall face down on the stones. With one last squeeze, the heart spilled its blood onto her, and he tossed it beside her body without remorse.

The male who turned around to look at her was not the face she'd arrived with.

Garrik's face had paled drastically until little color was left and blackened veins branched from his eyes, neck, and any piece of exposed skin outside his armor. His shoulders rose high when those endless orbs of night slammed shut.

Ten heart beats later, silver orbs reclaimed his eyes again.

Her High Prince stepped inches from her, blocking her view of the three dead bodies when he spoke. "From this moment on, remember that he is a memory. Nothing more."

When Garrik stepped aside ...

No.

Garrik intertwined their fingers. Anchoring her. His deep, warm voice waved over every frozen bone in her body, shaking her alive again as she stared into the face of her walking nightmares.

Into the eyes of Kaine.

"Tell him everything. Every single thing you have ever wanted to say. Twist the knife, make it hurt as he hurt you."

But Alora stiffened. Her sapphires flickered to Garrik.

"You think I will judge you?"

She squeezed her fists, fighting the trembling there. Saying nothing.

In raging Smokeshadows, beside Kaine, the female returned. Garrik stalked up to her and found his hand once again around her throat. "I have dreamed of the day that I take your chains and fasten poison-covered, sharpened hooks to them, hanging you by your skin while I cut shards of glass to every inch of your body. Your blood slowly dripping to the stones until there is no inch of your skin left split open and flayed from your body. *Just as you did to me.*"

The female's neck snapped at an odd angle before he threw her off her feet into the stone wall.

She reappeared, standing, breathing before him once more. Garrik slammed his boots one by one into her knees, bending them backward with distinctive snaps so she fell to the stones. His hands fisted into her hair, wrenching her head backward to stare up into his blackened eyes.

"I have ripped your fucking hair out section by section. Your bones bared before taking those spikes and driving them slowly into your skull. Your teeth I have shattered while still inside your gums so I can pull the bleeding shards out piece by piece. *Just as you did to me.*"

Garrik grabbed her by her teeth, pulling until her head split in two.

She reappeared.

He slammed her into the wall with a spine-splitting crack. Smokeshadows tendriled in his hands, revealing daggers. Each blade slowly tore into her abdomen with each word.

"I have sliced you open, making you feel every starsdamned cut. Every fucking touch. Killed you ten thousand times just to bring you back to life and start all over again. *Just as you did to me.*" He steadily drove a dagger into her heart. "And I have looked into your starsdamned devilish eyes—as you did every time you *fucked* me—while I drive my blade through your worthless heart. Over and over until I have shredded your body to pieces and no trace of who you once were remained."

Garrik's roar ripped through the room as his dagger shoved through her, cracking the stones of the wall behind. His body viciously trembled with a shuddering breath as he whispered, "Just as you did to me."

He didn't look at Alora when he spoke again. "Nothing you can say will be worse than what I have done and will do." He turned, meeting her watery eyes. "And if you cannot kill the memory, then you tell that fucking worthless piece of Elysian shit what you need to, and I will be your death-sword. Over and over, until you can take the blade and do it yourself." Turning to Kaine, Garrik towered over him, his voice a thing of death. "*Get on your fucking knees before your queen.*"

"I'm not—"

Garrik whipped his head to her. And by that very look, she spoke no further. Not wanting to be on the receiving end of the very wrath he was trying to contain.

Before her eyes, Kaine's body bent, slamming his knees into the bloody pools, staining his image of perfection.

In all the years she suffered, not once had he bent a knee to her, not even when he asked her to spend her life with him—and forsook lavishing her with a ring. Not once had she seen his clothing out of place or even a speck of dirt on his pants.

The poster of perfection and status now soaked in blood and stench and dirt like he forced upon her.

Garrik's veined hand fisted tight into Kaine's hair and tore his head mercilessly backward. Mahogany eyes beheld her strength and confidence.

Garrik's sword lifted in her hands. Somehow, she mustered the strength to guide it through the air and rest it at the hard lump of Kaine's throat.

Glowing specks of silver glistened in Garrik's blackened eyes, showing her that he was there—barely. He promised that he would be her executioner, if needed, but if she was entirely honest, would she be able to kill Kaine? Even if he was only a memory.

Hot tears blurred Alora's vision as she drew a ragged breath, struggling against the anguished tide rising within and threatening to rob her of her breath.

Her High Prince gave her a subtle nod, the encouragement she needed to speak.

The mighty blade reflected flames against Kaine's throat as her venom built and tingled inside her mouth.

Alora remembered every marble step her head had cracked on. Every drop of blood she slipped her hand in atop redwood floorboards. Every burn of a candle. Every night her body was a canvas and he'd painted her with his fists. Every starsdamned red rose.

The blade pressed against his skin, trickling a crimson line down to the collar of his perfect white shirt.

"I used to wonder what it would feel like to be loved and wanted by someone," she began. "For so long, I'd lie awake at night and dream of who would treat me the way I begged to be treated. I'd cower with every echoing footstep down the hall and dread the moment you'd walk through the bedroom door. When you'd take me, hard, uncaring how much I screamed and cried from the pain. How you enjoyed every moment of it to bring yourself pleasure.

"You stole pieces of me that I will never get back. And I don't want them back because I have grown stronger in their absence. I have replaced what you broke with something far greater. And though it may be a darkness surging through my heart and a fire gleaming in my soul, I do thank you for that, because without you, I wouldn't have known just how powerful I can be.

"I'm *not* your property. You do *not* own me. You never did. I just didn't know it until I was broken and brave and so much stronger than you will ever be. You wanted me quiet, but I will no longer let you steal my voice. You wanted me to submit to your every whim, but I will no longer kneel. *You kneel to me, now.* Your eyes don't deserve to look upon what I have become."

Garrik gripped Kaine's hair and ripped his head forward, slamming it into the stones. With a knee to the bloody pools, Garrik whipped his head up and gnashed his teeth. Still gripping Kaine's ebony hair in his fisted hand as he forced Kaine onto his palms.

Her High Prince remained before her, waiting.

Alora twisted the sword and rested it at the base of Kaine's neck. "My body isn't yours to own. My words aren't yours to steal. You are the worthless coward who beat the only one that loved you until that love emptied and hatred remained. I *refuse* to let you live in my mind any longer. I'm not the worthlessness you made me feel. I'm fucking fire and you're the ash beneath my feet, blowing away on a smoke-covered wind to the depths of your own miserable and pathetic life."

For so long—too damn long—Kaine kept her powers subdued by brutality and threats alone. But not today.

The iron of Garrik's sword began to ripple, cascading in a white glow until it went molten. Metal burst in beams of white, sizzling with a heat that far out-weighed a mere flame.

No. This was something out-worldly.

And she would make sure Kaine felt it. Felt what he was *so* afraid of.

As he fucking should be, Garrik's voice growled in her mind.

She pressed the burning blade's edge harder into Kaine's skin, searing it until it bubbled and blackened flesh began to steam.

"You no longer deserve a single thought. A single look. And the longer I hold my eyes to you, is one more moment you will steal from me. And I don't deserve for you to take one more starsdamned thing from my life. *Ever. Again.* If I ever see your pathetic, worthless ass in my shadow, because that's only where you'll ever be, I will unleash my fire, that you so deeply feared, upon *every single thing* you own until not even the dust remains."

Alora crouched, the worn leather of her armor creaking faintly with the motion. White flames burst down the blade until they swirled around Kaine's neck. She balanced on the balls of her feet, poised as if ready to spring forth in an instant. A restrained energy settled on her strong frame, and she held the half-crouched hover with feline grace.

"You've lost control of me. And this is me letting you fucking go."

Embered sapphire eyes met Garrik's endless abyss and his wicked, proud smile.

She nodded to her High Prince, her executioner.

Kaine's face slammed into the bloody pool before his skull caved in under Garrik's boot.

CHAPTER 55

G arrik lifted her into his arms, dawning them back the moment Alora collapsed and slammed into the stones beside Kaine's crushed skull.

Kaine wasn't truly gone. It was an illusion, but even so, it was the image of the male she once loved.

Kaine had heard it—all of it. Every single thing she had ever wanted to say.

And on that bloodstained floor, she decided that is where Kaine would remain. Forever locked inside a prison, never to return.

As the darkness swiftly carried them from that terrible place, she caught a glimpse of Garrik's eyes gleaming. Proud. Flashing in admiration and mixed with something else she couldn't discern.

They returned to her tent. The lantern being the only source of light dancing its white glow and shadows across the canvas. Outside, the thunderstorm had died, drizzling hushed taps of rain above them, offering the pleasing aroma of soaked plants, flowers, and trees.

Her eyes were shut, replaying every breath, every word, every menacing drop of Kaine's blood.

She was strong. Brave. More than he thought her to be. And this time, she left him behind wholly embracing that.

Never again would she cower at his face.

Never again would he take anything more from her.

Never again.

Alora tightened her arms around Garrik's neck, feeling the shift in her body returning from being smoke and shadow and swirling ash. And as his boots disturbed the soft furs on the wooden floor, she knew something deep inside her had been forever changed. Something mercilessly abandoned.

Not only deep inside. But as her arms clung to her High Prince, the immense weight that had dragged her deeper and deeper and deeper down inside herself. The weight that crushed her shoulders and bent her back to its breaking point. The weight that pounded her chest, unable to breathe … it was gone.

Never again. Her mind repeated, and she felt Garrik grip her tighter as if he too knew.

Never again.

"Hey, clever girl," Garrik's soothing whisper broke through her roaring silence. "We are home." A kiss so lovely and tender pressed into the top of her head. Calming. Reassuring. He was there, as he was in that dungeon. "Let's get you to bed."

But as he leaned his body over her bed, Alora pulled herself into him tighter.

Garrik's pleasing hum reverberated through her exhausted body. He turned without a word and walked across the fur rugs to the far side of her tent. As he drifted, his eyes fell on the white lion trinket sitting on a small table. With a gentle bend, he reclined on the emerald reading chair and pulled her body close.

After they left the Dawnspace, their armor was traded for what they wore before.

She didn't care to cover herself. Her legs possessed no strength to pull her knees under her crimson tunic. But Garrik's calloused hand brushed down the fabric and gripped the hem enough to pull the bunched-up layer down her thigh, covering her lacey underthings.

Alora shivered at the feather-like touch of his hand. It had her mind teeming.

Two thuds disturbed their silent breathing.

Garrik's legs spread long in front of him after he pushed his boots away from his feet. When she felt a tender brush against her cheek, her white hair tucked behind her ear, she leaned into his touch. Loving the way that gesture felt from his hand, Alora spoke in a soft return, "Thank you."

His chest vibrated in a low hum. "I thought it might bother you."

A smile crept up her face. "I don't entirely mean my hair."

Alora pivoted her head to look up at him. He was grinning, but not in that irritating smirk kind of way. It was nothing more than a smile, one she longed to see since after Alynthia's wall. One that she was certain she'd never see again.

It made her heart leap in the way that falling would.

Her fingers brushed a button on his tunic. "I don't understand how you can forgive me so easily. But I wanted you to know that I ... thank you."

Garrik's thumb lazily grazed against her thigh, cradling her across his lap. That smile slowly faded. "How could I not forgive you? It is so easy because I, too, have visions of those who haunt me. You saw"— Garrik's breath hitched—"the female at the wall. The illusion. She haunts me as Kaine haunts you. Your pain is raw. Just because you survived does not mean you stepped over a line of hurting and into being instantly healed."

"But I thought I was better. I thought I *was* healing."

"Progress is not linear, Alora. You can survive months without your pain, only to fall and shatter a moment later.

"My pain has haunted me for nearly fifty years. I have lived daily in the memories that touch my skin and keep me awake every night. I can be distracted for some time, thinking I have seen the last of them until one day, I smell something that reminds me of her, or see the sky's hue in flames, and my feet sting like they are burning. I hear a whip crack, the clamor of metal in the arena, and one of them will be standing in front of me, preventing my breaths. Demanding my attention before I am taken back to my pain."

He forced a hard swallow. "I feel the brush of fabric or wind against my skin ... am forced lay on my back even if it is bleeding because anything touching my abdomen is too much to bear." Garrik shuddered beneath her, closing his eyes to inhale a measured breath. "Healing takes time. You cannot expect yourself to be whole and mended in a day."

Alora rolled her lip between her teeth and dropped her eyes low. She was healing. And though she was marching with his Dragons, death looming over their heads with every step, she felt safe. But Kaine had haunted her for so long. Could what happened in the dungeon be enough to keep him away? How many more times would she need to return to that place until he was with her no more? After all, Garrik's visions still haunted him, and it didn't seem like what happened in the Dawnspace was anything new for him.

"How do I keep him from returning? Do ... do I have to go back there again?"

He was silent for a moment, face slightly paling before he rasped, "I wish I knew." The weight of his hand pressed harder into her thigh. "And if he does return, promise me that you will not shut me out. That you will run *to* me and pull my head out of whatever-the-fuck I am doing so I can help you."

She reluctantly nodded.

"We take it one day at a time, like all things. And if you ever desire to go back to that place, you need only ask. Until then, I think it is time you learned to protect your mind from unwanted intrusions. Even mine."

A SOLID WALL of burning hot flames stood between her and the gentle caress of shadows exploring the confounds of her mind. One crack in the flames, a shadow wedged through, escaping to wreck whatever havoc the whorl could.

"Try again," Garrik echoed somewhere in the distance, but she was focused solely on her flames. "One more time. Be an impenetrable wall. Allow nothing through."

Alora gripped his shoulders tighter, her legs straddling him in the chair as they both locked their eyes to one another, focusing on the echoing abyss over darkness and memories inside her mind. Garrik's hands firmly cradled the sides of her head as Smokeshadows bore into her mind, crashing relentlessly against a wall of flames extending high inside.

He was relentless with his advances. The tendrils viciously swirled on ruthless winds, expanding, splitting, and counteracting each of her flames' pursuit.

Behind her aching eyes, her fire fought him. Not one shadow could find a pathway through.

"Good girl, Alora." Garrik's hands cupped her temples as she blinked. "I want you to practice this every day. Until it is as simple as blinking."

She nodded, "Again."

"That is enough for tonight. You need to rest."

"I want to try again."

"You will hurt yourself. I see the pain behind your eyes. How does your head feel?"

Alora's mouth twisted. If she was entirely honest, her vision was spotting behind head-splitting pain. She inhaled, then breathed out in a frustrated sigh, crossing her arms as she leaned back. "Fine."

Garrik smirked, and his hands fell to her exposed thighs below the hem of her tunic.

She forced herself not to react. To not think about where his hands were. How they felt against her warm skin. Forced herself not to think of a darkened annulus or an old leather chair. Or how his lips felt against hers, which were now only a few inches away. And she certainly refused entirely the thought of how her thighs straddled either side of his muscular legs. How his alluring eyes pulled her in.

His thumb twitched on her thigh. It would take only one easy movement for it to slip under the hem of her shirt.

Alora *definitely* wasn't going to think about that.

Or the warm pulse that fluttered between her legs.

"Tell me what you are thinking about."

Oh stars. Could he sense her quickened heartbeat or see it in her eyes? Scarlet flushed her cheeks, and Alora quickly found anything— everything else in the tent more appealing. Anything but his eyes, the chiseled muscles of his solid chest, how his tunic draped perfectly down to his pants and ... his belt.

Garrik shifted his hips and arched a brow, waiting.

"I ... um..." *There.* The ripped fabric of his tunic, covering his death mark. The deep wound festered as it did hours before. She scrunched her eyebrows, lips taut. "You didn't put healing balm on these yet?"

He was silent.

She frowned. Turning to his other arm, Alora twisted it, exposing another deep wound on his forearm. With a bend at her side, she leaned over the armrest to the writing table where a small vial of Calla's healing balm sat after she had rubbed it on her bruise—which healed almost entirely now. She plucked it from the table and popped the lid open. Soft like velvet between her fingers, warming it with a quick rub, Alora placed a small amount across his forearm.

Silver followed each stroke like a wolf stalking its next meal.

"How did this happen?"

Garrik's face was unreadable. "I allowed it."

Alora shifted to his upper arm, separating the torn fabric and exposing his festering skin. Ever so gently, she pressed the balm deep.

Garrik's arm trembled with each stroke. Still, he watched her.

"Why?"

The hard lump on his throat bobbed. "I needed to feel something again. And I..." He shook his head, eyes rolling to the canvas above. "It does not matter."

"Don't do that. You asked me not to shut you out. Don't shut me out."

Something like panic flashed in his expression before he winced from the tunic, pulling away from the festering burn fused to the fabric. Before she could pull it completely away, Garrik's hand enveloped hers, stopping her completely.

His breathing went uneven.

The blackened abyss crawled over his eyes that had glazed over, inspecting her warm hand—her naturally colored, rounded nails—with the edge of his thumb. Tracing each one slowly in deep assessment.

But she didn't move. Didn't feel afraid. Didn't flinch away or tear from his hold.

Silver specks of glowing light dotted his eyes. The blackened abyss faded, and his body loosened. "Forgive me," he breathed, blinking out the remaining whorls in his eyes as he relaxed his hold on her hand, dropping his to the armrest. It rested there, knuckles blanching in a trembling, ruthless hold. "Please, continue."

"What is it?"

She looked into his eyes. The silver dulled as if they were screaming and felt everything of wherever they had transported him to. In the silence, Alora raised her hand.

He meticulously watched it draw near, head rolling away when the warmth of her palm slid under his tunic and met the ice of his chest.

She gently wiped the balm across the charred, peeling flesh.

Where before he hissed at the pain, Garrik's face now sat distant, in a hard line, looking back at her. His heartbeat, slow and unusual, found the quickened beat of hers as she stroked. Garrik's palm rose and scratched against the back of her hand until his fingers enveloped hers completely.

Then, she felt him. Trembling in a cascading shudder that wracked his entire body.

She felt him stiffen. Every hard and loose muscle tensed.

Still, he didn't release her.

"I can hardly stand the air that touches me," Garrik breathed. His body remained trapped in small, shuddering waves, and he squeezed her palm and pressed it harder into his chest. "But your touch—" Garrik shuddered. "Hers is ... so cold."

Like the night they'd spent in the sky, a thought rippled. But instead of her sparks, Alora willed her palm to heat without embers, pulsing soothing warmth, sinking it deep into his skin.

At last, a smile twitched on his face, only for a moment when he whispered, "You are so warm." Garrik pressed her palm harder against his skin.

He needed to feel something again.

Pain. Control. Warmth. A touch that he would allow.

Unimaginable agony overtook his. He dropped his head back to the headrest. Breathing deep. Breathing so deep and so slow and so fractured, like every memory was flooding through him and the pain of the burn on his chest somehow tethered him. Keeping him anchored there. A way back. And he was fighting behind his eyes and behind the trembling of his body to stay. Fighting against every touch and memory it brought. Fighting to replace the freezing, phantom hands on his skin with the warmth and gentle pain of hers.

Liquid lined Alora's softened eyes, looking at him in a way that resembled a broken heart. And a thought hit her with the force of a damning blow.

The dungeon. *It was a memory.* A place where she could inflict pain on who hurt her.

Somewhere, he could inflict justice on those that haunted and left him horrifically scarred.

"That place"—she struggled to pull her gaze from his chest and to his face—"the blood. It wasn't theirs pooled on the stones, was it?"

Garrik's face paled, and she knew.

The vague sentences he'd spoken. The insinuations of what horrors he had suffered. The idle stares into nowhere. Now seeing a bloody dungeon full of chains and cruel weapons. How his entire body seized up under her in Maraz and now the rigid expression on his face. How every single day she had watched as his hand would tremble and tug away the fabric at his abdomen.

Her scars were hidden deep inside, but his ...

Alora shuddered a sharp breath like broken glass.

Garrik didn't lift his head, didn't open his eyes. He only spoke in a tortured whisper. "No. Every last drop is mine."

They didn't need to exchange words—only silence. The language they both knew too well. It was in the screaming silence that their hearts always spoke the loudest. And that was enough.

Before Alora knew what she was doing, her arms weaved around his neck until his gray hair was pressed into her shoulder.

Garrik accepted her embrace without hesitation now. His corded arms encompassed her ribs, extending around her back until he pulled her in. When her legs wrapped around him, he pulled her impossibly close. Until his heartbeat slowly—unevenly—pulsed against her own.

Taut muscles spasmed on his back, and she pulsed warmth from her hands into him once more. Garrik cursed under his breath. "Please, speak to me. I need to know ... to hear it ... it is not"—Alora felt him shudder as his grip tightened—"her. Please."

"I'm here. I'm not leaving," Alora breathed, allowing the warmth of her arms to pulse across anywhere her skin touched. "I'm always here."

What else could she say? He was the one who had helped pick up so many of her shattered pieces. And now, the one who always took care of everyone else was shattering underneath her.

"You didn't ask for any of this." Alora's throat cracked. "None of this was your fault."

Her High Prince's breathing fell shallow when her fingers laced through his hair. She heard him whisper again, "You are so warm." Whispered as if it was all he could think. That line he hovered on of his past and the present. The only thing holding him there.

In gentle strokes, her fingers brushed circles within his silken hair. She never noticed how it shined against the light. At least ten hues of silver and gray streaked through it. It was enchanting. *Beautiful.* And his scent... Intoxicating. Hints of flowers and citrus, vanilla and oak on his breath. The metal and leather scent. It drew her in more times than she could admit.

Then, his voice went soft and low. In a way that longed to mask the words spoken but desperately pleaded to uncage them. "I crave death like a dying animal craves the life that is fading."

Alora jolted back at the bite of his words. She pulled his face from her shoulder. Lifeless, glassy eyes pierced through her entire inner being and collided with every shattering piece of her soul. The same dullness she'd gazed upon when he was locked in another world; those same eyes stared at her now.

Warm hands rubbed his cheeks. "Show me why."

"No. Let me enjoy this. You. If you would allow me—a fucking monster—to stay."

Darkness swirled in his eyes, and she thought she could hear thousands of pained screams echoing from them. Alora brushed his hair from his forehead. A sheen of icy sweat coated it.

"You'd have to fight me to leave out that door tonight. You're not a monster for what you're forced to do. I see it in your eyes, High Prince. *I see you.*" Garrik's eyes darkened as he meant to pull his head away when she held strong. "You hear me? *I see you.* Not whatever happened to you. Not what the stories say. Not what *she* did to you. Elysian will know who you are and what you've done for them. We will make them understand. We will."

"I am a plaything, Alora. A savage beast. I will never be anything more. Elysian deserves better. You all deserve better." The dancing glow of the lantern cast dark shadows over his cheekbones. "And I am so tired." Liquid-lined eyes drained of life as he added, "So fucking tired."

In all the words he didn't say, she knew what he meant. He fought every day for them, mostly in silence. Hidden behind an illusion of impeccable physical strength, beaming hope, and unimaginable power. A weight that, with anyone else carrying it, would've left them with a broken spine. But Garrik. He was the image of unwavering vigor. A force of shining assurance in a world that had been shrouded by evil for far too long. And he stood in the gap. He shouldered the burdens of Elysian. He faced them first, walking through doors so he could guarantee everyone behind him would make it out alive at a great cost to his own life.

Yet somehow ...

He believed *they* deserved better?

Alora's arms wrapped around his shoulders, embracing him tight. "Until that day when you see that *no one* could ever replace you ... one day at a time, High Prince. You've made it this far. One more day. And then tomorrow, tell yourself the same. We take this one more day, every day."

They were silent for ages. Holding each other, feeling each other's heartbeats. Then Garrik's shoulders fell as he whispered, "One more day."

"One more day," she repeated.

Her fingers trailed to the back of his stiffened neck. Massaging into the sore, knotted muscles. Dragging her fingers down his shoulders and upper back until she felt his body relax and head sink.

She smiled, loving that he very well, if only for this moment, found some comfort. Some tenderness. That she was able to be his solace and give back some of the safety he had offered her so many times before.

Garrik breathed a calmed moan.

Alora couldn't help but love that sound, too.

But at the same moment, her heart began to split.

Because all this time that she had been fighting ...

He was beaten and bruised and broken, too.

CHAPTER 56

D awn cast golden rays of breaking light over Garrik. He hadn't slept and was sitting in Alora's emerald reading chair. From the darkened circles under his eyes, she wondered if he'd even closed them once before daylight rose over Alynthia's peaks.

Through the night, she had looked to him from her bed when dreamless sleep would stir and shake her awake. There he stayed, reading that green book on a knee, his ankle resting across it. Two fingers pressed into his temple, holding him upright, exhausted eyes scanning the pages in the dancing lantern light.

Alora turned from him to find a few moments of further peace.

But when the sun's rays were warm and caressing her awake once more, he wasn't there. A small pearlsea flower rested beside the Blazebloom on her bedside table and a note written in his immaculate handwriting.

She brushed her fingers slowly over the coarseness, the ink as dark as Smokeshadows. No blotches, no marks of hesitation to be seen. This time, he was certain with his writing.

483

One more day.

She hummed, tracing each perfect line and swirl of the lettering.

It was a promise. *A written promise.* Not loose words that could be sung one day and fade to breaths the next.

A silver glow pulsated within her heart.

"One more day."

ALL MORNING, in scattered rainstorms, the Wingborne transferred the patrols, carrying and rotating out soldiers in their Dragon armor. No Ravens had penetrated their defenses, none were reported seen.

Jade's cutting gaze, sharp as the daggers she idly twirled between her fingers, met Alora's outside the war tent. Without hesitation, Jade pushed off the pole holding the tent erect and stalked through the mud across the short distance to her.

Guilt instantly rattled across Alora's every nerve as her stomach tightened.

"I saw Garrik leaving your tent this morning." Jade brushed her long, fiery, damp braids over her shoulder, green eyes meeting sapphires with something short of wrathful disdain clouding her features. "He was smiling. I haven't seen him smiling like that in ... a very long time." Her eyes flickered to the sky, resting there. At last, when she spoke again, it was laced with honest empathy. "Are you two on good terms?"

She wanted to tell Jade everything, to strip herself bare, loosen her tongue about Kaine. But Jade wasn't asking for an explanation. And from the way her knuckles whitened around the bone and melted coin necklace, Alora knew that Jade already understood.

Gentle raindrops pattered against her battle leathers, reminding her of the soft cadence on her tent last night. Reminding her of Garrik. His sword. The Dawnspace. His smile. "Yes."

Jade's hand fell from her necklace, wrapping around the pommel of her sword. "Then so are we." She turned without expression and disappeared inside the war tent.

Alora remained there, basking in the cool mist of the breeze.

"You caught her on a good morning."

Her heart leapt at the pleasantly thin, cheerful voice that cooed from beside her.

"It's raining."

A smile swelled her cheeks as she turned to Aiden. "Indeed," she said, chuckling at his blatancy.

Aiden tilted his head back, closing his eyes to the sky, allowing the rain to pebble on his scruffy chin. "Jade loves the rain."

And Alora wondered if that *love* went further than just the rain beholding him there. She shifted on her feet, feeling the mud squelch beneath her boots. That same guilt returned as she watched the musty breeze tickle his ebony hair. "I'm so sorry, Aiden. I didn't mean—"

"Aye, love. None of that." He held open his arms, fluttering the white tunic underneath his coat in the wind as he quickly beckoned her.

Alora instantly melted into him when her arms tightened around his neck, grateful for that half-breed heartbeat.

Aiden smiled until the skin beside his eyes wrinkled.

"How will I ever make it up to you?" Tears coated her eyes, dripping onto a brass button by his neck.

He cupped her shoulders, pulling away with a serpentine smile. "I can think of one way." Aiden winked, and Alora instantly shook her head, chuckling as if she read his mind. "I think you'd find it rather enjoyable to come in my tent."

Rolling her eyes and scoffing, she took a measured step forward, forcing their Captain back a step. With a stiff finger, she pressed it to Aiden's chest. An enticing grin dominated her features. "*I* think I'd much rather *come* in our High Prince's. His is much bigger." She winked. "Much more to enjoy." And she slapped his chest.

"Is that so?"

That enticing grin misted away.

She turned—slowly.

Garrik leaned on the tent post, arms folded and an ankle crossed over the other, towering over her with pure, primal male eyes.

And suddenly, Alora could only think about the scorching heat in her cheeks ... a different heat than that in his eyes. "How long have you been standing there?"

Garrik's answering smirk was brighter than her white flames. "Longer than you would like." Then he gestured with his head, summoning the remainder of his Shadow Order inside.

T**HE WAR TENT** was filled more often than the arena that day, as it always was the day before the army would move. The generals were quick to argue, and Garrik usually allowed them to discuss. But today, an urgency settled in her High Prince's eyes.

Once he spoke, his word was final.

She sat across from Garrik at the table, not against the canvas wall. Each time she entered, the seat had been empty, waiting for her.

His silver caught her sapphires more times than she could count. Each time, reminding her of the heaviness she'd seen the night before.

He looked tremendously exhausted.

Yet no one noticed. Or no one dared to say anything.

You should go rest. Surely these meetings can wait until tomorrow?

Garrik's eyes flickered to hers, but his voice didn't enter her mind.

Alora quickly closed her eyes and checked if her wall of flames was too high. It wasn't.

Should I start feeling myself to get your attention? she toyed, eyes narrowing on him.

Not even a twitch, accompanied by perfect silence.

Come on, play with me, say something, she thought to herself.

But he still remained silent.

Every meeting that followed, he remained the same, if not worse. And as the evening progressed, his eyes found hers fewer times. When she had the audacity, according to a thick blond bearded male six seats down, to speak out, Garrik's hand only rested on the map and tapped almost unnoticeably, as if in a daze which probably saved the generals life. His eyes burned into the table, concentrating on something until her boot *accidentally* knocked into his.

Brows pinched and lips pressed in a thin line, Alora shrugged and shook her head in silent question. Something was eating at him. Vexing him into an evasive state.

Her boot stirred him enough that he shifted his posture from lounging back in his chair to standing, towering over the room. "That is enough for today. General Realmpiercer expects you at first light," he ordered, nodding at Thalon to his direct right. "I require your full compliance to his orders in any absence of my own. Is that understood?"

The room erupted in nods and words of their fealty before Garrik dismissed them.

Alora hesitated and sat waiting for the room to clear. When the last disappeared through the canvas doors, Garrik reclined back in his chair, kingdoms away.

"Go to dinner. Rest early tonight, tomorrow will be a ... tiring day."

Tomorrow. The memory made her body viciously shudder.

"Is Nevilier—"

"No." There was a bite to the word. "Please, Alora. Go." Smokeshadows whirled in front of him and misted away atop a small pile of blank parchments. A quill and ink jar rested beside them.

Garrik didn't look up at her. He only danced the fingers of his right hand over the armrest as the quill lifted and began scratching dark lines into the first sheet with a tendril of shadows.

DINNER THAT EVENING WAS MOMENTOUS. Aiden had explored Alynthia and returned with satchels overflowing with fine meats, vegetables, breads, butter, cheeses, and the most decadent aroma of spices that they hadn't had the pleasure of enjoying in his absence.

A roasted red sauce bubbled in the iron pan while meatballs spiced with dried basil, oregano, rosemary, and thyme sizzled on a flat stone. Homemade pasta boiled in a pan while he grated a stiff cheese into a pile over a table near the fire. His bright face, cast in the fires dancing glow, had lit up when she walked into their firesite.

Everyone had been around the fire.

Everyone except Garrik.

When the pans emptied—and not one plate was set aside for him—she began to worry. The sun was falling into night, long since passing behind the last peak and welcoming in a golden moon. She waited at the firesite until all the others abandoned the warmth of the fire for their tents, and only then did she venture to her bed too.

Now, the soft sheets felt coarse against Alora's skin as she shifted atop the mattress, failing to find any position that brought relief. Although satisfied and full, thanks to Aiden, her stomach tightened with every frustrated adjustment she made to find comfort.

Her mind wandered recklessly, picturing Garrik as he was the night before. In the dungeon. Carrying her in his arms. Underneath her as they trained in her mind. In the war tent all day.

She entertained the thought as she traced her eyes over waved blackwood and the glass that sat inside. Her window danced with a single Smokeshadow tendril, carelessly beckoning to her to come and ask what she wished to see.

But the one thing she wanted to see ... she thought it inappropriate to spy and quickly turned her eyes away.

With a deep inhale, Alora pressed her head into her pillow, missing the comfort of a leather and metal scent, and closed her eyes, wishing for sleep that didn't come.

CHAPTER 57

H e was out there somewhere.

She could *feel* it. Some connection, like a tightened rope, pulled her every step.

Alora had waited, in the cover of the shadows, until he emerged from his tent. The burdens and torment of his day had been clear, and she ached to reach out and soothe it.

A sword sheathed in the scabbard on his back and one to his side, Garrik wore his battle leathers. Unusual. He never protected himself from war in his midnight trainings deep inside forests.

Something was *very* wrong.

It had been all day.

For miles, Ghost's white hair irradiated a faint prismed beacon through the mountain. Weaving slowly between towering pines, her steps were perfectly silent, as if Garrik was shielding each snap of a branch or crack of a stone.

By some mercy, Alora remained unnoticed riding Storm, who too seemed to understand the importance of their own cautious steps.

The darkness set an uneasy cover across the night. It didn't dance and didn't move as darkness usually did. Unsettled. Its pulse was heightened. Its touch was ominous. In its breath, it whispered caution.

Still, she followed him. Eyes pinned to the white beacon ahead—her guiding star.

Alora swallowed back the burning, rising bile in her throat.

Was he out there to ... die?

You promised one more day. And another after that. One more day, every day.

Is that why he had barely looked at her all day? Barely spoken a word?

No. She wouldn't think about that. Refused to entertain her reckless suspicion.

The tree branches webbed like a spider's labyrinth overhead. A thick canopy that allowed shards of the glowing, golden moon to peek through. Her eyes adjusted to each passing tree, ears meticulously listening for any sound the mountain offered.

Alora's eyes rolled to the skies after her High Prince was swallowed by a thicket of trees beyond a sleeping glen.

She sat atop the sloping hill, just inside the edge of ending pines, breathing in a cool lupine and valerian breeze dancing in from the north. The fluttering breeze disturbed her waved locks, tickling across warm skin until she tucked a strand away to bask in the magnificence. The stars glistened brighter, outshining the moon himself. Such beautiful swirls of dark royal waves in a way that resembled the deepest depths of oceans and held just as many secrets too. Dark amethyst and charcoal accompanied it, mixed and rippling around each star.

She'd never enjoyed gaping at something more than the night sky. Never felt comfortable in the scorching heart of the sun or light of day. But the night sky ... she imagined its comfort to be something like what home should feel like. Darkness had always allured her, called to her. The safest place she could drown in and lose herself entirely to. Dancing its shadows in the most exquisite perfect steps.

Such beautiful shadows.

A white speck emerged from the forest beyond the glen.

Ghost.

The saddle was empty ... no. It was entirely gone, along with every other piece of tack.

Alora straightened in her saddle, scanning the forest's edge with pinched eyebrows and sweat forming on her hairline.

Garrik hadn't emerged.

Storm loped down the hill, racing for Ghost, who in turn twisted her ears in their direction. Alora bounded off Storm in one easy fall, landing seamlessly in the grass beside Ghost.

"Where is he, girl?" *As if a horse could speak.* Alora shook her head, placing her hand between Ghost's eyes where a faint glimmer sparkled, brushing down her nose. "Where is he?"

SNAP.

A warm finger brushed across the empty gem casings on her obsidian dagger and pressed into the pommel.

Snap.

That makes ten.

Ten cracks in deep brush. Ten broken branches. Ten steps of something wandering the forest.

Sapphire eyes scanned the darkness.

Snap.

To her left. And closer than the last.

On light, calculated steps, Alora took cover behind the deadwood of a tall pine. Dagger resting at the hard spot between her breasts covered by leathered armor. Then, heavy footsteps. Careless and clumsy. Disturbing leaves and branches beneath. The steps were of no animal. Animals didn't walk like that. Whoever it was, they were on two feet.

Something deep inside her told her it wasn't Garrik.

Garrik's steps were measured. Precise. Hidden. He'd never allow himself to be exposed.

Whoever this was ... made her bones shiver.

She swallowed down another thought—he could be injured by whomever was lurking.

Her mind roared to follow as the footsteps trailed away. And as hers gracefully fell in quiet line behind the cracks of sticks and movement of leaves, Alora's heart pounded when the footsteps stopped, accompanied by the cold trickle of a mountain stream.

She narrowed her eyes on the darkness, shoving herself behind a tree, breathless. Shaken.

The blood drained from her face.

A Raven.

A glimpse, a mere glisten of something like glowing silver, was enough to determine as much. Only the High King's army wore silver.

And somehow, one of them—one with exemplary skill—found their way through the patrols.

Where is Garrik? A weight pulled at her heart and released it into a panic.

She knew what she had to do. If this Raven encountered Garrik, if they left her High Prince horribly injured somewhere, she had to know. Had to find him. And letting the Raven wander to Alynthia could be catastrophic.

A faint hook tugged at her spine. No longer a speck of dirt in a sea of Dragons. She was the claws. Sharp and ruthless and fearless. And though her mind fought against an incoming wave of Kaine's relentless taunting, she knew that everything laid in the balance of her dagger and her power.

Kaine wouldn't stop her today. *Not ever again.*

Alora only saw red as her feet glided across the forest floor.

Obsidian dagger drawn, its woven leather handle felt cold in her hand as she swiped it out to her side. Ready to strike. She stalked behind the crouching body at the stream. Her breath, slow. Embers, burning. Every muscle settled in perfect position; she was trained for this advance.

With a swift slice through the shadows, Alora's hand fisted into the Raven's thick hair, wrenching his head back to face the night sky as her dagger pressed cold to his throat.

The metallic smell of his blood teased her senses. She had sunk the blade a little too far.

Not far enough, though. She growled to herself.

Shadows shrouded his face, but in his darkened eyes, she could see the glowing reflection of the stars.

"Show me your hands or this dagger will gut you entirely."

The Raven didn't move.

"Hands. *Now.* Before I cut your starsdamned head off." She pressed on the dagger. The blade sunk deeper into his skin. A pleasing amount of blood followed.

And *now*, she'd bleed him dry to find Garrik, to save those she had spent months training to protect.

The Raven's hands still didn't move. But in the golden moonlight, she saw a twisted smile.

His cold, deep voice wickedly snickered. "*I dare you* ... clever girl."

CHAPTER 58

I ce enclosed her trembling palm, still woven through his hair. That all-familiar chill like death touched her hand, pulling the blade back slowly—carefully—until cold crimson dripped down the lump on *Garrik's* throat.

His hooded features were no longer obscured within the inky darkness, and familiar silvers glared back at her.

"Alora. Unless you wish to turn this into something more, I suggest you let me go." Garrik wolfishly grinned.

But her handhold pulled his gray hues tighter, hovering the blade there, and she realized that the silver she'd seen, that small gleam, must've been an illusion of his power.

He hissed and gritted his teeth, yet remained docile beneath her.

"I thought you were a Raven! I thought you were injured! *I could've killed you!*"

Garrik's grin widened, baring his gritted teeth under the pain of his taut hair. "Do not insult me. I am far better looking than any of those ilk."

Seething, Alora growled, "What in Firekeeper-filled-hell are you doing out here lurking in the darkness?"

"I should ask you the same. Did you not think I knew you were following me? You should know by now that you cannot hide from me. And as much as I am enjoying being on my knees before you, I do not have much time to make this pleasurable for you so—"

Garrik winced a jarring laugh as Alora wrenched his head back further. The skin of his neck stretched to its splitting point, yet his smirk grew wider.

"This little game you are playing will have to resume another time. There is not much time left. Let me loose, or will you need persuading?"

Alora's eyes flickered to her blade, where Smokeshadows whorled. Slowly, tauntingly, they swirled. Climbing across the jagged edge, daring her to stop them when white flames pricked from her skin and ignited across the embellishments, licking the shadows. The two powers intertwined, her fire dancing. His shadows whirling.

On close inspection, the sparkling embers in the flames flickered like stars inside his night-like darkness.

A wicked grin later, Alora's sapphires shot to him. "Careful, mighty prince. Don't you know it's dangerous to play with fire?"

Garrik's growl reverberated through his body and vibrated across her palm to her racing chest. "I am not afraid to get burned." He paused and smiled. "And I take considerable pleasure in fanning flames."

She leaned close enough to share breath. "You take pleasure in toying with me."

His eyes cut to her mouth before following their gaze back to hers. "I take great pleasure in anything that involves you." The tendril of shadow receded, misting away into his skin as his body relaxed below her.

That look in his darkened eyes ...

It sent molten sparks inside her veins.

Garrik, the ruthless, savage High Prince of Elysian, Lord of Darkness and commander of endless shadows, subdued by *her* hold. She wasn't naïve in thinking she held any power greater than those of his own. But their position burned something fierce inside her, as it did when she stood before her illusion of Kaine. And even if he was restraining himself, even if he could simply dawn or pull his head from her grasp, she knew that whatever shattered and repaired itself in her last night was fueling a new inferno within.

This was exhilarating. Power. Control. Fearlessness. A desire to be something more.

Something much more.

Could he see it in her eyes, too? A shift. Is that why, as he only pressed against her hand, he didn't overpower her and push her away? Those new embers in her eyes. The ones glimmering and teeming with newfound strength, where she would no longer picture herself as small—a particle of dust in the storm of her High Prince's Dragons.

And standing there, like that, she knew how high her head held and unmistakably noticed how her dagger didn't tremble in her grasp.

Alora loosened her grip on his silken hair. But Garrik subtly groaned in disappointment. "Pity, I hoped you wanted me to persuade you otherwise."

With a wry grin, her hand tightened once more, and he hissed with a pleased smile. This time, yanking him backward onto his back with a burst of air from his lungs.

He actually looked *surprised*.

In a swift motion, Alora twisted, threw her armored leg over his torso, and jammed a knee to his chest. Her obsidian dagger's edge rested on the shining black dragon carved into his armor, his roaring fiery insignia over every Dragon's heart.

Glowing with white embers, Alora's palm pressed into Garrik's shoulder. The armor lit up in her controlled burn.

A curse escaped his lips. "*Careful*, darling." A sharp warning. He wasn't playing anymore.

But she was. "It's you who should be careful. You may have devised this scheme and led me out here, but it's I who will end it. Afraid I'll overcome you?" The dagger pressed an indent in his armor. "The mighty High Prince, championed by one so ... *foolishly unprepared*."

Maybe it was adrenaline from the hunt or her nerves on edge because of Garrik's unknown condition. But stars, she felt like a ... *lioness*. Her roar had been silenced for far too long. Words ruthlessly shoved so deep inside and caged until hardly a breath could escape. Her claws ripped out and teeth dulled by years of hands that no longer controlled her.

Not anymore.

Never again.

Alora wanted him to push back. Wanted to feel herself release that tether she kept hold of for too long. Wanted to take on the wolf that prowled by her feet and guarded her nights.

But cold palms cautiously wrapped around both her wrists, and he pressed his body deeper into the dirt as if to restrain himself.

Garrik released a cautionary growl, "*Alora*. This is done."

"No." Her eyes glistened.

"I could hurt you." He growled again and moved to rise, but her knee pressed harder. "*Alora*."

495

In the glow of her embers, her eyes shifted to his.

Her High Prince tilted his gaze upward to pin her with his silver, starlight glimmered brighter in their shadows. She couldn't tell if they reflected her burning embers or the night sky. But the pale celestial flecks kindled strange fires that danced across his obsidian irises, as though the night sky itself wasn't only mirrored but contained in twinkling miniature behind that dark gaze.

"You can move when I say." Her eyes were fixed so sharply they could slice diamonds as she threw authority into her breathless voice.

Garrik's hair fanned around him against the dirt, pressing back with a tortured sigh. "What do you want, Alora? What is this?"

"Why are you out here?"

His eyes evaded hers, pivoting his head, looking into the distance.

The cold blade of her dagger brushed his cheek, the matte smoke embellishments touching his skin as she forced his head back to look at her. "One more day. You *promised*."

Garrik's tense face relaxed.

Something blazing and wet scorched down her cheek. Tears of anger as she shook out in a breath. "You. Promised."

"I know." His hand cradled her knee, thumb brushing above it. "And I meant it. I am not going anywhere. At least not until Magnelis is dead. Then, Destiny can decide." Alora's lip quivered, and she moved to speak, but Garrik's other hand brushed up her thigh and squeezed. "You will not be rid of me that quickly. I have to get you to Dellisaerin first." Another promise.

Alora frowned and bit back the countless words racing through her mind. "Then what are you doing out here, alone. And you sent Ghost away?"

Garrik swallowed. "I have a debt to settle."

"I could burn it closed." Alora nibbled on her cheek, watching him.

The scratch of his torn tunic held firm against his neck. The gash hadn't stopped bleeding since she punctured his skin nearly an hour before.

Garrik knelt by the calm, fresh stream, its water trickling slowly around smooth pebbles and forming gentle rapids. With a twist, the fabric released pink water and washed down the stream before he pressed it to his neck once more.

"Strange," was all he said. Eyes pinched and focused on thick dark lines of crimson across his empty hand. Mouth in a thin line, drawing his fingers together, the blood swirled and spread as he examined them.

"What's strange?"

"This bleeds like a mortal wound. One this shallow should not bleed so much." Garrik stretched his neck, allowing the fabric to press firm.

Alora crouched, running another ripped shard of fabric through the stream before stretching out her arm, offering it to him.

They made a fire next. A glowing orb of white flames and glistening sparks hovered through the air and fell into a stacked pile of branches that Garrik had collected. The glow illuminated both of them, casting dancing light across their skin. And in that dancing light, Alora's eyes nervously roamed from the wound to a long, raised ridge nestled on the side of his neck.

"Did that one bleed the same?"

Garrik's eyes flicked down as if he could see the old scar himself. "That one killed me."

She crossed her arms. "Yes, because you look entirely like a walking corpse."

"Why do you suppose I can transform into shadow? I am an entity, clever girl. I am not real."

"Funny," she mocked, and he smirked. But his eyes revealed something different. Garrik appeared nervous, scanning the fire, the stream, and trees around them. "Are you worried?"

"Of course not." His grin turned wolfish as the fabric released another long stream of crimson down the lump of this throat. But she could see that sudden flash in his eyes when it reached inside his leathers.

Garrik's head pivoted over his shoulder, gazing to Alynthia's dim light cast in the sky and cold peaks of the mountain. When his eyes met hers again, urgency rushed over his features. "We should move. There is not much time left."

Again, he said it. *'Not much time left.'*

But time for what?

"You're still wounded. We shouldn't be going anywhere."

"I have fought countless days while clinging to death's door. A stroll in the dark will not kill me. Come." Garrik rose to his feet before she could protest.

Her eyes widened in horror as he pulled a charred stick from the fire, its ends smoldering with glowing embers, trailing smoke in the movement to his neck. His bleeding wound sizzled against the blazing wood, and he held it there with eyes sealed shut before a pained hiss

497

matched the searing noise. From a small saddle bag, Garrik wrapped a long cloth several times around his neck before they began moving.

Every step. Every tree they passed. His eyes focused forward in silence as if he was tethered to something far ahead.

"Where are we going?" Alora shuffled around a tree branch that Garrik held aside for her.

"Just ahead, through those trees." The branch snapped back, and he found himself beside her.

The edge of the forest was mere steps ahead.

Blackened silhouettes of jagged pines were stark against a crystalline glow. Shards of prisms and light glares cast rays through the trees like the dancing auroras from what she imagined Evanoran—Kingdom of Crystal and Glow—would look like. As Garrik's rippling figure, monstrous in Dragon's armor, emerged from the trees in front of her, the light seemed to brighten, then swallowed him whole in a way a dying star faded.

She knew her eyes were reflecting every burst of light and unbelievable spectrum of color when she, too, emerged from the darkened forest. A sharp sting crossed behind her eyes from the sheer beauty of the glorious shine. Before her, a meadow pulsated with the magnificence of diamonds and crystals and gemstones.

Only, they weren't stones.

Flowers.

Millions of them. Radiating unimaginable light into the night sky. The aurora she'd seen within the darkened pines spurted and waved up to the stars in clouds of unspeakable colors—some she couldn't recollect even once experiencing.

And the *smell.* Sweet aromas mixed with citrus and berries, warm spices, and delicious wine. Hints of summer and spring, a fresh mountain brook, and the most tranquil scent of dirt after rain.

Tears welled in her eyes. Some from the pain of the luminance, but mostly by the perfection of beauty that rested before her.

Her world had been unimaginably cruel. Since she was an orphaned faeling, the drab colors of Telldaira, the dust and mud, even the faeries' cold and hard faces, Kaine's ruthless hands, earthen colors of sand and muddy-gray stone buildings surrounded her every day.

But *this.*

Ever since she was rescued from Telldaira, her world had been brightened, full of color, full of majesty and hope and light.

"I've never..." Alora's sapphire's glistened, holding back tears. "This is..." She gasped in a breath, unable to speak.

"Beautiful." Garrik stared into her eyes, feet from her, the luster of the flowers cast iridescent flares across his even-more-so enchanting face. "So beautiful."

"Yes." Eyes so wide the whites glowed, staring at him, too. She felt a soft brush against her forearm and squinted down.

Garrik's hand had lightly brushed her from where he stood, shoulder to shoulder.

Alora wondered if he knew of his touch. His willing and casual touch. But doubted it by the way his eyes were captivated.

"My mother treasured gardens equal to these. They were one of her greatest joys at the castle. She would devote most her days tending to flowers. Pearlseas were her favorite. They all died when she did. Magnelis never allowed them to be tended again."

A slender tendril of Smokeshadows stirred in his twisting palm. A sheen of pearl across layers of wave-like petals appeared. Garrik twisted the stem in his fingers with mesmerized eyes. Each tip of the petals was born in the foam of the sea and swirled like the swells within it.

Alora's throat constricted. Garrik's eyes were enchanted by the flower, but his face held a pain that she was all-familiar with.

Zyllyryon's Queen of Mist and Sea—High Queen of Elysian— Garrik's mother, died nearly sixty years passed.

Though Alora knew that not all rumors held any ground, it was said that she was overcome by a dying spirit. In her last days, she was merely a shell of the exceptionally breathtaking female she once was. Their revered queen, most kind-hearted and with a love for her kingdom unlike any other monarch in the histories, found herself with nothing else to give. Airathel had thrown herself from the tallest castle wall, leaving only her memory behind.

In the days following, Alora had worked in the tavern—many years before she met Kaine. The mourning was unbearable, even in her city. Heartache surged through the entire kingdom and had a choke-hold on her people. She could still picture the pearlseas flooding the streets, in every windowsill, on every table of the tavern in honor and remembrance of their High Queen.

Pyres were lit every night for a week, lifting their heartache and wishes to Maker of the Skies for her. And in the following days, High King Magnelis never once publicly mourned her death. She imagined the sea-blue smoke as if it were drifting to the sky in that meadow.

Garrik was still looking at the flower, its petals glistening in a twirling spin. "I miss her," he breathed low enough the breeze could carry it unnoticeably away.

Alora laid her palm on his smooth wrist, admiring the way the tendons felt as they moved.

"My mother did not seek a coward's exit. Her memory is stained by a false narration spun by Magnelis for his gain. I watched." Garrik forced a hard swallow. "My magic subdued, wrists bound behind my back, on my knees from the citadel as my mother was thrown from the castle walls by the High King's hands."

Alora's veins burst with spikes of grief.

"Magnelis gave the order to release me, and Thalon was commanded to cut loose my bonds. By the time I arrived in her gardens behind the wall, her body had been removed. Her flowers speckled with blood and pools of it remained. Magnelis forbade her name from that moment on. Never to be spoken again. All pieces of her were viciously obliterated from the castle, save for her wing. I secured that in an unbreakable, permanent shield. I would not allow her memory to be destroyed.

"She deserved much more. She endured Magnelis's treatment for far too long and protected me while she could. I watched her fight every-fucking-day to find a way to overcome him.

"But he had become High King overnight. Mother told me that armies rose around Elysian as if they had been resurrected from the dirt and stole her rightful reign. Her own armies fell before him without a glance of reverence to her authority. They marched, kingdom by kingdom, and seized great powers for him until not one remaining king or queen spoke against him. Those that had were replaced by someone who would bow to his claim of High King.

"My treatment was physically barbarous, but my mother endured a great deal more-so. The first time he laid his fucking hands on her in my presence, I released a shield so devastating the dining room crumbled and trapped Magnelis under the rubble. I shielded myself and my mother, but Magnelis was too powerful."

The flower twirled once more before disintegrating in a puff of smoke.

Garrik continued, "He had always been cruel, but my punishment for defending my mother was far more severe. I woke five weeks later, unable to move most of the shattered bones in my body, locked in a darkened cell in the depths of the castle. My guards were ordered to administer a drug to counteract my blood and break my body while unconscious, so when I woke, I would be powerless in my suffering. When he freed me, my mother's presence was forbidden. Locked away in her wing."

His face shifted from rippling anger to a softness in his eyes. He began to walk into the meadow, the glistening light beams of the flowers flashed across his scaled armor.

Alora followed, hands lightly grazing soft petals, watching him saunter slowly feet ahead.

He stopped, nearly crouching fully to the ground feet later. Observing a pearl petaled flower much like the one he'd been twirling. Grasping its stem, Garrik plucked it from the tuft of greenery it grew in and turned to her, outstretching his hand, beckoning her to take it.

She accepted it with a faint smile.

"I miss walks with her. From a faeling until the morning she died, I never tired of them. My mother was at such peace when her fingers brushed the petals and, *stars*, how her eyes ignited when I would pick one and offer it to her. Swirling teal and turquoise so bright in her eyes that outshined a glistening sea. My flowers, she said, were her truest treasures. Though her hands tended them, it was mine that considered which would be the honored chosen one. I would find perfection in the petals, one that reminded me of her vibrant and loving and kind spirit.

"What she did not know was that the flowers were where I felt at peace, too. Where I only found peace—with her. With something as simple as a flower. And she kept every one of them. Her rooms are overflowing. Each preserved like the day they were plucked. Vases overwhelm any surface they can rest on. When I am summoned to Galdheir, it is her wing where I find rest because mine holds too many painful memories. I feel her presence like she never was stolen from me. There, she still lives."

Alora deepened a breath. The sweet and tranquil aroma of the meadow pleasing to her senses. They walked, stopping a few times when her High Prince would survey a flower and leave it attached to its stem. She followed him in silence, surely teeming with the memories of his mother as he strolled.

But when the edge of the meadow released its last glistening rows, he leaned against a darkened tree, arms crossed and face taut once more.

"I need you to stay here."

"That's funny. I thought I heard you say that I need to stay here." Alora smirked and moved toward a clearing in the trees, ignoring him. Before she could pass through, Garrik's arm stretched across, gripping his broad hand into the bark, stopping her path.

From his stern expression, she stepped back.

"Not this time, Alora. The thing in these woods ... I cannot risk you falling to its schemes."

"And you can?"

A smile twisted across his face. "Are you worried about me, clever girl?"

"In your dreams."

Garrik breathed a laugh, crossing his arms before his head dropped low. "How could I expect anything else?" His smile pleasingly grew.

"Oh, I don't know, maybe from all that blood loss. You're going mad. I can't trust any of your decisions. Delirium and all." She smiled and fell back against the tree, facing him.

But Garrik's smile faded. That same muddy, dull look surfaced when his eyes roamed into the darkness beside them. Few heartbeats later, he stiffened, and his face transformed into one she'd seen many times. His High Prince face. The one that commanded armies. The one that gave orders and sat across a table from her making battle plans.

His voice was low. Severe. It carried authority and warning all the same. "There is one more story I must tell you," he cautioned and shifted against the tree.

"Kerimkhar once lived as a being who offered great gifts of mercy to the weak and powerless. Alongside his twin brother, suffering Elysian souls were presented a new life with little price simply because he thought they were deserving. His gift came with a knowledge of the past. While his brother, Allseeah, possessed a knowledge of the future.

"Those who long-suffered illnesses but still exuded kindness would die with grace. Others wronged and maliciously left for dead, clinging to the hope that they would be spared. And they might have been, too. It was Kerimkhar's greatest joy, his acts of mercy, his treasured gift for as long as Elysian has lived." Garrik's eyes drifted to the sky, the silver glistening in a far-off world.

"Allseeah dealt in destinies because he *is* Destiny. But he was far more knowing than Kerimkhar. His gift protected the balance of the future. Kerimkhar's mercies altered that.

"Five hundred years ago, Allseeah was approached by a young king by marriage alone. Not by noble blood. And he deemed the king's request unworthy.

"Kings hundreds of years prior were merely seen as someone who could seed a bloodline for a beloved princess. To offer an heir to her father's throne. This young guardsman was groomed his entire life for a duty such as this. Only a pawn in a game. The young princess fell in love with the male, convinced her father that royalty is not by blood alone but by heart.

"They married, and not long after, the king died, and the princess ascended her throne. But the young king felt weak, powerless. No one would bow to his empty blood—not a drop of true royalty within him. So the young king sought out Kerimkhar.

"Kerimkhar saw his past, saw the cruelty, and extended a generous gift of mercy. A wish he would regret. One wish that left him turned into a creature against his kind nature, imprisoned to this mountain for eternity by his brother for upsetting the balance."

Garrik speared her with a critical gaze.

"I do not want you following me, Alora. Kerimkhar demands cruelty as payment for his deals. Where once he flattered painless death, now he holds your soul for eternity. Your past will haunt you until he deems enough suffering as payment. Forever alone and locked inside this mountain. Faces are stolen and eyes are controlled to see what he cannot see. His trickery will find you wanting, digging his claws deep into your desires until you have offered him everything, even your own life."

Alora inhaled deep, extending her lungs to the pain point.

"I go alone." Garrik's hand fell to his sword. "I made a promise that I must keep."

"I can help—"

"You will be a distraction."

Alora frowned and Garrik dropped his expression in apologetic grief.

"My mind is sound and guarded, but if you are there with me, I will be swayed to keep you safe more than dealing with Kerimkhar's trickery. Please, do not make me ask twice. I need you to stay."

He was right—she hated to admit it. She only nodded, eyes drawn in nervous disappointment. "What if you need me?"

Garrik's eyes softened for a moment, then narrowed as he spoke. "No matter what you hear, do not come for me. Do not cross into the forest."

"I hate you for asking me this."

"I know ... I will return. I promise."

She stiffened. "Don't make promises you can't keep."

Garrik's eyes took her in. A look so long that quiet, unspoken words could translate into a chilling connection. His eyes. They seemed as if he thought this was the last time he'd ever see her again. Alora felt tempted to give into her every prickling nerve and tell him that she wouldn't stay. That she wouldn't allow him to do yet another thing alone.

But that look in his eyes.

It froze her solidly to the tree.

Her mouth opened to speak, but she didn't have enough time.

Garrik, without a word, pushed from the bark and grasped her cheek, thumb tracing a lazy circle. The calluses of his hand scratching against her porcelain skin as he leaned forward. Those icy lips brushed against her forehead as she closed her eyes, taking in the incredible feeling of him, of his power rippling underneath.

His lips hovered there, much longer than she expected, before he pulled away. But she didn't let him go far before her hand gripped his, stopping him.

"Alora." His voice was low yet unsurprised. "I need to go. There is not—"

"Much time. I know." She swallowed at the feeling of his lips beginning to fade away. "Why do I feel like I won't see you again?"

Garrik's sigh was devastating. "I have told you before. Wherever there are shadows, I will always be." Softly, Garrik's arms wrapped around her, folding her against him while she basked in his uneven heartbeat.

"Don't do anything stupid, mighty prince. We need you."

Icy fingertips gripped her chin, lifting her gaze to meet his. Garrik pressed another kiss to her cheek. But she couldn't fight off the sudden flutter in her heart or whatever pulled at her own lips.

Alora turned her head, brushing her own lips against his.

This time ... something was different. This kiss was ... different.

Felt different ... like the way she imagined a first kiss would feel like.

Garrik closed his eyes too. Unhurriedly—carefully—moving his against hers as his other hand cupped the small of her back. His lips moved as if he wanted to memorize every bit of her against him. Not lust, but something ... so much more radiated from his lips. It mystified her. Made her think that perhaps her flames were strong enough to ward off the cold and his shadows all-consuming enough to smother the heat in equal measure.

Until he slowly—painfully—pulled away.

Until her hand gripped his chest, silently begging. *Don't go. Please, don't go.*

"Wait for me," he breathed with a smile so unlike him.

Panic surged through her body as she held him there against her. Something critical flashed in her eyes, and she was frantic enough to say it. "Don't go." Tears lined her lashes. *"Please."* Desperation flooded the word as much as her heart.

Garrik's fingers laced through her hair and thumbs rested on her cheeks. That grin widened into the most beautiful smile she had ever seen, and she scorched it into her mind, never wanting to forget it. "Make no mistake, my darling, there is no reality in which I would not return to you." Garrik's thumb traced her lips. "The thought of never seeing you again ... feels like dying."

Before she could say a word, his lips pressed into hers.

Smokeshadows curled slowly around his body. She felt him slipping from her palms, no matter how hard she closed her fists on his leathers as he misted away. No matter how hard her lips clung to his.

He disappeared on a smoke-covered wind into the darkened forest—
the only way she couldn't follow him.

Something tickled her palm.

Alora mindlessly traced her fingers across her lips where his had just
been as she glanced down. Within her tightly closed fist, a pearl-petal
flower rested. She let her arms hang by her side, feeling all the blood
draining from her limbs, and held onto that flower as if it were a long-
lost, treasured, precious lion trinket.

She should have gone with him.

Why didn't she go with him?

CHAPTER 59

Rotting, cracked wooden boards twisted in a jagged path across the putrid swamp. Garrik was deep within the dark forest. And because of the ancient magic surrounding this swamp, he was only able to dawn to the edge of its waters.

He would have to cross by foot.

Overlooking the mist and fog that rose as far as his eye could see. Every few feet, torches were aflame, and the only movement was their reflection in the lifeless waters. Not even a breeze shuffled its stinking liquids. Decomposing carcasses and deadwood floated but never so much as twitched. It smelled like death. Worse than death. No corpses he ever had the displeasure of smelling had a stench quite like this.

And if the rumors were to be believed, this swamp was not only filled with decay.

But souls too.

Who knew the decay of stolen souls stunk so terribly?

Garrik fought back a wave of nausea while his boot took the first step on the creaking board. It instantly crumbled beneath his weight and caused him to stumble back. The water rippled where the wood fell, and underneath, something moved beneath the grime.

He twisted his mouth. Navigating this treacherous path was fools play. One slip, one ill-placed step, or rotten piece of wood, could be his doom.

The legends foretold that no living creature made the putrid waters its home. No. As lifeless and unmoving as the swamp was, so were the souls that remained trapped there. One brush of their essence and he would become one of them. Trapped for eternity and ruled by the immortal beyond its shores.

Seeking out Kerimkhar somewhere in this wasteland would not be easy, he knew as such, but did the pathway have to be so decrepit that he could not cross?

With no choice but to move forward by foot, Garrik took another wide step. This time, the wooden board groaned but held.

From the corner of his eye, he could have sworn he saw a shadow move. Only it was not a shadow. He controlled the shadows. Whatever this was scuttled away and remained cloaked within them.

It moved high above the trees. When he pivoted his gaze, it had gone still. Whatever it was. It was watching. Waiting.

The wooden boards made one last jarring turn around a half-sunken tree, rotting with algae growing up its trunk. At the pathway's edge, slick and sludge-covered stones were etched into twenty rounded and wide steps.

Two colossal stone pillars flanked the entrance parallel to the doors of a mausoleum. Hewn walls of unforgiving stone enclosed the top of the staircase. The crypt's double-doors shone pale alabaster, engraved with a visage of otherworldly, chilling beauty. A cruel smile curled upon male, carved lips, as though delighting in a sinister joke—forever captured as a herald of startling beauty and malevolence. It marked a boundary Garrik had no choice in crossing.

He stepped onto the stones and began his ascent. Beside the steps, ivory sand settled and disappeared far behind into the forest. But when his silver focused, the ivory was not dust at all. He had split open flesh, cut through limbs, and shattered bodies with airwaves enough times to recognize these ivory shards and dust fragments.

Bone.

The shore was swallowed in it.

Something like a deathly chill climbed up the back of his neck. Like an entity brushed his skin, or a presence was standing directly behind him. Garrik gripped his sword and slowly turned back to the water, his boots resting on two separate steps.

His breath went shallow.

The calm water that he slowly crossed, empty, without a trace of life. Now waited in the eerie, iridescent green glow of thousands of floating, staring, life-hungry bodies.

Souls ... they hovered, shoulder to shoulder. Waiting for him to return.

Not a chance in Firekeeper-filled-hell.

He would take his chances with Kerimkhar.

Garrik stood outside two doors made of dripping, gray *bones*, half-opened as if he was expected to walk inside. Self-preservation shot through his body, pleading with him not to take the steps inside and down the long dark staircase to where the myth of trickery awaited. But he had no choice.

A deal is a deal. And as he pressed his hands into the doors, a smile crept up his face when a Smokeshadow danced across his palm. Only the swamp full of souls had been guarded by magic. *Good.* He would need every ounce of his power to deal with the monster inside.

The door opened to a tunnel, and beyond that a staircase lined with

...

Garrik stiffened as he scanned.

Cleanly cut, severed heads lay within the stones. As if they were stones themselves, each face remained wide-eyed, fully whitened orbs, all with the same expression that tracked him as he walked. The faces. Each a payment for a deal in this very crypt.

Would his be laden in the stone too? Or would his soul be promised to serve after death?

At the end of the tunnel, a staircase descended into a crypt as long as Aiden's ship. The floor was broken in random pathways across shale-colored stones that were decrepit and broken. Between the vast spans of missing stones, glowing green water waited. Its depths flowed so deep, he could see the shattered stones of an underworld of decay. Bones of faeries and creatures so vile, flesh decaying from the bones, screaming faces of agony, and swimming creatures filled the pools.

Jagged stone columns and pillars jutted from the darkness down deep as if they were holding up the crypt, preventing it from falling and succumbing to the waters. Only when his eyes focused on the pillars did he realize it was not entirely stone he was looking upon.

More faces.

Preserved like they were still living. Still breathing.

And the eyes ...

Each one were turned up to the surface. To where he stood. And each one glowed red.

Garrik tore his eyes away from them. The longer he stared, the more it felt they were reading deep into his soul.

Above, those same faces lined the walls of the crypt. Barely a stone held them hostage as they, too, looked directly at him. Hanging from the crypt's ceiling, death and decay were all the same. Torn and molding tapestries fell.

But they were not the only objects swinging from the dripping ceiling. Bodies hung by rusted and dripping chains, their faces plastered with the same agonized screams as those underneath. Except their eyes. Each one of them glowed something fierce. There was not one ounce of light, save for the glowing pools and glimmering red eyes.

The room danced with rays of light as if the entire room was underwater. And those waters refracted sunlight in waves around him. Yet ... he breathed air.

Garrik sucked in a breath to be sure, before pushing the mind games aside.

At the far end, straight ahead and across the broken floor and pools of glowing green water, a figure stood on a crumbling dais. Robed in deteriorating charcoal rags, its darkened cloak sat over its head as prism-filled eyes speared his glowing silvers.

Kerimkhar.

He lifted his head and smiled with black rotting teeth and peeling gray skin. An unappealing sight to how the legends once described him and his brother. Two of the most handsome beings to ever walk Elysian. Now his greed and cruelty stained his true physical form just as horrendously as his heart.

Garrik's Smokeshadows cascaded from his shoulders and covered him in a cape of swirling smoke as he shoved power and defiance into his spine and stepped off the staircase.

Ten thousand voices echoed from around the hall as every mouth—above water and below—opened within the crypt. Garrik's senses blasted from every direction.

Then, Kerimkhar and his faces spoke, "Savage Prince. Heir of Darkness, Beast Made for Magnelis." The voices hissed at the High King's name. Young and old, ill and whole, male and female, spoke at once, "We've been waiting a long time for you."

ACKNOWLEDGMENTS

Can I thank potatoes for inspiring literally every firesite meal in the book? Where on earth would we be without potatoes? Or Damon Salvatore for inspiring Garrik's morally gray side and his drink of choice? Or Henry Cavil's voice for helping me write literally every piece of dialogue Garrik says (yes, I write with his voice; there's just no other way).

In all seriousness, there are so many people who, without you, this book would have never happened. I know it takes a village to accomplish certain things, but I never would have imagined that it'd take a realm. And, thank you, God, for the people who fell into my path because I would be nowhere without them all.

Before we go on, my crippling anxiety and people-pleasing is SCREAMING at me to let you all know that the following "list" by no means reflects your status of importance.

To the broken-hearted and those in abusive situations: You are strong. You are worth the air you breathe. You are important. You are worth it. Tell yourself "one more day." Your shattered pieces are what will help you fight. Remember what Garrik said? Flowers still grow after forest fires. Your story is not over. It's not! Please, I'm crying and begging. Hear me. You are loved, and this is not the end. Here is a sneak peek from book two because I love you that much... Place your hand over your heart and imagine these words speaking to you. "You feel that? It's still beating. And as long as it's still beating, you're still fighting. I know it hurts. I know you're tired of fighting. But you've made it through your darkest days—nothing has killed you. You will make it through this day." And if you are going through domestic violence or plans of suicide, please don't hesitate to reach out to me or our Nicolle May's Broken Hearts Facebook group. We will find you support and resources to get you out! You're never alone. NEVER. US Domestic Abuse Hotline: 1-800-799-SAFE(7233) Suicide Crisis Helpline (Text or call): 9-8-8 (For all other countries, don't hesitate to reach out and we will find the number for you.)

To Anny: (Que the tears... Yep, there they are.) How on God's beautiful Earth did I find one of the most important people in my life RIGHT when I needed her? You're my best friend. The one I leave thirty-minute voice messages to and can never get enough of yours in return. You're the reason I started writing this story... So YOUR DV story could be told, and so we could help others with trauma. This is all BECAUSE OF YOU! I didn't think I could do it. That my ADHD would win. But you told me that my ADHD is a superpower and not a mental illness. I want to say so much more, but at the risk of writing 172 more pages, I will just have to bring over some french fries and vegan chocolate and tell the rest to you in person.

To my Nicolle's Tribe: The ones who were there from the start. My cheerleaders. The ones who read the raw, unedited, horrendous first draft. Your input and ideas were infinitely valuable. A lot of your suggestions made it into the book and made it more than I ever thought it could be. So, to my alphas: Anny, Charlotte, Elizabeth, Lisa, Pheonix, Roxanne, and Sarah. And the ones who helped me refine the billionth draft. Who helped me developmentally before I sent it out to my editor. Who sent video reactions and made me squeal every time I saw that a new comment was sent to the Google doc. For the dopamine when I saw those comments because they were life. And for your chapter summaries, that helped me refine chapters and really pull the story together. My incredible betas: Ajay, Arielle, and Marley.

To Lisa: Aiden is yours. Forever yours! For my beautiful birthday present, to talking with you about roadblocks in book two, all the way to funding the amazing character art singles of my characters.

To Marley: You're my sister-in-kind. I would go into the Pits of Torgal to fight for you. You're constantly there, even when I am an anti-social awkward squirrel. I love you so freaking much. You not only had a huge hand in my book's success, but your help with my website, running my social media accounts, helping me figure out the characters' birthdays, sending me songs and encouragement, and just being YOU.

To Charlotte: Your pictures and displays of the book are STUNNING. From the very first picture, the original cover idea, all the way to the cover reveal party. Your work has brightened my life and enhanced my marketing efforts. I couldn't be more grateful!

To Ellie: My genius of an editor. The manuscript was good, but with you, it shot beyond the stars. Your editing was a work of pure MAGIC. Every clever editing suggestion, new scene idea, or simply just a brainstorming session with you made the book more than I could have ever thought it would be! And I am so incredibly excited to work with you for the rest of the series.

To Charity: My patient and kind formatter. It was a pleasure working side by side with you to put the prints and eBook together. The physical look of the book is better because you put your hands and expertise to it!

To Mageonduty: My hardcover art is to die for! And every single piece of character art you have drawn is so stunning. I can hardly stop myself from flipping through them daily. I am so so proud of your talent and awestruck by not only the beauty of the work but the beauty of your heart. So happy to call you my friend!

My Family: Mom, Dad, Adam, Melanie, Grandma, Geraldine, Henk, Chantal, Clayton, Dean, Nadia, and Peter. Firstly, none of you should be reading this book, especially not book two. And if you do, do NOT talk to me about it. Moving on... For the love, support, and check-ins. The excitement for every time I gave you an update. For believing in me and supporting yet another venture and the biggest investment of my life. Your prayers for success are a true treasure. I love you. I couldn't have asked for a better family.

To my PAs: Jessica, Marley, and Sarah. When my ADHD wouldn't let me write or create content all at once, you all stepped in. Marketing is hard, but with all of you, it was seamless. I never had to worry about a thing when you took over. I could physically feel the stress lift from my shoulders when I didn't have to worry about content creation and could focus on writing.

To Artscandare: After so many failed attempts with other cover companies, you came into my life and were by far the easiest and most understanding designers I dealt with! You made my vision reach perfection. My cover couldn't be more perfect!

To the readers: Those of you in Nicolle May's Broken Hearts Facebook group, anyone who shared, posted, or created reels, and those who screamed from the rooftops to others that they just HAD to read the book. The booktokers, bookstagramers, bloggers. For every DM and email, fan art, gorgeous photos of the book. Every honest and thoughtful review, the stars, and recommendations of the story to your favorite people. How could I continue Garrik and Alora's story without my incredible readers? I hope you know how important you are!

To BOMM and MTMC: Without your book tours, getting my name out there would have been near impossible—or took a lot longer! I had so much fun planning the tours and getting updates throughout the days we worked together.

To Amanda: Where do I begin? You have heard me cry and dish out every bit of fear I had as a new author. And you never made me feel like my emotions were too much, that my fears weren't valid. You heard me.

Actually heard me. And listened. You only needed to organize the BOMM (Book of Matches Media) book tour with me, but instead, you took my hand and led me through everything I would need. Not only that, but we share the same faith. You're so much more than someone who organized influencers to enjoy and post about my book. You're someone whose heart is there for indie authors. Who has a real and honest love for us. Every time I spoke with you, I left feeling ten thousand percent better and well cared for. You went above and beyond, and I am so so happy to call you my friend.

To my ARC readers: Your enthusiasm to read a brand-new author who you have never heard of had to be one of the biggest highlights of my career so far! Reading your threads and play-by-plays of what you read, seeing your favorite quotes, and falling in love with the characters was so mind-blowingly amazing, my heart could actually explode. Without you and every review, WLWMAS would not have had the success that it has so far!

Author friends: LJ Andrews, J.M. Kearl, Clare Sager, Ellie Race, and Lauren Biel. I found my tribe. Thank you for your knowledge of self-publishing and every moment of support. For every post allowed in your groups and for the behind-the-scenes chats. Your encouragement and stories kept me writing, kept me hoping and dreaming!

To Rick: I love you, loser. (I can hear you yelling from the basement, "Whatever, nerd.") Surprise, surprise. I'm crying—come here so I can soak your shirt like usual. When we met thirteen years ago, who would have ever thought that your Worship Arts graduate girlfriend would become your author wife? In our ten years of marriage, you have backed every single one of my life changes. From my big move to Canada to being stuck with me for the rest of our lives (mwahahaha). You've supported me each time I left my super successful jobs to focus on whatever current hyperfixation that inevitably led to now writing full time. And each step along the way, you've worked through snowstorms, long trucking halls, blistering hot summers, and physical labor that no mere man could do. Babe, words cannot express (crying harder) ... They will never be able to express how thankful I am for you. You literally saved my life when we met. Not figuratively. Literally. And now you work to support my dream. I just hope that one day I can give it all back to you.

And finally, to myself: I am SO PROUD OF YOU! You wrote a book! A WHOLE BOOK! YOU DID THAT!

DESIRING MORE?

CONNECT WITH ME!

Facebook Reader Group: Nicolle May's Broken Hearts

Goodreads: Nicolle May

Instagram: authornicollemay

Tiktok: authornicollemay

Facebook Page: Nicolle May

Email: authornicollemay@gmail.com